THE PRIEST

THE

PRIEST

ELLEN GUNDERSON TRAYLOR

WORD PUBLISHING
NASHVILLE
A Thomas Nelson Company

ISBN 0-7394-1865-3

Printed in the United States of America

To my mother,

Carol Gunderson,

who took this book to heart

The Lord said:

"My temple shall be called a house of prayer for all people!"

Isaiah 56:7 TLB

CHAPTER 1

October / *Tishri*

David Rothmeyer stretched his long legs and twisted stiffly in the molded chair of the airport terminal. Airplanes and waiting-room chairs were not made for people over six feet tall, he thought, and he exceeded that height by five inches. He had not been comfortable even in the first-class seat on the flight that had brought him to New York.

"You are related to the Philistines!" his Grandma Rothmeyer used to say. "On your mama's side!" That was the only way she could account for his quick growth and lanky stature as a child.

Rothmeyer smiled a little at the memory. For years he had barely thought of his Jewish grandmother; the past few days he had thought of her a lot.

Through the haze of the terminal's smogged-up windows, Rothmeyer saw that the fall sun was setting. Red-orange, it smudged through the huge chrome-and-glass room, seeming to sink into the dingy scarlet carpet. The flat-napped floor had been worn by thousands upon thousands of feet into definite paths, the widest and best traveled leading straight through the terminal to yet other terminals that would take travelers across the map; other paths, narrower but faded, led toward men's and women's rest rooms, a clutch of obscenely priced tourist shops, and an indoor "sidewalk" café complete with umbrellas that were never touched by sun or rain.

From this café the aroma of tobacco smoke and reheated

popcorn wafted over the gigantic room, and David's keen, hazel eyes flitted from the endlessly scrolling TV monitors suspended over his seating area to the bumping walk of the miniskirted barmaid who seemed to be the little eatery's only employee. Daring to leave his chair, his single suitcase, and his briefcase for a second, he adjusted the brown leather cap on his unruly shock of sandy-colored hair and approached the young woman. "I'll have some popcorn," he said, reaching for his wallet.

Casting her chewing gum from one side of her mouth to the other, like a cud-chewing cow, the thin-limbed barmaid thrust one hip forward, then rested her tray upon it. "We're out," she said.

David wondered how two words could reveal so much about character. Yet, they were so heavy with Bronx twang, so enveloped in snarl, that they instantly evoked the stereotype of the obnoxious New Yorker so repulsive to foreigners.

David was not a foreigner, but he may as well have come from a distant planet, so little had he in common with this female. Pushing his wallet back into his pocket, he returned to his seat without a word and wished he could hop the next plane back to Columbus, Ohio.

The sterile black and white chairs arranged in locked rows about the red floor reminded him of the checkerboard his grandfather used to put on the dining table each holiday evening. Every Purim and every Hanukkah when he was a boy, he and his family would wile away the sacred nights playing board games. This activity, of course, was indulged in only after his grandfather had recited the history and moral lessons of the feastday for the children. But David remembered the holidays of his youth more for the games and family closeness than for the pedagogy.

Still, it was not like David to give his childhood so much thought. His recent ruminations on his Jewish heritage were sparked by this trip and the invitation that had brought him to JFK airport.

Leaning back in his seat, he absently thrummed his fingertips on the chair's plastic arm. Since his flight had arrived early, he still had fifteen minutes to kill in this unfriendly place. Then he would take the escalator down to the lower level where his hosts were supposed to meet him.

He had mixed feelings about this imminent encounter.

Pursing his lips, he reached inside his tweed sport coat and pulled out a rumpled letter. How many times he had folded and unfolded, read and reread this document since receiving it a week before, he could never count, but it had become the focus of almost all of his thoughts.

He knew the contents by heart now, but he scanned it once again, trying to imagine the full import:

Dear Dr. Rothmeyer:

You have been referred to us by Rabbi Yitzak Schiller of Temple Beth Shalom, Columbus, Ohio, who speaks highly of your work as an archaeologist and your commitment to the Jewish community.

We are a committee of rabbinical and historical researchers, involved in a project of highest importance to the future of Israel and the welfare of our people. We have been seeking a practiced Jewish archaeologist and linguist to assist us in this project.

After investigating your credentials and your reputation, we are convinced that you would be a great asset to our endeavors, and we would like to meet with you in New York City on the afternoon of October 9.

Knowing that this date might be inconvenient to your duties at the university, we have already taken the liberty of contacting your department chairman, Dr. Kenneth Aronstam. He indicated that you have accumulated leave time during your tenure at the school, which could be used for research, if you choose.

To that end, we have also taken the liberty of enclosing an airline ticket to bring you to New York. We will pick you up at the appropriate terminal when you arrive.

Due to the sensitive nature of our project, we cannot divulge more than this. But trusting that a man of your scholarship and heritage could not reject an opportunity to be involved in research of monumental historical significance, and an opportunity to be of invaluable assistance to his people, we look forward to our meeting.

Sincerely,
Rabbi Horace Benjamin, Th.D.
Rabbi Menachem Levine, Sc.D.
Dr. Carl Jacobs, M.D.
Rabbi Uriel Katz, Th.D.

As always, David was impressed by the heavy, cream-colored stationery with its gilded letterhead. The quality of the paper alone, which revealed a fine watermark when held to the light, lent an air of authority to the contents. The credentials that followed the signatures were enough to raise the hair on the young professor's academic hide. However, he had never heard of any of these men, nor had he heard of the Temple Consortium, the agency they represented. In fine gold letters the group's name was embossed at the top of the page, and next to it, in the left corner, was an embossed menorah, the seven-branched candlestand that symbolized Judaism. Precise in detail, the little menorah, although only one inch tall, was so radiant its miniature candles may as well have been lit with real flames.

Naturally, when the letter had first been delivered to David's cluttered college office, he had scratched his head in bewilderment. Rabbi Schiller and Temple Beth Shalom were figures out of David's childhood. The old rabbi had officiated at his bar mitzvah over twenty years ago, but rarely since then had David set foot in the synagogue. As for his "commitment to the Jewish community," it had rarely been tested, except for the occasional playground skirmish, wherein he had retaliated against some childish ethnic slur.

And what did the consortium mean by calling him a "practiced Jewish archaeologist"? True, he was an archaeologist, and he was Jewish. But that was where the connection stopped. His expertise as a scientist was in cultural anthropology, but his studies, his fieldwork, and his digs had been primarily in the Mayan and Aztec regions of Central America. Never had he been to Israel. Never had he studied biblical or Hebraic archaeology, nor had he any interest in doing so.

Furthermore, it was quite disconcerting to think that there were strangers out there who had been "investigating" his credentials and reputation—that people he knew nothing of, knew a great deal about him!

Not the least bewildering aspect of the letter was its imposing nature. Not only did the committee, whoever they were, conclude that David would be interested in their mysterious project, but they had presumed to make airline reservations for him without so much as a by-your-leave.

Chagrined, David refolded the letter and put it back in the inside pocket of his jacket. Of course, he *was* sitting in the New York airport. He *had* left his cloistered classrooms and his tiny office to fly halfway across the country on an unknown errand. The letter *had* spellbound him, and he had thus far complied quite nicely with the demands of the document's drafters.

With a shiver, David pulled his jacket across his chest and crossed his arms. Maybe these people, whatever they were about, knew him better than he cared to think. Maybe he knew less about himself than he cared to admit. At any rate, he was on their journey, at their expense.

Ken Aronstam, who, in his mid-thirties, was the youngest chairman ever to head the anthropology department of Midwest University, had been of no help when David barged into his office waving the freshly opened letter. Looking up from a pile of grade sheets, Ken had slipped his wire-rimmed glasses down his large nose and shrugged. "I don't know who these guys are," he said glibly. "So they really wrote to you, huh? I thought their call was odd, but I forgot about it. You know, we get calls now and then from agencies, looking for cheap research help. Usually they want some starving grad student to do summer work, that sort of thing. I've never run into anybody who requested a Ph.D., and certainly not a Jew in particular. But I guess I just didn't think much of it."

"Have you ever run into people who would send a first-class airline ticket to someone they've never met?" David asked. "Doesn't sound like a lean outfit to me."

Scooting forward in his castered chair, Ken lifted his spectacles again to his eyes and reached for the ticket. "Let me see that," he said. Intrigued, he read the fare. "Five hundred and thirty-six dollars!" Handing it back to David, he blew on his fingertips, as if they were red-hot.

"Look at the letter," David replied. "Weird, right?"

As Ken perused the letterhead, his dark eyes grew wide. "Pretty classy, Dave!" he replied. Then as he scanned the contents, he frowned slightly. "Temple Consortium," he muttered, rubbing his neatly clipped beard. "I remember thinking it was a funny name when the guy called. But," he added, handing it back, "like I say, I didn't think much of it."

"Well," David said, "if it were just a letter, I wouldn't think much of it either. I'd probably throw it in the circular file and see if they called again. But this ticket . . ."

Turning it over and over, he stood before the desk in silent wonder. "Do you remember who called you?" he asked, glancing at the signatures on the bottom of the letter. "Was it one of these guys?"

Ken ran over the list and settled on the top name. "Benjamin," he said. "I'm pretty sure that's the one. It wasn't a secretary, but one of the rabbis themselves. And I remember thinking the name was as strange as the call. 'Horace Benjamin.' Quite the classic moniker!" He laughed.

"And ethnic," David added. Then, looking at the floor, he shrugged. "But I guess that's not so bad."

"I suppose it wouldn't hurt either of us to trek to synagogue now and then," Ken said. He placed his pen on the pile of grade sheets, then looked sideways at David. "How easily we forget who we are."

Rarely had David and Ken spoken of their mutual heritage. Each knew the other was a Jew, but when, in their far-removed world of freshman seminars and Central American file cards, did they have cause to talk about it? Oh sure, they told each other Jewish jokes and wished obligatory Happy Hanukkahs. But if any colleague had joked about their ethnicity like they themselves did, David and Ken would have labeled that person anti-Semitic.

David was about to leave, to ponder the mystery in his office cubicle, when Ken reached for the ticket once more.

"Just a minute," he said. "Let me see that again."

Reading down the figures, his eyes grew wider than ever. "Check this out!" he marveled. "Did you notice that this ticket is one-way?"

Quickly David grabbed it back, gawking at the fine print. "You're kidding!" he exclaimed. "I'll be. . . . It is!"

With a vacant stare, David slumped down onto the folding chair across from the administrator's desk.

"Looks like you have a deeper riddle than we thought," Ken teased.

When he saw that David did not appreciate his humor, he leaned back in his tilting chair and studied the young professor soberly. "What are you going to do?" he asked.

For a moment, David squinted at the ticket and the letter. At last, he jumped to his feet. "The whole thing's crazy!" he fumed. "I'm a teacher, not an international sleuth." He headed out the door. "They need a detective, not an archaeologist!"

It was just such words that turned Ken's crank. "What's the difference?" he called after him.

Stopping, David growled, "What did you say?"

"What's the difference?" he repeated. "Aren't a detective and an archaeologist pretty much alike?"

Exasperated, David returned to the office and poked his head in. "Are you suggesting I go on this snipe hunt?" he muttered, glaring down at him.

Ken shrugged, then picked up his pencil and doodled on his grade sheets. "Did you have something better to do this winter?" he inquired. "Look, you've got tenure and earned leave. You're due to present the committee with your plans for a sabbatical. Your grad assistants can cover your classes for you. Maybe this project could be a start—"

"I can't believe what I'm hearing!" David interrupted. "You know that whatever these jokers are up to, it's about as related to my field of interest as fish to bicycles!"

"Or the modern world to Mayan architecture?" Ken goaded.

With a scowl, David reentered the office, threw the documents on the desk and leaned across them, staring the chairman in the eye. "What is that supposed to mean, Ken? Are you saying I use my studies as an escape?"

Ken gave a fake gasp. "Would I suggest such a thing?" Then, more compassionately, he added, "No. Not always, Dave. But . . . ever since Susan . . . went away . . ."

That was a mean blow. It was true that for the past three summers David had buried himself in the ruins of an ancient village high in the Guatemalan mountains, as much to flee a broken heart as to outline a pottery history. The death of his precious wife and coworker, Susan, had nearly killed him, though it had also meant an end to her torment as a cancer victim. The childless couple had thrived on going on digs together and on studying the dust of the past. That dust had been David's healer after her passing, and he thought it was cruel of Ken to criticize him for it.

Wounded, David said not a word but turned again for the door. Sweeping up the letter and the ticket, Ken left his desk and pursued him down the hall.

"Look, Dave," he pleaded, grabbing him by the arm, "I didn't mean . . . I mean—maybe this is an opportunity to turn your thoughts elsewhere." Quickly he pushed the papers into David's hand. "Look. Don't make a decision today. Sleep on it and talk with me tomorrow."

With a sigh, David nodded. "Okay. But what about this crazy one-way ticket? How do I get home?"

"Take your Visa card." Ken grinned and hurried back to his grade sheets.

Hard to believe that conversation had taken place just a week ago, David thought. It seemed years since the inscrutable letter had arrived.

As "Muzak" floated through the mammoth terminal, blending with the sounds of travelers coming and going and planes whooshing on and off the ground, David hunched down in his seat and tried to relax.

The busy place hardly invoked serenity, however. The droning voice on the intercom, announcing arrivals and departures, and the ceaseless churn of escalators full of tired families and harried businessmen were hard to shut out.

David was about to pull his leather cap over his eyes for a forced rest, when a peculiar gathering of people drew his attention to one corner of the waiting area.

A group of Orthodox Jews were standing together in a cluster. They were dressed in plain black suits that buttoned to the neck, and wore various sorts of hats: broad, fur-rimmed platters, or little embroidered *yarmulkes*, like the one David donned on his rare visits to synagogue. Wearing striped prayer shawls, they faced the darkening windows that provided a ribbon of view toward the eastern sky, over rows of airport buildings, and they nodded and bobbed their heads in prayer, their lips moving in a low, murmured chant. Some held small prayer books, while others gripped their hands close to their chests.

Although they were gathered together, no one led them. Each was alone in his own world of meditation, eyes closed or lifted toward the east.

Toward Jerusalem, David thought, remembering the evening prayers that older men in his family had said.

Fascinated, the professor observed them. He could make out a few of the words they softly recited, the movements of their lips recalling certain phrases:

If I forget thee, O Jerusalem, let my right hand forget her cunning.
If I do not remember thee, let my tongue cleave to the roof of my mouth;
If I prefer not Jerusalem above my highest joys.

David had not thought of these words for years. He wistfully smiled, and a surprising sense of nostalgia settled over him.

But it was all too fleeting. A shuffle near the praying men broke in on his reveries.

A small boy, probably no more than four years old, had wandered close to the group and stood looking up at them in curiosity. This little fellow was also dressed in ethnic garb, but not of a Jewish variety. He was wearing an embroidered, striped tunic and a small boxy hat of like material. Noting the outfit, as well as the boy's dark hair, large, dark eyes, and olive skin, David deduced he was of Middle-Eastern heritage.

The little boy watched the praying Jews with wide, round eyes. Then tentatively, he raised a hand and reached for the tasseled fringe of one man's striped prayer-shawl. Giving a little tug, he got the man's attention, jolting him out of his meditation.

"Hi, mister," he said, his wee voice cheery and inquisitive.

The startled Jew stared down at the upturned face and smiled slightly. Gesturing toward the waiting area, he asked, "Where is your mother?"

Barely were the words out, however, before an olive-skinned man, with black eyes and blacker beard, swept across the room, grasped the lad's arm, and jerked him away. He barked at the boy and thrust him toward a woman who sat in one of the waiting-room chairs. Apparently the lad's mother, she was dressed in a long kaftan, her head and face concealed by a broad scarf.

The man gave her a spearing look and growled at both of them. Then, gesturing toward the Jewish group, he spat out a stream of epithets in Lebanese.

David's linguistic training picked up on the gist of the nasty phrases, as the angry man drove home to his son that these were "untouchables, the enemy, the Jews!"

The man's invectives were startling enough. But his voice, itself, was more so. Unusually rasping and coarse, it caused people to stop in their busy rush through the terminal to turn and stare at him.

The little boy now sobbed in his mother's arms. Glancing at the onlookers, the man said no more, just snapped his fingers and motioned for his wife and child to follow him. Together they joined the flow of foot traffic down the concourse.

Although the incident did not involve David, it took on special significance, both because of his trip and because of an incident he had just learned about that morning. As he had prepared to depart Columbus, David had caught a snippet on CNN about a bus being blown up in Tel Aviv. Arab terrorists were blamed. Of course, such news was all too commonplace anymore, and in the past it would not have overly concerned him. Lately, however,—ever since the Temple Consortium letter—he had been much more in touch with his own Jewishness, much more aware of the hallmark of his ethnicity, his thin, hooked nose.

As the Lebanese Arab and his little family passed by David's seat, the professor felt, for the first time in his life, the deep and terrible chill of racial fear.

Turning his head, he avoided eye contact. Once they were gone, he nervously cleared his throat.

A clock on the terminal wall said it was time to go downstairs. He felt strangely relieved as he descended the escalator, suitcase in hand.

He watched for a group of rabbis, who, like the men upstairs, should not be hard to spot. No such greeting committee was to be seen, but just as he reached the main floor a flash of evening sun reflecting off gleaming metal drew his attention to the street. Just pulling up to the loading area was a sleek limousine, the longest he had ever seen. Like a shining gray whale, it glistened beside the curb, its black windows inspiring mystery.

As David watched, the chauffeur jumped out, ran to the passenger door, and opened it. From the depths emerged a most unusual character, a man in a long black coat, wearing a wide black hat, beneath which dangled fluffy white curls. As this fellow straightened, facing the terminal, David was amazed by another tumble of curls that descended to his chest, a veritable snowfall of a beard.

From behind this figure emerged three other men, all dressed in black and conservative gray, all with distinctive hats: two broad-rims edged in ebony-colored ermine, and one the more common, skull-fitting *yarmulke*. All the men were bearded, their beards carved so that the corners were left long. Their hair was of varying lengths, but they all wore the traditional *poyis*, long ringlets on either side of the face.

The young professor from Ohio felt his pulse race again, but this time out of awe more than anxiety. As the men stood on the curb, they searched the terminal windows, then moved forward as a body to enter the building.

David clutched his suitcase nervously, and shoved the letter deeper into his pocket.

No one needed to tell him that the drafters of that invitation had just arrived.

CHAPTER 2

Father Ian McCurdy knelt in the soft brown dirt of his Oxfordshire garden, mulching his rose bed for winter. Although it had been ten years since he had worked in the Israeli desert, the moist soil of his English garden often reminded him, by contrast, of the long, hot days he had spent there. It seemed he could never get enough of the solace he found in his dark-earthed haven.

Leaning back, he rubbed his hands on his khaki work slacks, leaving streaks of soil on his thighs, and loosened the neck of his plaid shirt. It had also been a long time since he had worn his clerical collar, the mark of the priesthood that he was seldom called upon, these days, to practice. He wondered if he should put it on today.

Though he lived only a few miles from Pembroke College, one of the few Catholic institutions among the thirty-five campuses of Oxford University, he was emeritus and rarely lectured there anymore. He had not received a professional visitor in a long time. He avoided the thought that he should dress the part of a priest or a faculty member.

Ian McCurdy had never enjoyed standing on ceremony. It had been the bane of his existence as an Irish Catholic priest. That was why he preferred the realm of scholarship to the role of the pastorate, and he had buried himself in archaeology because it was the field of study most removed from the formal classroom.

Digging in his English garden had nothing to do with archaeology, however. He had cloistered himself in this quaint corner of Britain because it was as unlike the Judean desert as possible, its fertile dirt yielding no great finds, only the glory of roses and greenery.

No, he would not wear his collar. He would not even have granted the upcoming interview if the young journalist who made the appointment had not been the daughter of an acquaintance—his sister Emily's acquaintance, not his own.

His lips tightened in a line of resentment as he realized the power Emily had over him. She was his only living relative, and it was to indulge her that he had decided to break his vow of public silence and meet with a reporter.

Having lived as a virtual recluse for months, he knew it would be tempting to say too much. He must guard himself against that vulnerability. He had seen the media's warped coverage of his character and his life's work. It would be a longed-for relief to unveil himself, to stand before the world and cry out in his own defense. But this he must not do. He must phrase all responses carefully, to protect the dreadful secret that was his to bear, even if it meant he must go to his death unvindicated.

Father McCurdy brushed his gray-white hair from his round face and reached for the ash-tipped cigar he had set on a rock. Besides Emily, his cigars were another weakness he indulged. He took a long drag, then blew circles in the air and tried to clear his mind. The interview would not last long; he would see to that. When the young reporter left, she would wonder why she had bothered to come. Emily would be satisfied, and he would be none the worse for it.

A rattle of the gate behind told the priest his afternoon of solitude was ended. John Cromwell, his tall, thin-boned houseman, had entered the garden, looking for him.

"Your visitor is here, Ian," he announced.

Standing up, Ian removed his gardening gloves, dusted the dirt from his pants and put a hand on Cromwell's shoulder. "The dog returns to its vomit," he quipped in his Irish brogue.

Cromwell sighed. "How can you make light of this, Father? Did you see the morning's headlines?"

"I saw CNN," he replied. "Something about Allaman and the Deadly Duo."

Cromwell didn't like the priest's satiric reference to the very people who were disparaging him *and* the church before the world. "Allaman has come out with a full endorsement of Bailey and Lee's Deception Theory. How much more of this will you allow to go unchallenged?"

"Allaman has always been an atheistic maverick, looking for any opportunity to promote his heresies! Remember," Ian chuckled, "this is the same clown who insisted the followers of Jesus were a mushroom cult! He did the team the greatest of favors when he left Israel. Now," he said, rubbing his ample stomach, "fetch us a snack."

Britta Hayworth sat on the edge of a wing chair, notepad and pencil in hand, and breathlessly watched the parlor door. Any moment the elusive Father McCurdy would be entering the room, granting her a reporter's dream, the chance to interview an international enigma.

For weeks she had waded through stacks of journals and newspapers, reading anything she could get her hands on regarding the Cave Scrolls and the controversy surrounding them. Of course, most literate people had heard of the famous scrolls, discovered in the forties in the Dead Sea wilderness, at the ruins of the ancient settlement of Qumran. Most knew that they contained records of a mysterious sect called the Essenes, though that designation was now disputed.

When the public first heard of the scrolls, they were touted by the media as the archaeological find of the century. Along with their unique chronicle of Jewish culture before the sacking of Jerusalem by Rome in 70 C.E., they also appeared to contain proof that Old Testament scriptures that seemed to point to Jesus as the Jewish Messiah had not been "revised" after his death.

For four decades they had caused no end of embarrassment to scholars of the "modernist" camp, who had discredited the notion that Jesus was foreseen by Isaiah and other pre-Christian writers.

Now, however, the scrolls were back in the news, this time at the center of an unparalleled debate challenging the very foundations of the Christian world.

Father Ian McCurdy was at the center of that debate, though he did not openly participate in it and had made no public statement about the scrolls for nearly a decade. In fact, it was his very silence that had turned public scrutiny increasingly in his direction, for he was the senior member of the original team of scholars that first translated the scrolls.

Britta smoothed her tailored pantsuit, the "professional woman" attire she had adopted since she graduated from the casual college scene three years ago and entered "the real world." She knew she had a more credible image as a reporter when she dressed this way, and Britta, with her cherubic face and unruly blond curls, needed all the credibility she could muster.

Actually, twenty-four-year-old Britta came from a long line of newspeople, her great-uncle being a legendary photojournalist who had worked for the *London Times* during World War II. He had made an indelible mark on the profession by his risk-taking feats in the line of duty, even receiving the coveted George Cross for wounds received on assignment at Normandy.

Britta had always admired her uncle, visiting him twice during college breaks at his home in Nazareth, Israel.

Having been assigned to photograph the immigration of Holocaust Jews to the emerging nation of Israel in the postwar years, he had fallen in love with that land, and with a young Jewess, whom he eventually married there. From that time on he had divided his work between Israel and England, taking up full-time residence in the Holy Land upon retirement.

It had been Britta's lifelong dream to be as proficient with her writing as that heroic reporter had been with his camera. Presently, she worked as a stringer, a freelancer employed by the same legendary newspaper for which her great-uncle had worked. The *Times* already paid her more for her stories than most stringers received. If only she could impress them with one really big scoop, she felt she might have a chance at a regular position. This interview with Father McCurdy might be the break she had been looking for.

In preparing for this meeting, the reporter had read everything she could find on the enigmatic priest and had pumped his sister for details. Britta learned that he had earned a reputation for genius as a lecturer at Trinity College in his native Dublin, Ireland, teaching courses in archaeology. He had been courted by Oxford, hiring on at Pembroke, which specialized in Middle-Eastern studies, when he was only twenty-eight.

His scholarly interests leaned toward ancient languages, and his courses in Hebraic archaeology were always full of enrollees.

After the Cave Scrolls were discovered, Oxford sent him to Israel to work at the field site under the direction of the head of the archaeology team. Eventually, he spent more time in Israel than England, until his sudden and unexplained return to Oxford ten years ago.

He was now in his late seventies, and his mystique had only grown with his inaccessibility.

When McCurdy finally entered through the french doors leading from his garden and approached Britta across the parlor, she was surprised at his appearance. If she had gone out of her way to look professional, he looked anything but the part of a priest.

Father McCurdy drew a handkerchief from his back pocket, wiped his soiled hands once more, then reached out to greet her.

Britta managed to conceal her jitters and, poking her notepad under one arm, stood up, giving him a hearty handshake. "Father McCurdy," she said, "I'm Britta Hayworth, with the *Times*. Glad to meet you." She liked linking herself with the prestigious newspaper, regardless of her fledgling status.

McCurdy surveyed her quickly and deduced that this would be a quick and uneventful encounter. He need not have worried about an inquisitor who looked like Shirley Temple.

"A pleasure, Ms. Hayworth," he replied, using the generic title for sake of political correctness. Likely she considered herself a feminist of sorts, in her male-dominated world of ink and newsprint.

"I'm a bit of a mess," he acknowledged. "Would you like to talk in the garden?"

"I would," she said, admiring the sunlit grotto.

Cromwell brought them tea and cookies on the flagstone veranda, as they chatted about Ian's sister Emily and then his flowers.

Britta, eager to get to her subject, asked, "Did you do much gardening in Israel?"

McCurdy puffed on a fresh cigar and looked at her knowingly. *Clever*, he thought. *She's not new to this game*.

Before he could answer, she laughed and added, "But of course you were digging for other things than weeds when you were there!"

McCurdy blew smoke from the side of his mouth. "I'm sure you're aware of all the digging we did," he muttered.

"I have tried to educate myself," she said, pushing back a lock of her wayward hair. "The questions I would like to ask may be rather repetitious to you," she proceeded. "I hope you will indulge me."

He knew what Emily liked about this young woman. They were two of a kind.

"If they've been asked before, they've been answered before," he said, "and you've doubtless read anything I've had to say."

He had her there. He knew she'd never read any such thing, for none had ever been written.

She blushed a little. "Very well," she conceded. "Then, I do appreciate this opportunity. I will get right to the point."

Good, he thought. *Then you can get right back to London*.

"What do you think of the Deception Theory?" she began.

McCurdy's eyes narrowed. "You know what I must think! It fits in the same category as Allaman's poppycock book that claimed the early Christians ate 'magic' mushrooms! It's balderdash! Pure foolishness. And if I weren't a priest, I'd use stronger language!"

"How so?" she went on, jotting on a notepad.

"If you've read the Deception Theory, you know it essentially says that the Christianity of the Bible is a perversion of Jesus' teachings. It equates 'The Teacher of Righteousness,' referred to in the scrolls, with Jesus, and 'The Wicked Priest,' who was out to destroy the Teacher, with St. Paul."

McCurdy frowned at her as she wrote down key phrases. "The theorists," he went on, "say that the scrolls present the Teacher as an adherent of the Jewish law and that Paul, because he taught that the law was not the source of salvation, was a heretic. Hence, the Christian committee that was in charge of the scrolls hid this dreadful revelation from the world, for fear it would undermine the very roots of the Church, showing the Christianity of the New Testament to be a fraudulent distortion of Jesus' original doctrine!"

Britta scribbled quickly, wishing she had taken a shorthand course along with her writing classes, and trying to follow the priest's explanation.

"So," she mused, looking up from her notes, "the drafters of the Deception Theory claim that the Qumran writings are truer to the teachings of Jesus than those of the New Testament and that what the Gospel writers came up with was heresy?"

Ian nodded curtly. "They say that Jesus was essentially a Jewish teacher, with no intention to deviate from traditional Judaism. They say that Paul was the culprit who planted the idea that people no longer had to abide by the Judaic law and could be saved by faith alone."

He took a breath. "As for me," he reiterated, "if the Teacher and the Priest do represent Jesus and Paul, which I sincerely doubt, the Qumran doctrine is the heresy, not the New Testament!"

Britta, who had an Anglican and Jewish background, had not gone to church or synagague much and knew very little about the Bible. Looking up at the priest, she commented, "But isn't Christianity full of rules and regulations? What's the difference?"

McCurdy had not anticipated the interview to go in this direction. Sighing impatiently, he blew out more smoke. "Christianity as it is misconstrued, yes! One of the things I've always loathed about the priesthood is its rules and rituals. I think I would have liked Paul."

Then, leaning forward, he peered directly into the young woman's open face. "But this is not why you are here. You want to know if we were, indeed, covering up this . . . 'revelation.'"

Britta nodded. "Isn't that what everyone wants to know?"

Ian gave a chuckle. "Dear girl! If we wanted to cover up every pseudo-Christian line of thought, we'd have to burn every *Book of Mormon*, every

Watchtower magazine, and every book of Ellen G. White! They all teach salvation through works!"

"So," Britta marveled, "you're equating the monks of Qumran with certain sects of today?"

"They were Jewish traditionalists, that's all. No more sectarian than any Jew then or now. *If* their writings refer to Jesus and Paul, instead of outright rejecting Jesus as Messiah, they merely redefined him, like any good Mormon or SDA. That set them apart from the Jews who wanted nothing to do with him, just as they were already set apart from the temple in Jerusalem, which had become 'ceremonially' unclean. No, my dear, the Deception Theory is a bunch of wishful thinking, a contrivance to shame the Church!"

For a moment, Britta was at a loss as to how to proceed. To buy some time, she studied her notes. Finally, however, the source of her bewilderment took on focus: All of this had been much too easy.

Shaking her head, she found only one question to ask. "Father," she said, "when you come right down to it, there is nothing earthshaking in your answer. Why then have you avoided the press?"

Ian was caught off guard. He took the cigar from his lips and twirled it aimlessly. "Well," he grunted, "perhaps I didn't expect reporters to be so easily satisfied."

Ian's heart pumped uncomfortably. In being very forthright with her, confident in doling out doctrine, he had made it appear he had no real reason to hide from the press. He could have anticipated her next words.

Britta closed her notepad and looked squarely at him. "I sense, Father, that we have been dealing with a smoke screen. You say you have no secret. Yet, for almost half a century, the scroll team sat on their cache of parchments. It is believed that even today there are scrolls you have not released to the scrutiny of the scholarly community. What then *have* you been concealing?"

Ian squirmed in his patio chair. "Can't you just accept that I am an old man?" he offered. "I would like to live out my years in peace. I granted this interview to appease my sister, and I have nothing more to say. My original colleagues have nearly all died off. The scrolls are in the hands of our apprentices and the world at large. Some of our students have turned out to be renegades, making personal fortunes off absurd conspiracy claims. You have the scrolls. Go and read them. You'll see that there is nothing to hide!"

With this, he stood up, straightened his stiff knees, and bowed curtly to her. "Cromwell will see you out." He waved her off and turned to his rosebeds. "My garden is calling."

Britta rose and stuffed her notepad under her arm. "What about the rumors of other scrolls?" she called after him. "Scrolls not yet released to the public?"

By now, Cromwell was ushering her back through the house.

"Thank you for coming," he said, as he opened the front door. "It has been a long time since Father had such charming company."

CHAPTER 3

David Rothmeyer sat in the side seat of the glistening gray limousine as it sped from the airport into Manhattan. He had never ridden in such a vehicle before, and he appreciated its spaciousness, stretching his long legs into the center of the passenger compartment.

His hosts studied him quietly, obviously sizing him up.

One of them, the one whose name headed the signatures at the bottom of the mysterious letter, sat in the seat against the window separating the back of the limousine from the chauffeur. He made amiable conversation, discussing the weather and asking chatty questions, the answers to which David was certain he already knew: Have you family? Oh, you are a widower—so sorry. When did your wife pass away? You have been at Midwest for seven years? How do you like it? What classes do you teach? How many digs have you been on? etc. etc.

David replied to each question simply, directly. He knew that old Rabbi Horace Benjamin was trying to break the ice, but until the young professor knew what this visit was about, there would be a virtual iceberg between them.

It was the tail end of rush hour, which meant that this trip would be excruciatingly slow. Somehow, the chauffeur managed to maneuver the huge car through the traffic with a minimum of delays. The tedious pace, however, allowed too much time for silences between stabs at conversation.

David felt it was not the time to be asking his own questions. He thought that was best reserved for when they arrived at whatever their destination was.

The other three men in the car interjected pleasantries, but David found Rabbi Benjamin to be the friendliest. He was the awesome-looking gent with the cascading beard David had seen emerging from the limousine at JFK.

The rabbi struck David as almost holy. At the very least, the man evoked wonder and respect, not only by his appearance, but by his gentle voice and kind mannerisms.

David's linguistic background clicked in, once again, the instant the rabbi spoke. He noted that the gentleman had a thick Jewish accent, often ending his sentences on the downswing, rather than in the typical upbeat ending of American English: "You are a widow-*er*. We are so sor-*ry*." His speech did not have the nasal characteristic common to the Yiddish dialect, however. Instead, his distinctive talk pinpointed him as highly educated and refined, while a hint of the Queens/Brooklyn "r-dropping" was evident.

Actually, all the men but one spoke this way. They also used their hands more than the ordinary American. David's trained eye and ear allowed him to assess these things easily. In fact, it was second nature to him to make such analyses.

Of the four hosts, Rabbi Uriel Katz was the most reserved. He sat in the backseat between Menachem Levine and Carl Jacobs, whose broad, ermine-trimmed hats cast him in shadow. Rabbi Katz, more than the others, seemed engrossed in studying David, saying little and occasionally closing his eyes, as though to imprint something in his mind.

Perhaps because he was a slighter fellow than the others, or perhaps because he sank back into the seat, keeping his head against the headrest in a contemplative posture, Rabbi Katz seemed to blend with the background, and his silence lent him mystique. He wore an elaborate yarmulke embroidered in many colors, which was secured to his thinning hair with gold clips. He, too, had a beard, close-cropped and streaked with gray, though he did not appear to be older than forty-five.

His first name, Uriel, seemed rather ethereal, and David recognized it as the name of one of the archangels of folklore.

When he spoke, which was not often, his accent was distinctly foreign, that of an Israeli-born Jew. David figured he must be one of the first generation of Jews born in the newly established state of Israel after the exodus from the European Holocaust.

All of these facts made the man intriguing, though each of the hosts was part of the enigma that had haunted David since he received the letter.

The limousine had passed through the Queens-Midtown Tunnel, and as it sped up First Avenue, which was relatively free of congestion, it passed the United Nations Building.

David gazed out the car window at the sprawling structure, with its flags of many nations illuminated in the evening sky. Although he did not know where he was headed, he appreciated this chance to sightsee. As the car sped west down Forty-ninth Street, David's eyes were drawn up, up the sides of skyscrapers, and he wondered if they were near the building that was bombed in 1993.

"Are we close to the World Trade Center?" he asked, scanning the slit of horizon above the street.

Dr. Jacobs shook his head. "The financial district is on the southwest side of Manhattan," he said. "But we are not far from Rockefeller Center and Grand Central Station."

David perceived the pride in the man's voice. He evidently enjoyed showing off his city to an out-of-towner.

Passing block after block of New York's multistoried monoliths, the professor remembered well the day of the dreadful bombing of the World Trade Center. He had been home, making lunch in his small apartment kitchen between class sessions. The little TV on the kitchen counter was tuned to CNN when the regular news was interrupted by the special report of the explosion in one of the world's most famous skyscrapers. Shots of men and women being hauled out of the building on stretchers, blood-spattered victims hobbling between less wounded coworkers, and the cries of onlookers would remain forever a part of American memory.

He also recalled his gut reaction. Almost without thinking, he had called Ken Aronstam at the university and announced, "Ken, wait 'til you see what the Arabs just did in New York!"

It had taken the media much longer to draw that same conclusion. At first they had posited that either a gas line or a container of some other volatile substance in the mammoth skyscraper's subterranean chambers had malfunctioned, leading to the deadly blast. When that had not proven itself out, they had surmised that a disgruntled janitor or other manual laborer at the building had driven a bomb-laden van into the basement.

Only after clues began to trickle in as to the possibility of a terrorist attack had they begun to zero in on a violent Egyptian cult led by a blind Islamic holy man. The ensuing investigation revealed that the terrorists had been on the verge of fulfilling other plots, including the bombing of the Holland Tunnel during rush hour. Fortunately, that scheme had been intercepted.

Since then, any disaster that smacked of subterfuge opened immediate speculation that Muslim terrorists were the instigators, from the bombing of the Oklahoma City Federal Courthouse, to the TWA disaster over Long Island.

As for David, he was no genius of international politics, but quick reasoning had led him to suspect Arab terrorists the moment he saw the World Trade Center coverage.

"What makes you think it's Arabs?" Ken had asked him.

"Come on." David had laughed. "Think about it! If you wanted to get at the wealthiest and most influential Jews in the world, where would you go?"

Ken's silence spurred David to fill in. "You're thinking Israel, right? No way, Ken. The thickest concentration of Jewish power resides at the World Trade Center! Any anti-Semitic message delivered there will be heard loud and clear!"

So it had followed. The Muslim perpetrators had eventually been caught and tried, and their leader had been imprisoned. Interestingly, however, although the Egyptian cult was the same one that had been accused of assassinating a Zionist leader in this same city in 1990, no media commentary had ever given the explanation David gave. No one, he figured, had dared touch the obvious.

As David lowered his eyes from the tall buildings, he noticed how people on the street tried to peer through the darkened windows of the car in which he traveled. On the rare occasion that he had seen a limousine pass through Columbus, he had done just as these onlookers were doing: He had peered quizzically into the obsidian-like glass, wondering who the passengers could be. Celebrities? Tycoons? Now, David was the limousine passenger, and people were giving him the same unfocused stares he had leveled at luxury cruisers.

He felt foolish. The further he went into this conundrum, the more ridiculous it seemed.

David should have figured his hosts would not be quick to reveal much about themselves. As much as they knew about him, he was proportionately ignorant of them. It appeared that they intended to keep it that way, at least for a while. The first suggestion of this was the fact that they would only meet with him in a neutral place, not in a home or office.

Smoothly, the limousine veered toward the curb in front of the Waldorf-Astoria Hotel. As it pulled to a stop at the Park Avenue entrance, the hotel's crisply uniformed doorman rushed out and saluted the unseen occupants.

The chauffeur beat him to the passenger door, and as he let the rabbis out, he told the doorman to fetch a bellboy. In a moment, a sharply-groomed adolescent was unloading David's luggage from the trunk and taking it to the elevator of the elaborate, muraled lobby. All tips were paid by the chauffeur, and soon David and his hosts were escorted to a posh tenth-story suite.

David's modest salary had never allowed him to stay in such a place. Even if he had been blessed with a windfall, he would not have spent it on the luxury of a New York hotel. He would have used the money to fund a trip to some primitive Central American dig. Still, he could not help being impressed with the three-room suite. Crystal chandeliers and gilt wall sconces graced the ceilings and walls; bouquets of fresh flowers lent life and aroma to the room, and a marble-walled bathroom, which David could see through the arch beyond the vast bed, added a final touch of opulence.

David's wide eyes said the "wow" he was too dignified to say.

Then he spotted something that made his academic spine tingle. One low table beneath the parlor window was covered with books, some of them so ancient they could have been from the cloisters of a medieval monastery. Speechless, David walked toward the table, then stopped and turned to the rabbis gathered in the middle of the room.

"Go ahead, Dr. Rothmeyer. Look at them. They are here for you to study," Rabbi Benjamin said.

"Study?" David repeated. "Now?"

He walked to the table and gazed on the musty old volumes. Most of them were in German, some in other esoteric languages he vaguely recognized, like post-Roman Latin, Syriac, and ancient Aramaic.

Many of the books were half- or full-bound leather, with raised compartments on the spines and gold-tooled titles. Daring to touch them, he opened to pages of parchment and vellum, many of them illuminated, the designs intricate and elaborate. As David ran his hands over the priceless works, his fingers quivering, Rabbi Benjamin and the others drew near.

"We know you must be tired from your journey and all this strangeness," Benjamin said. "We want you to rest this evening and get a good sleep."

The kindly rabbi placed a hand on David's shoulder. "You must have a thousand questions. All in good time, my boy. Meanwhile, there is plenty here to amuse you."

Then, pointing to a stack of newer books and leaflets, he said, "Some of your questions will be answered by these." He picked up one pamphlet and suggested David start with it.

"This will tell you enough for now," he said. "We will meet you for breakfast in the hotel dining room at seven A.M."

As David glanced at the pamphlet, the rabbis left the room.

The professor did not think to say good-bye as he turned the little booklet over in his hands. At the top of the front flap was the same shining menorah that had graced the letterhead he received a week before. The pamphlet's title promised to explain some things: "Temple Consortium, Paving the Way for Messiah."

CHAPTER 4

Father McCurdy woke suddenly and sat up in bed, his heart racing. He had not had one of his recurring dreams of Qumran for months. It was clear why he had this one tonight, however. The interview with the young journalist had provoked old fears, old anxieties.

He reached out and pulled back the filmy curtain that gave him a view of his garden. Usually, the pleasant bower, especially when seen in the moonlight, salved any restlessness of his spirit, but tonight it only added to his agitation, making him feel quite alone in the world.

He swung his legs out from under the covers and shuffled to the kitchen. A mug of warm milk might relax him, he thought. The house was quiet. Only the ticking of the old wooden wall clock above the sink filled the silence.

Fumbling through the cupboard, he found a saucepan, poured in some milk, and warmed it to a steamy froth.

He had just sat down to the comforting cup when his dear friend and houseman, John Cromwell, entered the room.

"Father," he greeted him, "I heard you rustling about. Having trouble sleeping?"

"Sleep is not the problem," Ian answered. "It's what comes with the sleep."

"How Shakespearean!" Cromwell chuckled. "'To sleep. Perchance to dream . . .'"

"'Ay, there's the rub!'" Ian joined him. "Yes, yes," the old priest said with a shrug. "I guess Hamlet and I do have something in common."

Cromwell rubbed his bleary eyes, placed his spectacles on his nose, and went to the cupboard for his own mug. He was hesitant to say what he thought, but when he sat down, he couldn't help letting out a heavy sigh. He took a sip from his steaming cup and stared intently at the tabletop.

"Come, old friend," Ian nudged him. "You can say it."

"Well, it almost seems irreverent," John replied. "You know, Shakespeare and all. But I think you have Hamlet beat by a long shot."

"How so?" Ian asked.

"The Prince of Denmark bore only the secret of one royal murder and an incestuous conspiracy. You bear the burden of the world's future—the security of the entire planet!"

To a chance listener, such a declaration would have seemed melodramatic, even ludicrous. But to the two men sitting in the Oxfordshire kitchen in the dark of night, the statement was anything but absurd. It was altogether factual, an unearthly load to bear.

The two of them had borne it together for ten years!

Cromwell had never been to Israel. He had been caretaker for Ian's residence since the professor's early days at Pembroke College. In the 1950s, when Ian began to spend months at a time at Qumran, John had been his mainstay, keeping his home in his absence. Though one was Anglican and the other Catholic, the two had become fast friends, and the houseman had followed with interest letters sent from the Holy Land while Ian was working there.

When the letters became less frequent, the tenor less personal, Cromwell had chalked it up to distance and infrequent visits between the two men. Even the best of friendships must suffer under such strains, he figured.

But then Ian had returned, suddenly, unannounced, keeping close to the house and avoiding society. That was when the facts of Ian's trials in Israel became their mutual secret.

"Let's go to the parlor," the priest said. "I've never been good at talking in a kitchen."

The last embers of the October hearth glowed amiably on the grate. Two wing-backed chairs faced the warmth, and the flannel-robed gentlemen settled into them like monks in quiet cells.

Here, it always seemed, the world was not so much with them, though in this quaint corner of Britain, on this country road, well back from the flow of English life, there was little likelihood of eyes or ears within miles.

Beside the priest's chair were baskets piled with current issues of *Biblical*

Archaeology, the *Jerusalem Post*, *Mid-East Scholar*, and newsletters from a dozen Israel-based agencies, all more or less related to the fields of Middle-Eastern history and the Bible. Next to these were other baskets and boxes, stacked with issues of international newspapers and magazines, ready for the fire. Upon inspection, these publications would have revealed gaping holes, where articles had been neatly cut out and placed in scrapbooks that lined the shelves of Ian's study.

In that study, which was adjacent to the parlor beyond a set of glass doors, were older *BA*s and bound volumes of the *Jerusalem Post*. Ian never permitted those publications to be cut or altered in any way.

How many evenings the two men had sat before this fire, reading, clipping, and cataloging, was impossible to say. Once they had finished, even on summer nights, Cromwell burned the international papers in a barrel stove in the garden. And morning duties in the house included arranging clippings in the scrapbooks.

Ian figured that the young London journalist who had visited earlier that day had noted the horde of publications near the wing chairs. Undoubtedly her notebook contained an entry to the effect that he was still obsessed with the Middle East, and with developments in the arena he had supposedly forsaken.

Since the release of a good number of the scrolls for public consumption, and until the recent blast from Allaman and the Deadly Duo, the media had calmed down to a tepid simmer over the whole issue of the Cave Scrolls. Except for *Biblical Archaeology*'s ongoing pleas for the release of more information to the scholarly community, there had been only the occasional offbeat conspiracy theory to keep the matter in the public eye.

Every print medium, from the *New York Times* to the *National Investigator*, had made a stab at the mystery of the scrolls' contents. The latter posited everything from the secrets of alien spaceships and interplanetary flight, to the genealogy of Bigfoot as the great riddle that was being withheld.

The clamor on the part of Allaman and his cohorts was only one more in a string of suppositions trying to guess at what kept the committee from releasing its hold on the scrolls for nearly half a century. To Allaman's credit it must be conceded that this latest attack was the best thought out and most cleverly "supported" of the theories.

John leaned forward and prodded the embers with the poker. As he did, Ian reached under his ottoman for a back issue of *BA*. It, like all the publications received at this house, was addressed to J. Cromwell; the less Ian's name was associated with such matters, the better. He chuckled as he opened the magazine to a review of *The Cave Scroll Deception*.

"You know," he said, "I rather think it is a good thing the blockheads have gained such a spotlight. In time, their silliness will blow over. Meanwhile, the shakeup has taken the newsmongers off the scent of the trail."

Cromwell was astonished. "But, Father, what of the church? What of the integrity of—"

"Come, come, John," Ian interrupted. "In two thousand years nothing has prevailed against the Word of God. This sham of intellectualism is nothing new. Nothing new at all!"

Though Ian had many fine qualities, John liked this part of his priestly friend best of all. The two were of different creeds, but when it came to Scripture, Ian knew it inside out, and he knew the God of Christianity with a faith that never bowed in the face of challenge.

"You are right, of course," John said. Grabbing a hunk of the *New York Times*, he crumpled it for the fire, and Ian glanced at it thoughtfully.

"I must say, though," Ian observed, "those New Yorkers tend to give me a scare sometimes."

He took a cigar from his side table, bit off the tip, and held it close enough to an ember to light it, then put it to his lips and blew out a long breath of smoke. His mind drifting through the flames of the fresh fire, he relived one of his worst experiences as though it played on a screen before him.

"You are thinking of Father Ducharme," Cromwell surmised.

"The New York paper did not know how close it came that time," Ian replied. "Had the old fellow lived . . . well, perhaps things turned out for the best. . . . May his soul rest in peace."

John sat back and studied Ian's sad face. He knew what a harrowing few years Ian had spent with his mentor, the original master of the scroll committee, as that French scholar had destroyed himself with drink and madness.

"Never has a student loved a teacher more than you loved Ducharme," Cromwell said. "You did all you could—no one could have done more."

"But the paper was right," Ian recalled. "They guessed he went mad with some horrible burden, something he hid from the world." The priest's eyes glistened in the light of the fire, and he blinked back a tear.

Then he gave an ironic chuckle. "Such a legacy he left me! Shall I, too, go mad, John? Shall we go mad together?"

"Don't say such things!" Cromwell demanded. "Ducharme had too many weaknesses. You are stronger."

"True." Ian snorted. "I have no great need for wine or liquor, like my mentor. I have no penchant for female parishioners or for choirboys, like others I have known."

Cromwell gave a sad grin.

"No, John," Ian conceded, "I do not have those weaknesses. But to live with the revelation of the infernal scroll is enough. I think it was enough to produce Ducharme's madness!"

At this, John jerked violently. "Enough, Ian!" he exclaimed. "You are my employer, but you are also my friend. I will not have you tormenting yourself with things that will never come to pass, secrets whose finding out is as likely as . . ."

A long, deathly silence passed between them. The fire crackled, rising up in images of unspeakable misery and annihilation.

"As likely as the Holocaust?" Ian offered.

Cromwell shuddered. Sinking back into his chair, he put his hand to his lips and spoke no more.

"I must tell you," the priest muttered. "I am not afraid of the journalists *or* the conspiracy theorists. There are others, others more resourceful, more motivated than any hack writer. They are on a quest to fulfill their God-given destiny, and their quest requires my secret."

At this, he opened to the back of the old *BA* he had retrieved from beneath the ottoman. Pointing to a small classified ad buried on the last page, he handed it to his friend.

"If you doubt me, see here," he said.

"*Committee of Orthodox rabbis seeking Jewish archaeologist with background in linguistics for sensitive study. High pay and world travel guaranteed to qualified applicant. All references considered. Contact Temple Consortium, 36 Rebi Josef Street, Jerusalem.*"

The little ad was highlighted with the figure of a tiny menorah.

Cromwell's eyes went wide, the pupils large and dark. Peering over the rims of his spectacles, he asked, "You know these people?"

"I know of their work," the priest replied. "It would surprise me if they have not already found their linguist. They move very quickly when they set their minds to something."

CHAPTER 5

David's eyes felt dry as sand as he stepped from the elevator and entered the hotel's sumptuous Peacock Alley Restaurant. He had barely slept all night, poring over the maze of reading matter that his hosts had left for him.

For much of the early evening, he had been alternately fascinated by the esoteric materials and angered by what appeared to be a huge academic joke. Could it be that this entire episode was nothing more than an expensive and elaborate farce conceived by his coworkers at the university, some kind of scholarly prank to send him off on sabbatical with a gleeful "gotcha!"?

He knew better, of course. None of his coworkers had the kind of money it would take to pull off such a charade. No, the rabbis were for real. It was up to David to make some sense of the material they bestowed upon him, at least enough to ask intelligent questions in the morning.

Around midnight, he had decided to arrange the books and pamphlets in chronological order. Since the oldest volumes had no copyright dates, he had had to go by inference. This took time, since not all the writers were historians and dates seemed quite unimportant to them. He was able to deduce that many of the ancient books went back to about 1500 C.E. Some of these were written in Ladino, a blend of Spanish and Hebrew spoken by the "Sephardic" Jews living in Spain in the Middle Ages and later. Others were written in Yiddish, a blend of German and Hebrew spoken by the Jews of Eastern Europe.

Next he was able to pinpoint writings that dated close to these, encompassing nearly five centuries thereafter. To his bewilderment, the non-Hebrew texts were not Spanish, German, nor even European. These were Syrian, and full of lengthy discourses on Jewish law. The only thing they had in common with the first were long lists of genealogies.

Then there were pieces from a scholarly group in the Balkans, dating back as far as the early Renaissance, and first-century manuscripts from the famed rabbinical schools of Alexandria, Egypt.

Later writings were from the 1800s, during the rise of Zionism as a philosophy. Even more modern writers from Brooklyn, New York, and New Jersey added their two cents.

Sometime toward dawn, a theme began to emerge from the plethora of seemingly mismatched and haphazard material. While the writings spanned the gamut of history, law, and philosophy, all of them dealt directly or indirectly with the quest for one enigmatic figure. Some called him the Messiah; others distinguished him from the Messiah, referring to him as the heir to a great priesthood and calling him "high priest" of Israel.

Some volumes seemed to be repositories of that priestly ancestry, line-by-line tomes keeping account of his family tree. Others debated just what he would mean, whether he was real or symbolic, and whether he would ever exist at all.

Just before the front desk rang David's room with his wake-up call, he had lain down and fallen into a fitful sleep, replete with the smell of old paper, dried leather, images of shepherds and archaeologists and mitred priests. Like the tigers of Little Black Sambo, the cartoonish characters chased each other round and round the hotel room, until they dissolved into a buttery blur of pancakes and syrup that splattered into dawn's light when the phone rang.

Upon waking, David had a craving for flapjacks.

In a private, glassed-in dining room of the Peacock Alley Restaurant, the rabbis waited for David. Tall green plants along the crystal wall provided a screen against the bustle of customers who took seats in the main dining hall.

Rabbi Benjamin, seeing the professor had arrived, hailed him congenially, waving him into the quiet sanctum and pulling out a chair. "Good morning, Dr. Rothmeyer," he greeted, handing him the menu of strictly kosher dishes the rabbis had requested. "We trust you had a good rest."

All the hosts nodded and smiled warmly. Even Uriel Katz seemed a little less shadowy in the morning light that filtered through the room's tall windows.

David took a seat and sighed audibly. "Good morning, gentlemen," he said. "But I doubt you trust any such thing. You knew that anyone with my background would be awake all night with the stash you left me to sort through."

"Ah!" Rabbi Benjamin brightened. "You found the material interesting!"

David scowled at him and his colleagues. Leaning back, he gestured to the sumptuous surroundings. "It is obvious you are doing your best to impress me," he said, "courting me with the finest your city has to offer."

When Dr. Jacobs and Rabbi Levine only nodded proudly, David shook his head. "No, gentlemen!" he snapped. "Enough parlor games! You have had me on puppet strings for a week. Now it is my turn to ask questions."

Rabbi Benjamin grew grave. "Very well, Dr. Rothmeyer. I told you we would give you answers in time. Begin."

"Well," David said, "I know that through the night you had me on a scavenger hunt. One piece of information, if analyzed properly, could fit in with another and lead forward. But this hunt was more puzzling than most, because you never told me just what I was to look for."

The men glanced at one another, avoiding David's angry eyes.

"We gave you a clue," Dr. Jacobs said, the portly gent seeming genuinely concerned about easing David's mind. "Rabbi Ben told you to start with the pamphlet first."

David thought back. That gesture had seemed days ago.

"All right," he replied. "I'll grant that much. So you wanted me to deduce from that little bit of information that all of the material I would be reading related to this so-called 'paving the way for Messiah.'" His face flushed, he felt more the brunt of some ungodly joke than ever.

When the men only smiled quietly, he grew more agitated.

"You're not serious!" He gave a derisive laugh. "You people really think there's some great New Age about to dawn, and you want me to help you usher it in?"

Rabbi Levine jerked his hands up from the table, his long, thin face stern and corrective. "We don't use the term 'New Age.' That has the wrong implications!"

David rolled his eyes. "New Age, Golden Age, Aquarian Age . . . what's the difference? You don't really expect a scientist to take any of this seriously, do you?"

The men turned to one another and muttered quietly.

At last, Rabbi Benjamin reached out and touched David's arm. "Professor, true science does not avoid inscrutable matters. It does in fact embrace them. We hired you exactly because you *are* a scientist."

"Yes," Dr. Jacobs enthused, his round face red with ardor. "And a linguist."

"And an archaeologist!" Rabbi Levine added.

"And Jewish," Uriel Katz said somberly, his brooding eyes boring through David like those of an owl at night.

For a long moment, David was fixated upon this one man, at once fascinating and frightening.

Then Rabbi Benjamin's kind voice broke in. "Consider it all a great dig!" he said. "You may find nothing, but then again, you may come up with trowels full of treasure!"

David ripped his gaze away from Uriel Katz and shook himself. "But why?" he asked. "What is this all about? What is in it for all of you, if we learn something about this ancestry stuff and law stuff and Jewish stuff?"

Dr. Jacobs leaned forward eagerly, his ample paunch doubling over the table edge. "We will be able to build our temple!" he declared. "We will be able to build the temple that Ezekiel prophesied!"

Rabbi Benjamin hushed him and looked anxiously through the glass partition, into the main room.

"Temple?" David snorted. "Where? Jerusalem? Like . . . in the Bible? Come on! You can't be serious!"

Suddenly Uriel Katz filled David's sight. Like a cloud, the little man loomed larger, rising from his seat, pressing in close, his face directly in front of David's.

"There is nothing more serious in all the world than what we speak of, Dr. Rothmeyer! Nothing more serious for us, or for you, or"—he gestured toward the roomful of diners beyond the private chamber—"for all of humanity!"

David was stunned. Sitting back, he swallowed hard and watched mutely as Rabbi Katz sank again into his seat.

"And just what is it you want from me?" David finally managed to ask. "How do my 'talents' fit in with your quest?"

Horace Benjamin scooted close and spoke softly. "First of all, David, you must understand that we do not presume to search for the Messiah. He will come of his own accord, in his own time. What we want you to do is help us find our high priest. Without him, we have no use for a temple. Without a temple, Jerusalem is a crown without a star, the Messiah has no place from which to reign, and Israel is a dream unfulfilled!"

David stared at the rabbi mutely. From what Benjamin was saying, it seemed that if David accepted this assignment, he would be responsible for the world's future! It was more than his mind could absorb.

Flashes from his crazy nightmare darted to mind. His head fuzzy, he scanned the kosher menu. "Do they serve pancakes here?" he muttered.

CHAPTER 6

April / *Nisan*

Mel Wester settled back in the seat of his modest rental car and sped up Highway 95 out of Coeur d'Alene, Idaho. Drinking in the April green of the forested hills, he lowered the driver's window and let a sun-warmed breeze spill across him.

Just an hour ago, he had disembarked at the Spokane airport from a flight out of Los Angeles. Already he could feel the tension of twelve years on the Los Angeles police force, and the stress of five years of a high-profile legal case, easing out of his broad shoulders.

This would be the best move he ever made, he told himself. Leaving California to join his older brother, Pete, in the hills of Montana would forever change his life—might even save it.

"Should have done this long ago," he muttered, glancing at his early-forties reflection in the rearview mirror.

He passed through names on the map that had long peppered his brother's conversations.

Sandwiched between humps of rolling hills and verdant valleys, along clean rivers and lakes at the foot of tall, forested mountains, such towns as Hayden, Chilco, Athol, and off the beaten track, Rathdrum and Spirit Lake, were more than just bucolic villages. According to Mel's brother, they represented a mind-set and way of life that challenged the "sheeplike indifference of the apathetic masses."

If Pete was right, rusty junkyards and tacky R.V. parks belied the fact that deep thinkers lived here, "men and women who have clearly seen the truth of America's wretchedness and have removed themselves from it."

Oh, sure, yuppies had invaded the region, clearing forests for multi-million-dollar golf courses, erecting posh resorts with "wilderness" themes, "restoring" failed sections of the little cities into "old towns" for the marketing of "primitive art" and espresso.

"In the name of nature, they rape nature!" Mel snorted as he passed through one such restoration.

This statement was not original. He was quoting his brother. After all, who was Mel to criticize what he had accepted all his adult life? The L.A. scene was as far from "nature" as any scene could be.

But Pete had always been ahead of Mel when it came to truth seeking.

As he passed beneath the shadow of black bluffs to the west of Lake Pend Oreille and wound through dark evergreen bowers, Crosby, Stills, and Nash crooned on the radio, reminding him of his youth in Seattle, when he and Pete had decided to become hippies.

"Become yourself," the songsters implored, because the past was just a "good-bye."

Mel and Pete's parents had died a thousand deaths when the boys grew their white-blond crewcuts into braids and exchanged their button-down collars for beads.

With the encouragement of such mentors as CSN and the Grateful Dead, they had set out to abandon the establishment, donning the regalia of the counterculture, trying a little pot and marching against the war.

Then Mel had been drafted and went off to Viet Nam, serving in the final conflicts. He returned "without a conscience," Pete said, joining the L.A. police to fight all over again in the ghettos.

Pete, who had dodged the draft with a bad back incurred on the Queen Ann High School football field, had retained his integrity and carried his dropout spirit into the hills, first the Okanogan region of Northeastern Washington, and then, five years ago, the Bull River Valley of Western Montana.

Somewhere in those transitions, Pete had left off his childhood nickname and insisted on being known as "Peter," in the style of his hippie cohorts. After a while, Mel had adjusted to the new name. For years, his brother had been "Peter" to him.

Mel had noticed, however, that in the past few letters his brother had sent, he had reverted to "Pete." At first, Mel thought this was just evidence of middle-age mellowing, of a maturing comfort with his past that did not need counterculture posturing. But other things had changed in Pete's letters, and in his infrequent phone calls. Whereas Pete's antipathy toward "the establishment" in his younger years had always been pacifistic, his language was now more activist. He wrote and spoke about the government as the enemy in a way he had never done before.

No longer was there a Viet Nam to protest. Yet Pete's antipathy toward "the central bureaucracy" was more venomous than it had been even at the height of the war. And he mentioned gatherings that Mel wondered about, meetings with people who had never been pacifists and who seemed anything but hip.

Sometimes Mel wondered if Pete had become too chummy with some of the "rednecks" in the region, although he could not believe Pete would go far enough to actually befriend gun-toters.

Mel was looking forward to a life free of the violence he had known in L.A.—the race wars, the bloodshed, and the legal traps that could pin a racist rap on a good cop like himself. He would be happy, now, to live without a gun. He might learn to hunt for deer or elk, but he would never again point a gun at a fellow human being.

A prick of envy stabbed Mel's heart as he made his way farther into the outback of the Northwest. Even the names of the dirt roads that took off from the highway, disappearing into the mysteries of piney shadows and leading to overgrown, Emersonian hideaways, made him jealous: Homestead Road, Timberland Route, Remington Way, Granite Loop, Blacktail Road, Log House Way conjured up images of calming cottages and long-haired women in macramaed dresses setting up preserves from naturally grown gardens.

Mel knew it couldn't be that perfect, that utopian. Whatever the folks had here, though, it was better than what he had known, and he wondered why he had waited so long to seek it out.

Now and then, incongruous tourist traps with names like Ponderosa Condos or Big Valley B & B jolted him. An amusement park featured the Big Bear roller coaster and fake holdups by cowboy bandits on the miniature railroad that carried dazzled families through pristine groves. Eventually, though, such commercialism was less conspicuous than logging roads and real railroads. Taverns, posted as the spots "where good friends meet," replaced yuppie bistros. Horse trails through the brush were more frequent than jet trails overhead.

What seemed to Mel a peculiar blending of cultures led from billboards advertising "See the Wolf People—Gifts and Souvenirs," to a marquee announcing a Celtic harp concert; from a classy little sign pointing out an elite ski resort, to an Adopt-a-Highway marker, sponsored by a gospel mission.

Mel remembered the gospel missions in the L.A. area. Pockets of reprieve on hopeless streets, they served an admirable purpose, and although the cops trusted the managers to help them make a dent in the crime scene, the missions were also sad reminders of the depths to which men could sink, and the long way up they had to climb.

Mel wanted to be away from all that, never to return.

Somewhere near the Montana border, as the sun was beginning to sink and the heavens began to spread out in that phenomenon known as "the Big Sky," all vestiges of blatant commercialism seemed to fall away. Southeast, along Highway 200, which followed the Clark Fork River down the west side of the state, teepee burners—the smokestacks of shingle mills—spiked the sky, the only human counterpart to the tall tamaracks that graced the skyline. Wildhorse Saloon, Hoot Owl Saloon, and a dozen other such establishments sat alongside little chapels and Jehovah's Witness Kingdom Halls in the small burgs that dotted the road. Solar-paneled houses and earth berm holdovers from the back-to-the-earth movement of the seventies sat alongside roads like Deer Hoof, Moose Jaw, and Hope Route.

Montana was the only state in the union where, instead of "60" or even "65 Miles Per Hour," speed limit signs said "Reasonable and Prudent."

The wild west is alive and well, Mel thought, grinning to himself.

Yet, in this land of the independent cowboy, folks were savvy enough to use the government to their advantage. On the edge of one town, a ranch-style house sported a cage door on its garage. "This Pet Cougar Protected by Federal Law," a sign warned.

That sign was one of the markers Pete had told Mel to watch for. About a mile after that, the highway would bridge the Bull River, where it met the Clark Fork. Just before the town of Noxon, an unmarked road would take off from the highway east into the hills of the Kootenai National Forest. "I'll tie a red bandanna to a tree where you're supposed to turn," Pete had said. "It's a dirt road. Hit it before sundown, or you'll get lost before you reach the house."

Once, when Pete had lived in the Okanogan, he had given Mel similar instructions. He had been living in a wigwam at the time, as he built a stone house without benefit of power tools, deep in the sagebrush hills. On his one and only visit from L.A., Mel had indeed gotten lost. Had it not been for a kindhearted hippie who had come rumbling by in a VW bus, Mel might have spent the night with the rattlesnakes.

This time, he was running ahead of the sun. He would make it up the rugged road just in time for dinner. At the thought of the meal his brother would set out, his mouth salivated.

Pete's "significant other," Honey, who had been with him ever since his Okanogan days, had split a few months ago. Pete had not gone into the reasons why. But the couple, while not strict vegetarians, had learned together the marvels of homegrown gardens, herbs, and real nutrition. Even Mel, who had to have meat with every meal, came to admit that wonders could be worked with yogurt and tofu.

The red bandanna was tied to a white birch on a road between the Naughty Pine Tavern and a cute, cabin-style Baptist church. The narrow, bumpy road that cut a swath between dark woods became barely more than a trail as it ascended Cricket Creek. At last, a couple of crook-necked turns brought the rental car out of the woods onto a slope of ground that lay like an open palm before the house of Peter Wester.

"Good grief!" Mel sighed, as he saw the place for the first time. It was beautiful! And his brother, who earned a decent living as a freelance carpenter, had built it with his own hands.

A spacious log house, graced by a broad front porch, it was a true work of art. The big roof, which came down over the porch in a sweep of hand-hewn shingles, sported dormers for the loft Pete had told him about.

"You'll sleep there," he had promised, "like you've never slept before."

"It's quiet, huh?" Mel had asked.

"It's so quiet you can hear the quiet," Pete had bragged.

The porch posts were as elaborate as any machine-turned columns. They were each made from a single, twisted log, with gnarls and burls that looked like totem faces. Mel remembered Pete's letter, telling how he and Honey had hiked into the woods day after day, looking for just the right tree trunks for those pillars. When they had found six, they had called friends together to help them haul them to the house site, and with a big party, they had celebrated their placement.

Mel had not heard mention of those particular friends for some time. He wondered if they had moved away or if Pete just didn't see them anymore.

Stopping his car on the grassy slope, he turned off the motor and breathed in the quiet.

Soon, the quiet was outdone by an even better sound. Pete was on the porch, calling his baby brother's name. "Hey, Mel, ol' buddy! Welcome to the Promised Land!"

CHAPTER 7

Spring in the Montana hills brought cool evenings. Pete Wester grabbed a padded flannel shirt off a hook by his front door and bounded off the porch to greet his brother.

Though they were two years apart, the men were twin-like, with their husky builds and white-blond hair. Tall and muscular, they were distinguishable primarily by dress and hairstyles: Mel in citified slacks and sweater, his hair cropped close, while Pete, in jeans and plaid, still wore his hair long and tied back with red string.

The main mark of Pete's transition from pure hippiedom to the Montana outback was his new footwear. Whereas he used to wear sandals, he now wore cowboy boots, much more practical in the hills.

"How's the refugee from the asphalt jungle?" he asked with a smile, tiny crow's-feet about his eyes the only sign of aging in his youthful face. The two men enjoyed a brisk hug, and Pete took Mel's suitcase from the backseat.

"Good to be here!" Mel admitted.

"Come on!" Pete said, as Mel hung back, studying the trees and the sunset sky. Like a stained-glass dome, the red-pink glow hung over dark green spires.

"Gorgeous!" Mel said.

"Sure! But there'll be plenty of nights just like it. Supper's waiting."

The log house was as warm and inviting as Mel had imagined. His brother's craftsmanship gleamed in every cabinet, every rafter. With a sweep of his eyes, Mel tried to absorb it. A grand rock fireplace filled the entire south wall. Though it was April, the crisp mountain air called for a fire, and a small blaze glowed on the grate. The wood hues of the room were complemented by colorful Indian blankets draped over the loft rail and braided rugs on the floor, lending further warmth.

"Braided rugs!" Mel exclaimed. "In L.A., we don't see those even in antique shops."

Pete spoke softly. "They're not antiques. Honey made them."

Mel detected the sadness in his brother's tone and knew it was not the time to ask about her. "Something smells good," he said instead.

The kitchen was open to view, taking up the north end of the big room. A hallway led toward a pantry and another smaller porch in the back.

Between the kitchen and the fireplace, a steep set of half-log stairs led to the loft, which, Pete had told him, was divided into two bedrooms, with a bathroom in between. Filtering through the log posts of the banister, the glow of sunset descended through the front dormers.

The only other illumination was from oil lamps. Electricity, which was supplied only by a generator, was used sparingly, and none was in evidence that night.

Mel was glad he had sold off his few sticks of furniture and his Spartan kitchen supplies before coming here. Pete's home was fully equipped, and nothing Mel could have contributed would have been worthy of the place.

The ex-cop had arrived with literally all his worldly goods in his rental car: a few books, photo albums, and mementos in boxes, and a suitcase full of clothes. His old beat-up car had died, just before he left L.A.—a symbol, he had thought, that it was time to leave everything behind.

Pete bounded up the stairs with Mel's only suitcase. "I'll just set this on your bed. Make yourself at home. We can unload the boxes after supper."

Mel wandered past the dining area where a huge pine table was set for two. An old matte-black cookstove, the kind with shiny nickel decorations, warmed the north end of the house, radiating enough heat to take the edge off the chilly spring night.

Atop the stove, one huge kettle bubbled, and Mel, potholder in hand, lifted the lid. A savory steam escaped, and Mel made out hunks of colorful vegetables and potatoes simmering in a ruddy broth, with only a few pieces of meat for flavoring.

"Elk," Pete said, joining him. "I try to get one a year, and it makes enough for . . . well, more than enough for just me."

That was a comfortable cue to Mel that he could ask about Honey. Pete ladled up two big bowls of stew, and the men took seats on the table's split-log benches.

"Must be kind of lonely here without your lady," he said.

Pete dunked a piece of homemade wheat bread in his bowl and held it between his fingers a moment before taking a bite. "Sure, it can get that way. I keep busy."

"What happened?" Mel asked directly. "I thought you two would be together forever."

Pete shrugged, avoiding Mel's gaze. "I guess she got spooked."

"What?" Mel asked, wondering if he had heard right.

Pete chewed on the bread and swallowed hard. Aimlessly stirring his stew with his soup spoon, he appeared to try to look casual. "There's plenty of time to talk about these things," he hedged. Then rolling his eyes toward his brother, "What about you? Any more trouble from that case in L.A.?"

Mel took a bite of stew. "I think I kept you updated," he said. "I was vindicated. But five years of legal hassle and death threats took it out of me."

Flashes of the scene in the streets that had nearly cost Mel his life, let alone his job and reputation, swept over him even now. Never would he forget the call that came that evening, the last night he worked the force on a regular beat. A small all-night market in a Watts neighborhood, one of the most notorious black ghettos in L.A., had been held up. A routine incident, he and his partner figured.

They had not expected that one of them would die in an ensuing scuffle outside the market.

Surrounded by a group of foul-mouthed ruffians, the officers drew their weapons. Most of the boys backed off, but one of them, high on crack, made a lunge, knifing Mel's partner in the kidney. Jorey Evans, the finest cop in the racially torn city, had not lived to see morning, dying in the E.R. of the Angel of Mercy Hospital.

Mel had not been able to be at his side when he died, as he had stayed behind when the ambulance left, interviewing witnesses and writing up the necessary reports. That fact alone had been enough to ruin Mel's sleep for months. But it was his own eyewitness account that nearly cost him his own life.

It was customary for one white and one black cop to work the Watts beats. Jorey Evans had been a great officer and had built good relations, as far as they could be built, with the people of the streets. Mel had believed that everyone involved in the event that night, including his partner, was African-American, and he had written in his report that a young black man had wielded the death instrument.

When the case went to trial, however, the issue was not over whether or not the suspect in question had actually wielded the knife, but whether or not the report was trustworthy. After all, the defense lawyers argued, Billy Olivera, the defendant, was predominantly Chicano, not black. If Mel Wester could not report an ethnic identity correctly, how could he report a murder correctly?

By the time the trial came to court, all other witnesses had retracted their statements, undoubtedly frightened by threats from the neighborhood ganglords. Mel knew how that felt. He had received more than his share of the same threats from the same hoods. What the ganglords had not counted on was Mel's depth of devotion to his fallen comrade. If he had to die in the process, he would not give up his fight against the killer of his best friend.

Shaking away the awful images of that night, Mel focused again on his brother. "I guess I'm just lucky I never went through something like the Rodney King case, or"—he snickered—"the O.J. trial."

Then, remembering his brother's efforts in behalf of civil rights in their hippie days, he quickly added, "Don't get me wrong. I think those bozos were way out of line. Kicking the life out of a guy—they were no better than the street gangs! And that investigator on the Simpson case—wow! A smart cop doesn't use racial slurs. He deserved getting kicked off the LAPD."

Pete, who had seemed less than intrigued by Mel's comments, suddenly sat up straight. "You mean the detective who got shafted by Judge Ito?" he asked. "Did you know he moved to Idaho?"

"Yeah," Mel replied, wondering if Pete took pride in the fact. "I also heard the people of Sandpoint didn't want him."

Pete sank back, and Mel couldn't read him.

For a long while, silence passed between the two brothers. Mel could taste the awkwardness as easily as he could taste the stew. *What is going on?* he wondered. Had Pete changed so much that they couldn't even talk?

"Hey, bro," Mel said. "For years you gave me no end of grief for being a cop. Do I detect some kind of admiration toward that racist fuzz?"

Pete removed his napkin from his lap and set it on the table, then rose and began clearing the dishes.

His silence was disconcerting, but Mel did not press the issue. Instead, returning to a previous subject, he asked, "So, what about Honey? What did you mean, she got 'spooked'?"

Pete stood at the sink, his back to Mel. At last, he turned around and faced him squarely. But once again he ignored the direct inquiry.

"You've come to the right place, baby brother," he said. "This is the 'last best place,' you know. And not just because we escape things here."

Mel listened respectfully. He knew this part of his brother, this serious side, this pedantic side. He had been on the receiving end of many a lecture through the years, about social ills, war, poverty, racial injustice, and the right way to live. He was ready now to hear it again. Whatever Pete had to say, he felt it would be worth hearing.

He did not know that this time it would scare him. Always before, Pete's lectures had pricked his conscience or made him rethink his life, even make drastic moves, like this one to Montana.

Never before had Pete's opinions made him recoil.

"We don't just escape things here," Pete was saying. "Not me, not my friends, not anymore. We have not just removed ourselves from the wicked world. We are now prepared to do something about the wickedness!"

"Prepared?" Mel said. "How so?"

Pete came closer and leaned on the table, his fists pressing down like axeheads. "By first being aware of the enemy," he said, peering deep into Mel's blue eyes. "By not being so naive as we have been. By not believing that there are no such things as classes or good wars or races."

A shiver went through Mel. He was not sure what all this meant, but he did not like the sound or the feel of it.

At last, he swallowed and managed to ask once more, "What spooked Honey? Why did she leave?"

Pete stood up straight and looked out the window, in the direction of the road which could not be seen and the highway that led to the outer world.

"Have you ever heard of Ruby Ridge?" he asked.

CHAPTER 8

Peter Wester stood on the cedar deck of his log home, a steaming cup of coffee in hand, and breathed deeply of the cool morning air. The sky over the Bull River Valley was vivid blue and cloudless where it stretched between the cathedral-like grove that covered his acreage. He watched the sky for a moment, hoping that the old bald eagle would appear again, the one he'd seen a hundred times since moving there five years ago.

In the house, his brother enjoyed a deep sleep, and would probably not set foot out of the loft for at least another hour. Pete had not had the heart to tell Mel that their solitude and the quiet of the retreatlike grounds would be broken in a couple of days.

Before Mel had left Los Angeles, Pete had been notified that the committee might need his house for a "gathering." Pete had attended such events in Idaho. He knew they usually came together quickly, people involved in the network being notified sometimes only hours beforehand. He had not known for sure that the "gathering" at his house was a go until Mel was on his way to Montana.

Maybe it was providential that his brother had arrived at this time, Pete thought. Meeting his new connections might be the best way for Mel's education to begin. After all, Big Brother Pete carried only so much weight with Mel. There were things the ex-cop would need to learn from other sources.

The tall, Nordic-looking Westers were stubborn fellows. They had come to blows more than once as youths. In their late teens, they had seen eye to eye on most things, but Mel had always been less comfortable with the revolutionary scene than Pete had.

When Mel went to Viet Nam and then became a cop, Pete had nearly given up on him. Still, the two were fast friends, and Pete knew it would take more than politics to truly separate them. Now that Mel had moved to Montana, Pete hoped he would hear him out on his newest beliefs, accept his latest comrades and give them a chance.

Actually, the tenets of Pete's current faith were not so new. They had been growing in him for a long time, and when he analyzed them, it seemed that, although they involved tolerance of a more militaristic mind-set than he would have once embraced, they were the ultimate outgrowth of his hippie days.

He grinned sardonically. When he thought about it in light of Mel's arrival, he realized that his new views actually embraced many of the things he used to criticize his brother for espousing.

Pete walked out on the grass, and after placing his coffee cup on a low rock wall bordering a flower bed, he stretched in the sunlight. His azure eyes mirroring the heavens, he watched for the eagle but kept his ears pricked for the sound of a radio on the front porch, the ham radio that was, apart from a small transistor Walkman, the only technological connection he allowed himself with the outside world.

When he had first met the folks who would be coming to his house, their leader, Jim Fogarty, had been pleased to learn he was a ham operator. Fogarty had used him many times as a relayer for messages to and from members of the brotherhood in distant places.

Usually, the voices on the ham radio were American, but some had foreign accents. The messages were often a jumble of code words. Pete had tried to decipher the code, for his own curiosity, but had never been able to figure out more than a few phrases. He had never asked questions, though. He respected Fogarty and felt rather privileged that, when the leader was in the area, he used the house as headquarters.

A few days ago, an Irish-sounding voice had told him to expect a message today. It was supposed to come before ten A.M. He hoped it would come before Mel got up. He preferred to take the message in private.

Sitting down on the rock wall, he sipped his cup of coffee and studied Honey's outdoor handiwork. She had landscaped the yard. He wished she were here to give it the feminine touch. He tried to keep up the flowers, but they didn't do so well without her.

As the coffee-cup's steam drifted into the cool air, so, too, did Pete's thoughts drift to Honey. Nothing did so well without her, he admitted.

Suddenly the radio emitted a garbled bunch of static. Pete lurched, spilling his coffee. He darted across the lawn, fumbled with the headset, placed it quickly over his ears, then picked up the microphone.

"Cricket, here," he said, giving the code name that referred to his location on the nearby creek. "Over."

The static was thick. That could indicate either bad weather somewhere in transit or radio interference from anywhere on the globe.

Even when the voice became clear enough for Pete to make out, it was an odd one. Not only was it obviously foreign, the accent recognizably Middle Eastern, but it had a raspy, grating quality, not accountable to bad transmission.

Between bouts of interference, Pete could make out several of the code words that had become familiar. "Eagle-eye" was one, and "happening" was another.

Pete had heard these terms often enough to figure that, in context, they meant, "This message is for Fogarty." Eagle-eye was Fogarty's code name.

The next terms, however, were a mystery: "Relay to Swastika. Bailey's Bug is a go."

Strange, Pete thought. *What in the world could that mean?*

As he listened to the coarsely spoken phrases, he scribbled them quickly on a piece of note paper. The riddle in combination with the unforgettable voice gave him the heebie-jeebies.

The last line of the message added to the mystery: "Cedars ready to drop on Shekinah."

Pete hastily wrote it down, then heard, "Over—out," followed by loud static.

As he sat pondering the scribbled notes, the bald eagle he had awaited came swooping out of the mountains and circled on soft currents over the property.

"Eagle-eye happening," Pete muttered, a chill working down his spine at the thought of the voice.

Suddenly a sound from the house caught him off guard. Mel had come downstairs and was standing in the front doorway.

Pete shook himself and quickly put the message in the pocket of his flannel plaid shirt. Standing up, he feigned sunny cheerfulness. "Heckuva morning, huh, bro?" he greeted. "How 'bout some scrambled eggs?"

CHAPTER 9

Spring brought a different sort of beauty to the Holy City, Jerusalem, than it did to the hills of western Montana.

David Rothmeyer had never anticipated that he would spend a spring in Israel. Of course, when he had committed to working with the Temple Consortium six months earlier, his university colleagues having accepted his application for earned leave, he had not anticipated any of the strange twists and turns his life had taken since.

But here he was, in the capital of Judaism—the capital, in fact, of three world faiths—and the international hub of contentious politics.

The fact that, three days ago, Arab suicide bombers had set off explosions at the busiest intersection in the city, killing themselves and several civilians including tourists, was testimony to the perpetual strife that flared over every inch of Israel's soil, and over Jerusalem in particular.

The Holy Land had been contended for by the children of Abraham, today's Arabs and Jews, since the days of the patriarch, each claiming the right of inheritance. Jerusalem, its spiritual and geographical capstone, was the most highly prized gem and was the central focus of Muslim and Jewish jealousy.

Then, since the time of Jesus, it had been the faith-heritage of Christians the world over, and no end of bloodshed, in the name of the cross, had occurred on its soil.

David strode down one of the narrow streets of the Jewish Quarter this bright April morning. A bag of hot bagels dangled from one hand, and he gripped a stack of file folders with the other.

He was learning, after half a year here, that life in this strife-torn city had a way of going on with amazing normalcy, despite confrontations. He might have been walking across the campus in Columbus, Ohio, carrying a pile of lecture notes and grade sheets, and balancing a cinnamon roll picked up at the Student Union Building. But he had developed a taste for bagels since coming to Israel, and he was not presently teaching classes at Midwest.

He was mentally preparing, however, for an academic presentation.

He hurried to the cloisterlike apartment that the rabbis had reserved for him in a wonderful old house that had become his home away from home. His employers were to meet him there in a few minutes, having flown in from New York to look in on him and see how he was progressing with his assignment.

He had been up since dawn, getting ready for the meeting, thinking through just how he would explain the steps he had taken in his research and what the results had been. An hour in an open-air coffee shop had been a welcome reprieve, but even there he had pored over notes and outlines. There was no more time for preparation.

The yellow-white rock of the Old City pavement was already warm with morning sun. Palm trees threw stripe-like shadows across the awnings of little shops as he rushed by. Jerusalem was all abloom with flowers that did not grow in Ohio, succulents and poppies that would have been more at home in the California hills.

David's work had not allowed him much time to admire the city. The reading material that the rabbis had provided in the Waldorf-Astoria hotel room had been shipped to Jerusalem along with the professor. It had taken him months to go through the material and to make enough sense of it to produce an outline of the contents.

The rabbis had sufficiently explained their goals so that he knew what to look for and what questions they were trying to resolve. What he had not realized, however, was just how involved his research would be, until he saw that the building in which he lived was the repository of an enormous library of such books.

If he had been asked to provide a description of his job, he would have had to say that he was like a scribal monk, secluded in a stone building, writing and researching night and day. He was no prisoner, but he was not permitted to call his colleagues back home or to share what he was learning with anyone outside the select circle from New York.

Sometimes he resented his isolation. But Israel, as far as he had observed it, was a fascinating place, and no one was holding him against his will. Besides, he had been hooked the night he was left alone with the old books in the New York hotel.

His suite of rooms was part of an ancient house located along the southern wall of the Old City, the central portion of Jerusalem that bore the most history. The wall against which the house was built was a conglomeration of stones from several periods—Crusader, Byzantine, and along the lowest layers, rubble from the days of Herod and the Romans. Often, when David approached the place, he was transported back in time, as he wondered what stories the stones could tell if they could speak.

The house, which was also the residence for the Temple Consortium, bore no sign over the entry. The path that led to it veered off one of the narrower streets. Several stone steps led to a barred gate. Vegetation concealed most of the building from the view of passersby. In fact, it would be easy to miss its presence altogether, if one were not looking for it.

The first time David had come here it was with Rabbi Benjamin, who had accompanied him to Israel to help him get settled.

"This house dates to the time of the Crusades," the rabbi had told him. "Of course, the invaders simply built upon the rubble of the city they overran, so the foundations probably go back much further, as is true of most places in the Old City. You will be living with the ghosts of millennia past," he said, with a wink.

Now holding the bag of bagels in his teeth, David took out the key he kept in his pocket, opened the gate, and let it swing back with an antiquarian creak. He had learned the hard way always to lock it behind him. One evening a bunch of street kids had entered the yard, tearing up the flowers so lovingly tended by Anya, the immigrant housekeeper.

Anya, a plump and pleasant old woman, had recently arrived in Israel from Russia. For a time, she had made her way by playing a violin on Ben Yehuda Street, where the terrorists had set off the recent bombs. She spoke only a smattering of English and a rough version of Hebrew. The rabbis considered her no threat to their business and, because she knew how to cook kosher, hired her to keep the place.

David rarely conversed with her, other than to praise her for the sweet Russian breads she was fond of presenting him after a day of baking in the antique kitchen.

He opened the front door, a tall thick slab composed of half a dozen cedar boards and fitted with heavy iron straps. Like the gate, it moved with a groan of age, and David stepped into the cool sanctum of the lobby.

David had grown quite fond of the strange old house, which was more like a series of ascending caves than a man-made building.

As were all the rooms of the house, the entryway was furnished with massive antiques—a coat rack, a side table with a beveled mirror, and heavy straight-backed chairs that looked as if they could have been brought overseas by the Crusaders.

David tossed his keys on the sideboard and took the next steps three at a time, rushing to his apartment up a winding corridor that was a series of stairs and landings leading past the parlor, the kitchen, and several private rooms. Passing a large vaulted chamber lined with books on shelves that reached to the ten-foot ceiling, he stopped short.

To his dismay, he could hear voices coming from his suite, the last one in the house. Making the final turn up the stone hallway, he jockeyed his bagels and files under one arm while he smoothed his breeze-blown hair and straightened his rumpled shirt, recalling with chagrin that he had not changed it since yesterday.

If you aren't the epitome of the absent-minded professor! his wife used to tease him.

Placing his hand on the door's handle, he took a deep breath, then entered the apartment.

His friends—for indeed, some degree of trust had grown between them—sat around a table in the front room of the suite. Spread out on the tabletop was a roll of paper, composed of several smaller sheets taped end to end. The roll was so long that it ran onto the floor in overlapping waves.

The men, intent on studying the paper and talking excitedly among themselves, did not hear David come in.

Clearing his throat, he greeted them. "Rabbis! I guess I'm tardy for class!"

Looking up, they returned his greeting, and Horace Benjamin rose to meet him. Of the four men, Horace was David's favorite, and the two shook hands warmly.

"Professor!" Benjamin said. "Welcome. My colleagues and I have been looking at your work. We are amazed at your accomplishments!"

"Yes, I see you have been reading the chart," David noted, placing the files and the bag of bagels on the sofa. "Can you interpret my scrawls? My wife always said I should have been a medical doctor, my handwriting is so bad."

Dr. Jacobs chuckled at this. "Well, I for one am used to interpreting such scrawls, as you say. It is the science of your work that is truly gratifying."

David stepped up to the table and surveyed his handiwork with a flush of unconcealed pride. "I guess I have been busy, haven't I?" he said.

Upon the wide ribbon of paper David had drawn a chart. One long line ran across the top, composed of dates going back into antiquity on the left, and up nearly to the present toward the right. Below this, a complex series of lines looking like trees spread across the pages, a veritable forest of branches. Upon each branch was a name, and each branch connected to other branches, down to the trunks where yet other names were recorded. Probably one hundred of these trees made up the chart. The trunks, branches, and most of the names had been filled in with black pencil, although each tree also contained names written in red. Some of these red names were connected horizontally through time by another line, which was also red.

David had made such charts before, though never anything this detailed, when he had traced pottery styles or other artifact types on time lines. Such tools were used in archaeology to unravel the history of a culture or to see its inter-relatedness to other groups, as represented in its handicrafts.

But this chart did not deal in pottery styles. This chart dealt in human names. Family names.

The effect of the dark red line across the expansive charcoal forest was that of a bloody ribbon, a stream of blood on a background of history.

And in truth, it *was* a bloodline.

As David traced his finger across the crimson strand, the men pressed in close about him, Rabbi Benjamin and Dr. Jacobs almost blocking his view, while Dr. Levine and Rabbi Katz leaned from the far side for a better look.

Their bushy beards and side-curls dangled on the paper, and they adjusted their spectacles, taking it all in with wonder.

Nearly breathless, they asked the silent question.

"Yes," David said, "this is the Cohen line. To the best of my knowledge thus far, all the records you have given me play out this way."

As they all knew, the name "Cohen," and its many cognates, were derivatives of the name "Kohath," the patriarch from whom Moses and his brother, Aaron, were descended. From the time that Aaron was installed as high priest of Israel, his male descendants, through his firstborn son, were set apart for priestly duties. They came to be called the "Kohathites," or "Kohanim."

Any quest for a legitimate heir to the high priesthood must follow that line, which in modern times was called the "Cohens."

The rabbis let out a collective sigh, like men who had gazed on the contents of a royal tomb or who had just lifted the lid on a treasure chest.

"So," Rabbi Benjamin said, "the records are incredibly intricate. To think, our people have kept their genealogies this perfectly!"

"The *Cohen* people," Rabbi Katz interjected. "Not every Jewish family can claim as much."

"Of course, of course," Dr. Levine muttered. "But what race of people has survived the centuries and the vagaries of history like the Jews?"

"Yes—*all* the Jews!" Dr. Jacobs asserted. "It may be true that the Cohens—including the esteemed Katzes," he said with a bite, "have been more particular. But the mere fact that the Jewish people still exist at all is a wonder!"

Rabbi Katz only crossed his arms and rolled his eyes.

"Gentlemen," Benjamin said, "this is no time for the eternal quarrel. Let's keep peace for now."

But Rabbi Katz was only more piqued. "Let us hope the quarrel is not eternal," he spat. "Did we not hire Professor Rothmeyer just so the contest would be resolved, once and for all?"

Horace Benjamin drew back and blew softly through pursed lips. "Must you see all this as a contest, Uriel? Is it not God's will we are seeking, and not the glory of some human bloodline?"

At this, Katz looked aside, avoiding Benjamin's eyes. But his pride was still evident by his clenched fist.

David took all this in silently. Always it was like this, when the rabbis came to visit: little squabbles and power struggles that led nowhere. After witnessing several such interludes he surmised that Katz was greatly invested in the outcome of his studies.

David realized, not only from his recent research, but from his Jewish upbringing, that there were many names related to the line of the Kohanim, or the Cohens. "Katz" was one of them, being a contraction for two words: Kohen, meaning priest, and Zadok, meaning righteous, rather like "Kodak," of camera fame.

Uriel Katz apparently had reason to believe he had a greater stake in the findings of this study than that of other people with his rather common surname.

Actually, it was not impossible that Dr. Levine, being in the line of the Levites, the priestly tribe from which Aaron and his brother Moses were descended, could potentially be in the line of the high priest. Even Dr. Jacobs, being lumped with the patriarchy of Jacob, who was the original "Israel" and who was the father of *all* the Jewish tribes, could potentially be of the same lineage.

However, since their names were part of broader branches, and were not specifically Cohen, they apparently had less at stake in the outcome.

As for kindly old Rabbi Benjamin, there was no possibility that he was in the priestly line. The tribe of Benjamin was distinct from that of Levi and had never had a priestly function. Perhaps this helped him to maintain his objectivity and to fulfill the role of moderator, with which he seemed to be invested.

Actually, as far as David could see at this time, the possibility that Katz, let alone the others, might be in the true high priestly line was no greater than it would be for any one of the millions of Cohens throughout the world. But David had been hired to narrow down the search, and he had spent the past six months working toward that goal.

Despite their ongoing sparring matches, the men seemed to be pleased with his work.

Benjamin, in an effort to redirect their attention, perused the chart again. The long red line, which connected the various historical segments, was not a continuous strand. Here and there, large gaps showed up, before the line resumed again and went on in relative wholeness for years at a time.

"As we would expect, there may be places where the chart can never be complete," Benjamin observed. "The gaps come exactly where they must be."

"Yes," David said, pointing to a vague area dated around the sixth century B.C.E. "The period of the Babylonian Captivity, for instance, is a hazy one, although copies of scribal records brought back by the returning exiles have helped somewhat."

Passing his hand to the right, David pulled the paper and smoothed out a section from the eleventh century C.E., and following. "There is also quite a set of discrepancies that arises in the period of the Middle Ages. I am sure most Jewish scholars, yourselves included, are aware of the ethnic split."

Katz stiffened, and the others looked at one another knowingly.

"You speak of the social division between the Sephardic and Ashkenazic families," Benjamin surmised.

Again, Katz tensed. "Far more than *social* division!" he exclaimed. "We Jews divided along every imaginable line: political, religious, scholarly . . ."

David sensed another debate coming. Intervening, he stopped it before it flared. "Gentlemen," he said, "I do not know what issues divide you, but my job would go easier if you brought cooperation to our meetings, rather than constant quarrels."

The men quieted, and David tried to bring them together. "Regardless of your individual roots, you are all scholars," he said. "Now . . . shall we proceed?"

Directing them again to the paper, he pointed to the area nearest the end. "Of course, we all know that the Holocaust of this century caused monumental losses to the recordkeeping of our people. I do not know how you wish for me to address that issue. I have really done nothing with it, to this point."

Rabbi Benjamin nodded. "We have much to tell you about work in that arena," he said. "For now, are there other periods you wish to point out to us?"

David moved the paper again so that the generations nearest the Roman period were on the table.

"Here is one of the most difficult sections," he said, pointing to the first century. "As would be expected, following the destruction of Jerusalem in 70 C.E., during the great Dispersion, there is a lot of information missing."

Then, gesturing to the back wall of his parlor, he reminded them of the books they had provided. "I was able to find some help from the records of the Jabnians, of the first century."

A look of grave concern clouded the professor's face. "Despite those clues," he said, "it will take keys of information, which I am not sure we will ever find, to legitimize the rest of the line."

The rabbis hung on his words.

"What I am saying, gentlemen," David explained, "is that, up until 70 C.E., when the temple was destroyed, we can pretty much accept that the Jews had done their homework. We will probably never find records any better than what they had, to fill gaps existing at that time—such as the Babylonian period. When they installed a high priest, unless they were capitulating to some outside pressure, they went by the best records known, records that we will not be able to top."

Rabbi Benjamin nodded. "There were, of course, spurious installations during the time of the Hasmoneans."

"And later, during the Roman occupation," Rabbi Levine said. "Anything to please Caesar."

"That's right," David said. "We can see this in the broken lines around the time that Annas and Caiaphas were the temple chieftains. Always, there were those who maintained the true records, and sometimes impostors were deposed."

"Very well," Rabbi Katz said, anxious to move on. "We are aware of this. So, what you are saying is that the gap we must be most concerned with comes around the time of the temple's destruction. Up until then, we must rely on the wisdom of the genealogists of the day."

"I think we can do no better," David said.

Dr. Jacobs jumped in. "And, after that time, without a good record of the first century, anything we deduce must be held in question."

David crossed his arms and studied the men carefully. "I guess you answered that when you first contacted me. If you felt you could trust tradition from the time of the Dispersion, you never would have hired me."

At this, he began to roll up the scroll, again toward the time of the temple's destruction. "In fact," he said, "you probably could have saved me a lot of time and energy by having me trace the line from 70 C.E. on, and leaving the first half to history. You surely knew that the only real controversy arises after that point."

Rabbi Benjamin smiled sheepishly. With a shrug, he turned his palms upward. "You have us there, David."

"So," the professor said with a half-smile. "This has been a test? I suspected as much. Well, it's your money, gentlemen. Pay me for wasted effort, if you will."

"Wasted?" Rabbi Levine marveled. "Surely not, David! No study of our past is wasted! Besides, how did we know but what you would turn up something new?"

David shrugged. "Okay. Let's get back to the record." He placed a finger at a point on the scroll. "There was a lot of controversy going on for two hundred years or more before the fall of Jerusalem," he said. "The split in the records is phenomenal!"

Again, the men bent close, gathering around the paper. David observed them closely. The factious splits that preceded the Roman invasion were familiar to the scholars.

Rabbi Benjamin looked at David inquiringly, his bright eyes studying him with keen interest. "This is the time of the great division in the temple administration. Have you read much about the Essenes, Dr. Rothmeyer?"

"Those were the fellows at Qumran," David replied. "I suppose everyone has heard of the Cave Scrolls. Of course, I came across many references to them in my study here."

Katz jumped in. "Then you may know that the temple priesthood came under sharp criticism at that time. In fact, the people of Qumran may have been disgruntled priests themselves, who left the sanctuary because of the corruptions they witnessed."

David nodded. "That is one of the theories. It might explain their apocalyptic views, the insistence that the world was divided between the Sons of Light and the Sons of Darkness, and that a great war would soon be waged between the sides."

"Well, for our purposes," Dr. Jacobs offered, "there was undoubtedly a huge dispute over which priests were legitimate and which were impostors."

David rubbed his chin. With a shrug, he said, "There certainly are confusions in the genealogical records of that time. As to direct references to the heir to the priesthood, however, I found nothing in any of the quotations from the Qumran scrolls."

At this comment, the men glanced at one another furtively. David perceived, in the thick, awkward silence, that they wished they could say something but dared not.

"What is it?" he asked. "Have I hit on something?"

Benjamin hedged. "There may, or there may not, be such references."

A chill worked across David's shoulders. He realized, now, that they knew much more than he did, and he felt like a mouse between the paws of four cats.

Drawing back from the table, he scrutinized them with sparking eyes. "Now, hold on!" he said angrily. "What kind of game are you playing? You obviously know something that I do not—something essential to my work. If I thought you had nothing better to do, I could believe that you took me away from the university as part of some perverse need to toy with a stranger! Before I go another step, I want you to come clean with me!"

Dr. Jacobs and Rabbi Levine glanced covertly at one another, and Katz cleared his throat. Gesturing to the sitting area of David's parlor, Benjamin directed everyone to find a chair.

When they were seated the old fellow took a long breath, blew it out softly, then began speaking. "Of course, as you surmise, there are things we know from years of dealing with these matters that you could never have known. You have quite accurately deduced that what is essential to our goals is information from the Temple period. Yes—the time of the Essenes and other radical groups who asserted that the priesthood was corrupt."

David sensed a pronouncement coming, but when the rabbi was only silent, he knew he must prompt him. "Let me guess," he said, half in jest, "we are on the prowl for some mysterious lost scroll. Ah! A story for the tabloids! 'Secret Jewish Group Discovers Genealogy of Christ in Desert Cave.'"

But the rabbis did not laugh.

Dr. Jacobs, his usually good-natured face tensing with soberness, stared at David from across the sitting room. "You do not know how close you come to the truth," he said. "We do not seek the Messiah's bloodline, but we seek the next best thing. And, yes, there is the distinct possibility that there is a scroll—probably from Qumran—that will give us what we need."

David's eyes grew round with wonder. "You're serious," he marveled. "But weren't all the scrolls finally released to the public just recently? They're available to be read by anyone who is interested."

Rabbi Levine lifted one eyebrow. "So it would seem. So certain people mean for it to seem."

David ran the damp palms of his hands down his thighs. "Now, let me get this straight. You believe that all the hubbub about the scroll committee and its sequestering of the scrolls is not really resolved? You believe there is still some material hidden away?"

Katz would have the last word. "We not only believe it; we know it to be the case. And we want you, Dr. Rothmeyer, to help us track it down!"

CHAPTER 10

The Daisy Pub in the old square of Oxfordshire was relatively quiet. Most students who had not gone home for Easter break were outside, enjoying the serene beauty of the university town—the wide greens between the campuses or the sloping banks along the River Cherwell, where rowboats dotted the water.

Britta Hayworth, the young reporter from the *London Times*, and Emily McCurdy, sister to Father Ian McCurdy, were having lunch in the pub. This was one of Emily's favorite places at Oxford, and since she did not visit England often, she always had her choice of rendezvous.

The last time Britta had been in Oxford was over six months earlier to meet and interview Emily's brother, a feat achievable only because the elderly Irishwoman had arranged it.

Emily was a longtime friend of the girl's family, and Britta held her in great esteem. She had been a Red Cross nurse when Britta's great-uncle Reginald had been wounded at Normandy during assignment as a photojournalist there. Emily had tended to him during his recuperation at an army hospital in France, and then she had been transferred to Germany, ultimately helping in the evacuation of the Holocaust death camps when the survivors were freed.

Britta, having grown up with stories about Emily's and uncle Reginald's experiences in World War II, had decided as a child that she would be a heroine, if she could. Though no great opportunity had presented itself, she was determined to serve humanity grandly, if the chance arose. So it was that a twenty-four-year-old, moppet-curled blond and a tall, dignified woman in her seventies sat together that day in a pub, chatting over tuna on rye and drinking Guinness.

Dark, polished oak beams and wainscoting, accented by gleaming brass bar rails, sconces, and hardware, and soft, multicolored light from Tiffany lamps lent a warm and endearing mood to the place. Conversation was easy, backed by the strains of folk music, laughter, and the hypnotizing plunk-plunk of cue balls and pinballs. They were in England, but it was easy to forget this when a sign on the wall, advertising Bailey's Cream, asked, in letters four inches high, "Is There Any Irish in You?"

After half an hour of girl talk, catching up on Emily's Dublin garden and Britta's latest fashion spree in London, the conversation inevitably turned to their common interest, Reginald. It was no secret that Emily and Reg, as he was usually called, had once been "a thing." Their romance, which blossomed during Reg's stay at the army hospital, had been brief and was interrupted by their duties. After Reg had recuperated, he had been whisked away on another assignment, and Emily had been transferred to Germany.

Correspondence had kept the fire of their feelings alive for years. But like so much in the wake of war, their relationship had been a casualty of long separations and stress, and was now a fond memory. Reg's meeting of a young Jewish Holocaust survivor, his eventual marriage to her elder sister, and relocation to Israel had eliminated any hope of Emily reuniting with him. But the Irishwoman still cared about Reg and always asked after him.

"He is doing well," Britta said. "I got an e-mail from him last week. His grandson, my second cousin, recently celebrated his bar mitzvah. Reg scanned me some photos of the event. Quite the party!"

Emily shook her head. "I still cannot imagine your uncle marrying outside his faith. Why, my Catholicism versus his Anglicanism was one of our stumbling blocks. And then he went and married a Jew!"

Britta smiled wanly. She did not understand why religion of any kind should be an impediment to love.

"Apparently Aunt Deborah was not a devout Jew when they met," she said. "She converted to Uncle Reg's faith before they married."

Emily sighed. "I guess you told me that before. Then, why . . ."

"Why did my cousin celebrate his bar mitzvah?"

"Yes, especially as an adult. Don't they usually go through that rite at twelve or thirteen?"

"Cousin Zachary embraced some new form of Judaism," Britta said with a shrug. "I really don't understand it, but Uncle Reg seems quite proud of him."

Emily leaned back from the table and chuckled. "How do you keep it all straight?" she asked. "I thought it was difficult in Ireland. All we have to worry about are the Catholics and the Protestants!"

The two laughed together, and Britta was relieved at Emily's good humor.

Then, Emily grew more sober. "Speaking of the Jews, as I've said before, I came to admire them greatly when I worked with them in Germany. I don't know much about their religion, but many of those who survived the camps were inspiring." She took a sip of Guinness, then continued, "Did you know that one of the ways in which the Jews kept their traditions and the memory of their Scriptures through all they endured was by writing them in secret places?"

"Secret places?" Britta repeated. "What could be kept secret in the camps? Besides, they had no paper, no way to store anything."

"Ah, but they were resourceful! They did have the clothes on their backs, clothes given them by the SS. Using bits of charcoal from fires the guards had them build, they wrote on the insides of their prison garbs, inside their shoes, or on the thin blankets of their bunks. If the guards came across these scrawls, they ignored them, having no respect for Hebrew and considering it nothing but childish scribbling. I remember how some of the survivors clung to the rags that held these precious documents—the remnants of religious and ethnic history they had risked everything to record."

Thinking back, she recounted a particularly memorable scene.

"I recall coming upon a little group of huddled prisoners, intent on unearthing a pile of the very rags I have described, near the foot of one of the guard towers. Apparently, they had been in charge of burning the clothes of the prisoners when they became louse-infested or if they had been removed, for any reason, from the bodies about to be burned in the ovens. In their unique position, they had been able to rescue many of the clothes that bore these documents I speak of, and had stashed them in a small pit dug when the guards were not looking—a pit right under the noses of the SS!" She smiled wanly. "I think they got some pathetic sense of enjoyment out of that trickery."

Britta was intrigued by this account, and covertly reached for her notepad. "What else do you remember?" she asked.

Emily looked at her suspiciously. "Why? You aren't thinking there's a story here, are you? Child, there are millions of such tales from the Holocaust. This one is nothing."

Britta shrugged, placed her notepad on the table, and scribbled a few words. "You never know," she said. "I just like to keep notes on any possibilities. I doubt I'd ever do anything with it, but it might get me thinking about other story ideas."

Emily looked at the girl with almost as much admiration as Britta bestowed on her. "If grit has anything to do with it," she said, "you're sure to win the Pulitzer someday!"

The reporter smiled. "I don't know. The really great stories seem to elude me."

Emily knew she was referring to the interview with Ian.

"I remember your saying that my brother was not much help," she said. "Well, at least you got in to talk with him. You're the only reporter he's even opened the door to."

"And I have you to thank for that much," Britta said. "He, of course, denied that there was any story to be had at all. I went away with nothing."

Emily looked down at her plate. "I wish I could have done more—"

But Britta interrupted her. "No, I take that back," she said. "I did come away with something—a feeling that your brother is still hiding something. He was so adroit at handling the Deception Theory that I was left wondering what all the mystery is about. I was left with the sense that there *is* a mystery, though not the one everyone has been pursuing."

Britta had spoken little with anyone about her experience with Father McCurdy. She had told her editor she had reached a dead end with the story. Still, a persistent hunch nagged at her.

Emily was clearly in the dark. She gave no hint that she knew anything of her brother's doings. "What about another interview? I could try—"

"No," Britta said. "Thanks, anyway. I wouldn't know what to ask him if I did see him again."

Then, purely from politeness, she inquired, "I hope he is well. Are you enjoying your visit with him?"

"I am," Emily replied, brightening. "But he is going to London this afternoon. He'll be gone when I get back to the house today and won't return until tomorrow."

Britta looked at her friend quizzically. "Why would he leave home when you are here for a visit?"

"Once a year, he has an appointment at the British Museum to look in on his cubicle."

"Cubicle?" Britta said. "What cubicle?"

Emily explained. "Oxford professors, particularly those who deal in history or languages or, as in Ian's case, archaeology, may use study closets at the museum. They are usually assigned them for the length of their tenure here.

They may work there privately or with students, with access to the materials in the Hall of Manuscripts."

Britta was intrigued. "And Ian has one of those cubicles?"

"Yes," Emily said. "He is still emeritus, and may keep the cubicle so long as he checks in annually, though I doubt he ever works with students at the museum anymore."

"So," Britta said, "these cubicles . . . are they exclusively for the use of the ones who are assigned them?"

"Oh yes," Emily said. "It is quite an honor to have one. And it is almost like a vault, accessible only by the assignee or his assistants."

Britta leaned back and cocked her head. The wheels of journalism were whirring in her brain. "Does Ian have assistants?" she asked.

Emily laughed. "Oh no. Not any longer. What would he need graduate assistants for when he no longer has classes? But Ian is a proud member of Oxford. And I never knew an Oxfordian to give up his privileges lightly. In fact, he never misses going to that cubicle punctually this time of year. If he overlooks using it by this deadline, he must relinquish it to a more active member."

Britta tried not to ask more questions, though her instincts were humming.

"So, you will be keeping house with dear Cromwell?" she guessed, remembering the dignified fellow.

Again, Emily shrugged. "No—Ian is taking John with him. They always make this annual trek to the museum together."

CHAPTER 11

The next morning, Britta was back in London. She had spent a leisurely afternoon with Emily, visiting the shops in Oxford, then had caught one of the late-night buses back to the city.

Leaving her apartment early, she took one of the underground trains heading for the British Museum. Sunlight stabbed her eyes as she emerged from the tube station at Tottenham Court and hastened down Great Russell Street. The spring day was cool and crisp, almost fallish, though the trees were brilliant green.

The reporter figured that Father McCurdy and John Cromwell would have arrived at Victoria Station too late to go to the museum before closing time. They would probably waste no time this morning, however, making their way to the great complex and its fabulous library. She intended to be there when they arrived, even if she did nothing more than observe their level of tension.

The British Library, housed on the ground floor of the immense museum, was best known for its manuscript hall. Called the "Manuscript Saloon," the main room covered a good city block, its ceiling soaring to the height of three stories. Each wall of this and adjacent rooms was lined floor to rafters with leather-bound volumes, each one handwritten. Those manuscripts on the higher shelves were reachable by long ladders and catwalklike galleries.

Astonishing as this collection was, the contents of glass cases, arrayed along the floor, were the most breathtaking. Many of the greatest documents in the history of humanity could be viewed here, from the Magna Carta to the original score of Handel's *Messiah;* from the Codex Sinaitica, the oldest manuscript of the Holy Scriptures, to the poems of Coleridge and Shelley.

Pausing at the museum's main desk, Britta reserved the use of one of the library's reading rooms. Since the museum had only just opened for the day, there was no waiting list.

As she made her way through the Manuscript Saloon, she skirted Handel's score on the way to the Medieval hall. She had been there more than once in her life as a Londoner, but she stopped on a double-take, amazed at what scraps of paper filled the case next to Handel's great oratorio.

Scrawls and doodles from jam sessions of the Beatles were on temporary exhibition, accorded equal honor with Beethoven and Bach. "I Wanna Hold Your Hand" was on display across the aisle from "The Unfinished Symphony."

Chuckling to herself, Britta shook her head and entered the huge chamber of illuminated Medieval manuscripts. A door led from this hall, down narrow corridors through which no one was permitted to go without a pass, to the offices and staff lounge, and then to the reading rooms, or students' rooms, of the library. She assumed that cubicles such as Emily had described, assigned to scholars like McCurdy and his Oxford cohorts, were probably nearby.

After showing her admission slip to the guard at the door, she went down one hall until she came to the main reading room of the manuscript collection.

Here she was obliged to check her purse, while she told the attendant what she wanted to see. She had given much thought to a plausible alibi for being there.

"I'd like to see William Blake's *Europe*," she said.

The man looked at her from his perch behind a high desk. He was old, balding, and smelled of ancient leather, like the volumes on shelves behind him. Britta wondered if he had known Blake personally.

Peering down his long nose, he said, with a sniff, "Of course, the original is housed in the archives. The best we can do is let you see a rare imprint."

Britta glanced down the gleaming oak table that stretched from the desk to the far side of the room behind a low oak partition. There were no other students or readers here. "That will do," she said, imitating a version of scholarly haughtiness.

The attendant reached under his desk and pressed an unseen button, releasing the lock on the partition's gate. Britta pushed against the gate and entered the room. She took a seat facing the entry, in the hopes that, should McCurdy arrive, she might see him. She had a hunch that the scholars' cubicles were down yet another hall visible behind the warden's desk.

After she had taken her seat, the attendant picked up a phone and spoke softly into it, ordering the book she wanted brought in from the stacks.

Since there were no other patrons present, Britta felt free to speak to the man.

"Sir," she called out to him, "is it possible to reserve a study carrel? I have heard that there are such rooms available to researchers."

The attendant looked down the table toward her, obviously unused to conversing freely in the quiet sanctum. Pursing his lips, he sniffed again. "Are you on the faculty of one of the Queen's colleges?" he asked, his doubtful tone thick as London fog.

"Uh, no," Britta replied. "But I *am* with the *London Times*."

The man lowered his wire spectacles and eyed her skeptically. Nonetheless, he seemed to mellow a little. "I see. And what use would a reporter have for a cubicle?"

At that moment, a delivery boy entered the room, bringing Britta's copy of Blake's *Europe*. The attendant waved Britta over, and she took the book, returned to her chair, and placed the volume on the felt-covered stand that sat on the table before her. Carefully opening it, she pretended to survey the art-nouveau etchings and Blake's fine, swirling penmanship.

"Well," Britta continued, "say there was a hunt for a missing Blake plate and we needed to research the history of the piece and its various owners. We might need more than a day or two in a reading room to do the work."

There. She had not lied. She had only presented a possibility.

The attendant seemed to be impressed, his interest piqued. Still, he maintained his stiff demeanor. "In such a case," he said, "you could apply for an extended reservation. But assignments are quite limited."

Britta looked up at the old fellow with a melting smile. "I see," she said, repeating his earlier phrase. "Now, say that our research was of a highly sensitive nature. Say that we wished to be assured that our research materials were available only to us for that certain period of time."

The man took her persistence as evidence of her sincerity. "You want to know about security measures here?" he said. "My dear girl, the museum prides itself on its impeccable guardianship. Whatever a scholar needs is reserved in his—or her—name, until the research is done."

Now Britta was getting somewhere. "Very well," she said. "And what of materials the researcher might wish to bring into the library? Are there ways of storing such items?"

"Oh, indeed," the man answered, beaming with pride. "Each carrel has its own strongbox. The researcher may rest in perfect confidence that all materials are safe day and night."

Britta's cheeks warmed. She could hardly believe her own cleverness. If her hunch was right, she hardly even needed to see McCurdy's arrival. She certainly did not need to test him with questions—not at this point, anyway.

What purpose could the emeritus professor have with a permanent cubicle, and with a strongbox, if he was not hiding something there?

Britta stood up from her seat and gently closed the Blake book. Taking it to the attendant, she smiled again and told him she would speak with her editor about the library's superior service.

"Come again," the man said with a nod.

As Britta slipped down the hall from the reading room, she kept her eyes open for McCurdy and Cromwell.

The timing was perfect. She had just reached the door at the head of the hall, when the Irish priest shuffled in, his houseman close behind him.

Feeling quite confident now, she hailed him. "Why, Father McCurdy!" she exclaimed. "Fancy seeing you here!"

Father McCurdy stopped abruptly, wavering on his feet. John Cromwell nearly collided with him from behind and then held on to him to lend support.

"M-Ms. Hayworth," the priest stammered. "What are you doing here?"

Britta laughed lightly. "So much for 'howd'ya'do,' " she teased. "Perhaps I should ask the same of you. After all, I am a Londoner visiting a London museum, and you come from seventy miles away."

McCurdy blushed, and John intervened. "How pleasant to see you, Miss," he said. "I hear that you were visiting our fair village only yesterday."

He had her there. "Yes," she said. "I spent the day with Emily."

A long span of awkward silence passed between the three, the two men studying Britta for any hint of suspicion and she surveying them for the same. Each side awaited questions that did not come.

"Well," McCurdy finally said, stepping sideways past her, "charmed, as always."

"Charmed," John echoed.

"Greetings to your sister," Britta returned. And with that, she exited.

McCurdy looked up at his friend, his face white as paper.

"Now, Father," John said, "do not be concerned. What can the girl know?"

The priest glared down the hall angrily. "I am going to find out," he said.

Making his way to the reading room, he approached the high desk.

The attendant greeted the professor warmly.

"Professor McCurdy!" he said. "I was only just yesterday looking at your file! You've just crept in under your deadline again!"

"So I have," McCurdy grumbled. "Say, old fellow. Was there a blond woman in here just moments ago?"

The attendant glanced down the table to where Britta had sat. "Nice girl," he said. "Do you know her?"

"I know her slightly," the priest replied. "Did she have business here?"

"So it seems. She wouldn't say much, but it seems she's on the trail of a lost work."

McCurdy froze, his heart thundering. "Lost work?" he repeated, his throat dry. He reached up and gripped the edge of the tall desk, as flashes of his beloved scroll, the despicable, damning scroll, careened through his head.

"Yes," the man said. "Watch for it in the *Times*."

CHAPTER 12

Pete Wester paced the broad porch of his Bull River home, checking his watch and keeping his ears pricked for the sound of approaching vehicles.

Pete had broken the news to Mel, over breakfast two days ago, that they would not be enjoying their solitude for long. They would be receiving company this afternoon, a large group of people, who would probably be staying for a while.

Mel had asked a lot of questions. Pete had fielded them pretty well, explaining as much about the upcoming gathering as he could without frightening his brother away.

"You used to enjoy hanging out with my hippie friends when you came to the Okanogan years ago," he said. "These fellows will seem a little strange, but give them a chance. You may learn something."

Mel, who remembered the spontaneous parties Pete had taken him to, had actually responded with relief. "Hippies?" he replied. "I'm glad to hear you still know a few. I can handle hippies!"

Apparently Pete had not made himself clear. "No—I don't mean these guys are hippies. I mean, you learned to appreciate the weird friends I had once. These guys are weird in a different way. Some are ex-hippies, but most of them wouldn't claim that identity any more."

Mel was thoroughly confused, but he quit asking questions, content to wait it out and make up his own mind about the visitors.

The fact was, Pete didn't know what to expect completely, himself. He had entertained Jim Fogarty and a few of his upper-echelon cohorts whenever they had used his premises as their headquarters. He had taken the mysterious messages that crackled off the ham radio. He had long ago bought into the anti-government rhetoric of Fogarty and his Freemen when he attended meetings at a camp in Idaho. But he had never hosted a large gathering of such people. So, apart from preaching the doctrines of the revolutionists, there was not much he could say to prepare Mel for what was coming.

And he chose not to preach. He figured Mel would get his eyes opened quickly enough.

When Mel had called from Los Angeles, saying that he wanted to come to Montana, Pete's first urge had been to short-circuit his plans, to make up some excuse why his baby brother shouldn't come. But, on second thought, he had decided it might be an opportune time for Mel to learn the truth—not only about Pete's new life, but about the realities of the world.

Mel was in the house, washing up the lunch dishes, when Pete stopped his pacing and cocked his ears toward the road. "I think they're here," he called through the screen door.

Mel wiped his hands on a towel and stepped outside. Up from the woods through which he had driven the other night, Mel heard the sound of rumbling engines. "Gosh, sounds like an army!" he said. "What are they driving, anyway?"

Pete grinned nervously. "I think it's the hogs," he said.

As the distant rumble became a roar, and then an earthshaking thunder, Mel's eyes grew wider and wider. Suddenly, like black knights on metallic warhorses—rather stubby, and very hairy knights who rode with their knees to the saddle horns, their helmeted heads at an obtuse angle—a dozen leather-clad bikers burst out from the forest. Several of them had riders behind them, skinny women with windblown hair held down with bandannas and glistening chrome studs stamped all over their skintight pants.

"Hogs," Mel sighed. "I get it. Harleys."

Pete shrugged, trying not to show his embarrassment.

Mel leaned close. "You've got to be kidding, Pete," he said through gritted teeth. "These are your new friends?"

"Don't let the extremes throw you," Pete said. "They always take the lead, but they're not the leaders."

As the bikers rumbled into the yard, they tipped their machines and circled in front of Pete's cabin, kicking up the dust of his driveway.

Mel noticed Pete wince, and he shook his head, wondering what he had gotten himself into. The last time he had seen Harley hogsters had been in the ghettos of L.A., a part of the culture he had hoped to leave behind.

As the hogs quieted to a thumping chug, seeming to function on one cylinder apiece, other vehicles came into view. One after another, they entered the yard and parked along the edges of the open area.

Most of the rigs were pickup trucks, the majority at least seven years old, Mel guessed, many older, showing the scrapes, dents, and bent fenders of rough wear. Almost all of the trucks had rifles on back-window racks, and some carried loads of firewood or hay bales. There were absolutely no foreign makes among them.

Mel gawked at the incongruity of the gathering on the lawn. What in the world, he wondered, could a bunch of gangsters have in common with farmers and ranchers?

His capacity for amazement was about to be further stretched.

As men in baseball caps labeled Cenex, John Deere, and Budweiser piled out of the trucks, their middle-aged, overweight wives, and passels of kids clambering out with them, a little caravan of VW Bugs and buses arrived.

From these vehicles—apparently the only sanctioned foreign make—a peculiar group of folks emerged. Coming close to Mel's image of the perfect back-to-the-earth female, thirty-something women in long dresses appeared, their straight hair woven into braids and their smocked bodices jangling with beads. Their menfolk, many wearing tie-dyed T-shirts, ambled up to the farmers, shaking hands as though they spoke the same language, while the women joined the farm wives, bearing linen-covered platters and picnic baskets.

Food, food, food was carried from the vehicles—canned goods, pickled goods, breads, pies, and meat ready for barbecue.

Pete certainly did not have the means to feed this crew, Mel thought, so it was a good thing the visitors had come prepared. The women had brought tablecloths to spread on the ground, and a few tables made of boards and Pete's sawhorses were set up on the grass, but the tailgates of all the trucks would be needed to accommodate the fare.

The arrival of the gathering was not really a processional, but the various contingents did tend to come in clusters. The next bunch were of a different stripe altogether than the first three. These arrived in battered four-wheel-drive rigs and were dressed military style, in camouflage or army surplus olive drabs. They were skinheads, their pates, as well as their faces, clean-shaven and their bare forearms boasting Nazi tattoos.

Among all these sorts, there were those who were less noticeable. They were small-town folks, for sure, Mel thought: loggers, mechanics, shop owners. There were no yuppies here, no rich people, and no white collars.

Still, Mel could make no sense of the diversity. What neo-Nazis could have in common with ranchers, or bikers with New Agers, he could not imagine.

Although Mel did not know it, this diverse processional was only the prelude to the arrival of the grand master of them all.

As the people greeted one another, the women laying out the food and the men talking bikes, guns, planting, or taxes, the mood was one of quiet eagerness. Mel noticed that they all watched the woods, listening, just as Pete had done, for the sound of another rig.

At last, as though the timing was deliberate, a shiny vehicle flashed into the open: a dark blue, four-wheel-drive Suburban, glistening with a recent wax job, whitewalls slick and chrome sparse but gleaming. This rig, with its dark windows, looked as if it might be armored.

Everyone stopped talking as the car pulled into the center of the green. But the moment the front passenger emerged, the crowd burst into cheers.

Mel watched over Pete's shoulder as Jim Fogarty stepped into the sunlight. Taller by a head than most of the men present, he was attired to match his car, in dark, uniform blue. Crisp pants and shirt with epaulets gave him an official look. His collar-length white hair and neat beard were accented by a blue beret.

The crowd clapped and hoorayed.

When he motioned to the backseat of the car, calling forth a newcomer, the onlookers grew hushed.

This man was also tall and bearded, with shoulder-length hair pulled back in a black ribbon. He wore camouflage shirt and pants and thick combat boots, and Mel thought he saw the bulge of a shoulder harness beneath his padded vest.

As he was introduced, he stood straight, chin raised, not disdainfully, but with supreme self-confidence.

"Ladies and gentlemen," Jim Fogarty announced, leading the stranger into their midst, "this is our friend from Germany, Monte Altmeyer. I know you will show him your warm, all-American hospitality."

The people were utterly thrilled. Mel sensed that they had heard much about this fellow and had come from great distances just to meet him.

In respectful groups, they came forward, reaching out to shake Altmeyer's hand and expressing gratitude for his coming.

Mel nudged Pete. "Who is this guy?" he asked.

"Altmeyer?" Pete said. "Just one of the great social geniuses of our time! You've never heard of him because keeping a low profile is a key to his success."

CHAPTER 13

Eating and conversation took up the afternoon. The aroma of barbecued hamburgers lured Mel into the throng, which by midday had grown to about two hundred. Pete took him from group to group, introducing him as his ex-cop brother from Los Angeles, who had given up the ghetto and the concrete to find some peace in Montana.

Mel did a lot of listening throughout the afternoon. He did not need to ask many questions. Once people knew who he was, they seemed eager to fill him in on their viewpoints and reasons for being there. As they did so, he picked up on recurring themes—beliefs and experiences held in common. After hours of taking in their expressions of personal anger, political frustration, and social hatred, he began to see that it was indeed plausible that such diverse types could come together.

Window stickers and bumper decals on pickups, buses, and even on the fenders of the Harleys expressed the sentiments on which the people elaborated: "I Love My Country, but I Fear My Government," was popular among the pickup trucksters, along with "Return Prayer to the Schools So the Kids Can Pray for the Government—It Needs It!" Then, there was a new slant on an old classic: "America—Love It, but Don't Pay Its Taxes!"

The bumper stickers on the buses were still as counterculture as during the sixties, only more militant: "Nuke the

Nukes—Over the White House"; "Ban the Bomb but Bomb the IRS"; or "One More Long-hair Who Don't Care to Share—Keep America for Americans!"

Mel could not help but grin at the one that said, "Beam me up, Scotty! The taxman's after me!"

The most radical of all, however, were the hogsters. "Revenge Ruby Ridge" and "Wacko about Waco" were tame compared to "OK City—Only the Beginning" and "You Ain't Seen Nothin Yet," emblazoned over a silhouette of the Murrah Building in flames.

Mel wandered through the crowd, paper plate in hand, munching on his second hamburger, unaware that he had drawn his shoulders into an avoiding hunch, subconsciously trying to appear inconspicuous.

Passing one more cluster of VW buses, he glimpsed an intriguing sticker: "Zap Zog." He stood looking at it, wondering if it was something from a Star Trek convention. Zog must be some alien planet, he thought, and the owner of the bus was probably a comic-book collector.

He did not realize how alien he, himself, felt in this environment until someone tapped him on the shoulder. As though he had been shocked, he lurched, sending his plateful of food flying to the grass.

"Sorry, ol' buddy," one of the ranchers said as he turned around. "Didn't mean t'spook you."

Mel's face burned. "That's all right," he muttered, amazed at his own jitters. A couple of pet dogs raced over from a family rig and made quick work of the spilled food.

Mel drew back as the flannel-shirted rancher helped him brush crumbs off his clothes.

"So yer Pete's brother," the man said. "Hank, here, Hank Dwyer."

He stuck his hand out, and Mel, first wiping mustard off his fingers, returned the gesture. "Nice to meet you, Hank. My name's Mel."

"Hear yer from L.A. Wow, is that a sty, huh?"

For some reason, although Mel agreed completely, the description of his former hometown seemed a bit insulting. "It has its problems," he said.

"Phew-eee, yeah!" the man laughed. "I guess! All them spooks and spicks! And they call 'em minor-tees. Why, the white race is the minor-tee in them places!"

Mel shrugged and made an innocuous grunt.

Hank motioned toward a dull brown crew cab around which five young children played, and called a woman over to join them. Mel noticed that she seemed to have forgotten to take a couple of rollers out of her salt-and-pepper hair.

She came obediently, straightening her cotton dress as she walked. She had a neat, work-hardened body, but her veined legs would have looked better in pantyhose, Mel thought. He didn't know they even made bobbysocks anymore, but she wore white ones, unselfconsciously rolled above the ankles of her black loafers.

Mel noticed that Hank's truck proudly bore the emblem of the Montana Militia, with the initials A.C.E. stamped in gold foil. Mel had already met several ACEs and knew the letters stood for All Citizens Equal.

Hank introduced his wife, Lucy. "Mel here's from L.A.," Hank told her. "I was just tellin' him he made the right decision, comin' to Montana. Keep the races sep'ert, we always say." He drawled on, "L.A. ain't fer the white man anymore. Heck—prob'ly never was. We took it from the spicks, and the spicks always wanted it back. Good riddance, I say!"

Lucy laughed softly, the gap of one missing tooth marring what might have been a pretty face. "Not that we got anythin' against anybody," Lucy chimed in.

"Heck no!" Hank said. "It's just best to keep the races to theirselves, don't you agree?"

Mel gave no reply, only a twitch of a smile.

"At least we ain't farmers," Lucy said. "Geez—they gotta work with the wetbacks every harvest!"

Hank grunted. "Yeah. Let the wetbacks work, I always say, just don't let 'em shake theirselves off in my backyard!"

At this, the man whooped hilariously. Soon, others were gathering around, wondering what the gag was.

"Thorny here's from Spokane," Hank said, drawing a man to the front of the group. "I bet he has a few things to say about wetbacks!"

"John Thornton," the new fellow said, thrusting out his hand. Then, he threw in, "I think Hank's confusing Spokane with Yakima. We don't have wetbacks in Spokane—just niggers!"

Again, the air was filled with raucous laughter.

Mel cringed. He had worked the beat for years in "nigger" territory. His best friend, Jorey, killed in the line of duty, had been a black man.

Thornton went on. "Yeah. Spokane used to be a nice little town. Could leave your car on the street, your screen door unlocked. If there was any niggers, they knew their place."

Hank nudged Thornton in the side. "The good ol' days, eh, Thorny?"

"You bet."

"Gone fer'ever," someone else chimed in.

Mel was growing agitated. He knew if he didn't break away soon, he would lose his temper and say something not in his own best interests.

Glancing over the heads of the group, he pretended that his brother was calling to him from the porch. "Hey, guys," he said, "I'll get back to you. Pete needs some help in the kitchen."

Hank and Thorny nodded, then went back to their conversation, as Mel made a quick exit.

Of course, Pete had not really called him. In fact, he did not see Pete anywhere. What he did see was a group of skinheads watching him from a corner of the yard. He nodded to them, but moved toward the house quickly, not needing to hear what they had to say. Their message could only be more offensive than that of the farmers and ranchers, which, to Mel's way of thinking, was inflammatory enough.

"Hey, friend," someone called as he started up the steps to the porch.

Wheeling about, Mel froze. A man the size of a mountain was approaching from the driveway, having left the huddle of bikers who were never more than a few feet away from their machines.

Mel gulped. "What's that?" he said.

"I said, 'Hey, friend,'" the giant repeated.

Mel had never seen anything like this fellow, not in all his years working with toughs on the L.A. streets, not in an entire career in the worst parts of hell.

This man was seven feet tall, if he was an inch, and his grizzled hair hung down his back almost to his waist. It was nearly as long as his bushy beard, which came to his belt buckle. He was dressed all in black leather, which is to say that what clothes he wore were of that material. Apart from skin-tight pants, he wore little. Only a short vest covered any part of his upper body, and the vest did not meet in the middle, but flew back with each step, revealing a torso that could have been a sampler for a tattoo shop. His bulging, rock-hard arms were covered with hair, but tattoos were visible even there. Mel noticed one in particular as the biker stuck his thumbs in his belt loops and eyed Mel up and down. "Born to be Wild," it said.

Mel had no doubt about it.

"Bored with the clodhoppers?" he asked, spitting a stream of tobacco on the bottom step.

Mel dodged the saliva and cringed. "Clodhoppers?"

"The farmers—the cow-pokers," the big fellow replied, nodding his head in their direction.

"Oh—yeah," Mel said. "Nice folks . . ."

The biker only looked him up and down again, like a butcher sizing up a piece of meat.

"So," Mel said weakly, "what brings you people here?"

As soon as he'd asked this, he regretted it. He was curious, indeed, as to what a bunch of hogsters would find important about such a meeting, but he didn't really want to engage this guy in conversation.

"I hear yer from L.A.," the biker said. "I guess you think all Harley riders are Hell's Angels, huh? Well, let me tell you, we ain't got no part with them jokers. They're nothin' but junkies and junk dealers, y'know. A real syndicate, that's what they are, into pimpin' and the whole nine yards!"

Again he spat on the ground, this time having courtesy enough to aim away from the steps.

He removed his thumbs from his belt loops, wiped saliva from his lips, and stuck out his hand. Mel shook it, having no other choice, and tried not to be obvious as he wiped his own hand on his pants leg.

"Willard's the name," the big guy said.

Mel grunted his own name. "So, you fellows aren't anarchists?" he quipped, trying to be facetious.

To his grave concern, the big guy's face clouded. Mel couldn't tell if he was angry at the question or just didn't understand it.

Mel would have explained, but Willard huffed, "Libertarians, that's what we are! Not right wing, not left wing—just the ultimate freedom fighters!"

Mel tried not to stare at the man's tattoos, but saw one that indicated he had served in the U.S. Army. "I suppose some of you are vets," he surmised.

"Some?" Willard spat again. "All of us, man. Ain't hardly a one that ain't, 'cept our ol' ladies!"

This last reference caught the attention of the bikers and their girlfriends. The women began to amble over, and the men followed.

"You gettin' mouthy again, Willard?" one of the women teased. "Leave this poor bugger alone. He mighta been headin' for the john."

"I was just tellin' him we ain't no antichrists," Willard said.

A number of the bikers looked quizzically at one another.

"I . . . I said 'anarchists,' not 'antichrists,'" Mel corrected, unable to keep from smiling.

Willard drew closer than Mel liked and looked down at him threateningly. "You laughin' at me?" he growled.

"Back off, Willard!" one of the male bikers warned. "Sorry, mister," he said, nodding at Mel. "Willard here wouldn't know anarchy from an anchovy if it bit him on the behind!"

By now Mel had overcome his desire to flee. He was intrigued by this strange lot and wondered what made them tick.

The second biker, who was much smaller than Willard but impressively built, black bearded, and notably tattooed, stuck out his hand. "Crossley," he introduced himself. "Hear you were a cop."

Mel's hackles rose. He wondered if the fact of his background made him their target. Reticently, he shook the biker's hand. "Willard says you guys are freedom fighters."

The men straightened proudly, and the women raised their chins or draped their arms through the bikers', apparently proud to be in the men's shadows.

"Heck, yeah!" Crossley replied. "I guess that about sums it up."

Mel glanced over at their gleaming hogs. "So tell me," he said. "Those stickers on your bikes—do you really mean that?"

The men turned to see what he was referring to.

"You know," Mel went on, "'OK City—Only the Beginning,' or 'You Ain't Seen Nothin Yet . . . ' You mean that?"

Crossley sneered. "Would we advertise it if we didn't mean it? Look, Melvin," he said with a snarl. "That is your name, huh? It's one thing to talk politics, like the farmers, or wear tattoos, like the skinheads, it's another to be willin' to lay down your life for what you believe."

"Yeah," one of the women joined in, her hands on her hips, "we got sick a long time ago of hearin' how this farmer lost his farm to the international agriculture monopolies or how sweet Suzy-Q got aced out of a job by affirmative action. Our boys are willing to take affirmative action of a different kind. That's why we're here today, 'cause Fogarty brought in this Altmeyer, a die-hard activist!"

The woman raised a clenched fist, and her friends cheered.

"We ain't like the New-Ager quasi-White Supremacist survivalists who don't know whether to wait for the Hale-Bopp comet or lie down on the Nuke Train track," another added. She snickered over her shoulder at the hippies. "We ain't waitin' for no one to save us, man. We're takin' action now!"

Mel darted another look at the VW vans. "Say," he said, "is Zog related to Hale-Bopp?"

Again, the bikers looked quizzical. Then, the light dawned. "Zog?" someone said. "Oh—Zog! You saw the Zap Zog sticker! Zog is the Zionist Occupied Government! The U.S. government, man! The world government!"

"Yeah, and the bankers—the Jew bankers!"

Mel was bewildered, and looked it.

Crossley, who seemed to be the leader, shook his head. "You gotta be kiddin', man. Are you really that out to lunch? Surely you know that the Jews run the world! Man—come to think about it, I guess that's what brings all of us together—farmers, ranchers, New Age freaks, skinheads. The one thing we all agree on—the one thing we all know for sure—is the nature of the enemy."

Mel bristled. "You mean, the main thing that unites everyone here is that you're anti-Semites?"

Willard drew close to Mel again, breathing on him from his towering height. "Who you talkin' about? We ain't against no semis. My dad was a trucker!"

Crossley grabbed Willard by the arm and pulled him aside. "Keep a clamp on it, Bozo!" he snarled. "We ain't talkin' about semis or truckers. We're talkin' about Jews!"

Willard was dazed, then comprehending. "Oh—yeah! The Jews—we all hate 'em. Need to start with the Jews. We all see that real clear!"

CHAPTER 14

Dusk brought a chill to the Bull River Valley. After the long afternoon of barbecue and "fellowship," the men began to gather up wood for a bonfire, apparently to be built on Pete's driveway.

Mel found his brother, who had spent the day in a round of fetch and carry, serving Jim Fogarty and his henchmen their umpteenth cups of coffee on the broad porch. "Hey, Pete, look at this," he said, drawing him aside and pointing to the wood gatherers. "Do you want a fire on your property?"

Pete observed the activity with apprehension. "Gee, I guess it's okay," he faltered.

Mel heard the hesitation in his brother's voice. "You have the last say, don't you?" Mel challenged him. "This *is* your property!"

Pete shuffled. With a glance back toward Fogarty, who sat sprawled like Saddam Hussein on one of the handmade deck chairs, he muttered, "Let it go. Jim's managed plenty of bonfires."

With this, Pete hurried off on yet another errand, and Mel watched him helplessly. He hardly recognized his elder brother anymore. He used to be so strong, so opinionated and "in charge." What had these people done to him?

As stars appeared in the purple canopy above the treetops, someone set a torch to the tall stack of brush and pine logs. Hank, Lucy, Thorny, and their friends gathered just beyond the brightest part of the firelit circle, their kids scrambling for blankets strewn on the grass and sitting cross-legged in anticipation of something.

Gradually, the rest of the crowd congregated as well, always leaving room before the fire. Resting on the porch rail, Mel leaned against one of the posts, expecting that some show was about to be staged.

Whatever was coming up, however, his attention was grabbed by the sight of the skinheads along the crowd's shadowed boundary. He saw yellow armbands on their camouflage sleeves, something they had not worn earlier. He did not need to stare to recognize the emblem stamped boldly upon the saffron ribbons: The Nazi swastika was impossible to misconstrue.

Mel's stomach tightened, the hair on his arms rising in goose flesh. He knew now, more than ever, that he wanted nothing to do with these people. Pulling on the plaid jacket Pete had loaned him, he peered over the crowd toward his car, which was parked by a small outbuilding at the far side of the yard. Slipping silently from the porch—unnoticed, he hoped—he headed for the darkness that ringed the group, intending to skirt the edge.

Suddenly, however, he was stopped in mid-escape by the sound of a whoop and a cheer, accompanied by the wild strumming of guitars, the jangle of tambourines, and the piping of flutes.

Hidden in darkness, he stood spellbound by the sight of twirling women and wild-haired men bounding into the firelight. It was the bus contingency, the New Agers, leading the crowd in song.

On cue, the people began to clap and sway, to tunes Mel had heard before. The assortment of music, however, was as odd as the assortment of people. How they managed to find common meaning between "If I Had a Hammer" and "Onward Christian Soldiers," or "The Battle Hymn of the Republic" and "The Times They Are A'Changin'" was a wonder to Mel. But they sang them all with equal gusto, their mood swinging from brotherly love to religious zeal to social defiance, without missing a beat.

Mel wondered, in fact, if they were paying any attention to the lyrics. When Peter, Paul, and Mary had hammered out "love between my brothers and my sisters all over this land," they had surely never worn Nazi armbands. And when the old North had sung the Civil War "Battle Hymn," they had never dreamed that leather-clad bikers would someday declare, "In the beauty of the lilies Christ was born across the sea, with a glory in his bosom that transfigures you and me!"

Incongruous as all this was, however, Mel was further appalled by other armbands, other emblems. The bikers, he noticed, now sported their own ribbons, black with white silhouettes of raised fists.

He had been a preteen when the Black Panthers had been on the move in the sixties. He remembered that their symbol had been the black fist. The meaning of the new White Power emblem was unmistakable.

Mel could have stayed. It might be his only chance to see such a gathering firsthand. Until now, he had seen such things only in movies and on news footage. Probably these events took place far more often than the average Joe had any knowledge of, but he doubted he'd ever be so close to one again. And he could stay for his brother's sake. For the first time in his life, he felt like Pete needed him—like his big brother could be in big trouble.

But Mel wanted nothing more than to be out of there and down the road, back to the pit of L.A. or the lethargy of Spokane, or anywhere but here, before anyone missed him.

He was almost to his car. Only one hurdle of Harleys, moved aside to make room for the meeting, stood between him and freedom. He was fumbling in his jeans for his car keys, when a shadow suddenly loomed through the moonlight across his path.

Frozen, Mel looked up, and up, to the leering face of Willard, the brain-dead biker.

"What's yer hurry?" the giant growled. He had planted his feet wide, straddling the path. From behind him came Crossley.

"Hey, ol' buddy," the pack leader spat, "you wanna miss a good show?"

"I—I forgot my glasses," Mel lied. "In—the glove box," he said, pointing toward his car.

"Don't think so," Crossley said. "Top Cops don't wear glasses."

What had made Mel think he could fool guys who knew the law well enough to stay outside it?

Willard planted an arm across Mel's shoulders. "Now, we wouldn't want you to miss anything," he snarled. "You just come back with us."

Mel stumbled along beside Willard, or rather, Willard dragged him, back toward the throng.

By now the dancers were really wild, the women in their ankle-length calico skirts, colorful scarves, and long beads, the men in striped vests and silky pants bounding around them. One of the women carried a large American flag on a long pole. As the crowd sang "Hooray for the Red, White, and Blue," she waved it over their heads, while the men, some of whom were old enough to have burned similar flags in the seventies, strummed and banged away on their guitars.

As Mel cringed under the pain of Willard's grip, another woman flashed into the light, twirling round and round as she tied a scarf around her forehead. To Mel's horror, it was yellow, like the skinheads' armbands, and also bore a swastika. As she danced, the crowd cheered wildly, until what seemed the ultimate irony took place.

One of the skinheads, representative of the rightest of the rightwingers, jumped into the circle with her, symbolically joining his ideology to her leftist agenda, and the two spun together until the people were nearly frantic with joy.

Crossley leaned close to Mel. "Amazin', ain't it?"

Mel's throat was dry, and he pulled against Willard's hand. "You bet," he said with a grimace.

Willard finally let loose of him, and Mel rubbed his shoulder.

"I—I guess I have to admit," the cop said, "I don't get it."

Crossley exchanged a knowing look with his sidekick. "Surprisin', huh?" he said. "Well, think back. You remember Rajneesh?"

Rajneesh . . . Rajneesh . . . the word was familiar. "Oh, yeah," Mel recalled. "The commune in Oregon."

"In Antelope, Oregon," Crossley said. "They renamed it for their New Age swami, remember?"

It was coming back to Mel now. He remembered how in the eighties, a far-out group of New Agers had followed an East Indian guru to the tiny town of Antelope and had completely taken it over, driving out the locals. They had then brought in busloads of homeless people from big cities—mostly runaways, drug addicts, and the like—and had proceeded, under the guise of giving them shelter and food, to turn them into a bunch of programmed zombies.

The last he had heard, the Rajneeshis had disappeared when their leader was sent packing back to India and his thugs were incarcerated for a plot to poison the water system of a nearby city.

Crossley reminded him, as if it were something to be proud of, that the Rajneeshis had renamed Antelope's town dump "Adolf Hitler Landfill."

Mel's skin bristled. Now that he thought about it, he remembered seeing photographs of the Rajneeshis wearing Nazi armbands for the benefit of the media. Finally, it was dawning on him: The frailty of philosophy was that, in the extreme, extremes were compatible.

Around and around the hippie woman and the skinhead danced, while the mesmerized crowd absorbed their harmony of hate and glutted themselves on it.

Mel had enough presence of mind to see that Jim Fogarty was now standing. Doubtless, old Eagle-Eye would use the fervor of the hour to give a mind-numbing speech. The L.A. cop braced himself, knowing there was nowhere to run.

Fogarty came down off the porch and stood in the firelit circle. As the dancers fell at his feet, the crowd received him with wild applause.

Throwing his arms wide, he shouted, "Welcome to the Promised Land!"

Mel cringed again. His brother had greeted him that way only two nights ago.

At the time, it seemed he had entered a perfect world. Now that world was the Twilight Zone.

CHAPTER 15

Jim Fogarty was a credit to his race, so his father had always said. Fogarty came from a long line of Aryans. His great-great-grandfather's racial ethic, instilled at birth, had been passed on through the Fogarty line at great price, beginning with the losing of the Civil War. And one of the Fogarty ancestors had been a founding father of the KKK in Georgia.

Jim was carrying on a torch handed to him with firm expectations. He must work valiantly, as had his forefathers, to bring about the purifying of the Great Race and the founding of a New Jerusalem in a new Promised Land, sanctified for the rebuilding of the Aryan Nation.

Tonight, as he stood before the bonfire on this piece of the New Heaven, he was a striking figure. Tall and white—even his once blond hair had turned a gleaming silver—strong, defiant, and intelligent, he was the perfect example of his ideologically perfect man.

He had earned his nickname, Eagle-Eye, by virtue of his cold, steely gray eyes, which seemed to penetrate the people in any crowd as if sifting it for impostors. More than once, when giving a speech at just such a rally as this, he had been known to single out those who were there under false pretense. He had an uncanny ability to ferret out hypocrites, reporters, undercover agents, or just plain party-crashers and humiliate them to the point of leaving.

If humiliation did not force them out, there were always

men in the crowd, like Willard and Crossley, who were willing to make any gate-crashers wish they had never shown up.

Tonight, Eagle-Eye was in fine form. As the flames leapt and crackled behind him, he stood like a crucifix, arms spread, his shadow stretching and contracting hypnotically against the ground.

The dancers, who had brought the spectators to a fever pitch of anticipation, slowly rose from the places where they had collapsed and eased back into the crowd, leaving Fogarty the sole focus of attention.

The audience was already under his spell, ready to believe anything he said.

Mel was not very familiar with White Supremacist dogma. He knew that Hitler had taught the doctrine in his speeches to enormous rallies of Brownshirts at Nuremberg, and throughout the "Fatherland." He knew that the Ku Klux Klan, with its cross burnings and lynchings, had spouted a variation on the theme.

He also knew that in the years since the Civil Rights Movement, new groups had arisen, groups who harped on a spectrum of political grievances, all of which, they believed, could be blamed on what they called "subhuman" races, of whom, they asserted, Jews were the archetype.

Not until that day had Mel realized the extremes bound together by the racist teachings. Still, he did not know much about the particular beliefs that had spawned the likes of Fogarty.

Fogarty's leadership style, which had won for him the esteem of these diverse groups, capitalized on the themes that drew them together and minimized the points on which they differed. One of his favorite teaching techniques was to give a mini-history lesson at each rally, complete with maps and charts, slanted in a way that would never have been accepted in any university or anthropology department.

A hodgepodge of evolutionary theory, religion, and mysticism, it amounted to nothing more than wishful thinking, convincingly presented. But as Mel was about to learn, it was eagerly embraced and supported with all sorts of personal "evidence" by those who wished to blame their disappointments on convenient scapegoats and those who wished to believe they were part of a superior race.

Before Fogarty began speaking, he led the crowd in one last song. Building on the euphoria already generated by the previous songs and floor show, it was set to the tune of "The War Song of the Army of the Rhine" and was called "One Race Über Alle."

Mel tensed as the song commenced. Perhaps Willard sensed his reaction, for, pretending to place a brotherly arm about Mel's shoulders, the big fellow squeezed until the ex-cop thought his shoulder blades would crack. An unspoken reassertion of power, the gesture reminded Mel that he had no choice but to stay put and listen.

"Fogarty wrote this, hisself!" the giant said, bending close to Mel's ear. "Ain't it glorious!"

As the song ended, Mel saw tears in many eyes.

Suddenly Fogarty boomed out, "Brothers and sisters, is it not a blessing to be part of the Great White Race?"

Choruses of amens and yeah-mans echoed his sentiment.

"Have you ever asked yourself," he cried out, "'Why me? To what do I owe the privilege of my birth?' Have you ever asked yourself why you were favored not only to be born in this country, but to be born with white skin and superior intelligence? How is it that we were blessed to be born part of the Super Race, when others are born in poverty, cursed from birth with the inability to better themselves because of their genetic makeup?"

The people nodded, and Mel wondered if they ever looked at themselves in mirrors. If Lucy and Hank and Willard were part of the Super Race, the world was in hopeless shape indeed. But Mel dared not reveal his thoughts, not even with a roll of the eyes or the tiniest of smirks. Super Willard would as soon crush him as hear logic, though Mel doubted he would recognize logic if it slapped him in the face.

Fogarty's question had sounded rhetorical, but he actually intended to answer it. "Well, dear brothers and sisters," he went on, "let me tell you why you, and not others, were so blessed."

This was a cue, for from the shadows near the porch, two of Fogarty's henchmen appeared, carrying a large easel between them. They set it on the driveway, in plain sight of the crowd, then threw back the cover of a large tablet.

The first page was a colorful map of Europe and the Mediterranean. Across the top half was a band of reddish pink, with bold arrows flowing southward through continental Europe and fading as far as Persia and even India. "Expansion of the Pre-Germanic Nordics—1800–100 B.C.," it was labeled.

The audience shuffled for a view, some coming closer to the fire and sitting on the ground, as Fogarty's assistants shone large flashlights on the map.

"Here, my friends, you have a quick layout of the origins of the Aryan race. Strong, robust, 'barb-aryan,' the Norsemen were bred to endure extremes of climate. By the law of evolution, only the fittest survived the harsh world of the North," he said, running his hand across the regions of Scandinavia and upper Russia. "And by the laws of nature, they maximized human potential!"

The crowd hung on his words, many of them nodding, even clapping one another on the backs, apparently considering themselves to be examples of the lesson.

Spreading his fingers wide, Fogarty next drew his hand down the European continent toward Italy and then did the same toward Mesopotamia and India. "You see here that your forefathers brought their blood into the Roman and Eastern worlds, through conquest and subjugation of inferior races. From those lands, civilization arose, along with all the arts and sciences we have today. This was all due to the influence of the Super Race!"

Mel let out a sigh. By now, Willard and Crossley were caught up in the teaching and did not notice his agitation. *Where had Fogarty learned his history?* Mel wondered. Even grade-school children knew that civilization had arisen in the Fertile Cresent of Mesopotamia and Egypt, had been perfected in Greece and Rome, and had then spread to "barbarian" Europe. Fogarty had it backward.

The silver-haired orator was relentless. "Let me tell you," he continued, "our forefathers did not accomplish all of this by interbreeding with subhumans!"

At this, a loud cheer went up from the crowd. Men stomped and women clapped.

Next, Fogarty flipped to a chart of various types of monkeys, trailed by humans representing supposed levels of evolution. "Let's change gears," he announced, "from history to biology. All you ranchers out there, you breed cattle, right?"

Men like Hank waved their hands and whistled.

"Tell me," Fogarty said. "What happens when you breed a thoroughbred with a donkey?"

"A mule!" the men shouted.

"Why not a thoroughbred?" Fogarty asked.

The men looked at one another and shrugged, until one of them shouted, "Because water seeks its own level!"

"Exactly!" Fogarty said. "In the rules of breeding, refined traits always bow to primitive ones!"

The crowd oohed and aahed, their faces lighting as though full of insight.

"And now," Fogarty drew them on, "what happens when you cross a white man and a Negro?"

"A mulatto!" someone answered.

"A white man and an Indian?"

"A half-breed!"

"A white man and a Jap?"

No ready name came to anyone's mind. At last, Willard hooted, "Somethin' nobody wants to see!"

The crowd loved this, and Fogarty gave Willard a thumbs-up.

The litany could have gone on, but someone cried out from the middle of the crowd, "What about the Jews? Are they white or what?"

The crowd mumbled, some shaking their heads and others shrugging, until Fogarty flipped the chart again.

Here he displayed a drawing of a tree with a snake wrapped around it and a woman holding an apple.

"Neither!" Fogarty declared. "The least of the low, the spawn of Satan—the Jews cannot be accounted for except as the offspring of Eve and Lucifer!"

Obviously awestruck, the crowd clapped again, not asking for the proof of such a statement.

Fogarty drew closer to the people, now, looking at them with such sincerity, they hushed with reverence. "My dear friends," he went on, "the reason you have been blessed with your heritage is because your forefathers had the foresight to keep themselves pure! You are the result of the pure Aryan will. And you are the foundation of the New Aryan Nation!"

Exultation swept over the crowd, and there were more congratulatory handshakes and back-claps.

"The future of our beloved race has been entrusted to your care," the leader challenged. "Upon the hills of the great northwest, we will establish a pure land, free of inferior beings, the New Israel!"

Mel could hardly believe his ears. What was this about Israel? A New Israel in the Northwest?

"Rejoice, Lost Tribes!" Fogarty cheered them. "Your wanderings are over! You have come to the Promised Land, and your time is at hand!"

Mel had not a clue as to what this was all about. It sounded about as ludicrous as belief in the Hale-Bopp snatch, by which disembodied souls would have been transferred to a higher planetary existence.

He had no opportunity to question Fogarty's statements, however, for suddenly Mel felt the eyes of the crowd upon him. Then he saw that Jim Fogarty, himself, was giving him the eagle-eye.

Mel's heart thrummed with fear. Did Fogarty sense his hypocrisy, did he know he was not a true believer? The Aryan leader studied him for a while, and the crowd was breathless.

Strangely though, Mel had the feeling that Fogarty was not suspicious. He sensed that Fogarty was actually admiring him.

"Ladies and gentlemen," the leader proceeded, "in a few moments, our guest, Monte Altmeyer, a prime example of German manhood, will be speaking to you. Before he comes, however, I want to say that we are honored tonight to be hosted by two of the finest specimens of Aryan blood I have ever laid eyes upon."

Mel glanced around, wondering who Fogarty was referring to. He noticed that everyone was still looking at him, and Fogarty's eyes had not shifted.

Without taking his gaze from Mel, Fogarty lifted his hand and waved someone up from the shadows. "Pete Wester!" he called. "Come out here! And you, the other Mr. Wester—yes, you . . ."

He was pointing at Mel.

"Come up and join your brother!"

Willard and Crossley, standing on either side of Mel, snapped amazed looks toward him. Mel swallowed hard, barely registering what was happening.

When he saw Pete come out from the porch, joining Jim Fogarty in the firelight, he knew he had not misunderstood. The Aryan leader was calling him forward as a representative of Nordic manhood.

Both brothers were red-faced as they came to the front, Mel from sheer embarrassment and Pete, most likely, from awe.

"Ah, see there!" Fogarty declared. "Only the white man can blush! Only the white man, Adam, was made in God's image—Adam, which in Hebrew means 'red face.' No other race can claim such a trait! Therefore, no other race is divine!"

Mel did not hear all of this. His head was buzzing with fear and humiliation.

Fogarty now had one brother on each side, an arm about each man's shoulders. "Have you ever seen truer specimens, ladies and gentlemen?" he shouted. "Hair blond as sunlight, eyes fair as the sea, skin white as birchwood! And tall! Aren't they tall! And strong!"

Mel wanted to run. He felt like a slave up for sale.

"All the qualities of perfect manhood, if ever I saw it!" Fogarty repeated. Then, turning to Pete, he gave him a special endorsement. "And brave!" he said, displaying the host proudly. "You all know what Pete did to keep himself pure!"

At this, many people in the crowd clapped and whistled, but Pete shook his head and whispered in Fogarty's ear.

Mel wondered what special heroics his brother was being praised for.

"Like a true Aryan!" Fogarty went on. "He is not only brave, but humble! He doesn't want me to praise him publicly!"

Now the people clapped and stamped more loudly. "Go, Pete! Go, Pete!" they hollered.

Mel noticed that Pete was avoiding his gaze. Whatever Fogarty was about to announce was something Pete did not want his brother to hear.

But there was no stopping Eagle-Eye. Proud as a cigar-passing papa, he sang his disciple's praises. "Your host, Peter Wester has given one of the ultimate sacrifices in his devotion to the Super Race. This man used to cohabit with a Jewess. When he learned the truth about her despicable race, he chose to endure the heartbreak of sending her away, rather than continue to soil his own body with hers. Yes, my friends, he cut the filth of that relationship from his heart and stands before you today, a clean Aryan man!"

The dazzled crowd applauded, whistling and cheering the shamefaced Pete.

Mel was dumbstruck. Visions of the sweet and beautiful Honey ripped at his heart. Honey—sent packing. Honey—the best thing that had ever happened to Pete Wester—kicked out of the Promised Land.

CHAPTER 16

Mel paced in the dark behind Pete's house. The party out front was breaking up, and he waited for his brother to be done with his guests for the night.

As soon as Fogarty had released the brothers from center stage, Mel had disappeared into the house. Being one of the heroes of the evening, no one questioned him. Even Willard and Crossley left him alone.

For an hour, he seethed with anger. It was probably a good thing he had a few minutes to cool down before confronting Pete. He would have decked him if he had gotten to him sooner. As it was, he was still fuming when Pete sheepishly came looking for him.

The last song of the evening had been sung, and the last cheer for the Great White Race had been whooped. Mel had missed Monte Altmeyer's talk, but he figured he could live without it.

The crowd was dispersing to campsites about the yard when the screen door on Pete's back porch creaked open, sending a shaft of yellow light across the garden patch behind the house. "Little Bro," Pete called, "you out here?"

Mel clenched his fists and growled through gritted teeth, "I'm here, Pete. Just long enough to hear where Honey is, and then I'm gone!"

Pete stepped off the porch and joined Mel in the dim light. When he spoke, his voice was dry, as though he were talking through cotton. "Look, Mel," he began, "I know you think I'm scum."

"You got that right!" Mel muttered, turning on him with a vengeance. "How could you? How could you send Honey away? That garbage about her leaving because of Ruby Ridge—that was just a smoke screen, wasn't it?" Flashing angry eyes toward the treetops, he snarled, "Pete, how could you buy all this trash about races and bloodlines? Where's your brain?"

Pete sighed. "I can't expect you to understand," he said. "You haven't learned all the stuff I have. You haven't seen what I've seen—my friends losing their homes, their ranches. You haven't read the stuff I've read. Give it time, Mel. You'll see. . . ."

Mel stared at Pete in disbelief. "You've actually bought the idea that Jews control the world?" he fumed. "Everything's a big conspiracy? Tell me," he challenged, "how did Honey conspire against you? You lived with her for nine years! Did she grow horns or a tail in that time?"

Rolling his eyes, he spat, "Besides, when did you figure out she was a Jew? I don't remember anything like that ever coming up before. Her last name—Aronstam—is that Jewish? I never would have known it was Jewish. So what does it matter, anyway?"

Pete stuck his hands in his pockets and looked at the ground. "It didn't matter, not years ago. I wouldn't have cared if Honey was a black African. I loved her, Mel—you know I did!"

Mel's eyes burned with exasperation. Blinking, he fought tears. He knew it was no use asking Pete to explain. Whatever had driven him to his desperate act, it must have been based on rhetoric such as Fogarty spewed. There was no reasoning with the irrational.

Gritting his teeth, he tried to listen. "So, what happened, Pete? What finally convinced you to send her packing?"

Pete grew very quiet, and Mel wondered if he would speak at all. For a long while, he gazed deep into the woods. Finally, his voice soft, he said, "Lots of my friends, the ones I used to run with, turned to farming and ranching after their partying days. You remember Cy and Michael, and the others?"

Mel remembered. They were the ones who had helped Pete build his house. Still hippies in their hearts, they had been forced to grow up when families came along, little by little giving up their marijuana and their footloose lives to earn a living from the soil. A lot of them had worked as parttimers or itinerants in the orchards and fields until they could afford to buy land and go into business for themselves.

"Sure, they were good guys," Mel said.

"Well, most of them are gone now, forced out by the agricultural conglomerates—forced out by the banks in hard times. Their farms are now owned by international monopolies, Mel. There is hardly such a thing as the family farm anymore."

Mel shook his head. "All in the last ten years?" he asked. "How did all that happen?"

Pete tensed his jaw. "Well, brother, that's where I'd have to start preaching my heresies. I don't think you really want to hear any of that."

Mel tried to be patient. "I see," he said. "That's where the theories about the Jewish bankers come in. Well, let me tell you, coming from the ghettos in L.A., I've known a lot of bankers and a lot of slumlords. They sure aren't all Jews, and no matter what they are, some of them even have hearts. Besides, as I recall my history, the very word 'ghetto' comes from the hellholes where the Jews had to live for centuries. They sure haven't all been wealthy or powerful."

Pete shrugged. "You're not going to listen, I know that. This thing's a lot bigger than either of us can understand. It's international, Mel."

The ex-cop glared at Pete. "So much for that, Big Brother. I want to know about Honey. What pushed you over the edge?"

Pete took a deep breath. "I had been going to a lot of these meetings. Honey never came. One night, when I got home, she was already in bed. We had had words before I left. I couldn't understand why she wouldn't ever go with me, why she couldn't see the truth behind what my friends were saying. Well, I was just putting a log on the fire, and I reached up to the mantel to get the matches."

At the memory, his face twitched. "You remember Honey's music box? The one she always kept above the fireplace?"

Mel nodded. "Sure. It was really special to her."

"Well, I accidentally knocked it off the mantel. It fell to the hearth and broke apart." Pete's hands shook. "I can still hear the tune playing over and over while I tried to pick up the pieces."

Mel felt his sadness. "'The Blue Danube,'" he said. "Sure, Pete, I remember."

"I took the parts to the kitchen table," Pete went on. "I was hoping I could get them back together and that Honey hadn't heard the crash or the music. As I fumbled with the sides of the broken box, the bottom came off in my hands, the part that the little crank sticks out of."

"Yeah, go on," Mel said.

"Well, there in the bottom was a piece of cloth. At first I thought it was just some padding, insulation or something, for the sound box. But when I took it out, meaning to rearrange it, I noticed it was something odd." Pete stopped, his eyes moist and red.

"So . . . what was it?" Mel prodded him.

"It was a little rag, a funny little thing. It was kind of a grayish yellow and shaped like a star—not just any star, Brother. It was a Star of David. You know, a Jewish star."

Mel didn't make much of this. "So? Probably some holiday ornament she made when she was a kid. You know, some little-girl memento?"

Pete sighed. "I wish," he said. "No, it was more than that. I looked at it real close, and it had funny writing on one side. I can't read Hebrew, of course, but that's what it was. All crimped and jagged, like whoever wrote on it had a shaky hand. And the writing was old, you know, like it had been there for years. Besides, the rag was dirty, not a nice little decoration the way you're thinking."

Mel shrugged. "Are you telling me that finding a Jewish star in your lady's music box was enough to turn you against her?"

Pete glared at his brother. "You'd like to think I'm that stupid, wouldn't you? No, Mel, I didn't want to think anything bad about Honey. It's what she told me that finally left me no choice."

Mel listened as Pete recounted that strange night.

"The crash woke Honey up, and she came out to the kitchen to see what had happened. When she saw what I had—the little rag—she suddenly got real weird."

"Weird?" Mel repeated. "How so?"

"She came over to the table and grabbed the star out of my hand. She started to cry, and I thought she was mad about the music box. But it wasn't the box she was upset about. It was the rag. Man, you'd think I'd broken into her diary or something! She said it was something very private and that no one was supposed to touch it! She said it was a secret and not to tell anyone about it."

Mel looked quizzical. "That doesn't sound like Honey. She was always real level-headed."

Pete nodded. "Exactly. Now, you're beginning to see how weird this was. Anyway, after that, things changed between Honey and me. We'd never had secrets from each other—at least, not that I'd known about. Suddenly it seemed like Honey was real fidgety. Whenever I'd talk to her about the Militia or what I was learning, she'd get real antsy—paranoid-like. Finally, one day, I put two and two together. I started to think about her name. I remembered how Moses, in the Bible, had a brother named Aaron. And then, I realized: Aronstam had to be a Jewish name!"

Mel tensed. Pete knew what he was thinking.

"Now listen, brother," he said defensively, "I swear to you that's not what broke us up. No matter what I've come to believe, I never would have sent away the woman I loved because of her last name—not if Fogarty himself held a gun to my head. But, it was Honey; it was the way she started acting, like she had this big secret and she wasn't safe with me anymore. She stopped entertaining our friends, the ones I was bringing home from the meetings. And she kept a close eye on them whenever they were in the house. I swear, that funny little rag had come between us!"

Mel frowned. "So, is that what pushed you to send her away?"

Pete took awhile to answer. It seemed to be hard for him to find the words. "I don't know if you can believe me," he finally said. "But I didn't send her away because we had problems or because she had changed. I sent her away to protect her."

Mel was doubtful. "Sure!" He sneered.

Pete glanced toward the house, as if fearing eavesdroppers. "Listen, bro," he said, "did you know it's possible to believe certain things and yet fear the ones who preach them? Well, I've come to believe a lot of what the Freemen preach, but sometimes I think they take it too far. I don't know where to draw the line. I think they're onto something with the racism stuff. But I happen to be in love with a Jew. In fact, sometimes I don't know who the enemy is. I'm one mixed-up guy, Baby Brother. I'll tell you this—when push came to shove, I sent Honey away because Fogarty is a dangerous man. As much time as he spends here, with his scary thugs, I knew it wouldn't be long before he'd learn about Honey, maybe even find that crazy rag. So I sent away the one I love, and I'm harboring her enemy."

Mel was incredulous. It occurred to him, not for the first time, that Pete had lost himself, that he was behaving like a programmed freak from some kind of cult. "Man, you're in one strange position!" he said, taking him by the arm. "Did it ever occur to you that it was a lie that sent you down this slippery slope? Why don't you just follow your heart, man? We have to get out of here and go find Honey!"

Pete looked confused, as though two voices were speaking in his head simultaneously. At last, he nodded, like he was about to take Mel up on the idea. But, before he could say anything, the screen door creaked again on the back porch.

In the light from the house's warm interior, Jim Fogarty stood, tall and gleaming with his frosty hair. "Hey, fellas," he called. "My men and I are having a private meeting with Monte Altmeyer. Come on in and join us. He wants a few choice folks to hear what the future holds."

Pete and Mel stood hesitantly in the yard.

Again, Fogarty motioned to them enthusiastically. "Come on," he called. "How often do you get to glimpse the inner workings of the world?"

The two brothers tried to look impressed as they walked toward the house. When they reached the door, Fogarty clapped them on the backs. "Welcome to the inner circle, boys!" he exclaimed. "You've done yourselves proud!"

CHAPTER 17

Honey Aronstam walked down the hall of the anthropology department at Midwest University, reading the various names on the office doors. The receptionist had offered to call her cousin's office to announce her arrival, but Honey told her it was to be a surprise.

"I haven't seen Ken in years," she said. "I just happen to be in town, and I'd like to say hi."

Actually, Honey didn't want her name being spoken over any telephone. She had come to think that the less her whereabouts was revealed by any electronic device, the safer she would be.

Honey had never gone out of her way to look attractive, but she was a natural beauty. Wherever she went, heads turned. Her dark hair fell in natural waves, and she wore it that way, without pins or barrettes. Only a touch of lipstick brought extra color to her light olive complexion and big, brown eyes. With Honey's looks, even in her mid-thirties, less was best.

Now, more than ever, she wanted to be understated. She preferred the backwoods look that worked best in the Montana hills to anything flashy or trendy. Because she was in a big city, she had worn her one really nice dress. Even it was nothing fashionable, an old Gunne Sax that she'd had since the eighties. The last time she had worn it had been to the wedding of friends in Thompson Falls. She had often thought she would wear it if she and Pete ever formally took vows. That had never happened, and now she figured, it never would.

Honey clutched her small travel bag, the only one except her large shoulder purse that she had brought with her from Bull River. Passing door after door labeled "Graduate Assistant" and "Graduate Fellow," she finally came to the last two in the hall.

The door to the right was shut tight, the frosted glass panel on the top showing no sign of interior light except what came from some outside window. "Dr. David Rothmeyer, Professor of Ancient Cultures and Linguistics," the door was labeled. Below the name was taped a note written with black marker pen: "On Sabbatical."

Straight ahead was the office Honey was looking for: "Dr. Kenneth Aronstam, Department Chairman."

That door, too, was shut, but warm yellow light shone through its frosted glass, and the receptionist had assured her that the chairman was in.

Honey smoothed her flowered dress, then knocked on the door.

"Come in," her cousin called.

He sounded so professional, she thought, not like the kid she'd grown up with.

Slowly she opened the door, stuck her head inside, and waited for Ken to look up.

Busy as always with a pile of papers, he did not immediately respond, until she stepped in and placed her travel bag on the floor. "Come in, come in," he finally said, motioning to a chair, but still not raising his head.

When he did at last glance Honey's way, he gasped in surprise. "Honey!" Jumping up from his swivel chair, he took one giant step and reached for her, lifting her slim body off the floor and hugging her tight. Then, as if remembering his professorial image, he put her down, shot a look toward the door, and shut it.

"Honey, girl!" He laughed and hugged her again. "What on earth brings you here? Did some grizzly chase you out of the mountains?"

Honey laughed with him. "No such luck, Ken," she said. "I wish it were just a bear that drove me out."

She had intended to keep her first moments with her cousin lighthearted. But, suddenly, feeling the comfort of his presence, she let down her guard, and tears welled in her dark eyes.

Holding her at arms' length, Ken studied her sad face. "What is it, cousin?" he asked. "Here, have a seat."

He led her to the folding chair upon which so many people had sat through the years. A department chairman filled many roles beyond that of administrator, he had learned, from tutor to diplomat to psychological counselor. He had a hunch Honey's needs surpassed any he had dealt with thus far.

Honey was Ken's favorite relative. The two had grown up together, children of two brothers. They had gone to school and synagogue school together, had enjoyed the post–Viet Nam era together, with all that the holdover hippie culture afforded the young. They had even gone to this very university together, before Honey, whose real name was Clarissa, adopted her "back-to-the-earth" name and took off for Seattle.

Ken had met Pete a time or two when he visited Honey on the coast. He had liked the offbeat fellow well enough, but he had worried that he was unstable, fickle in his devotion to various causes, and he wondered if Pete was good for Honey. When Ken had heard from her, during the holidays or on his birthday, she had always seemed happy, and so he had hoped for the best.

"So, what's going on?" he asked, handing her a tissue from the ever-ready box that chairmen learned to keep near their desks. "If Pete's turned mean, I'll—"

Honey sniffed and wiped her eyes. She felt foolish, showing her emotions this way. "No, no," she said. "Pete's not mean. A little crazy," she said, with a half-smile, "but not mean."

Ken said nothing, knowing she would tell him what she wanted to.

She took a deep breath, wondering just where to start. Of course, she had thought about this long and hard ever since deciding to come to Columbus.

"I'm going to ask a strange question," she said.

Ken nodded. "Okay."

Honey looked around the little office, got up, and glanced out the window, then turned to him.

"Is it safe to talk?"

"Safe?" Ken shrugged. "Anything you say is safe with me."

"No, I mean really safe. Like . . ." She nodded toward the walls.

"What?" Ken laughed. "You mean bugged? You wonder if my office is *bugged?*"

Honey blushed. "I told you it was crazy," she said, taking up her bag and making as though she would leave. "Maybe I shouldn't have come here."

Ken lurched forward. "Now, *that* is crazy!" he huffed. "What is this all about, Honey? Are you in some kind of trouble?"

With this, Honey broke down. In a gush, all of her pent-up fears came tumbling forth.

"Oh, Ken, you have no idea! Pete . . . he fell in with some bad people! I don't know if I'm in trouble or not. I only know that I can't be too careful, and I must seem like—really flipped out!"

"What kind of people?" Ken asked, frowning.

Honey sighed. "You know how Pete was always hopping on some bandwagon, always into some cause or other? Years ago, I loved him for that, for the caring and daring it represented. He seemed like a leader, but after years of being with him, I learned that he could be taken in . . . you know—duped."

"So," Ken tried to interpret, "he's in with some bad folks, and you're in danger?"

Honey fidgeted. "I—I don't know. That's part of the problem. If I knew for sure, maybe I'd know what to do. But Pete thought I might be in danger, so—" Her chest heaved with a sob. "He sent me away!"

Ken tried to envision it. He knew that Honey had been happy with Pete, happy in those beloved hills he had never been privileged to see. In the cards and letters she had sent over the years, she had expressed her excitement about what she was learning, as well as her hopes for the future. He knew she wanted children and suspected that the lack of them created a hollow spot.

But for her to leave Pete and Montana must have taken something traumatic indeed.

"What kind of people, exactly, is he involved with?" Ken asked.

Anxiously, she spoke of the Militia, of Fogarty, and of the rallies. She spoke of what they had done to Pete's head and how he talked, now that he had been swayed by Fogarty's awful lies. "Fogarty wooed Pete by giving him a special job," she said. "Lots of evenings he sits by his ham radio on the porch, and he waits for messages."

"Messages?" Ken repeated. "What sort of messages?"

"I never heard them very clearly. I'd usually be in the house, doing dishes or something, when the crackling and the popping would start. Pete would tense up, grab a pad, and get ready to write. I swear, the words were some sort of code! They didn't mean much to me at all. But the voices, that's what weirded me out! They were usually foreign, although some were Southern. But the foreign ones, they sounded like they were Arab—or some type of Middle Eastern. Then, there was this German voice, and once or twice a voice that sounded Irish."

Ken's eyes grew wide. "You've got to be kidding!" he muttered. "You poor kid. No wonder you're scared to death!"

Honey lowered her head, and Ken handed her another tissue. "You understand, then? You don't think I'm nuts?"

Ken leaned back in his chair and cupped his hands behind his neck. He blew out softly and shook his head. "From what you describe, you'd be crazy not to be scared!" Leaning forward again, he gazed at her intently. "I know you don't have a TV at your house, but you've surely been in touch enough to think those sorts of connections might insinuate trouble."

Honey swallowed hard. "Of course, Ken. We get the paper when we go into town, and we have a transistor radio. We're not hermits!"

Ken sensed her defensiveness. "All right. You've suspected anything I could suggest. Pete's got himself hooked up with some group much bigger than any stateside militia. Sounds like this Fogarty's using Pete's naiveté and his enthusiasm to rope him into being a go-between."

Honey's hands were cold. She tucked them against her lap.

Ken observed her pale look. "Now," he asked, "how are *you* in danger? What happened to make you think they would come after you?"

The woman shook her head. "It all seems too far-fetched. It seems like something out of a movie. Maybe I'm imagining all of it."

"Nonsense," Ken said. "What you've told me so far is only too believable."

"Okay," Honey sighed. She set down her purse, and reached for her little travel bag, setting it on her lap. She opened it gently, and drew out an envelope. She placed the envelope on the professor's desk as tenderly as though it were a Fabergé egg, then smoothed it with a caress.

"Here," she said. "This is what it's all about."

Ken looked at it quizzically and gave her a questioning glance.

"Go ahead. Open it," she said. "Just be careful."

As he picked up the envelope and peeked inside, he frowned.

"I have never shown this to anyone before," she said. "My dad gave it to me when I enrolled at the university. I think he knew he would not be here much longer. He said I was grown up and ready to take care of it."

Ken pulled out a little piece of yellow, ragged cloth, about three-and-a-half inches long and cut in the shape of a Star of David. He studied it in bewilderment.

Honey's father, his uncle, had died of lung cancer shortly after Honey entered college. Having lost her mother not many years before, she suffered a long bout with grief, but she had never told Ken about the strange gift.

"Is this what I think it is?" he marveled.

Honey nodded. "It's a Jew badge, worn by our great-grandfather Aronstam in the camp at Dachau."

Ken was stunned. It had been a long time since he had heard reference to his great-grandfather, who, as a very old man, had been liberated by American GIs when they freed Holocaust survivors.

"Great-grandpa Aronstam?"

"That's right," she said. Then, reaching out, she gestured to him to turn the star over. "Look at the back side."

Ken did so, and his eyes grew even wider.

"What the . . ." He pulled it close to his face. "This looks like Hebrew!" Glancing up at his cousin, he saw that she agreed. "Do you know what it says?"

Honey shook her head. "Great-grandpa sent this to the family by means of the Red Cross the day he was set free. It went to his eldest son, our grandfather, then to my dad, because he was the oldest."

She continued, "The instructions were that it was to be a family secret until"—she stopped and looked at Ken quite sincerely—"until we could show it to a wise man in Jerusalem."

Ken blinked. "Wow! That sounds pretty strange. Are you sure you have that right?"

"I heard it more than once. My dad told me several times. It was real important to him, so it's always been very special to me. That's why I hid it. I kept it in the base of a music box all these years, and never told a soul—not even Pete."

Honey gazed out the window, her thoughts in the Bull River Valley. "You know," she said, "I don't think Pete ever really realized until just recently that I'm Jewish. For all the years we spent together, and as close as we seemed to be, we never talked about much of anything deeper than politics, gardening, and natural foods."

Ken smiled at her sadly, then scratched his forehead. "So let me guess," he said. "Pete found your star, and with his connections, he got scared."

"Exactly!" Honey exclaimed. "How did you know?"

"Pete's no dummy," Ken asserted. "He recognized a Jewish secret when he saw it. No one would have to read Hebrew to know that this is old, and probably a message of some kind. In the circle Pete runs in, a secret, especially a Jewish one, can have international significance."

As Honey pondered this, Ken surveyed the cloth like a hungry man at a bakery window. "What I wouldn't give to study this out!" he declared. Then, looking disappointed, he added, "But I guess I don't meet Great-grandpa Aronstam's specifications."

Honey did not reply, her mind still on her predicament.

Observing her, Ken scooted his chair close and patted her knee. "Pete was wise to send you away," he said. "Not only do you have a Jewish name, but you were hiding something Jewish. His new friends were always going to be snooping around your house. He knew you'd never destroy that cloth, and short of that, there was no other answer."

Honey looked amazed. "I-I don't know," she stammered. "I never thought of all that."

"No?" Ken replied. "You may not have it all figured out, but you've sensed the danger of your position." Then, with a wink, he asked teasingly, "Why else do you look for bugs in people's offices?"

Honey grinned, the tension easing a little, despite the realities that seemed to be settling in.

"So, what should I do?" she asked. "I don't have much family left. I've been on the run for months—Seattle, Wyoming, staying with friends. Can you help me?"

Ken Aronstam was a secularist and a rational scientist; he claimed no particular religion. But ever since David Rothmeyer's invitation to Israel, he had been thinking more and more about his Jewish heritage.

This visit from Honey pricked him in more ways than one.

Clearing his throat, he tried not to sound too grave. "You know me, Honey," he said, "old 'science brain.' I've never believed in God or fate. But I have to admit, this little cubbyhole of an office is attracting strange vibes these days."

Honey listened respectfully. After what she'd gone through, nothing much surprised her.

"Believe it or not, you're not the first person to come through here lately with a Jewish secret. One of my top professors was contacted a few months ago by some Jewish agency looking for help with a mysterious project. In fact, right now he's in Jerusalem working for them on something so sensitive that he can't even tell me about it! To avoid questions, we put a note on his door saying he's on sabbatical, but actually, he's only on earned leave, not even under our auspices at this point."

Honey raised her eyebrows. "That is peculiar," she said. "I wonder what the mystery project is."

"Who knows?" Ken shrugged. "Well, so much for the cloak-and-dagger stuff," he said with a laugh. Grabbing for an address book and a notepad, he began to jot something down.

"This does give me a thought, however," he said. "Do you have a passport?"

Honey was baffled. "It's with the personal papers I brought from home. Why?"

"Is it still active?" he asked, busily writing away.

Honey shrugged. "Yeah, sure," she replied. "Pete and I went with his brother to Costa Rica a few years ago. Why?" she asked again.

"What would you think of going to Israel?" Ken inquired, looking at her over the rims of his glasses.

Honey was astonished. "Israel? Me?" she gasped.

Ken sat up from his desk. Trying not to frighten her, he said firmly, "Cousin, I do believe you are in danger. You need to leave the country, and Israel is a natural. It's where Great-grandpa Aronstam said the star should go, and you could find safe harbor there."

Honey's brain was whirring. "S-safe harbor?" she stammered.

Ken tried to ease her fears. "Sure," he said with a smile. "After all, according to Great-grandpa, Jerusalem is where the wise men are."

Shoving his notepad across the desk, he pointed to a name and address in the Old City. "Now that I've heard your story, I understand your fears of being followed. I don't think we should notify anyone," he continued, "but I want you to hook up with my friend when you get there. If there ever was a wise guy, it's David Rothmeyer!"

CHAPTER 18

Rabbi Horace Benjamin never felt more in his element than when he was walking down a street in Jerusalem's Old City. Although he was not a proud man, he always held his head a little higher and wore an expression of sincere satisfaction.

People passing him could not help but take a second look. He was used to tourists, in Jerusalem or in New York, taking pictures of him as he strode along in his long black suit and wide, flat hat. Had he been dressed in red, he would have resembled a Santa Claus, save that he had no round belly. His friend, Dr. Jacobs, filled that requirement better than he. But Benjamin's bushy white hair with its long tendrils, and his glorious fatherly beard, which hung nearly to his waist, were eye-catching indeed.

Unlike many of his colleagues, Benjamin did not avoid the eyes of the public. He did not keep his face downcast or don the aspect of a preoccupied mystic, which in too many cases was not indicative of holiness, but a ruse to shun interaction with humanity.

Nor had he ever been known to take offerings from naive seekers of blessings, as was the habit of some of his fellow rabbis.

Benjamin was an Orthodox Jew, of the Hasidic type, his roots going back to the followers of Israel Ben Eliezer in southeastern Europe during the eighteenth century. Known as Baal

Shem Tov, the "Kind Master of God's Name," Eliezer taught the suffering Jews of the southern provinces to seek joy in everyday things, that God loved them, and that the Mosaic Law was made for them, not them for it. Certain aspects of the Cabala, an ancient mystical and magical interpretation of the Scriptures, wove their way into Eliezer's teachings, so that, between the mixture of joyfulness and mystery he brought to religion, his followers gained a new understanding of the word "Hasidic," Hebrew for "pious."

Dancing and singing, which were frowned upon among the scholarly Talmudists of northern Europe, enlivened Hasidic celebrations, making them gay and bright. Hasidism spread like wildfire across the spiritual desert that was legalistic Judaism. After a while, the Hasidic approach to religion was the Judaism that the world recognized, and it came to be considered the main form of orthodoxy.

It was true that in the centuries that had passed since Baal Shem Tov, Hasidism had lost some of its gaiety. It had fallen back into a form of legalism that sometimes made it indistinguishable from the rigid teachings of northern Europe. The all-embracing love for mankind exhibited by Eliezer was often nearly extinguished among some sects of Hasidism.

Yet, there was still a fascination for the Hasidics that drew people to observe and even to envy them—to lift cameras in the streets of New York and Israel and snap photos of them, to marvel at their animated debates in the restaurants and marketplaces, and to honor their devotion to God.

Horace Benjamin was among the most sincere of Hasidics. David Rothmeyer did not know much of the history of his sect, but if he had been asked to name the warmest and kindliest man he had ever met, he would not have hesitated to name the rabbi.

David walked proudly beside Horace today, his long stride matching the rabbi's enthusiastic pace as the old fellow led him down a cobbled street toward Temple Mount.

Rabbi Benjamin had taught David a few things about that sacred mountain. Jews called the area of the Wailing Wall, or Western Wall, "Temple Mount," because that was the site upon which the ancient temple of Judaism had once stood. Presently controlled by Arabs, the platform now occupied by the Muslim Dome of the Rock was once the foundation of Solomon's and Herod's fantastic edifices. The building that stood there now, housing the rock on which Jewish sacrifices were once offered up, was one of the most sacred mosques in the Islamic world. And the Muslims did not even acknowledge that the sacred ground was related to Jewish history.

While living in Jerusalem, David had taken many a trek to the Western Wall. He had witnessed Jewish festivals at the high stone structure, which, since the destruction of Jerusalem in 70 C.E., was the only remnant of Herod's vanquished temple, and which was, itself, merely a part of an ancient retaining wall.

"Wailing Wall" was a fitting nickname, for Orthodox Jews were known to spend long hours literally wailing there for the lost pride of Israel. Also, they prayed there for the day when their temple would be rebuilt, a "house of prayer for all nations" as the Bible promised. Along with this, their prayer was for the coming of the Messiah, who must one day reign from the Holy Mount.

The mount was known by various names, especially Mount Moriah, meaning "Wisdom Teacher," and Mount Zion. It was from this second name that the term "Zionism" arose, the political movement that had given birth to the new state of Israel, making it possible for men like the rabbi to even go there.

Benjamin's colleagues had returned to New York City, and he had stayed in Jerusalem to help instruct young rabbinical students at the Consortium's seminary or "yeshiva." He spent some of his nights at the school, and had met David at his apartment door this morning, promising to show him things he never dreamed of.

David hastily showered and dressed, while the rabbi visited with Anya in the kitchen, feasting on her cinnamon rolls for breakfast.

Now, as they walked together, the rabbi was radiant. "Prepare to be 'blown away,' " he said, chuckling at the use of slang.

"Where are we going?" David asked.

"To a gallery," Horace replied.

David was disappointed, and his face showed it. The rabbi laughed again. "Not just any gallery, David. This is the gallery of the world's future!"

The professor had no idea what this meant, but realizing Horace was enjoying the intrigue, he asked no more questions.

The street down which they walked, like most of the streets in the Old City, did not accommodate cars. It was ancient and narrow, and was solely for foot traffic. But it was one of the grandest of the Jerusalem avenues, its buildings full of intriguing history.

Much of the architecture was from the Crusader period and then the Ottoman, that time in which the Turks nearly wiped out all Christian advances in the culture, along with Judaism. Evidences of the British Mandate period lay farther out, along the newer streets and broader avenues beyond the Old City walls.

Ahead, wide, banistered stairs led to the courtyard of the Wailing Wall. From the vantage point of a large veranda at the head of the stairs, one could take in a fabulous view of Temple Mount, the Kidron Valley at its foot, and the Mount of Olives beyond.

Rabbi Benjamin stopped, as was his custom, long enough to breathe a prayer upon viewing the holy site. David waited respectfully, removing his leather cap and bowing his head.

The rabbi then took him by the arm and, with the excitement of a young boy, he said, "We go this way." He pointed down a narrow lane that ran left off the veranda, paralleling the distant Western Wall.

A few doorways down the street, a little sign hung over the entry to a tiny set of descending stairs. "This is it!" the rabbi announced.

David would never have noticed the sign or the stairs had he not been directed to them. "Temple Jewels Exhibition," it said, and then in smaller letters beneath: "Temple Consortium, 36 Rebi Yosef St., Jewish Quarter."

David fumbled with his cap, not knowing whether to put it on or leave it off. Although Horace continued to wear his rabbinical one, David decided, in the split second before he was ushered into the place, that it was probably not fitting that he wear a hat in a building that housed "Temple Jewels," whatever that meant.

A small reception desk at the front lent the air of a typical tourist trap, complete with pamphlets and books for sale on the history of the exhibit, commentaries on the Scriptures regarding a prophetic rebuilding of the temple, little packets of slides, and knickknacks such as miniature menorahs.

Rabbi Benjamin introduced David to the young women who handled the reception desk and sold the trinkets. Then he said, "This way, my friend," and led David toward the central hall.

Above the doorway that opened onto the exhibit itself was a huge oil painting, an artist's conception of a glorious building. Awesome in detail, the dreamscape lifted the soul and the imagination. From a gleaming, alabaster court, a fabulous edifice arose, its aquamarine facade reflecting the light of heaven and the gleam of many candlestands. In proportion to the small figures who peopled the court, the building appeared to be several stories high. These people were garbed in elaborate robes and turbans, like actors in a Mideastern pageant.

"What is this?" David asked, pausing long enough to gaze on the work.

Rabbi Ben beamed. "That is what our temple will look like when we build it," he replied.

David studied the painting in amazement. Positioned about the temple court were ornate furnishings and various implements that the professor assumed to be ritualistic. A gilt-framed plaque beside the painting announced that these items were on display in this very exhibit.

"So," David marveled, "this gallery is about plans for the temple."

The rabbi nodded. "Not just the plans! The exhibit shows much of the actual work we have done to this point."

Looking at his watch, Benjamin said, "Why don't you wait here, while I go and fetch our guide?" Then gesturing down the hallway, he suggested, "There are several items on the wall that will introduce what you are about to see."

As the rabbi hurried off, David scanned a short history of the Jewish yearning for a temple, which was displayed in easy-to-read posters and articles, illustrated with scenes from the Bible, from the wanderings of the Jews, and from the reestablishment of the nation in 1948.

Under a poster of a Jewish family gathered about a Passover table, David read: "The hope of the rebuilding of the temple was conceived on the very day of its destruction, nearly two thousand years ago. Throughout those centuries, the Jewish people have never forgotten the temple. On our holidays we pray: 'Build your house as at the first, set your temple on its foundations, allow us to see it built, and make us joyous in its establishment . . . '"

The words reminded David of his childhood and of the many such feasts he had celebrated with his family. Indeed, he remembered reciting that very prayer and wondered, now, why it had never much impressed him.

He was gazing at the poster and at the prayer, lost in thought, when the rabbi returned with another gentleman. "Dr. Rothmeyer," Horace announced, "I want you to meet Rabbi Shalom Diamant, curator of this gallery. He is going to take us on a little tour."

The guide was dressed in more modern clothes than Horace's but wore a yarmulke like that of Uriel Katz and was bearded, as were all the Orthodox Jewish men David had met.

"Glad to meet you," said David, shaking the rabbi's hand.

"I am happy to show you around, Dr. Rothmeyer," Diamant began. "I have been following your work with keen interest for months."

This should not have surprised David. He knew that his whereabouts and his activities were monitored by numerous people he had never met, just as his credentials and background had been scrupulously investigated by the Consortium. Nevertheless, the reminder of that fact gave him the same sense of uneasiness he had experienced countless times since committing to this assignment.

He should have also anticipated that the "gallery" to which Horace had brought him would present him with yet more surprises, but he never could have been completely prepared for what he was about to see.

As the three men stepped through the arch that led to the first display area, Shalom Diamant launched into a monologue that he had apparently given often. His affection and enthusiasm for his topic were not blunted, however, by repetition.

Directing his guests toward a reproduction of the bas-relief from the Arch of Titus in Rome, he said, "We all know that the temple of Israel was destroyed in 70 C.E. at the sacking of Jerusalem by Rome's General Titus. We see here a depiction of Jewish slaves being forced to carry away items from the temple as booty for the conquerors. The great menorah that lit the court, the silver trumpets used by the Levites . . . these things and many other treasures disappeared during the destruction of Jerusalem."

David nodded. Many memories were pushing through the cobwebbed years that had separated him from his upbringing. He remembered reciting the mournful refrains of the Jewish prayer that stated, "It would be a delight unto my soul to walk barefoot upon the desolate ruins that were your holy courts."

As he followed the curator through the exhibit, he was surprised by a strange sensation of otherworldliness.

"The dream of rebuilding the temple spans fifty Jewish generations," Diamant was saying, gesturing emphatically. "It has been cried out upon every continent, sea, and ocean. The prayer for its rebuilding has been spoken in all human languages, and in all places, from synagogues to yeshivas, from prisons to ghettos, from homes to fields, each day for two millennia of exile!"

He had now led David and Horace into a room lined with tall, glass-fronted cabinets. Before directing them to the contents, he went on, "After seemingly endless centuries of peril and persecution, the dream of the actual reestablishment of the temple has taken on new hope with the return of the people to the Land of Israel and with the rebirth of the Jewish state.

"Twenty-seven hundred years ago, the prophet Isaiah declared that one day there would stand on Mount Zion a 'house of prayer for all people.' On that day, 'God will be king over all the earth!'" Diamant's eyes glistened behind his horn-rimmed glasses, and he clenched his hands together in front of him.

"Dr. Rothmeyer," he said, "the Temple Consortium was founded to fulfill God's command to build him a temple. For years, we have been researching the materials, measurements, and design of that temple as described by the Torah, the prophets, and our traditions. We have also been researching the sacred vessels, implements, musical instruments, and priestly garments necessary to the temple rituals. What I will show you now is the result of that research."

Inside the tall cabinets that lined the room were cups, platters, and censers of various types, all made of brass and fine metals. Gleaming beneath indirect lighting, they showed the finest of craftsmanship.

As the professor listened to Diamant's description of their purposes and uses, he was incredulous at the scholarship that had gone into the work.

Cups for the measuring of wine, water, oil, and grain, according to the specifications of Moses; vessels for the preparation of flour and other ingredients for the making of grain offerings; tongs for the carrying of coals to the altar; a huge copper wash basin and stand constructed after the biblical ordinance for the washing of hands; decanters, spices, incense trays . . . on and on the display went.

One showcase held little jars of spices, the result of intensive research into the components of temple incense. Another held little vials of substances for the making of the dyes that would be used for the fabrics and vestments of the court. Although he was taken aback by the fact that some of the implements were related to animal sacrifices, he had seen enough of such things in the world of archaeology that he did not, just now, question it.

In an adjacent room, the most magnificent of artifacts resided: a seven-branched menorah, as tall as a man, made of beaten brass. "This is only a model," Diamant said. "The one that will stand in the Holy Place, before the entrance to the Holy of Holies, will be made of pure gold, just as in the days of Solomon!"

David was no jeweler, no dealer in precious metals, but he knew that such an artifact would be utterly priceless.

Reminded of the letter he had received that had sent him on this adventure, its logo being a small, golden candlestand, he was astonished, trying to imagine the expense and dedication that must be going into the making of all these items. "This is incredible!" he exclaimed. "Why hasn't the world heard about your work?"

The two rabbis looked at each other and smiled feebly.

"Our work is not 'politically correct,'" Diamant replied. "The media barely acknowledges the right of Israel to exist, let alone what we are doing here."

Horace shrugged and lifted his palms to heaven. "The fact that this little agency resides here at all is a miracle," he said. "We are well aware that we have many enemies who would squash us, if they got the chance. In fact, there is no reason why they have not wiped us out of Jerusalem, except for the protection of God."

David had to agree. The consortium was brazenly situated mere meters away from the Dome of the Rock, the Arab sanctuary. Only the Western Wall courtyard separated it from the footstool of Israel's enemies, and there were no guards stationed anywhere nearby.

As he considered the exhibit's location, however, and as he stood surrounded by evidence of the temple's preparation, facts began to coalesce in his mind. Suddenly a fearsome understanding flooded David's consciousness, and with it a fledgling appreciation for the tremendously sensitive nature of the rabbis' work. Dumbfounded, he felt like a child on his first day at school.

Diamant, noting his awestruck expression, asked, "What is it, Dr. Rothmeyer? Are you all right?"

The professor shook himself and stared at his guides. "Let me get this straight," he said. "The Temple Consortium wants to rebuild Israel's lost temple where it once stood, right?"

The rabbis nodded, glancing at each other as though they knew what David's mind must be processing.

"That is right," Horace said. "Mount Zion."

David waved his hand and shook his head again. "Okay, okay!" he exclaimed. "But that is the present site of the Dome of the Rock. Correct?"

Rabbi Diamant followed his train of thought. "Also correct, Dr. Rothmeyer. Mount Moriah or Mount Zion. The two are one and the same."

David closed his eyes, actually feeling the blood drain from his face.

Rabbi Benjamin stepped closer to him. "Surely you knew this!" he exclaimed.

The professor opened his eyes again, feeling quite foolish. "I-I did . . . and I didn't!" he stammered. "I mean, somehow, despite my upbringing, despite years of watching CNN and thinking I'm informed, the sensitive nature of this situation has gone right over my head!"

The rabbis smiled sympathetically.

"You are not alone, David," Diamant observed. "Many intelligent, educated people have missed what goes on here. The fact is that the Arabs, and their Dome of the Rock, now occupy the sacred mountain where the most holy place in Judaism once stood, and where, the prophets tell us, it must stand again!"

Rabbi Benjamin showed untypical surliness when he said, "We can hold the news services liable for such lack of understanding! They do not tell the rest of the world why there is such jealousy between the Arabs and Jews over that tiny piece of real estate. But it is, indeed, the piece of property over which all Middle-Eastern conflict arises!"

David shrugged. "I am certainly vague on it all!" he confessed. "I thought most of the squabbles were over the Palestinians being edged out of their ancient territory."

The rabbis were not surprised at this admission, but Diamant's blood began to boil. "Of course!" he exclaimed. "That is all you have been told. But tell me, where will the Jews live, if there is no Israel? The Palestinians now own Bethlehem and Hebron, and will not be satisfied until they own all of Jerusalem, to make it *their* capital, not ours! The Arab world stretches from India to Libya, and from Bosnia to the Sudan! Do they really need more of the speck of dust that the world conceded to the victims of the Holocaust? Why doesn't CNN show a map sometime?"

Rabbi Benjamin placed a calming hand on Diamant's shoulder, then turned to David. "Dr. Rothmeyer," Horace said, "we did not expect to speak of such things today. But perhaps it is good we are doing so. After all, everything we are about relates to the bigger picture."

David nodded gravely. "I would say 'relates' is an understatement. I would say that the minute you and your agency set foot on Mount Moriah to build anything, it could spark—"

He shuddered, and Rabbi Benjamin filled in, "World War Three? Yes, David, we hear this objection every day!"

The professor was speechless, his body tingling with fear. At last, finding his voice, he observed, "I do not recall discussing any of this with the committee. It must seem strange to you that this has not hit home with me before. But do you really think I want to be part of something with such horrific international ramifications?"

Hearing this, Rabbi Diamant glared at David and then at Rabbi Benjamin. "You told me he was a secular Jew, Horace. But you didn't tell me he was against us!" he spat. In a huff, he turned on his heel, as though to leave.

"Shalom!" Horace pleaded, grabbing the curator by the arm. "Be patient! Put yourself in Dr. Rothmeyer's place. He has not been as close as we are to all of this. Now that his eyes are opening, we must expect this reaction!"

Not for the first time, David was observing Rabbi Ben's peacemaking abilities. This time, however, the professor himself was on the receiving end of the rabbi's diplomacy.

Diamant calmed enough to turn around and faced David with doubtful eyes, while Horace focused on the professor's concerns. "Please don't be hasty in your conclusions, Dr. Rothmeyer," he said. "Although you are not part of our 'orthodox' camp, I trust you do have a heart for Israel, or you would never have come with us this far."

The tightness in David's chest eased a little, and his hands, which had been balled up in fists, loosened.

He took a deep breath. "I suppose that is true," he admitted. "But this whole aspect of things does give me pause. . . ."

Benjamin nodded. "And so it should," he said. "We would not want you to be part of our efforts, if you took them lightly. It is good that you see the larger implications so that, if you proceed, it is with full understanding."

David might have asked why that "full understanding" had not been shared with him earlier. He knew, though, as they probably did, that if it had been, he never would have signed on.

Rabbi Benjamin was not one to preach, but his next words did prick David's conscience. "Dr. Rothmeyer, we looked long and hard for a man of your stature. We do feel God led us to you. Won't you at least see the rest of the exhibit, meet a few more people? And try to do so with the eyes of faith. Then, if you still feel you made a mistake . . . we will understand."

David looked around the display area. "I can do that," he replied, his voice smaller than he intended.

Rabbi Diamant reacted stiffly, obviously not certain that he wanted to spend more time with this heretic. But Benjamin, grasping the curator by the elbow, gave him a look that convinced him to go on.

"This way," Diamant said, his tone clipped.

Directing David to a display of musical instruments, he stood beside a dark wooden stand on which several silver trumpets were arrayed. Returning to his role as guide, the curator said, "You will note that these items are patterned on instruments shown in the Arch of Titus, which we saw earlier. The arch shows the slaves hauling off instruments just like these." Beside the trumpets were gleaming, handcrafted harps of fine Israeli hardwoods, small enough to be carried but large enough to produce an impressive sound, as Diamant demonstrated, running his hands across a set of strings.

Gesturing to the trumpets and harps, he said, "Hundreds of these instruments are being constructed for the use of the musicians in the new temple courts. Four thousand of these wonderful harps are being made, even as we speak, for the use of the temple choristers, the Levites."

Despite his perplexity, David could not help but be impressed, once again, by the craftsmanship and scholarship of the consortium.

He followed Diamant into another room, where they stood before a display of garments to be worn by the priests in the court. Diamant explained that hundreds of such garments were being made. In one corner of the room stood a huge computerized loom and a spinning wheel for the making of thread. The difficult pattern called for in the robe, headdress, belt, and pants of the priestly garb was based on ancient writings, and Diamant explained that the only weavers who seemed capable of reproducing it were from a Native American tribe.

"Research is still underway," he said, "for the identification of the precious stones of the high priest's breastplate, the twelve of which are meant to represent the twelve tribes of Israel."

It was as David stood in this room, where a faceless mannequin wore the first attempt at the reproduction of the high priest's garments, that he suddenly experienced something for which he had no name.

Only moments ago, he had been ready to run from this entire assignment. Fear, confusion, and anger had gripped him. Now, something beyond emotion filled his heart. Perhaps it was that brush with the divine, which mystics call "revelation," or perhaps only the jolt of facts coming together, so that, in one bullet of time, the meaning of his life was condensed, readable, foreseeable.

Whatever it was, it made his hair stand on end, for it relayed to him, in terms nothing short of supernatural, an interpretation of all the strange events that had befallen him since receiving the letter in Columbus.

Above the display of the priestly garments was a sign quoting the words of a traditional Jewish prayer: "Return priests to their service and Levites to their songs and music, and return the people of Israel to pleasant places, and there we will ascend and be seen and bow down before you."

David was mesmerized. Long and hard he studied the words, letting them sink into his bewildered heart, as they had already blazed through his spirit.

"Return priests to their service and Levites to their songs . . ."

Right there, in black and white, was the purpose for which he had been hired by the consortium. He, David Rothmeyer, bored professor of Central American antiquities, lonely widower, sorely empty of faith of any kind . . . *he* had been singled out of humanity to find the Keeper of the Temple's flame, the one who would govern all that went on in the only-dreamed-of Holy Place.

Why? he wondered. *Why me?* Surely he did not merit such a calling! Surely, he had never even believed in such things!

"Dr. Rothmeyer," a voice jolted him. "Dr. Rothmeyer, we have more to show you."

David looked into Rabbi Benjamin's smiling face, sensing his empathy.

"Are you ready for another glimpse of eternity?" Horace asked.

David's knees were shaky. "Stay beside me, Rabbi," he said softly. "I am not used to walking on streets of gold!"

CHAPTER 19

Shalom Diamant and Horace Benjamin led David briskly through a narrow back corridor of the consortium exhibit. According to a sign over the hall's entrance, they had left the public area and were now entering into the institute's private offices. Little cubbyholes, marked "Consortium Administrator" and "Secretary," were empty of people. David figured the administrator's office belonged to Rabbi Diamant. They passed a small room labeled Staff Lounge, where a pot of coffee sent off a stale aroma.

At last, they descended another small flight of stairs, which took them briefly outside to a lovely flowered patio whose high wall blocked a view of the Western Wall courtyard. Leading back into the basement of the institute was an open doorway, from which could be heard low voices.

"Step this way," Diamant directed the professor.

David, taller than anyone else here, ducked into the entrance and found himself in a long room full of workers seated at tables lined with computers. Flickering screens jumbled with words and images, nimble fingers flying over keyboards, contrasted strangely with piles of ancient books and the musty smell of deteriorating scrolls.

"What is this?" he asked, more amazed than ever.

"This is our research room," Diamant said.

Leading him toward one work station, he introduced David to a young colleague who was probably still of yeshiva age, his face not yet bearded, though he probably coaxed his peach fuzz each morning. Bushy tendrils of hair groomed into side-curls laced the edge of his face, and a small, crocheted yarmulke covered ample hair where in older fellows a bald spot might be hidden.

"This is Samuel Goldstein," Diamant said. "Samuel, meet Dr. Rothmeyer."

The young scholar pushed his chair back and thrust out a hand never hardened by outdoor work. "Glad to meet you, Dr. Rothmeyer," he said with a smile. "We have been waiting for you to come."

At this, about a dozen young men, ranging in age from mid-teens to thirties, stopped working and smiled at him. Several of them wore thick glasses, possibly the result of years before back-lit screens.

David nodded to them, and Diamant said, "Samuel is our chief computer guru, but all these fellows are indispensable."

Samuel smiled again, a blush bringing color to his pale cheeks.

"Sam," Diamant directed, "can you bring up a page of the floor plan?"

"Sure," Samuel replied, and with lightning speed, his deft fingers tickled the keyboard, scrolling through several screens and menus until he came to one boldly headed "Master Plan/Temple Layout."

David had seen such programs on computer screens in deluxe hardware and home-supply stores in Columbus. He had never owned a home but found the displays, usually in the kitchen-cabinet section, fascinating to watch.

Samuel ran the cursor around the courts of the computerized blueprint, clicking here and there to enlarge various chambers. "Here we are," he said with a chuckle, "standing in the Holy of Holies!"

David grinned broadly, and Rabbi Horace nudged him. "Enjoy it this way, David. No one except the high priest will ever enter the real thing."

David remembered his synagogue school teacher showing the class a layout of the temple on a flannel-graph when he was about seven years old. He remembered how the teacher had emphasized that in the times of the temple, the inner chamber beyond the Holy Place, the Holiest of the Holies, was visited only once a year, on the Day of Atonement. On that day, the high priest entered by himself, after going through intricate ritual cleansings, and there he offered up prayers for the sins of the people.

If that priest had even so much as a sinful thought when occupying the sacred room, he could die in an instant. No one would be able to go in after him, for the Ark of the Covenant and the Glory of God resided there. For that reason, he wore bells on the fringes of his robe so that the people outside could hear his movements. If the bells were silent, they would know that he had collapsed. For that eventuality, he also wore long cords on his garment, which trailed behind him beneath the curtain that separated the sanctuary from the adjacent court. Lesser priests could pull his dead body out from the chamber by means of those cords.

"But," the synagogue school teacher had said, "we have no record of this ever being necessary. The high priests must have been quite holy indeed."

All of this flashed through David's head in a second of remembrance, just as much of his childhood had returned to him during his work with the consortium.

"I don't see the Ark of the Covenant," he observed, leaning close over Samuel's shoulder. "Shouldn't it be in the center?"

Samuel glanced up at him. "We are looking at a rendering of Herod's temple," he said. "So far as we have been able to determine, there was no Ark present at that time."

David stood up and shrugged. "Of course," he said. "I saw *Indiana Jones!* The Ark was taken to Africa, right?"

The rabbis grinned, and the young scholars laughed. "You believe the movies?" Diamant said, his tone once more challenging. "Surely you are too much a scholar for that!"

David's face grew red. "Well, where *is* the Ark? Does anyone know? Will you have it in your new temple?"

Horace sensed David's embarrassment and stepped in again to cover for his handpicked professor. "Of course, the Ark of the Covenant is not Dr. Rothmeyer's specialty, Shalom. Let's not be hard on him. From what we've seen of David's work, if we were to assign him to the quest for the Ark, he would find it in short order!"

Again the roomful of computer jockeys chuckled. But this time, they were more respectful.

David's face was still red, not because he was ignorant regarding the Ark, but because he doubted he deserved Rabbi Benjamin's glowing endorsement.

Shalom continued. "Speaking of your work, Professor—assuming you will be staying on—you will be collaborating closely with our staff here."

No one could miss Diamant's sarcastic tone. The young men did not know what was behind it, but Horace glared at Diamant, and the curator backed down.

Leading the professor about the room, from work station to work station, Diamant continued. "The consortium utilizes cutting-edge technology in all of its research for the coming temple. Architects and engineers feed data from the Talmud and other ancient writings into our data banks, to prepare these blueprints, the clothing designs you saw upstairs, the formulas for the dyes, the identity of the metals and precious stones for such things as the priestly vestments, and so on.

"We have been fortunate," Diamant explained, "to have the help of experts from all over the world in setting up our data bases and keeping current with the best programs for our work."

He had brought David to the last work station, this one larger than all the others, and staffed by three men, each with his own computer. "Gentlemen," he said, "meet Dr. Rothmeyer. David, you will be working especially closely with these young men, for they are sorting Jewish genealogies from all over the world."

One by one, the staffers shook David's hand, introducing themselves as Clement, James, and Shofar.

David was not one to categorize people, but if he had seen these fellows on any street corner in the world, in any café or on any bus, he would have pegged them instantly as computer nerds. Complete with horn-rimmed glasses, pocket protectors, and rumpled shirts, they fit the image of the classic lost-in-cyperspace soul, though distinguished by their side-curls and yarmulkes.

Their work station was cluttered and old paper coffee cups and bagel wrappers were strewn about. But David had been around enough of such fellows at the university to know that those trappings could be the sign of sheer genius.

"Glad to meet you, Dr. Rothmeyer," they said, almost in unison.

"These fellows have been following your work with more than cursory interest," Diamant said. "What we want to do now is begin to feed the findings you have compiled into the work they have been doing on current family lines."

Clement, who headed the team, joined in. "Dr. Rothmeyer—"

"Call me David," the professor offered. Then, glancing sideways at Diamant, he added, "Since we *are* going to work so closely, let's not be formal."

Clement nodded appreciatively. "David," he said, "do you read the *Jerusalem Post?*"

"I guess I have been a lax patriot," David confessed. "Until I came to Israel, I rarely saw a copy."

"Well then," Clement replied, "you might not be aware that, for years, the agency has run ads in the international edition asking Jews to send the names and family information of any Cohens they might know of. We have been compiling this information into our data banks, and now literally have millions of names, both living and dead of the Cohen line, in our computer library. As we follow up on the leads, we are also able to create family trees, going quite far back."

Now Shofar jumped in. "You might be surprised at how many amateur genealogists there are out there. Among Jews, genealogy is quite popular, because we are so anxious to reconstruct our lost history and create a feeling of roots for ourselves."

"Yes," James added, his small dark eyes even smaller behind his thick lenses, "did you know there's even a site on the Internet specifically for Jewish genealogy? We have found all of this to be of enormous help."

Rabbi Benjamin joined in. "Of course, not all of the genealogy information we receive is applicable to the high priest. But we also need hundreds of qualified personnel to fill the lesser priestly stations in the temple courts. Any information we receive on the Cohen families is useful to that end."

David shook his head. "I was not aware of any of this work," he replied. "It sounds fantastic! So, how does my research add to yours?"

Clement explained, "What we have lacked was a scholar who had the breadth of your linguistic background. All of us here are knowledgeable in Hebrew, and some of us know a smattering of Greek and Aramaic, though those studies are confined mainly to the Septuagint and related writings. When it comes to the plethora of languages with which you are knowledgeable, we are in the dark."

Clement rubbed his chin hairs. "In fact, Dr. Rothmeyer, there are not even computer programs to aid us when it comes to some of the ancient, lost languages of the Diaspora. Judaized Syriac, for instance, or barbarized Roman Latin—where would we ever come up with such things?"

Horace beamed behind David, taking in this praise as though it were his own. "So," he said, leaning around the professor, "you see why you were chosen? Your education and experience have singled you out."

As Rabbi Benjamin gave this endorsement, Rabbi Diamant was steely jawed. When Horace saw this, he nudged him in the ribs.

"Uh, your ethnicity also qualifies you," the curator muttered.

David, heedless of this interaction, was caught up in his own thoughts. He felt as if he were standing on the edge of a high precipice. "So, now you are ready to begin meshing the information I have researched, in the hopes of finding links that may lead us forward to—" The professor stopped, awed by the concept.

"To lead us to the right one," Horace filled in. "To the one who should be priest!"

David felt another tingle cross his shoulders, just as he had felt upstairs when he stood before the display of priestly vestments. It seemed inevitable that he should have come to Jerusalem. Despite all misgivings, he found himself irrevocably drawn to this project.

"I guess I never realized that my background was so unique," he marveled. "I've been engrossed in Mayan and Aztec studies so long, I never thought of applying such knowledge to my own heritage."

He paused and fought that thrill again. "Or to the future of my people."

CHAPTER 20

Two evenings later, David sat on the veranda of his thousand-year-old house, looking over the Hinnom Valley, which paralleled the Old City's southern wall.

Except for Anya, the housekeeper, who was in her own apartment, David was alone in the medieval building. Rabbi Benjamin was spending the night, as he often did, at the consortium's yeshiva, a seminary where young Cohens were trained for priestly duties.

The sun was just setting, casting a coral glow across the modern high-rise hotels and clustered apartment houses of the opposite ridge. Beautiful as the contemporary buildings were, they lacked the character of the Old City, but they were nonetheless a part of the history of Jerusalem, exemplifying the growth and the youthful spirit that typified the modern state of Israel.

One of David's favorite parts of Jerusalem was the section that lay between the high-rises and the Old City wall, leading up from the Valley Hinnom to the new section. It was an artists' colony, full of studios and shops, its quaint buildings of yellow brick and stone terracing the hillside between ribbons of flowered gardens.

Over a century old, it had a noble history, for it represented the first Zionist attempt to develop a residential area beyond the city walls. The brave little village had been named Yemen Moshe, after Moshe Montefiore, a wealthy European

Jew who poured much finance and personal risk into the dream of an Israeli homeland. Despite its hopeful beginning, however, it quickly met with failure, as wandering bands of Bedouin marauders made life for its inhabitants impossible. Creeping back inside the Old City walls, the dreamers gave up Yemen Moshe but never abandoned the dream of Israel.

A testament to the courage of those pioneers, Yemen Moshe had left its mark on the landscape. One of its most prominent buildings stood in sharp contrast to the fortresslike architecture of the many conquerors and cultures that had defined the look of Jerusalem. A windmill, used for the grinding of grain in that early colony, stood witness to the influence of those nineteenth-century Europeans, its charm lending permanent testimony to the melting pot of domesticity that was the Israel of the returning Jews.

David feasted on the beauty of the hillside village as sunset pulled a crimson brush across its canvas. But when he looked over the Hinnom Valley, he also thought about less romantic periods of Jewish history.

Valley Hinnom, meaning "Valley of the Children," was so named for the atrocities that had scarred it. In the times of ancient Canaan, worship of Molech, god of the pagan natives, had been observed there. This worship involved the sacrifice of children upon huge bonfires on the valley terraces. With the snuffing out of those young lives, generations of potential Jewish families had been sacrificed in that valley, just as surely as they had been extinguished by the German Holocaust.

It was a sad part of Israel's story that she often took up the practices of her neighbors and forgot the laws of Moses and the warnings of her prophets.

Sometimes, when David sat there of an evening, looking over this haunting view, he could almost imagine he heard the cries of those little souls as they entered the fire.

And then, there were other stories that fit exactly with the view he loved.

One of those was a story of another David, the great king for whom so many Jewish men, himself included, were named. The tale went that King David used to walk upon the rooftop of his palace when the nights were warm. Situated farther to the east and just below Temple Mount, on a parallel with David's residence, the king's palace commanded a view quite similar to that which the professor enjoyed.

One evening, as the king walked there, his eyes fell upon a beautiful woman bathing, as was the custom, in a bathing tent, upon a distant rooftop. Just how much of her loveliness he was privy to, no one could say, but it was sufficient to set his soul on fire with desire.

The legend of David and Bathsheba was one of the most well known in

Jewish and biblical lore—how he had sent for the woman, lying with her despite the fact that she was a married woman, wife of one of his best soldiers; how she had become pregnant with his child; how David had summoned her husband, Uriah, home from the warfront in the hopes he would lie with his wife and claim the child as his own; how the valiant Uriah would have none of such luxury when his comrades were in danger; and how, at last, fearing exposure, David had sent the man to the front lines of the battle, fully expecting him to die.

King David, having added murder to adultery, spent much of his remaining life paying for his sins. But ultimately, Bathsheba, whom he took as wife, gave birth to Solomon, the king who would build the temple and bring Israel to the position of a world power.

From pondering the mystery that was Israel, the professor's thoughts turned to his work. He had just spent a full day entering his long paper of family trees on several computer disks, with a genealogy program provided by the Consortium. The next day he would take the disks to the institute, where Clement and the others would begin weaving it into their own findings. Although he was exhausted from his work, he was excited to begin the intermeshing of the separate researches. As much as he loved the history of Israel, he was also fascinated with its future.

Would they actually be able to pinpoint a single individual after all their work was done? Such a dream seemed very unrealistic. Yet, David knew that in this age of global communication, computerized language, and the ability to trace the most minute movement of people and events, it was just possible that they could succeed.

Still, there were great gaps that they might never be able to fill. One of the major obstacles was the Holocaust period. Even if they could say with some certainty that the line of the high priest could be defined through the eons previous, that period alone had produced a chasm in recorded knowledge that might never be bridged.

David closed his eyes and found his heart whispering something like a prayer. For the professor, this was a new experience. He had not truly prayed for years.

Even when his wife had died, he had not been able to pray. His heart had been too broken, his spirit too dark, to believe in anything. Now, however, he found himself thinking of the future in a new way.

And he thought of himself differently. He had a purpose and a work that was important, though he did not fully understand it. He had a growing sense of wonder in everything he did, in every new encounter.

"God, guide us," he whispered. "If you are really out there, if you really have a stake in all this Israel stuff . . . well, just help us out."

For such an educated man, for such a man of the world as David considered himself to be, he felt quite inept as he prayed. Though he could sort through tomes of ancient languages and deduce reams of genealogy—though he was a *linguist*, of all things!—he had a difficult time finding the right words when it came to prayer.

Opening his eyes, he shot a glance heavenward, like a little boy, wondering if anyone had heard him. He believed that, somehow, he *had* been heard. And he felt good.

Well, back to work, he thought, as he turned to the laptop computer on the patio table. Being single, he kept late hours and did some of his best work at night.

As he clicked a key, engaging the screen's backlight, something caught his eye on the roadway that hemmed the Old City wall, the highway that ran through the Hinnom Valley.

A taxi was just pulling up to let a passenger out at the foot of the wide stone walkway that led from the road to the Jaffa Gate. David watched as the occupant emerged from the cab.

Long-haired and lovely, a woman of about his own age stood beside the taxi, fumbling through her shoulder bag for change to pay the driver. The cabbie was opening the trunk and pulling out a single travel bag.

David noted that she almost grabbed the bag from the driver, as though she did not want him handling it. Mostly, though, he noticed her loveliness.

Smiling, he considered the fact that this was no bathing beauty on a housetop, but he had a fresh appreciation for just what that ancient monarch might have felt that long ago night. This woman was beautiful, as Bathsheba surely must have been. Though David had no power to summon her, he would have if he could.

Through the soft night air, it was actually possible to make out the words spoken below. At first, the professor figured his fantasies were playing tricks on him when he heard the woman speak his name. Leaning over the balcony, he listened closely to the quick conversation that passed between the driver and his fare.

"Dr. Rothmeyer?" he heard the man say after the woman had paid him. "I have no idea, lady. As for any temple agency, that is located in the heart of town."

The woman held out a scrap of paper and looked up the walkway toward Jaffa Gate.

"But I was given this address. You say this is the closest entrance to reach that street?"

"That's right, lady," the cabbie said. "But you won't find any consortium there. Not that I know of."

The woman looked very tired. She thanked the driver and began walking up the ramp.

"Sorry, lady," he called after her. "I would drive you there"—he gestured toward his old Mercedes—"but the streets are just too narrow."

The woman waved back to him. "That's all right," she called. "I'll find it."

"The streets are quite safe," the driver added, "but don't linger."

David knew he had heard his name. Who in the world was this woman, and why was she coming to see him?

"Just one more of your many mysteries," he muttered, speaking to the spirit of Jerusalem, from whom he had come to expect surprises.

Suddenly it occurred to him that he had not put on a fresh shirt that day. He rushed to the bathroom, smoothed his hair, and splashed cold water on his face, then hurried to his closet for a nice pullover.

If Bathsheba was coming to visit, David would be ready.

CHAPTER 21

David listened from the doorway of his apartment as Anya answered a buzz from the front gate. After dusk, the gate to the residence was always locked, and so the woman who had come from the cab could not approach the main door.

The cavernlike corridor that led down several flights of steps, past private rooms, the kitchen, and the parlor, to the main entrance, acted like a megaphone, sending Anya's voice through the multistoried house.

"Who is it?" she inquired over an intercom.

"Hello," the woman replied. "I am a visitor from the United States. I have come to see Professor David Rothmeyer."

Anya, obviously protective of her house and its occupants, hesitated. "It's quite late, Miss," she said, in her broken English. "You come back tomorrow?"

There was a long pause before the woman answered, "I was told I could find help here. I was sent by Dr. Kenneth Aronstam, of Midwest University. He is a friend of Dr. Rothmeyer. Is it possible to at least speak with the professor?"

At the mention of Ken Aronstam, David jolted. Who this could be and what she wanted, he had no idea. But if she knew Ken, David could not turn her away.

Rushing down the stairs, he called, "Anya, it's all right. I'll speak with her. Let her in."

The housekeeper shrugged and turned aside, letting David press the button that deactivated the gate lock.

"Hello," David called over the intercom. "This is Professor Rothmeyer. Come in. Meet me in the lobby."

Within seconds, the beautiful creature whom he had admired from the veranda was standing in his house. Obviously tired and looking a bit overwhelmed, the woman put out her hand and said with a sigh, "Dr. Rothmeyer, I'm so glad to find you. I just arrived in Israel today from Columbus. I took a bus and then a cab from Tel Aviv. I hope I am not imposing."

David shook her hand, looking her over carefully. "You were sent by Ken Aronstam?" he repeated.

"Yes," she said. Then, flustered, she added, "I'm sorry. I didn't introduce myself. My name is Clarissa Aronstam. I am Ken's cousin. Most people call me Honey."

"And what brings you to Israel?" he asked. In a fleeting deduction, he knew it had to be more than tourism that would send a woman straight to his door on the day she entered the country.

Honey set her travel bag on the floor, and David could see the weariness in her face, more weariness than would be produced even by a long plane flight and jet lag.

"Now it's my turn to apologize," he said. "Here, let me take your bag." He bent over to pick it up, but Honey grabbed it as if it were gold—just as she had earlier, David thought.

He straightened and gestured to her to follow him. "Anya," he directed, "please fetch Ms. Aronstam some tea."

The plump housekeeper looked the visitor over suspiciously, then hastened toward the kitchen.

"Honey, is it?" David said. "Why don't you come sit in the parlor? You must be very tired from your trip."

"Thank you," Honey said and followed him back up the hall.

The parlor of the great old house was always cool. The massive stone walls kept all heat at bay, so there was always a fire burning in the hearth.

"Have a seat," David offered.

Honey chose a large armchair but did not really relax. She perched on the edge of the cushion, tightly holding on to the handle of her travel bag.

As Anya came bustling in, setting a tray of tea and cookies on the footstool, David poked the embers of the fire, then sat across from the woman, trying not to stare. She was, indeed, quite beautiful, even more so in the glow of the firelight.

It had been years since David had given any woman more than passing scrutiny. Ever since Susan's death, he had believed the part of himself that needed a woman had died with her.

"So," he said, trying to think in strictly friendly terms, "are you in Jerusalem for business or pleasure?"

Honey bit her lower lip and watched the fire. "Neither," she said softly.

She seemed to be on the verge of tears.

"Dr. Rothmeyer—" she said, taking a big breath.

"Call me Dave," he interrupted.

"Dave," she complied, "I must seem very peculiar. Actually, I am quite harmless. But I am not here as a tourist, and I have no real business. Actually—"

She paused, and her shoulders shook. "Actually, my cousin sent me to Israel to get me out of a scrape."

David studied her, a bemused expression on his face. What could Ken mean, sending a troubled woman to him? Whatever Honey's problem, Ken must have realized David would have no time to serve as rescuer.

He sat forward and poured her a cup of tea, then handed it to her as he pondered how to respond. "I don't understand," he said. "Did Ken think I could help you?"

Honey smiled wanly. "I believe he thought Israel could help me—you know—in some grand sense of destiny. . . ." She shook her head. "Oh, I don't know! Ken didn't know either. But he said my problem put him in mind of what had brought you here. And he said I'd be safe here."

David was more bewildered than ever, and Honey could see she had only confused him.

"Truly, Dr. Rothmeyer—Dave," she went on, "I am as puzzled by all of this as you must be. I never dreamed I would come to Israel. But then I never dreamed half the things that have happened to me in the last few months!"

Now this sounded familiar. It echoed feelings the professor had had many times since receiving the Consortium letter. His life had taken turns he did not even know were possible, and he still did not know what they were all about.

"Let me get this straight," he said, rubbing his chin. "Something happened to you in the States that Ken believed warranted your coming to Israel? Ken actually sent you here and gave you my address?"

"That's right," she replied. "He made the flight arrangements. Even put it on his own credit card!"

David shook his head. "You *must* have been in trouble!" he joked, knowing that his friend was tight with money.

"It's a long story," Honey said with a sigh. "He wanted to call you, but thought it best if I just showed up unannounced. He thought it would be safer."

David noticed the woman seemed to shiver, though the room was warm enough, and she cradled her teacup in her hands as though thankful for its heat. Suddenly he read more than exhaustion or bewilderment in her eyes. He read fear, an emotion he had experienced in connection with this assignment only once, the day he sat in the airport in New York, awaiting his hosts. It had shot through him when he observed the Arab with the raspy, hate-filled voice telling his little boy that Jews were "the enemy."

For the first time in his life, in that moment, he had experienced ethnic fear. Whatever Honey was afraid of, her look of intimidation reflected similar feelings.

Reaching out and patting her hand, he said, "I can tell that what you need right now is rest. Whatever has brought you here, you are a friend of my best friend. We can talk about all of this in the morning."

Honey blinked back tears and nodded with relief.

As she finished her tea, the professor went to fetch the housekeeper again. "Anya," he called, "please make up a room for Ms. Aronstam. She will be staying the night."

Late the next morning, David was sitting on the veranda, making entries in his laptop computer for yet another disk that he would take to the institute, when Honey appeared. He was pleased that she looked somewhat refreshed. Though it was always a tough transition to change time zones, it appeared she had slept quite well, possibly assured of her safety for the time being.

"Good morning!" he greeted her, pulling up a seat at the table. "I was just about to have some breakfast. Won't you join me?"

"Yes, thank you," Honey said as she sat down.

David could not help but notice how radiant she was in a bright yellow dress, her face aglow in the sunlight.

He quickly shuffled his papers into a file folder and, knowing he should not be too trusting, turned the computer screen so that only he could see its contents. After all, he did not know this woman, and he was under obligation to the committee to consider the security of his work.

In fact, he had given a lot of thought to just how generous he should be with this stranger in opening the house to her. He would learn what he could about her that morning and then decide if he should bring her business to the attention of Rabbi Benjamin. No matter what her problems were, he could not let her stay more than a day or two without the committee's approval.

Anya served them the traditional Israeli breakfast of fresh fruit, vegetables, eggs, cheese, and bread. As they ate, they chatted about inconsequential things—the weather and her plane flight.

David found himself enjoying her company and realized anew how devoid of warmth his life as a widower was. Grief had supplanted memories of human companionship, and he was surprised at how the mere presence of a young woman in his home enlivened his spirits.

Honey looked at his laptop with curiosity. "I've never had a computer," she said. "We didn't even have a TV where I came from."

David gave her a quizzical look, and she suddenly realized that he assumed she lived in Columbus.

With a laugh, she filled him in. "Oh, I didn't tell you . . . I don't live in Ohio anymore. I actually come from Montana." Then, with another laugh, she added, "Not that Montanans don't have TV. My S.O. and I don't have it where we live, but only because we choose not to."

"S.O.?" David said, again baffled.

"Significant Other," she replied. "I guess that's better than calling him 'my man,' like some of his friends would."

David processed this information quickly and was again surprised at his own reaction. Deflated, he thought, *So, she's spoken for. She has a relationship, and she's letting me know up front.*

"I guess so," he replied, trying not to sound disappointed. "So, you must live in the wilderness?"

"It would seem like wilderness to most people," she said. "Actually, there are a lot more remote places in the world, and even in Montana. But we like it there. It's quiet . . . peaceful . . ." Then, looking wistful, she added, "At least, it used to be."

David figured she was alluding to the troubles that had caused her to flee.

He felt quite awkward. He was not used to dealing with people's feelings or problems. He had had enough of his own in recent years and had found it comforting to lose himself in academics, avoiding any interaction that involved the problems of others.

After an uneasy silence, he asked, "Is that why you left? Things got bad for you in Montana?"

It took no more than this to bring tears to Honey's eyes. Fighting them, she tried to look composed. At last, she sighed, as though resigned to unburden herself. "Listen . . . ," she began, "Ken sent me to you because I told him some things that made him think my safety was at risk. He told me you are a bright guy and that, with your connections here, I might find some answers."

"Go on," the professor said.

Taking a deep breath, Honey began to pour forth her entire story—telling David about Pete, about her history with him, about the strange things he was involved with, and at last, about the old star and the crisis that had convinced Pete to send her away. By the time she reached this point, she was alternately sighing with relief, wiping away tears, and shuddering for fear of her situation.

David, overwhelmed, could only listen in amazement, questioning her when she skipped something he needed to know to help him understand. By the time she got to the part about the music box, he was leaning with both elbows on the table, chin in hands, in rapt attention.

As she dabbed at her eyes, yet one more time, he tried to make sense of the whole story. "Okay," he said, "let me see if I have this straight. Pete, and now Ken, as well, think that this little star you have may be something risky for you to own. Neither of them knows what it's about, but Pete thought it was dangerous enough to warrant your leaving home, and Ken thought it merited your coming all the way to Israel?"

Honey sighed. "Sounds crazy, I know. But it was also important enough to my great-grandfather that he went out of his way to get it out of Dachau and into my family's safekeeping for all these years. And it was his expressed wish that we would show it to no one until we could show it to a 'wise man' in Jerusalem."

David leaned back, his eyes sparking with interest. Although it appeared, from Honey's longing references to Pete, that she was not available, her story was intriguing enough to keep his interest.

"Well," he said, "I don't know that I fit requirements of the 'wise man' type your great-grandfather referred to. But I do know a lot of astute, scholarly Jews. Perhaps we could get one of them to look at it." Of course, he hoped he himself could see the little scrap of cloth that had precipitated this mystery. But he did not presume to ask for the honor.

"It's in my travel bag," Honey said. "I'd be happy to show it to you. I'm not sure what my great-grandfather meant by 'wise man,' but you have fine credentials. Ken told me so. Won't you see what you can make of it?"

David brightened. "Well, sure, if you think it's all right. Maybe I can at least help you with the language."

Honey was up and to the door of the veranda before he quit speaking. In a flash, she returned with a large manila envelope. She sat down, shuffled through the manila envelope, then drew out an old letter and placed it on the table.

"Before I left Columbus, I went by my aunt's house. She still lives next door to where I grew up and has some of my family things in storage. I dug through my dad's old papers and found this letter from the Red Cross."

She pushed it toward him. "The star was wrapped inside when the family got it."

David opened the letter and quickly perused the note. It was written on letterhead with the logo of the British Red Cross. It related the same story Honey had given, of the old rabbi and his wish that the star reach his family. "Rabbi Yitzak Aronstam wishes you to keep this private," the note said, "until you can show it to a 'wise man' in Jerusalem.

"At your service," the note ended, and was signed, "Emily McCurdy, R.N."

David glanced up at his guest, handing her the letter. "Did your family ever meet this Nurse McCurdy?" he asked.

"No," Honey said. "As far as I know, we've just done as she said, and left it at that. I have no idea if she's even still living."

At last, Honey brought forth the scrap of cloth and tenderly spread it out.

David's eyes widened. It was, indeed, a "Jew badge" like countless others to be seen in old photos of the period and in museums of the Holocaust.

"May I touch it?" he asked. He felt the same sort of thrill he used to get on an archaeological dig when finding a rare artifact.

"Of course," she said. "The writing is on the back."

David lifted the scrap, tingling with the knowledge that this cloth had witnessed horrors and events he had only read about. Ever so carefully, he turned the piece over, laying it again on the table, and studied the scrawls on the back.

He pushed his computer to one side, lowered the screen so that she could not see his work, then excused himself. "Let me get my magnifier," he said, and quickly ran to his apartment.

Coming back, he leaned over the table, just as the rabbis had leaned together over his long genealogy, and he peered at the cloth through the reading glass.

"The words have faded," he said, "and the substance they are written in has smudged badly. It appears to be charcoal."

Honey nodded. "I am sure he had to use a piece of charred rock or wood, don't you think?"

"They certainly wouldn't have allowed a prisoner to have a writing implement," David agreed.

Continuing to study the piece, he easily lost himself, as he always had, in the joy of such a find. "It's amazing," he said, "how well preserved this is. Considering the primitive nature of the writing tool and considering the natural degeneration of cloth, no matter how well stored. Even in only half a century, it should have blotted and absorbed the charcoal more than it has."

"The family cherished this," Honey said proudly. "Until just recently, I kept it in the safest place I could think of."

"You did well," David said.

Continuing his analysis, "The writing is indeed Hebrew—actually sort of a Yiddish version. You see, even Hebrew script varies from place to place in the Diaspora. A good paleographer, or ethnographer, could tell us exactly where your grandfather came from, by the style in which he wrote his Hebrew characters."

Honey was not sure what a paleographer or ethnographer was, but she got the general idea. "He came from Frankfurt," she said. "I always wanted to go to Germany."

By now, David was not paying much attention to Honey. He had already retreated into the comfort of his calling, having registered deep inside himself that Honey was not for him. Still, he felt a kinship with her, a mutuality based on their interest in Jewish history.

"Interesting!" he exclaimed, his breath fogging up the magnifier. Standing up, he looked at her quizzically. "This cloth seems to refer to some location, perhaps at the death camp."

"What?" Honey asked. "What are the words?"

David leaned over the cloth again and said, "Here, write this down." He shoved a notepad and pencil her way.

The note consisted of five crimped lines. Although the writing was tiny, it was legible enough to interpret. " 'Third row from the bottom,' " he read, " 'back left corner, fourth brick from the end.' "

Honey wrote quickly. "What in the world?" she said. "Sounds like a treasure hunt."

David had thought the same thing but was too reserved to say so. "I doubt they had any treasures at Dachau," he said.

Honey lowered her eyes. "So, is that all?" she asked.

"No, there are two more lines. Hebrew is a kind of ancient shorthand, and it's possible to cram a lot in a small space." As he mulled over the translation, suddenly his scalp tingled and the hair on his arms stood up.

"What is it?" Honey asked, seeing his look of genuine amazement.

"I don't know what we have here!" he replied. "But I read similar words only yesterday. 'Build your house, O Lord. Return priests to their service and Israel to its House of Prayer.' "

CHAPTER 22

Pete Wester leaned back in the passenger seat of his brother's rental car, trying to sleep. He and Mel were somewhere south of Billings, Montana, in the thick of a rainstorm, driving down Interstate 90.

Little conversation had passed between them since they had turned south toward Wyoming. Once they had reached the Y in the roads at Billings, which offered the choice of traveling directly east, toward North Dakota, or turning off this way, they had relaxed a little. If anyone had been following them, unless the tracker saw their quick exit south, the chances were fairly good that the Westers had lost them at the junction.

Until that point, however, the two men had done a lot of talking, and a lot of looking over their shoulders and in the rearview mirrors.

Taking turns with the driving, they rehashed what had gone on at the meeting to which Fogarty had invited them, the one held after the campers and the dancers had gone to their campsites and bedrolls. That meeting had revealed things to them, secrets that Fogarty would only have shared with men whom he believed to be True Aryans, things too fearsome to speak in public or within earshot of anyone who was of doubtful allegiance.

Even as the two brothers spoke of it in private, within the cocoon of the car, they sometimes hesitated, as though ears beneath the car or in the bushes that rushed past the windows, might hear them.

Pete and Mel were on the run.

The meeting of Fogarty, Monte Altmeyer, and their stooges had lasted until the wee hours. The Westers, captives of Freemen hospitality within Pete's own domain, could do nothing but play along.

For Pete, the situation had been quite troublesome. The fact was that, until only hours before, he would have been proud to be included in Fogarty's inner circle. Things had changed for him when Fogarty called him into the limelight, praising him for something he abhorred, for supposedly breaking up with Honey because she was a Jew.

As he caught Mel's look of shock and disgust in the firelight, he had suddenly seen himself for the confused, fragmented person he really was. He had known, then, that no matter what he thought to gain by joining forces with the Freemen, he would lose his soul in the process, just as surely as he had already lost the love of his life.

He would have run away with Mel that evening, on a quest for Honey, if Fogarty had not intercepted them. Instead, he and his brother had been forced to endure hours more of White Supremacist diatribe as Fogarty and his men took over the living room and held their clandestine gathering.

Unable to communicate freely with each other, the brothers had decided independently that, as soon as that group broke up, they would flee. What they had not anticipated was what they would become privy to during those hours with the brotherhood.

Monte Altmeyer, they learned, had been involved with Freemen, the KKK, and several other White Supremacist groups within the U.S. for years. As a former officer in the German army, he was a skilled military trainer, specializing in guerrilla tactics and terrorist techniques.

Something of a mercenary, he had hired himself out to terrorist groups in the Middle East and in Ireland, and now worked a circuit of militia compounds throughout the United States.

He was well known in Idaho, where he had served as a trainer at Aryan Nations survival camps. His firelight talk in Pete's front yard, the one that Mel had missed as he paced and fumed behind the house, was intended to enlist trainees for a new camp Fogarty was establishing in the hills near Montana's Canadian border.

None of this information was particularly shocking or disconcerting for Mel and Pete. It was not until Fogarty and the German began alluding to certain activities instigated or orchestrated by Altmeyer, activities that had been spin-offs of the camps, that the brothers realized just what they were dealing with.

Pete had brought Fogarty and his friends their second pitcher of beer when the more sensitive information began to emerge. The warm fire and the liberating effect of alcohol led them from speaking in general terms about the greatness of their cause to recounting memories of their favorite feats. They went from horror stories of abuses by the Internal Revenue Service to reminiscences of their own clever tax evasions; from stories of playground skirmishes to tales of skinhead rumbles they had participated in; and finally, from tales belittling "subhuman" races, to accounts of beatings, lynchings, cross-burnings, and church burnings.

At last, as the night wore on and they felt embraced by camaraderie, they filled Mel and Pete in on some of their more daring escapades.

In the gloom of the rain-streaked highway, as he pretended to sleep, Pete shivered, recalling the first mention of Oklahoma City and the Murrah Building. Even now, after he and his brother had gone over and over what they heard, it was hard to believe they had hosted murderers in their midst.

Yes, Altmeyer had been involved in the Oklahoma City bombing! Not directly, not hands on, but he had been one of the masterminds of the coup. It was an awful, chilling fact that Monte Altmeyer had helped plan the disaster from its inception. In fact, he claimed to have conceived of the idea, though there were others who challenged him for that credit.

Woven between these proud confessions was the fact that the ones whom juries had convicted of direct responsibility for the "most horrible crime ever perpetrated on American soil" were actually only naive pawns of greater minds. Certainly not innocent of all involvement, the two who had been pinned by the courts as the primary criminals had only been shoved to the forefront by Altmeyer and other comrades, left to take the rap for actions beyond their own scope or ability.

However, even these revelations had not come close to the horror of the next disclosure. Pete's stomach knotted each time he thought about it. The federal government and state agencies close to the crime had actually managed to strong-arm the courts into denying the defense that would have brought forth evidence of higher responsibility. The two convicted saps who believed they were serving some grand cause, however misled, had been betrayed, not only by their own patrons, but by the governments who were supposed to protect the public.

In fact, for reasons that Pete still didn't understand, it appeared that the government and the Militia, as well as the government and the terrorists, were actually unlikely accomplices.

Pete had never loved the government. From his hippie days until now, he had held the Feds and the state suspect of all sorts of complicity with evil. What he had not realized, until just hours ago, was that the ones he admired, the ones who were supposed to be undermining that establishment, were in league with that very establishment!

And in that one sweeping encounter in the living room of his own home, Pete had also begun to see that the Militia honchos visiting the property were only one tiny link in a network that spanned the globe!

Pete, eyes still closed, could see himself now, sitting on the porch of his handcrafted home, behaving just as naively as the two convicted dupes must have behaved, as he took radio messages and faithfully passed them on to Fogarty. He cringed, now, to think what those messages might have contained, couched in code and transcribed by his ignorant hand to bring about who-knew-what.

As the boasting Fogarty and Altmeyer let their tongues wag on, they had actually revealed that the direct, hands-on perpetrators of the Oklahoma City bombing had been foreign. The public had been kept oblivious to the fact that witnesses at the Murrah Building that fateful day had observed men of Middle-Eastern appearance drive that bomb-laden van into the parking lot. Furthermore, government agents had apparently been aware that some atrocity was being plotted, for they had shown up hours beforehand, making a cursory "inspection" of the grounds and the building with bomb-sniffing dogs.

Fogarty and Altmeyer had chuckled together over the blindness of "the people," citizens whom the Militia were supposedly trying to help with their antigovernment activity, citizens who dumbly took whatever came forth from government memos and from the press as "truth," citizens represented by the 168 who had died that horrific day!

It was the middle of the night before the men grew weary of boasting. Before they crept off to bedrolls strewn about the floor of Pete's living room, they had made oblique references to "other victories," but they had not gone into the details.

Pete and Mel, disappearing upstairs to their beds in the loft, were left to surmise what other ghastly secrets, what other plots, had been set into motion by the network.

Unlike the men downstairs, Pete and Mel had not gone to sleep. Pete, creeping into Mel's room, had waited with him until they heard the sounds of snoring. Together, they had crammed a few clothes and necessities into one backpack, then climbed out the loft window to the back porch roof, jumped to the ground, and skirted the yard to Mel's car.

They were not much surprised when Willard and Crossley, again playing the role of sentinels, stopped them in the shadows.

"Fogarty and the crew need more beer," Pete explained. "We're going into Thompson Falls. There's an all-night market there. Is there a problem?"

Giving an unspoken dare, he rolled his eyes toward the house as though to say, *If you doubt us, go interrupt Fogarty's meeting.*

"Why both of you?" Crossley asked, eyeing them suspiciously.

"Well, Mel's car is near the edge of the yard," Pete replied. "I guess we could wake up all the campers to move their rigs, so I could get my pickup."

"Can't you take the car without the cop?"

Pete shrugged, pretending to think this over, while Mel jumped in, "Can't do that, boys. It's my rental."

Crossley sneered. "'Course! Wouldn't wanna strain the rules, eh, Top Cop?"

"I suppose Mel could go by himself," Pete suggested coyly. "I'm sure you can trust one of the LAPD to return if he says he will."

Willard looked very perplexed, but Crossley gave a warning pose and shook his finger at them.

"Okay, boys," he said. "But just see that you *do* come back. Hear?"

Pete gave a flippant salute, and Mel headed for the car.

Just as Pete turned to follow, Crossley growled. "Hold it!" He nodded toward the backpack. "Watcha need that for, if yer comin' back?"

Pete looked bemused. "This?" he said, pulling his pack off his shoulder. "Just returning some empties. Need all the cash I can get."

Willard stood behind a scowling Crossley with his arms crossed, but neither of the toughs made a move to stop the brothers as they piled into the car.

Once Pete and Mel were away from the property, they had breathed a little easier.

Mel's first words, after they reached the main road were, "Well, where do you suppose Honey is?"

Pete had already given this much thought. "I have a hunch she would have gone to stay with friends in Cheyenne. She kept in close touch with a couple who moved there from the valley. She's never contacted me, but I think that's a likely bet."

"Maybe you could call and see if she's there," Mel suggested.

Pete thought that was not such a good idea. "I'm probably the last person she wants to hear from," he said sadly. "Besides, if we give notice that we're coming, she might just hightail it. Once we get there, maybe someone can tell us if she's moved on."

"What about Ohio?" Mel asked. "Wasn't she from there originally?"

"Yeah," Pete said, "but there's not much family there anymore. Her folks are both dead, and she didn't have any brothers or sisters."

"Okay," Mel agreed, putting his foot to the gas, "Wyoming it is!"

After speeding down the highway, through the hamlets of Noxon, Trout Creek, and Belknap, the two brothers stopped only in Thompson Falls to get gas and then had taken off again, cutting over to I-90 on a back road, and heading for Missoula.

They knew that when they did not show up at the house within a reasonable span of time, the bikers would get suspicious. Undoubtedly, Fogarty had been roused and told of their escape. In fact, several trackers would probably have been sent after them, heading in various directions: west toward Spokane, south toward Missoula, east toward Great Falls, maybe even north toward Calgary.

But by the time all this was set in motion, the brothers would have been well on their way to their destination.

Now that Mel's snappy rental car had left Montana and entered Wyoming, Pete tried to put his mind at ease. He had time now, in the dark loneliness of his own thoughts, to think again of Honey.

Sorry, Girl, he thought, his eyes moist with feeling. *You gotta know I love you. Please know I love you. . . . I'm coming Honey Girl, coming to find you. . . .*

The image of the little yellow star flashed before him, peeking out of the music box like a premonition. Pete drew his jacket close, trying not to shiver.

All at once, it seemed pieces of the puzzle began to form themselves into a believable theory. All the anti-Jewish rhetoric of the Freemen to which he had been exposed for months took on ever-widening dimension.

"Good gosh!" he suddenly cried out, lurching upright in the seat.

Mel jerked the steering wheel, causing the car to skid on the wet pavement and nearly sending them into a ditch.

"What the . . ." Mel spat, grappling the car back onto the road. "What's the matter with you, brother? You want to kill us?" Glancing over at Pete, he saw that his face was as pale as death.

"That's it!" Pete cried again. "That's the connection!"

Mel, wondering if his brother was in the thick of a nightmare, reached over to shake him. But Pete lurched aside. "I'm awake," he said. "I may be more awake than I've ever been!"

"What do you mean?" Mel was flabbergasted.

"It's suddenly come to me," Pete said. "Something I've been missing all along!"

"Have you totally lost it?" Mel barked.

"No, listen," Pete went on, gesturing wildly. "Remember, Fogarty said that the Oklahoma City thing was actually pulled off by Middle-Eastern types?"

"Yeah," Mel replied.

"Well, think about it! What is the one thing the Militia, the Arabs, and most terrorist groups have in common?"

"Hatred of the Jews? Hatred of Israel?" Mel guessed.

"Exactly! Now carry this a step further. If it's true that the government is in cahoots with these people, or at least isn't pulling the plug on them, it has to be benefiting somehow from their activities."

"I don't follow," Mel said frowning. "How would the government benefit? Why wouldn't they want to squash anti-Semitism, once and for all?"

"Oil, man! Arab oil!" Pete was really wound up. "It all makes sense now! You don't bite the hand that feeds you, that keeps your industries running, that keeps the wheels of commerce humming. You don't fight the oil merchants!"

Mel tried to sort through the logic. "So, if the Arabs blow up a federal building, they get away with it because the Feds are afraid to stop them?"

"Exactly!"

"But"—Mel paused—"how does that relate to Israel? Why would the oil merchants blow up a minor fed building? How does that have anything to do with Jews?"

"Terrorism, man!" Pete declared. "That's the nature of the game! Confuse the world, scare us so we are afraid to move. Keep us wondering when the next 'random act' will take place."

Mel shook his head and watched the road silently for a while. "I don't know," he said sighing. "Sounds awful far-fetched. I don't get how it all ties together. If what you say is true, I don't see how random terrorism is going to accomplish anything for anyone."

Pete sat back and scratched his forehead. "Think like a terrorist," he said. "If you want to accomplish something but do it somewhat secretly, what's the best way to keep people off your heels?"

"Distract them!" Mel exclaimed. "Yeah, I remember the gangs in L.A. using that tactic! They'd lead the cops on a wild-goose chase down some alley, while the baddest of the bad pulled off some dirt."

"Except this time," Pete said, "the cops are helping them out."

The two digested that for a while. Then Mel added, "But bad dudes always want it known that they are bad—powerful, you know. The gangs never denied everything. They'd leave clear trails often enough that the neighborhood lived in fear of them."

"Okay," Pete said, "so terrorists will sometimes claim responsibility. Like the IRA in Ireland or the PLO in the Mideast."

"Right . . ."

"And we always know who their target really is, no matter who they aim at?"

"Yeah," Mel said. "Like, the Cryps hate the Bluds, or the IRA hates the Protestants, or—"

The men looked at each other with mutual insight.

"Or the Arabs hate the Jews!" they said together.

The car passed over the wet road in swift silence, only the hypnotizing slap-slap of the windshield wipers and the whirr of the rain-spattered tires accompanying their thoughts. Suddenly an awful possibility dawned on them.

"Pete," Mel said, "do you suppose this is the case with other crimes, like the TWA disaster? Or the World Trade Center?"

Pete's hands grew cold. "You mean, like some are unaccountable, no good reason behind them—to throw the world off the trail?"

"And some are directly related to the big hatred!"

"Geez!" Pete gasped. "The World Trade Center was traced to Arabs! I never thought about it. If you wanted to get at the wealthiest, most powerful Jews in the world, the Trade Center is a natural!"

Mel nodded. "Makes sense to me!"

Pete clenched his fists. "Well," he said, "I don't know about Israel, but I am afraid for one little Jewess. These guys are tenacious and vindictive. They probably suspect Honey's hung around their agenda long enough to be a threat. We've got to find her, bro, before Fogarty and Altmeyer track her down!"

CHAPTER 23

The state of Ohio, perhaps more than any other, was a microcosm of American history and traditional values. Probably no town in the United States typified the heartland more than Columbus, the state capital. Eight Ohioans, two of them from Columbus, had served as U.S. president, and one native son had been the first man to set foot on the moon.

Pete remembered Honey's fond accounts of her state's achievements. As he and Mel drove I-70 into the heart of the Scioto Valley, with its agrarian ambiance, its middle-American feel, he wondered if Honey had ever had to battle anti-Semitism while growing up.

He doubted it. As far as he knew, having lived with her for nine years, religion played little part in her life, and certainly no ethnic cords bound her to Judaism. Most likely she had never given her heritage any more thought as a child than she did as an adult, and most people, like Pete, would not have recognized her name as particularly Jewish.

In fact, now that he thought of it, she had always decorated the house at Christmas with a tree selected from the back portion of their property and had often talked of how wonderful it would be to have children creeping down the stairs on Christmas morning. Though, for both of them, Christmas had related more to Santa and his chimney crawling than to Jesus of Bethlehem, Honey had never made an issue of Hanukkah.

Pete reached into the backseat and pulled his pack into his lap. Fumbling through it, he found a tattered address book, hastily snatched from the guest-room desk as he and Mel had left the loft. It contained current and scratched out addresses and phone numbers of Honey's friends and relatives, going back to her college days, as well as entries which the couple had made over the years.

"I remember Honey saying she grew up in a posh district of Columbus," Pete said. "When we first met, she talked a lot about how materialistic her family was and how she had escaped all that by joining the back-to-the-earthers."

Glancing through the windshield, he saw a highway marker reading, "Capitol Building, High Street Exit, 3 miles."

Above that sign was another that jogged his memory. "Pull over here," he said to Mel. "I think we're close."

Leafing through the book, he found her parents' crossed out address, as well as that of Honey's aunt, Jessie Aronstam, who had lived next door.

After the deaths of Honey's parents, years ago, her childhood home had been sold, and when she moved to Seattle many of Honey's family possessions had been stored at her aunt's house.

"Yeah, here it is!" he said. "She lived on Scioto River Drive in Arlington Heights. That was the fancy suburb she left behind."

"Okay," Mel replied. "That sign says Arlington Heights Exit. I guess we'd better turn off here."

As the car veered down the off-ramp, leaving a view of the "Hat Box Capitol," the headquarters of the state legislature with its famous flattened dome, Pete ran his hands down his blue-jeaned legs, then snapped a look at himself in the visor mirror.

"Calm down," Mel said. "If she's at her aunt's, she'll probably fall into your lovin' arms without a second look."

"Sure," Pete sighed. "She'd just as soon point a shotgun at me."

Mel laughed.

At this point, the brothers had been on their quest for four days, driving and catching sleep in turns, fighting bad weather that made travel slower than they liked. They had been hung up in Cheyenne, looking for Honey's friends. At last, they had learned that she had been there more than once in the last few months, but had been too nervous to stay.

"The last time she was here, she said she was going back east," the Wyoming friends had reported. "Something was eating at her real bad."

"Look," Mel went on, "if Honey wanted to hide from you, she never would have told her friends where she was going. She hopes you'll find her, bro, can't you tell?"

The section of Columbus known as Arlington Heights was a grand departure from the city's "Cowtown" nickname. Street after street of lovely brick and clapboard houses recalled the colonial tradition, with its Greek Revival and Saltbox styles. Tree-lined avenues fronted gorgeous parks and playgrounds and world-famous golf courses.

Pete wondered which schools Honey had attended, and smiled to think of an adolescent girl in long skirts and beads, flaunting tradition in this conservative environment.

He saw a lot of churches, but no synagogue. There had to be at least one, he thought, in a city of this size. He wondered if, as a girl, Honey had ever attended one.

In no time, Mel had found the river and the broad avenue that wound along it. Looking over at Pete's address book, he compared the number of the house with addresses on the street.

"We're close," Mel said. He slowed the car to a crawl, and the two men peered out the windows, reading the golden numbers on the porches.

"There!" Pete said. "That must be it!"

Mel pulled the car to a stop in front of a tall white Colonial, complete with pillars capped by a Federalist porch roof.

"Wow!" Pete sighed. "She preferred our log house to this?"

Mel clapped his brother on the thigh. "What did I tell you?" he said. "Hang in there."

Pete looked at the houses on either side of the Colonial. "That must be Honey's aunt's," he said, pointing to the one that matched her address in the book.

Suddenly aware of just how disheveled he looked and how worn out, with dark circles under his eyes, Pete ran a quick hand through his long blond hair, retied his ponytail, and reached for the car door. "Well, here goes nothing," he said, stepping out onto the sidewalk.

As the two men approached the porch, a woman's voice halted them. "Hello! May I help you?"

Walking toward the corner of the house, sprinkler hose in hand, a gray-haired woman in a prim gardening smock, her face shielded by a wide-brimmed straw hat, hailed them from the side yard.

"This must be Aunt Jessie," Pete told Mel.

"Hi!" he called to her. "I'm Peter Wester, from Montana. I'm looking for Honey Aronstam. Has she been around?"

The woman turned the hose spigot off, then looked the men up and down, lifting her chin defiantly. "Clarissa isn't here. And from what she tells me, she's better off without you!"

Pete winced. "Well, ma'am, I sure wouldn't do Honey any harm. You must be Aunt Jessie, right?"

The woman put down her hose but did not remove her gardening gloves or reach out to return Pete's offer of a handshake.

"I'm Jessica Aronstam," she said.

"Well, Honey has always spoken highly of you," Pete said diplomatically.

Aunt Jessie's face softened a little. "She's a fine child," she said. Then stiffening, she added, "What is it you want, anyway?"

Pete glanced at Mel, as if for support, then answered, "Honey and I had words—maybe she told you. I just want to patch things up."

Mrs. Aronstam hrumphed and turned the water on again. "Not likely," she said. "You wouldn't go sending your thugs after her, if that's all you wanted! Why don't you people just leave her alone?"

"Thugs?" Pete said. "What thugs?"

Mel stepped forward, his cop instincts suddenly clicking in. "Ma'am, Mel Wester," he said, putting out his hand. The woman ignored him, but he spoke firmly. "Look, ma'am, whatever you think of Pete, he would never hurt Honey. He's come a long way to find her, just because he cares. Now you're telling us someone else has been here? Looking for her?"

Aunt Jessie turned the water off again and studied Pete. Perhaps his evident sadness and concern convinced her to be less suspicious.

"Look, young man," she said, "you know the family never approved of you."

Pete frowned. "I suppose not," he muttered. "But none of you ever went out of your way to know me, either."

Jessica sniffed. "Well, it's too late for all that now. And I'm afraid you're too late to find Clarissa. She was in a hurry when she left here. Wouldn't even sit down to have coffee with me, and sure didn't tell me where she was going."

Mel tried to focus. "Ma'am, back to the 'thugs.' You say some guys came here before us?"

The woman sighed. "I shooed them away, you can be sure. We don't want that sort hanging out in Arlington Heights! My bridge club was due anytime, and I would have died a thousand—"

"Ma'am!" Mel interrupted. "What did they look like? The men who came by here?"

Jessica shuddered. "Pretty horrid, I'd say. Driving their big motorcycles right up on the lawn! Look!" She gestured at some tire tracks left in the smooth green turf of the Aronstam yard.

"Bikers?" Pete gasped. "How many?"

"Two. They were ghastly fellows," Jessica went on. "One of them was a giant! Seven feet tall if he was an inch! And he looked like something out of a freak show!"

"How long ago?" Mel asked, absently rubbing the side of his hip where, in his cop days, he had kept his gun.

"Yesterday afternoon," she replied. Then looking suspiciously at them again, she added, "Come to think of it, they also asked if anyone else had come looking for Clarissa. Are you saying you know them or you don't know them?"

"We know them all right," Mel said. "They were looking for us, as well as for your niece. But their reasons weren't friendly!"

Pete, frustrated with dead ends, stepped closer to the woman and looked down at her demandingly. "Mrs. Aronstam, Honey could be in really big trouble. These guys you saw are no good, and they mean no good for her! Do you have any idea where she took off to?"

Now the woman grew grave. "I-I don't," she said. "Clarissa's in trouble? She's not just running from a broken heart?"

Pete's mind registered this as a ray of personal hope. He couldn't think about that now, though. "Yes, ma'am. Big trouble," he reiterated.

Mrs. Aronstam shook her head, her eyes suddenly brimming with tears. "I wish I knew where she went!" she exclaimed. "Oh, Lord, what shall we do?"

Pete stepped up and touched her arm. When she did not recoil, he slipped his own arm about her shaking shoulders.

Sobbing, she declared, "I never told those hoodlums anything. They were scary, but I played dumb, you can be sure! As far as I knew, I told them, Clarissa was still in Montana!"

Pete spoke comfortingly. "That's good, Aunt Jessie," he said. "You did real good!"

The woman heaved a huge sigh and gestured to her home. "They looked at my house," she recalled, "as though they were about to ransack it! But then, the big one refused, telling the smaller one I reminded him of his grandma."

She gave a wan smile, and the two brothers smiled with her.

"Is there anything you can tell *us* about where Honey might have gone?" Mel implored.

"All I know is she came straight here from visiting my son at the university three days ago. She rushed into the house, and I followed her around, trying to chat, while she shuffled through a bunch of my brother's old papers."

Pete translated. "Your son would be the professor, the head of the anthropology department at Midwest?"

"Yes, that's right," she answered, reaching into her smock for a handkerchief and rubbing her red eyes.

"And your brother was Honey's dad?"

"Yes," she said again, seeming to appreciate Pete's informed status. "I couldn't get her to relax or visit awhile. She was bent on finding something. And as soon as she found it—" She gestured with a whisk down the street. "Off she went!"

"Maybe your son knows something. Do you think?" Mel asked.

"Maybe," she said, hesitating. "I asked him about their visit, but he didn't say much."

"Thanks, ma'am," Mel said, catching Pete's eye and moving toward the car. "You've been a great help."

Pete followed Mel to the car and jumped inside.

"Let's go do some digging in the anthro department!" Mel said, starting the engine and flooring it.

"Exactly!" Pete replied. "Spoken like a true cop."

CHAPTER 24

The Wester brothers hurried across the broad-lawned campus of Midwest University feeling out of their element.

"So, these are the college students of today?" Pete laughed as he looked around at the young people who spilled across the quad, rushing for classes. "They look like babies!"

"They could be *our* babies!" Mel replied. "We like to think of ourselves as eternally young. Guess what! We're getting old!"

Pete smirked. "I'll tell you this," he said. "I sure used to handle a few nights without sleep a lot better than I do now!"

Finding a map of the campus in a glass-fronted sign, they located the anthropology department and headed that way.

"Aronstam will never tell us anything, you know," Pete said. "Honey probably gave him an earful, and he'll keep her as far away from me as possible!"

"I thought of that," Mel returned. "What I want to do is find out when the good professor has classes so that we can go by his office when he's not there."

"And what do you hope to accomplish by doing that?"

Mel shrugged. "I don't know. But I never got to play detective on the force. Might as well take a crack at it."

Pete followed obligingly as Mel led the way to the fine old building that housed the social sciences. Greek Revival in style, it was the typical grand university edifice, complete with ivy-covered walls.

Finding the anthropology wing, the two men tried to appear casual as they entered the front office.

Mel was almost disappointed at the ease with which they made their way past the secretary's desk and down the narrow hall that led to the staff offices. Apparently they had arrived at coffee-break time, and no one was overseeing the reception area.

"Even if we do find the right office, what will you do then?" Pete whispered, following Mel like a shadow, darting sideways glances at closed doors.

"Are you asking if I'm flying by the seat of my pants?" Mel inquired. "What would *you* do?"

In no time, they stood where Honey Aronstam had stood only recently, but this time the office was closed and no light shone through the door's opaque, rippled glass.

"'Dr. Kenneth Aronstam,'" Mel read. "So here we are."

The two stood nervously together, ears pricked for the sound of anyone entering the hall. It seemed that anyone not on coffee break must be in classes just now. They were quite alone in the office quadrant.

"What if he comes back? What will we say?"

"He'd recognize you," Mel said. "So that can't happen!"

Pete sighed and shook his head.

"What are you doing now?" he asked, incredulous that Mel had actually placed a hand on the doorknob. "It's locked."

"Oh yeah?" Mel said.

To Pete's amazement, the door was opening, creaking back ever so gently under Mel's guidance.

"Gads! You're crazy!" Pete croaked.

"Like a fox!" Mel replied, shooting another look down the hall and sliding inside the office. He pulled Pete in, then slipped the door shut again, letting the latch click.

Pete stood in the dimly lit office, wondering how they would explain themselves if caught, as Mel did a once-over on the cluttered desk.

"What do you think you'll find?" Pete muttered, teeth clenched.

"Maybe nothing—maybe something," Mel replied. "If this guy's like the typical harried professor, he probably doesn't put stuff away real often."

Pete fidgeted nervously with his belt loops.

"Come on!" Mel snarled. "Get with it! See what you can find!"

Pete, keeping his ears tuned to the hall, sidled up next to Mel and scanned the desk. Suddenly he jolted as if he would jump out of his skin. A red light was flashing on Aronstam's phone.

"Cool down!" Mel spat.

Pete, trying to ignore the light, turned and fumbled through papers on a nearby table. Suddenly he started. "Mel!" he gasped. "Look at this!"

The cop peered over his brother's shoulder and let out a soft whistle.

"Okay, Pete! Okay. You've got it!"

In the Montanan's sweaty hand was a rumpled note, something the professor must have hastily scratched out when he met with Honey. It regarded airline departure flights for New York and Israel, the flights for New York having left three days ago. At the bottom was a credit card number, along with a reservation control number and Clarissa's name, with an arrow connecting it to one of the flights.

As the men scanned the note, the light on Aronstam's desk suddenly stopped blinking. From down the hall, they could hear a woman, probably the secretary, saying, "Dr. Aronstam, here's your mail. And there's a call for you, about the faculty meeting. Do you want to take it here, or in your office?"

"I'll take it in the office," the professor answered.

Pete quickly shoved the note in his pocket, as he and Mel slipped out of the room. Aronstam could just be seen coming down the hall, absorbed in reading his mail, as Mel jerked Pete sideways.

Everything went black, as Mel pulled him into a tidy broom closet.

"So far, so good," Mel whispered.

As Pete stood quaking in the dark, he wondered why he had always been considered the crazy one in the family, and not his younger brother.

CHAPTER 25

Clement, James, and Shofar, the genealogy researchers of the Consortium's computer lab, huddled around a central monitor in their work station. David Rothmeyer stood with them, waiting eagerly as his disks were integrated into the massive bank of data stored in the computer's memory, data regarding family lines of Cohen Jews, compiled from around the world.

"It will be interesting to see how your findings collate with ours around the time of the early Middle Ages," Clement said, his dark eyes looking small but bright behind thick glasses.

"Why that period?" David asked, watching the screen and listening to the soft shifting of the hard drive.

"We have found prominent strands that seem to repeat themselves, being updated or added to in thirteenth-century Germany. They wane during times of persecution, as during the massacres of our people that accompanied plagues and the like . . ."

"Like the Black Plague," James filled in. "Lots of Jews were killed or had to flee, as scapegoats, blamed for the coming of the epidemic."

"Right," Clement said, "and of course they lost track of their roots. Family history sinks to a low priority at such times."

David nodded. "So, what about these strands you found?"

"Well," Clement went on, "in several of the genealogies that incorporate these lines, there is reference to earlier generations having come out of England. Some even trace the line back into Britain at the time of the Crusades."

"Specifically, following the First Crusade," James added.

David tried to interpret. "You are saying that there is a strong indication that the priestly line can be traced through England and then on into Germany?"

"Quite possibly," Clement replied. "Most Cohen genealogies are pretty sketchy, marvelous as they are compared to other family records. The records of this particular Cohen family, however, are quite insistent on a priestly link, and it crops up more frequently in their records than in those of other families, indicating that they retained the idea, longer than other Cohens tended to, that they had a special, priestly calling."

David was amazed. "You mean, you actually received information like this from people around the world, regarding their ancestry? What form did it take? Letters, manuscripts, what?"

James responded enthusiastically to the question, his nasal voice higher than usual. "It's like a treasure hunt. You never know what people will find when they start digging in their attics, their old trunks, or in the basement stacks of old libraries."

Shofar jumped in. "Family Bibles, even Christian ones, are a great help."

James watched the screen flicker, as it continued to collate information.

"What these records are lacking is a straight line to a present-day heir," Clement said. "They all fade away into dead ends or claim only distant kinship to the *zadokim*. What we need is a definitive connection to the priestly line of Zadok."

David knew this. One of the first things he had learned in this quest was that not every Cohen male had the potential of being in the priestly line. Candidates must be narrowed down to descendants of David's and Solomon's priests, whose names were Zadok. No Cohen of certain earlier branches, such as those descended from Eli or Abiathar, could be considered, because those particular priests had been guilty of actions that disgraced their office, or were not descendants of Aaron's eldest son, a necessary qualification.

As the computer whirred and clicked away, David hoped all was well at his house. He had seen to it that Honey Aronstam had something to do that day, away from the residence, away from his notes and files. He had made a reservation for her with a little tour company and had sent her off to see the sights of the Holy City, then had asked Anya to keep an eye on her if she returned before he got back.

He had not yet told Rabbi Benjamin about his peculiar visitor, as the old fellow was at the yeshiva when she arrived. But he knew he must do so before the rabbi learned of it independently.

For now, he tried to keep his mind on the business at hand.

"It will take quite awhile for all of this to dovetail," Shofar said, pulling up a chair. "Here, have a seat. I'll get you some coffee."

David sat down, and Shofar returned a few moments later with a steaming cup of coffee. David took a sip, then said, "According to my research, there have been so many contending parties throughout our history, I don't see how any particular genealogy will prove to be definitive."

James nodded. "Possibly, Professor. But we must begin somewhere."

"Of course," Clement agreed, "every group that cared at all about such matters has had its favorites through the years. The Cabalists and the Hasidics, for instance, have always contended that some mystic from their ranks must be the chosen one. The Talmudists have the superior scholarship behind them and are convinced that only a great scholar can be priest. Between the Sephardics of Spain and the Ashkenazaics of Eastern Europe, the chasm has always been so great, they could not agree on anything, much less who should be called righteous."

Shofar snorted, that strange little nerdish laugh that David had found typical of computer pros. "Then there are the Reform Jews who think this is all immaterial and deny the literalness of it all," he said. "So far as they are concerned, it is sufficient that Israel as a whole has a priestly function in the world. They spiritualize everything down to broad maxims and vague generalities."

"For our purposes," James added, "Reformism is irrelevant. If we did not believe in a literal priesthood and a literal high priest, we would not be doing any of this." He blew a good-bye kiss toward the computers, and the others laughed.

David was still ambivalent. "All that aside," he said, "if there is no link going back to the last known priest, an actual priest who served in the actual temple, how can we prove anything?"

The young men kept their eyes to the screen and did not answer. So David went on: "Besides, who *was* the last legitimate heir to the priesthood? One of the last priests of record was Caiaphas, in the time of Jesus, and even his credentials are suspect."

"Oh, more than suspect!" Clement declared. "We know for sure that he was not a legitimate heir!"

David was stunned. He had not expected such a firm response.

"What do you mean?" he asked. "I found nothing in my work that discounted him completely."

The three jockeys looked at one another nervously and then back at David.

"Didn't Shalom Diamant show you the lab?" Clement asked.

"Lab?" David repeated. "You mean the one where they have been researching the dyes for the garments and such?"

The young scholars drew aside, whispering together and glancing over their shoulders at the professor, until he felt uneasy. Finally, seeming to have reached a consensus, they came back to him.

"Surely Shalom means to show you this," Clement said. "He must have overlooked it."

"Show me what?" David asked.

"Go on, Shofar," Clement directed. "Take him in there."

Shofar jerked his head toward a door at the back of the computer room, indicating that David should follow him. Bemused, the professor complied, leaving James and Clement to watch the monitors.

The low door opened on a dark chamber, and David was obliged to duck his head as he entered. Shofar flicked on a bank of fluorescent lights that spanned the close ceiling, and the professor blinked his eyes.

Amazed, David looked around at a room that stretched quite a distance beneath the old city street above, its floor superimposed on the pavement of yet another street that was centuries older. The temperature of the room was surprisingly moderate and even, not cavelike or dank. David noticed dehumidifiers and an elaborate temperature-control system. He stared, mystified at long, polished chrome counters, beakers, bunsen burners, centrifuge machines, high-powered microscopes, and other high-tech lab equipment.

Shofar answered David's wide eyes.

"This is the Consortium's science lab," he said. "The research in here is way out of my league, I assure you. In fact, the geneticists only come here about once a month."

"Geneticists?" David marveled. "What does the Consortium need with geneticists?"

Even as he asked the question, he felt the hair on the back of his neck stand up. He suspected the answer and was not sure he liked it.

"They have been studying the chromosomes of Cohen males for a couple of years now," Shofar replied. He realized such news might be startling, and tried to be casual. "They've made some fascinating finds."

"Chromosomes?" David croaked. "How are they acquiring chromosomes?"

Shofar gave a quick history of the relatively young project. "A scientist in Haifa has collected saliva samples from Cohen volunteers by swabbing the insides of their cheeks. His volunteers were from three separate countries and were not directly related to one another. Running various tests on these samples, he and his colleagues have determined that Cohens across the board share a variation of the Y chromosome, aligning them as descendants of Aaron."

David frowned, skeptical. "Come on!" he grumbled. "Is that really possible? Aaron lived thirty-five hundred years ago!"

Shofar shrugged. "Those are the findings. What can I say? I am no scientist!"

Suddenly David's assignment was more than politically sensitive. It had taken on Orwellian overtones. "Let me guess," he said. "When we come up with our candidate, he will be subjected to this genetic test?"

Shofar shrugged again. "Let's call it a 'confirmation,' not a 'test.'"

Then, leaning back against a counter and crossing his arms, he looked at the professor quizzically. "Have the rabbis ever told you what such candidates were put through in the old days, when Israel cared enough to keep meticulous records?"

David shook his head.

It was evident that Shofar liked telling this story. Clapping his hands brightly, he began, "There used to be a great room in the Temple Cloisters, called the 'Hall of Polished Stones.' It is described in the rabbinical writings as quite a fabulous chamber.

"Anyway, there was a committee in Jerusalem that sat daily in that hall interviewing and looking over hundreds of candidates for the lesser priestly stations in the temple. These candidates had to produce detailed genealogies on themselves, proving their bloodlines, before they would even be considered.

"Then, there were copious doctrinal questions and scholarly questions they must answer. Finally, if they passed those tests, they were submitted to rigid physical examination."

Shofar's eyes flashed with intrigue. "Now get this," he said. "If a candidate's genealogy was flawed, he was publicly shamed by being dressed all in black with a veil over his face and was permanently removed from the court! If his genealogy passed the test, he was examined for physical defects, of which there were 162 that could disqualify him!"

The professor was appalled. "I can't imagine such treatment being tolerated today!" he exclaimed.

Shofar lifted his hands. "If we find a candidate for high priest, he will have to be physically pure, for sure. His line must be proven, and his theology must be straight. So what if he must produce a little spittle? Is that so bad?"

David laughed. "I guess not," he said. Then, looking about the room, he added, "Speaking of the old days, we were talking about the high priest, Caiaphas. Was there something in here you wanted to show me regarding that period?"

Shofar beamed. "There sure is!" he replied. "Step this way!"

Taking him to a large table at the back of the room, he said, "The people who come to this lab to work are some of the most highly respected scientists in the world, and they are of several disciplines: genetics, nephrology, and anthropology. Together, they have made one of the most astounding discoveries of all time!"

David raised his eyebrows. "What you've already told me is astounding enough! There is more?"

"Much more," Shofar replied. "See this?"

He directed David to a glass case, locked with a heavy clasp. The lid was edged with a latex seal that meshed with another along the top of the box itself. Inside the case was a control that kept the temperature and humidity of the contents constant, its little flashing light registering each fraction of variation.

Upon a glass tray in the bottom of the case was a pile of yellow-gray dust and shardlike fragments.

David, with his background in anthropology, recognized the material instantly. "Bone?" he said.

"Exactly," Shofar answered. "But not just any bone."

"Of course not," David agreed. "It appears to be quite ancient. From some tomb?"

"From the casket of Caiaphas," Shofar replied reverentially.

Suddenly it came back to David, information he had read in science journals. He remembered that archaeologists in Jerusalem had claimed to have found a burial box in their digs near Temple Mount and that the box was engraved with Hebrew letters spelling out the name of the ancient high priest before whom Jesus of Nazareth had stood trial.

"Good Lord!" he exclaimed. "Are you telling me that these are the very bones of Caiaphas?"

"The same!" Shofar answered, breaking into a smile.

As David bent close to the case, he was trembling both inside and out, with the feeling he experienced only upon some great, professional find. He had to hold his hands against his chest to keep them calm.

For a long while, he stood before the case, mesmerized. Then he drew back and tried to collect himself.

"Okay! Okay!" he replied. "So, I get it! You mentioned that nephrologists are on the team, right? They've been working with the geneticists, right? And they have run tests on these bones?"

Shofar nodded. He knew the professor deduced the rest.

"So," David went on, "Caiaphas is ruled out as a *zadok?*"

"You have it!" Shofar said.

David was incredulous. "This is the most amazing thing I've ever heard of!" he said. "So the turmoil of the late Temple period was justified. The rebels who claimed the priesthood was corrupt were absolutely right!"

"They were!" Shofar exclaimed, delighted to be teaching a teacher.

David wanted to linger over the glass case, but Shofar headed back for the door. "We'd probably better get out of here," he said. "If Shalom finds out I broke all of this to you . . . Well, I'm sure he wanted to do it himself."

The professor followed but dragged his feet. "I wish I could meet with the lab team," he said wistfully. "I have a hundred questions."

"Perhaps you shall," Shofar said, clicking off the light and shutting the door behind them.

Again, they stood in the computer room, David's head whirring like the computers themselves.

As they rejoined James and Clement, David rubbed his hands together. "So, going back to the revolutionists in the temple . . . some of them left to live in the wilderness—the Essenes of Qumran, for instance."

"You would know all of that better than we," Clement said. "But we've always suspected that the people at Qumran were revolutionaries."

"Aha!" David shouted. "So, that is the final missing link. We may find everything we need from that point on, but without a record from the revolutionists themselves, we won't have a clue who the last legitimate heir from the Temple period really was!"

Clement shook his head. "Sad, but true. We can only trust that all our work here is not in vain."

As the men stood in silent contemplation of this reality, the computers suddenly went silent, the whirring tapering off to a final click. The central screen flickered, and the windows changed in rapid succession, until a block of intricate information flashed to life.

Clement, Shofar, and James bent close to the monitor, with David right behind them.

"Wow!" James sighed. "Do you believe it?"

"What? What?" David gasped, wedging between them.

"It's practically flawless!" Clement exclaimed. "Your information, your months of research findings mesh almost perfectly with the current genealogies! There is a line, clear as day, running through England! Now, we just need to trace it forward to someone living today."

"Yes," James said, "and then backward, to someone who lived in Caiaphas's time, someone robbed of his priesthood and nameless to history."

The three computer jockeys stood up and stared at David.

"Back in your court!" James said. "Good luck, Professor!"

CHAPTER 26

As David hurried home, his mind buzzing with the information he had received at the lab, he hoped he was making it back before Honey returned.

The moment he entered the house, he intended to contact Rabbi Benjamin at the yeshiva where he had spent the night. He must tell him about his guest from Montana and get some guidance as to how to proceed with her. Rabbi Ben would also be fascinated, he was sure, with the woman's story, and might want to meet her.

As the professor opened the massive old door, however, he knew he was too late. Voices coming from the parlor cued him that the rabbi had already come home and was talking with Honey at that moment.

David cleared his throat nervously as he entered the room, hoping the rabbi would not consider her presence a dreadful security breach. When Horace Benjamin glanced up, greeting him with an effervescent smile, he relaxed a little.

"Dr. Rothmeyer," the rabbi called out, "did you expect to keep this delightful creature all to yourself?"

David sauntered in, trying to look nonchalant. "I see you have met Ms. Aronstam," he said. "I was just going to call you and ask you to come make her acquaintance."

"Well, that I have!" the rabbi replied. "And she has a fascinating story!"

In front of the rabbi, spread out on the coffee table, were

the Jew badge and the Red Cross letter that Honey treasured. It was obvious that the rabbi and the woman had already spent enough time together for her to share her mystery.

Honey spoke up. "I hope you don't mind, Dave. I got back from the tour about two hours ago. It was wonderful! Thank you! What a marvelous city this is! Anyway," she enthused, "the rabbi came home, and well, here we are. . . ."

She gestured to the artifacts excitedly. "Dave," she said, "I do believe I have found my 'wise man.' Rabbi Benjamin seems to believe I was meant to come here!"

David pulled up a footstool and sat down. "I'm relieved, Rabbi," he said. "I was afraid you would think I was out of line letting Honey stay here, considering our work."

He then looked at the woman apologetically. "Sorry, Honey," he said. "But we have certain reasons to keep matters here private."

Rabbi Benjamin leaned back and chuckled. "Don't worry, David. I have already told her."

"What?" the professor marveled. "But I thought—"

"You thought right," the rabbi interrupted. "Our work is sensitive, no doubt about it. But I have lived long enough, and closely enough to spiritual things, that I think I know supernatural intervention when I see it."

David was stunned, and Honey's eyes grew wide.

"S-supernatural intervention?" she stammered.

The rabbi looked at the two of them intently. "Let me give you an example," he said. Then turning to David, "I will be very surprised if you tell me your findings did not mesh with what Clement and his boys have put together."

"That's true!" David exclaimed. "It was almost too perfect!"

Horace nodded matter-of-factly. "That is the way it has been all along with this project, Professor. Not to minimize your scholarship or the work of the computer experts, but it seems quite clear that you are being assisted by powers beyond yourself in all your endeavors."

The professor thought long on this, then conceded, "I would be a fool to claim otherwise."

Honey took this in silently. Such an approach to things was foreign to her. Her spirituality had never gone beyond an appreciation for nature, for mountains, and for human ties. The closest she had ever come to any spiritual quest had been when she and Pete attended an Indian sweat lodge where, they were told, they might see visions. Even that quick dip into otherworldliness had been only a faddish exploit, and they had returned quickly to contentment with mundane things.

Now, here she was—she who had never graced the inside of a church, and who had attended synagogue only as a child—sitting in the Holiest of Cities, at the feet of a great rabbi. That rabbi had just revealed to her a quest much greater than anything she had ever dreamed of—the quest for the one who would serve as leader in the ultimate reestablishment of Judaism.

She glanced down at the little star that had never meant more to her than a cherished responsibility—a responsibility which she did not even understand—and she sensed, for the first time, the hand of destiny.

The rabbi was looking at her now. "And you, young lady, can you say that you have not been led here? Can you say that your coming to Jerusalem is mere happenstance or that the emblem you have protected all these years might not be something very sacred?"

Honey quivered, gripping her elbows tight to her sides. "I-I don't know," she admitted.

The rabbi accepted that and went on. "Now, Professor, I suppose that you are wondering what all of the findings in the lab portend. They can only take any of us so far, but we still have unanswered gaps."

"Truer words were never spoken!" David agreed. "We seem to be fleshing out several centuries quite nicely. There is a strand that leads strongly through England, but the Holocaust period is still sketchy, and then—" He stopped and shook his head. Sighing deeply, he added, "Then, even if we were to find a modern descendent of the firmest line, without proof going back to the Temple period, we cannot prove a thing!"

Rabbi Benjamin nodded. "Shalom meant to show you something related to that issue," he said, "the day he gave you the tour. We ran out of time after we visited the computer room. Perhaps he would not mind if I showed you."

David figured it would do no harm to tell the truth. "I believe I know what it is," he said. "Shofar took me into the science lab."

The rabbi did not take this news as cheerily as he had taken the news of David's having a houseguest. "What?" he barked. "Shofar had no right! That is highly confidential. . . ."

But then, he caught himself. "Listen to me," he said sheepishly. "Have I not just been preaching supernatural guidance? So," he sighed, "you saw the bones?"

Honey jolted. "Bones?" she croaked.

The rabbi laughed softly. "Sounds terrible, eh? Actually, such things are quite common finds in archaeology. Recently, diggers under the auspices of the Jerusalem Antiquities Authority unearthed a very special casket, marked with the name of Caiaphas."

Honey drew a blank. She had heard of the trial of Jesus, of course, but she could not have named Pilate or Herod or Caiaphas, before whom he had been tried.

Quickly the rabbi filled her in. "Caiaphas was one of the last recorded priests before the destruction of the temple in 70 C.E. Actually, he probably did not live that long, as he is referenced as being in office at the time of Jesus, and later discharged by Rome about 38 C.E."

Again, Honey was out of her element. "I never went to Sunday school," she said. "For sure, when I attended synagogue, which wasn't all that often, they never taught about Jesus!" David, seeing Honey's puzzlement, explained, "What is important about Caiaphas is not only his involvement with Jesus, but also the fact that there was a lot of foment at that time, about the legitimacy of the officiating priests. There were sects that had broken away from the temple and then went off on their own to worship away from what they considered to be graft and pollution in the priesthood."

The rabbi explained. "We were able to run DNA tests on the bones of Caiaphas, at least the bones that were in his casket, which we must assume were his. What we found was that he does not fit the chromosomal specifications that would have marked a legitimate heir. Since he was undoubtedly typical of the high priests of the time, appointed by Rome rather than by Jewish law, we can safely deduce that the revolutionists were right. Those filling the office of high priest, until the time of the temple's destruction, were certainly not there legally."

The men were not certain Honey got the gist of what they were pointing out. They were pleasantly surprised when her big brown eyes got even bigger, and she said, "So, this genealogy thing depends on your finding a reference to a legitimate heir way back then?"

The rabbi leaned back and clapped his hands on his thighs. "Exactly, Ms. Aronstam! That is the quandary we face, no matter how brilliantly we piece things together otherwise."

Honey was on a roll, and she began to appreciate the thrill of the chase. "So," she went on, "we have a double mystery, like a candle burning at both ends! We have to find the ancient link, and we have to find the modern one!"

She gazed at her star again. "We have to fill in the blank from the Holocaust. . . ."

Rabbi Benjamin studied her pensive face with compassion. "I could be entirely wrong," he admitted, "but I have a strong hunch that your little star and the message it contains ties in with what we are seeking. Whether or not it relates directly, I cannot imagine that a scribe at Dachau would have risked his life to lead us to anything, unless it was very important to Judaism."

David and Honey looked at each another, sensing the kinship of their mysteries. "Well, Rabbi," she said, "I have come this far on this strange journey. I am willing to go further."

"Of course, Rabbi Ben," David added, "you know that I am committed to the entire venture. What would you like for us to do?"

Nodding gratefully, Horace picked up the letter that accompanied the star and noted the signature at the bottom.

" 'Emily McCurdy, R.N.'," he read. Then glancing up at Honey, he asked, "You say your family has never contacted this woman?"

"Not to my knowledge. I'm sure my dad would have told me."

The rabbi thought a moment, then reached into the pocket of his long black coat. Pulling out a little address book, he said, "It so happens that the International Red Cross has been very helpful in our genealogy work. Some years ago, they began a program of soliciting and gathering information on the families of Holocaust victims. We have been able to incorporate much of their findings into our own research."

Again, David was amazed at the complexity of the Consortium's networking. It seemed he learned something new about it every time he turned around.

The rabbi continued, "If Nurse McCurdy is still living, I am sure the Red Cross can help locate her. We can then hope she will assist you to follow the clues to the treasure buried at Dachau."

David and Honey knew the implication. "Help *us*?" David said. "Are you saying that Ms. Aronstam and I should go to Germany?"

The rabbi gave a wink. "Did you have something better to do?" he asked.

CHAPTER 27

Pete and Mel Wester were not world travelers. Except for one flight to Disneyland with their parents when they were in grade school, and one vacation with Honey to Costa Rica, about seven years ago, they were relative novices. Mel had flown only between cities on the West Coast, and Pete had taken a few turns in crop dusters.

A transoceanic flight was new for both of them, and the one they were on now was not for pleasure. They were running across the world to find Honey and bring her home safely.

After hiding for half an hour in the dark, stuffy broom closet near Ken Aronstam's office, they had at last been able to escape, unseen, from the anthropology department of Midwest University. After a restless night at a dumpy motel on the outskirts of Columbus, they had managed to catch a couple of standby seats on a flight to New York, and then, after several long delays, to Europe. Taking what was available meant they would have to fly into Munich and hope for another set of standbys heading for Israel.

It was not due to any pre-planning that they each had passports. Since Mel never intended to return to L.A., his was among personal documents in the glove box of the rental car. Pete's was in the little binder where he kept his tattered address book and other papers, and which he had hastily stuffed in his backpack before fleeing Bull River.

Flying into darkness for most of nine hours made for an arduous journey, but the brothers felt lucky to have made it this far.

Ever since they learned that Willard and Crossley had gotten off their scent when they turned south toward Wyoming, the bikers apparently having proceeded straight to Ohio, the brothers had breathed a little easier.

It was also comforting to think that the bikers had lost Honey's trail. Mel and Pete were hopeful that the hogsters had accepted defeat and that no tracer was following any of them further. Tenacious as the Militia could be, there seemed no reason to expect that the brotherhood would consider them worthy of an international chase.

Despite in-flight movies, too many trays of food, and the discomfort of too little legroom, Mel managed to catch up on much-needed rest.

For Pete, however, the worst part of the journey was the dead time, for it allowed him to ponder his past. Disquieting scenes tumbled through his erratic sleep, as he relived his fight with Honey and then the agony of sending her away before they could patch things up. On waking, he wondered if she understood, at all, that he was trying to protect her and if she would ever be able to forgive his crazy involvement with the Freemen.

He also pondered the meaning of his work for Fogarty. How many messages had he taken off that despicable ham radio, never knowing what he was relaying or what plot he was aiding? This question had tormented him ever since the all-night meeting in his own home, when Fogarty and Altmeyer snickered over the mayhem they had conceived and carried out over the years. The ugly, unmistakable sense that he was no smarter, no better than the idiots who had aided in the orchestration of the Oklahoma City bombing nagged at Pete's soul.

Gazing out the window at the depressing darkness, he rehashed the messages he could remember, wondering if there was any way to intercept their outcome. But he always came to the same dead end: If he could not even interpret the coded phrases, how could he fight against them?

Somewhere over the mid-Atlantic, as the screen at the head of the cabin gave a computerized depiction of the plane gliding over the English Channel, he found himself dwelling on the last message he had received, the morning before the gathering descended. He remembered that the first words from the strange, grating voice were "Eagle-Eye happening." That phrase, obviously meaning "this is for Fogarty," was the most oft-repeated one in all the messages he received. But what came after was a total mystery to him. Something about "Swastika," "Bailey's Bug," and "Cedars," he recalled. Then, strangest of all, the last word: "She . . . she . . ." what was the word? Yes—"Shekinah!" he remembered now. Try as he might, he could not recall the rest of the message.

Suddenly, however, something did occur to him, and he stiffened reflexively at the thought, bumping his dozing brother as he did so. Mel grumbled and turned over, breathing down Pete's neck.

What came to mind was that the shirt he had worn the morning he took that message was the same one he was wearing now. In their clandestine attempt at packing, he and Mel had not been very selective regarding what they stuffed into the backpack. But Pete had made sure to bring his favorite flannel plaid.

He also remembered that, on the morning when he received the message, he had hastily scratched out the words on note paper and stuffed it into the pocket of this very shirt. Was it possible that the note was still there?

Trying not to disturb his brother further, he reached into the pocket. His fingers tingled as he felt the scrap of paper. Gingerly he pulled it out and reached overhead to flick on the dome light directed at his seat. Very carefully, almost afraid to look, he opened the paper and read the words.

A chill of dread moved up his neck. "Relay to Swastika. Bailey's Bug is a go. Cedars ready to drop on Shekinah," the message said.

He had no idea what "Bailey's Bug" or "Cedars" could mean. It occurred to him, however, that "Swastika" was probably the German, Monte Altmeyer. Eagle-Eye Fogarty was not necessarily meant to understand the message, but to serve as intermediary to get the message to Altmeyer.

This made it most likely that the message was of international significance, for Fogarty was only an American White Supremacist, while Altmeyer was a multinational mercenary. It also seemed all too likely that the term "ready to drop on" could mean "ready to bomb."

Pete's throat went dry, and he lifted a shaking hand to turn off the light. Enveloped in gloom, he felt like the loneliest soul in the universe; suspended between earth and heaven, he felt unfit for either.

Yet, what could he do? Not only was the entire message a riddle, but he had never heard the word "shekinah" before and would not even know whom to ask for an interpretation.

He could try to find some government agency that might help. But after everything he and Mel had learned about terrorists and their collusion with the authorities, he did not think that was such a good idea.

All at once, however, it swept over him that he had not relayed the message to Fogarty! In the excitement of the gathering two days later, and all of his duties as the host, he had forgotten to pass the word on to Eagle-Eye!

Perhaps there was some saving grace in that fact. Perhaps, whatever the plot was, he had helped to delay it. Perhaps . . .

Oh God in heaven! he prayed. *Let it not be too late. Help me put a stop to this thing—whatever it is!*

Pete was not used to praying. He had never been a believing man, beyond the nebulous warm fuzziness that came over him when he walked through the woods or thought about how vast the universe was. He had always figured he was a good guy, as good as any, and better than some. If there was a God, he figured that might count for something.

Now, all of a sudden, that kind of assurance seemed awfully tenuous.

The fact was, he was probably no better than Fogarty. In fact, he had, until just the last couple of days, thought Fogarty was great. Now, he thought him demonic. He went numb all over as he realized he had been a member of his camp—politically, spiritually, physically.

Pete's eyes grew hot and teary, and a sense of panic engulfed him. Choking, he took a deep breath to calm himself, then looked out the window. Dawn was coloring the sky gold and pink, and he could see the European mainland in the distance.

Soon, they were flying over the lush green hills of Germany, which were dotted every few miles with glorious castles, a world-class chessboard, reminiscent of the many conquerors and kings who had staked out claims on the Continent.

History never changes, Pete thought. *There have always been mighty men who used pawns to fulfill their ends. I am just a pawn—one little pawn—Help me, God, if you are there, to break one link in the chain of evil.*

CHAPTER 28

The next flight from Munich to Israel would not depart for another four hours. Pete and Mel had been waiting to catch standby seats since eight o'clock in the morning. It was now noon. If the four o'clock flight did not have room, they would have to consider finding a hotel in Munich for the night, then face another round of waiting tomorrow.

On the flight to Germany, Pete had read an article in one of the seat pocket magazines claiming that this airport had now surpassed the extravagant castle of Neuschwanstein as the country's leading sightseeing attraction. Although it had made an impressive scene as they approached it, its glass-sheathed control tower meeting the sky nearly eighty meters above the twin parallel runways and its single terminal spreading out over one full kilometer, Pete and Mel quickly wearied of hours confined to its sleek, luminescent interior.

Views out every window were, except for the continual landings and takeoffs of giant winged carriers, gray and depressing. Built on the Bavarian bogland, the airport landscape was dismal most of the time.

"Looks like we're stuck here at least for the afternoon," Mel said as he read yet another news magazine and watched the waiting area's TV news in German. "Let's take that 'moving sidewalk' down to the shop area."

Antsy with boredom, Pete agreed.

The brothers left the gate where the Israeli jets came and went, and hopped on the human-sized conveyor belt that eased them through a nearly endless, neon-art lined corridor to the main lobby. Here, at least, they might wile away some time in the gaudy little shops that were intended to rob tourists of their dollars, yen, and marks before they even made it downtown.

One huge checkerboard of black-and-white squares, the floor of the main concourse spread out as far as the eye could see, beneath banners and signs luring spendthrifts into temptation. Starting at one end of the lobby, the two men said little as they ambled from one shop to the next.

Mel suggested they should each buy a new shirt, having packed so little in their haste to depart Montana. When they saw the price tags on simple T-shirts, however, they decided against it.

Since their early-morning in-flight breakfast had worn off long ago, the brothers stopped for pizza-by-the-slice and groaned as they had to pay out the equivalent of four American dollars apiece. They sat on shrub-lined benches, making quick work of the "meal," then had white-chocolate yogurt for dessert.

A couple of hours later, one more flight had arrived from Israel, and the big jet was undergoing ground check and refueling, awaiting the takeoff, which, space permitting, would finally take the men to the Holy Land. They would not know, until the last passenger had boarded, whether or not there was room for them. But, they decided to return to the gate. "Maybe we can catch a catnap in the waiting area," Mel suggested.

Shuffling through the x-ray line once again, they picked up Pete's backpack, their keys and wallets from off the belt, and made their way back toward the El Al gate, whose planes, with the blue Star of David on their tail fins, represented aviation in the modern state of Israel.

The number of the gate was still some distance down the broad corridor when Pete suddenly stopped short, grabbing Mel by the arm, and staring straight ahead. "Am I dreaming?" he asked.

Mel followed his gaze down the long hallway, and his mouth fell open.

It took several seconds for their minds to register that they were not imagining what they saw.

Honey Aronstam and a tall, lanky stranger were standing in the corridor before the El Al waiting area, shaking hands with two women, one a dignified-looking older woman and the other a curly-haired blond.

None of this computed; none of this made sense. "That's Honey—no doubt about that!" Mel exclaimed. "What's *she* doing here?"

Whatever the answer to that question, another blazed louder through

Pete's already tormented heart: Who was the fellow she was with, and had he replaced the Montanan?

Pete ducked into a coffee shop close enough to watch the group, and Mel stepped in with him. "What's with you, brother?" Mel grumbled. "Are you going to let her get away?"

Pete's face was red with a tumult of feelings. "She's with someone!" he muttered. "What would I say?"

Mel sighed, exasperated. "When did you become such a wuss? So what if she's with someone? She belongs with you!"

Pete ran a hand through his long blond hair and smoothed his rumpled flannel shirt. Taking a deep breath, he looked back at Mel as if to say "Wish me luck" and reentered the corridor.

Slowly he walked toward the group, who seemed to be introducing themselves to one another, and then he stood by silently, waiting for Honey to see him out of the corner of her eye.

After what seemed a very long while, but was really only seconds, during which Pete ran hot and cold, sweaty and chilly, the woman who owned his heart glanced his way.

The look that came over her face was at first disbelief, then bewilderment, then . . . Pete could not be sure what it was.

Surely a thousand questions raced through her mind: How had he found her? How could he have tracked her down? Was he an enemy agent, here at Fogarty's command? And, was that Mel with him? What was Mel doing here?

It was fear that Pete read in her face. But just as quickly, it seemed to be replaced by a softer emotion. Did she see how he felt? Did she see that he was tormented, that he loved her? That, however he had found her, it was love that had brought him looking?

Suddenly she trembled. The man with her reached out to steady her. "What is it?" he asked, darting an anxious look at the two strangers. "Who are these guys?"

"Honey?" Pete cried, stepping toward her.

Rothmeyer started to intercept his advance, but Honey whispered, "It's okay, Dave." Leaning on the professor's arm, she looked at Pete as though the moon lay between them.

"What are you doing here?" she gasped.

Pete's eyes were moist, and he choked as he answered. "I was on my way to Israel to find you, Honey. I would have crossed the world, if I had to. Don't be afraid of me, Honey. I'll never hurt you again!"

Honey Aronstam knew Peter Wester too well to be fooled by a lie. She knew he was telling the truth and could hear by the sound of his voice the agony her loss had caused.

Stepping forward, she let him hold her, and for just a moment, they forgot they were in one of the world's busiest terminals. Oblivious to the churn of engines outside, the murmur of voices inside, they were lost in each other's embrace.

Tenderly, Pete lifted Honey's face to his and kissed her as though his life depended on it.

CHAPTER 29

David Rothmeyer glanced in the rearview mirror of the van he had rented at the Munich airport. Past his own bewildered reflection were faces totally new to him.

Only one of them had he come to know a little in the past few days: Honey Aronstam. He felt he could trust her. As for the others, he had only been scheduled to meet Emily McCurdy, the former Red Cross nurse who now sat in the passenger seat. The rest had been thrust upon him by chance and by wills other than his own.

He did not see that he had any choice but to let the strangers come along, at least as far as the hotel where he had reserved two rooms.

Britta Hayworth had accompanied Nurse McCurdy, the Irishwoman said, as her "companion." David could understand that a woman in her seventies would not want to travel alone and so did not take issue with the young woman's inclusion. He would decide if she should come with them to Dachau the next day, after he got to know her through the evening.

To David's mind, as he glanced at Britta, who sat in the van's second seat, she was pleasant enough company, with her upbeat personality and winsome smile. *Not bad looking, either,* he thought. A little young, barely older than most of his students at the university. But, then, he was not over the hill himself.

As for the men who sat on either side of Honey in the

backseat, the long-haired one draping an arm over her shoulders, the professor had no real qualms. Honey had already told David enough about Pete that he was prone to believe the two brothers had literally stumbled into her in a mad dash to save her in Israel.

There was no mistaking the love that sparked through Pete's eyes as he gazed down on the sweet woman. And Mel seemed like an honest sort, as baffled by the events he was caught up in as all of them were.

None of the newcomers needed to know the particulars of David's mission—he and Honey had already agreed to that. As far as Emily and the others knew, this entire venture simply revolved around the mystery of the badge, and the desire of some agency in Israel to know what it meant.

Though it was spring, evening brought a dank chill to the dusk that settled over the Munich bogland. David was glad to find the hotel before darkness descended, and he pulled into the parking lot with relief. He was ready for a good night's sleep and pleased to see that, as usual, the accommodations were first-rate.

The Consortium never spared expense when it came to lodgings, David thought. This was a four-star hotel, its sixteen stories rising up from an elegant boulevard in shining, black marble panels.

"I'll go in and see if they can upgrade us to larger rooms," David said, as the Westers hopped out and began to unload the baggage.

By the time he had reregistered the three women in one suite and himself with the brothers in an adjoining one, bellhops had loaded the suitcases and backpacks on a brass cart and were headed to the sixth floor.

As the group followed the baggage in a separate elevator, David assessed their level of weariness. Nurse McCurdy and Britta had done no more than a major commute across the English Channel, Emily coming from Dublin and Britta from London. He and Honey were not too much worse off for having flown from Tel Aviv to Athens and then into Munich in one day. The Westers, however, looked pretty worn out. David could not have known just how worn out, for he did not know that they had been on the run for days, from Montana to Wyoming, to Ohio, and then overseas.

"You fellows feel up to a good meal before hitting the sack?" he asked.

Even given their state of exhaustion, neither of them was about to turn down such an offer. "Sounds good!" Pete said, and Mel nodded.

As the elevator door opened on the broad, carpeted corridor that led to their rooms, the group agreed to meet back in the main floor dining hall at seven.

"Dr. Rothmeyer," Britta called after the professor, "I've been wanting to ask you some questions. May I sit with you at dinner?"

David turned to her in surprise. "I would be flattered," he replied, a little nonplussed.

At this, she approached and thrust a business card into his hand.

"Thanks so much!" she said, leaving him to gawk at the impressive, embossed card: "Britta Hayworth—Staff Correspondent—*London Times*."

Britta tried not to behave like a reporter as she sat across from Professor Rothmeyer that evening. The low-keyed dinner was meant for relaxation. But this was a chance she had never dreamed of, to be able to talk with another highly respected archaeologist—Father McCurdy, of course, having been the first.

When Emily had told her about the summons to meet Dr. Rothmeyer in Germany, the young correspondent saw an opportunity for two story possibilities.

She had brought all her charms and powers of persuasion to bear on her elderly friend, convincing her that she would be wise not to travel alone, and that the story of the old scribe at Dachau could be the one that would help put Britta in line for a regular slot with the *Times*.

The young reporter did not let on that the second story, and really the more important one to her mind, related to Emily's brother and the probability of a secret scroll. If David Rothmeyer was working for an Israeli agency, he must know something about the Cave Scrolls and the controversy surrounding them. Perhaps, just perhaps, he could shed some light on the mystery of Father McCurdy's skittish avoidance of the press.

She realized she would have to be coy in her approach to the topic, not wishing to offend Emily with her obvious opportunism. As for Rothmeyer, if he chose to be closemouthed, well, she had run into that before.

Britta had given much thought to how she might broach the topic of the scrolls. It had come to her that a direct involvement of Emily in the conversation would be the best way to avoid the appearance of scheming.

After the hotel waiter had taken orders around the table, Britta, sipping from a goblet of white wine, began, "Dr. Rothmeyer, my friend Emily is the most amazing person. Sometimes I think she should have been the journalist and not me!"

David observed Britta quietly, wondering what it was about himself, lately, that he was so aware of attractive women. He had been caught off guard by the pleasant intrusion of Honey Aronstam into his life, surprised at the magic her presence had worked on him, and disappointed when he learned how unattainable she was. Now, here he was, again, quite conscious of the magnetism of a pretty woman.

Certainly he had associated with many attractive females, both at the university and even in the field—young coworkers, instructors in the anthropology department, even students in his classes. None of them had ever particularly intrigued him.

As for Honey Aronstam, he had concluded that her allure had to do with the setting in which he had met her, the romance of Israel and Jerusalem, and her kindred interest in things Jewish, as much as her evident beauty and sweetness.

How should he reason with himself about Britta Hayworth? He had not spent enough time with her to have any good reason to give her a second thought, especially since, for David, good looks were not "good reason." Yet, in the few hours since he had met her, he had already thought about her more than a second time.

As she reiterated that she was a journalist, he came up with a probable explanation. At the elevator, she had placed a *London Times* business card in his hand, and he had been duly impressed. This was a professional woman, a peer.

Though she was young, her curly blond hair and cherubic face reminding him of a child star, she was adult enough to have made inroads into the staff of one of the world's most prestigious newspapers. He had always respected determination and strength in a woman, and this was evidence of those qualities.

In keeping with Britta's topic of conversation, he asked, "I suppose you are referring to Ms. McCurdy's involvement in this mystery?" He nodded courteously toward the elderly nurse. "If she is like me, she can be close to a wonderful story and not have the slightest idea how to capture it on paper." Then, more pointedly, he added, "I assume that is what you have in mind—turning our little mystery into a feature article?"

Britta blushed. "Guilty as charged," she said.

David glanced down the table toward Honey, who was not deaf to the conversation. He could see that she appeared uneasy at the thought of a possible involvement of the press.

"It remains to be seen," David said, turning back to Britta, "if there is any real story here at all. So far, we have only an old badge with a few scrawls on the back."

Britta took a bite of her salad and lifted her chin. "Dr. Rothmeyer," she said, "your agency would not have sent you to Germany if they believed there was nothing important to be had here." Then, smiling coyly, she added, "I wouldn't mind if I was on hand for some great find."

Emily, appearing to sense Honey's tension, tried to mediate. "The professor is right about journalism. I knew, when I met Rabbi Yitzak years ago that he was a wonderful character and that he had served his people. But I never could have made a news story of those facts."

Britta shrugged. "I suppose it remains to be seen if I can either. First, I should have the good professor's permission to exploit him in this way."

David gave a fleeting glance toward Honey. Trying to be diplomatic, he said, "If I were to be exploited, Britta, I can't think of a more charming exploiter than yourself. You must understand, though, that I am representing a group. This is not 'my' story, to be told to just anyone. This is Ms. Aronstam's story, and it is my agency's story. For now, we have reason to keep the press at arm's length."

Far from putting her off, this kind of statement was just the sort that got Britta Hayworth's investigative nose twitching. "And why is that?" she asked, wishing dearly that she could take notes.

David pulled back and looked at her cautiously. "Aha," he said, "an interview. No, Ms. Hayworth, I will not get into the nature of the agency or why it does anything it does. It is enough that you know Emily's side of things."

The nurse only looked bewildered. "I really have no 'side,' as you say," she replied. "I simply helped an old, dying man at Dachau by sending his family his precious badge."

Britta turned inquisitive eyes toward her friend. "Didn't you wonder about the writing on the back of the cloth?" she asked.

Emily shook her head. "You must realize that we were dealing with hundreds—no, thousands—of prisoners. I have no idea how many I helped in such a way, getting messages to their families, and all. The thing that was noteworthy about Rabbi Aronstam was how we found him that day."

Honey Aronstam had never heard the full story of the rabbi's rescue, and she leaned forward eagerly. "Emily," she said, "please, do tell us how you met my great-grandfather! I have always wished I could have known him."

By now, the waiter was placing meals on the table, the pungent aromas of brautwurst, sauerkraut, hot potato salad, and whitefish in herb sauce competing for attention with the topic of conversation. Digging into the hearty German cuisine, the diners nonetheless hung on to Emily's words, as she gave an account of that distant memory.

"I could never begin to describe the camp or the horrors we came upon. I will try to tell you, though I shiver even now to think of it."

Her eyes were misty as she paused, and David knew she was reliving in a moment the gruesome scenes she had managed to bury beneath years of passing time.

"The American GIs and the British troops who entered with us that day had just loaded the last of the survivors onto the backs of big trucks. They hung like skeletons to the side racks, staring through sunken eyes across the compound where they had endured the worst of hellish nightmares."

Forgetting for the moment about her food, Emily set down her fork and wound her fingers together, nervously weaving them in and out. "I was at the end of the barracks nearest the ovens. . . ."

The young people listened somberly, almost forgetting their own meals.

"We had just found a few survivors lying on the ground near the path that led to the deathhouse. They had apparently been scheduled to die that afternoon and were already close to expiring from cold and malnutrition. The troops were lifting their frail, nearly weightless bodies onto their own shoulders, carrying them out, sometimes two at a time, toward the trucks."

Again, she paused. Her voice cracked as she continued, "Suddenly one of the GIs shouted at me to come help him with something. I glanced up toward the oven house, and he was trying to carry an old man—the rabbi—away from the place. It seems he had come upon him, scrambling about at the back corner of the deathhouse. You'll see the place tomorrow, Dr. Rothmeyer. Anyway," she went on, "as he brought him out, the GI told me that he had found the old fellow madly pushing against the back side of the building. It seemed he was fixated upon one row of bricks and sat there, bony and frail, pounding and pressing upon them for all he was worth, as though—" She paused, as if a light had gone on in her head. "I never thought of it before, but it was as though he was trying to close something in!"

Honey quivered, setting her fork aside, and Pete reached for her hand.

"Did the old fellow say anything about what he was doing?" Mel asked.

"There were only two words that I could make out. He kept repeating 'Schuh,' the word which I believe means 'shoe,' just like we would say."

David nodded. "That's right."

"'Schuh!' 'Schuh!' he kept saying. And then something like 'dampen.'" Emily shrugged. "I don't recall anything else. You see, many of the people we rescued that day were talking out of their heads, if they were talking at all. We really gave none of this any mind at the time. The only other thing I remember about that episode was the old fellow thrusting his feeble fist into my hand and releasing his crumpled badge. 'Get this to my family,' he said, in English plain enough that I could understand."

Honey looked sadly at the tabletop and blinked back tears. "My poor great-grandpa," she said with a sigh. "The only things I know about him are what my father and grandfather told me. He was some sort of record-keeper—"

"A scribe?" David interrupted.

"Yes, I guess so," she said. "What in the world could he have been doing behind that building?" Her voice was husky as she fought back tears.

Emily turned to her, reaching out and patting her arm. "I learned a little about him, once he gave me the name of his son and his whereabouts. Some of his fellow prisoners walked with the GI and me to the truck, where the poor old soul was to be carried out. The folks on the truck greeted him with a bit of energy, something rare in their condition. When we got him into the rig, they cradled him between them, trying to offer him warmth. The people who walked with us said he was an important man, something of a village historian. That is really all I know."

As her voice trailed off, the table was very quiet. Even Britta, for once, was speechless.

Pete took a handkerchief from his hip pocket and handed it to Honey, who dabbed her eyes. At last, David broke the silence.

"Well, I'm no literary critic, but your way with words certainly gives a picture," he said. "If a story does come of this, our journalist would do well to quote you."

Britta agreed, her blue eyes filled with admiration. For a long while, nothing more was said at the table, as each absorbed the sad legacy of inhumanity.

Britta was not so insensitive as to lunge forward with her investigation at this moment, but she would at least prime the pump for later efforts. "As I said earlier," she noted, "Emily should have been the journalist. But then, she is not the only one in her family to be blessed with a fine mind. You might be interested to know, Dr. Rothmeyer, that Emily's brother is a professor like yourself."

"Really?" he said. "Where does he teach?"

Emily brightened. "He is emeritus now, Dr. Rothmeyer. But he still lectures, now and then—at Oxford!"

The last two words were spoken with evident pride, and David could not help but be impressed.

"Oxford!" he exclaimed. "And what is his area?"

At this, Britta looked at Emily as though the thought were new. "Archaeology!" Britta sang out. "Isn't that something, Emily? To think, they are in the same field!"

"Why, that's right!" Emily thrilled. "Perhaps you've heard of my brother, Professor. Ian McCurdy?"

David was stunned. The name blazed forth from his academic background like the name of Freud from the annals of psychiatry or Darwin from the field of anthropology. "Ian McCurdy!" he exclaimed. "He is your brother?"

"The same!" Emily replied, sitting up tall and straight.

"*The* Ian McCurdy who was on the Cave Scroll committee?" he marveled.

Britta pretended to be astonished at all these coincidences. "Right!" she said. "Isn't this something? The sister of one of the greatest archaeologists sitting at dinner with yet another great archaeologist!"

"Yes," Emily agreed, "this is amazing, indeed! And to think, Britta is the only reporter who has ever gotten an interview with my brother. He's quite mum, you know, about his work at Qumran." Then, pausing and thinking a moment, the woman seemed to have hit on an incredible irony. "In fact, you two men have a great deal in common, even for your profession! Israeli archaeology . . . tattered writings . . ."

David looked at Emily with a fixed expression. His face did not show the sifting and sorting that was going on in his brain, the amalgamation of facts and seeming coincidences that were surely not happenstance.

Then, not knowing whether to be angered or intrigued by the suspicion that posed itself to him, he turned intuitive eyes on Britta.

"I've read about the controversy regarding the Cave Scrolls," he said, slowly. "I know that the scroll committee hid them from the public for decades, but that's all I know, Ms. Hayworth. Were you hoping that I knew more?"

Guilty as charged! ran through Britta's head again. This time she did not admit her duplicity. Instead, with the deftness that could one day win her a Pulitzer Prize, she rallied, making the best of an awkward moment. "I must confess that the possibility did occur to me," she said. "Perhaps we can help each other in our quests."

Then, in a fit of inspiration, she added, "Wouldn't it be something if our two quests were one and the same?"

CHAPTER 30

More than most places on earth, the backdrop of Upper Bavaria fits its history. Frequently fogged over, the dismal terrain suits the spirit of what transpired there a generation ago. As the traveler passes through boggy stretches, gray and dampish cold, it is possible to believe the ghosts of Dachau and its numerous satellite camps might still linger there.

Indeed, through the headlights of trains and cars along the soggy grasslands, spirits have been seen. Whether sparked by people's imaginations, enlivened by the facts of the area, or whether true phantoms of agony and despair, these spectres are sometimes observed in the striped workclothes of the camp inmates—skeletal, piteous, hands outstretched to the speeding vehicles, as if asking passage away from a horror long past.

Perhaps no odder assortment of travelers ever wended through that bogland than the passengers in David Rothmeyer's rental van. From separate corners of the earth, from places as far distant and unlike as the Montana outback, the cobbled streets of Dublin, the metropolis of London, and a middle-American university in Ohio, they had been thrown together by what seemed more and more to be orchestrated events—events not of their own making.

That morning, they had picked at a hotel breakfast, feeling mixed emotions about the day's venture. David and Britta were, of course, eager to see how the mystery unfolded. Honey was apprehensive about going to the site of misery so closely connected to her family, and Emily had trepidations about returning to the place of nightmarish memories.

As for the Wester brothers, Mel's experience was closer to that of a tourist than any one of the others'. Pete, however, was a jumble of nerves, not ready to see what his Aryan brethren claimed never existed. He knew now that it must have existed, that the story handed down to Honey could not be a lie. He would go along quietly, fists clenched, shame-laden, but ready as he could be to see the truth.

None of the crew had slept well. David had tossed and turned all night, wrestling with an overwhelming sense of destiny. As if sent on a celestial roller-coaster ride for the past several months, he felt more keenly now than ever that something beyond himself was pulling him from one tidbit of information to another.

It was as though some invisible hand had been guiding him when he did not even seek guidance. Along the way it would stop and point a finger at a particular line of type, thrust him into some undreamed of conversation, or even fly him across landscapes he had seen only in books, depositing him here and there as the nameless spirit deemed necessary.

Oh, he knew now what that spirit was. It had to be God. Nothing else could have brought him this far. And he had even learned to pray—tentatively, hesitantly—but truly. Where it was all leading, and why, were the ongoing mysteries.

At times, the information he was now gleaning in his abstract delvings had nothing to do with his own skill as a researcher. It seemed to be planted just where the powers above knew he would dig.

The night before, he had been most confounded by one phrase dropped at dinner. It had jolted him at the time, but he had not digested it until later, as he lay in bed, tossing and turning. Emily McCurdy had related that Rabbi Aronstam's friends at the camp called him their "village historian." This fact, coupled with Honey's recollection of her great-grandfather's being a "scribe," had teased Rothmeyer's imagination all night long.

If this information was true, then whatever the rabbi was hiding at Dachau must relate to Jewish history. *A record of some kind!* David thought. The badge the old fellow had passed on to his family, with its cryptic references to rows and bricks, absolutely had to be a key to the exact bricks he was found working at the day the GI found him.

David tingled every time he considered the possibilities of what the old man had buried there. It could be nothing more than a personal account of his miseries in the camp, but if the man was a scribe he would not have been writing about personal matters.

It had to be some kind of a record.

Again, it could be no more than a list of names of his fellow villagers who had died in the camp. This would be a useful thing for families to have, and for future generations to refer to. But David had been on this assignment, this mission, long enough to have seen the celestial orchestration at work. He felt, to his very core, that he had been brought to Germany as one more step toward the fulfillment of the quest he had been assigned.

Maybe this was faith, he thought. He was beginning to believe that faith was not just an ethereal form of wishful thinking. It was not clairvoyance. He was beginning to see that faith was a certainty.

Faith was the substance of things hoped for, the evidence of things not seen.

Now, where had he heard that line? He would have to ask Rabbi Benjamin when he got back to Israel.

Of course, having worked in the field on countless digs, it had occurred to him that whatever Aronstam had been secreting away that day might have deteriorated beyond recognition. Particularly in this damp climate, it would be miraculous for any form of writing material to survive, walled up in a cold, moisture-riven wall for over half a century.

The old rabbi himself must have been concerned for such things, David thought. As he pounded on the wall, repeating the enigmatic "Schuh," "Schuh," he had also been moaning "daempfen," the German word for "damp." And then, what form of writing material had he been attempting to preserve? If the little badge was an example, with its coalish ink, it would be a wonder if anything legible remained.

Still, as David drove through the foggy morning, heading northwest out of Munich, he did so with a sense of anticipation. He felt certain, based on his experiences all along the way, that he had not come here for nothing.

Gripping the steering wheel resolutely, he peered through the mist and listened to the diesel engine of the German car. There was precious little other sound to cue in on; his passengers were amazingly quiet, each obviously lost in thoughts of his or her own.

The van was nearing the middle-sized burg of Dachau. The low, gray sky seemed even gloomier here. Even though it was late spring, the greenery was less than lush.

No one spoke as the car followed the street signs toward the encampment that lay on the outskirts of town. David wondered if his passengers were struck, as he was, with the fact that life went on here. Houses and yards were typical of homes anywhere else in middle-class Germany. Playsets with swings and seesaws testified to the fact that children grew up here, played, and went to school. Businesses operated, cars streamed down busy streets, people greeted one another on the sidewalks, as they would in any city.

The professor was profoundly disconcerted that the locals could eat, laugh, and sleep here. *Do they think about it?* he wondered. *What do they do with the fact that such a travesty happened on their soil, or that the compound still exists, a perpetual reminder of Aryan guilt?*

As he maneuvered the van onto the main boulevard that led to the memorial, David's stomach tightened. There, beside the road, was evidence that the Germans were not alone in their ability to "move on." A bright red and yellow billboard, an advertisement for a world-famous American burger chain, flashed its commercial message even here.

"I don't believe it!" he exclaimed, pointing to the sign. "Do you see that? Does that strike you as tasteless?"

"Tasteless, indeed," Emily said tersely. The others in the van shook their heads and muttered their disgust, while Pete, his jaw tense, eyed the sign incredulously.

At last they came to a long, high wall that stretched for several blocks along the street. Gray like the sky, it bore no emblems, no words upon its concrete facade. Atop the wall were several rows of barbed wire, and spaced every hundred yards or so were towers, their empty windows staring out upon the world like the eye sockets of dead giants.

"This must be it," Mel called out from the backseat.

All heads were turned, the passengers leaning toward the side of the van that passed closest to the wall. Beyond Mel's simple statement, no one said a word.

David Rothmeyer had visited the Holocaust Museum in Jerusalem. So had Honey, on her one-day tour of the Holy City. Profoundly moving as that had been, the museum was only a reproduction of scenes from the nightmare. This, however, was reality—reality based on memory, to be sure, but as physically present a reality as anything could be.

The impact it would have on them would be beyond definition, past description.

They made their way to the parking lot designated for visitors and piled out of the van. Honey reached for Pete's hot fist. Glancing down at her, he loosened his grip and let her slip her small hand into his sweaty palm. Britta walked quietly beside Emily, who was already choking back tears. David and Mel walked silently together, listening in amazement as Emily began, already, to relive that long ago day.

"This is where the trucks pulled in," she said, pointing to that very parking lot. "It was from here that we got our first glimpse of the emaciated bodies clinging to the iron gate. I can see them now!" she cried.

Stopping in her tracks, she shuddered, her face pale. "Oh, Britta," she gasped, "I don't know if I can go in!"

Britta grasped her close, and Mel reached out his protective hand to steady her. "We're with you," he said. "You can lean on me, if it gets too tough."

CHAPTER 31

The camp at Dachau was laid out simply, constructed for one purpose: the incarceration and extermination of human beings.

Beneath the now-vacant gaze of the first guard tower, the visitors freely entered an open gate, a gate through which prisoners were once ushered against their will.

As they moved along the walkway leading to the interior, they passed between the high gray exterior wall and a barbed-wire fence. Just beyond the fence was a deep trench.

Honey paused, looking at it quizzically. "What was the ditch for?" she asked.

"It was to keep the prisoners from reaching the fence," Emily replied. "They approached it only on penalty of certain death. Guards watched for trespassers from their turrets, submachine guns at the ready."

To the immediate left, upon entering, one long, wooden building sat watch over the huge, rectangular compound. Emily recounted that the Spartan structure once housed the SS, the ruthless officers who oversaw the enforced labor and eventual death of thousands. "Some of the Nazi officers hid in that building when the Allies invaded," she said, "but it was not much of a fortress."

Leading directly perpendicular from the headquarters was a pristine, graveled aisle. Emily walked with the group to the head of the path and with a sweeping gesture, explained,

"Along each side of this corridor, the bunkhouses stood, containing wooden beds three levels high, like stalls on a slave galley."

Only two reconstructions remained of thirty-four bunkhouses, which, according to the diagram on a sign, were spaced in dreary, symmetrical balance down that wide path. Just the foundations of the others were visible, the buildings having been so run-down, the sign said, that they had to be demolished.

The Dachau that David and his party observed was a horribly clean place. All remnants of its gruesome past had been raked and shoveled and purged away, much as Lady Macbeth scrubbed at her guilty hands until they wreaked of cleanliness.

In the remaining starkness, the visitors were left to form their own images of the atrocities that had taken place here. It was as if, with the cleansing, a slate had been handed to them, not for the rewriting of history, but for the envisioning of it personally, privately, with whatever memories or imagination each might bring to it.

Nor was there any chance that imagination could overstate what had happened there. Not even Dachau survivors were capable of overstating it.

The starkness of the camp hit Emily McCurdy full force. The horror of that long ago day blazed at her from every open walkway, each exposed foundation. The souls she had seen that day were present in the extreme—the blood, the waste, the disease, and the brutality. She wished there were something to interfere, some professional guide, some taped lecturer whose account would take the edge off her memories. Had there been, she could have said, "Yes, that's good, but not good enough. That's close, but not close enough. I remember it differently."

The blending of her experiences with someone else's could have diffused the emotional impact.

It occurred to her that, in leaving Dachau to the imagination, the German people had displayed wisdom. A degree of absolution had been attained by their stark presentation of their history, their refusal to couch it all in explanation or description.

Only one area of the compound was devoted to images. The headquarters now housed a photo gallery, life-size black-and-white ghosts of the horror that had transpired here.

Though visitors were allowed to come and go freely from the compound, to wander from site to site unhindered, and though there were no guards or custodians scrutinizing their movements, the professor did not want to draw attention to his group by acting differently than most who came here. "We're not just visitors," he said, "but I think we should begin with a tour of the gallery."

Emily took a few hesitant steps into the place and broke into a dewy sweat. It was not so much the hideous depictions spread out through several long rooms that troubled her. By now, there were few people in the civilized world who had not seen such pictures in newsreels of the era and in the endless repetition of war movies and documentaries. Rather, what squeezed her heart and tripped her pulse was the knowledge that Nazi officials, the evilest and cruelest of humanity, had lived and worked within these walls.

Taking Britta aside, she begged off. "I'll wait for you outside," she said, her face pale.

Britta offered to accompany her, but she would not allow it. "I'll be fine," she insisted. "Go see the photos. I saw the real thing."

Quickly she passed back through the entryway and into the dismal yard, leaving Britta to rejoin the others.

As for David, while his mind was centered on the task at hand, he was drawn to the depictions, compelled to take in the horror of the photos. The captions, mostly in German, were obviously directed at the conscience of the offending nation, but the photographs spoke for themselves.

Every horror, from mass shootings at the edge of great pits, to burial mounds of twiglike corpses, was covered in the gallery. Scenes from one of the dormitories showed that the building was devoted to scientific and medical experimentations so grisly in nature as to bring tears to the women's eyes and cause David's stomach to churn.

One chart was of special interest to David and the others, for it outlined the various types of prisoners who had been incarcerated here. The visitors were surprised to learn that Christian Scientists, Jehovah's Witnesses, homosexuals, writers and artists who had offended the regime, and many others were taken captive and held in special bunkhouses. One dormitory was devoted solely to Catholic priests who had spoken out against Hitler. The SS took special pleasure in sending these men off to the experimentation lab.

For each type, there was a special badge, homosexuals designated by pink triangles, for instance, or political prisoners by orange ones.

In each case, however, if a captive fell into any of these categories, and was also a Jew, an extra triangle was added to his badge, to form a Star of David. It was apparent, from the photos, that for such prisoners, existence in the camp was made all the more miserable.

At last, as the little group made its way to the concluding photos in the gallery, the scene shifted. These photos, in full life-size, were of the Allied troops entering the compound, of their carrying the prisoners to the waiting trucks, and of their driving the SS at gunpoint off to prisons and trials of their own.

"This is what Emily described!" Britta gasped as she gazed upon one photo of Red Cross nurses lending assistance to the GIs and other allies. "Do you suppose she's in this picture?"

Mel, Pete, and the others gathered before the photo, scanning it carefully.

"How would we know?" Mel asked. "I'm sure she's changed a lot in fifty years."

David glanced out the window of the gallery and spotted Emily sitting bleakly on the front steps, apparently lost in thought, while other visitors came and went.

"Come on, guys," Honey said. "We should join her. She looks pretty miserable."

David led the group through the door at the far end of the building. Silently they crossed the yard to the nurse's side.

Pete, having said nothing throughout the entire tour, stepped up to Emily and placed a trembling hand on her shoulder. When she glanced his way, her face pale and wan, he found the courage to speak.

"Miss McCurdy," he said, his voice husky and tight, "I feel I don't deserve the honor of being in your company today. For a long time I believed those who say none of this here ever happened." He gestured to the vast compound and the fearsome towers. His eyes welled with tears, but he forced them back.

"I just want to say that I'm sorry," he went on. "It's one thing to deny the history books. It's another to deny your friends, and"—he turned to Honey—"your loved ones." He gave a deep sigh. "I don't know if I'm ready to see the rest, but I know I'm ready to believe. No—I *do* believe! And, well, I just want to ask your forgiveness."

Emily studied Pete's handsome Aryan face. She did not know this young man, but she knew he had been duped by one of the grandest lies of all time.

Reaching up, she patted his hand where it rested on her stooped shoulder. "My forgiveness is not necessary," she said. "Just pray that you can do something, from now on, to dispel the myth."

Then, rising, she smiled sadly at David. "Well, Professor," she said, "shall we move on? We came here to find something, and hopefully whatever we find will bring some healing."

At the back end of the compound, a little bridge led over the deep ditch that ran the circuit of the place. Passing through another gate, the group wended their way through a bower of fir trees and green bushes that, with their inviting look, were strangely out of place here.

This had never been meant to be a showcase. In fact, the Nazi regime had meant to hide their gruesome business from the world. But in designating the site a war memorial, the German people had done what they could to make the place minimally tolerable. Perhaps this pathway necessitated some kind of buffer, something to soften the ghastliness of what the brick buildings ahead represented.

But there was no real way to soften the horror of what that path led to.

Within the bower, three buildings stood, each one bigger than the last, as the ultimate work of the death camp demanded more and more space, more efficiency for its execution. These buildings housed the ovens, the final repository for thousands of unfortunates.

One end of the longest building contained the shower room, where prisoners thought they were entering for a bath. Though legend had it that these showers were never used, not even to gas the prisoners, that was no credit to the Nazis. If it was true that they were never employed, it was only because the SS had decided that such duplicity only wasted time. Better to execute the prisoners at gunpoint and move their bodies quickly into the incinerators.

As Emily made her way up the path and through the trees, she knew what she was about to see. Silently, she turned to Mel. The big, rugged policeman stepped to her side and offered her the strong arm he had promised.

"Thank you," she whispered, leaning on him.

For the first time in her seventy-six years, she felt frail. Emily had always been grateful for her good health and for her robust stature, which defied her age. Today she trembled like an old woman, and her heart beat like that of a bird caught in a net.

Suddenly Honey let out a little cry and buried her face on Pete's chest.

As Pete observed the unthinkable, his face was white as death.

The group stood before the largest of the buildings. Its great doors stood wide open, revealing two immense furnaces, each with its iron doors agape. There was no mistaking the fact that their tunnellike maws were built for corpses, the bottoms of the coffin-shaped oven liners outfitted with sliding iron stretchers for ease of deposit.

Mel placed a quivering hand to his lips. He had seen morgues in Los Angeles. As a cop it had been his distasteful duty to identify murder victims. Many times he had watched as slab doors were opened and bodies were pulled out on gurneys much like the platforms in these ovens.

But, never had a morgue, in L.A. or elsewhere, been outfitted to receive bodies the way Nazi ovens were. In front of the furnaces, on a beam that spanned the room, were suspended hefty iron pulleys, complete with huge hooks. A black-and-white sign attached to the beam explained in cryptic German, English, Russian, and Italian: "Prisoners were hanged from here."

Emily patted Honey's back. "The day I arrived here, GIs were taking bodies off those hooks. The ovens were still smoldering, but those poor folks at least received a proper burial."

Britta's eyes stung, but not from tears alone. "There is a stench to this place!" she moaned. "Is it what I think it is?"

"It must be," Mel replied. "After half a century!"

Emily pulled back and walked again to the pathway. Turning about, she gazed at the scene and stepped back in time. She could see the GI hailing her from the corner of the oven house.

She pointed in that direction. "That is where the soldier called for me," she said. "He had found the old rabbi around back."

David turned his attention her way. Despite the horrors of this place, the quest he was on took over. "Can you show us?" he spurred her.

Emily nodded. Mel offered to take her arm again, but she squared her shoulders and shook her head. "I'm all right," she said.

David glanced around the area and, seeing no other tourists, said, "We're alone now, but we don't want to be caught." Turning to the big ex-cop, he suggested, "Mel, how about standing out front here? If anyone comes along, let us know. We'll try to be quick."

Mel nodded and walked casually over to the first oven house, pretending to read a brief history posted there.

Adrenaline coursing through his body, David followed Emily as she led him and the others around the far end of the largest building, to the back side.

Pointing to the corner, she said, "This is where the rabbi was, sitting on the ground, pushing on the wall."

The spot she designated was overgrown with vines. "Here?" David asked.

"Yes, but the wall was bare back then," she replied.

David knelt on the ground and shuffled through the pocket of his tweed jacket. He pulled out a small notebook, opened it, and found the translation of Honey's badge.

"'Third row from the bottom, fourth brick from the end,'" he read.

He tingled as his eyes fell on the last lines of the directions, but he did not read them aloud: "Return priests to their service and Israel to its House of Prayer."

Like a surgeon, he called for the necessary implement. "Honey, the trowel, please."

Honey reached into her shoulder bag and pulled out a small, pointed tool, which David, in preparing for this assignment, had packed from Israel.

The archaeologist was now in his element. He deftly pulled the tentacles of a vine away from the old wall and ran the trowel down the face, looking for anomalies.

Pete, Emily, Britta, and Honey leaned close, breathing over his shoulder.

"Aha!" he said. "Look at this!"

Along the edges of the very brick designated by the badge, there was no mortar.

"This brick was removed at one time," he said, "and then it was replaced, but not sealed in."

His proficient eyes scanning the adjacent bricks, he noted, "It appears that three others were handled this way. See?" He placed his hand on the face of four contiguous bricks, two on top of each other.

Gently, he eased the point of the trowel between the mortared bricks and the one named on the badge, third row from the bottom, fourth brick from the end.

Suddenly Honey gasped. "Dave," she cried, "do you see that?"

The brick David worked with had some kind of etching on it. He ran his hand over the face and removed loose dirt.

The wide-eyed group leaned closer.

"This is it!" David exclaimed. "Can you believe it?"

There, plain as could be, was a Star of David, scratched into the red clay.

Honey knelt down beside David and ran her fingers over the precious mark. "My great-grandfather must have put this here!" she marveled.

"No doubt about it," David agreed.

Quickly now, he worked the trowel deep into the seams that separated brick from brick. Round and round each edge he worked the tool, pulling ever so gently as he did so, to ease the first brick out. Then, after placing the trowel on the ground, he used his fingers to loosen the brick further, until he had pulled it nearly all the way forward.

As his friends watched, he gave the final tug—and held the brick in his hands. "Here," he said, handing it to Honey. "This is yours."

The woman took it and cradled it to her chest, her eyes welling, while David continued to the other three rectangles, breaking them free and removing them, one at a time.

Now was the moment of truth. All five of the seekers were kneeling, as though in obeisance to the gaping hole in the wall. No light shone through, as the bricks apparently abutted an inner wall, forming only a facade. As the group peered into the opening, they let out a collective sigh.

"Wow!" Pete exclaimed. "Look at that!"

Against the inner wall, where connecting mortar should have been, was a wide green piece of rubber. Flat as a sheet, it was shaped like the silhouette of a foot and was graced with broad straps and rusty buckles.

"It looks like a boot!" Britta gasped.

Emily gripped the edge of the opening and stared at the strange, flat object. "Why, it *is* a boot! The kind the SS wore on rainy days! A lot of them were wearing these over their shoes the day we entered the camp!"

David hurried now, trying not to be clumsy, running his fingers down the edge of the rubber to loosen it from its fifty-year-old burial site. Gradually, he was able to ease it out. As he did so, the top edge separated, revealing that both sides were present. The sole, they saw, had been removed so that the rubber was like an "L" shaped tube.

"This must be the 'Schuh' the old rabbi kept mentioning," Emily said.

"He was worried that it would get damp," David recalled. "So, it must contain what we are looking for!"

Drawing the boot onto his lap, he leaned on his heels and pried it apart, ever so carefully. "Move back a little," he said. "Give me some light."

For a moment, the onlookers complied, but just as quickly pressed in again.

"Yes . . . yes!" the professor marveled. "There is something here!" Spreading the top of the boot wide, he turned the opening toward the group.

"What is it?" Pete urged.

David reached into the boot and pulled forth a dingy piece of fabric. It was rolled in a skin of transparent oilcloth, but through that layer could be seen the dark gray stripes of a prisoner's clothing.

"Where would he have gotten a boot and an oilcloth?" Britta marveled.

Emily was enthralled. "The troops used to keep their paper money in oilcloth. Perhaps the SS did too. The rabbi must have come upon a piece of it!"

"Crafty old fellow!" David said with a chuckle. "He must have scavenged for this stuff for a long time. Now it remains to be seen if the rabbi's protective measures preserved his treasure!"

"Take out the fabric!" Britta cried. "Is something written on it?"

David gingerly unwrapped the oilcloth and pulled out the roll of striped cotton. "There's something here, all right!" he replied, loosening one end of the roll to reveal some jagged figures. "Looks like Hebrew!"

But just as he was about to unfold more, Mel appeared at the corner of the building. "Better hurry," he called in a hushed tone. "There's a group of schoolkids coming into the area with their teachers. Must be some kind of field trip."

David quickly rerolled the cloth and stuffed it into the oilskin. "I don't think we need the boot," he said, secreting the little parcel in his jacket.

Honey picked up the trowel and placed it in her shoulder bag. Then, despite David's assessment, she picked up the boot, a souvenir of her great-grandfather's bravery, wrapped the brick in it, and deposited it in the same bag.

David, catching her covert move, gave her a wink, and she smiled shyly.

"We'll have to read the rabbi's message back at the hotel," he said, taking Emily by the arm. "Careful. Don't trip over those vines."

CHAPTER 32

The mood in the van as the six travelers headed back to the hotel was quite different than it had been upon their arrival at Dachau. Though the experience of seeing the concentration camp was unspeakably sobering, the thrill of their find and the anticipation of learning its contents enlivened the spirits of the group.

Heading straight for David's suite, the little entourage fidgeted as the professor fumbled for his keys and unlocked the room door.

After casting their coats on one of the beds, they huddled anxiously around a table under the window and watched as David sat down, brought forth the parcel, and began to open it.

The morning fog had lifted somewhat, and sunlight, the first they had seen since entering Germany, filtered in glorious stripes through the venetian blinds. Emily drew the curtain cord and raised the slats, permitting the light to spill across the table. A distant view of the Alps went unnoticed by the preoccupied guests.

Before unrolling the oilcloth further, David glanced up at Honey, who stood breathlessly gazing at his still hands. "Perhaps you should do this," he offered. "After all, this is *your* property."

Honey smiled gratefully but shook her head. "Go on, Dave," she replied. "This is your quest, as well as mine."

The professor turned his attention to the parcel and pulled back the oil-cloth carefully, unrolling it a little at a time until the striped cloth inside lay on top. Although he had handled many precious artifacts in his career, none had merited such respect as this one. Whatever this cloth contained, whether of use to his search or not, it had been created at great risk to the writer.

Gently, he unrolled the striped material as his companions bent close. He was reminded of the day the rabbis huddled with him around the long genealogy scroll in his apartment.

As he began to analyze the writing upon the fabric, he was first of all amazed at the condition of the piece. "The letters are still intact!" he said. "It is Hebrew, perfectly preserved!" Scanning it with the eye of a scientist, he went on, "The ink is of the same composition as that used on the badge. It is a crude, charcoal material, probably made from water mixed with scrapings from burnt wood, and applied with some sort of quill. My guess is that the rabbi made a pen from a piece of stick or a feather. That the writing has held up this well is utterly amazing!"

David's friends glanced at one another.

"Very interesting," Mel sighed. "But what does it say?"

"Yes, yes," Emily spurred David on. "Tell us the words!"

David bent close over the cloth and tried to read it. "Britta," he said, "if you'll look in my briefcase, over by the bed, you will find a magnifying glass. Would you get it for me, please?"

Britta hastened to comply.

"Here," she said, sliding it under his nose.

Holding it over the fabric, he gazed at the first line for so long, the group began to fidget again.

"What does it say?" Britta asked, trying to be patient.

"This starts out as a prophecy and then seems to become a chronicle," David said. "It follows the same pattern of many things the rabbis gave me to read when I began my search. Let's see . . ."

He paused again, and the group shuffled.

"Aren't you reading it backward?" Mel asked.

"Hebrew goes from right to left," Honey said, proud of her new knowledge.

Mel shrugged, looking a little embarrassed, but busied himself pulling up several chairs. They all sat down, except for Pete and Honey, who stood riveted with interest directly across from David.

"It begins something like this," he said. Haltingly, in broken syllables, starting and stopping, he interpreted the tiny figures:

Sons and daughters of Jacob, all you who suffer under the hand of desolation, take heart! The time is coming when Israel will be reclaimed and the land will be yours forever, and your children's forever.

Honey reached for Pete's hand, and he cradled it close to his heart.
"Now, here the chronicle starts," the professor went on.

Let all those who seek to rebuild the Holy Temple pay heed to the story of Israel Ben Kahana.

At this, he stopped and looked up at Honey. "Does the name mean anything to you?" he asked.
She only shrugged, and shook her head.
Going on, he read:

Many are those who say, "Behold, the priest! He is here or he is there. When the Temple is rebuilt, this one or that one shall light the lamps and offer the offerings and enter into the Holy Place to accept atonement for the sins of the people, after centuries of their wanderings. . . ."

David's voice broke. Incredible as it seemed, it appeared that what he was about to read had to do with his exact quest!
Britta, who sat beside him at the table, reached out and touched his arm, squeezing it softly. Moved by her gesture, he glanced her way and, for a fleeting moment, their gazes met.
"I take it this is what you were hoping to find?" she asked.
For once, David sensed that Britta's interest was genuinely personal, her question not part of an interview.
When he turned apprehensively to Honey, the only one present who knew the nature of his assignment, the woman nodded to him, as if to say, "I think it's safe."
"Britta," David replied, focusing on the pretty blond, "the subject matter is related to my work, true enough. I guess we'll see how related as I read on."
Tremulously, he continued his deciphering of the cramped letters:

But I tell you, there is a line, unbroken since the time of Aaron, brother of Moses, and from the time of the House of Zadok, of the reign of David and Solomon, which line is the only true one. . . .

David stopped and breathed out softly. "Wow, the old fellow knew the necessary qualifications! None of the non-Zadokite line were levitically pure."

The five listeners glanced at one another again, having no idea what he was talking about. However, they remained silent, not wanting to break David's concentration.

Holding the glass at an angle to enhance the sunlight upon the fabric, he said, "The letters are hazy here. There's a bit of old mildew."

Then he went on:

Many have claimed to be in that line, to have inherited the priesthood. But only one is worthy to be called High Priest, and his heritage has been protected from defilement. He will be a descendant of one who was rescued out of great destruction, who was taken from Jerusalem at the time of its overwhelming.

"When would that have been?" Britta asked. " 'The time of Jerusalem's overwhelming.' "

David sat back a moment. "My first hunch is that he's referring to the Roman invasion of 70 C.E. But he could also mean any number of later conquests. Maybe he will tell us."

The writing was laid out in narrow columns, much like the writing on a scroll. The professor bent over the fabric again. "The letters are so incredibly small!" he noted. "It must have taken the rabbi weeks to compose all of this, especially in secret. I can guess where he started and stopped on different sessions, and even how he must have been feeling on different days."

Honey withdrew her hand from Pete's grasp and leaned on the table. "Really?" she marveled. "You can do that? How?"

David pointed to one section that had bigger, freer lettering than the others. "See here," he said. "This is obviously a single session. On this day, your great-grandfather either felt pressed for time, and wrote hastily, or he was in a lighter mood than usual. Or, maybe it's the subject matter that has him more enthused."

At this, he read:

Now, as to that day of overwhelming, it was a great and terrible day, and it lasted for eighty-eight years. But it was a time of rescue, for it was at this time that the soldier who wore a cross spared the young Kahana and took him across the seas.

The professor sat back again and slapped his thighs. "Yes!" he cried. "The Crusader period! The rabbi is excited to relate to us that the subject of this drama was rescued by a Crusader and taken to Europe. This phrase, 'soldier who wore a cross' has to refer to a Crusader, and we know that the period of the Crusades lasted for exactly eighty-eight years!"

Britta absorbed David's enthusiasm. "So, you are investigating the Crusades?" she guessed.

At this, Honey laughed softly. "Dave," she said, "do you really think it would do any harm to tell everyone what you're after? Maybe Britta would promise not to make a headline of it just yet."

Mel nodded. "I'll tell you, I'd sure like to know what this is all about. I'm just a guy off the L.A. streets. I promise you, I won't tell anybody!"

All of them chuckled over this, and David lightened up. Looking at Britta, he raised his eyebrows.

"Of course, David," she said. "I won't make anything of it, not without your approval. You can trust me."

The professor was surprised by this unprecedented move on the reporter's part. Pondering her offer for a moment, he at last reached out a hand to shake her outstretched one. "It's a deal, Ms. Hayworth," he said.

Then, with a sigh, he gave a brief explanation of his work, emphasizing the sensitive nature of the quest, but giving no details of the genealogy.

"And so," he summarized, "you can understand that the search for the high priest of Israel is rather like the search for the catalyst to the apocalyptic age! We don't really have any idea where such a quest will take us, or the world around us."

Britta looked back at her friend, Emily, who listened to the professor's tale with an intensity as profound as her admiration of the old rabbi.

"Well, Emily," Britta mused, "it appears we got ourselves into much more than we bargained for."

"I'd say!" the nurse exclaimed.

Pete nodded empathetically. "I don't think any of you could be more surprised by all of this than I am. I sure never dreamed that looking for Honey would take me on the biggest trip of all time!"

The others laughed, and then David bent once more over the writing. "Let's move on, shall we?" he said. "I want to know where the rabbi is taking us next."

Eagerly, the onlookers listened as David read further:

Pay heed, you who have ears . . .

David glanced up at his audience. "The old prophets were great ones for lines like that. I guess the rabbi took after them."

Then, thinking of Honey, he quickly added, "Nothing against your great-grandfather. As the villagers said, he was their historian, and this is the way Hebrew historians write."

Honey hushed him. "Dave, it's okay. I'm just touched to get these glimpses of my ancestor. He must have been quite a guy!"

David nodded, and went on:

Pay heed, you who have ears. Israel ben Kahana was but a boy when the soldier who wore the cross took him to England.

The last word rang strangely through the room.

David raised his eyes for a moment, wondering if any of them could know how awesome such a declaration was.

"England!" he cried. "The computer analysts in Jerusalem told me there was a strong strand of genealogy going through England! The word the rabbi uses here is only a Hebraic approximation. There is no word for England in Hebrew. It is England, though—no doubt about it!"

Britta, particularly, was fascinated by the writer's claim. After all, she was British, and it was amazing to think that this cryptic account related to her homeland. "Are you saying that the blood of the high priest might flow in the veins of some unknown Englishman?" she marveled.

"I'm not saying that," David corrected. "Rabbi Aronstam says that. And he apparently bases his story on an ancient legend."

He read on:

Let it be understood that the true priest will be found among the people of Britain.

David stopped and said, "That's another approximation." Then, he continued:

His line is that of Cohen, of the town of Castlemont-on-Wandermere.

At this proclamation, Emily McCurdy suddenly lurched forward in her chair. "Cohen?" she gasped. Then turning to Britta, "Do you suppose . . ."

Britta's heart thrummed. "David," she said, "my family on my mother's side are Cohens. Is it possible—"

David tried to be kind. "Anything is possible," he said. "But you must understand that Cohen in Jewish circles is like Smith in English or American circles. 'There are more Cohens,' my grandmother used to say, 'than there are bagels in New York City!'

"And, while the modern-day Cohens are related ancestrally to the first high priest, Aaron, they are not all high priest material!"

The group laughed, and David added, "It appears likely, though, that, since Kahana is a root-name of Cohen, whoever we find will be called Cohen, or something related to Cohen."

Britta sighed, and Emily sank back into her chair. The young journalist patted Emily teasingly, "Now, now, Emily, just think. If you had married Uncle Reg Cohen, you might be the mother of the high priest. Would you really want that responsibility?"

Emily laughed heartily. "You always see the bright side," she said.

The others did not know the meaning of this private allusion. When it was not offered, Honey suggested, "Read on, Dave."

"Hm," David mused, "the writing here is quite cramped and hurried. Maybe our rabbi was under some pressure to finish this thing."

> *The hour grows short. Let it be understood, when Israel goes about the business of rebuilding her sanctuary, and when the priest is found, he will be an heir of Israel ben Kahana. And his credentials will be proven thus: The pedigree of Israel ben Kahana extends back to the time of the first overwhelming, when the holy scribes moved to the desert. There they protected the ancestor of Kahana, and this is his name. When you shall find that record, the name shall be written therein, to prove what I write. The name therein shall be "Gabriel ben Zadok," and thus the line shall be complete.*

David sat hunched over the fabric for a long while, as the others tried to make sense of what he had read.

The professor shook his head. "Let me see," he said. "'The first overwhelming' would most likely be the Roman invasion of Jerusalem in 70 C.E., and—of course! The holy scribes who went to the desert could be the Essenes! The ones who wrote the famous Cave Scrolls!"

Now it was Britta's turn to jolt. "Really?" she cried. "You mean the scrolls that Emily's brother worked on? What do they have to do with this?"

David sat back and rubbed his chin. "Now don't misunderstand," he warned. "I am not drawing any conclusions here. I could be all wrong about the first overwhelming and the scribes. It's just an educated hunch. You see," he said, his eyes bright, "the people of Qumran believed that the only pure Cohen line, the only Cohen branch worthy of the high priesthood, were the Zadoks."

When the group looked bewildered, he explained, "The Zadokites were the high priests of David's and Solomon's time. Zadok means 'righteous.' After that period, the priesthood was corrupted."

Britta's mind was whirring. "Back up, David," she pleaded. "I don't understand what the rabbi is saying."

Mel, who had no background in any of this, did have a quick, discerning mind. "It's simple," he said. "The old guy is telling us that we will know the right person for the job of high priest because his ancestry goes back to this Kahana kid. And the ultimate proof of everything the rabbi is recording will be in the fact that the Kahana kid is related to the last recorded heir, this—Gabe—what is it, again, Doc?"

David liked Mel's street-savvy analysis. "Gabriel ben Zadok," he repeated with a grin.

"Right," Pete jumped in. "You've got it, brother! Honey's great-grandpa was telling us, or whoever found his note, that the genealogy would be complete with those two links—the Kahanas of England and the Zadoks of—where, Doc?"

"Qumran is a fair guess," David chuckled.

"Okay! Okay!" Pete exclaimed, totally caught up in the treasure hunt. "Then, we just have to find the Cohen of Castlemont, right?"

"No, that's not all," Mel countered. "We also have to find the Gabriel record. Right, Doc?"

"Seems so," David replied, amused that this quest had now become the focus of four new people.

"So . . ." Honey asked, "where do we look for that?"

Britta gave a little gasp, and all eyes were on her.

"What is it?" David asked.

The young reporter had turned to Emily in amazement, and the older woman stammered, "Britta, are—are you thinking what I'm thinking?"

CHAPTER 33

The next day, the little entourage that had visited Dachau departed Munich on two separate planes heading to opposite points of the compass.

The threesome from Montana took an El Al flight to Israel. When Pete and Mel accompanied Honey through airport security, she placed her shoulder bag on the x-ray conveyer belt so reluctantly that she raised the suspicions of the attendants. They had riffled through it thoroughly before they let her pass.

Finding nothing of interest other than an old boot and a red brick, which must have mystified them, they disregarded the precious treasure that lay wrapped in oilcloth with her wallet, her passport, her brush, and her lipstick. Shrugging to one another, the attendants had waved her on.

She sat now in the center row of the 747 as it took off from Munich on the noon flight, safely ensconced between the Wester brothers. In a few hours, they would arrive in Israel, where Honey would release her precious document to Rabbi Benjamin and his Consortium colleagues for analysis.

Meanwhile David, Britta, and Emily were on a plane to England in the hopes that Father McCurdy would receive them.

What inspired this unplanned trip on David's part was a strange story Britta had shared as the group was gathered around the table in his hotel suite.

He had just finished deciphering the words on the striped cotton rag, and they were discussing the missing "Gabriel Ben Zadok" record, when the two Britons lurched as though hit by an electric current. It seemed that a sudden hunch had gripped both of them regarding a possible key to the genealogy. That hunch related to Britta's experiences with Father Ian McCurdy.

The group already knew that she was the only reporter to whom the elusive archaeologist had granted an interview. What not even Emily had suspected, until that moment, was Britta's intuition regarding his elusiveness.

"I felt I had reached a dead end with your brother," Britta told Emily, "until the day you and I had lunch at the Oxford pub. I knew he was hiding something, based on the way he avoided my questions in the interview, but it wasn't until that day that I began to suspect what it might be."

Emily had bitten her lower lip, trying to think back. "What did I say, Britta? I can't imagine—and I wouldn't want to betray Ian."

Britta hastened to assure her she had done no such thing. "No no, dear," she said. "There was no betrayal. Do you recall telling me that your brother and his friend, Cromwell, were going to London the next day?"

"Why, yes, I did. But what—"

"Well, you told me that he was going to visit his study carrel at the British Museum, that Oxford professors are assigned such places for research."

Emily was bewildered. "I don't see—"

"You also told me," Britta continued, "that he visits it only about once a year, just to keep his tenure. It was then that I thought, 'Why would an Oxford don need a study carrel when he is no longer regularly teaching or researching?' From my meeting with your brother, he did not seem the pompous sort who would want to maintain such a privilege out of pride."

Emily laughed. "Ian? Absolutely not! Sometimes I wish he were not so humble."

"Very well, then. Perhaps you can see how my reasoning led me," Britta went on.

David and the others followed her logic closely, caught up in yet another mystery.

"Knowing a bit about the British Museum, I realized that it is a great repository of ancient writings. Though I had not ever heard of it housing any of the Cave Scrolls, I thought it would be a logical place for a linguistic archaeologist to work on such a thing, perhaps even keep such a find safe and secure."

David's intuition clicked in. Recalling how Rabbi Katz and the Consortium leaders had said they believed there was Cave Scroll material yet to be divulged, he jumped in, his eyes wide with possibility. "Are you saying you suspected Father McCurdy was sitting on an unreleased scroll? Are you thinking that the scroll committee never released all of its findings?"

Britta nodded excitedly. "That's exactly what I thought, and still do think, Professor. I knew, as I spoke with him, that there was more to his evasiveness than fear of exposure on the issue of the Cave Scroll Deception Theory."

Pete, Mel, and Honey did not know what this was and looked quizzically at her. But David knew. He had read all about it in various journals.

Quickly he explained. "For a while there, the media was full of the theory that the Cave Scrolls had been kept from the world by the scholars who worked on them because the scrolls might contain something destructive to Christianity. Ongoing scholarship has pretty much debunked that notion," he said, "but McCurdy's avoidance of the press, as the only living member of the original team, keeps the rumor active."

"Exactly!" Britta said. "Thanks to pressure from his sister, I was able to get an interview, and felt quite fortunate. But when Father McCurdy answered my questions about the Deception Theory as adroitly as he did, I began to wonder why he had avoided the press for so long—especially if he could deflect that rumor with a few words."

Diplomatically, she told Emily, "When I asked him that very thing, he seemed to be cornered. I did not mean to make him uncomfortable, Emily. But he was quite nervous, and soon enough, I was ushered to the door by Cromwell and left to ponder it all."

Emily smiled and patted Britta's hand. "It's all right, dear. My brother has been a riddle to me for years. I never did understand why he never returned to Dublin after he retired from Oxford. Now it makes more sense. The faculty there is really quite cloistered, you know. It is quite a chore for the press to climb inside those ivy-covered walls."

David thought a moment. "So, Britta, let me complete the circle of reasoning. It seems that my reference a moment ago to the desert scribes of Qumran may tie in here. Is that what you're thinking? Are you saying that Rabbi Aronstam's reference to the genealogy being composed and protected by the desert scribes could be related to McCurdy's secret?"

Britta held up her hands. "You *are* a fast thinker! That's precisely what I was driving at. But let me tell you more."

Pete and Honey leaned over the table, breathless, while Mel listened with the ears of a cop accustomed to unraveling clues.

"The day after Emily and I had lunch, I went to London. Sorry, Emily," she said, "but I didn't think you needed to know. Anyway, I suspected that your brother was going to pop up at the museum, and so I reserved a slot in the reference room and watched for him. Sure enough, he came in, with Cromwell in tow. Before he got there, I had pumped the reference librarian for information about the research carrels. Just as I had expected, they were used for storage of research materials, as well as for work. In fact, the attendant told me, the ones designated for the Oxford professors are even outfitted with lockable safes!"

Mel nodded eagerly. "So, what happened when McCurdy arrived? Was he shocked to see you?"

"Shocked?" Britta laughed. "Indeed he was! He went white as a sheet, and Cromwell needed to hold him up!" At this, she glanced again at Emily. "Sorry."

The older woman looked a little sad but shrugged her shoulders and sighed. "My poor Ian," she said. "He put himself in this position. I just want to know why."

David spoke reassuringly. "Perhaps we can find out why, Emily. And maybe in so doing, we can help your brother. He apparently carries a very heavy burden, something no one should do alone."

The nurse smiled gratefully. "Are you saying we should go to him?"

The professor nodded. "One call to Jerusalem, and we will be on our way. Honey, if you will take the Dachau parcel to Rabbi Ben, we can try to track down this end of things, okay?"

David, Britta, and Emily agreed not to notify Ian of their coming. It would make him too skittish and give him a chance to cover himself.

Though Emily had pangs of conscience, she put the quest above misplaced loyalty. Whatever Ian had hidden for nearly half a century, it was time, she thought, that he let it go.

CHAPTER 34

Gatwick Airport was fogged over in typical British fashion when David, Britta, and Emily arrived. Deciding that they would wait until morning to catch the bus that ran day and night between London and Oxford, the three got off the airport train at Victoria Station and took the subway to South Kensington, the terminal nearest Britta's apartment.

David considered his good fortune in being thrown, by fate or whatever forces were leading him, into the company of the young English woman. This aspect of his ongoing adventure was, to this point, the most charming surprise.

The more the professor got to know the perky reporter, the more he liked her. He had come to understand that her blunt, businesslike manner, when he had first encountered her in Munich, was pure professionalism. When she allowed herself to be simply sociable, she was delightful.

The three travelers would stay at Britta's walk-up apartment for the night. A short jaunt from the subway station, it lay on a narrow, cobbled street, typical of many London neighborhoods. A renovated townhouse with classical white trim and slender columns, it had been transformed in the 1950s into four flats, one on each floor and one in the basement. The reporter's flat occupied the top level.

When Britta opened the door to her little suite, David was captivated. Nothing gave a better glimpse into a woman's soul than her own residence, he thought. It was there that she revealed, in her furnishings, the colors of her walls, the paintings she had hung, and countless other details, a personality not always observable to an outsider.

While Britta could be brusque and businesslike when going after a story, she revealed a much softer aspect in the way she had decorated her apartment.

Mauve and pale beige were Britta's colors. Her home was casual and modern, in contrast with the classic design of the building. But there was no chrome or black leather in Britta's contemporary abode, a style often found in the apartments of young professionals who put on minimalist airs. Britta's furnishings were of Danish teak and other golden-hued hardwoods, the polished oak floors warmed with large, neutral area rugs. Color was reserved for wall racks full of Franciscan earthenware, its splashes of irises and peonies repeated in full curtains gathered on brass rods across the french doors of the third-story balcony and in throw pillows piled about the floor.

Gilt-framed landscapes of the English countryside were the only other wall decor, except for a large, flowered wreath that encompassed a collection of personal photos depicting family and friends.

The professor was instantly at home, and Emily turned perceptive eyes upon him as Britta took their coats. "She has a lovely way with things, hasn't she?" the elder woman said.

David only nodded, his pleased expression speaking for him.

"Why don't you put your baggage here by the couch?" Britta suggested, guiding David across the room. "I hope you don't mind a sleeper sofa. There are twin beds in my room, which Emily and I can share."

"The sofa will be fine," David said. "I think I'll be able to sleep on a rock by bedtime."

Britta turned to the gas-powered grate in her small hearth. "It will take me only a moment to light a fire, and then I'll fix something to eat!"

She flicked on a switch near the mantel, and instantly a welcoming blaze lit the fake logs in the fireplace. "*Voilà!*" she said, and turned to her guests with a little laugh.

"That's wonderful, Britta," Emily said, taking her own bags to the bedroom. "But we don't expect you to cook, not after traveling all day."

David shook his head emphatically. "There must be wonderful restaurants in this neighborhood," he said. "I saw all sorts of exotic cuisine advertised as we were walking here. Let me treat you both."

But Emily deferred. "I'll tell you what I'd really like," she said. "A nice cup of tea and a little nap. If you'll permit me, Britta, I'll just forage in your cupboards. But I think the two of you should go out for a nice meal."

David liked the sound of that, thinking there could be nothing more desirable than to spend the evening alone with Britta.

But she was not so sure. "I don't like to leave you, Emily. Are you certain . . ."

"Positive!" Emily insisted. "Just show me the way to the teapot!"

The old, lantern-shaped lamps of Kensington Avenue were just coming up as Britta led the way to one of her favorite haunts. She and David had decided they wanted something light, after sitting on a cramped plane all afternoon and downing too many snacks.

"You'll love this place!" Britta said gaily as she pointed to one of the basement windows of a corner townhouse. The window, set deeply into the old stone foundation, was enclosed by a decorative iron fence. Bright geraniums added a splash of color to what could have been a dingy hole.

"The entrance is around the corner on the back side of the building," Britta said.

The block on which the building sat was shaped like a piece of pie, the building itself three-sided and taking up the tip of the triangle. Britta guided David to the narrow, brick stairway that wound down to an open door. Soft, happy music floated up from the cellar, along with the smells of onion soup and pasta sauce.

A bright red sign showing a chubby chef in a tall hat read "Vincent's."

"The after-work crowd has probably left by now," Britta said. "I hope we can get a table."

As David stooped inside the low door, Britta glanced up at him and giggled. "I tend to forget how tall you are!" she said.

The restaurant was really more of a diminutive café. *Any number of people would constitute a "crowd" in this place*, David thought. Fortunately, there was a spot near the door, and the couple slid onto benches, facing each other across a dark wooden trestle table.

The main piece of furniture in the room was a short bar, along which four men and one woman sat, their feet resting on a brass rail. The matron of the place, who also served as the bartender, hastened out to greet Britta the moment she entered.

"Good evening, Miss," she said, her words thick with a Cockney accent. "Back from the Continent so soon?"

"Yes, Martha," Britta answered. "This is my associate, Dr. Rothmeyer."

She turned to him. "Do you like onion soup? It's wonderful here." When he nodded, she said to the woman, "We'll each have the soup."

The woman nodded, her plump cheeks bright like an elf's. After serving each of them a glass of red wine, which she always assumed people wanted when they ordered her onion soup, she bustled into the kitchen, where she also served as cook.

David peered into the cavelike room where the culinary work was done. "And where is Vincent?" he asked, seeing no one else back there.

"I'm not sure there is such a person," Britta answered with a laugh. "I think Martha is the jack-of-all-trades in this place."

David raised his glass and tapped the rim of Britta's drink in a toast. "Nice to be here," he said. "Vincent or no Vincent."

For the first time since he sat with Britta at the table in Germany, where the group had examined the rabbi's scroll, his eyes locked with hers. He thought he read in her warm gaze that the attraction was mutual.

"To tomorrow," Britta said, leaning her glass toward his.

"To tomorrow," he repeated, "and to Father McCurdy."

Britta smiled, and David set his drink down, then cleared his throat. "I have been wanting to share some thoughts with you," he said. "Ideas have been tumbling around in my brain ever since you told me about McCurdy and the possibility that he is in possession of Cave Scroll material."

"Yes?" Britta said, leaning across the table.

"It's been a long time since I paid much attention to the story of the scrolls and their controversy. But I recall that there was one document in particular that sparked a good deal of interest when it was discovered, in the early fifties, I believe. It was called the Copper Scroll. Have you heard of it?"

Britta thought back. "Yes, of course. All of the others were written on leather."

"That's right. In fact, the Bedouins who discovered them originally sold some of them to a shoemaker in Bethlehem, who thought he could use them in his shoemaking business!"

"I read about that!" Britta said. "But there was one that was made of metal, and the scroll team had a great deal of trouble even figuring out how to open it."

"Right," David replied. "It was frozen shut with corrosion. They finally cut it open with a small electric hand saw, mounted on a slide."

Britta nodded thoughtfully, then asked, "So, what does that have to do with Father McCurdy?"

"Well, follow me, now," he said. "Do you remember what the Copper Scroll was all about?"

Britta frowned for a moment, then suddenly brightened. "Yes, I do!" she replied. "It was a list of treasures. The scholars thought it might be a list of things taken from the temple before the Romans arrived, and hidden about the countryside for protection."

"Yes," David agreed. "It's thought that the directions to the various treasures might be in some kind of code. Anyway, so far no one has been able to decipher it. And, according to some estimates, that treasure, if all put together, would constitute enough to pay off my country's national debt!"

"Good Lord!" Britta cried. "That much?"

"That's what they say," David repeated.

Britta shook her head. "I still don't see how that relates to Father McCurdy. What are you thinking, David?"

The professor was about to speak, but stopped short as the waitress-cook-bartender returned to the table, placing two steaming bowls of onion soup before them, with a pewter plate of hard rolls.

Nodding to the woman, David thanked her and waited for her to leave.

Then speaking softly, he went on. "The fact is that the Copper Scroll contained more than a list of treasures and their locations. It also contained an enigmatic reference to yet another Copper Scroll, which, it seems to indicate, would give the key to the code that conceals the treasure locations!"

Gasping, Britta sat back and gawked at the professor. "Do you know what you're implying?" she asked. "You are saying that Father McCurdy may be sitting on the key to the greatest treasure on earth!"

David's heart beat faster, echoing her excitement. "Well, it's as possible as anything else I can come up with," he asserted.

Britta's hands went limp, and she rested them in her lap. "Very well," she managed at last. "Let's assume you're right, that this secret of Father McCurdy's relates to gold and jewels and wealth unimaginable. Lovely as that would be, what does it have to do with your assignment, with what's truly important here?"

When Britta asked this question, David felt himself melt inside. With that one inquiry, she revealed more about her character than many women would do in years. She showed that she had a true sense of values, that what she deemed important was not money or material treasures, but the sort of spiritual quest that David's assignment represented.

For a long moment, he only stared at her, saying nothing.

At last, growing uncomfortable, she squirmed. "What is it?"

"You are amazing!" he said. "Most women would stop at the gold and silver thing! That would be enough for them, and they'd be off on a chase for the golden goose!"

Britta's eyes grew wide. "Perhaps some would," she agreed. "Priests and prophecies and that sort of thing are more to my liking. Besides, I don't think Father McCurdy gives a fig about material treasures, either."

David looked down at his soup, wondering why he was lingering over a bowl of broth when what he wanted was to scoop a far more delicious morsel into his arms.

He swallowed hard and forced his thoughts back to the topic at hand. "I'm glad to hear that," he said, "because that makes what I'm thinking even more plausible. If your Father McCurdy has the scroll I believe he might have, it probably contains another treasure list. That list would not be of lampstands and golden bowls and trumpets. It would be a list of names—the genealogy that the desert scribes hid, the one Rabbi Aronstam referred to! If I'm right, Britta, Father McCurdy hordes a find that will usher in the millennium!"

Britta was amazed. "Really?" she croaked. "But why would he want to hide such a thing?"

"I hope we'll find out tomorrow," he said.

Quietly the two ate their meal. David's mind was whirling with possibilities—and not only regarding the scroll. He was also thinking about a very different treasure. In Britta he had found something more precious than anything the world could offer him.

He planned how he would manage to hold her hand on the way back to her apartment. The attainment of that sort of treasure did not require a map. It only required courage.

CHAPTER 35

Although Emily McCurdy had never married, never lost her heart to anyone after Reg Cohen, she was good at matchmaking. It was clear, however, that her services in that area were not going to be necessary to get David Rothmeyer and Britta Hayworth together. She had done enough in seeing to it that they had had dinner alone together the evening before. Beyond that, there was nothing she needed to do, because the spark that flickered between the two was growing into a nice enough flame all on its own.

On the bus ride from London to Oxford, the two women suggested that David ride next to the window, since he had "never been privileged," as Britta teased, to see the English countryside before. She sat beside him, pointing out the highlights along the way, and Emily sat across the aisle, enjoying their interchange.

David did not reach for Britta's hand in the presence of so many passengers. But she could still feel the warmth of his touch from the evening before, when, as they walked back to her apartment, he had brushed her fingertips with his and gently slipped his strong hand around hers.

Though surprised by this gesture, Britta had not pulled away. She felt herself eminently comfortable with the professor.

Amazing, she thought now, how much could be said without words! She, who made a living with ink on paper, would have been at a loss to describe the instant bond that that simple move on David's part had created.

Today, as she leaned close to him, naming the hamlets and old churchyards that dotted the knolls, the streams that crisscrossed the rolling green hills, recounting bits of history marked off by hedgerows and ancient roads, she enjoyed the feel of his tweed-jacketed arm against her own and took pleasure in studying his strong profile against the window.

If any part of England could win the undying admiration of a visitor, it was Oxford. As the bus pulled into the modern sector that defined the entrance to the city, it was clear to David that Oxford did not languish on the laurels of its academic reputation. It was a thriving, bustling place.

The university, itself, was actually an amalgamation of thirty-five separate colleges, each one an architectural gem. The bus passed broad greens and expansive rock-walled gardens fronting buildings rich with the ambiance of tradition, and at last parked in front of the quaint pub where Emily and Britta had had lunch not long before. As the passengers disembarked, the two women glanced at each other.

"Hard to believe our last conversation here portended such an escapade!" Emily commented.

Britta agreed. "And it may be only beginning!"

"We will need to take a cab to my brother's house," Emily said. "It is quite a distance out of town."

David crossed the parking lot where the bus sat waiting for its next load of passengers to return to London. Other buses churned in and out of this lot on a schedule of fifteen-minute turnarounds, and eager cab drivers lined up just as regularly to take visitors to whatever part of Oxford they wished to see.

Hailing one of the cabs, David gestured to the women and they all piled in.

"Windham Road," Emily said. "About five miles out, and then a turn to Crossing Creek."

David loved Emily's lilting Irish accent. Coupled with the quaint English place names she called out, it charmed him.

"I wish I could spend some time here," he said. "I know already that I'll want to return."

Britta nodded. "And so you shall," she insisted. "We will see to it, won't we, Emily?"

As the cab wended through the cobbled streets of the ancient village, the two women pointed out the old pub where C. S. Lewis was known to join his colleagues most every day after classes; Blackwell's Bookshop, which was actually housed in several buildings and was said to contain two miles of stacks; and the great bell tower of Christ Church College, where each evening the bell pealed 101 times for each of the first year's enrollees.

"Ah," Emily said, pointing to a cluster of antiquarian stone buildings directly across from Tom Tower, "that is Pembroke College, a rare Catholic institution in this Anglican stronghold. Its specialty is Middle-Eastern studies. My brother is an emeritus member of the faculty and can often be found in the faculty lounge, like a proud member of some British men's club!"

"Do you think he might be there today?" David wondered.

"Usually not on Fridays, Professor," she replied. "He likes to get a start on his weekend gardening on Fridays."

Britta recalled her visit to Father McCurdy's home. "He is a master gardener, David. To see his place, you'd think that gardening was his profession, and not archaeology!"

Emily nodded. "He always says he was born to dig. I guess he just transferred that instinct to the flower beds when he retired."

The cab was now crossing Oxford's River Isis, the upper reach of the Thames, where the university's famous intramural rowing races were held. Britta, whose interests were more literary, pointed to the gentle green slope that led down to the water.

"They say that's where Lewis Carroll told Alice the stories that became *Alice in Wonderland*," she said. "Remember the dream of the rabbit and the rabbit hole? It was against that tree that little Alice supposedly fell asleep and then began her adventure."

David smiled. "Well," he said, "let's hope the chase we're on leads to more than a Mad Hatter's Tea Party. I'd hate to go back to Jerusalem hearing Rabbi Ben shout, 'Off with his head!'"

Britta and Emily laughed with him. But, as the cab passed beneath a tunnel-like covering of ancient oak branches and turned down a winding lane toward a distant cottage, the professor felt a little like Alice must have felt. He only hoped he was on the trail of something real, and not a bizarre fantasy.

Ian McCurdy leaned on the handle of his garden hoe, peering down at his rose bed. This time of year, the weeds seemed to leap from the black, turned soil even as he looked on.

"I am getting too old for this," he called over his shoulder. "The chickweed moves faster than I do."

John Cromwell set a tea tray on the glass-topped patio table. "Come, Ian. Take a break," he said. "The weeds will still be there when you return."

Father McCurdy removed his gardening gloves, the fingers of which were worn through, and he wiped a light sweat from his brow, leaving a smudge of dirt above his eyebrows. Just at that moment, the cab from Oxford could be heard pulling into the front drive.

"Oh, heavens!" the old priest fumed. "Not another salesman! How do they find us way back here? Send him away, won't you, John? I'm in no mood for chitchat."

"Shall do," Cromwell replied, and hurried off.

When instead of giving a rebuke at the front door, John was heard to greet someone cheerily, Ian drew out his handkerchief and wiped the soil from his face. Who could be coming to visit, he could not imagine.

In no time, Emily bustled into the garden, greeting her brother robustly.

"Emily!" Ian exclaimed. "You are back from Europe already? Why didn't you let me know you were coming . . ."

Then his voice suddenly dropped as he saw that Emily had brought company with her—not just any company, but the bold young reporter from the *Times*.

Seeing her, the old priest went clammy. The last time he had laid eyes on this girl, she had been at the British Museum. That day he had been convinced that her appearance there was not happenstance, and the reference librarian had revealed that she was on some nameless mission regarding an obscure manuscript. Ever since then, Ian had believed that she might have deduced something about his secret, and he never wanted to be confronted with her again.

When Emily had phoned from Dublin, telling him that she had been summoned to Germany on a Red Cross matter, he had not questioned her. She was an independent woman, who had maintained ties with the service organization. His only concern had been for her traveling alone, and when she assured him that her friend, Ms. Hayworth, would accompany her, his fear for her safety was assuaged. Since his sister knew nothing of his precious scroll, there was no danger that she would reveal anything to the reporter.

"Ms. Hayworth," Ian muttered. He bowed slightly to her and pulled up two chairs for the ladies.

John was flustered, however. Standing in the doorway, he gestured to his friend. "We have yet one more coming," he called. "He is just now paying the driver." He disappeared into the house and returned a minute later with David Rothmeyer.

Emily jumped to introduce her guest. "Ian, this is Professor Rothmeyer. He was in charge of the investigation in Germany," she said. "David, this is my brother, Father Ian McCurdy."

David crossed the patio, his lanky arm outstretched in greeting. Ian quickly wiped his dirt-smudged fingers on his handkerchief and the two men shook hands.

"Father McCurdy, this is an honor!" the professor exclaimed. "I never expected to meet such an eminent member of the Cave Scroll team!"

Ian looked at him curiously. "Glad to meet you, I'm sure," he said, offering him a seat. Confused by this unexplained visit, he asked, "And just how is it that you happen to be here? Did my sister so charm you that you had to follow her home?"

The little gathering laughed together, and as Ian and John offered tea all around, Emily filled her brother in.

"The two of you have much in common, Ian," she said. "Dr. Rothmeyer is an archaeologist, like yourself. And a linguist! Not only that, but his present interest is in Israeli archaeology."

"Is that so?" Ian marveled. "And how do you happen to be working on a Red Cross matter?"

When Britta suddenly spoke up, McCurdy looked at her coolly. "Father," the young woman said, "David has been dealing with old Israeli records, attempting to piece together a puzzle that spans centuries—not unlike the work you did at Qumran."

Such a pronouncement, especially coming from the nosy reporter who had been a source of untold anguish, put the old priest on guard. "I doubt it is anything like the work we did at Qumran," he answered tensely. "That was a localized phenomenon, and our findings related to a specialized sect."

Then looking at David, Ian added, "I'm sure you have read all about it in the journals, Dr. Rothmeyer."

"I have read some," David said, his thin face tightening. He wished Britta might be a little less spontaneous. Better to lead into this thing more subtly. The matter had been introduced, however, and David knew it was up to him to smooth the way.

"Father McCurdy," he said, "Ms. Hayworth's analogy may be an overstatement. My work may be nothing at all like yours, but when Britta spoke to me of her talk with you, I got to thinking that you might at least have some leads for me to follow."

Ian sat back and considered the two intruders carefully. So, the reporter had told the professor of her attempt to interview him. Feeling slightly cornered, he grew agitated. "Dr. Rothmeyer," he began, his voice dry, "as you know, I have kept away from questions for years. Unless your interest relates specifically to the Cave Scrolls, I have little to offer you. And even if I did have, I doubt that I would."

Ian's manner, as contrasted with David's, was anything but diplomatic. The professor was not surprised. He had read enough about Ian McCurdy and his way with inquisitors to expect no spontaneous fellowship.

But David could fire back rapidly, when a situation demanded. Facing the priest squarely, he replied, "What if I were to tell you that I think my assignment is linked directly with what the Essene scribes were all about? What if I were to suggest that I suspect there are things yet to be found in those ancient caves, if they have not been found already, that bear directly on my quest? Would you speak with me then?"

The priest sat back and studied David long and hard. At last, after clearing his throat, he tried to keep steady.

"I don't believe you've told me who you are working for," he said.

David's answer sank into Ian's heart like a harpoon. "I have been hired by an international agency called the Temple Consortium. Have you heard of it?"

Father McCurdy jerked a sideways glance at his secret-sharer, his sole confidant, John Cromwell. John's face was suddenly pale, a mirror of his own.

He was sure that John was thinking of the same thing he was: the little advertisement they had read months before in the *Biblical Archaeology* magazine, the one announcing that a committee of Orthodox rabbis was seeking a Jewish archaeologist with a background in linguistics for sensitive study.

Noting that Ian's hand was shaking as he put down his teacup, John did just as he had the day they ran into Britta Hayworth at the British Museum. Stepping up behind him, he reached out a comforting hand, to support him. And just as he had done when Britta Hayworth came to the house for her interview, he tried to usher the visitors out.

"This is all quite intriguing, I'm sure," Cromwell said stiffly. "But the good Father is not feeling his best today. Perhaps it would be better if you all came another time."

Ian gazed across his garden, his mind wandering along the flowered hedge. His jaw tensed, and David thought he saw the glimmer of tears along his lashes. Reaching up, the priest patted his old friend's hand, where it rested on his shoulder.

"It's all right, John," he said with a sigh. "One cannot evade the world forever, can one? Let me hear what the professor has to say, while you fetch us another pot of Earl Grey."

CHAPTER 36

Ian McCurdy had carried a burden, the intensity and weight of which defied description, for nearly half a century. Like anyone with a grave secret, he had lived in relentless fear of exposure.

For the last decade, ever since the outcry demanding the release of the Cave Scrolls to the public and permission for other scholars to analyze them, he had endured a growing sense that it was only a matter of time before his secret was dragged out of him.

Fleeing Israel upon the death of his beloved mentor, Father Ducharme, ten years ago, he had hoped to deflect the scrutiny of probing questions. But his lot had been so solitary, so foreboding, that he had at last drawn one other soul into his dilemma: John Cromwell, a strong man, who was able to help carry the weight.

He was forever indebted to John, not only for commiserating in his horror, but also for shielding him from the public, a task that Cromwell had performed admirably.

When Emily finagled an interview for her friend Britta, a crack developed in Ian's defense, which, with the subsequent encounter, spread out in fissures, like the crazing on a priceless piece of pottery. Ian knew that Britta Hayworth had seen through him, when the rest of the world's media had only shrugged in helpless frustration and given up trying to break him.

Afternoon was drawing on, the sun settling in a hush over Ian's garden, as David Rothmeyer finished telling of his quest for the priestly heir. It was a tale worthy of the interest of the world's most auspicious archaeologist, and Father McCurdy listened in rapt attention.

At last, when the adventure had been told, when the story had taken them from Ohio to Jerusalem, from the computer and genetics labs of the Temple Consortium to Honey Aronstam's star, and from Israel to Dachau, Ian felt the hands of fate clutching in an ever-tightening grip about his heart. The exposure he had feared for so long now faced him, in the hopeful gazes of the visitors. They believed he could provide the crucial link in the chain of the genealogy, and they were about to ask for it.

Cromwell was in the kitchen, preparing to serve the guests dinner, for they had stayed well past the time that they should be sent away without the offer.

Ian drew a long cigar from his pocket, bit off the tip and lit it, puffing circles into the dewy air of the Thames Valley evening.

"So," he asked the pregnant question, "what is it you want of me, Dr. Rothmeyer? You have not come to Oxfordshire and you are not sitting in my garden only to tell me this tale."

David glanced at Britta, and Emily nodded encouragement.

"I think you already know what we are after, Father McCurdy," David replied. "You must realize by now that we believe you are in possession of the very material that will answer our needs. We believe that not all of the scrolls have been released and that you might very well hold the key to the greatest find in archaeological history!"

Father McCurdy blew smoke out softly, more circles that vanished slowly into the mist. "Go on, Dr. Rothmeyer," he said, feeling somewhat like the mouse *and* somewhat like the cat in a game of cat and mouse. "Surely you surmise something more specific."

David ground his teeth behind closed lips and wondered whether to despise this old fellow or admire him to the hilt.

"Very well," he replied. He took a deep breath, then finally said, "I believe you possess the Second Copper Scroll, the one referred to in the first, the one that gives the key to the treasure list. I believe, based on Rabbi Aronstam's reference to the desert scribes, that the Second Copper Scroll must also contain the name of the extant high priest, the one whom the Essenes held to be genuine. That, indeed, would be the greatest of the treasures they possessed!"

Ian stared into his garden for a long while. His face looked older than it had in years. Emily reached out to him with tender concern, but he shook his head. "It's all right," he said, patting her hand. Then, standing up stiffly, he gestured to his visitors to follow him into the house.

"The nights are always cool in Oxfordshire," he said as he led them inside, "especially in this old stone building. John and I make it a practice to sit by the fire in the evening."

Calling to Cromwell, he asked, "John, while I talk with our guests, would you be so good as to bring us our meal by the hearth?"

John poked his head out of the kitchen, giving his friend a worried look. When Ian nodded to him, he shrugged in compliance.

David was astonished as they passed by the office that sat adjacent to the parlor. Beyond the old French doors, reams of newspapers and magazines were kept in perfect order. Stopping long enough to peer through the beveled glass, he saw thick binders that he assumed were filled with clippings. Every handwritten title he could make out related to the field of archaeology and Middle-Eastern affairs. And it appeared that the ceiling-high bookshelves lining the room contained book after book on the subject. It was the most amazing private resource collection that David had ever seen.

The professor's scholarly heart thrummed at the sight. How he wished he might spend the next few years learning at the feet of Ian McCurdy!

Britta, seeing David's entrancement, pulled gently on his sleeve. "They want us by the fire," she said, smiling sympathetically.

As Cromwell seated the three travelers by the crackling grate, placing standing tea trays before them, he drew near his old friend and peered over his spectacles at him. He sensed that he was about to divulge what the two of them had spent their life's blood to protect. *Do you think this is wise?* his eyes seemed to ask.

Ian glanced up at him and nodded toward a little plaque on the mantel. The others did not notice this gesture, but John fleetingly read the inscription, a verse from Ecclesiastes that some parishioner had given Ian years ago: "To everything there is a season, and a time to every purpose under heaven."

"'A time to keep and a time to cast away,'" Ian added in a whisper, as John bent near.

Cromwell finished laying out the china, then shuffled hesitantly back into the kitchen. Behind him, he could hear Ian begin to talk, and he stopped a moment, looking up at the sunset sky from the kitchen window. As his ears were tuned to the sound of his dear friend's voice, he also hoped for a word from that heaven.

"Give him wisdom," he prayed. "And bless his tired old heart."

Ian glanced about the room at his guests. A tremor passed through his body, which no one present could miss.

"I have never told a soul what I am about to tell you," he said, his voice resigned. "No one, except Cromwell." Then, looking pointedly at David and Britta, he said, "Dr. Rothmeyer and Ms. Hayworth, you are quite aware of the controversy that has boiled around the Cave Scroll team. Well, let me tell you something about that."

He sat back in his armchair and chose his words delicately. "In keeping the scrolls to themselves for nearly half a century, the team members were accused of everything from egotistic possessiveness and exclusivity to defrauding of a public trust. In the past few years, they were accused of conspiring against the secular world to keep some horrid and damning revelation about Christianity under wraps."

David and Britta nodded, knowing the recent media circus the scrolls had inspired.

"I will say that, on the part of some of the international team members, some of those accusations are valid. There was academic pride involved. When a scholar is given a work to do and when he spends years of his life doing it, he begins to feel that the work and the findings are his own. He can easily forget that he is supposed to be serving the realm of knowledge. I will not deny that, on the part of some of my colleagues, an unfortunate possessiveness set in. Of this, they are guilty as charged."

David appreciated his honesty, and Britta listened respectfully.

"Concerning the accusation that they withheld something devastating to the Church, I think that has been sufficiently laughed away by serious thinkers. Not one shred of reliable evidence supports that theory, as I told Ms. Hayworth months ago." He studied her for a reaction, but she gave none.

"As for myself," he went on, his voice stronger with the unburdening, "I bore with the accusations quietly, not because I was egotistical or exclusive or possessive, and certainly not because the scrolls contained something that would destroy my faith!"

Ian gazed sadly past David, past Britta and Emily, as though his mind wandered through a distant time and place. "Where shall I begin?" he asked with a sigh. "I must begin by telling you about my mentor, Father Ducharme, the original custodian of the scroll team."

David had read about Ducharme. Much mystery shrouded the enigmatic scholar, who had descended into a pit of alcoholism and seeming insanity before his death a decade ago.

"I was next in command, under Ducharme," Ian said, "and I was his closest disciple. All along the way, he invested the most important aspects of the scroll studies to me, and he trusted me with the most sensitive tasks."

The listeners could see, from Ian's wistful expression, that he had loved the man dearly.

"I want to put to rest, here and now, the notion that Ducharme was a maniac. Ms. Hayworth," he demanded, "if you insist on making a news story of all this, please do the justice of righting that unfair accusation."

Britta's face grew warm. Out of respect, she again said nothing.

"If any lesser man had borne the burden Ducharme bore, he would have cracked much sooner," Ian went on. "I swear, I have come close to the edge many a time myself."

By now, John had returned, bringing steaming bowls of soup and placing them on the tea trays. In the firelight, his face showed the lines earned by years of stress.

Ian continued, "I will never forget the day—it seems a lifetime ago—that Ducharme called me into his room at the Institut Biblique, the scroll repository. Father Ducharme lived with the scrolls day and night, his private quarters being right next to the scriptorium where they were laid out."

Ian fidgeted with his soup spoon, too engrossed in his story to eat. "He told me that one of the students who helped with the dig at Qumran, a college intern from the States, had brought him a container the day before. It was a clay jar, like the others in which so many of the scrolls were buried. We had a policy that student interns were not to open the jars but were to bring them to the archaeologists directly."

Ian's tone picked up momentum. It was evident that the excitement of that find still came over him whenever he thought of it. "Well," he went on, "Father Ducharme had opened the container and instantly recognized the contents as a second metallic scroll, much like the first, which had raised such interest. It was fortunate, he told me, that the jar had been brought to him and not to one of the other team members, for, as he came to discover, the scroll was of a highly sensitive nature."

Father McCurdy's face twitched as he recounted this. "Ironic," he said. "Ducharme at first felt it was a godsend that the scroll had fallen to him. Later, I am sure, he cursed the day he first laid eyes on it. In truth, it became the death of him."

David felt for old Ducharme. It was evident that the possession of this document had posed no end of testing for him and his disciple. Still, eager to push on, he asked, "So, Father McCurdy, are you admitting that Father Ducharme bequeathed this very scroll to you, that it is in your possession?"

Ian gave David a bleak look. "Do not be so eager, young man, to get hold of the devil's tail. I tell you, it will whip you about without mercy!"

David was stunned.

"Now," Ian said, "let me back up a moment. Regarding my colleagues, upon whom so much censure has fallen: You must understand that some of them always felt they were dealing with classified material. These scholars kept quiet, never rising up in defense or otherwise answering critics, doling out their translations, publishing their books and papers, keeping the wolves at bay because they believed that part of what they had come to know was so potentially dangerous that, if it were wormed out of them, it could usher in . . . Armageddon."

This last phrase shocked the listeners. Britta's eyes went wide with amazement, and David reached for her hand as if by reflex.

"Armageddon?" Emily croaked.

Ian disregarded their horrified expressions. "There were literally hundreds of scrolls, you know. But it was the Copper Scroll that the team felt had the most awesome implications," he explained. "Due to its fragility, it was not cut open and unrolled for four years, but the archaeologists could tell from the reverse impressions of words readable on the outside that it contained a treasure list. Its discovery tainted their view of all the documents, and they held some of them back until such time as their studies led them to feel they were not so volatile.

"Gradually, they published their findings and ultimately the scrolls themselves were released. Even the Copper Scroll, itself, was laid bare to the world. But the furor would not calm down."

Britta needed clarification. "Was the Copper Scroll considered dangerous merely because it contained a treasure list?" she asked.

"Mainly," Ian said. "But not just any treasure! It appeared to contain a list of the treasures of Herod's temple, stored away throughout Israel for safekeeping as Rome's threat of invasion became imminent. The team feared its publication would lead to a scramble by treasure seekers that could devastate the fragile terrain of their ongoing dig."

Then, sighing softly, he added, "More important, they feared that, with the jealousy that continually raged between the Arab world and Israel, delivering up such sensitive material might spark another spate of terrorism, or even war. As it turned out, the Palestinians of Jordan, directly across the river from Qumran, now claim that they should have equal rights, or even predominant rights, to the dig sites and all that derives from them, particularly since it was a Bedouin boy who made the initial find."

He referred, they knew, to the widely celebrated story of the young Arab shepherd who threw a rock into a desert cave, and the resounding "clunk heard round the world," as it hit the side of a scroll jar.

Father McCurdy scratched his head, his brow furrowed with concern. "I must add, also, that the possibility of hidden riches was not all that made this a touchy issue. As you have indicated, Dr. Rothmeyer, the Jews hope to find the key to the treasure list because it is related to their future temple, the one they wish to build on Mount Moriah. Most likely, if the treasure itself is ever found, it will contain artifacts from Herod's magnificent complex, as well as revenue for the temple's operation!"

The old priest looked at David squarely. "Do you understand," he asked, "that the Jews wish to rebuild the temple on the very site now occupied by the Arab Dome of the Rock?"

David grimaced, remembering how horrified he had been when, on his first day at the Consortium gallery, he had realized the international fallout that could come from such a move.

"I do understand, Father McCurdy," he said. "And I also know that the Arabs will never sit still for such a thing!"

Ian leaned forward and studied the professor's pensive face. "Yet you continue to do what is required to bring about the new temple!"

David shrugged. "I am not a religious man," he said. "But, I seem to be"—he hesitated—"appointed."

Ian sat back in amazement. Considering their mutual dilemma, he suddenly wondered if he had more in common with this young man than academics: a mutual sense of fearsome responsibility.

For a long moment, there was silence, until Britta broke in. "Concerning Father Ducharme and some of your scroll committee, she said, "it seems to me that they should be applauded, not criticized! They held out for decades against—"

"Unending pressure," Ian filled in. "Yes, Ms. Hayworth, pressure from all quarters, academic and political. What finally convinced the committee that they could let go without ushering in World War Three was the fact that they believed there was no key to the Copper Scroll. It was, they decided, indecipherable. Any attempt to locate the treasure would only end in frustration."

David sat back and crossed his arms. "Yet, you and Ducharme knew differently!" he concluded. "The metallic scroll which Ducharme possessed was, indeed, the Second Copper Scroll, the one that could unlock the treasure hunt of the ages!"

"And the inevitability of another Holocaust," Ian muttered.

John Cromwell stood in the kitchen doorway, listening in on the conversation. When Ian made this statement, his face grew deathly white. Suddenly he rushed to his friend's side. "Can't you leave him alone now?" he barked, glaring at the visitors. "This is enough for tonight!"

Ian grasped John's flailing hand and held it close. "It is all right, my friend," he rasped. "It was inevitable that this time should come. Since my will is being forced, I must accept it as God's doing."

"B-but Ian," Cromwell stammered. "What of the dangers, what of the horrors?"

As Ian shook his head, his shoulders slumping for lack of an answer, John confronted the guests again. "Should you have any doubts about it, it was not self-interest that made Ian keep his secret. It was altruism, of the purest and holiest sort. Make a note of that, Ms. Hayworth! For years, Ian McCurdy has literally laid down his life for the good of humanity. I hope and pray that whoever is next in line to deal with his despicable treasure will have as good a heart!"

"I will keep all of that in mind, Mr. Cromwell," Britta replied quietly.

Now, Ian turned to David again, scholar to scholar. "Dr. Rothmeyer," he said, "you came here in hopes of finding clues to the priestly line. Perhaps the scroll contains such information, but I have never read it."

David was perplexed. "You mean, you have not read the scroll?"

Father McCurdy smiled wanly. "Not all of it. Strange, eh? Well, let me explain. When Ducharme discovered that the scroll was indeed a key to the treasure list, he asked me to help him translate. Many a night, he and I sat up in the scriptorium, when the others had left for their apartments and hotel rooms. We employed a little circular saw like the one that was used on the first scroll, and bit by precious bit opened the second. But as we got to the end, the metal was so crimped and our work was so arduous, that, without the help of the rest of the team, we felt we could not go further.

"For months at a time, we would ignore the project, involved in other things. Then, as outside pressures worked on Ducharme, as the dread of what he knew increased, his drinking and his demoralization grew as well. I feared to let him near the document. At last, we ceased work on the scroll altogether. After a lifetime of toil in Israel, Ducharme died, poor soul, and I returned to Oxford. Taking the scroll with me, I managed to get the metallic cylinder through customs by showing the officials my card from the Department of Israeli Antiquities. I never returned to Ireland," he said, looking at his sister, "because I was too public a figure. I wished to spare you, Emily, the onslaught of the Press."

Emily's eyes welled with tears. Drawing nearer to Ian, she embraced him sadly.

David shook his head in wonder. Even though he had come this far, actually gaining a confession from the notorious priest, there was no certainty that he had found anything firm to help him in his mission.

Ian must have read his disappointment, for in the next breath, he was giving him hope. "I do not understand why I am being forced, no—led, to help you, Dr. Rothmeyer. The goals of the Temple Consortium are not in keeping with what I believe. The Consortium is not Christian! And they wish to rebuild the temple, with all its antiquated rituals, its offerings and its laws, and its blood sacrifices, for heaven's sake! Not only do I fear the international fallout from the Consortium's plans, but none of their sacrificial system fits with my understanding of the New Testament, which says that Jesus was the ultimate and final sacrifice!"

David knew little of Christian doctrine. He knew precious little, in fact, of his own heritage. "I do not know what to say, Father," he said with a shrug. "That is not my realm. My duty is to get a piece of Israel's past back to its homeland."

The old priest was haggard, defeated. Slump shouldered, he bit his lower lip and choked back a mist of tears.

"I don't know," he said, heaving a huge sigh. "I can only say that I am cornered by a severe but gentle force. Stay the night, my friends," he offered, managing a resigned smile. "We have plenty of room in this lonely house. Tomorrow we will go to the British Museum. I will exhume the battered piece of metal, and we will hop a plane. All of us, yes, John? Yes, Emily? If I am to return the document to its rightful owners, I want to meet them."

CHAPTER 37

Monte Altmeyer paced the glossy hardwood floor of the Wester house in Bull River Valley, Montana. Jim Fogarty sat slumped before a meager fire on the mammoth stone hearth, avoiding Altmeyer's furious face.

"I don't know! I just don't know!" Altmeyer repeated over and over, in his harsh German accent. "I trusted you with some extremely sensitive information, Jim. What made you think you could trust Pete Wester?"

Fogarty's henchmen sat outside on the porch, taking in the cool morning sunlight and listening to Altmeyer rave on. Ever since the Wester brothers had disappeared, the leadership of the White Supremacists had been in tumult.

As soon as it became clear that the brothers were not returning, Fogarty had awakened the camp and announced that there was a security breach. The campers had been interrogated, first as a group and then individually, as the leaders tried to determine if anyone present knew anything about the vanished Westers. What were they up to? Where had they gone? Had they said or done anything to indicate their plans? As this questioning went on, Fogarty's boys ransacked the house, searching for clues of any kind.

By noon, the only hint as to their possible destination was an envelope with Honey's Aunt Jessie's return address, and a vague recollection on the part of Lucy, Hank's wife, that Honey had once spoken of Columbus. On the strength of that,

Fogarty and Altmeyer had sent Crossley and Willard off on the wild goose chase that dead-ended in Ohio.

When the second day of the gathering failed to offer any of the lectures or training that had been promised, most of the campers had folded up their tents and packed their rigs in disappointment, if not disgust. Though they did not blame the leadership for this turn of events, they left downhearted, wondering how far their grand cause had been set back.

Only a handful stayed behind, including the "old ladies" of the biker contingent, willing to help with the ongoing search. The leaders had done all they could think of, from this remote spot, to track down the escaped Westers. In addition to sending out Crossley and Willard, other bikers had been deployed, who had headed for major points west, north, and south. Ham radio communications were relayed to and from contacts across the country.

One such communication from Wyoming said word had it that the two had visited friends of Honey in Cheyenne. But where the brothers had gone from there, no one seemed to know.

As for Honey, there was less information about her. If she had gone to Wyoming, she had long since fled. And when she left Bull River, she had taken almost every shred of material that might give a clue as to her destination. Aside from that one envelope, found in a trash basket, no personal address book, no passport, no diary, nothing of any kind was found in the house that would leave a hint of her background or where she might have gone.

One by one, all the tracker groups had returned, empty-handed. Even Willard and Crossley had returned. Short of roughing up Mrs. Aronstam in Columbus, or vandalizing her house for clues—neither of which the two bikers were willing to do—they had no leads.

They sat, now, on the sunlit porch with the henchmen, bone-weary and defeated.

Despite their tough exteriors, they winced as they listened to Altmeyer's diatribe.

"What made you think you could trust this Wester?" Altmeyer demanded, pounding his fists against his thighs and tromping across the floor. "Were you so blinded by his Aryan looks that you could not doubt him?"

Fogarty slumped further into the wing chair that faced the hearth. "He seemed a simple sort," Fogarty grumbled. "He was easily led. He never questioned any of the communiqués he received. He always followed through on anything I asked of him. Why should I suspect him?"

Then, self-defensively, Fogarty sat up and spat, "It was that brother of his! Everything was going fine, until he came along. He must have planted ideas in Pete's head."

With this, Fogarty's eyes flashed, and he continued, "Yeah, that's it! I'll bet Mel Wester was a plant! He comes from California, right? A cop, right? Put it together, Monte! He was sent here by the ATF!"

Altmeyer stopped his pacing and glared down on Fogarty. "Another government conspiracy, Jim? Come on! Do you really believe all that hogwash?" His foreign accent wrapped strangely around the colloquialism.

Fogarty was caught off guard. His brow crinkled, and he squinted confused eyes at Altmeyer. "Believe it?" he cried. "I teach it every day! What? You *don't* believe?"

Altmeyer looked at the floor and shook his head. "That's right, Jim," he said with a sneer. "I forgot! An FBI agent behind every bush, the CIA beneath every bed!" Then stepping up to Fogarty, he grasped his jaw in his hands and squeezed, forcing the big Aryan to face him squarely.

"Do you not get it? Do you not see, after all these years?" he growled. "*We* are the conspiracy! *We* control the ATF, the FBI, and the CIA! Or had you forgotten!"

With this, he released Fogarty's head and sent a stream of spittle hissing into the fire. Then, his voice low and rolling like thunder, he added in Hitlerian phrases, "We have only one true enemy, Fogarty! Have you lost sight of that? We need to concern ourselves with only one grand task: the extermination of the Jew-devils! This is not just a political war, Jim! If it were, we would not have the allies we have, in every corner of the globe! I would not have been sent to Libya, to the Philippines, to Tokyo, to Belfast! I would not have trained thousands, of every political persuasion, in the guerrilla arts, if this were just a political war!"

He took a deep breath. As if Fogarty needed to hear more, he reminded him, "And it is not just a race war! This is something greater than the sum of both. This is, to borrow a phrase from our Arab friends, 'Jihad! Jihad! Holy war!'" Then, throwing his arms wide, he added, "Why, even the Bible says, 'Israel is a stumbling block to all nations!'"

For a long while, the room was quiet. The men on the porch, ears tingling, strained to hear more.

But Altmeyer had said enough. Too much, perhaps. One could not be too careful, he realized. One never knew who one's friends were, or one's enemies.

Not for the first time, Fogarty felt small. Though he was an imposing figure, with his gleaming silver hair and his six-foot-four physique, he always felt like a peon when Altmeyer was around.

In their circles, Fogarty *was* a peon. His little realm of Aryan Nations, White Supremacy, Militia, and Freemen was but one small cog in a gigantic machine, a machine whose tentacled network spanned the globe. Sometimes, he thought he had a notion of how great that machine was. But when Altmeyer was around, he was easily reminded of just how vague his understanding really was.

When Altmeyer talked this way, Fogarty tried to comprehend. But for Jim and his like, this *was* a political war and a race war. He was lost when Altmeyer talked *Jihad*. He had never had the courage to ask him to explain how anything could be bigger than races and politics; he had not wanted to reveal his ignorance. And, actually, he did not want to know the answer.

For Fogarty, political war and race war were enough. If there was, in truth, some greater struggle going on, it was on a plane he did not need to enter. Besides, Altmeyer was right about one thing: The focus of all these wars was the extermination of the Jews. If that could ever be accomplished, the race war, the political war, *and* the Holy War, whatever it was, would be won.

"Okay, okay," Fogarty said, submitting like a dog on its back. "I hear you, Monte. Holy War, for sure."

Altmeyer tried to calm himself. Sitting down across from Fogarty, he spoke in measured tones. "About this Wester," he said, "are you sure he gave you all the messages that came through?"

Fogarty thought back. "As sure as I can be of anything," he replied. "Why?"

Altmeyer looked out to the porch and lowered his voice. "I was expecting a message from Belfast," he said. "Anything come through?"

Fogarty shrugged. "Not that I know of. Since Wester left, different fellas out there have been monitoring the radio."

Standing up, Fogarty went to the screen door and called out to the porch, "Any of you guys get a communiqué from Ireland?"

Collectively, they shook their heads, and he returned to the hearth. "Nothin', Monte," he said.

Just as Fogarty was about to throw another log on the dwindling fire, Willard pulled open the door and entered the room.

"Uh, I'm not sure if the voice was Irish," he said. "Sounded like a Ay-rab to me. And it was awful raspy-like." He held out a scribbled note. "I wrote this down earlier. 'Scuse the spellin'."

Altmeyer rose from his chair and, with a furious glare, tore the paper from Willard's motor-oil-stained fingers.

"When did you think you might give it to me?" he growled.

As Altmeyer silently interpreted the scrawls, his hand shaking so that the paper fluttered, his face turned red with rage: *Eagle Eye happening. Relay to*

Swastika. Bailey's Bug must be used. Potency waning. Called you a over a week ago. Cedars heading for Shekinah. Why didn't we hear from you?

By now, the men from the porch had entered the room, wondering what was going on. As Altmeyer digested the note, the veins stood out on his forehead.

Eyes darting around the room, he surveyed the gathering. "How did I ever fall in with such a bunch of fools?" he cried. "If you represent the Great Aryan Race, Whitey doesn't stand a chance!"

Fogarty's face reddened. Turning on Altmeyer, he shot back, "Now, hold on there, Monte! Wester may have betrayed us, but these fellas here are freedom fighters from the word go!"

Altmeyer fumed, "Get off the soapbox, Jim! We are not dealing with farm takeovers and mill shutdowns now! This message goes way beyond that!"

He waved the note under Fogarty's nose without letting him read it.

Fogarty scowled. "What's going on, Monte?" he snapped.

Altmeyer read the paper again, his face clouding even more. He crossed the big room to the front windows and glared off into the distance, as though his mind traveled the highway beyond the trees and farther.

"How long ago did the Jew woman leave Bull River?" he asked the roomful of onlookers.

There was some subdued discussion. No one seemed sure of the answer.

"She never came to the meetings except a couple of times with Wester," Crossley recalled.

Fogarty scratched his head. "I remember coming by here late last fall," he said. "She was here then. But the next time I came through, on the way to the holiday gathering in Idaho, she was gone. Yeah," he remembered, "I came through to pick up messages on the way to Hayden Lake. Wester was pretty bummed out and asked to hitch a ride with us. That's when I figured out he'd sent her packing!"

Altmeyer considered this. "So," he said, "she left at least four or five months ago."

Fogarty and the others agreed.

Altmeyer started pacing again, looking at the note over and over. "And now we learn that Wester received a communiqué that he never gave to us."

Fogarty answered weakly, "Looks like it." Then holding up his hands, he shrugged. "I swear, I never thought he let anything fall through the cracks. He was always real quick to mention any messages he'd gotten."

The German flashed dubious eyes at his underling. "Qualify that statement, Jim," he barked. "You have no way of knowing what he might have failed to tell you. Meanwhile, he could have been collecting and keeping all sorts of information meant only for the brotherhood!"

Fogarty looked at the floor. "I see your point," he said. "I guess I assumed he was *part* of the brotherhood."

The German glowered. "Once again, you assume too much! Did it occur to you to even ask him if there were any messages when we arrived here?"

Fogarty avoided the leader's furious gaze. "A lot was happening," he argued. "The crowd . . . the visiting . . ."

"The applause! The attention!" Altmeyer shouted. "It is hard to focus, Jim, when you *are* the focus!"

Jim hung his head. Turning to the fireplace again, he slumped into a chair and stared at his feet. He had been thoroughly put in his place, reminded, once again, that he was a small cog in a machine whose size he did not comprehend.

"Let us, as you Americans say, cut to the chase, shall we?" Altmeyer continued. "You may be right about the idea of a 'plant,' an 'infiltrator.' But I think we are dealing with a trio of them. And they are not from the U.S. government."

Fogarty glanced up. To his relief, Altmeyer's angry eyes were no longer on him. The German was pacing in front of the windows again, the note clenched tightly in his fist. The bikers, their girlfriends, and the assorted holdouts from the gathering watched him silently—fascinated, admiring, or just plain mystified.

"What we are dealing with here is an *Israeli* agent and her henchmen!" Altmeyer announced.

Fogarty was stunned. "Israeli?" he croaked. "How does Israel fit with any of this?"

Altmeyer's patience had been strained to the limit. "You ask ignorant questions because you are shortsighted!" he growled. "Must I remind you why the Arabs help your people? Or why the government does so little to stop them?"

Altmeyer shook his head in disgust and wheeled on all of them. "There is a much more important agenda than your anti-American Separatist dogma. In the big pond, you people are mere amoebas!"

The bikers shuffled, looking at one another in confusion.

Crossley, at last, spoke up. "Tell us, Monte. What's all this about Arabs and Israel and Belfast—and what's shakin' down, anyway?"

Altmeyer liked Crossley. He was uneducated, but not dumb.

"That is the burning question," the German replied. "There is something very big about to happen, and I'm afraid Wester knows enough to intercept it."

Grabbing a pad of paper and a pencil off an end table, he scrutinized the biker. "You know how to operate the ham radio?" he asked.

"Sure!" Crossley brightened.

"Good. I need you to make some contacts," the leader commanded.

As Altmeyer jotted down some call letters, one set for his contacts in Belfast and another for a computer expert who could hack into airlines reservation lists, he turned to the demoralized Fogarty. Fishing for something to commend him for, he said, "Jim, I know you picked this place because it is remote. Excellent. But where can I find a fax machine?"

Jim shrugged. "Thompson Falls, I guess."

Fogarty was dumbfounded when Altmeyer snapped his fingers at Willard and ordered, "Warm up the Suburban. I will need a ride to town as soon as I get through to Ireland!"

CHAPTER 38

It was the middle of the night in a hotel room near Heathrow Airport, London. The occupant had not slept since arriving there on a commuter plane out of Belfast earlier in the evening.

The man who occupied the room had spent his entire stay, to this point, in prayer, much of it on his knees, facedown on the little prayer rug that he carried in his suitcase everywhere he traveled.

Bowing over and over, he touched his forehead to the carpet, sometimes staying in that facedown posture for protracted moments, his head pointing due east, toward Mecca, most sacred of all Muslim cities.

Mammed Kahlil was a religious Arab, particularly when he knew his next few hours might be his last.

He had never become used to risking his life in the cause of Islam. He knew that those he worked for thought he was immune to fear, so close had he come to death in his many international escapades. But the possibility of his own demise never rested well on his shoulders.

Mammed was a professional "terrorist." He did not use that term, preferring to think of himself as a "munitions and counter-intelligence expert." Unlike some others, he was not a freelance mercenary, working for whomever would pay him the most. He was a devoted Muslim, believing thoroughly in the cause of the fundamentalist Arab agenda, which included the right of the Palestinians to a formal homeland, the elimination of the State of Israel, and the extermination of all Jews.

Though Mammed lived in New York City, he was Lebanese by birth and went by the code name "Cedars," for the famed forests of his country. He liked the irony of his code name, for, while the famous king of the Jews, Solomon, had used cedarwood from Lebanon in the construction of his Jerusalem temple, three thousand years ago, it was one of the purposes of Mammed's people to forestall all possibility of such a temple ever being built again.

It had been a victory of supernatural proportions, they believed, when almost fourteen centuries ago the Arab world had claimed Mount Moriah, the site of Solomon's vanquished temple, for themselves.

Their prophet, Mohammed, had symbolically laid claim to the place, they were taught, by ascending to heaven from Mount Moriah's flat top. For centuries, a mosque had stood there, the Dome of the Rock, commemorating Mohammed's "night ride" to heaven.

Yet now the Jews, hereditary enemies of the Arabs for four thousand years, wished to reinstitute their ancient system of worship on that site.

Mammed had a long and impressive record of international terrorism to his credit. He had helped to mastermind many a plot directly or indirectly aimed at Israel or her supporters. The world at large saw the increasing frequency of such atrocities, not knowing that most of them were not random at all, but part of a networked scheme.

Not even Mammed, himself, knew all the players or the plans. But he believed in what he was doing, enough to lay down his life in the grand cause.

A few years ago he had fumbled one assignment badly, setting off a container of toxic gas prematurely in a Jerusalem bus station and not fleeing before the fumes attacked his throat. Though he survived, his voice had never been the same.

There had been talk among his superiors of retiring him from his work. Their fear was that his speaking voice could draw attention to him, and the one thing no hired terrorist could afford was unwanted attention. To blend into crowds, to go about his business anonymously like a slippery shadow, was the ideal.

However, Mammed was so good at what he did, his employers were willing to risk using him, and so he had learned to speak as little as possible when on assignment.

At prayer, however, he did use his voice. This night, he invoked the protection and guidance of Allah, gesticulating and beating his chest until the sweat ran off his dark forehead.

The next day he was flying to Israel, where he was due to pull off a direct hit on the very soul of the temple movement. Never before had a violent act been so directly and publicly aimed at this Jewish endeavor.

Eight years ago, one of the heads of the Zionist movement, a figure prominent in the temple agenda, had been assassinated in New York City, by the very same Islamic group that ultimately bombed the World Trade Center and whose plot to bomb the Holland Tunnel was intercepted. But even those acts of terrorism had not been seen as attacks on the temple movement, for the world as a whole was still blissfully unaware that the Jews even had such an itinerary.

Tomorrow, the world *would* know, Mammed thought. Tomorrow, everyone would know that an agency of that movement had been attacked. Tomorrow, the world would question not only why the attack, but they would also begin to question why the Jews had such an inflammatory agenda.

Mammed knew he might not be alive to see the publicity. He might never be privileged to see the outcome of his own sacrifice, or the pressure it would bring from all quarters against the Jews; Mammed might not live to see his heroism rewarded.

As he bowed again to Allah, he prayed for his wife and little boy. He had not seen them for almost seven months, and the last time he had left them, for this "one more trip away from home," he had spoken roughly to his child.

The memory of that last interaction, a moment that should have been a loving farewell, still haunted him. He and his little family had been waiting in the JFK airport terminal for his flight to Belfast. His child had wandered too close to a group of Jewish men at prayer and had innocently spoken to one. When Mammed found him, he had rudely jerked the child aside and growled at him in Lebanese, forgetting to keep his coarse voice low. "No, no, Faisal! Bad! These are wicked men! Enemies, Faisal! Jews! Not to touch! Not to speak!"

The boy had burst into tears, drawing even more unwanted attention to Mammed than he had already drawn to himself, and so he had snapped his fingers at his wife, commanding her to follow him as they departed down the concourse.

Mammed had never forgiven himself for treating his son that way. He only prayed he would have an opportunity to make it up to him. And he also prayed Faisal would grow up to despise the enemy as he did. "Let me redeem myself," he prayed. "Let my actions tomorrow bring glory to Allah in my son's eyes."

On Mammed's bed, the suitcase from which he had taken his prayer rug lay next to a smaller bag, a toiletry clutch. Although it contained shaving lotion and other necessities, it also contained a small glass vial, wrapped in washcloths, holding one of the most lethal substances ever concocted.

"Bailey's Bug," it was called. Irish scientists, agents of the IRA, had created it. A form of anthrax, it was specially formulated for use in close quarters, for decimation or destruction of narrowly targeted populations. It had been successfully tested on barnyard animals in the farming area outside Belfast. Tomorrow, it would be directed against a very specific human group: the handpicked arm of the Jewish Temple movement.

For nearly seven months, Mammed had been in Belfast, training IRA subversives in the finer points of terrorism, one of his roles as an international "munitions and counter-intelligence expert." The contract between Mammed's superiors in Beirut and the IRA in Belfast designated that the formula for the new "bug" and a sample thereof would be given to Mammed in exchange for his services.

He would have gone to Jerusalem a week ago, but the go-ahead had not been received by a German contact in the United States, Monte Altmeyer, the master terrorist who had trained Mammed and many of his compatriots.

When the Irish formulists warned that the "bug" had a half-life that would be quickly waning, and that it must be used before its potency failed, Mammed's superiors decided to wait no longer.

What had befallen Altmeyer, they did not know. He had last been heard from before departing for some "survivalist" camp in the American outback. As was typical of such outposts, there was no way to reach him except by ham radio, and there had been no reply from him in response to Mammed's last two messages.

Dawn was just creeping through the hotel room window when Mammed finally gave up his prayer vigil. Petitional tears were still wet on his olive-complected cheeks, and he was rolling up his little carpet, when he was suddenly electrified by the ringing of the room's telephone.

As always, Mammed had requested a room with a fax/phone, a rare luxury for which he paid a premium. Before answering the ring, he set down his prayer rug and watched the lights on the machine. It was not a call coming through, but a fax communication.

To his knowledge, the only people who knew his location were his superiors in Beirut and the IRA agents in Belfast. The read-out for the incoming number, however, had a United States country code and an area code unfamiliar to him: 406.

Quickly, the fax printout scrolled up from the paper guide. Mammed bent over the machine, reading the heading on the paper, as the printing continued. "Thompson Falls Midnite Mini-Mart," he read. Brow knit, he grumbled, "Where on earth?"

In his business, it was a fact that communications rarely came from private phones, cellular phones, or private fax machines. Even e-mail was avoided. Messages were often funneled over pay phones or pay faxes in train stations, airports, or hotel rooms. But he could not imagine why he would be getting something from an all-night market in a town he had never heard of.

Until he saw more of the cover sheet.

"Aha!" he exclaimed. "Thompson Falls, Montana! It must be near the militia camp!"

Quickly, he ripped the completed fax from the machine. If this was from Altmeyer, it had taken some doing on his part to track Mammed down. It must be important. Holding the paper as steadily as he could in trembling hands, he read the memo:

> Hello, Cedars. This is Swastika. Got your whereabouts from Ireland. We know about bug. You must move quickly. Hope this reaches you before you head for Skekinah. There has been a leak here. Your message of last week fell into wrong hands. Computer tap at JFK confirms spies headed for Israel. Beware of two American men—twinlike, tall, big, blond, blue-eyed, one short-haired, one long-haired; and one petite American woman, long dark hair, dark eyes; possibly traveling together. Appear to be Israeli agents. Jihad, Cedars. Be safe.

Mammed's mouth was dry as sand as he finished reading the fax. Tremulously, he folded it and put it in his day-planner.

He picked up his watch from the nightstand and realized his non-stop flight for Tel Aviv would depart in two hours.

Then he finished rolling up his prayer rug, drew it to his lips, and kissed it.

Unlike some of his fellow Muslims, he did not think of the seventy virgins he would receive in Paradise, if he died as a martyr. Instead, he stroked a photo of his wife and son that he carried in his suitcase and prayed that he would see them again.

CHAPTER 39

As the El Al plane bound for Israel taxied down the airport runway, its gigantic engines blasting beneath its wings, its proportionately tiny rubber tires spinning toward liftoff, Father Ian McCurdy watched the passing landscape as if in a dream.

The old priest had spent most of the past decade in some form of prayer, either consciously or subconsciously invoking the protection and the will of God in his attempt to save the world. Today, he felt as though those prayers were at last leading him on a tangible path. For some reason beyond his comprehension and against his better human judgment, against everything he held to be consistent with his beliefs, he was being guided to turn his scroll over to its original owners.

As he sat on the crowded 747, his dear supporter, John Cromwell, beside him, he cradled the scroll on his lap.

When he left Israel ten years ago, he had packaged the fragile document in a soft roll of linen and created a formfitting liner for a large valise, hollowed out to the exact dimensions of the wrapped scroll.

Despite the fact that he had kept it all these years in a study carrel at the British Museum, he had never taken it out of the container for research, had never done more than open the little safe that protected it, peering in once or twice a year to be sure the valise and its contents were still there.

This morning when he and his traveling companions had

checked through the x-ray machine at the airport, he had been detained. The image of the metallic scroll caused no end of concern for the check-in attendants, who, due to the increased potential for terrorism, were much more cautious these days than a decade ago. Against Ian's protests, they were ready to open the briefcase then and there, in front of the world, and rifle through its delicate contents.

Fortunately, with the help of David's credentials from the Midwest University anthropology department, and Ian's own faculty card from the Oxford archaeology department, they were able to forestall the search.

Ian had not let go of the valise since retrieving it from the x-ray conveyor belt and refused even now to "place it in the overhead bin or beneath the seat" as the stewardess gave her loudspeaker instructions. Instead he hid it beneath a flannel lap robe provided by the airline for sleeping passengers and hoped the stewardess would not notice.

Emily, Britta, and David shared the center row of three seats, across the aisle from Ian and John. As the plane at last rose into the air, Ian watched from his window seat as the pavement retreated, grew tiny, and was finally lost beneath a wisp of clouds.

Soon the British Isles were no larger than a hand, and the greenness of his native Ireland could barely be made out across the Irish Sea.

For the first time in a long while, Ian had dressed in his priestly garb, a long black cassock and pants, black buttonless shirt, and white, backwards collar. Emily had commented on how dashing he looked, but he had only dressed this way in honor of the duty he was about to perform.

Leaning back against the headrest, he closed his eyes. For years, he had followed the development of the Temple Consortium. Though he never visited its gallery, he had read many articles and seen many pictures of the implements, the garments, and harps being made there.

As a student of the Old as well as the New Testaments, he was very familiar with the nature of the worship and service that had taken place for centuries in the temple of ancient Israel.

Based on the layout of Moses's wilderness tabernacle, which had traveled everywhere with the Israelites in their wanderings before they entered the Promised Land, the temple's focal point was the Holy of Holies, which housed the Ark of the Covenant. Outside the Holy Place, where the priest entered once a year to make atonement for the sins of the people, daily sacrifices were made in the courtyard. Thousands upon thousands of animals were killed there every week, he knew. The calculations made by some scholars concerning the amount of blood that must have flowed from Mount Zion into Jerusalem's underground sewers was staggering.

As much as it troubled Ian to be turning over a list of treasures that could bring the jealousy and hatred of the world against Israel and could possibly usher in the greatest battle of all time, it troubled him even more to think that he could be helping to take religion backward, to the pre-Christian era. *I don't understand, I don't understand,* he thought as he sat with his eyes closed. Yet, he also knew that the prophets, Jeremiah, Ezekiel, Isaiah, and others, had declared thousands of years before that one day Israel would build a "house of prayer for all nations." The prophecies were quite specific regarding its structure and functions. Anyone in touch with world events could see the buildup of the Arab nations against this eventuality.

Why, the Scriptures indicated that Jesus himself would one day reign from Mt. Zion, and his people would recognize him for who he was.

Ian cringed at a horrid notion. Could it be that Jesus, establishing himself as ruler over Israel, would consent to reign over a place where the blood of goats and rams ran through the stones, and the smoke of sacrifices filled the air?

He thought not!

But, about this incongruity, Ian had thought too much and too long. For years, he had wondered about these enigmas in the Scriptures. He could not figure it out, and he knew of no one who had.

All he knew, here and now, was that he was being carried along on a wave of inescapable fate. He was taking the scroll back to Israel, and he was about to turn it over to hands responsible for Israel's future. He could do nothing, now, but trust that the prayers he had delivered up for a decade had not led him astray.

As his four companions were carried, with him, on the wings of destiny, they were all silent, each deep in thoughts of his or her own.

Apart from John Cromwell, who knew Ian's struggles and shared them, David Rothmeyer had the most vested interest in the scroll. If it did, indeed, contain a vital link in the genealogy, the goal of his assignment would be all the closer to fulfillment.

As the plane flew over the English Channel, Britta studied David's pensive face, reading his nervous anticipation. Reaching over, she clasped his hand in hers, and smiled up at him.

She was about to lean his way with a whisper of reassurance, when the rattle of a food cart drew their attention to the aisle. Stewardesses were making their way slowly up the walkway, handing out little trays of kosher breakfasts.

It seemed there was enough time for David to make a quick trip to the lavatory before the cart reached their seats. "I'll be right back," he said, giving Britta's hand a squeeze.

Quickly he made his way back to the rear of the plane, and finding that the lavatory door read "occupied," he waited beside it, stooping under the curved ceiling, which was too low for his tall frame.

The cart was almost to his row of seats when he at last heard the toilet flush in the little cubicle and the sliding lock sign slapped to "vacant."

As the door opened, he pulled back farther and waited for the occupant to exit. The instant this happened, David did a double-take: He had seen this character before.

He might not have remembered just where he had encountered the dusky fellow, or why the sight of him was troubling, had the man not given a cursory, "Pardon me," as he slipped past. The sound of those two words, rasping and strangely coarse, recalled to David the scene in the JFK terminal. This was the Lebanese man who had chastened his little son for speaking to a Jew!

That day, for the first time since childhood altercations, David had felt ethnic fear. Though the man had not looked his way, the professor had been stunned by his expressions of hate.

Today, once again, David was alarmed by his presence. Though he had no reason to be suspicious of the man, he struck an anxious chord in David's spirit. As the professor slipped into the lavatory and washed his hands at the little sink, he relived the scene in the New York airport with a shudder. Never before had he seen such hatred in a man's face, as this stranger directed at the praying Jews. Jews were the "enemy," he had told his son. "Not to touch! Not to speak!"

Feeling clammy, David ran a damp paper towel over his face, closing his eyes. *Why,* he wondered, *would a man who loathed Jews to that degree, be traveling to Israel?*

CHAPTER 40

Later that evening, Honey Aronstam stood at the rooftop balustrade of the house where she had first met David Rothmeyer. It was from this vantage point that the professor had first set eyes on her as she emerged from the taxi upon arriving in Jerusalem.

Now she was the one watching for a cab, this one due to arrive any moment, bearing the professor and Britta Hayworth, Emily McCurdy, and two men whom she had not met. Behind her, seated at the table where David often worked with his laptop computer, sat Pete and Mel. Downstairs, in the parlor of the big house, other men had also gathered.

The rabbis of the Temple Consortium were all there, waiting together in the medieval chamber for the arrival of Ian McCurdy and his priceless scroll. Anya, the housekeeper, bustled about, serving them sandwiches and pouring pot after pot of coffee.

The mood all through the house was one of tense anticipation, of the long-dreamed-of climax to an arduous search.

When David had called from Germany with news of the successful procurement of the Dachau document, Uriel Katz, Carl Jacobs, and Menachem Levine were already headed to Jerusalem from New York. Rabbi Benjamin had reported to them on the findings of the computer lab, and they were eager to look in on that work. They had not known about the German material until they arrived, and felt it was divine timing that they should have come just now.

Amazed at such a windfall, they anxiously awaited the integration of the Aronstam document into the genealogical chain.

It had not taken long for the new information to be collated into the data files. Since the lab had already determined that there was a strong British strand in the line, the document made the evidence even stronger. It remained for the sorting through and discarding of millions of names to narrow the field.

Several strands within the British records stood out as possibilities, but one by one they were eliminated as dead ends, as the computer programmers manually entered information that continued to pour into the institute.

Honey breathed in deeply of the sage-scented air wafting up from the Hinnom Valley. During her brief time in Israel, she had learned the pleasure of such evenings, when soft, warm breezes blew across the rooftop.

Pete watched her from behind as she stood at the rail, admiring the willowy form that never failed to please him and the thick, wavy hair, which flew free in the air's gentle currents. He believed that the best thing he had ever done was to take Mel's lead and go in search of this woman. Never again, he was determined, would he let her go.

His fondest desire now, was to get her back to Montana, to the beloved home he had built for her with his own hands. How he hoped that wonderful house was still standing, that the Militia had not revenged themselves against him by destroying it! But even if he must build a new place, deeper in the outback, far from the reach of ruthless men, he would see to it that she was never put in danger again.

And once this escapade was resolved, he planned to give her her heart's desire, a beautiful wedding.

For now, he felt as she did, that they must see this venture through. He and his brother had become as caught up in the mystery of the quest as anyone else.

Below, in the parlor, the four colleagues of the Consortium chatted together, their conversation sinking, as was too often the case, into a sparring match. Rabbi Benjamin listened helplessly as, once again, Uriel Katz fumed over the ongoing quest.

"I cannot think that the true line leads through Britain!" Katz declared. "Oh, I can see the possibility that it paused there for a while, but for the data to say that it stopped there is just very hard for me to accept!"

Dr. Jacobs sat back in his armchair, rubbing his protruding stomach after feasting on too many of Anya's treats. "And what will you do if the record proves you wrong, Uriel?" he asked.

"You all know that I believe, along with thousands of like thinkers throughout our history, that the first mark of a true priest is scholarship. Of course, not all the great priests were great students. But, surely, the highest of the priests must first be devoted to the Torah, the Talmud, the Mishnah . . ."

Menachem Levine sniffed and turned perceptive eyes on his disgruntled colleague. "Come, now, Uriel! What we all know is that you have set out to prove that the line devolves through Eastern Europe, through Northeastern Europe, to be exact. You and your fellow Talmudists will never be happy unless one of your cold, literalist scholars is put in charge of things!"

Dr. Jacobs, who was usually quite jovial and accommodating, was less generous that evening. "Let's face it, Katz!" he spat. "You are determined that anything less than the declaration of a Katz as the successor is unacceptable! Your fondest desire is to see yourself, yes, *yourself*, installed as priest! You have even created an Internet web page, of all things, setting out your credentials before the world!"

Katz stiffened. "I did not create that page, Carl! You know that very well. It was my students at the Brooklyn synagogue who did that. It has been quite the embarrassment, actually!"

Rabbi Benjamin intervened. "Now, gentlemen, let's be gracious to one another. As for myself, I would be pleased to see Uriel gain the post, if God wills it. He is a great mind."

"If not a great heart!" Menachem muttered.

Jacobs chuckled at this, but Uriel was chagrined. "Horace!" he growled. "How did you come by these two?"

Rabbi Benjamin shook his head. "You could do with some sweetening, Uriel. Your poor wife will vouch for that!"

At this, the other two laughed aloud.

"Now, now, Uriel. I mean no harm," Horace said. "But I do agree that there is more than scholarship and orthodoxy that qualifies a man for this position. We will probably be quite surprised when God presents us with the chosen one!"

"Aha!" Uriel fumed. "There we go with the orthodoxy thing again. Are we not all orthodox here? But, then, I forget . . . you tend toward the Cabalist teachings, don't you, Horace?"

Rabbi Benjamin, coming from a long line of Southeastern Europeans, had been reared in the tradition of the mystics who followed Eliezer Ben Tov. As a result, he did respect certain aspects of the Cabala, believed to be a code for deciphering untenable portions of Scripture.

"I will not debate with you, Uriel," he asserted. "Let us just remember how God surprised Israel with the choice of King David. He was nothing more than an unschooled shepherd. Probably dirty and puny, at that!"

"Amen!" Carl chuckled.

"Well spoken," Levine cheered.

For the moment, Katz had been put in his place, though not the place he thought he should fill.

Meanwhile, Honey, looking down from the roof, spied a taxi cab pulling up to the curb.

"I think they're here!" she cried, turning to Pete and Mel. Then, watching the passengers emerge, she declared, "Yes, I see David, Britta, and now Emily. With them are the men from England! Go tell the rabbis!"

Mel jumped to do her bidding, and Pete joined her at the rail, slipping his arm about her slim waist. "I can't believe we're here, waiting for the greatest find of the century!" he said. "How do we rate?"

Honey smiled up at him. "I've stopped asking that question," she said. "Somehow we got plopped into the middle of all this. I have to believe there's a good reason for it!"

"Well," he said, "I can see why you'd be here. Your star was a key in the whole search. As for me . . . well, I just hope I can help."

Honey perceived the regret in his tone, sorrow for past involvements and causes. She slipped her hand in his, where it rested on the rail.

"I don't know much about God," she said. "I used to think about him some, when I walked through the woods on our property or sat by the stream. But now I think he's a lot bigger than all that. I don't think anything happens without his say-so. If you want to help, I'm sure he'll find a way to let you." Then she smiled lovingly. "Besides, just your being here has already helped *me* a great deal!"

The sound of the front door intercom drew the two lovers from the rooftop, and hurrying down the hall, they joined the rabbis in greeting their friends.

"Gentlemen," David began, "this is Father Ian McCurdy, his sister, Emily, and his friend, John Cromwell, from Great Britain. And this is Emily's friend—and mine," he said wistfully, "Britta Hayworth."

Pete and Mel took their jackets and luggage as Anya ushered them into the parlor.

"Come, come," Rabbi Benjamin offered. "Rest by the fire! Father McCurdy," he said, stretching out his hand, "I am honored to meet one of the world's great scholars." This last phrase was for Uriel's benefit, who needed a reminder to accept the man.

At this, Uriel, too, shook Ian's hand, and Carl and Menachem offered their warmed-up chairs.

"Gentlemen," Ian said, bobbing his head in a bow, "the pleasure is mine, I am sure! I have followed your work for years. I hope I can be of some assistance."

In his arms was the precious valise from the British Museum. He had not let it go, even once, since leaving London.

Rabbi Ben deduced the contents and did not immediately offer to relieve him of it. "You have brought the scroll?" he asked gently.

"I have," Ian replied. "Perhaps you can understand my insistence on transporting it personally. It has long been a part of my soul."

John Cromwell swallowed hard as Ian said this. No one else could possibly know how true that statement was.

"Father," Horace said, "you may rest assured that we will not take it from you against your will. Although we believe it belongs in Israel, you must let God tell you what to do. After all, he apparently entrusted it to your keeping for all these years."

Ian was stunned by this sympathetic observation.

For a long, silent moment, the two clerics stood face to face on a small, oriental carpet before a Jerusalem fire. Etched before the golden blaze in long black frocks, both with snowy hair and guileless faces, they looked more alike, than unlike.

CHAPTER 41

The next morning, the house was bustling with joyous activity, as all the company from across the world anticipated the outcome of the day's findings.

Honey was helping Anya clear the breakfast dishes from the dining room, where the four rabbis, the Catholic priest, John Cromwell, Emily, Britta, the professor, and the three Montanans had devoured a large meal.

In a few moments, all the men but Pete and Mel would be going off to the Consortium's computer lab, where, in the security of the underground workroom, the scroll would be unveiled.

Since women were not allowed in the Consortium lab, Honey, Emily, and Britta were discussing with Pete and Mel a day-long tour of the city, under the escort of the Wester brothers, when Rabbi Benjamin ducked his head in the room.

"Come join us," he said. "We're going to say a prayer over the day, before we depart."

Honey wiped her hands on a napkin and left the chores to Anya. Together, the five guests followed Rabbi Benjamin to the parlor, where David and the other rabbis waited.

"Let's join hands, shall we?" Horace said, gathering his friends and colleagues in a circle. Silence descended on the group.

Rabbi Benjamin looked around at his fellow clerics. The rabbis, all except Katz, had their eyes closed, their heads bowed. Horace noted that Uriel's face was a bit clouded and thought perhaps he was uneasy with the ecumenical spirit. Thinking it best to ease his comrade's mind, Ben said, "Uriel, would you do us the honor of invoking God's blessing on our day?"

Katz glanced at Horace in pleased surprise, then closed his eyes and cleared his throat.

"Hear, O Israel," he began, "the Lord our God is one God. There are no others. God of our Fathers, bless our endeavors. Bring to light the ways of righteousness and guide us to fulfill your will on earth. Help us to establish your sanctuary, once more, among men of all nations. And may your Shekinah glory dwell again among us!"

To this, everyone said "Amen," and the men clapped one another on the backs, like soldiers ready to enter the fray.

But one of the guests had been stunned by the prayer, wondering if he had heard the words correctly.

The scholars and the rabbis were gathering up their briefcases, heading for the front door, when Pete rushed up to David and drew him aside. "Excuse me, Professor," he said in a low voice, "may I see you for a moment?"

David glanced at his exiting coworkers. "Now?" he asked. "What is it?"

"Maybe nothing," Pete said, feeling foolish.

David read deep concern in the Montanan's eyes. Calling to Horace, he said, "I'll be right there, Rabbi. Go on. I'll catch up with you."

Then, turning to Pete, "I'm all ears."

Britta and Emily had left for their room, to get ready for the day's tour. Only Mel and Honey lingered behind.

"What's going on?" Mel asked, joining his brother.

Honey, seeing that Pete's face had gone white, slipped up beside him, too.

Pete's voice was dry. "Like I say," he repeated, "it may be nothing. But . . ."

"Go on, Pete," Honey spurred him.

"Well," he said, "when the rabbi prayed, he used a word I've been wondering about. I know this will seem crazy, but, Professor, can you tell me what 'Shekinah' means?"

David was bewildered, and not a little annoyed at what seemed an unnecessary interruption to a crucial schedule.

"'*Shekinah?*'" he repeated. "Well, Pete, I don't know why you're asking, but *shekinah* is the Hebrew word for the glory of God, which the Bible says used to fill the Holy of Holies, the inner sanctum of the temple, when the Lord would descend. '*Shekinah,*' 'Glory of God.' Why?"

Pete understood David's impatience. "Bear with me, Professor," he said.

"Maybe Honey told you—I used to take messages for the brotherhood, off the ham radio." Quickly he related the incident of the Arab voice coming over the receiver, and he pulled the crumpled note from his wallet, where he had transferred it from his shirt pocket days ago.

David scanned the note, and as he did, his eyes grew round with fear. " 'Ready to drop on Shekinah'!" he read.

He looked in dismay at Honey, who grabbed the note and gawked at it. "Oh, no!" she cried. "This sounds like a threat to the Consortium. 'Shekinah' is also the name of the yeshiva where the rabbis are training young men for priestly duties in the future temple!"

"Yeshiva?" Mel asked.

"Seminary!" David explained. "Yeshiva Shekinah, 'School for God's Glory,' houses and trains the very finest young Jewish scholars—Levites and Cohens—for roles in the future sanctuary! Rabbi Ben is an instructor there."

Honey clutched Pete's arm. "Did you say the transmission was from an Arab voice?" she asked.

"I'm no language expert," Pete replied. "But it sounded Middle Eastern." Then, feeling helpless, he added, "The only other thing noteworthy was the voice itself—extremely coarse and raspy."

Now it was David's turn to lurch. "What did you say?" he gasped.

"The voice, it was—"

"Okay! Okay!" the professor said. "I hear you."

"What's wrong?" Honey cried.

"Like Pete said," the professor muttered, "it may be nothing, but I've run into a guy with that sort of voice more than once now. He's definitely Arab, Lebanese by his language; he's an international traveler; he hates Jews, that's for sure! And—"

He paused, making the others edgy.

"Go on, Professor!" Mel exclaimed.

"He's probably in Israel, even as we speak," David replied. "I saw him on the plane heading here!"

Dread filled the American foursome as they all drew the obvious conclusion.

"What shall we do?" Honey groaned.

David pondered this, his palms sweaty. "We don't have enough to go on to alert the authorities," he said.

Pete and Mel glanced at one another, each knowing what the other thought about such "authorities."

"What about the rabbis?" Honey asked, her face full of fear.

David shook his head. "Again, since it could be nothing, I don't think we should disrupt them and their guests. Not today, of all days!"

Honey nodded. "What then?" she implored.

David thought a moment. "Since nothing happened during the night, maybe our fears are unfounded. But we can't be too careful."

Looking the Westers up and down, he said, "Maybe it's providential that you guys are here. You look like you could handle most anything. Mel, you've got street smarts, and Pete, you'd recognize the guy's voice if you heard it. Why don't you two hang out near the school for the day? Watch for a burly guy, dark hair, dark beard, dark complexion."

The Westers did not hesitate. "You've got it," Mel said, and Pete gave a thumbs up.

"Honey," David went on, "you can lead them there. I'll go join the rabbis, like they expect me to. Once you get Pete and Mel oriented, which shouldn't take long, come back and get Britta and Emily out of the Old City. Tell them you're taking them to Ben Yehuda Street for a day of shopping. Tell them you'll do the sightseeing thing tomorrow, because Pete and Mel decided to help at the lab. Okay?"

"Okay!" Honey agreed.

David grabbed his briefcase off the parlor sofa and headed for the door.

"Glad you came along, fellas," he called back to the Westers. Then, surprising even himself, he stopped and added, "Maybe God knew we needed you!"

Yeshiva Shekinah sat on one of the typically winding, narrow streets of Old Jerusalem, several blocks away from the Temple Jewels Exhibit. Pete walked so fast, he appeared to be leading the way, as Honey gave directions and Mel followed.

"I never overlooked giving Fogarty a message—never until this time," Pete said. "Now I'm glad I did!"

Honey hurried to keep up with the long-legged Pete, pointing this way and that as they turned corners and descended the crooked, terraced streets of the town. As Pete unburdened himself, she listened respectfully, seeing in him the crusader spirit that had attracted her to him years ago.

"I can't explain," he went on. "I've just had a spooky feeling about this note ever since I remembered it being in my pocket—like, like . . . well, like it was meant to be that I didn't deliver it. Like, maybe, it was a—"

"A warning?" Honey guessed.

Pete shrugged. Seeing that Honey was out of breath, he stopped a moment. "I don't talk to God much, not since I was a little kid. But on the plane, when you were asleep, Mel"—he turned to his brother—"well, it just kind of settled over me that I should shoot a prayer up about this thing. Dang, guys, I'll just say it! I told God I'd like to help if I could, you know, do something to make up for—"

His face turned red, and Honey touched his arm.

"I understand, Pete," she said.

Mel, feeling out of his element, cleared his throat and said, "Bro, you know I'm with you. Where is this place, anyway?"

Honey pointed to one more corner, and once they had rounded it, they saw that it dead-ended at a plain little house, two stories high, probably dating back to the same era as David's place.

"That's it," Honey said. "Rabbi Ben showed it to me once, when we went out for an evening stroll. He didn't take me inside, of course. Women aren't permitted."

A small sign, not in the least ostentatious, was the only adornment on the heavily carved door. *Yeshiva Shekinah* was all it said, in unimposing letters.

Decoration was sparse; a couple of large flowerpots, filled with red nasturtiums, one on each side of the door, provided the only splash of color. A wrought-iron bench sat to one side of the tiled porch, which was little more than a step.

"Check it out," Pete said to Mel. "If anyone wanted to do damage here, there's only one way to enter, and the high windows on the top story are covered with grille work. It would take a fairly powerful bomb to blast through those rock walls!"

Mel surveyed the scene, much as he would have done at a crime scene in a Los Angeles alley. "No, look," he said, pointing to a small flight of stairs barely noticeable behind an iron gate to the side of the building. "A lot of these old places probably have only one door, but I'll bet they use the rooftops for patios, like in the older apartment houses in big American cities—and like where David is staying. There's probably a way in through the roof."

Honey was amazed. "You're right, Mel. Pretty clever. Actually, you can walk from house to house on the roofs. It's like a thorough-fare up there."

"You mean, people aren't freaked by strangers crossing their roofs?" Pete asked.

"Well, all I know is, David and I took a walk with the rabbi one evening to see the city lights come up. We went along the rooftops like we were on a sidewalk. No one asked any questions. They just nodded and said hello as we passed by. You could see entrances to the floors below."

"Wow, strange!" Pete said. "The closest we get to that idea is Santa Claus on Christmas Eve!"

The three laughed, but Mel was still speculating, analyzing the building and the street that dead-ended at the front door.

"One of us could go up on the stairs, and one of us could stay out front," he said to his brother. "But how would we explain ourselves, if the students see us? Tell you what," he suggested. "We passed some little shops not too far back. How about if we hang out there and keep checking the street? Chances are probably about fifty-fifty that anyone wanting to 'drop' something, like the note says, will approach from the street anyway."

Pete shrugged. "Sounds like a plan," he agreed. Then, turning to Honey, he gave an anxious nod. "Okay, kid," he said, "you get out of here!"

Honey shot a worried look at the school and then rushed toward Pete, embracing him and burying her head on his shoulder.

"You be careful!" she said, then sighed, "I need you, Pete!"

CHAPTER 42

David arrived at the institute just in time to enter with his associates. Smoothing his hair, he tried to look calm, to focus his attention on the task at hand.

The computer lab was a whirl of activity when the men arrived. Clement, James, and Shofar were madly collating reams of names that continued to pour in from respondents to the Consortium's request for Cohen family histories.

"Good morning, fellows," Rabbi Benjamin greeted them. "I have brought some very important guests."

Clement stood up from his work station, where he had just clicked the enter key to deposit about a thousand names into the main computer's spinning brain. When he saw his four bosses, he snapped to attention. "Good morning, Rabbis," he said, nudging James, who nudged Shofar, so that they, too, snapped alert.

"This is Father Ian McCurdy, from Oxford, and his coworker, John Cromwell," Horace announced.

Having anticipated this visit, the programmers' expressions were full of admiration.

Clement thrust out his hand, at the same instant as his companions, so that three eager hands waited for Ian's attention. Shaking each in turn, the good Father smiled.

"Quite the greeting committee!" he said to Rabbi Benjamin.

Stepping up to the computer bank, the Oxfordian studied

it with amazement. Reams of paper flowed steadily from printers, each sheet laden with charts and columns of names, dates, and places.

"So this is the result of your work?" he asked. "All of these are Jewish histories?"

"That's right!" Clement said proudly. "We are very close to drawing some important conclusions!" As the computer master spoke, his eyes were locked on the valise in Ian's arms. He was hesi-tant to ask the obvious question, but turned eagerly to Rabbi Benjamin.

"Yes, Clement," the rabbi answered. "This is the scroll, the one we always hoped to find."

Clement rubbed his hands together, like a hungry man over a feast, and his two companions pressed close to his back, peering around him at the marvelous find.

"The back room is ready," Clement said, looking longingly at the door to the adjacent laboratory. "Rabbi Diamant opened it last evening for the geneticists. They put all their work away so that you could have free reign. I—I certainly would like to see the scroll. . . ."

Rabbi Benjamin glanced at his colleagues. Uriel Katz looked askance at such a notion, but Levine and Jacobs welcomed the participation.

"You'll be working with the results," Horace said. "You might as well see the unveiling."

Elated, Clement turned to his envious companions. "You have plenty to do," he said. "I won't stay long."

At this, he took a key from his pocket and opened the back room, then flicked on the bank of lights that ran the length of the subterranean chamber.

The last time David had seen this place, it had been the repository of the bones of Caiaphas, ensconced in a hermetically controlled case. Now that case was nowhere to be seen, probably secreted away for further study, and all of the lab equipment used for that work had been lined up neatly on a side counter.

The long, stainless steel table in the center of the room was open for use, the geneticists having thought to set out a little circular saw, a surgical tool the men might need for their task. This lay beside a roll of white butcher paper, which they thought the linguists might want to spread on the work area.

"How surgical!" Ian said. "I feel as though I am about to submit my child's body for autopsy!"

The rabbis did not know whether to laugh or console him.

"Sorry, lads," the old priest said. "Just a bit of the dry Irish wit!"

Surveying the room, he sighed. "Goodness! If we had had such facilities at Institut Biblique we could have worked on those scrolls much faster."

Rabbi Benjamin hated to press him, but he reached out his hands, silently asking for the parcel. "May I?" he asked.

"Oh—of course," Ian replied. "Here, let me set it down."

The priest walked to the lab table, ready to deposit the scroll. But before he did, David, who was now centered on the work at hand, grabbed the roll of butcher paper and handed Clement one end. "Here," he said, "help me spread this out."

Clement, honored to be part of the procedure, quickly pulled the end free and, while David held the roll, draped a large sheet across the table. Quickly, David cut it with his pocket knife, and Clement, finding a roll of tape, secured the piece to the metallic surface.

"Now?" Ian asked.

"Now," David said.

Ian glanced at John Cromwell, as if for reassurance.

John nodded, and the priest set the valise on the table. "David," he said, "would you do the honors?"

The professor had thought that he could never be more nervous, more awestruck by a professional assignment than he had been when he had looked at Honey Aronstam's star. Then, the day he exhumed the document from the brick wall at Dachau, he had believed there could be no greater privilege.

Now, he was about to open the most sought after of all the Cave Scrolls, the one whose portent could reach from across the centuries to shape the destiny of the world!

As he pressed the lock buttons on the valise, the metal tabs flicked up with a snap. Gently, he lifted the lid with its form-fitting liner.

There, snuggled in its linen wrap, was the scroll.

He turned again to Ian, who nodded the go-ahead.

David rubbed the fingers of both hands against his thumbs, like a safecracker about to work a dial. Gingerly, he lifted the linen swaddle from the case and set the parcel on the table.

Next, he turned the bundle over and over, unrolling the linen wrap, until an ancient metal cylinder was exposed.

Ian stepped up to the artifact reverently and gazed upon it with a sigh. "Hello, old friend," he said, "old enemy. We meet again."

Cromwell stood by silently, wondering how Ian would bear up. When the priest stepped away, stalwart and unflinching, John breathed easier.

David gestured to Ian to begin taking apart the pieces that had been fit together after the original cutting.

"No, no, Dr. Rothmeyer," he said. "I am much too old and shaky for such close work. Be my guest."

David swallowed hard. If his colleagues only knew what anxiety he was feeling after learning about the possible terrorist threat, they might not trust him to be less shaky.

Piece by piece, the professor began to lay out the shards of corroded copper, side by side so that they formed a recognizable document, reading from right to left.

The rabbis leaned close, trying to make out the antiquated Hebrew characters.

"See how the language has changed!" Ian said. "It will take some getting used to, as the forms of the letters alter with time. What you are looking at is stylized in the writing form popular in the first century C.E."

It had been years since Ian had worked with such material, but he had given many a lecture at Oxford, explaining how paleographers and linguists determine the era in which a piece is written.

His voice showed the enthusiasm of a true scholar as he proceeded. "It is apparent, also, that this was written by somebody other than one of the Qumran scribes. Their handwriting and their use of language were quite precise and educated. Whoever wrote this is probably the same fellow who wrote the first Copper Scroll, likely a coppersmith, hired to do the work, and possibly borderline illiterate. He would have been copying a script written out on some other parchment and would not have understood much of what he wrote. We can see this from his misspellings, jumbling of characters and, sometimes, outright skipping of words."

The rabbis were amazed at Ian's analysis, but David was familiar with the analytical process and only admired his astuteness.

"It is marvelous that you can deduce so much from what, to the layman, is merely a bunch of graffiti," Dr. Jacobs observed.

"Rather like the pharmacist reading the doctor's prescription?" Levine teased.

Jacobs grinned, but Uriel Katz was more somber. "So, Father McCurdy," he asked, "is this, in truth, a key to the treasure scroll?"

Ian nodded. "It appears to be. We never implemented it. As I told David, Father Ducharme and I worked on this privately. We were under much duress as we did so, and we could only do so much. We never analyzed it in detail with reference to the first scroll. Because we were familiar with that document, though, it became obvious to us that this one was directly related."

Horace Benjamin shook his head in amazement. "Is it possible, Father, that there would be references here to the lost treasures of the Holy of Holies? The Ark of the Covenant, for instance?"

The priest looked at the floor. He had always feared such speculations, for he knew the international skirmish they could create. He answered carefully. "Anything is possible, Rabbi. As I say, we were not after any treasure. We were simply trying to interpret what we had found, though we did not complete that task."

At last, after David had spread out the copper shards in the puzzlelike arrangement, what was left of the scroll was the crimped core Ian had spoken of, the remnant that he and Ducharme had feared to tamper with.

"There, Dr. Rothmeyer," Ian said, "if your genealogical reference is in this scroll, it will be in that section. We saw nothing of the sort in the first part."

David's hands were sweaty as he reached for the diminutive, battery-powered circular saw. "Clement," he asked, "could you please bring me a paper towel from the sink?"

As Clement obeyed, Uriel Katz scrutinized the scroll and rubbed his forehead. "Now let me be sure I understand our thinking here. We are hoping to bring together the references in the Dachau document with scribal notations in this scroll? If we find a reference here to the first-century priest mentioned by Rabbi Aronstam, that should verify his contention that the line goes through a Jew who was taken to England during the Crusades. Am I right?"

"That is right," David replied. "The Dachau document says that the line of Israel Kahana, who was raised in England, descended from a certain Gabriel Ben Zadok, one of the 'righteous' Cohen priests. It says that the legend will be verified if a reference to Gabriel can ever be found and that this reference was recorded by desert scribes, presumably of Qumran fame."

"So," Katz went on, "bear with me. We are also saying that if such and such can be proven, it only remains for some modern line to be linked with this Englishman, and, *voilà*, we will have our candidate!"

No one present could miss the sarcasm in Katz's tone.

Neither David nor Ian knew how to respond, but Rabbi Benjamin was used to dealing with his obstreperous colleague. "'*Voilà*' indeed," he said pleasantly. "Can you imagine a more definitive trail of evidence?"

Katz had never grown accustomed to Horace's way with him: always able to squelch him, yet remain kind in the process.

Levine, however, was more blunt. "Step back now, Uriel. Let Dr. Rothmeyer work," he said, pulling Katz away from the table.

David cleared his throat tensely and held the saw in crimped fingers.

Pushing the little button on the side, which would disengage the motor the moment he let up on it, he set the saw to humming.

With a high-pitched squeal like that of a dentist's drill, it bit into the first thin layer of the tightly wound core. Bit by Bit, David worked through the coiled layers, removing a strip at a time and placing them beside each other, like pieces of onion skin.

"Beautiful!" Ian whispered. "You are a craftsman!"

David worked through the last layer, and when he had unraveled the final characters, placing the last thin section next to the others, the men gathered around the table. All of them knew Hebrew, whether in this archaic script or in the words of a freshly printed Torah. Scanning the frail shards, they looked anxiously for the necessary reference.

"Clement," David called, drawing an overhead lamp close to the table, "do you have a magnifier?"

Clement rummaged through a drawer in a nearby cabinet and quickly produced a reading glass.

Looking somewhat like Sherlock Holmes, with his tweed jacket and serious, thin face, David Rothmeyer read as quickly as possible through a long list of explications on hiding places and the meanings of words in the first scroll.

At last, with a thrill coursing through his entire body, he thought he had fallen on something. "Father McCurdy," he said, handing the priest the glass, "look at these lines, just before the benediction! Do they say what I think they say?"

The rabbis moved collectively closer, trying to get a view while not disturbing the paleographers. "Have you found it?" Rabbi Benjamin asked in a whisper.

Ian began to read the vague, corroded letters of the section David pointed out. "Much of it is missing," he said, "but I can make out certain familiar phrases."

Slowly he pieced together a few words for the listeners. " '*Asher ba'u habrit hahadashah. . . .*' " Then he interpreted, " 'The people of the community of the renewed covenant.' "

David nodded agreement. "Go on," he said.

"There is a rusted place here," Ian said, "but I see the next phrase as '*halakah bene sadoq.*' "

David nodded again. "I agree, 'the law of the sons of Zadok'!"

The rabbis were astonished. "The priestly line!" Dr. Jacobs exclaimed. "It is talking about the priestly line!"

"It seems so!" Ian affirmed. "Now here, what is this?" he asked, squinting through the magnifier. "Again, there is something missing. But the next recognizable phrase is *'rebi saddiq'*!"

He glanced up at the onlookers, and as one voice they shouted, "Righteous Teacher!"

Dr. Jacobs and Rabbi Levine grasped each other in a hug.

"They are speaking of the Teacher of Righteousness! The one so often heralded throughout the Cave Scrolls! He was the leader of the commune!" Levine recalled.

"So it would appear!" Ian said, trying not to overanticipate. "But, let us go on. . . ."

Again, he squinted through the glass and read the adjoining words. Suddenly his old eyes grew wide, and the magnifying glass wavered in his hand. David grasped it from him, fearing he would drop it on the scroll.

"You *do* see it!" David cried. "I am not imagining this?"

The old priest rose up stiffly, straightening his back and gazing speechlessly at the American.

"What? What?" the rabbis cried. Even Uriel Katz was unable to resist the drama of the moment. "Tell us what it says!" he exclaimed.

Ian ran through the phrases in his mind, filling in the missing parts to make a likely composition.

"I do not feel we are out of line at all, gentlemen," he finally said, "in making the following interpretation. This is the culmination of the document, the place where the drafters give their credentials. They are put just before the closing benediction and would read something like this:

"'The law of the sons of Zadok, the people of the community of the renewed covenant, and their Righteous Teacher or Rabbi . . .'"

Here he paused, his entire body atingle. John Cromwell patted his back and whispered, "Go on, Ian."

"'. . . their Rabbi, Gabriel Ben Zadok'!"

At the sound of these words, the ultimate proof of the monumental quest, the rabbis were ecstatic. Jacobs and Levine hugged one another rapturously, and began to dance around, singing, lifting their old knees and stomping their feet, clapping their hands and twirling like boys at a bar mitzvah.

Reaching for Rabbi Benjamin, they drew him into their jig and then held out their hands to draw the others in. Suddenly the entire group, even a previously reticent Uriel Katz, was caught up in celebration, singing and dancing around the metal table.

David, John, Ian, Clement—all of them—laughed and clapped, spinning around the priceless scroll in unleashed joy.

Perhaps, centuries before, the drafters of that document had prayed for this day, when the scroll, prepared under great duress and hidden at great risk, would serve the purpose for which it was created. Perhaps they even dreamed it would be celebrated in this way, received with great joy, for the door it would open on the future and the new day it would usher in.

CHAPTER 43

Mammed Kahlil was used to pulling off his violent acts under cover of darkness, or at least, in the confusion of crowds.

However, this assignment was different. It called for daylight, for the Islamic forces behind it wanted it to receive immediate media focus. And because of the layout of the dead-end street and the yeshiva building, chances were that he would not be able to sneak away unnoticed.

But he was prepared for that eventuality. He was prepared either to die and go to Paradise, where he would be received in honor by the Prophet Mohammed, or to become a bull's-eye of media attention for the Islamic cause.

So long as he was successful in destroying the Jewish school, where youngsters were trained as functionaries in the planned temple, he would please Allah.

Mammed had spent the night in Tel Aviv, and took a cab to Jerusalem in the morning. Dressed in casual attire, he could have been a tourist, a Lebanese businessman, or even a secular Jew. Though his skin was darker than that of most Jews, if he did not speak, he knew he should go unnoticed in the Orthodox neighborhood where the school was located.

Apart from the directions to the yeshiva, which he had received from his employers and committed to memory, he also bore in mind Altmeyer's description of the blond American men and their dark-haired female accomplice. If anything was going to interfere with Mammed's duties, it would be a threat from Israeli counterintelligence.

Bright noon sun flooded the narrow lanes and twisting streets of the Old City as Mammed wended through the marketplace nearest the school. In a small leather case, the strap of which was over his shoulder, was the precious vial full of Bailey's Bug. Mammed held the bag beneath his arm, close against his body, like a tourist might hold an expensive camera case.

He walked through the bazaar as nonchalantly as possible, at the same time considering the volatility of the vial's contents. Though the lid was securely tightened, he could not be too careful in avoiding jarring the bottle. Too harsh a bump from a passing pedestrian or a clumsy stumble over a crack in the lane could spell disaster.

As he skirted clusters of tourists and shoppers along the way, he also skirted his enemies. This was an Orthodox Jewish neighborhood. He was reminded of this every time men in black suits and broad-rimmed hats passed him, chatting together in Hebrew, keeping their eyes to the ground.

How he hated them! How his pulse pounded as he moved ever closer to vengeance.

Ahead he could see the sign for the street that led to his target.

He could feel each beat of his heart now, thrumming, pushing adrenaline through his body. He wondered how many more times it would beat, before it was silenced for eternity.

It had been two hours since Honey had left Pete and Mel in the marketplace near the yeshiva. The Westers felt awkward as they lingered near the corner of the little side street leading to the school. Trying to look like tourists in the small shops lining the adjacent block, they feared their extended "visit" there was beginning to attract notice.

Pete had tried on five pairs of sandals, declining to buy anything, while the anxious shop owner jabbered away about the fine quality of the cheap leather, and Mel had downed his second cup of thick black coffee and a prune pastry at the neighborhood café, when they joined one another at the intersection for the umpteenth time.

"Maybe we should come back this evening," Pete finally said, as they stood at the corner. "If anything's going to happen, maybe it'll be after dark."

Mel was prone to agree. "The professor and the rabbis will be done at the lab soon enough. Dave will probably think it's okay to tell them about this situation, once their research is finished. Maybe they'll want to contact the authorities."

"Yeah," Pete agreed. "Maybe we're in over our heads. Or, like we keep saying, maybe there's nothing to any of it."

Just as he admitted this, however, he noticed a peculiar look come over his brother's face. Seeing that Mel was focused on something behind him, Pete turned around and followed his gaze. "What is it?" he asked.

Mel had observed the behavior of countless drug dealers on the streets of L.A., countless ganglords trying to look harmless as they ambled through the hood, nodding innocently to the patrol car as it passed by. Something in the demeanor of an oncoming stranger was similar.

"What do you suppose he's all about?" Mel whispered, nodding in the stranger's direction.

His words were more of a statement than a question. As Pete observed the enigmatic fellow, whose description matched that which David had given, the hair stood up on the back of his neck.

The Arab, who had stopped at a fruit stand, pretending to survey the wares, had not yet noticed the Americans.

"Look at how he babies that bag of his!" Pete muttered.

Mel ducked into a small trinket shop and pulled Pete with him. Hiding behind a rack of posters, he spoke softly. "Bro, how about you head on down toward the school? I'll stay at this end of the block, and let's see where he goes."

Pete did not need to think about it. Moving out just before the Arab began sauntering down the street again, he walked calmly but quickly toward the yeshiva. Mel, shielded by the posters, pretended to read a guidebook as Mammed drew near the corner.

As Pete arrived at the school, he was horrified to find that the door to the building was ajar. Two young students sat on the bench by the step, sunning themselves in their cotton vests and debating something they studied. Oblivious to what transpired, they sparrred jovially, their dark side-curls bobbing as their animated heads shook.

Casting a quick look over his shoulder, Pete saw that the Arab had not yet rounded the corner. Quickly, he approached the yeshivites, trying not to startle them.

"Hey, fellas," he hailed them. "You don't know me, but I think you'd better get inside!"

The students looked up at the American with wide eyes then, glancing behind him, suddenly darted into the building and pulled the door shut with a slam.

Pete, wheeling about, saw the Arab approaching.

It was a stunned Mammed who, upon rounding the corner, laid eyes on the big, blond informant. Stopping dead in his tracks, his olive face paled, and he nervously drew his bag from under his arm.

Pete stuck his thumbs in his belt loops and rocked back on the heels of his boots. "Howdy, stranger!" he said, in his best John Wayne. "New to these parts?"

Fumbling with the mouth of the bag, Mammed began to reach inside. At that instant, however, another American voice called out, "Don't even think about it!"

Shocked, Mammed wheeled about, ready to flee, but the instant his eyes landed on Mel, approaching from the head of the lane, he did a double-take.

Though he had been given the Westers' descriptions, they were an awesome duo in the flesh. With their unusual white-blond hair, their husky builds, and their Nordic height, they appeared like warrior angels, ready to smite him.

In a fit of rage and fear, Mammed grabbed the bag from his arm and began to swing it over his head, like an ancient sling. "Stand back!" he cried in a Lebanese accent. "This is Allah's will! You interfere with the will of Allah!"

The two brothers, seeing that he was not going to go down easily, began to circle him, darting the purse as it whizzed overhead.

Meanwhile, the young men of the yeshiva were gathering on the roof, going out through the top-story hatch and lining up along the balustrade. Thirty or forty of them had gathered before Pete looked up and saw them bunched precariously along the parapet.

"Back, fellas!" he shouted up at them. "This guy's dead serious!"

Mammed was working himself into a frenzy, the purse continuing to cut the air above his head. With a crazed expression, he lunged repeatedly at the Americans.

"Jihad!" he cried. "Jihad! Holy War against all Jews, and all lovers of Jews! Allah is the only true Glory! Death to the Shekinah!"

Hearing his ranting, people were drawn to the little street from all corners of the neighborhood. Soon a large group gathered at the intersection, many of them hurling Jewish epithets at the Muslim.

Distracted by their catcalls, Mammed glanced their way for a split second—just long enough that Pete was able to catch the handle of his whirling purse, like the rope of a whizzing tetherball as it spins around a schoolyard pole. Tearing it from the Arab, he took him off balance, and Mel was able to tackle him to the ground.

Instantly, the mob rushed forward, spitting and hissing at the terrorist.

Mel grappled with the would-be assassin until he had him facedown on the cobblestones, then locked the man's arms behind him, just as he had done to many a culprit on the Los Angeles streets.

"Back, back!" Pete warned the mob. "This is a very dangerous bag!" He held it carefully before him, and the crowd fell over one another in their rush to get away.

As Mel took off his belt, using it to tie up the Arab's wrists for lack of handcuffs, the Muslim continued to spew forth his venom.

Pete, meanwhile, had taken the bag to the bench outside the school and proceeded to open it gingerly.

Bringing out a little bundle that lay in the bottom, he saw the glass vial, and broke into a sweat. He was astonished that it had not been damaged in the fracas, but did not think he should handle it further, and placed it on his lap, afraid to make another move.

Meanwhile, more people were arriving on the scene, pushing through the crowd, amazed at what they had come upon. But these were not strangers. These were friends, and when Pete glanced up, he heaved a grateful sigh.

"Honey!" he cried. "You were supposed to stay away from here!"

Britta, who had come with her, hung near David as he stooped to help Mel.

Clustered about the ex-cop and the Lebanese were the rabbis. As the professor helped Mel bring the Muslim to his feet, the rabbis rushed into the school. Seeing that no harm had been done, they called to the rooftop gathering, telling the students it was safe to come down.

Honey, flying to Pete's side, slumped down beside him on the bench. "I couldn't stay away any longer!" she cried. "Oh, Pete, if anything had happened to you . . ."

Suddenly she noticed the vial he cradled and deduced immediately the nature of the attempted assault.

"Don't touch it!" Pete warned. Then, ever so tenderly rewrapping the container in its cloth, he slipped the bundle back into its purse. "Now, I think we have something to show the authorities," he said.

Honey looked up at her handsome man, tears welling in her eyes. "Do you know what you have done?" she sighed. "You have saved the choicest sons of Israel! You have saved Israel's future!"

CHAPTER 44

Ian, Emily, and their dear friend John Cromwell sat in the back of a silver-gray Mercedes limousine, as it sped out of Jerusalem and up the highway toward Tel Aviv. With them, in the side seat, was Rabbi Horace Benjamin, who was accompanying them to the airport.

For the second time in his life, Ian was fleeing Israel under a spate of media harassment.

Within a few hours of Pete and Mel's dramatic intervention at Yeshiva Shekinah, newspeople had descended on David Rothmeyer's house. Word had quickly reached the news hounds that the two heroes were staying there, having been seen entering the place after their bold escapade in the Old City. The Jerusalem bureau of CNN was at the site almost as quickly as local TV news crews, ready to flash the story across the globe.

After the scholars at the Consortium gallery had completed the analysis of the copper scroll, David had broken the news of Pete's message and the possible implications. The rabbis, anxious to go to the yeshiva, had sent Father McCurdy and John Cromwell back to the house under Clement's escort, asking the Britishers to wait there.

Unfortunately, when the CNN staff arrived at the house, demanding an interview with the American heroes, someone had caught a glimpse of Ian inside and recognized him as the notorious press dodger, the famed head of the Cave Scroll team.

Instantly the reporters were on him, clambering over him in the lobby, thrusting microphones in his face, demanding to know what connection he had to the Wester brothers.

Rabbi Benjamin, with the help of David and John, had managed to move the reporters out, then had tried to calm the shaken priest.

"I'll be all right," he said, catching his breath. "I'm just having a bad case of déjà vu."

Emily, left waiting at the old house, when Britta accompanied a distracted Honey back to the yeshiva, had heard the account of the rescue as one wily reporter managed to get to the Westers. She, also, was shaken.

"Ian!" she cried. "What's going on around here? I'm not sure I like any of this!"

Ian sympathized. "I know, I know! I think we've served our purpose in Israel. It's time to go home!"

After an unsuccessful attempt to persuade Ian to stay, at least until the computer collation was done and a more definitive conclusion could be gained from the information in Ian's scroll, Rabbi Benjamin had phoned the airport, making plane reservations on a night flight to London.

After saying farewells to David, whom he hoped to meet again, and to the rest of the American contingent, whom he had only just gotten to know, the old Oxfordian, his sister, and John Cromwell made a hasty departure.

Britta, with her love of a good story, had contacted the *London Times* about a potential feature series and had been assigned to stay on. So she hugged Emily fondly and promised to meet up with her at the Oxford pub when she returned.

Now, as the limousine cruised up the main highway that connected the length of Israel, Ian took what he believed would be his last glimpses of the Holy Land.

Leaning back in the leather seat, he let out a sigh. "I hope you know, Rabbi," he said, "I have a great love for your country. My desire to leave is not a reflection of my feelings for this land and its people."

Horace smiled at him with understanding. "Why do you think we keep such a low profile, ourselves, when we are here?" he said. "The entire political and spiritual climate is so sensitive that, given our agenda, our lives are in jeopardy all the time!"

"I suppose you speak mainly of Arab-Israeli tensions," Ian said. "But I am sure there are many Jews who would not welcome the idea of a return to the old ways—of the restoration of ancient rituals, for instance."

The priest had picked his words carefully, but the rabbi knew what he was referring to. "You speak of the return to animal sacrifices," Benjamin surmised.

The Oxford scholar nodded vehemently and Emily winced squeamishly. "I tried to tell David, and I am sure you must realize, that I consider this aspect of your plans to be utterly antithetical to my beliefs," Ian declared. "Not only do I spurn the notion on the grounds that I consider it a reversion to a more primitive role of religion, but it also flies in the face of New Testament teachings, the teachings, my friend, upon which I base my life!"

Rabbi Benjamin replied with energy, "Father McCurdy, not only am I not surprised by your statement, I would be surprised if you said otherwise. I realize that much of what the Consortium has undertaken, in its efforts to duplicate the ancient covenental forms of worship, is not only unChristian, but antithetical to much of modern Judaism."

Ian leaned toward the rabbi with a puzzled scowl. "Why then do you proceed?" he asked bluntly.

Before the rabbi could answer, however, Father McCurdy anticipated the response.

"I know," Ian said, "you are going to quote Jeremiah and Ezekiel, and you are going to refer to the vast body of prophecy that seems to indicate that such a temple and such worship must be reinstated at the coming of Messiah."

Horace smiled. "You are right," he said. "But I was also going to ask you why you have participated to the degree you have, if you are so opposed to what we are doing."

The luxury sedan hummed its way up the road, carrying Ian away from a venture that had been the biggest conundrum of his life. Sighing again, he glanced out the window at the passing terrain upon which the most fabulous dramas of human history had been enacted.

"You have me there," he confessed. "I have asked God that question a hundred times. Perhaps I will never know the answer."

Horace closed his eyes, as if he had something to say, but did not know how wise it was to say it. He remained in that attitude for so long that the others began to wonder if he had fallen asleep.

At last, smoothing his fluffy white beard with his wizened hands, he cleared his throat and said, "Ian, I am going to tell you something I have never had the nerve to tell anyone else. It is certain I would not share this if my colleagues were within earshot."

The three passengers glanced at one another, mystified.

"Let me begin by saying that, as much as I admire my colleagues, we do not always agree on everything. You know what they say about us Jews." He laughed. " 'Where there are two of us there are three opinions!' "

Ian echoed his laugh, and Emily felt less tense.

"Well," Horace went on, "if any of them knew, especially Uriel Katz, just how many friends I have among the Messianic contingent, they would probably disbar me from my position!"

"By 'Messianic' you mean 'Christian' Jews?" Ian asked.

"That is one way of saying it. They call themselves 'Messianic' for two good reasons. One: They believe in Jesus as the Jewish Messiah; and two: The term 'Christian' has too many evil connotations among Jews who have been persecuted. After all," he reminded them, "the mass of Germans during the Holocaust and the greatest of the persecutors throughout modern Jewish history have called themselves 'Christian.' "

Ian was aware of this and nodded sadly. "That is an irony, and a shame," he said. "Jesus was a Jew, and so were all of his followers. Certainly, he never would have endorsed such horror!"

"I believe you are right," Benjamin agreed. "Part of what I want to tell you, and what I have rarely admitted to anyone, is that I have a great deal of respect for Jesus of Nazareth. You might be surprised to know how many of my fellow scholars and thinkers feel the same."

Ian was surprised and showed it.

"But let me continue," Benjamin went on, "before I lose my nerve." At this, he took a deep breath and shot a glance back at the retreating highlands that cradled the Holy City.

"You might also be surprised to learn how many of my fellow rabbis are now participating in Messianic congregations. The Messianic movement is, to be frank, enormous in Israel and among Jews of many lands. It has the potential of the great evangelistic movements that took place in Europe and America in the nineteenth century!"

Ian studied Horace's expression curiously. "Rabbi," he said, "it sounds to me as though you, yourself, have been giving a lot of thought to the claims of Jesus. Is this what you are leading up to?"

Benjamin shrugged. "I may as well confess, I have even attended meetings once or twice. There is a Messianic congregation that meets every Wednesday evening at the YMCA in Jerusalem."

Ian was astonished. "Across from the King David Hotel?" he cried. "Why, Horace, the Y has been a bastion of Christian presence in Israel since the British Mandate!"

"So it has," the rabbi agreed. "Well, I got real brave and went to the meeting there. I tried not to draw attention to myself, but . . ." Again, he stroked his patriarchal beard, and the passengers chuckled.

"You would look like a rabbi even if you showed up in blue jeans!" Emily observed.

Horace agreed. "Then you see how much courage it took on my part to set foot in the place!"

Growing very sober, he went on. "The fact is that my own background is not so rigid as that of Katz and his ilk. He is a Talmudist of Eastern European descent, though he was born in Israel, and lives in Brooklyn. He, like his ancestors, prides himself on a very strict and literal view of Scripture."

Cheerfully, he added, "As for my background, my people are Hasidic, also from Eastern Europe. We take a deeper view of Scripture, one that allows for a lot of things the Talmudists cannot abide. Add to that the fact that I have also been trained in the Cabala. Do you know what that is, Father?"

Ian was familiar with the term. "Cabalism looks for hidden and mystic meanings in the Scriptures, am I right?"

"Exactly!" the rabbi said. "And we find them!"

Ian considered this. "So, how does that relate to the Messianics?"

Benjamin's face took on a look of awe as he related his experience with the strange congregation.

"The first night I attended one of the meetings," Horace explained, "the speaker was a Cabalist! He believed in Jesus as Messiah, and spoke at length of the years he had spent using the Cabalistic approach to his scripture studies. He claimed to have discovered that the name of Jesus, or *Yeshua*, is encoded throughout the Scriptures and is intertwined with references to Messiah, especially in those portions we call Messianic prophecy!"

"The name of Jesus?" Emily marveled. "How so?"

Benjamin spoke in a hush, obviously moved by the profound topic. "It is literally woven into the fabric of the ancient verses, each letter spaced perfectly in patterns and predictable arrangements in the orginal Hebrew text! I have looked at the material myself, and he is right! It is all there, just as he said!"

Ian was astounded. "Is it also to be found in the sections dealing with the future of Israel, for instance in Jeremiah?"

"That was the most astonishing part of the matter!" Benjamin exclaimed. "The very books that speak of the reinstating of Israel as a nation and of the worship on Mount Zion are interwoven with the name of *Yeshua!* Jeremiah, Ezekiel, Zechariah, Isaiah, Daniel—all of them!" The rabbi's eyes were full of zeal, his hands clasped ecstatically before him.

"So," Ian reasoned, "if this is true, are you thinking that your colleagues may be misconstruing their duties? Are you saying that the blood sacrifices may not be necessary?"

Benjamin stared at the floor of the limousine. "I have never voiced this to anyone," he confessed, "but I do wonder that very thing. Perhaps the encoding is a riddle, meant to direct us to Yeshua, as the ultimate sacrifice! If so"—he shrugged and lifted his hands—"many of the preparations that have already been made may ultimately be unnecessary—the vessels for blood, the training of the young priests in the execution of sacrifices, and so on." At last, with a sigh, the rabbi concluded, "In any case, the great majority of our preparations are perfectly useful. And so, I go on with my work."

Ian agreed. "Particularly the work of locating a high priest!"

"That is correct," Horace said. "The prophets are quite clear that there must be an officiating administrator in the temple, even though Messiah will be the King."

Ian sighed and leaned back in his seat. Suddenly it seemed there might be light at the end of the tunnel he had entered on blind faith. "Well," he marveled, "then perhaps you have answered another question that has been nagging at me."

"What is that?" Horace asked.

"I had no idea what a movement this Messianic thing was," he admitted. "However, I knew that, through the centuries, many Jews have been absorbed into the Church. Many Jews do not even think much of their ethnic heritage and consider themselves to be Christian by creed. My question, Horace, is this: What will you do, if, when you find the rightful heir, you discover that he is a Christian?"

Horace closed his eyes again. Then opening them, he pleaded with Ian, "Pray for us, my friend. The possibility you have posed is not at all remote. There are those among my colleagues who would disqualify such a person without a second thought. Pray that we will have ears to listen and hearts to discern the will of God."

CHAPTER 45

Over the next few days, the media bombardment of the old house where David lived waxed and waned, but never completely abated.

Though Pete and Mel Wester had offered no information that would keep the press coming back, any new bit of evidence regarding the incident or those involved sparked a fresh flurry of reporters smothering the street outside the house, sitting on the ancient gate, thrusting mikes at anyone who came or went.

The story the Westers gave was simply that they were American tourists who happened to be in the right place at the right time. The Arab had looked suspicious, Mel was trained in spotting suspicious characters, and *voilà*, they were able to nab him.

In the interim since the would-be assassin was wrestled to the ground and turned over to Israeli authorities, however, the international intelligence community had come up with personal profiles on the Westers, and even on Honey, which cast them in a very different, much more complex light. Bits and pieces of this information leaked to the press, just enough to keep them salivating and lunging at anyone who came near the house.

It was quickly learned, for instance, that Pete and Honey were from Montana, one of the U.S. hotbeds of Separatism. This tidbit immediately launched a full-scale investigation into their political backgrounds. When it was learned that they were somehow linked with White Supremacist groups in their area, there was no way that the press was going to leave them alone.

Yet, the Westers had rescued a Jewish community. They had intercepted an Arab terrorist on a mission to seek and destroy. And Ms. Aronstam had a Jewish name! This did not fit with the doctrines it was assumed they would espouse.

Coupled with this was the fact that they were staying in Jerusalem with members of the most right-wing movement in Israel. Then, to top it off, the head of the notorious Cave Scroll team, which had been accused of anti-Semitism, was guesting with them.

The facts, as they emerged, made for a banquet of contradiction and confusion that fed the talk shows, the evening news, and the tabloids for days.

One theory that emerged was that they were U.S. counter-intelligence agents, posing as Militia members or Freemen, yet actually spying on Arab activists! But even that notion did not tie in with Ian McCurdy's presence.

And what about this American professor, David Rothmeyer? Both he and McCurdy were linguistic archaeologists. Were they working on something together?

Of course, all of this attention and speculation caused no end of concern and fear on the part of the Consortium rabbis. They who had attempted for years to keep a low profile were suddenly under international inquiry.

It had not taken long for the media to piece together the fact that the seminary the Westers had rescued was under the auspices of the Temple Consortium. This had never been a hidden fact, any more than other activities of the temple movement had been hidden. Indeed the Consortium had created a public gallery to display all the artifacts and explain the hoped-for construction of a new temple.

What was covert was the search for the high priest.

That must be kept from the eyes of the world until such time as the man could be ushered safely into his place as Israel's religious representative. Until that time, there were too many enemy forces who would attempt to intercept that find, to circumvent the resurrection of Israel's sacred system.

At last, something happened that alleviated the tensions in the house, at least temporarily.

One evening, as David, Britta, Honey, and the Westers sat with the rabbis enjoying one of Anya's fabulous dinners, the front gate intercom buzzed.

"More reporters," Horace grumbled. "When will they ever quit?"

David stood up and went to the door. "Go away!" he shouted over the speaker. "We have nothing for you!"

This time, however, the reply was a surprise.

"Dr. Rothmeyer?" a dignified voice called out. "We are not members of the press. We have, in fact, just sent the press away. We are agents of your country, Dr. Rothmeyer. We have been sent by your government to ask some questions."

Just enough of this response could be heard from the dining room that the company stopped eating and listened.

"Agents?" Rothmeyer repeated. "One moment."

David hurried back to the dining room and stood in the doorway, looking to Rabbi Benjamin for guidance. "Did you hear?" he asked.

"We heard," the rabbi said. Then, glancing at his colleagues, who looked mystified, he rose up and went with David to the lobby.

After introducing himself over the intercom, the rabbi objected, "You have no right to place demands on us. Although we are American citizens, we are here on international business, living in an Israeli house. You have no right—"

Cutting into his defense, the agent's voice called out again, "Reverend—uh, Rabbi—you are correct. We have no papers from the Israeli government giving us entrance to your house. However, if you will only let us in, we think you will find that we mean no harm. In fact, we only mean to help."

Putting his hand over the intercom, Rabbi Benjamin whispered to David, "Go outside and look at their credentials. Ask them if they are armed. If they are not, let them in."

Moments later, two tall, middle-aged men in dark suits, bearing briefcases and badges identifying them as members of the Central Intelligence Agency, entered the house.

Rabbi Benjamin, not offering to shake their outstretched hands, simply asked, "What is it you want? Whom do you wish to see?"

"We want to see the Wester brothers and Ms. Aronstam," they replied.

"Who doesn't?" the rabbi said, in his best Yiddish twang.

Then, leading the men into the parlor, he sent David to fetch the three.

The moment the three Montanans entered the room, Honey looking intimidated and the brothers angry, the agents tried to reassure them.

"Agents Morris and Dalton," one of them said. "Please, be assured that we are here for your benefit."

Pete, who had never trusted authority, smirked and Mel nudged him. Honey pressed close to Pete and grabbed his hand.

"Mr. Wester," Morris said, confronting the long-haired Montanan, "you are quite the international hero."

Pete returned the agent's gaze suspiciously but said nothing.

"We have been sent to take you home, Mr. Wester, you and"—he nodded to the others—"your brother and Ms. Aronstam."

At this, Pete bristled. "Why should I go home?" he spat. "I've done nothing wrong, and I have not made the personal decision to go home just yet."

Dalton, the other agent, stepped in. "Mr. Wester," he said, "you must surely know that we are aware of your past involvement with the Aryan Nations and similar organizations."

Pete's face went red. "It's all over the news! How could you miss it? What no one seems to realize is that I'm done with that bunch!"

Mel placed a brotherly hand on Pete's shoulder, and Pete clamped his mouth shut.

"In that you are mistaken," the agent went on. "We think you have proven a new loyalty. You risked your life, and so did your brother, to save an Israeli school. Rather than doubt your intentions, the world seems to be siding with you. And so are we."

Pete breathed out through pursed lips. "So," he muttered, "what do you want? Why do we have to go home?"

"We believe that with your background, you would be a great asset to your government in tracking down and curtailing the activities of American terrorists."

"Possibly even *international* terrorists," Morris added.

Pete did not need an explanation of that last statement. Having taken radio messages from many foreigners, and having been present the night Fogarty and Altmeyer talked about their international connections, neither he nor Mel were surprised by the agent's assumption. Besides, the CIA network undoubtedly knew about their recent trip to Germany and probably had speculated wildly about it.

As for Dalton's allusion to the U.S. government, Pete gave a sardonic chuckle. "My government?" he growled. "My government is in league with the Militia and their sort up to its eyeballs! I don't trust you guys any more than I trust Fogarty or Altmeyer!"

The agents, to Pete's surprise, were not rattled. "We thought you might feel that way," Dalton said. "So we've brought you something that might help convince you we mean well."

He reached into his valise and pulled out a large, white envelope, emblazoned with the seal of CNN.

As Pete opened it, the agent explained. "We've already told the talk shows they can have you for as many interviews as you care to do. If you have dirt on the U.S. government, now's your chance to tell the world!"

Pete's hands trembled as he unfolded an invitation to appear on *Larry King Live*.

Honey and Mel read the note in amazement, as the agents added, "Rest assured, if what you have to say sounds at all plausible, there will be a full-scale investigation, the likes of which our country has never seen!"

Pete looked into the faces of the two emissaries. Maybe he did read sincerity there, he thought. "What about Fogarty and the others? How do we know we'll be safe?" he asked, drawing Honey closer.

The agent clamped his briefcase shut like the door of a prison cell. "We intend to see them behind bars!" he said. "As to any danger their followers might pose, we will grant you full protection, until you tell us otherwise."

Pete sighed. "I sure would like to see that scum locked away!" he said.

"Very well, then," Morris granted. "We are here to offer you safe passage home, at the expense of the American government."

"And full immunity for any improper involvements lurking in your background," Dalton added.

Pete turned to Honey and Mel. "What do you think?" he asked.

Mel nodded. "We're with you, bro, whatever you decide."

Honey squeezed his hand. "It looks like God has more work for you to do," she said with a smile.

"All right," Pete said. "When do we go?"

As soon as it was heralded that the Montana Contingent, as they were now being called, had returned to the U.S., the talk shows were abuzz with more speculations. Even in Israel, people could not turn on their televisions without encountering some new report related to the Westers.

Shortly after they left, information regarding the substance that the terrorist had intended to drop at Shekinah came pealing across the airwaves.

"A New and Even More Lethal Strain of Anthrax!" it was touted. "Developed for Use in Confined Areas, for the Decimation of Specific Populaces, Schools, Churches, Synagogues!"

The formulation had been traced to Ireland and was called "Bailey's Bug."

Scientists, analyzing the formula under highly controlled conditions, had found that it was viable outside its container for only moments and then was harmless. It seemed to be designed for use in concentrated areas, such as bus stations and other gathering places, making its detection and interception more difficult than the weapons of mass destruction intended for larger populations.

"No One Is Safe!" the press blared to the world. "Beware of all Suspicious Activity!"

One evening, David and Britta sat alone in the parlor of the old house, watching the international news on television. The rabbis were on the rooftop, enjoying the warm evening air.

David was about to turn off the TV, having had his fill of speculations about the terrorist attack when suddenly, flashing on the screen was a scene of a beautifully wooded property somewhere in northwestern America. Scruffy-looking characters in handcuffs were being dragged from a large log house, past a row of Harley motorcycles strewn across the yard.

"American agents of the Bureau of Alcohol, Tobacco and Firearms arrested several members of the White Aryan Nations in Montana today," the news anchor announced. "Led to their hideout by the owners of the property, the Americans who intervened in the recent attack on the seminary in Jerusalem, agents stormed the remote house and broke up a standoff of about a dozen Militia members."

David lurched forward. "Look at that!" he cried. "That must be the Wester house!"

Britta's eyes were wide, her mouth agape. "And those must be the honchos Pete worked for!" she exclaimed, as the screen changed.

"Heads of the group, James Fogarty of the Montana Supremacists, and Monte Altmeyer, German international mercenary, had fled the scene by the time agents arrived," the moderator continued, "but they were caught by roadblock in the small town of Thompson Falls."

The TV showed armed ATF agents handcuffing a tall, silver-haired man and a dark fellow in army camouflage. Spread-legged, they leaned against a black Suburban as the agents frisked them.

Then, switching again to the Wester house, the news coverage returned to the drama of the Bull River arrests.

"I think I see Honey!" Britta exclaimed. "Isn't that she with Pete and Mel . . . look, back behind the bikers!"

Sure enough, as the hogster contingent, the only members of the Fogarty bunch who had remained at the vacated Aryan headquarters, were hauled away, they spat profanities and made obscene gestures with the fingers of their handcuffed hands. These obscenities were directed at a trio of onlookers, who stood on the porch of the log house, watching them go with faces of relief.

"Honey looks happy!" Britta observed. "Wow! She sure has a story to tell!"

David glanced at Britta. "Always the reporter!" he said with a laugh.

"Sure," she replied. "But, just think, if I didn't have a nose for news, I never would have met you."

David's heart raced. Glancing toward the hallway, he made sure that no rabbi or housekeeper was nearby. Then, for the first time since he had held her hand in the London street, David made a closer move. Bending toward the blond-haired darling, he cupped her face in his hands, and kissed her.

CHAPTER 46

June/*Sivan*

It was the time of the Feast of Pentecost in Jerusalem, the ancient and traditional holiday celebrating the first harvest of the year. Pentecost, meaning "fifty days," indicated that the festival was to take place seven weeks after Passover. It was the highlight summer event throughout Israel.

The celebration was like the Sabbath, in that no work was to be done, and families offered their rabbis small loaves of barley bread in commemoration of the harvest and in gratitude for the provisions of God.

All male Jews were supposed to attend services on this day. In Jerusalem, many congregations held special gatherings in the court of the Western Wall.

Though Britta had not been raised as a Jew, she rose with the sun this Pentecost morning, full of excitement for the day. She had plans to meet her relatives from Nazareth, Great-uncle Reg and Great-aunt Deborah, who were coming down to Jerusalem for the festival.

She had contacted her uncle when she first arrived in Israel, but, given the sensitive nature of her involvement there, she had put off a visit until things calmed down.

The *Times* had kept her in Israel, as she followed up on a feature series that grew out of the Wester saga, and she had been here for several weeks now, staying at the Consortium house.

It seemed to be perfect timing that Uncle Reg should be

coming her way now, for the world press had taken its focus off the Consortium for the moment, as it followed the Wester story across the seas.

Meeting David and Rabbi Benjamin for breakfast on the balcony overlooking the Hinnom Valley, Britta was radiant in a simple pink dress, her hair reflecting the golden light of morning and her cheeks flushed with the blush of love. She could scarcely believe how lucky she was, to be in the most amazing city on earth and to be sharing it with a wonderful man like David Rothmeyer.

"Sleep well?" David asked, pouring her a cup of coffee as she sat down.

"Very!" Britta said.

Actually, that was not true. She had tossed and turned all night in her room, savoring thoughts of the professor, as she had done too many nights since they had first shared a kiss.

Rabbi Benjamin glanced up from his Sunday edition of the *Jerusalem Post*. Had the enamored couple looked at him, they would have seen a knowing twinkle in his eye before he ducked, smiling behind his newspaper again.

"Good morning, Rabbi Ben," Britta said. "This is a wonderful day! I'm going to meet my Uncle Reginald at the Western Wall. He's coming down to celebrate with Zachary, his son, who attends a synagogue here."

"How nice," Horace replied, putting down his paper again. "I did not know you had family in Israel."

"My uncle—actually he's my great uncle—was a famous photojournalist during World War Two. He moved here after doing a photo-documentary on Holocaust immigrants. His work inspired me to become a journalist."

Then, dropping her voice a little, she gave a girlish giggle. "Would you believe he and Emily McCurdy were sweethearts during the war?"

The rabbi raised his eyebrows. "It is a small world," he said.

Then, as an afterthought, he asked, "Is your family Jewish, Ms. Hayworth?"

"On my mother's side," she replied. "We were raised Anglican. Uncle Reg married a Jewish woman, but even she is one of those . . . how do you say it—"

"Messianics?" the rabbi guessed.

"That's it!" Britta said. Then with a little shrug, "I really don't understand all of that. Somehow, they work it out, mixing the two religions."

"So," the rabbi inquired further, "your uncle's son—Zachary, is it? Is he Messianic, as well?"

Britta nodded. "I believe so. He has been studying Judaism for years, even made his bar mitzvah. But I think he attends meetings in a Christian building."

Horace made no issue of his thoughts regarding the Messianics. He had shared his views with Ian, but David and Britta were not theologians. Besides, he did not wish to get into a discussion of something that, if Uriel or the others were to overhear, could cause dissension on such a bright and glorious day.

"Are the others going to join us?" Britta asked, glancing down the steps that led to the rabbis' bedrooms.

"They were up hours ago," Horace replied. "They should be returning soon. They went to the Wall to do morning prayers before dawn."

Britta was amazed. "Such devotion!" she said. "I don't think I could ever get up that early."

David laughed. "Rabbi Ben and I never went to sleep," he said. "We were at the computer lab! Clement thinks they may have an answer today!"

Benjamin leaned across the table. "Don't tell the others," he said. "They would not approve."

Britta shook her head. "What's to disapprove?" she asked.

"They would accuse me of working on a holy day," he said with a wink. "The way I see it, the computers are doing the work. We only feed them!"

David and Britta stifled grins, not fully understanding his rationale, or the need for it.

"So," Britta asked, "what has the lab been working on since they received Honey's and Ian's material? I thought it all fit together quite nicely."

"It did," David replied. "Since then, it has been a matter of weaving in the mass of e-mails, faxes, and letters that continue to pour in from around the world, from people wishing to offer what they know of family histories. The lab has come quite close several times to a final genealogy. Always, though, there is something not quite perfect. We hope it is only a matter of time before an exact match comes in."

Suddenly their conversation was interrupted by another buzz at the front gate. From down the winding stairs, they could hear Anya answering the intercom. Soon, she was admitting Clement, the computer master, to the lobby and led him to the veranda as she brought the group a tray of breakfast.

When the young scholar explained his visit, however, no one cared about food.

His eyes bleary from a night in front of monitors, he carried a sheaf of paper in one hand, along with an airmail packet. "Rabbi! Professor!" he cried, tossing the papers onto the table. "I believe we have it!"

"The final list?" Benjamin gasped.

David scooped up the computer material and perused it, while Clement explained: "We were just sorting through a pile of mail we received a few days ago. Since the strongest line we had found runs through Britain, we decided to only look at postmarks or e-mails from that area, hoping to narrow the chore. We came upon this airmail package, from some elderly woman in Chesworth, England. When we collated her information into what we already had . . . *bingo*! It was there!"

Britta and Rabbi Benjamin left their seats and huddled over David's back, reading the letter. Written in the cramped characters typical of old folks' handwriting, it was nonetheless very detailed and well documented.

"Who wrote it?" Britta asked, reaching for the envelope and glancing at the return address.

"Dahlia Knight," David said. "What a name!"

"Dahlia?" Britta repeated. "I have a distant cousin named Dahlia, on my mother's side. Could it be?"

As David and the rabbi scanned the letter's contents, Britta was deep in thought, "In fact . . . I remember mother saying how Dahlia is into genealogy, big time! She has always kept copious records, writing for pictures of all the family weddings, asking for the names of every newborn, every new in-law! Apparently she used to bore the family stiff every time they visited, dragging out photo albums and reciting the family tree!"

David pulled an older letter from the packet, one with a broken wax seal. As he read it, his eyes grew wide. "Listen to this!" he exclaimed. "The old woman says that this letter, handed on by her great-grandparents, refers to a tradition of the '*kohen zadokim*', the righteous Cohen, going way back in her ancestry. She says that the ancient family manor is called Castlemont on Wandermere!"

Benjamin jolted. "That is the name the Dachau document gives as the Kahana home in England!"

David nodded affirmatively.

Then, with a sharp breath, the professor turned to Britta. "Have you ever met this Dahlia?" he asked.

"No . . . why?" Britta replied.

"Well, she's never met your Uncle Reg, but she seems to know about him. Claims that Reginald Cohen, a photographer, is descended from that line!"

Benjamin and David studied Britta's awestruck face. "Uncle R-Reg?" she stammered. "A high priest?" She did not know whether to laugh or cry, and stared at the letter, stunned.

"Now, dear," Horace said, "if your uncle is the one she refers to, he is probably much too old to take up the mantle of such leadership."

David nodded. "Besides," he said, trying to be gentle, "didn't you tell me that your uncle was wounded in the war, that he walks with a limp?"

Britta sighed. "Yes. Does that also disqualify him?"

Horace nodded. "It would, Ms. Hayworth."

Then, suddenly a light flashed through his old eyes. Glancing at Clement and David, then focusing on Britta, he exclaimed, "You said he has a son? A Cohen male?"

Britta gasped. "Zachary! Zachary Cohen! My second cousin!"

David folded up the papers and reached for his ever-ready briefcase. Stuffing them inside, he stood up and looked to the rabbi for the go-ahead.

Horace gestured toward the door. "May we accompany you to the Western Wall, Ms. Hayworth?" he asked. "We'd like to meet this fellow."

CHAPTER 47

Sunlight flooded the gigantic Western Wall plaza as Britta, Rabbi Benjamin, Clement, and David made their way down the stairs leading from the Old City.

Against the wall, in fenced courtyards on either side of a low divider that separated men from women, hundreds of worshipers sang, prayed, and read the Scriptures together, remembering the bounty of the earth and the blessings of heaven.

As always, the men's court was much fuller than the women's, as entire congregations of Jewish males representing many synagogues throughout Israel and around the world met in clusters about the pavement.

This holiday was almost as joyous as Passover, which coincided with the Christian celebration of Easter. It had little of the somber reflectiveness of Yom Kippur, when the nation remembered its collective and individual sins.

For Britta, who had never witnessed this Jewish festival, the sight of dozens of groups dancing and singing as huge, decorated cylinders were carried into the men's court—containers for the Torahs of the many congregations—was awesome indeed.

Old men, in flat black hats or woven yarmulkes, decked out in striped prayer shawls, leaned against the wall, praying in hope-filled tones for the coming of Messiah and the peace of Jerusalem.

Younger men sat on chairs, hunched together over portions of scripture, reading to one another and praying, their heads uniformly covered with skull caps and their ringlets bobbing with the rhythmic movements of their heads.

On the women's side of the divider, young ladies helped older ones to find places where they could fit small folded pieces of paper into the cracks of the wall's ancient stonework. Each slip contained a prayer, personal or universal. Every crevice of the retaining wall—the only remnant of the ancient temple—was so stuffed with notes that it was a wonder one more could fit in.

The group from the Consortium did not immediately enter the plaza, but stood on the stairs while Britta tried to locate her uncle.

Rabbi Benjamin handed David a prayer shawl which he had grabbed when they left the house. "Here," he said, "you'll need this."

As David spread the shawl over his shoulders, Britta suddenly brightened.

"I think I see him!" she said. "Over against the other wall!"

Rabbi Benjamin and David followed her pointing finger to a sizable group of people gathered away from the fenced-off areas. This was a mix of men and women, some dressed in traditional Jewish garb, and others not. They stood near the tunnel used as a priestly storehouse in ancient times, listening to an animated speaker as he addressed the flock.

"Shall we join them?" Rabbi Benjamin suggested.

The four crossed the plaza, then stood on the edge of the crowd, not wishing to interrupt the meeting, though some of the people recognized Horace and greeted him warmly.

"For the Messianic Jew, Pentecost is a double blessing!" the congregation's rabbi declared, his arms spread wide and his face radiant. "This is not only the festival of the firstfruits of the ground, but we remember that the Church was born on Pentecost Sunday! On that day," he cried, "the Holy Spirit descended on a gathering of those early Jewish Christians, in a house not far from here, and empowered them to preach the gospel to all nations!" Then gesturing toward Temple Mount, he proclaimed, "On that day, the apostle Peter preached in the court of the Gentiles, and his followers echoed his proclamations about *Yeshua*—Jesus, the Messiah—each speaking in a new and foreign tongue, so that people of the many nations gathered there could receive the story in their own languages! On that day," he cried again, "three thousand of our fellow Jews were ushered into the kingdom, receiving the word of truth and affirming that Jesus was the Anointed One, the one sent for the redemption of Israel!"

For the moment, David wasn't concentrating on the rabbi's message. He was scanning the gathering, looking for someone special.

He did not know what the man would look like, but he knew that, somehow, he would recognize him. As he walked around the perimeter of the meeting, his eyes fell on a dark, handsome man of about thirty, who sat casually on a ledge at the foot of the wall, his prayer shawl thrown loosely over one shoulder and his head bowed in contemplation of the message.

What struck David about this fellow was not only the sincerity of his countenance, but also his peaceful appearance. It occurred to the professor that he looked a little like artists' conceptions of Jesus that he had seen in Christian homes. David was also impressed that the young man seemed to sit apart, as though he enjoyed worshiping God one on one.

As the professor stood watching this stranger, Britta tugged on his sleeve. Wheeling about, David found that she had been joined by an older man and woman, who embraced her on either side.

The elderly gentleman was perfectly British, David could see. Tall and dignified, he leaned on a cane. His beautiful wife was clearly Jewish, her olive complexion framed by a fall of wavy, silver hair.

"David," Britta said, "meet Uncle Reginald and Aunt Deborah."

David thrust out his hand and shook theirs eagerly. "I am very happy to meet you, sir!" he said, focusing on the tall Cohen.

Reg greeted him with curiosity. "Britta tells me you wish to meet my son?"

"I do!" David replied. "Is he here?"

It was no surprise to the professor when the tall Briton pointed out the very fellow whom he had been observing.

"Thank you!" David said.

Shaking Reg's hand again, he nodded respectfully to Britta's aunt, then excused himself, and crossed the court to the place where the young man was seated.

For a long moment, he stood waiting for him to glance his way.

When the meditator did at last lift his eyes from his prayers and found a stranger gazing on him, he was bewildered. "Hello," he said shyly.

David's heart raced as he drew closer to the man.

"Zachary Cohen?" he said. "My name is David Rothmeyer. You don't know me, but I have been looking for you for a long time!"

THE ORACLE

ELLEN GUNDERSON TRAYLOR

WORD PUBLISHING
NASHVILLE
A Thomas Nelson Company

THE ORACLE

A NOTE FROM THE AUTHOR:

This book and its predecessor, *The Priest*, are works of fiction. However, they are based on actual events and characters existing today. I encourage the reader to keep abreast of current events, which confirm the scenario of both volumes on a daily basis.

If you have any questions regarding these works, please feel free to contact me by e-mail at:

porthole@digisys.net

and visit my Web site at

http://ellentraylor.com

God Bless You!

ISBN 0-7394-1865-3

Printed in the United States of America

To my husband,
Richard,
historical detective
par excellence

and

To my parents,
who could have been
writers.

BACKGROUND STORY TO *THE ORACLE*

David Rothmeyer, a young archaeology professor, received a cryptic invitation to do secret research for a mysterious Israeli group calling themselves the Temple Consortium. When he accepted, he had no idea that his research, if successful, could trigger a world crisis of unprecedented proportions.

The Consortium was eager to possess a missing Dead Sea Scroll that they believed would reveal the genealogical line from Aaron and would pinpoint the identity of Judaism's true high priest. With the authentic priesthood in place, they would be able to rebuild their Temple and, for the first time in almost two thousand years, reinstate their ancient Levitical worship in its pristine form.

But powerful forces were determined to block David's research: Islamic groups because it would mean destroying the Dome of the Rock, the sacred Islamic shrine that occupies the holy ground where the Temple must be built; and a rightist militia group in Montana with a white supremacist agenda that marked Judaism as a threat to Western civilization.

As David pursued leads from Dachau to Oxford to the caves of Qumran, it became apparent that many lives were in grave danger and he must depend on the help of a small group that providentially formed around him, a group that included ex–white supremacist Pete Wester; his Jewish girlfriend, Honey Aronstam; and his policeman brother, Mel; Oxford scholar Father Ian McCurdy, who for nearly fifty years had hidden away the explosive document that was the key to David's quest; McCurdy's sister, Emily, who as a World War II Red Cross nurse had preseved a crucial Jewish secret; and Britta Hayworth, a beautiful and persistent British reporter.

When David was ultimately successful in locating the legitimate heir to the priesthood, the cornerstone of Israel's future, he realized that the fate of civilization hinged on the results. His discovery could usher in the Apocalypse and the end of the world as he knew it . . .

CHAPTER 1

Lamar Jackson pressed his small body back into a corner of the booth at the all-night fast-food restaurant. Wadding the tattered cuff of his man-sized flannel shirt into one fist, he swiped it across his teary face and tried not to sniffle.

The burger shop's swing-shift busboy was getting close, the sound of his push broom sweeping down the aisle toward the front door. Any second he would be aiming for the base of Lamar's booth. There was no way he would fail to notice the little fellow huddled there.

Lamar drew his knees up to his chest, his feet propped on the seat, and hid his face in his too-long cuffs, trying to be invisible.

The sound of the broom and the busboy's plodding steps stopped short. "Hey, kid. You been here all night?" the teenager grumbled. "Ain't I told you, you can't hang out here? It's nearly mornin'. Better git!"

Lamar lifted his eyes to the bigger black boy. The night help in this place was used to shooing Lamar away. Sometimes his mother showed up to haul the child off. But that would have been hours ago. It appeared she'd forgotten him this time.

The busboy had never gotten used to Lamar's plaintive face. His big, wide eyes, dark as midnight, the whites contrasting sharply with his dark skin, had a winsome appeal. Always, they were sad eyes, pleading, though the child himself never begged.

"You hungry, I 'spose," the busboy guessed. Leaning on his broom, he studied the frail youngster. "Don't yo' mama never feed you?"

The child did not reply, but his eyes did turn fleetingly toward the kitchen. Though he could not see it beyond the seat's high vinyl back, the smell of coffee brewing and biscuits baking made his stomach growl.

The busboy sighed. Glancing at the front door, and seeing no customer at this predawn hour, he nodded his head toward the counter.

Quick as a cat off a fence, Lamar hopped off the bench and ran down the aisle of the vacant shop. The busboy followed, ducked into the kitchen, and, within seconds, produced a small white sack with the logo of the burger chain.

"Now, you git! Hear?" he commanded. "And don't you stop to look in that bag 'til you're down the street!"

Lamar smiled, his teeth white as the whites of his bright eyes. Heading for the door, he turned to wave good-bye, nearly colliding with a customer just entering the store.

The busboy quickly pushed a button on the cash register, causing the drawer to open with a ding, and pretended to drop money in the till, as though he had just made a sale. Shutting the drawer, he nodded at the incoming diner as Lamar flew out the door.

"Mornin', mister," he said. "How can I help you?"

Lamar scurried down the street, following a route he had taken many a morning of his young life.

The clean, beautiful buildings of this section of Washington, D.C., glowed rosy in the spring dawn: towering modernistic structures of steel and granite with tinted windows, intermingled with older, more elegant architecture. Office buildings, silent and austere in the prework hour, and hotels with sleepy doormen in sharp uniforms on guard for the earliest limousine, represented a strata of society to which Lamar was a stranger and likely always would be, though he was born in their shadow.

Despite the fact that he was a native of the area, they disregarded him and everyone like him. He was too young to grasp his social status, but, with age and continuing experience, his position on the lowest rung of the social ladder would become clear to him. For now he lived one day at a time, thinking mainly of where he would get his next meal, and, as sunset arrived, where he would sleep.

Many a morning he had made his way down this broad, angling avenue that led from the fast-food shop to a gigantic train terminal. He did not remember the first time he had made this journey. Probably his mother had carried him this way when he was too small to walk; he did remember how she had held his hand time and again, guiding him across the wide street and through the grassy expanse of parkland he traversed now.

Blocks ahead, he would come to an immense circular roadway that went round and round a fabulous fountain. Behind that fountain, mountains of terraces and stairways led to the gargantuan depot with its green-copper-and-crystal dome, where, it seemed to Lamar, all the trains in the world and all the subways in the world converged.

That was a safe haven for the likes of Lamar and his mother. People did not notice them there, did not question them; some even paid coins to keep them from bothering them. Lamar was old enough now to go there without his mother. On mornings like this, he had no choice but to go alone, for his mother was not able to come.

Breathing hard from his quick sprint down the avenue, Lamar could no longer ignore the gnawing at his ribs. The aroma from the warm fast-food bag made him salivate. Choosing a tree in the grassy park, he glanced shrewdly about and, seeing no one near, plopped down between two large roots.

Ravenous, he tore into the sack and pulled out two hot breakfast sandwiches. Todd, the teenager at the burger shop, seemed to know that Lamar liked sausage muffins without egg best. Maybe he had found discarded yolk on Lamar's plate on the rare occasions when he had fed him in the store. This morning, Lamar would have been hungry enough to eat even the egg, but Todd had given him sausage muffins with cheese, and the little boy dove into the food with gusto.

Leaning back against the tree, he gobbled and smacked until the hunger pangs subsided. He could hear his mother say, "Have some dignity, chile!" He was not sure what "dignity" was, but he couldn't muster it when he was hungry.

Savoring the last hunk of the second sandwich, he noticed that Todd had slipped something extra into the bag. As he dipped his hand inside, his face beamed. "No way!" he whispered, blowing a soft whistle of breath. He pulled out a slim wrapper, in which was a succulent, crispy potato cake, and he dove into it as though he had eaten nothing for days.

Todd was hip, Lamar thought. In fact, he was his hero. Lamar hoped maybe he could be like Todd someday, wearing a white cap and pushing a broom in an important place. It was a worthy dream, and he often indulged it.

But now he was thirsty. Todd, in his hurry, had not given him any juice.

Across a path, a drinking fountain promised to quench Lamar's thirst. The fact that an old man slept in front of it, his head propped on the ledge at its base, his feet covered with newspaper, did not faze Lamar. He was used to stepping around such people. This time of year, they slept most anywhere, needing little shelter. In winter they curled up on the steam grates set into the sidewalks, keeping warm in bunches, until driven away by building attendants each morning.

Lamar remembered sleeping that way a few times, cuddling under his mother's thin coat, as she huddled over a grate. He was not afraid of one old tramp by a drinking fountain.

Gingerly, he stepped around the dozing vagrant. Reaching the far side of the fountain, he jumped onto the ledge and pushed the big chrome button on the faucet. Pulling himself up on tiptoe, he slurped the cold water between his lips. The old fellow at the base roused at the sound and muttered something, tucking his feet up with the newspapers and turning over.

Even from the height of the fountain top, Lamar could smell the liquor on the old man's breath, the vapors that exuded from his clothes and his entire body. It was an odor to which Lamar was accustomed, for his mother often smelled that way.

His thirst slaked, Lamar jumped down from the ledge, tossed his empty bag into a trash canister, and proceeded down the parkway. His mother had taught him to dispose of garbage in the big waste cans that were everywhere in D.C. She said that if she ever had a house, it would be tidy.

Proceeding toward his destination, Lamar neared the elaborate Victorian train station. There was always activity around the place, but early morning was the quietest time, as commuter routes from Arlington, Alexandria, and cities as far away as Baltimore were less traveled at that time.

Lamar skirted the fabulous fountain that formed the centerpiece of the circular drive in front of the station, the gigantic, lounging statue of Neptune, with his mermaid consorts, staring down at him with an austere expression.

He hurried up the station's broad granite steps and, avoiding the eyes of the custodian sweeping the lobby floor, ran for the escalator that took him to one of the lower subway levels. There he could find a safe corner, away from the other street people, where he could watch the sleek trains that whizzed to a stop in the cavernous tunnel and unloaded well-dressed passengers from worlds and ways of life he could only imagine.

Anytime he came here he watched for one passenger in particular to emerge from the 5:02 train on weekday mornings. More often than not, his expectation was rewarded.

The person he watched for was of special interest because he represented everything Lamar thought greatness must be. Lamar had learned his name, Calvin Jefferson, when he had seen his picture on the front page of a newspaper at Todd's fast-food place. He had observed him many times as he got off the subway train, dressed in a fine suit, briefcase in hand. A tall black man with touches of gray in his hair, but a youthful face and athletic build, he carried himself with a dignity Lamar rarely saw in the streets.

Each morning, when the man exited the train, he followed the same routine, walking to the newspaper machine near the rail line, depositing several coins, opening the door to the box, and taking out the morning paper. Quickly he would scan the front page, then fold the paper, stuff it under one arm, check his watch, and head for the escalator.

Lamar had always figured he was a man of importance. His mother called such people "white shirts," though this man sometimes wore shirts of pale hues, or with thin colored stripes.

The day Lamar had learned the man's name, he had been pictured on the front page of the *Washington Post*, flanked by a couple of soldiers whose hands he held proudly in the air.

All three men had broad smiles, but the two soldiers looked as though they had been beaten up.

Lamar, who could not read, stared at the newspaper, which had been left on the table by some customer. He had not seen the man at the train station for a few days and was amazed to see him in the photo.

When Todd came by, bringing his secret ration, Lamar had pointed to the picture. "Who's that?" he'd asked, placing a finger on the central figure.

Todd had bent over the table, studying the photo.

"Oh, that's one brave man," he had replied. "That's Senator Calvin Jefferson, and he just rescued those guys from prison in a foreign country. They're soldiers, and the enemy was gonna kill 'em if Jefferson hadn't helped out!"

Lamar's eyes grew wider as he looked at the picture, his little mouth forming an amazed "Oh."

"Yeah," Todd went on. "Senator Jefferson travels all over the world, trying to patch things up between folks. I guess you'd say it's his callin'."

Lamar looked quizzical.

"*Callin'*," Todd repeated. "You know . . . like what he was born for. He's been tryin' to make peace between folks since the days of Martin Luther King!"

Now, that was a name that needed no introduction. Lamar had heard of the civil rights leader all his young life, and he knew what he stood for.

Todd's linking of Senator Jefferson with that auspicious black hero had sealed his importance in Lamar's mind. Many a morning, he rushed to the train station, just to catch a glimpse of the man with the "callin'."

Lamar did not know that not everyone had such high opinions of Jefferson as Todd expressed. The senator was, in fact, quite a controversial character, particularly because of his approach to politics in foreign countries. Many people, especially those of the southern state he represented, wished he'd just focus on their own interests, and "keep his nose out" of matters that didn't concern them.

But the little boy who watched for him this morning knew nothing of all that. To him, the man was a symbol of everything a black man could become. The child, who did not even know who his own father was, had come to identify personally with this stranger.

Once, the senator had smiled at him! Yes, one morning, as Lamar had observed his early hour routine, the man had caught a glimpse of him where he sat snuggled between a phone booth and a waste can, his knees drawn up under his chin, and his wide, worshipful eyes following his every move.

"Hi, young man," Jefferson had greeted. A sad expression filled the man's eyes as he looked about the empty platform. "Where's your mama?" he asked. "You alone, child?"

Lamar's voice, when he found it, was a tiny whisper, so that the man drew near and bent over him.

"What's that?" he asked.

Lamar nervously pointed to the women's rest room across the tiled hallway. "She in there," he lied.

"Ah," the man said, smiling again. Reaching out, he patted Lamar on his wooly head and said, "You come here often?"

Lamar nodded. Then, remembering that loiterers were not welcome here, he abruptly shook his head. "No, sir . . ."

Senator Jefferson stood up and eyed him doubtfully. Then, looking at his watch, he said, "You take care, now. Hear?"

The boy nodded, and as the senator departed, Lamar saw him cast a dubious eye toward the women's lavatory.

Ever since then, Lamar had avoided being seen by the senator. Though he craved another word, another touch from the man, he didn't want to be questioned, and possibly evicted, from the warm, sheltering station.

It had been a couple of weeks since Lamar had seen the senator. He knew this probably meant he was on some faraway journey, to some place on earth with a name hard to pronounce. In his ignorant small-boy way, he tried to keep track of the man, often asking Todd if he had seen a picture of him in the paper, or if he had read anything about him.

He had learned, over the months of watching the senator and of talking to Todd, that Jefferson traveled widely, taking care of his "callin'."

Lamar hunkered down on the floor at the end of a platform bench this morning. No one sat there, and he had a nice view down the tracks. The clock on the hallway wall said five o'clock. Lamar didn't know how to read time, but he knew the position of the hands just before the sound of the 5:02 train screeched into the tunnel and came to a stop.

Just on time, the sound of the approaching train could be heard from the dawn light at the end of the dimly lit passageway. Lamar's pulse surged as it always did when the train arrived. Would Jefferson be here this morning?

The big, shining conveyance sped like a robotic snake into the tunnel, whisked to a stop, and throbbed for a quick moment on the rail, its side doors flying back, depositing a few dozen commuters onto the platform.

There he was, the senator! Dressed today in a crisp, khaki-colored sport suit, he went, as usual, to the paper stand, reached into his pocket for his coins, and began putting them in the slot.

Also, as usual, all the other commuters hurried for the escalator, momentarily leaving the senator the sole occupant of the platform.

As Lamar's admiring eyes followed his every move, however, the routine was suddenly broken. Down the hallway, just beyond the door to the women's rest room, another door burst open, this one to the men's lavatory. Before Lamar or the senator could comprehend their movement, a group of four young men, all with shaved heads, heavily tattooed arms, and dressed in army camouflage, barged through the hall, skidding to a halt beside the paper stand.

Grasping the senator, they wrestled him to the floor. As one held a hand over his open mouth, stifling his cry, another kicked him repeatedly in the side with his heavy combat boots. A third drew a gun from beneath a speckled green jacket and buried it in the senator's rib cage. A silencer muffled the gunshot as he pumped a round into the man's body.

Lamar, horrified, choked back his own cry, and hunched invisibly beside the bench. The fourth skinhead grabbed for the senator's valise as the other three dragged the body toward the rail pit.

"Hurry!" growled the one who held the valise. "Git 'im down there!"

With a heave, the three men tossed the limp body into the pit, and then, clapping one another on the back, their faces spread in gruesome grins, they followed the fourth down the hallway and disappeared into a utility elevator.

Lamar, shaken to the core, jumped up from his hiding place and raced to the edge of the rail pit. "Sen'tor!" he cried. "Mama!"

Sprawled across the tracks was the corpse, an oozing red gash growing wider and spreading blood down the front of the khaki jacket.

From the dark tunnel the sound of the 5:10 blasted Lamar's ears.

For a split second the boy considered jumping into the pit and trying to pull the body off the tracks. But he knew such a feat was beyond his strength.

Slumping to his knees, he stared helplessly at the oncoming engine and cried out loudly.

But no one heard him. No one waited for the train, which would only be stopping here to let people out, and the engineer, guzzling on a coffee-thermos, neither saw the body nor registered Lamar's cry beyond the racket of the wheels.

Lamar clamped his hands over his eyes and squeezed them tight as the computerized train barreled toward the body. Blood splattered up from the pit and onto the platform as the corpse was crushed.

By the time the doors of the commuter train opened beside him, Lamar was oblivious. Having fallen into a merciful faint, he did not know that sprays of blood were on his own clothes and face.

The train was already speeding away when the horrified passengers, who had just emerged onto the tunnel platform, saw the child. Several of them whisked him to the security office and alerted the guards. Others, peering down onto the vacated tracks, spotted the unrecognizable body left mangled by the wheels.

Not until Lamar Jackson was capable of relating what he had witnessed, would anyone but he know that it was Calvin Jefferson who lay there, the victim of escaped assassins.

CHAPTER 2

Professor David Rothmeyer was having trouble concentrating on the pile of grade sheets stacked on his cluttered desk. Warm spring sunlight spilled in shafts through the tall maples outside his office window, streaking the thick, manicured lawn of the Midwest University quad with chartreuse stripes. It was a glorious afternoon, far too glorious to be spent cooped up inside.

Though he dutifully attempted to make headway through the paper pile, his mind kept wandering. When he was not watching clusters of students hurrying for final exams across the arbored grounds, he was distracted by a small gold-framed photo that he allowed to stare at him from a bookshelf beside the window.

The face gazing out from the frame was winsome and sweet, set off by a tousle of yellow curls. The blue eyes betrayed an almost impish quality, befitting the charming character of the young woman. But, David knew, she was no imp. Britta Hayworth, while a delightful personality, was also a serious professional.

It had been nearly a year since he had made her acquaintance. The circumstances under which he had come to know her had revolved around the most intriguing and unforgettable experiences of his life.

While he should have been working on his papers, he found his thoughts drifting relentlessly back over the adventure that had brought her across his path. This wandering of the mind was nothing new. In fact, Professor Rothmeyer, Doctor of Archaeology and Ancient Languages, had not been the same man, and his interests had forever been changed since the events that he had dubbed his "Jerusalem experience."

Britta Hayworth had been only one of the colorful and intriguing figures who had filled those most exciting days. A young reporter for the *London Times*, Britta had been investigating an enigmatic member of the original Cave Scroll team when he met her. David himself had been enlisted by an equally mysterious group called the Temple Consortium to track down the genealogy of the High Priest of Israel, third-millennium descendant of Aaron, brother of the prophet Moses.

David's quest had taken him from this college town of Columbus, Ohio, to New York City, to Jerusalem, to Dachau, Germany, and Oxford, England. His quest had introduced him first to the eccentric rabbis and scholars of the Consortium, and had eventually led him to the very Catholic priest whom Britta was investigating. Along the way, other unlikely alliances developed and at last, through a series of insights and findings, some so "coincidental" as to raise the hair on the back of his neck, he had found the man whom he believed to be the designated descendant of Aaron.

Before that assignment, David had been a rather bleak figure, a recent widower inhabiting a lonely bachelor pad near the campus, burying himself in the academic world of ancient Mayan and Aztec artifacts. Nine months a year of classrooms, broken only by summer forays to Central American digs, had become his existence. And a dreary existence it had been!

All that had changed the day he received a strange letter from the Consortium, inviting him to meet them in New York. That trip, and its ensuing international escapade, had introduced him to the Temple Movement, the Jewish effort to reconstruct the ancient lost temple of Israel destroyed by the Romans in 70 C.E. That movement, he had learned, had global ramifications that involved not only Arab-Israeli tensions in the Middle East, but a network of terrorist organizations around the world.

David had fulfilled his assignment, despite the fact that he and his coworkers had narrowly escaped being targeted by a militant Islamic radical.

Months away from the quiet, predictable pace of the college classroom, following on a quest suited to the likes of Indiana Jones, made it difficult for David to gear down. Every day since his return to the mundane world of textbooks and seminars, he wondered what it had all meant, why he had been singled out for one of the most amazing feats of scholarship ever achieved. Not only had it aroused interests he did not even know existed, not only had it taken him on a journey of mind and spirit of unprecedented significance, but now that it was over, he could not even share it with the world!

He had been sworn to secrecy upon taking the assignment, and now, having succeeded, he could not write a scholarly paper about it, he could not lecture on it, he could not even tell his best friend, department chairman Kenneth Aronstam, about his adventures.

The secret saga was the sole provenance of the strange bedfellows who had linked up during those months. Since parting, the group had kept in touch through letters, cautious phone calls, and even more cautious e-mails. They had learned to respect the fact that their movements and communications might be traced. But they were determined to stay connected.

David smiled wistfully at the gold-framed picture of the little blonde. Standing up from his desk, he reached for it and stroked the glass tenderly. Britta, a Londoner, lived an ocean away. While she and David often discussed visiting, their schedules, and their budgets, never allowed it. He hoped to fly to England this winter to visit her over Christmas break.

On the same shelf, next to Britta's beaming face, were other photos sent to him by the friends of his adventure. One was a snapshot taken on a wooded property far in the Northwest. Smiling out at him from that picture were two fair-complected men and one stunning dark-haired woman, arms entwined as they stood in front of a wonderful log home in the Montana outback.

Next to that photo stood yet another, taken at the headquarters of the Temple Consortium in Jerusalem. Pictured were Ian McCurdy, the old Irish Catholic priest whom Britta had researched, and beside him stood a tall, elderly Englishman and the priest's sister, a fine-looking gray-haired woman.

In a fourth photo were the four heads of the Consortium: Rabbi Menachem Levine, Rabbi Uriel Katz, Dr. Carl Jacobs, and the beloved Rabbi Horace Benjamin.

David chuckled and shook his head at the rabbis' shining faces. Their smiles belied the countless times he had witnessed their quarrels, their bickerings that sometimes bordered on hatred.

Jolly Dr. Jacobs, his spirit as ample as his round middle, beamed from the picture, his arms propped on the shoulders of his bearded colleagues, Rabbi Levine and Rabbi Katz. Menachem Levine, a serious scientist, had a studious look, though still pleasant. And Uriel Katz, an eminent theologian, appeared, as always, less than comfortable within the community.

David's brow knit quizzically as he considered this strange little fellow, whose stinging words and critical nature were, more often than not, responsible for sparking the group's quarrels.

Inscrutable as Katz was, however, his difficult temperament was offset by Rabbi Horace Benjamin's diplomacy. Of all the people David had worked with during those months, Rabbi Ben, with his wondrous snowy hair and chest-length beard, had been the most enjoyable. In the professor's estimation, the kind and fatherly man represented all the best that a cleric of any religion should be.

It had been weeks since David had heard from any of the Consortium members. Although their institute had every technological convenience, the rabbis avoided the use of e-mail, convinced that their communications must be shielded as much as possible from the prying eyes of computer hackers, foreign or domestic. They preferred snail-mail, and even avoided the telephone. Their rare letters divulged few specifics regarding their ongoing work, and all that David had ascertained was that they had spent the intervening months grooming the new high priest for his future apocalyptic work.

Among David's little photo gallery, one picture was conspicuous for its absence. There was none of the man who had been the object of the professor's quest, the one whom all the evidence, after it was finally accumulated, proved to be the true heir to the Aaronic priesthood.

A quiet fellow in his early thirties, Zachary Cohen was one of the younger generation of Jews born in Israel after the Holocaust and World War II. Of all the professor's memories, of both his Jerusalem experience and his entire lifetime, his first encounter with Zachary would always be preeminent.

He had found him on Yom Kippur in Jerusalem's Old City at the Western (or Wailing) Wall, the only visible remains of Israel's ancient temple. Even now, the mere thought of that day gave David goose bumps.

Nearly as soon as he had found him, however, the Consortium had whisked the young man into its own protective embrace. David knew that the rabbis had taken Cohen to New York, to study with them, but where he was now, and what he had gone through since, the professor could only guess.

Certainly, David had never been allowed to photograph him. Such a thing had not even occurred to him, and if it had, he would not have made such a request.

Zachary Cohen was a secret, to be kept for whatever purpose and plan he would submit to, and for whatever future lay ahead for Israel.

David still pictured him clearly, however, in his mind's eye. The recollection of that handsome face, with the piercing dark eyes, the dark beard and gentle expression, was forever emblazoned on the professor's consciousness. Had he never been assigned the task of finding him, had he never known the stranger at the Wall was destined to fulfill such an auspicious spiritual role, he would have sensed he was special on first introduction, for there was an indefinable and undeniable mystique about him.

The professor tried to clear his head of these captivating ruminations. He stretched his lanky frame and yawned, gazing out across the quad. Most of the students had now disappeared into classroom buildings, leaving the grounds quiet. His grade sheets beckoned to him from the disarray on his desk, and he ran a hand through his raggedy shock of sandy hair. Time for a trip to the barber, he thought. Maybe when he was done with this detestable pile of work, he'd fit that in.

David had never fussed over himself. He had relied on his wife to do that. But she had died four years ago, and he limped along, awkwardly filling in where she had left off in his life and his world.

During his Jerusalem experience, with its attendant journeys and unfolding drama, he had found joy and meaning he had not known since her passing. In fact, he had to admit, he had never known such fulfillment, even before her death, as he had known while working for the rabbis.

Leaving the tiny photo gallery, he returned to his desk and sat down with a sigh. In determination, he dove into the grade sheets, not to be pulled away from them again.

But just as he began to make some headway, a knock at his office door jolted him. Peering around the slightly open door was the department secretary.

"Phone call, Professor," she said, pointing at a blinking red light on his telephone. "It's for you."

David groaned. "Not now, Shirley. I'm way behind here. Please take a message."

The middle-aged woman only shrugged. "I tried, Dr. Rothmeyer. But they insisted."

"*They?*" he grumbled. "Who?"

"It's a conference call, Doctor," she replied. "Seems rather serious."

David scowled. "Okay," he said, waving her off. "Thanks, Shirley."

As the secretary pulled the door shut and departed down the hall, David wondered what could be so urgent. If Ken Aronstam needed to meet with him, he would have simply barged into his office. If the college president or board of regents needed him, they would have called him to the administration building.

Bewildered, he picked up the receiver.

"Rothmeyer here," he said.

"David!" came a chorus of voices.

Instantly he knew who spoke his name.

"Rabbis?" he exclaimed. "Is it really you? This is great, just great! I haven't heard from you in ages!"

The four voices, or more correctly three (for as usual Rabbi Katz was more withdrawn), expressed delight at this personal contact.

"Yes, yes!" Rabbi Ben expostulated. "It is wonderful to speak this way!"

What Shirley had mistaken for a "conference call" David immediately ascertained to be a klatch of enthusiastic old fellows huddled about one phone handset, all jostling to hear and be heard. Not only that, but he envisioned them leaning into some phone booth on a busy street, for he could hear the sound of traffic in the background.

The last David had known, they were in New York City, their hometown, where they had brought Zachary Cohen.

"Well, Rabbis? To what do I owe a long-distance call from the Big Apple?"

Rabbi Ben chuckled. "Nothing at all, my boy!" he replied. "We are not calling from New York!"

"No." Rabbi Levine laughed. "We are right here! And we want to see you!"

David was incredulous. "Here? In Columbus, Ohio?" he marveled.

"That's right," Carl Jacobs got in. "Is there a good kosher restaurant where we could rendezvous?"

David could barely grasp the news of their arrival, let alone think of such a place in Columbus.

Rabbi Ben saved him the trouble, however.

"We will come to you," he announced. "Stay put, David. You are in the anthropology building of Midwest University, right? How hard can that be to find?"

CHAPTER 3

David hung up the phone and surveyed the mess atop his desk. He figured the rabbis had called from downtown, which gave him several minutes to do a hasty cleanup.

He quickly pushed the various paper stacks into neater piles and plopped books on them as paperweights; then, turning to the floor, he picked up crumpled castoffs that had missed the wastebasket.

It had been four years since his wife's premature death, but even now he could imagine her teasing smile at his being caught in typical untidiness.

After tamping the last of the trash into the basket, he tucked in his loose shirttail and glanced out the window. The rabbis had not yet appeared when he caught his own reflection in the sunny window and smoothed his flyaway shock of hair.

The first time he had seen the rabbis had been through another window, one at JFK airport. Emerging from a huge gray limousine, they had made a daunting impression on the bewildered professor.

But there was no time for more memories. Across the quad, on which faced the oldest and grandest of the campus buildings, the little huddle of rabbis came trekking.

David straightened and crossed his arms, laughing to himself. His heart warmed at the sight of Rabbi Ben, who, as always, led the group with a confident stride, his long black coat and broad-brimmed black hat a stark contrast to his flowing white beard and hair.

Dr. Jacobs and Rabbi Levine walked close behind, taking

in the sights with wide eyes, nodding genially to passing students. Then, as was to be expected, Uriel Katz followed up the rear, a little distant from the others, in a more somber, colder world of his own.

All at once, as David watched their approach, it occurred to him that their sudden reentrance into his life might herald the advent of some new adventure. For certain, they would not have come halfway across the country just to pay a visit!

It also occurred to him that their meeting with him in this Midwestern shrine of academia might draw unwanted attention to them and to himself. If his colleagues were to see them entering his office, or to know that he conversed at length with such an unusual group, he might have an uncomfortable amount of explaining to do. Fact was, all that his department associates knew of the "sabbatical" he had taken last year was that he had been on a dig somewhere in the Middle East. Though Ken Aronstam knew he had gone to Israel, not even he knew the nature of David's Jerusalem experience.

As for the rabbis, surely they would not want the attention of inquisitive minds intruding into matters already quite sensitive in nature.

Suddenly protective, David threw up the window sash. "Rabbis!" he hailed them. "Up here! I am here!"

The rabbis stopped in the middle of the walkway and found him leaning out of the second story. Jubilant, they waved back to him.

David smiled nervously as a few students turned to follow their gaze.

"I . . . I will meet you out front!" he said, gesturing toward the entryway steps. "Wait there."

David left the window agape and rushed from his office, past the desk of the secretary, who observed him in bemusement. Down the main hall and out the front door he flew, to find his New York friends just approaching the stairs.

"Gentlemen," he greeted them, "how marvelous to see you!" He returned Rabbi Ben's open arms with a warm embrace and shook hands with the others. "It is much too fine a day to meet in a stuffy office. Come," he suggested, leading them to a set of benches beneath a glorious willow tree. "Let's sit here."

A dense row of hedges separated the tree and benches from the nearest walkway. David felt reasonably safe conversing here. When each of the men had made himself comfortable on the deep, slatted seats, David studied their familiar faces.

"How good to see you!" he exclaimed again. "What brings you to Columbus?"

The four rabbis exchanged quick, uneasy glances. Rabbi Ben was the first to speak. "We all know one another too well to waste time on pleasantries,

David," he said. "You realize that we admire your work, and that we could never thank you enough for all you did for us on your last assignment."

Indeed, David did know them well, at least as well as they would allow him to. He also knew that Rabbi Ben was not one to waste words—that every syllable he spoke was chosen carefully.

"My *last* assignment?" David said. "It was my *only* assignment, gentlemen."

Dr. Jacobs smiled broadly, and Rabbi Levine looked at the ground. Uriel Katz interjected a sober "So far."

David had been down such a road before. "All right, my old friends. You do not need to beat around the bush. I did not figure you came to Columbus for the fun of it. But I must tell you up front, I cannot take on any other . . . what did you call it, Ben? Assignment? I am a professor at this university, and I have already used my sabbatical. I must stick to teaching!"

This last assertion may have seemed a bit too emphatic. Ben's eyes twinkled. "Ah, but you have summer vacation coming up, do you not?"

David was flustered. His heart tripped and his palms were clammy. One part of him resented their easy intrusion into his predictable world. Another part—the part that had a hard time concentrating, the part that loved to look at the photos on his office shelf—longed to cry out, "What can I do for you? Where do you want me to go? What mystery do you wish for me to solve?"

"Uh, yes . . . ," he faltered. "Summer is coming. But I usually take students to Central America over summer quarter."

Even as he voiced this objection, that adventuresome part of himself recoiled at the thought of another vacation spent on a freshman dig.

Again, the rabbis exchanged glances, and David felt a strong sense of déjà vu.

"Now, don't tell me you have already gone to the department chairman!" he grumbled. "Ken wouldn't let you twist his arm again, would he?"

David remembered all too clearly how the prying rabbis had learned of his pending sabbatical, how they had taken the liberty of contacting Ken Aronstam and finding out just when the professor might be available to work for the Consortium.

"No, David," Rabbi Ben said. "We have not interfered with your schedule. But," he said with a sly grin, "do you really want to waste the summer digging in Indian graveyards?"

The professor nearly laughed with him. In mock offense, he said, "As I recall, you sent me off to dig in a Jewish death camp. Was that so much better?"

Despite the grisly reference, the little group chuckled among themselves, and Dr. Jacobs leaned back, his round belly shaking with laughter. "Oh, but didn't we have a fine time?"

Looking at him, David recalled how the jolly man and Rabbi Levine had danced in the laboratory the day the fabulous Second Copper Scroll was opened, the day it confirmed the identity of the man David had been hired to find. In an instant, a kaleidoscope of memories flashed through his mind, somewhat like the reports of those who say that, in a near-death experience, their entire lives flash before them.

He remembered tracking down the elusive Irish priest, Ian McCurdy, at Oxford; he remembered going with him to the British Museum, where he had kept the long-sought scroll in hiding for nearly half a century. He remembered unearthing another fragile document behind the oven house of Dachau, and he remembered translating it before the awestruck eyes of dear friends who had joined him from Ireland, England, and Montana.

David nodded his head with a sigh. "Yes," he conceded, "it was a grand time!"

Of course, those adventures had not come without a price. All those who partook in them had been in danger from the beginning, from forces determined to squelch their quest.

David cleared his throat and tried not to be swept away. "At least in the Andes, I am not risking my life at every turn," he objected. "I don't relish the idea of being the focus of international fallout."

But all of his objections were useless. He knew, as well as the rabbis, that the offer of a challenge such as he had taken on before was too exciting to be rejected.

The elderly gents offered no argument, only letting him ponder his own words a moment. At last, rolling his eyes, he shrugged. "Very well, my friends. Tell me what this is all about! Am I to track down the genealogy of the anti-Christ?"

He meant this as a sarcasm, but Dr. Jacobs shook his head. "Why would we want to know such a thing? The prophets say such a man will appear in his own time, and we are in no hurry to help him!"

"No," Ben said, "but surely you can guess what your next assignment should be. Surely you realized you were only taking a break from the obvious during this school year."

David knew what Rabbi Ben meant. He had often wondered if his work on the Second Copper Scroll was finished.

"You have me there!" he admitted. "Do you think I have not hankered to get my hands on that document again? If it told us who the high priest should be, what else might it reveal?"

The men nodded. "So," Levine said, "you understand our need of you,

Professor? Due to the sensitive nature of the scroll's contents, you and only you should have control of any work done on it."

"Yes," Jacobs agreed, "you have proven yourself worthy of our confidence. We cannot entrust its revelations to just anyone. And," he spoke almost in a whisper, "the time has come to decipher the scroll, all of it!"

Never would David forget the thrill of that day in the Consortium laboratory, when he was given the task of peeling back the first onionlike layer of the ancient copper artifact. Father McCurdy had worked in secret with his mentor, Father Ducharme, in cutting the scroll into fragile strips half a century before. Due to the dangers under which they had worked, they had never been able to analyze the contents, except to confirm that they were a key to another copper scroll, one whose existence and contents had been revealed to the public in the 1950s. That document contained a list of treasures hidden by the Jews before the destruction of Jerusalem in 70 C.E., the treasures of the Temple of Israel, which could easily equal the wealth of many of the world's modern nations! But it had been written in code, and no one but Father McCurdy and Father Ducharme had known of the existence of its key.

Still, David was puzzled by this sudden reentrance into his life of the enigmatic Consortium. His brow knit quizzically, he asked, "But, gentlemen, why have you come to me now? Why did you not enlist my talents in deciphering the rest of the scroll when I was still with you?"

Rabbi Ben leaned close. "We knew the time would come when we would need you once more, for the scroll undoubtedly reveals clues to the whereabouts of items essential to the fulfillment of our temple worship. However, our energies, since the day you led us to Zachary Cohen, have been in protecting him and training him for his future duties. It was not until a few days ago that we knew we must move hastily into the rest of our quest."

At the mention of Zachary Cohen, David grew very quiet. Not a day had passed since he had found him at the Wailing Wall that he had not thought of him, that he had not wondered what became of him, where he might be and what he might be going through.

With awe, David dared to inquire, "Have you been working with him all this time in New York City?"

It did not surprise him when the rabbis chose to sidestep this question.

"We are not at liberty to tell you his whereabouts, David," Levine answered.

Rabbi Ben nodded. "In time, you will meet him again. He needs you, just as we do."

From the rabbi's tone of voice, David sensed he should ask no further questions about Zachary Cohen, at least not now.

"Very well," he said. "I am pleased to be of service to him." Then, reflecting, he asked, "So, what happened a few days ago that has prompted your contacting me at this time?"

Afternoon was waning. The campus was growing quiet as students went to their dorms to study or to the cafeteria for supper. The sun was at a low angle, sending mellow shafts through the willow branches.

A hush had descended over everything, so that before Rabbi Ben answered David's question, he looked about the grounds to be sure he spoke in private.

"We believe that the Second Copper Scroll may help lead us to the whereabouts of certain artifacts essential to our priestly worship. We felt we had ample time to devote to our work with Zachary, before we would need to start out on the quest for these things. But something has happened which leads us to believe we may not have so much time as we had hoped."

David absorbed the tension of the rabbi's mood. "And what is it that has happened?" he asked again.

"You have undoubtedly heard of the dreadful assassination of Senator Calvin Jefferson," Ben said.

David frowned. "Yes, of course. That figures in here?"

Carl Jacobs spoke carefully. "We believe it may," he said. "The men who murdered him may be agents of certain enemies of Israel."

David quickly sorted through what he knew of Jefferson. "Enemies of Israel? But why?" he asked. "Jefferson was not necessarily pro-Israel, any more than he was pro-Palestinian. Was he?"

"You are right," Rabbi Levine replied. "But we have reason to believe that he was transporting something of interest to our purposes when he was murdered, something which our enemies would do anything to possess themselves."

The professor was confounded. "Now wait a moment," he said. "This is getting into very dangerous territory! I thought you wanted me to unravel a scroll, not get involved in a criminal investigation." Throwing up his hands, he deferred. "No thanks, old friends. I think I'll pass on this one!"

A cloud settled over Rabbi Ben's face. "Would it help if we told you there was a witness to the murder? Someone whose testimony might prove helpful to all of us?"

David was more bewildered than ever. "They have a witness?" he asked. "I have not read this in the papers."

"He is under government protection, Professor," Rabbi Levine said. "A six-year-old boy, who could become the target of terrorists."

CHAPTER 4

David's small apartment, a few blocks from the campus, was usually no tidier than his office. Today, however, it had been cleaned by a couple of college girls whom David had hired to do housekeeping once a week. As the professor put the key in the lock and, opening the door, turned on the light, he was glad for the timing.

The rabbis were with him. They had treated him to a meal in town, choosing carefully for themselves, from the Italian menu, a few items that fit with their kosher diet. He had invited them to spend the rest of the evening with him, as there was still much they had not been free to discuss in a public restaurant regarding their plans.

As David entered the room, he bent down to collect the day's mail, which the landlady had deposited in the letter slot of his door. Tossing it on the small sideboard near the coat closet, he did not bother to look through it but turned his attention to his guests.

"Rabbis, make yourselves comfortable," he said, waving them into the living room as he hung their coats and hats on a hall rack. "It's not much, but I call it home."

"Very nice, Professor," Dr. Jacobs observed, looking at the collection of photos and memorabilia David had displayed throughout the room. Photos from summer digs spanning several years dominated one wall. Spread out on a chest beneath were small artifacts he had retrieved from sites in the Andes. Above a stereo cabinet were framed certificates showing David's academic degrees and awards for various teaching assignments.

David's more personal photos, to which the rabbis were not privy, were reserved for albums in his bedroom. After his wife had died, he had moved into this bachelor pad, in the hopes he might be able to move on more easily without the constant reminders that their mutual home fostered. On his bedroom dresser was his favorite photo of her, standing beside him at the foot of a great Mayan pyramid.

There was, however, a picture of Britta in the living room, a shot similar to the one he had in his office. And, again, there were photos of the friends he had met during his Jerusalem experience, including one of Rabbi Ben shaking hands with Father McCurdy in front of the Temple Consortium Gallery door in Jerusalem's Old City.

"What a wonderful man!" Rabbi Ben said as he leaned over Dr. Jacob's shoulder, studying the photo. "Have you kept in touch with Ian, David?"

"I received a Hanukkah card from him last winter," David replied. "And we e-mail sporadically. We never discuss anything very . . ."

"Sensitive?" Rabbi Levine filled in.

"Good word," David said. "Actually, communications between all of us have been cautious, haven't they?"

Uriel Katz nodded. "As they must be," he said.

The evening was wearing on, and David could tell that the rabbis were anxious to discuss important matters. Directing them to the sofa and two easy chairs, he drew up a dinette chair and sat with them.

He would have questioned them further about Senator Jefferson and the young witness to his murder, but the rabbis had made it clear, after first broaching the topic, that they were not free to tell him more. They assured him that if matters developed to link his work with that subject, as they thought they would, he would know more in time.

"Let me recap where we left off before supper," he began. "First, you want me to continue with the translation of the Second Copper Scroll. But to what end, gentlemen? If the First Copper Scroll is any indication, we are going to be dealing with a multitude of clues to a multitude of treasures, strewn all over who-knows-where in the Judean desert."

"And perhaps elsewhere," Dr. Jacobs said.

David raised his eyebrows. "Very well . . . so what is your goal? Are you hoping to track down every artifact rescued from Jerusalem before the Roman invasion? That would surely be an impossible feat, even for the likes of our clever group!"

The rabbis mirrored his smile.

"Certainly, we do not expect any such thing," Rabbi Ben replied. "Whatever was hidden by the Essenes or similar rebels, there is no way it would all be traceable after two millennia."

"No, not even if we come up with a way to decipher every clue!" Carl Jacobs exclaimed. "Two thousand years of wanderers, tourists, and archaeologists have come and gone in Israel, and the landscape itself has changed countless times! Wadis have flooded and reflooded, caves have fallen in, erosion has taken its toll."

"Not only that," Rabbi Levine added, "but even if we could understand every word of the scrolls, we might never be able to pinpoint the locations they refer to."

David sat back and threw up his hands. "Why even begin, then?" he asked. "It sounds like a futile effort!"

Rabbi Ben was sympathetic. "It does," he said with a sigh, "but there are two reasons why we must try. First of all, our dream of a temple is dependent on us locating at least two of the artifacts, and second"—he paused—"we must have faith that God would not have restored the scrolls to us if they would lead only to a dead end."

David had become used to thinking of God while he had worked for the rabbis and with Father McCurdy. Not only did each of these men speak freely of him, but David had experienced things during his Jerusalem adventure that could not be accounted for, except as divine intervention.

The professor swallowed hard, goose bumps rising on his arms as he felt the familiar tug of a power beyond himself. He had learned better than to resist it.

"All right," he said. "So what are the two artifacts we are especially concerned with?"

The men looked at one another with awe-filled expressions. It was obvious that they were about to touch on something so sacred that they almost feared naming it.

Rabbi Ben began. "Do you remember the manikin in the Consortium Gallery?"

The gallery housed a fabulous collection of implements and furnishings made by artisans of the modern Temple Movement. Replicas of the golden candlestand and the silver trumpets, finely crafted harps, and many other items associated with rituals of the future temple were on display there. How would David ever forget the faceless image of the high priest that modeled special vestments fashioned on a one-of-a-kind loom, garments whose design was based on tradition and on writings going back to the Torah? The frock of the high priest was to be seamless, and of such a unique pattern and weave that the only artisans capable of re-creating it were of the Navajo nation in Arizona!

"Of course, I remember," David replied softly.

"Then you must also realize that the priest's most important piece of attire was missing."

The professor remembered discussing this on one visit to the gallery.

"You mean the breastplate?" he deduced.

"Exactly!" Uriel Katz exclaimed. "Although our scholars might be able to come close to re-creating the breastplate, it would be infinitely preferable for us to locate the original!"

"Especially since it is such a hallowed object, having sheltered the very hearts of generations of Israel's high priests!" Levine added.

Rabbi Ben was very somber. "Besides," he explained, "there are certain attributes about the breastplate that remain a mystery."

The old gents nodded together, Dr. Jacobs twining his fingers over his stomach and leaning back with closed eyes. Uriel Katz, his own owlish eyes boring into David, asked a deep question.

"You have heard of the *Urim* and *Thummim*?"

David thought a moment. "I remember the phrase from my childhood days in synagogue. As I recall, they were some sort of counters or die for predicting the future."

Uriel was taken aback. "You make them sound like crass tools of a fortuneteller!"

Rabbi Ben looked sharply at Uriel and shook his head. Then, turning again to David, he said, "You do well to come that close in your definition, Professor. Most people would have no clue regarding them."

Katz looked at the floor, his face reddening as Ben continued.

"But Uriel is right to be so careful," he went on diplomatically. "The Urim and Thummim were apparently some sort of implements for divining the will of God. They were used by the high priest in moments when the leaders of Israel, say a king or council, needed direction in some great matter. No one knows just what they looked like or just how they were employed. But we do know that one of the names for the breastplate is *ephod*, which seems to mean 'a pouch.' It would seem that the high priest's breastplate was like a large pocket, in which were carried, at all times, these two small items."

The professor's mind sorted back through his years of learning in the field of archaeology. "I do not mean to diminish these sacred objects," he said cautiously, "but similar items have been found in other cultures, both modern and ancient. In Greek lore, for instance, the Oracle at Delphi apparently used some sort of divining device to answer petitioners' questions."

Out of the corner of his eye, David could see Uriel squirm uncomfortably with the comparison. But he went on, "In the tombs of the kings and priests of the Mayans, we have found small pouches of bones and counters lined with hatch marks, which were apparently put to similar use. And then, in the Far East, there has been, for eons, the divining of tea leaves and . . ."

Dr. Jacobs cleared his throat, trying to be friendly as he intervened between David's analogies and Katz's growing peeve.

"Certainly, the culture of the Bible overlaps with cultures all around the Middle East, and surely mankind has carried on traditions handed down in various forms across time. All around the world, after all, people are related to one another and have learned from one another," he said.

"However," Katz objected, "there is only one God and only one Truth! The sacred Urim and Thummim cannot be mimicked, though other nations and people have surely tried!"

Rabbi Ben rubbed his hands together, eager to bring peace. "No one disputes that, Uriel," he said. "Which brings us to our very point: that if we wish to conduct the priestly office in the future temple in keeping with its original purpose, we must locate the original Urim and Thummim, wherever they are!"

David was feeling more and more at home with his old friends. How often he had witnessed their sparring, even participated in it!

"So," he said, "you have told me one of the things we seek. But there are two?"

Rabbi Ben was glad to change the subject. Perhaps the second would be less volatile.

"The other item we need is actually a substance, and is probably in a small container, a vial perhaps. It is known as the Ashes of the Red Heifer. Have you heard of this?"

David nodded. "I remember seeing photos in the Consortium Gallery of a young red cow which had been bred in Sweden. You told me that this was an attempt to produce a flawless red heifer that could be used in temple ritual. But," he said with a shrug, "I was not clear as to why this was necessary."

Rabbi Ben went on. "In the days of Moses and Aaron, a perfect red heifer was burned as a sacrifice. She had no white hairs and no defects of any kind. Her ashes were used from time immemorial to sanctify the altar of sacrifice and, indeed, to sanctify the Temple itself!"

David was astonished. "The ashes of a single animal were used all those years?"

Rabbi Levine explained. "We believe that as the ashes of the first heifer diminished, a portion of them were used to sanctify another beast, and so on, so that there was always a sacred heifer available."

Dr. Jacobs went on, "Unfortunately, if we cannot locate the original vial, we are reduced to having to breed another perfect heifer. Several attempts have been made, in Sweden, as you saw, and elsewhere. We have come quite close, and more than once we have thought we succeeded. But then . . ."

He looked quite dismal, and Rabbi Ben stepped in. "Always, just as we thought we had cause for rejoicing, the creature has turned out to be flawed." He held up his hands as though in surrender. "It seems we have no choice but to find the real thing!"

David was amazed. "And when is the last recorded incident of the original ashes being used?" he asked.

The rabbis were chagrined. "We lose track of the ashes about the time of Jeremiah. There is a tradition—and it is nothing more—that he hid the ashes somewhere in the Dead Sea region, or took them across the Jordan, about the time that the Babylonians were sweeping across the Holy Land."

David restrained himself from laughing. "You're kidding!" he said. "That is centuries before the time of the Copper Scrolls! Are you hoping that they give clues to the whereabouts of something that long lost?"

The rabbis were not fazed.

"That and the breastplate . . ." Rabbi Ben answered. "The breastplate of the high priest is not mentioned in the Bible after the time of the early monarchy, except for a possible reference in Ezekiel."

David had learned a lot of Jewish history in his time with the rabbis. "Ezekiel?" he hooted. "The time of the Babylonian Captivity? That's not much better than Jeremiah!"

Rabbi Katz shifted angrily in his seat. "Perhaps our visit is wasted here," he growled. "Horace," he addressed Rabbi Ben, "I implore you to reconsider . . ."

"Now, Uriel!" Ben interrupted, holding up a hand. "I know what you are about to say, and my answer is a firm 'No!' David has served us too well in the past. Just let him digest all of this in his own way."

David avoided Uriel's glowering eyes and shook his head. "I am sorry, gentlemen," he conceded. "When all has been said, you know I am with you. It is just so . . . so far-fetched!"

Ben smiled wanly. "I seem to recall your saying something similar when we met with you at the Waldorf Astoria, when we first told you of our quest for Zachary."

David remembered all too well his reaction to that initial meeting.

"Touché," he replied. Then, heaving a sigh, he asked, "So, where do we begin?"

Rabbi Ben's eyes glowed with the same glow he always got when he thought of the Holy City. "The scroll still resides in the laboratory in Jerusalem. We wish to send you there, David, as we did the first time. You may stay at our house in the Old City, just as you did before, and you may use the laboratory freely."

"Will you be with me?" David inquired.

The men seemed disappointed to deny his hope.

"There is nothing we would love more," Dr. Jacobs answered, "except that we feel constrained to stay with Zachary. He is doing well in his studies, but we feel uneasy about leaving him, even for this little while that we are in Columbus."

David interpreted. "Do you feel he is in danger?"

"Let us just say that his security is our priority," Jacobs answered. "He is due to return to Israel very soon to complete his studies, and that will give us even more cause for concern."

The professor understood that the heir to the high priesthood could be the subject of enemy forces.

"I mean no disrespect," he said, "but do you feel you are capable of such surveillance? It sounds to me like Mr. Cohen needs a bodyguard."

The men agreed. "That would be wonderful," Rabbi Ben assented. "But we know of no one we could trust with such an assignment."

The men were making ready to depart, standing up from their seats and taking their coats.

"We will call you in the morning," Ben said. "We are staying at the Hyatt Regency tonight. If it meets with your approval, we will make arrangements for your trip to Israel at the end of the school year?"

David could scarcely believe he was agreeing to such a thing once again. But how could he do otherwise? "Very well," he said.

As he walked the rabbis to the door, his eyes were caught by a piece of mail on the sideboard. A cream-colored envelope with silver type announced that it had come from Montana.

"What's this?" he said. "It appears I have news from our friends in Bull River!"

"Honey Aronstam?" Rabbi Ben guessed.

"Pete and Mel?" Dr. Jacobs added.

David opened the fancy envelope carefully. "This is not their typical stationery," he said jovially. "Do we have an announcement?"

Sure enough, the lacy card inside announced that Pete and Honey were to be married in a month. "Wow!" David laughed. "After a decade of living together, they are finally tying the knot!"

The professor's mind flashed to the photo of his Montana friends, which he had in his campus office. Beautiful dark-haired Honey and her boyfriend, Pete Wester, stood closest in that shot, with Mel, Pete's brother, alongside.

Pete's life had been changed even more dramatically than David's by his own Jerusalem experience. A former member of the Montana militia, he had been a supporter of the Aryan Nations agenda until his eyes were opened and his heart forever changed by the racists' targeting of his Jewish girlfriend, and an epiphanic visit to the site of the Nazi concentration camp at Dachau.

Mel, his policeman brother, had left Los Angeles to find peace in Montana, never dreaming he would end up doing international detective work.

And Honey . . .

David thought fondly of the first time he had seen her, a woman on the run for her life from the radicals whom Pete had befriended. David could have let himself fall in love with Honey, had she not belonged to Pete.

He was glad now that things had turned out the way they had in that department, for otherwise, he might have overlooked Britta.

As for Peter, David knew that the Montanan had had some rude awakenings during his association with the white supremacists. Nearly losing Honey as a result of that involvement must have made him rethink a lot of things, not the least of which was how seriously he should take his commitment to her.

"Well, gentlemen," David said with a chuckle, "you will probably have one of these invitations waiting for you when you get back home. What do you think of a trip to Montana before I head off to Jerusalem?"

The rabbis were flustered, Rabbi Ben most of all. "Oh, how wonderful it would be to see their wedding!" He sighed. "But that is impossible!"

Again they thought of Zachary and their need to be with him.

Grabbing their coats and hats from the hall rack, the men lined up at the door, ready to bid David good night, when Dr. Jacobs noticed another piece of mail on the sideboard.

"What is that?" He laughed. "Something else from Montana?"

David took a postcard from the pile. A humorous old-timey photo on the front showed a cowboy riding a horse that hauled behind it a shabby wooden outhouse on wheels. "Movin' On" was the caption.

On the back, Mel had cryptically written: "Hey, Dave, do you think they could use a new campus cop at Midwest University? Post this prominently on some main bulletin board: 'Ex-cop-turned-Montana-transplant looking for work.' Happy as I am for Pete and Honey, I think there's not enough room in this big house for a bachelor brother. Mel."

Like all the others in the Jerusalem saga, Mel Wester had been transformed by his experiences there, even becoming a true American hero in the process. When he and his brother had heroically intervened to protect a Jewish boys' school in the Old City from an Islamic terrorist, they had won themselves notoriety in the U.S. press and around the world.

Suddenly, as David read the postcard, an idea blazed across his mind like a prophecy.

"Rabbis," he announced, "I think I've found a bodyguard for Zachary Cohen!"

CHAPTER 5

Honey Aronstam sat in a pool of sunlight that filtered through the tall bull pines and onto the veranda of her spacious log home in western Montana. It was one of those crisp mountain mornings when the ground was still damp from a soft nighttime shower, but the trees and all around them luxuriated in the light of a pure blue heaven.

In a broad, raised flower bed, which ran the length of the veranda, interrupted only by the split-log steps, a parti-colored mix of pansies flourished. Honey had been thrilled when she discovered that her pansies had survived the winter, springing up in eager bunches as soon as the weather began to warm. She had lived in this place for nearly ten years but had never seen such a thing. It was true that this winter had been exceptionally mild, a holdover from flukish tropical air movement that had the world in a topsy-turvy climatic pattern. Still, for any annual floral breed to survive in Montana was noteworthy.

Honey held a steaming mug of fresh-brewed tea on her lap, her feet tucked up beneath her and covered with her long skirt, as she sat in a pine rocker. She surveyed her prized pansies and spoke congenially with an older woman who sat on the porch swing a few feet away.

"Now, why do you suppose the petunias didn't live?" she asked. "They aren't much different from pansies, as I see it."

She might have asked such a question of any of her women neighbors, just to make friendly conversation at the market or as they passed on Main Street in town. But when she asked it of Roberta Barrett, she expected a knowledgeable answer.

Honey did not entertain many visitors. Her home was located several miles out of the tiny burg of Noxon, up a winding, primitive road off the highway. Roberta's visit was not casual, and conversation was precious.

"All the ladies are talking about their flowers this spring," Roberta replied. "Lots of them say their pansies lived through the snow. As for petunias, they aren't quite as hardy a breed as the Spanish-colored pansies. They're doing a lot with flowers in England, I've read. They have developed several strains of common flowers that live through the cold falls and winters there. Maybe the ones we're getting here are related."

Just as Honey had expected, Roberta's answer was well considered and meaningful.

Roberta was a Mennonite. She never went anywhere without her little white cap, what she called her "covering." She was a thin, angular woman, very prim in her traditional shirtwaist dress of gray muslin. But she was not a rigid sort. She was a very amiable person, whose philosophy and religion undergirded rather than overrode her love of people.

When Honey had moved to Montana with Pete, a freelance carpenter, they had purchased their twelve acres of property from Roberta and her husband. The original Barrett homestead, settled a couple of generations ago, lay on the back part of Pete and Honey's land, and included a one-room cabin. Though the younger couple had little use for the tiny house, Pete kept it in good repair, as a tribute to its history.

Mr. Barrett had passed away shortly after Pete and Honey arrived, and Roberta, whose home lay on adjacent farmland, was their closest neighbor. Not to say that they saw each other often. The two houses were a good mile apart, the Barrett home being at the far end of sprawling acreage that covered half the Cricket Creek hillside.

Still, Honey and Roberta were fast friends, and Honey, a city girl, had learned much about the "back-to-the-earth" lifestyle from the woman. Of course, Roberta would not have called it by such a name; being raised a rural Mennonite, living off the land was as natural to her as breathing.

Roberta was a marvelous cook and baker. She made a nice side-income designing, baking, and decorating cakes for weddings and other celebrations. Honey had asked to see her portfolio of designs so that she could place an order for a wedding cake.

Pete and Honey were to be married on the front lawn of their rustic home. Though Roberta had been here many times, and had once owned the property herself, she said she always came up with the most suitable creations when visiting the site of an upcoming event.

"I can see why you want an outdoor wedding," Roberta said, gazing up into the spire of pines that sheltered the yard. "This is what I think a cathedral must look like."

Honey had often made such a comparison in her own mind and smiled in agreement. "My favorite color is green," she said. "That's one thing I love about our home here . . . all the greenery. So my wedding colors are to be hunter green and cranberry."

"Perfect!" Roberta said. "I was hoping to use green in the cake decoration. And with the brilliant colors of your flower garden, cranberry will work well."

She leaned out from the porch swing and flipped through several of the laminated pages in a three-ring binder that lay open on a small log table. "Here," she said, pointing to a favorite design. "Can't you see this in your colors? With a background of white frosting, of course."

Roberta referred to a three-tiered cake scalloped with ropes of dark green ivy, secured with cranberry-colored roses.

"I love it!" Honey exclaimed. "But could you change the roses to pansies?"

Roberta sparked to the idea. "Much more fitting for your place!" she said. Glancing around the perimeter of the yard, she added, "And how about I change the ivy to ferns?"

Honey liked that. "Wonderful!" she said.

But the cake was topped with a traditional figure of a bride and groom. Honey looked at it askance. "How about, instead of the couple on the top . . ."

Roberta eyed her knowingly. "I figured you wouldn't go for that," she said. "What would you think of replacing them with two larger flowers, one lying against the other?"

Honey thought a moment. "Better yet, how about a small log house in frosting, with a bouquet of small pansies resting against it!" she exclaimed.

Roberta laughed. "Do you think Pete would like being represented by a log house?"

"Sure!" Honey said. "Strong and durable. That's my Pete! Besides, look at the place he built for us!"

Roberta shrugged. "I guess it would be pretty enough. Okay."

Honey paused. "The only other thing I'd like is if the white frosting was not real glaring . . . you know?"

"You'd prefer a cream color?" Roberta guessed.

"Exactly! My dress is antique lace, and the wedding invitations were also off-white," she said.

"Very well," Roberta said, closing the binder. "That was painless."

Honey offered her another cup of tea, and Roberta gratefully let her refill the mug that sat on the table.

"If you would like, I can come the morning of the wedding and gather up some of your flowers and ferns from the yard for bouquets. I would love to help you decorate!" she offered.

Honey appreciated the suggestion. Roberta undoubtedly knew their finances were tight, and that such a thing would avoid a huge florist bill.

"I can't think of anything nicer!" she replied. "I want to keep the setting as simple and natural as possible. In fact," she said, her eyes brightening, "you know the old pinwheel quilt that hangs from our balcony rail?"

Roberta had seen it many times. "Your grandmother made it, right?" she recalled.

"Yes," Honey said. "I would love to work it in to the wedding. You know, 'Something old . . . something new . . .' "

" 'Something borrowed . . . something blue . . . ,' " Roberta recited. "But that usually applies to the bride's outfit. Surely you don't plan to use it as a shawl!"

Honey laughed. "Of course not!"

"What then, will it be the tablecloth? You wouldn't want frosting to get on it!"

"No," Honey said, swinging her legs to the porch and placing her tea mug on the table. She sat on the edge of her rocker and looked at Roberta intently. "You know that I am Jewish," she said softly.

Roberta had wondered when this topic would arise. She had wondered if Honey's heritage would enter into her wedding. But it was a sensitive subject for both of the women to address, due to the fact that one of Roberta's sons had joined ranks with a local group of Aryan Nations disciples, one of the most outspoken and activist of the anti-Semite "brotherhoods" in the Northwest.

Roberta's voice was sweet as she answered, "Of course, Honey. Everyone hereabouts knows that now."

She referred to the media attention Honey, Pete, and his brother, Mel, had received last year, when the two Westers had intervened in an attempted attack on a Jewish boys' school in Jerusalem. The brothers had quite possibly saved the lives of several dozen trainees of the Israeli Temple Movement, bringing that movement into prominence and exposing links between the Arab terrorist who perpetrated the attack and a network of terrorist organizations around the world. That network had brought the public eye full circle to the white supremacist agenda in the United States, and particularly in the Idaho-Montana region.

"I doubt there's a soul in this valley who didn't see all of you on those talk shows!" Roberta went on. Then, looking at her hands folded peacefully in her lap, she sighed. "Honey, if you're worried that I'm uncomfortable with your . . . your background . . . well"— she took a determined breath—"you just think again! Haven't I always been your friend? It doesn't matter to me who anyone's ancestors were, or what their bloodline is!" Roberta was almost angry at the thought. "No, ma'am!" she exclaimed. "Don't go judging me by that fool son of mine! I love him, but he is a shame to the family!"

Honey thought back to all the clandestine meetings she had seen conducted on this very property, in her very own house. Her beloved Pete had been a member of the "brotherhood" before he was brought to his senses by their targeting of Honey, whom he had not even realized was of Jewish heritage.

Roberta's son, Ron Barrett, had often attended such meetings, though he had moved to Spokane long before the Wester story broke.

Honey was grateful to hear Roberta's proclamation, though it did not surprise her.

"So," the Mennonite woman asked, "what does any of this have to do with your grandmother's quilt?"

Honey leaned back, her face shining with anticipation. "Well," she said, "Pete and I decided that we would have a civil ceremony, officiated by a justice of the peace. But even though Pete is not Jewish, he is open to having a few touches from the traditions of my people."

"Okay," Roberta said. "But the quilt?"

"You know that Jewish couples are married beneath a canopy," Honey said. Then, drawing her hands through the air above her head, she smiled broadly.

"You want to use the quilt as the canopy?" Roberta deduced. "How lovely!"

"Especially since it was my grandmother's," Honey enthused. "She would have wanted me to have a Jewish wedding."

Roberta chuckled. "Yes, but I suppose she would also have wanted 'you should marry a good Jewish boy!'" she said, doing a fine imitation of a Yiddish grandmother.

Honey laughed out loud. "That's wonderful! Wherever did you learn to do that?"

Roberta shrugged. "I have more talents than cake making," she teased. Leaning toward the table, she closed the binder and gathered up her notebook. "Well, this will be an event none of the neighbors will want to miss! How often do we have a Jewish wedding in this area?"

Honey gave a sly smile. "And how often do we see rabbis in Bull River?" she asked.

"What?" Roberta exclaimed. "I thought you were going to use a justice of the peace!"

"We are," Honey asserted. "But just yesterday I learned that some of our Jerusalem friends are going to be attending the wedding! Can you believe it?"

Roberta set the notebook down again and looked at her younger friend in amazement. "Are these the leaders of the Temple Movement we saw on TV? The ones at the boys' school?"

"The same!" Honey said. "I sent them invitations, but I never dreamed they would actually come. And not only them, but also the professor we stayed with! He is coming with my cousin from Ohio, who happens to work with him at the university."

"Oh my!" Roberta cried. "You will need all sorts of help . . . cooking . . . baking . . ."

Honey could see that there would be no stopping her friend from welcoming all of this strange collection with open arms. "You must promise me you won't tell anyone about the rabbis' coming," she said. "Pete and Mel are concerned for their safety."

Roberta grew somber. "Of course," she acknowledged. Then, back to her love of planning. "Now, where will everyone be staying? Do you have room for them all?"

Honey nodded. "We plan to put some of them in the old cabin," she said, indicating the homestead. "I think Dr. Rothmeyer and my cousin would enjoy staying there."

CHAPTER 6

The last time Mel Wester had driven the route between Bull River and Spokane, he had just come to the Northwest by plane from Los Angeles. Today he was returning to Spokane, but he would not be going back to L.A. He was going to Spokane's international airport to pick up his friends, the New York rabbis and David Rothmeyer.

As Honey had told Roberta, all of these people were coming for the wedding, along with her cousin, David's department chairman, Kenneth Aronstam, whom Mel had never met.

All the way from Montana, Mel had replayed in his mind the events of his short time in Jerusalem and Germany, when he had entered into arenas of investigation and experience that had forever changed his life. Upon returning to Montana from Israel following the whirlwind of attention the press had given the Wester brothers, Mel had found life a bit too humdrum. Ironic that this should be so, for he had come to Montana from the asphalt jungle of a cop's beat in L.A. to find peace and tranquillity. Now the silence of the hills and the absence of excitement were taking their toll on him.

This trip from the Montana outback, and the chance to reunite with his friends-in-adventure, was a welcome break.

It was a bright day of late spring as he made his 130-mile journey to eastern Washington. The weather in this part of the Northwest had a way of turning straight from the cold of winter to the heat of summer with little intermediate mildness. Mel pushed a switch for the sunroof of his red four-wheel-drive Suburban to let the sunlight pour in. The hot air outside the car whipped through, ruffling his yellow-white hair. When he had first moved to Montana, he had worn a cop's regulation crew cut. He had let his hair grow out gradually during the past year, but it was still much shorter than his brother Pete's ponytail.

Although the open road felt wonderful, Mel was cautious in his little escape. He and his associates had spent months under the scrutiny of the government and the press. There was also the ongoing threat that their enemies might be watching, eavesdropping on their communications, even following them. Such fears had waned somewhat with the passage of time, but even now Mel glanced in his rearview mirror out of habit, watching for any car that might appear to be tracking him.

The woods and hills of Montana might have afforded more freedom than did the bigger cities where the rabbis and the others lived, but the seeming liberty of the wilderness could be misleading. Pete and Mel did not fool themselves with any misspent hope that the handful of Aryan Nations aficionados who had been rousted from Bull River had left no followers behind.

In fact, the two brothers had grave doubts about the security of the rabbis entering that domain. When Honey had gotten word that the Jewish scholars would be coming to the wedding, Pete had expressed his misgivings. But Honey had been so crestfallen, he had let the matter drop. Mel and he had simply agreed that they would be on guard for anything suspicious surrounding the event, and Honey had agreed to tell no one but Roberta of their attendance before the big day.

The interstate through Spokane passed over the bustling city and the deep-cut, tree-filled river valley in which it lay, before turning sharply up Sunset Hill toward the flat, open plain that formed the western rim. Veering north, Mel's car followed the green highway signs that led to Fairchild Air Force Base, Geiger Field, and the international airfield.

Mel had seen some impressive airports in L.A., New York, and Frankfurt. Spokane's was about the size of Tel Aviv's, but uniquely lovely, with its terminal's modernistic swept-wing roofline and a multi-tiered parking garage linked to the main building by an arching skywalk. Passing through the laser-eyed tollgate, he lowered his window and grabbed his parking ticket when it was spit out by the machine. Round and round he drove, up the garage's spiraling ramp, finally reaching the parking level that shared the skywalk.

As Mel got out of his vehicle and locked the door, he scanned the area. Most of the spaces were full, but there were no other people to be seen at the moment. His police training had taught him to watch for anything out of place, a shadow where there should be none, a flicker of movement on the periphery of his line of sight. Shifting from one foot to the other, he studied the outlines of the massive concrete pillars supporting the level above.

He saw nothing to give him concern, and so proceeded to the skywalk. Again, except for a young mother and her two small children returning to their car, there were no customers in the elevated corridor, and nothing unusual to be seen out the windows, which gave him a view of the taxis and passenger-loading area below.

As Mel descended the escalator to the main entrance of the terminal, he scanned the lobby. David Rothmeyer and Ken Aronstam were to meet him here, having arrived on an earlier flight.

The moment he spotted the professor, Mel's face broke into a broad smile. Dr. Rothmeyer represented the best of humanity, Mel thought. It was no cliché to consider him "a gentleman and a scholar."

The professor and his friend, Aronstam, were standing with their backs to him, examining a wall map of the area, probably figuring out what route they would be taking to get to Honey's home. Mel approached them from behind, and called out, "Hey, Dave! How's it goin'?"

David wheeled around, recognizing the voice, which brought a smile to his face as well. "Mel!" he exclaimed, thrusting out a hand. "How good to see you!"

As the two shook hands, David introduced his friend. "This is Professor Aronstam, but he'll probably let you call him Ken," he said with a laugh.

Ken nodded and returned Mel's handshake.

"So you're Honey's favorite relative!" Mel said. "She speaks of you often."

"I guess I'm like a big brother to her," Ken said. "I had to come see to it that Pete does right by her."

This was said only half in jest. Mel could not miss the protective tone behind the words.

"Pete's a good guy," Mel said in his own brother's defense. "Sometimes he's just slow on the uptake."

Ken could have said something about ten years being more than slow, but David intervened. "The rabbis think the world of both you Westers," he said. "Honey could do worse, as I see it."

This seemed to take the edge off the men's introduction, and David added, "Speaking of the rabbis . . ." Gesturing up the broad ramp that led to the arrival-departure area, he suggested they head for the gate where the old scholars would soon be disembarking.

Finding the designated waiting area, they read the scrolling monitor suspended over the check-in counter. The line for the flight out of New York, via Salt Lake, indicated that the plane would be on time, and as they stood there, an airline attendant stepped behind the desk. After tapping on the microphone, he announced, "PanWorld Flight 219 from Salt Lake will be arriving in ten minutes. Those departing on PanWorld Flight 420 for Honolulu may check in now."

In compliance, several waiting passengers went to the counter, vacating their seats. Mel, David, and Ken sat down to wait for the rabbis.

As they watched the comings and goings of planes on the runway, Aronstam broached the topic that had troubled the Westers.

"Pardon me if I've been propagandized about your region," he said, "but isn't Montana a rather dangerous place for the likes of the rabbis?"

David cleared his throat. Ken seemed determined to step on Mel's toes at every verbal turn.

But Mel took the observation in stride. "First," he replied, "Montana is not exactly 'my region.' I moved there about a year ago, from L.A. Pete and I were raised in Seattle."

That established, he went on, "However, it is unfortunate that the media colors 'The Last Best Place' as a hotbed of separatism. That movement is a bleak minority in Montana, just as the gangs are a minority in L.A. Most of the folks I have met in Big Sky Country are as kind and humane a lot as you'll find anywhere. It's just that the troublemakers give the entire region a bad rap."

Aronstam was appropriately thoughtful. "Still," he said, rubbing his chin, "you have to admit, crackpots like Ted Kaczynski wouldn't have lasted long elsewhere."

Mel bristled. "Kaczynski's insanity was bred in California and fine-tuned at Berkeley. It just so happened that he needed anonymity to pull off his stuff, and people can find anonymity in rural places."

Rothmeyer squirmed uneasily in the black vinyl seat. He had gained experience as a peacemaker with the quarreling rabbis, but he had not anticipated needing to step into the role so soon.

"Maybe we should just give the place a chance," he said to Ken. "Let's draw our own conclusions when we get there, okay?"

Aronstam shrugged. "Works for me," he said casually.

There was a span of cool silence as more planes taxied in and out beyond the window. Joyous people greeted other joyous people arriving at gates up and down the long room, families embraced, others said good-bye, tearfully or wistfully. Most everyone was dressed in casual Northwestern attire—blue jeans, sweatshirts, flannel shirts, denim. Here and there a business suit was seen, but for the most part, the style was inconspicuous.

Observing this, Mel admitted, "I will give you this much: the rabbis are going to stick out like sore thumbs anyplace from here to Bull River!"

David and he laughed together, and even Ken, who had only seen the rabbis on TV during the media blitz, nodded. "I guess that's what I was driving at," he said. "I just hope they don't endanger themselves with unwanted notice."

All three of them could agree to this. But, however noticeable the rabbis would be, there was nothing the three younger men could do about it.

The rattling of the desk attendant's mike hailed the arrival of their plane: "PanWorld Flight 219 from Salt Lake to be unloading at gate C."

A big-bellied plane with the logo of PanWorld Airlines was just pulling to a stop at the loading tunnel. Mel, David, and Ken stood up and walked to the roped-off aisle where the passengers would enter.

"They'll probably be among the first to disembark," David observed. "They always fly first-class."

As he said this, several well-dressed yet casual passengers walked out from the loading ramp, greeting those who awaited them. David, who was taller than his companions, watched over Mel's and Ken's heads for the first sign of the rabbis.

His eyes were peeled for four peculiar hats—two gray fur-trimmed fedoras, one black fur-trimmed broad-brim, and one multicolored yarmulke. He did not notice four other hats, very different from those, as they entered the aisle. It was not until the milling crowd in the waiting area grew hushed and then began to laugh softly among themselves, that he identified the objects of their attention.

Nudging Mel, who was beside him, he sighed. "Good grief! What can they be thinking!"

Here came the rabbis, not done up in long black frocks and rabbinical hats, but outfitted like actors in some B western movie. They wore cowboy hats and bright plaid flannel shirts; flashy new low-heeled boots, which in their unbroken state appeared to be rather uncomfortable; and crisp blue jeans fresh off some rack in Salt Lake. With their incongruous beards and long hair, they could have been sidekicks to Tom Mix or Gene Autrey, had they not been so spotlessly attired.

"David!" Rabbi Ben hailed, waving conspicuously to the embarrassed professor.

Only Uriel Katz looked chagrined to be done up in this way. Red-faced, he ducked behind the others, who seemed oblivious to the gawking crowd as they proudly sallied forth.

As they were introduced to an astonished Ken Aronstam, grabbing his hand and shaking it exuberantly, one of Dr. Jacob's side curls, which he, like the others, had tucked up beneath the rim of his Stetson, popped out and dangled freely against his cheek.

Rabbi Levine reached up quickly and poked it back in for him. "Watch that, Carl!" he grumbled. "We don't want to draw attention to ourselves."

CHAPTER 7

As Mel's flashy red Suburban made its way up the highway between Spokane and Coeur d'Alene, Idaho, it carried the most unusual passenger load of any vehicle within the Inland Empire. Two professors of anthropology from a prominent Midwestern university, accompanied by an ex-cop from L.A., were incongruous enough. Add to that the presence of four New York Jews, rabbis at that, and the mix went beyond odd. But put the rabbis in their cowboy getups, and the scene would have been a challenge for a *Mad* magazine cartoonist to capture.

Mel was glad that he had stopped to fill the gas tank at the Flying J on the Idaho-Washington border before arriving at the airport. At least he wouldn't have to stop again before they were well into Montana, and should the rabbis step into some minimart along the way, there would not be many people to observe them.

Before they had left the airport, Mel had loaded his passengers' luggage into the back of the rig, having brought the car down from the garage to the loading area. As he did so, Rabbi Ben had taken David aside, a serious look on his venerable old face. "This friend of yours," he said privately, indicating Ken Aronstam, "how much have you told him about your work for us?"

David understood his concern. "Very little, really," he replied. "The department gave me leave to do research in the Middle East. The fact that I have not presented any paper on it yet is not unusual, so I have not been questioned much. Of course, Ken, like all my colleagues, saw the media coverage of our little scrape over there. But so far as they know, I was just doing archaeological research for you."

The rabbi seemed relieved but not surprised. "I knew you would be discreet," he said. "I am glad Dr. Aronstam has not pressured you."

The fact was, Ken Aronstam knew better than to pressure David Rothmeyer. His own experience with this Jerusalem matter had been cloaked in mystery and sensitivity from the beginning. Though he had, to this point, been on the periphery of David's adventure, he had known from the day the rabbis' strange letter arrived at the university, seeking to enlist a "practiced Jewish archaeologist" in a matter of "highest importance to Israel," that his best friend was about to become involved in more than a "research project." He had, in fact, collaborated with David in a rather vague wording of the proposal for the sabbatical, presenting it for the committee's approval as a "dig underwritten by Israeli archaeology authorities."

When Ken's own cousin, Honey Aronstam, ended up being the focus of the same enemies who wished to thwart David's work, the entire convoluted drama became personal. To this day, Ken did not understand it all, but his analytical mind had, of necessity, been stretched to accommodate the fact that there were forces at work behind the scenes that could not be explained scientifically. Whatever he might have speculated about Rothmeyer's involvement, he esteemed his colleague enough not to press him for what he suspected were "classified" answers.

David placed a reassuring hand on Rabbi Ben's arm. "I know that your greatest concern is for the safety of Zachary Cohen," he said softly. "You may be certain I have never breathed a word of our quest for the high priest to Dr. Aronstam or anyone else."

Rothmeyer was not the only one whom Rabbi Ben questioned before they left Spokane. As the professors and the other rabbis piled into the car, Ben stepped up to Mel, who was just closing the back doors where the luggage was stashed.

"Melvin," he said, "you know that I respect your experience as a policeman. I am sure you must be aware that our enemies are quite adept at various surveillance techniques."

As Rabbi Ben said this, he looked furtively at the shiny Suburban in which he was about to be taken into unfamiliar territory.

Mel got his gist and nodded. "Rabbi, if you're worried that someone might have planted some sort of bug in this rig, you can put your concerns to rest. It is outfitted quite nicely with surveillance tech of its own. If anyone were to touch this car, it would send off an alarm that would shake three counties! And"—he pointed his thumb at his own chest—"the only one who can deactivate that alarm is yours truly."

Rabbi Ben heaved a satisfied sigh. "That is what I wanted to hear, Mel," he said with the smile. At this, he joined Ken Aronstam and Menachem Levine in the car's middle seat.

Uriel Katz and Carl Jacobs sat in the rear and David had the front passenger seat. As Mel hopped behind the steering wheel and buckled his shoulder belt, the others followed suit, and the Suburban wheeled out of the loading area and toward the highway.

Once on the road, Mel glanced in the rearview mirror, again looking for suspicious cars behind him. But this time all he saw was a collage of cowboy hats. Though this was a spacious automobile, the wide brims of the rabbis' new headgear bumped together, and the tall crowns nearly brushed the ceiling.

"Rabbis," Mel said respectfully, "would you mind removing your Stetsons while I drive?"

The four old fellows looked uneasily at one another. Uriel Katz was more than happy to comply and whipped his hat off in a flash, plopping it disdainfully in his lap. The others also complied, but fumbled with their side locks, which fell instantly down to their cheeks.

"Thanks, fellas," Mel said.

Carl and Menachem held their hats awkwardly on their knees, fingering the rims and casting sideways glances out of the car windows. Rabbi Ben sat straight and tall, at least pretending not to be troubled when people in a passing auto stared at him. As though it were the most natural thing to do, he tucked his side curls behind his ears, giving the cue to the others to do the same.

Uriel snorted, at first resisting, but when Ben glared back at him, he, like his colleagues, concealed his distinctive ringlets.

Like an ad for L.L. Bean, the men each wore a plaid flannel shirt, but even in this getup they showed separate tastes. Rabbi Ben's color scheme was a subdued black-and-cream-colored flannel, and Levine's was also a muted beige tone. Carl Jacobs' shirt, though, gave the impression that, being loosed, however briefly, from the constraints of his traditional habit had been a tempting invitation to self-expression. His shirt was a wild red variation on the plaid theme, with embroidered green cacti on the yoke, and his wide-brimmed Stetson sported a flashy pheasant tail fan on the band.

As for Uriel Katz, even in this garb he was the epitome of conservatism. He had selected a plain dark brown flannel, with only a hint of a black plaid. Perhaps even he, however, satisfied a secret yen for self-expression in the addition of a tasteful bolo. The sliding clasp on the plain black braid was a silver Star of David. Mel was amazed that he had even been able to locate such an adornment.

The driver could not see the men's boots, but recalled all too well that they were classic cowboy footgear, complete with pointy toes and elevated heels. He remembered Carl Jacobs' as especially noteworthy, being made of glistening black-and-white snakeskin. More memorable than that, however, was the sight of all four men trying to walk in these boots, which, even had they been broken in, would take weeks to get the hang of.

At last Mel could contain his curiosity no longer.

"Okay, Rabbis," he said, "are you going to tell us where you got those outrageous clothes? And why?"

David winced. Though he had sometimes been confrontational with the old fellows, to hear someone else do so made his face redden.

Menachem was taken aback. "Outrageous?" he replied. "I should think you would be pleased that we are trying to fit in!"

Uriel leaned over Menachem's shoulder. "I told you we overdid it!" he growled.

Menachem only frowned, but Carl seemed not to be put off by the interchange. "We went shopping in the Salt Lake City airport," he called from the rear seat. "We had quite a high time!"

Mel glanced in the mirror at Carl Jacobs' round, shining face. He obviously still reveled in the experience, like a child on a holiday spree. As Mel envisioned the four men selecting their strange clothes and trying them on in the dressing rooms of some tourist trap, he stifled a grin.

But Rabbi Ben was somber. "Do you think we chose unwisely?" he asked.

Mel was chagrined. "I . . . I guess we are just used to seeing you in your traditional habits."

David turned to the elder gentlemen from the front seat. "I think the more important question Mel asked is 'Why?' Did you think you should not wear your Hassidic garments in this region?"

Rabbi Ben was sincere when he replied, "We did not wish to draw undue attention to ourselves. We feared people might recognize us from all the times we were shown on television."

Mel and David looked at each other in sheepish surprise. Why hadn't they thought of that?

"Oh," the professor said. "That makes sense."

A span of uneasy silence filled the car as it whizzed up the interstate toward the Idaho border. Some soft grumbling passed between Uriel and Carl, and some sharp looks were thrown their way by Rabbi Ben. Otherwise, the group was tensely quiet.

At last, Ken Aronstam broke in. "I know, from my younger years in synagogue, that the Hassidim are quite . . . shall we say . . . particular about their appearance." It was obvious he was choosing his words gingerly. "I would like to know how you justify such a break with tradition, even in light of the dangers you mention."

To this, Rabbi Ben had a well-honed answer, the readiness of which showed he had given the issue much thought before making his decision.

"The Torah does not make any direct comment about clothing," he replied, "other than to forbid men from wearing women's attire, and vice versa. The Torah does mandate that men and women dress modestly, so as to avoid anything revealing or suggestive. Beyond that, we are not bound, and, indeed, in cases where we might invoke danger or hostility, we are free to . . . shall we say . . . blend in."

"Blend in . . . yes, that is good," Carl echoed.

Rabbi Levine added, "You see, there is a difference between tradition and law."

Ken smiled wanly. "I see that you have given this much consideration," he said. "Your people are known for their scholarship, and even in this, you have lived up to it."

David heaved a small sigh. Ken was now playing the diplomat, and he hoped he enjoyed it. David had learned the role well and was glad to trade off for a while.

Rabbi Ben seemed pleased with his reply but was still concerned. "Perhaps, after all, as Uriel says, we did overdo it."

Rabbi Katz sat up taller at the acknowledgment.

But Carl was disappointed. "Oh, I don't know, Ben. The advertisements in the clothing store said such clothes were for the 'Rough-and-Tumble West.' "

Mel, unable to contain himself, laughed aloud. The rabbis were taken aback, but when Menachem lifted his elbows, holding his hands in fists as though taking up a horse's reins and bouncing up and down on the seat, the entire carful of men came undone.

Laughter filled the Suburban as it wheeled through Coeur d'Alene. And when the passengers in another car looked at them wide-eyed, Mel gave them a thumbs-up.

"Montana, rough and tumble!" he called. "Here we come!"

CHAPTER 8

Zachary Cohen stood at a third-story window of a sumptuous home in upstate New York. It was well past midnight, but the bed in his sleeping quarters had not been used this evening. In agitation, he paced before the window, his shadow moving across the yellow patch of light cast from his desk lamp onto the broad manicured lawn far below.

He missed the old rabbis, who had been his constant companions for the past year. He missed Israel, where he had been born and where he had lived all his life, until the fateful day when David Rothmeyer pinpointed him in the courtyard of the Wailing Wall as the designated heir to a priesthood he had never craved.

He missed his family—his father, a decorated World War II journalist, and his mother, a survivor of the Holocaust—whom he had left behind in Jerusalem to come to America and study for what the rabbis insisted was his destiny. Most of all, just now, he missed his church congregation, one of the many young Messianic assemblies that had sprung up in the past few years in Israel.

Zachary Cohen was one of the first generation of Jews born on the soil of the reborn nation of Israel, a nation that had had no place on earth for two thousand years except in the hearts of its people. He was also a Messianic Jew, a member of a movement so new and so untried compared to the millennia of Jewish history, that relatively few on earth had heard of it or paid any attention to it.

Zachary liked to call himself a "completed Jew." Most of

his fellow countrymen resented the phrase. Since when, they argued, are Jews "incomplete"? But Zachary and others like him believed no Jew was truly fulfilled until he or she had found the Messiah. Why else did the Jews "wail" at the Wailing Wall, praying for the revelation of Messiah and the fulfillment of Israel?

Zachary and his ilk, of which the growing number was so great in Jerusalem that the Orthodox considered them a definite threat, believed that Messiah had already revealed himself two thousand years ago. Messiah, they asserted, had a name and a history, and one-third of the earth's population already acknowledged him as the Anointed One. His name was Jesus, son of Joseph of Nazareth—or as the Messianic Jews liked to call him, Yeshua Bar Joseph.

One way of putting it was that Zachary was a "Christian Jew." The label, to many, seemed an oxymoron—a phrase that attempted to reconcile two irreconcilable spiritual and historical concepts.

But for Zachary, Messianic Judaism had resolved the conundrum of his personal heritage, the teachings of his Anglican Christian father, and the legacy of his Jewish mother.

Just now he did not think about all of this. Rubbing his neatly bearded chin, he thought about yet another riddle, the one he had yet to resolve, the one he had never dreamed could even exist . . . until that fateful day.

Nothing for Zachary Cohen had been the same since the professor had approached him at the Wall. He would never forget the awestruck look on the man's face when he came up to him where he sat praying, calling him by name and introducing himself. "You don't know me," the tall, thin stranger had said, "but I have been looking for you for a long time!"

Within moments Zachary had been surrounded by the rabbis of the Consortium. He had often heard of the Temple Movement. He had visited the Temple Gallery, where the implements for the dreamed-of temple were on display. He had seen the garments of the future high priest. But he had never personally identified with any of it.

That day he had recognized Rabbi Benjamin. He had seen him when the old fellow made surreptitious visits to the Messianic services when the congregation met at the YMCA across from the King David Hotel. Rabbi Ben had been like Nicodemus, Zachary thought, an orthodox leader of Israel who had crept out to visit Jesus at night when his fellow Jews would not see him.

Rabbi Ben was a closet Messianic Jew, Zachary realized, grinning at the analogy. He may have aligned himself with the movement in his heart, but he still hung back. What held him? Doubt, confusion, fear?

We have those feelings in common! Cohen mused.

It occurred to him that, though he had made some lifestyle changes, he was still holding back. He had left Israel, crossed the ocean, and was now holed up in a "safe house" in upstate New York. But in his heart he was only more confused than he used to be, more uncertain of things he had, after long, hard searching, come to accept as truth.

Zachary nervously ran the fingers of both hands through his thick shock of black hair. He stopped pacing and gazed out across the gracious estate where he had resided for the past year. He could not have asked for a finer place to be "protected."

The owner of this house, which was actually a mansion, was a member of the board of directors of the World Trade Center in New York City. He was one of the wealthiest Jews on the planet, and he was devoted to the cause of Israel, both the Zionist secular agenda and the orthodox religious one. While not strictly orthodox in his practices, he supported the Temple Movement and the dream of a spiritual state.

His name was Marlon Goldstein. He had been a close friend of a martyr of the cause who was killed by radical Islamists in New York City a decade ago. Ever since then, Marlon had been devoted to helping stamp out international terrorism, especially as it targeted Israel. When the World Trade Center was bombed in 1993, he had opened his home to witnesses whose testimony ultimately led to the arrest of the Arab radicals responsible for the atrocity.

His home had become a first resort for the protection of those who were potential targets of Israel's enemies. He had outfitted it with state-of-the-art countersurveillance equipment that would detect anyone or anything coming within a quarter mile of the estate's eight-foot-high stone walls. Sensitive monitors inside could trigger yet other devices that alerted guards stationed about the perimeter and within the compound. The Goldstein mansion was indeed a "safe house," more elaborately appointed than Camp David.

Not only was this place safe, it was a haven of luxury. Zachary's eyes settled on the glistening aqua water of an Olympic-size swimming pool about a hundred yards across the lawn. Its shining water was illuminated by submerged lights, and ringing the pool were lovely white cabanas for dining and lounging, complete with saunas and changing rooms.

The house itself was almost beyond description. Zachary had never dreamed such places existed. The main wing had a dozen bedroom suites throughout its three stories, each suite fully self-contained with kitchenette, fireplace, and entertainment center, to say nothing of the exercise rooms and balconies with hot tubs attached to each.

Zachary had never even seen the entire estate. He had no idea how many buildings the grounds contained, how many guest houses, dining halls, pools, fountains, garages, or patios. He only imagined that it had to come close to fulfilling what the mansions of heaven must be like.

But this was not what kept him awake tonight.

Leaving the window, he looked through bloodshot, sleepy eyes at the plethora of papers and documents strewn across his desk. The rabbis had left him a pile of assignments to complete: readings in Jewish texts so obscure that few of the most learned Israeli scholars had ever heard of them. The ones he had been left to tackle during the rabbis' absence were replicas of scrolls written centuries ago in Alexandria, Egypt. They were treatises on priestly ritual that only a handful of souls had bothered to peruse since the fall of the Temple to the Romans in 70 C.E. The scribes and teachers of the law who had fled Jerusalem at that time, settling in Alexandria, had believed the nation of Israel would be reestablished quickly. Surely the Temple would be rebuilt within a generation, perhaps even sooner, they fondly trusted.

When enough dust of time had settled on those ancient writings, and when the ravages of history had dispersed the people of Israel across the globe, the dream of the Temple had grown dingy, the luster of hope dim and distant. There had been little reason to resurrect study of such inapplicable documents.

But then the rise of Zionism and the rebirth of Israel, which it fathered, had resuscitated the dream of the Temple, and with that dream came the need to revive such studies.

For half a century, these writings and others like them had been devoured, debated, and digested by a few Jewish teachers and students in the *yeshivas* of modern-day Israel. Zachary Cohen had never attended a yeshiva. He had gone to Hebrew school at the local synagogue as a teenager, when he had struggled through his phase of identifying with his Christianized mother's Jewish heritage. Beyond that he had not been much of a scholar.

Tonight he had been reading about the high priest's use of the "urn of ashes." He had gotten to the part where a fresh young heifer, "without spot or blemish," was to be purified for sacrifice by the sprinkling on of the ashes from a previous heifer, which in its turn had been purified, and so on back to the time of the first heifer that Aaron blessed.

All of this was for the Day of Atonement, which, the rabbis told him, he would one day oversee.

Tonight, as he had read about the sacrifice, his stomach had churned. He could accept everything the rabbis told him about his supposed hereditary priesthood . . . everything but the notion of animal sacrifice.

When they spoke of this, and when he read of it, he rebelled.

He had come to believe in Jesus' atoning death through much personal struggle. He could not—would not—believe that the death of Christ was insufficient.

When he had disputed such things with the rabbis, Uriel Katz had been his most vehement opponent. Carl Jacobs and Menachem Levine had been a little less adamant, at least being open to the possibility of various interpretations of Ezekiel and other prophets who said that sacrifices would be part of the future temple.

Only Rabbi Ben had offered any real support of Zachary's view, and that support had been given at some personal risk to the old man.

Zachary would never forget the first time the issue had been addressed. It had happened the first time the rabbis had spoken with him.

The day Rothmeyer located the young man at the Western Wall, the rabbis had asked if he would accompany them to the Consortium headquarters in the Old City. Bemused, he had agreed to do so, but only because he figured he could trust Rabbi Ben.

Imprinted forever on Zachary's mind was the scene that had ensued once he was guided to the house, then led up the ancient winding steps and into the antique corridor. The massive oak door being closed and secured behind him, he was taken into the parlor, and the rabbis, talking all at once, attempted to explain themselves. While Uriel Katz was more reserved than the rest, and David Rothmeyer added only occasional commentary, the information doled out was overwhelming.

Snatches of the presentation stuck in his memory like arrows, still targeting his soul with fear, doubt, confusion, and wonder. "Consortium . . . priesthood . . . genealogy . . . Rothmeyer . . . research . . . Copper Scroll . . . Father McCurdy . . . Oxford . . . Honey's star . . . Dachau . . . computers . . . laboratory . . . England . . . Crusader knight . . . Zadok . . . Kahana . . . Kohn . . . Cohen . . . Reginald Cohen . . . Zachary Cohen . . ."

Layer by layer, like skin off an onion, the story unfolded, until, in the space of fifteen minutes or less, the young man felt as though he had entered the Twilight Zone.

Incapable of digesting what had been presented to him, Zachary's initial response had been to stand up from his armchair, turn for the door, and wave them all off as a bunch of quacks.

But Rabbi Benjamin had followed him to the parlor door. "Please, Mr. Cohen," he had implored, "we have only so recently found you . . ." He looked over his shoulder at his friends' distraught faces. "Do not go . . . not until we have had a chance to speak our case better to you. After all these years of searching for you, we have done a poor job of preparing to actually find you. We must sound like raving fools, yes?"

The old man stood before the handsome young Jew with his hands clasped, as though he were praying.

Zachary's heart softened. "Rabbi," he said, "you of all people know that I could never be a part of what you suggest."

The other men studied their colleague quizzically, and Uriel Katz seemed to bristle with sudden suspicion. Zachary picked up on this, and seeing a flash of desperation in Rabbi Ben's eyes, realized the others were unaware of the old scholar's covert visits to the Messianic services. Although Zachary did not know him well, he considered the rabbi a likable fellow, and did not want to cause him trouble.

Turning to the group, he covered quickly. "All of you must know, having found me with the Messianic Jews, that I could never join you wholeheartedly. Why, you propose to restore all the old ways . . . the old rituals . . . do you not?"

Of course they did, and Rabbi Katz was the first to express reticence. "I told you that we could not accept just anybody . . . no matter what the genealogies say!" His voice was atremble with seething self-vindication. "What can we be thinking to bring a Messianic Jew into this!"

"*Bring him into this?*" Jacobs growled. "The *records* bring him into this, Uriel! What would you do with the *records*?"

Rabbi Ben, sensing an altercation on the rise, held up his hands. "Gentlemen . . . gentlemen!" he called. "Let us not do this now, not in front of our guest!"

David had sat on the edge of the sofa, looking at the floor with his arms crossed, consternation and defeat upon his face. But Rabbi Ben was not about to give up so quickly.

Taking Zachary by the elbow, he led him to the door where he had stopped him from going just seconds before. "Tell you what," the old man said, "we realize we have pulled this off badly. Will you let me take you to lunch tomorrow? Perhaps things would go better one on one."

"Horace!" Rabbi Katz cried. "What are you up to?"

"Enough, Uriel," Rabbi Ben replied, wheeling about with a warning look. "Give the boy some peace!"

Zachary was utterly bewildered. "I . . . I don't know," he stammered. "I suppose I could do that. Sure."

And so matters had proceeded, with Rabbi Ben always being patient, always willing to look for common ground.

Walking Zachary to the front entrance of the old house, the rabbi had reached out to shake his hand, and with that gesture made a statement that was to be the theme of their relationship from that day forward.

"Give it time, Mr. Cohen," he had said. "Give it prayer. If it is meant to be, God will show you."

Tonight, as Zachary pondered for the hundredth time the inscrutable riddle of the past year, he remembered those words. How often they had carried him through the turmoil of this mystery!

Standing by his desk, he caught his own reflection in a gilt-framed mirror that hung on the wall. The image was of a brooding young man, shadows of weariness and etchings of stress too early marked on his handsome face.

Closing his dark eyes, he breathed the same prayer he had breathed countless times: "Yes, Lord, I will give it time. But nothing is clearer today than it was a year ago." Some of the tension eased out of his broad shoulders, and when he opened his eyes he felt better. He went again to the window and opened the lower sash onto the moonlit yard.

As he did so he noticed that Marlon Goldstein's dogs were barking in the kennel that bordered the east wing. The sharp-eared Dobermans only barked when someone was approaching the estate, attuned to noises the human ear would not pick up as quickly.

Zachary peered through the silvery darkness toward the main gate of the walled compound, which could be seen from his vantage point. Headlights were coming up the curving drive beyond the wall, pulling to a stop at the electronically activated entry. Apparently, whoever approached had been given the go-ahead to enter, for as the car pulled to a stop, the gates swung open. A long black limo eased onto the estate grounds, following the driveway all the way up to the front entry.

Zachary could hear the main door open and then voices beneath the awning that sheltered the sprawling porch. Leaving his room, he stepped onto the third-floor mezzanine, from which he could see all the way down the winding staircase that led to the lobby. The butler was at the door, and a group of uniformed men was entering the house.

Zachary immediately determined that they were police of some sort, perhaps government officials—CIA, FBI—he could not know for sure. Greeting them was Marlon Goldstein.

"How is he doing?" Zachary heard him say.

"He is a little frightened," one of the officials replied. "But he slept some on the way up from D.C."

Zachary leaned over the mezzanine rail, trying to see to whom they referred. Marlon Goldstein had knelt down on one knee, as if to speak with someone very small.

"We have a nice room for you," he said. "You will be safe with us."

Urged forward from the huddle of officers came a small boy, a black child about six years old.

"Lamar, is it?" Marlon continued, holding out a hand.

Lamar Jackson looked at the floor, as though afraid to speak.

"Geoffrey," Marlon said to the butler, "do we still have some of that peppermint ice cream?"

The butler smiled. "Yes, sir," he replied.

"Would you like some ice cream, Lamar?" Marlon asked.

The boy brightened, and as Zachary watched, the butler led the child toward the kitchen.

CHAPTER 9

Zachary Cohen stepped back from the mezzanine rail as Marlon Goldstein's young guest went with the butler to the kitchen. He was careful not to be seen as he peered down into the lobby from the darkened landing, eavesdropping on the agents as they spoke with the host. It was easy to hear their subdued voices as they carried up the three-story rotunda to the skylights that capped the spiral staircase. He could not make out the full content of their conversation, but he caught phrases expressed in urgent tones, the implications of which were chilling enough.

He had heard of the assassination of Senator Jefferson, which had taken place nearly a month ago, and tonight the man's name was repeated several times, along with such words as "witness," "police," "poor little kid," "terrified," "traumatized," "grateful," and "protection." As the agents turned to leave, each of them shook Goldstein's hand, and Zachary thought he heard one of them say, "Maybe you can get him to talk."

Goldstein saw the men to the door and, once alone, stood for a long while in the lobby, as though deep in thought. At last, he seemed to have an idea, and glanced up the stairs to the mezzanine on which Zachary stood. Just as quickly, he turned and went into the kitchen, was gone for a few seconds, and then returned, heading for the stairs.

The young Israeli hastened back to his suite and stepped inside, drawing the door closed. He could hear Mr. Goldstein climbing the stairs and figured he was coming for him, though he could not imagine why.

Looking at his unused bed and the mess on his well-lit desk, he realized there was no concealing the fact that he had been awake when the young boy arrived. He did not have to let on, however, that he had overheard anything.

Goldstein must have stood outside Zachary's door for a couple of minutes before deciding the light that showed through the crack at the floor meant the guest was awake. At last he knocked.

Zachary went to the door and opened it, trying to look surprised.

"Mr. Goldstein!" he greeted. "What are you doing up at this hour?"

Marlon Goldstein was a distinguished-looking man, tall and handsome, with clear olive skin and salt-and-pepper hair. He could not have concealed his Jewishness from the least observant viewer, his symmetrical features dominated by a large, hooked nose, and his dark eyes intelligently piercing.

"Mr. Cohen," he said apologetically, "I am sorry to bother you, but I saw that your light was on. I thought it might be all right if I spoke with you."

"Of course," Zachary agreed, inviting him into the room. "I was just studying, which seems to define my life these days."

Goldstein entered the room and noticed the open window. Stepping toward it, he watched the limousine depart, taking away the officials who had brought Lamar Jackson from Washington, D.C. "See that?" he said, directing Zachary's attention to the gate. "The men in that car are CIA agents. You know that Senator Calvin Jefferson was killed?"

Zachary gestured to a pile of newspapers on the sofa. "I've been following the story," he said.

Marlon quickly closed the window and drew the blind. "Mr. Cohen," he said, soft urgency in his voice, "you and your colleagues have entrusted me with information of the most sensitive nature. I am sure that I can do the same with you?"

Zachary felt the prickle of rising hair on the back of his neck. Knowing that Goldstein's main concern was always the welfare of Israel, he asked, "Does this relate, somehow, to the interests of my country?"

Marlon hesitated. "My educated guess, and the guess of the police, is that it very well might," he affirmed. "Senator Jefferson was involved for years in attempted mediation between Israel and her enemies. His murder could very well relate to that work in some way."

Zachary made a quick deduction. "And the men who just left . . . they are part of the investigation?"

Marlon nodded. "They . . . and an eyewitness they brought with them."

The Israeli did not let on that he had seen the visitor, but he knew that Goldstein must refer to the child who was in the kitchen. He hedged. "And who is that?"

Marlon was fidgety. "May I?" he asked, gesturing to the sofa.

"Of course," Zachary replied, pushing aside the papers strewn on the velvet couch. "Please, sit down."

Goldstein took a deep breath. "The CIA brought a young boy, a little street kid from D.C. He is here now, and he will be staying here as a protected witness of the state. It seems he was the sole observer of the crime, but he has been badly traumatized by what he saw in that subway station. Though a child psychologist has been working with him since the murder, so far he has only been able to tell that he saw Senator Jefferson pushed onto the tracks. He freezes up when asked for any more information."

Zachary shook his head. "Poor kid," he said. "Where is his family?"

"Like I say," Marlon repeated, "he is a street kid. Apparently lived, quite literally, on the sidewalks. He took the police to where he had last seen his mother, and . . ." The man looked sadly at the floor. "The street people who knew him said his mother had been found stone-cold dead early that morning. From all accounts, she was a heavy drinker, and sometimes added crack to her regimen."

Zachary sat down on the other end of the large sofa and slumped against the arm. "Wow!" He sighed. "That kid's been through it!" Shrugging, he said, "You certainly have my confidence, Mr. Goldstein. But what can I do to help?"

"First," Goldstein said with a smile, "you've been my guest for nearly a year. Please call me Marlon."

Zachary agreed. "And call me Zack," he said.

"Very well, Zack," Goldstein obliged. "The boy's name is Lamar Jackson. He is presently eating peppermint ice cream with Geoffrey. I would like to put him in the room next door to you. We are going to provide him with anything he needs—new clothes and all—as long as he's here. Meanwhile, if you hear him in the night, maybe you could check on him. He might have trouble sleeping."

Zachary was pleased to assist. "He won't be the only one with that problem," he said. "I've been quite a night owl lately."

Marlon seemed to understand. "I suppose it's strange not to have at least one of the rabbis for company."

Zachary nodded. "They're demanding old fellows," he said with a laugh, "but things seem awfully quiet without them."

Goldstein gave a bemused chuckle. "Somehow, I can't imagine them in Montana. They said they were going to that isolated log house shown on CNN last year?"

"That's what I understand," Zachary replied. "The whole thing appears rather risky to me, but Rabbi Ben insisted God would not want them to miss this wedding."

Marlon shrugged. "If Rabbi Ben says that, who are we to question?"

As they had been talking, Zachary had not heard the butler and the boy coming up the stairs. When Geoffrey knocked on the door, Marlon jumped to get it.

The door opened to reveal the youngster hiding behind the butler's leg. Geoffrey drew him around in front and, bending over him patiently, presented him to Goldstein.

"How was your snack?" Marlon asked.

The boy gave a shy smile.

"Lamar," Goldstein said, "we want you to meet a very nice man." Gesturing to Zachary, he said, "This is Mr. Cohen. He will be right next door to you all night. You will have a wonderful room and a comfortable bed, but if you become afraid, Mr. Cohen will be right here to help you."

Zachary, not at all sure of his childcare skills, wondered what he had gotten himself into. But as he studied the boy's big eyes and sweet face, his heart melted. Drawing near, he offered his hand to the child, who took it hesitantly. "Glad to meet you, Lamar," he said, shaking the soft little hand. "You may call me Zack. We're going to be great friends. Okay?"

It must have been four in the morning when Zachary finally drifted into a fitful sleep. Images of Senator Jefferson in his trademark trim suit and tie haunted his dreams. Repeatedly those images were disrupted by the imagined sounds of a careening subway train and the screeching of wheels. Always the crunch of metal against flesh was followed by the nightmarish screams of a small boy.

The Israeli was not to be graced with more than a couple of hours of such "rest" before the imaginary became real. The screams in his dreams awoke him, and as he lay there in a sweat he was still hearing them. The little boy next door was having his own nightmares, and the cries Zachary had incorporated into his dreams came from the child's room.

Throwing back his covers, Zachary rushed to Lamar's room. Not bothering to knock, he opened the door and bolted to the boy's bed.

He reached for the lamp on the nightstand and, turning on the light, found the child tossing about, kicking his little feet in a tangle of sheets.

Firmly, Zachary shook Lamar's shoulders. "Hey, little guy," he said, "it's okay. I'm here!"

Lamar gradually emerged from the all-too-real scene of the murder's reenactment. Seeing Zachary's kind face, he sat up and threw his arms about his neck.

Zachary had never been embraced by a child. Awkwardly, he returned the hug and held the boy tight until his trembling subsided.

"What is it, Lamar?" Zachary pleaded. "What did you see? Do you want to tell me about it?"

The little boy's face glistened with tears, and his teeth chattered. "Bad men!" he cried. "Bad soldier men!"

Zachary drew away enough that he could study his expression. "Soldier men?" he asked. "What did they do?"

Lamar wept. "They hurt Sen'tor Jefferson!"

Zachary ran a hand over the small wooly head. "What did they look like, Lamar? Can you tell me?"

The boy shook his head violently.

For a long while, Zachary alternately held him and coaxed him, but the boy utterly refused to say more. When Zachary finally got him to relax enough to lie down again, and reached to turn out the light, the boy stopped his hand.

"You want the light left on?" Zachary guessed.

Lamar nodded. "Yes, sir," he said. "The spiders will get me!"

Zachary tried to interpret this, and assuming he referred to bugs and vermin in the D.C. streets, he said, "There are no spiders here, Lamar. This is a good house."

But the boy shook his head again. "No . . . the bad soldiers will get me! They have spiders on their arms!"

CHAPTER 10

Stone-cobbled Rebi Josef Street ran from the veranda overlooking Western Wall Square and wound narrowly between ancient, compactly arranged storefronts. It was shaded from the midday heat of Old City Jerusalem. Tall, slender palms filled in between squared-off rooftops, and where the sun might have scalded the pavement, potted plants in hanging baskets, suspended from the exposed ends of roof rafters and from overhanging balconies, provided shade.

Laad Girzim was grateful for the relief from his hot journey. He had left Amman, Jordan, the day before yesterday, and after being detained at the Allenby/King Hussein Bridge checkpoint, where he had been obliged to sleep in the way station, he had entered Jerusalem at midday.

Ever since the assassination of U.S. Senator Calvin Jefferson, all border-crossing stations between Jordan and Israel had been under heightened security, and anyone coming or going from Amman had been of special interest to the guards. Though the world had no real clue as to who had killed the senator, everyone suspected a Middle Eastern connection. After all, he was returning from an ambassadorial assignment in that part of the world when his life was snuffed out, the full history of his mission dying with him.

Laad could have easily crossed the border if he had shown the badge he usually carried with him, the one proving that he was an employee of the royal palace of the king and queen of Jordan. The queen, however, had insisted he not show any such credential during this journey, and that he present himself as a commoner on a business visit to Jerusalem. Laad, with his quick step and no-nonsense attitude, could pull that off, though his thick glasses and serious aspect gave him away too easily as a scholar.

Scholars were politically suspect these days, what with the raging controversy over who owned what rights to archaeological sites on Israel's West Bank. Classic digs, such as the communes of Qumran and En-Gedi, just west of the Dead Sea, had long been the domain of the Israel Antiquities Authority. Since the ceding of that region to the Palestinians, oversight of those areas was highly contested.

Laad, with his dark Arabic looks, coupled with his studious appearance, had been given the third degree upon entering Jewish territory. Jordan's recently widowed queen had feared this but had no one else she could trust to get a certain parcel into the right hands in Jerusalem.

The enigmatic queen had long lived with the tension created by her late husband's friendship with Israel. The king had been the sole member of Arab royalty in the twentieth century to take concessionary, if not outright, pro-Israeli stands when it came to matters of land and peace. Though he had always been careful to respect the opinions and decisions of his fellow Arab dignitaries, he had incurred the animosity and even the hatred of many in the Muslim world.

Then, just before his death, he had developed an embarrassing friendship with an American evangelist. He had gone so far as to allow the flamboyant, longhaired preacher to hold Christian crusades in the capital of Jordan itself!

Even now, as Laad walked the last few steps toward his Jerusalem appointment, he shook his head at the thought. What could the king have been thinking? Had his failing health robbed him of the great genius that had guided him through many a tricky political shoal?

Laad remembered the times when he had seen more than grief on the lovely queen's face in those last months. He remembered the telltale signs of frustration and chagrin that she found difficult to hide, as she had taken on the burden of diplomacy her husband left to her.

Then, at last, there came the unfathomable moment when the queen called Laad to her stateroom. Laad had been in that auspicious chamber but a few times in his career as Caretaker of the King's Treasures. He was the curator of a fabulous collection of Jordanian valuables that had been handed down from generation to generation of Arab sheiks, long before the modern monarchy. Housed in an enormous wing of the Amman Palace, the treasury was one of the wealthiest in the world. Thousands of gifts from visiting dignitaries, jewels and gold exacted in tribute, the boon of conquest and the spoils of war from ages past lined the walls and aisles of several stories.

And Laad was in charge of it all.

Quite an accomplishment for a young man who had struggled to gain an education in the inhospitable region of Petra, the red-rock city of desert fame. At his grandmother's insistence, he had gone to public school in a nearby village. Then, working as a tourist guide within the confines of his strange native town, he had earned enough money to go to college in Amman, where he had excelled in history and caught the attention of his teachers. Ultimately, he had also caught the attention of the queen, who was seeking a curator for the royal collection.

Less than a decade later, just weeks ago, Laad had been summoned to her stateroom, where he had been given the strangest assignment of his career. He was to locate a certain artifact, which the king had designated in his will was to be sent to America. It was to be couriered there by an American, and it was to be delivered to a certain group of Jewish rabbis in New York City.

Just what this artifact represented, the queen said, even she did not know. She had only been told, by her dying husband, that it had been in the possession of his ancestors since time immemorial, and that it had always been called the "Jeremiah Box."

The king had seen the box only once in his life, when, as a child, his father had taken him through the archives of the collection. Winding through labyrinthine aisles of dust-laden acquisitions, he had led the boy, pointing out the most auspicious treasures and explaining the history of those he found most intriguing. The young prince had found this foray among ancient artifacts less than exciting. But he did remember his father stopping before one low shelf, bending down and picking up a strange-looking box. Intricately carved, it was smaller than a shoebox and the deeply etched design on the lid and sides was full of dust. His father had held it reverently and had blown softly on the dingy cover, releasing a hazy cloud of soil.

"This deserves better treatment!" he had snapped at the curator who accompanied them. Taking a silky kerchief from his vest pocket, he had gently wiped the container, revealing the soft sheen of ancient cedar wood. As he did so, the prince's eyes had widened.

"I see an animal!" he had exclaimed. "What is it, Papa?"

He referred to a depiction on the lid, of a creature whose eyes had probably been inlaid with precious stones in days gone by. The stones were now missing, and the box appeared much neglected, having gouges and rubs in many places.

"It is a cow," the king had said. With this, he removed the lid, revealing only an empty interior, hollowed out to hold a bottle of some sort. "The use of this box has been long forgotten, but I remember that my father showed it to me when I was your age, just as his father showed it to him and I am now showing it to you. He said that it had been taken from our enemies for the glory of Allah many centuries ago. He said that we must never let it leave our land, for in the day that we do, our enemies will begin to triumph over us!"

The prince had absorbed this message in sober silence. He knew that his father had brought him to the treasure house primarily to give him this instruction, that it must never be forgotten, and that he should pass it on to another prince one day. Having said this, the king bent down and, after wiping dust from the shelf, returned the artifact to its place. Then, turning to the curator, he had repeated in firm tones, "Take care of this treasure! It deserves better treatment!"

As years went by and the prince became king, he rarely thought of the mysterious box. Out of sight, out of mind. Then, too, as he grew older, he tended to doubt that a mere box could be a talisman regarding international affairs.

Laad did not know this whole story. Only the queen had been privy to the king's boyish encounter, and even she did not understand why, as he lay dying, the box had become so important to him.

For Laad, the assignment of finding the box in time for Senator Jefferson's visit, of bringing it to the queen and placing it in her protection, had been of paramount priority. Just locating the artifact had taken several days. Apart from the queen's description, he had nothing to go by. The item had doubtless been cataloged simply as "a cedar box," one of many in the king's cache. Nowhere in the inventory was anything listed as a "Jeremiah Box."

Finally he had found it, still sitting on the shelf where the former prince had last seen it. Once again, it was laden with years of dust and neglect. To Laad's bewilderment, it contained absolutely nothing, its interior simply lined with an ancient, brittle piece of velvet, form-fitted to the carved-out interior. He did note that the hollow in the box, both in the lid and the base, was shaped like a bottle, and he wondered what container once rested there.

But he had not been assigned to figure this out. He had only to deliver the box to the queen, who received it with bemusement. Though she did not say so, he could see that she wondered what could be so urgent about getting this to America.

Laad had not been privileged to meet Senator Jefferson. The man's visit to Jordan was unusually brief, as diplomatic missions went. He had spent only a day in Amman, as a guest at the palace, and then he had left for home.

The entire world knew what had happened after that. The untimely demise of the energetic and aspiring senator had come as a shock to his friends and detractors alike. That the senator had been given the mysterious box was a fact known only to Laad, the queen, and whomever the queen might have seen fit to tell.

Apparently someone in Jerusalem was supposed to know, because today Laad was on a mission to meet with him.

As he hastened down Rebi Josef Street, he gripped a small valise under one arm, his hands sweaty with the heat and with nervous tension. He studied the little shop signs that hung over various entryways until he came to one on the right, over the door of a building that backed onto the very edge of the high bluff overlooking Western Wall Square. "Temple Gallery," it said.

Laad felt a twang of discomfort as he stood before this doorway. All his life he had been taught to avoid contact with Jews. He had been taught that a good Muslim had as few dealings with the enemy as possible. He remembered how his father, a trader in Petra, had actually spat upon the ground after any transaction involving Jewish tourists, though he did, of course, treat them with effusive courtesy to their faces.

Now here stood Laad, ready not only to deal with Jews but to set foot in a Jewish sanctuary. He was not certain what the Temple Gallery was, but he knew it was not Muslim!

Clearing his throat, he straightened the *kuffiyyah* on his head, a skullcap a bit larger than the traditional Jewish yarmulke, and the distinguishing hallmark of an Islamic Arab.

Nervously, he stepped down the few stone steps to the sunken doorway and entered the sanctum. Once inside, he was surprised to see that this was a shop as much as a holy place. His eyes quickly swept around the room, trying to make sense of what he saw.

Above an archway that apparently led to the gallery proper, was a large gold-framed oil painting depicting the court of a magnificent building. The structure, which rose several stories from a parti-colored pavement, had a facade of aquamarine and was fronted by massive columns. In the court before it, men dressed in long robes performed some sort of ritual, the smoke of lampstands and censers wafting about them as they bent over an altar.

Laad's eyes grew wide as he tried to decipher what he saw. Then he read the sign that hung below the great painting: "Temple Consortium—Paving the Way for Messiah."

The Arab's knees grew weak. How he wished he could turn and run! But the queen had sent him here and he must go through with his assignment. *Just give them the parcel and be gone!* he told himself. *This won't last long*.

His private pep talk was interrupted by the voice of a clerk at the counter, a fine-looking young Jewish woman. "Are you Mr. Girzim?" she asked, using English as most Middle Easterners did when speaking with foreigners.

Laad jerked into the moment. "Uh . . . I am," he said. "I am here to meet Mr. . . ."

He could not call up the name, so frayed were his nerves.

"Mr. Diamant?" she filled in. "He is waiting for you. He expected you yesterday," she said pleasantly.

At this, she headed down the corridor that led to the gallery. In mere seconds a businesslike man entered the foyer.

"Mr. Girzim!" he greeted, hurrying forth to meet him. "I am Shalom Diamant, curator of the gallery! How good of you to come! Did you have trouble on your journey?"

Laad detected polished courtesy in Diamant's demeanor. The host, who wore the skullcap that was the Jewish counterpart to the kuffiyyah, was apparently quite practiced at trying to put people at ease. If he was uncomfortable with the introduction of a Muslim into this sanctum, he did not betray it.

Laad also saw how quickly the man's eyes landed on the valise beneath his arm. He did not reach for it, but he was obviously quite eager to see its contents.

The Arab returned his handshake. "I was detained at Hussein Bridge," he said. "I had to sleep in the bus station."

"So sorry," Diamant replied. "I know things are very tense at the border these days. Come, come," he said, directing him toward the gallery. "Let's visit in my office. Would you care for some coffee?" Then, thinking how hot and tired his guest must be, he offered, "Or something cold to drink?"

"That would be good," Laad said.

As the visitor followed the host to the office, he cast sideways glances at the displays they passed, bewildered by what they contained. Here were polished brass vessels, there was a row of magnificent hand-carved harps, here was a case of small vials containing dyes of many colors, and elsewhere were furniture and utensils for which Laad had no explanation.

"I will be happy to take you on a tour, as soon as you are rested," Diamant said, noting the guest's fascination for what he saw.

Laad, likewise noting his host's interest in the valise beneath his arm, realized that Diamant's main concern just now would not be for his enlightenment. Following him into the office, he set the case on Diamant's desk.

"I really do not have time for a tour, as grand as that would be," Laad said, exhibiting his most pleasant face. "Shall we get to the point of our meeting?"

Diamant placed a glass of iced tea before his guest and rubbed his hands together. Laad took a cold swig, then unlatched his valise.

"Sit, sit," Diamant said, pointing out a chair in front of the desk and seating himself across from him. The host watched in silent anticipation as the Jordanian sat down and opened the case. Drawing out a manila envelope, Laad handed it to the curator.

"May I?" Diamant asked, reaching for it with quivering fingers.

"It is yours, Mr. Diamant," the emissary replied. "A gift from my queen."

The Jew fumbled with the metal tabs and pulled back the envelope flap. Pressing the sides, he made a mouth of the opening and peered inside. Two pieces of cardboard lay together, and he pulled these out, removing the top one.

There lay a glossy colored photo of the artifact that the king of Jordan had desired to send to America.

Diamant lifted it tenderly and held it to the light. Wide-eyed, he turned to Laad, his voice constricted with awe.

"So . . . this is the . . ."

"Yes, sir," Laad answered his unspoken question. "The Jeremiah Box. Our queen fears it led to the death of Senator Calvin Jefferson."

CHAPTER II

Mel Wester breathed deep of the pine-scented air as he walked through the moonlit woods of Pete's property. Following him up the trail was Rabbi Ben; together they headed to the cabin that had been the original homestead of the Barrett family.

Roberta Barrett, Honey's Mennonite friend, and her husband had been the last couple to live there before their growing family demanded larger quarters. They had sold the old cabin, along with a dozen acres to Pete when their children were grown and gone and Mr. Barrett no longer wished to work the land.

The cabin, which sat at the back of the Wester property against a wooded hill far removed from the main house, was now visible a good distance up the trail. It was an inviting sight. Soft light from a lantern suspended on the porch cast a warm glow across the front, and in the light the silhouettes of several men could be seen, the noise of their jovial fellowship floating out on the night air.

"Sounds like they're having a high time!" Ben said with a chuckle.

"A finer bachelor party has never been thrown!" Mel laughed.

It was the night before Pete and Honey's wedding. Ever since the rabbis had arrived two days ago, Pete and Mel, along with David Rothmeyer and Ken Aronstam, had camped here. Honey and Roberta had stayed in the big house, where the older woman busied herself helping prepare for the big event, and Honey saw to the needs of her guests, the rabbis. Honey slept on the sofa, Roberta on a cot nearby, and the rabbis in the bedrooms upstairs.

But tonight the rabbis, dressed in their "Montana clothes," would stay up late with the groom-to-be, best man Mel, and the professors.

Rabbi Ben and Mel were arriving late because the rabbi had wanted to make a phone call to New York. Except for Mel's cell phone, which had a limited range, there was no telephone at the Wester residence, so Ben had not contacted Zachary or spoken with Marlon Goldstein since the rabbis had left for Montana. Mel had driven him into the nearby town of Noxon to use the pay phone at the all-night convenience market.

Ben had been obliged to speak on a phone located on the wall near the rest rooms. Mel did not know whom he was calling, but it seemed to be taking a very long time as the ex-cop waited in the Suburban outside. When Mel saw the old fellow step up to the counter, where he spoke with the clerk, he decided to go inside and hurry things along.

The clerk, whose bemusement over Ben's Yiddish accent and incongruent appearance was ill-concealed, wrote down a phone number on a scrap of paper and handed it to the elderly gent.

"What's happening?" Mel inquired.

"A friend in New York wishes to fax me something," Rabbi Ben said. "I need to give him the number."

The rabbi returned to the pay phone, spoke quickly, hung up, and came back to the counter.

As the odd trio of characters waited, the attendant eyeing Rabbi Ben with a curious smile and the rabbi pretending not to notice, the fax-phone finally rang. Together the three watched as a single sheet eased out of the machine below the cash register. Mel picked up on the rabbi's tension at that moment and distracted the clerk, asking him to show him where the Fritos were. The clerk left the counter just as the contents of the paper began to appear, and once the sheet was out, the rabbi bent his tall frame over the countertop and grabbed the paper from the feeder.

Mel detained the clerk long enough for Rabbi Ben to give the fax a hasty once-over. His face yielding no clue as to the nature of the contents, the rabbi quickly folded the fax and tucked it into the pocket of his plaid shirt.

All the way back to Bull River, Rabbi Ben had been deep in thought. Mel did not question him, and the rabbi spoke little, but when he did, Mel sensed an edge of urgency in his voice, an excitement that even the upcoming wedding would not account for.

The main thing the rabbi seemed to be concerned about as they had driven back from Noxon was the trustworthiness of Dr. Aronstam. It seemed to trouble him that Ken was not a part of the original team who had been involved in the quest for the Copper Scroll. The fact that Ken was

Honey's closest relative led Rabbi Ben to ask Mel half a dozen questions about him.

"Has Dr. Aronstam ever been to Israel? Do you know what his political inclinations are? Has Honey ever shared with him what we did in Jerusalem?" and so on.

Mel had to plead ignorance on all counts, though he doubted Honey would have been forthcoming on matters she knew to be of a sensitive nature, even with her cousin.

"Why do you ask?" Mel had queried as they pulled onto the rough dirt road leading from the highway to Pete's house.

Rabbi Ben had conceded, "I have some very important news which I want to share with my colleagues, all of you . . . except . . ."

"Except Ken," Mel surmised.

"Do you think he can be trusted? These matters must not wait!"

"You know," Mel replied, "Dave seems to think very highly of him. They are the best of friends, from what I can see. I'm sure Dave is pretty selective in his choice of buddies."

At this, Rabbi Ben eased up a little. "Yes, of course," he said. "David is a man of discretion." Then, his face relaxing into a smile, he added, "David is a good man . . . the best."

Mel read in this acknowledgment an endorsement of Dr. Aronstam. If people could be judged by their associations, Ken had spoken well for himself. As to the important news the rabbi had, Mel figured he wished to share it just once, in the hearing of the group.

The cheery sounds of laughter and joking grew more distinct as the two latecomers approached the cabin. Most of the trek up the trail had been sufficiently moonlit that no flashlight was necessary, but the woods were thicker the farther they went, so Mel took a penlight from his belt and helped illumine the path for himself and his companion.

He was savoring the thought of a cold drink and warm camaraderie on this spring night, his mind far from any sort of trouble, when something drew his eyes toward the summit of the hill. He could have sworn the flash of another light had appeared and, just as quickly, disappeared up along the ridge, which only mountain lions were known to frequent.

Stopping dead in his tracks, Rabbi Ben nearly colliding with him, Mel raised a finger to his lips. "Shhh . . . listen," he said. "Do you hear anything?"

The older man, whose hearing was not as keen as it once had been, shook his head. "Just the fellows on the porch," he said. "Why?"

"Did you see something . . . up there?" he asked, pointing toward the tree line.

"No," Rabbi Ben said, "but you are giving me a fright. What did you see?"

Mel stood still a while longer, his head cocked toward the ridge. At last, sensing his companion's eagerness to move on, he shrugged. "Nothing, I guess."

More quickly now, the two men hastened toward the cabin. The rabbi, though in amazingly good condition for his age, was winded from the hike in his unfamiliar boots. Mel's heart beat faster than usual as well, but not from exertion. He could have sworn he saw something on the hill, and considering the identity of his housemates, any unknown in the dark beyond was unwelcome.

Roberta Barrett had not had so much fun since she was a teenager. Having grown up in an ultraconservative household, her social activities had been closely monitored, and had been limited to church functions and summer camp frolics. She fondly remembered late-night giggles with her girlfriends at Mennonite camps, long after the tent meeting was over and tearful prayer sessions had burned out at the altar rail. Tonight reminded her of such occasions.

Honey sat against the arm of the sofa in the fire-lit living room of her grand log house, cuddling beneath one of her handmade quilts, her knees drawn up under her chin as she chatted gaily with her friend. Roberta, having forsaken a rickety cot, lay on a sleeping bag spread atop a bearskin rug before the fire, her head propped up on her hand as she listened to Honey's dreams for the future.

The fire was more for effect than necessity. The evening was cool, as evenings tended to be anytime of year in these mountains, but it did not really demand a fire.

Roberta smiled as she listened to Honey's rehearsals of her beloved's fine points. Yes, Pete was tall; yes, he was strong; yes, he had provided well for her; yes, he had proven himself one of the bravest of men; yes, yes, yes. It was hard to believe, listening to this litany, that Honey and Pete had been together, essentially in a common-law marriage, for a decade. The way Honey spoke of him, she sounded like a love-struck maiden.

Then Honey dreamed of the children they would have. She told Roberta she wanted a "passel" of them before she was too old to put such hopes to rest. Roberta wished for her the fulfillment of all her hopes and gave no comment as to the likelihood or unlikelihood of them.

A bowl of popcorn sat on the floor between the women. Occasionally one of them would pop a handful mouthward, but the snack had long ago grown cold as they chatted into the wee hours.

At last, as the orangey shadows grew shorter and the room cooler, Roberta stretched and yawned. "Well, dear girl," she said, "I would dream away with you 'til dawn, but we have a mighty big day tomorrow. You'd better get your beauty rest, or you'll be less a blushing bride than a sleepy one."

Honey grinned and brushed a strand of her long dark hair from off her face. "You're right," she sighed. "Sleep tight, Roberta."

The two women snuggled down into their respective beds, their minds drifting easily into delicious slumber. Somewhere between one and two in the morning, however, they both awoke again. Anxiously, Honey pulled her legs from beneath the quilt and tiptoed to the fireplace, stirring it to provide a little light.

Roberta's eyes were wide open, and she watched Honey, breathless.

"Did you hear something?" the older woman asked.

"I . . . I think so," Honey replied, kneeling down beside her. She was about to replace the fire poker into its holder but thought better of it. Gripping it firmly, she stood and, bundling her nightgown close to her chest, crept quietly to the front window. "I thought I heard something fall on the porch."

"Me too," Roberta whispered. Joining Honey at the window, she held tightly to her taller friend's elbow, peering around her to the moonlit veranda.

For a protracted moment, they stood together, squinting through the dark, trying to see something . . . anything out of place.

Nothing. They looked at each other, sheepish grins on their faces.

"Aren't we the pair!" Honey laughed softly. "We're acting like a couple of adolescents."

Feeling easier, they turned for their beds, to try sleep once more. But just as they settled down, they tensed again.

"Listen!" Roberta said. "What is that?"

Somewhere in the black distance, perhaps down the hill . . . it was difficult to tell in these echoing highlands . . . some sort of motor hummed, like the purr of a large, droning bee. "Sounds like a chainsaw. Who'd be cutting wood at this time of night?" Honey muttered.

Roberta cocked her head. "No . . . not a chainsaw. That's a bike . . . a motorcycle. Maybe a couple of 'em!"

Honey swallowed hard. "Coming or going? I can't tell."

Roberta shrugged. "Hard to say in these hills. No, wait . . ." Her eyes grew wide, the whites shining in the moonlight. "I think it's circling, like it went toward the highway, and now it's, maybe, on one of those trails off into the woods. Oh, I don't know!"

Honey quivered and hunched down beneath her quilt. "Boy, I sure wish Pete was here!"

Roberta agreed, but then, seeing Honey throw back the quilt, second-guessed her nervous friend. "Don't you even think about it!" she said. "Don't go trekkin' after Pete! Morning will be here before we know it. We're better off to just stay put!"

CHAPTER 12

The bachelor party that the men threw for Pete could have been anticlimactic; after all, Pete's relationship with Honey had long ago crossed the line from "live in" to "common-law marriage," by most people's reckoning. But the decision to put the stamp of formality on the arrangement said a lot for the change that had taken place in Pete last year. And the party reflected his joy.

His entire world-view had been altered by his brief and hellacious foray into the world of the Aryan Nations. He had nearly lost Honey for all time, not only as a partner but as a living being. The anti-Semites with whom he had been trafficking would have killed his beloved, had she not managed to flee to safety.

Pete considered Ken Aronstam and David Rothmeyer to be heroes in the utmost meaning of the term—Ken for getting Honey out of the country and into Israel, David for seeing to her safety once she made her way to his doorstep in the Holy City.

The rabbis, of course, were all part of the drama that had taught Pete the exact nature of the bigotry to which he had submitted. When Pete's heart and eyes had been opened to the horrors of the Nazi regime during his visit to Dachau, he had decided that if he could ever win Honey's trust again, he would marry her, in the full legal and spiritual sense of the term.

Tonight Pete felt like a king on a throne as he sat in one of the hand-hewn log chairs on the porch of the old homestead cabin. This was his domain, and tomorrow he would make Honey his legitimate queen.

What finer kingdom to hand to a woman? he thought as his eyes swept past the porch to the gentle darkness beyond. And what a night this was! Towering pines caught the sounds of the men's laughter in a soft sway of breezed branches. The warm glow of the hissing lantern enveloped all of them in a camaraderie of joy and serenity, the rabbis looking especially casual in their western getups.

Roberta had sent a pitcher of icy lemonade to the cabin before she and Honey settled in to spend their own "girls' night" together. The tart beverage made its way around the porch, passed from hand to eager hand as the men talked and joked together. A bottle of fine Manhattan wine, brought by the rabbis from New York, rested in an ice bucket, awaiting the toast that would culminate the evening. But on this tepid spring night, lemonade tasted awfully good.

Pete knew nothing of the interlude at the all-night market. He did not notice how Mel kept an eye on Rabbi Ben, wondering when and if he would speak of the communiqué received on the fax machine.

From Mel's perspective, it seemed the old rabbi was amazingly convivial, considering the sober mood he had displayed earlier. Perhaps he was testing the waters, fishing for Ken Aronstam's reaction, when he brought up certain memories from Jerusalem, held in common by the others present.

"Dear old Anya would have loved to work with Mrs. Barrett on the wedding," Rabbi Ben said to Pete. "You do remember our wonderful housekeeper at the house in Jerusalem?"

Pete smiled. "Of course," he said. "Great cook!"

The old rabbi glanced casually at Ken. "Have you ever been to the Holy City?" he asked the professor.

Ken frowned slightly. "I have never had the privilege," he answered. "Dave has been all too sparing in telling me about it."

Ken was on to the old detective. His answer was just what Rabbi Ben needed to hear. The older man gave a satisfied sigh and continued, "Our Dr. Rothmeyer is an honorable man. I am sure there is much he wished to tell you, Dr. Aronstam. You must suspect that your friend's experience there was of a monumental nature."

Ken's face twitched into an uneasy smile. He did not say a word, only nodded.

Rabbi Ben had a way of bringing things to a sudden hush. This was one of those moments. The group, which only seconds ago had been raucous with joking fellowship, was now quiet.

Rabbi Ben placed a hand over his heart, and, looking deeply into Ken's eyes, spoke in a low voice. "I also believe you are now in our company, and we are in yours, for reasons as yet unseen."

Carl Jacobs, Menachem Levine, and Uriel Katz knew what was coming. Their colleague was about to bring Dr. Aronstam into the brotherhood. He was about to share with him information heretofore possessed only by those who had the "Jerusalem experience" in common.

They reacted in different ways to Rabbi Ben's imminent inclusion of this newcomer: Dr. Jacobs gave a friendly nod, Rabbi Levine smiled cautiously, and Rabbi Katz squirmed in his customary, disapproving way.

"Horace," he said in a controlled snarl, "be careful now . . ."

The elder rabbi lifted his chin and gave Uriel a direct stare. "It is all right," he replied. "Trust me, Uriel."

Then, returning his focus to Ken, he said, "I am not going to give you the entire history of the group's experience together. I am going to leave that to David." Looking at the archaeologist, he said, "At your convenience, Dr. Rothmeyer, will you please tell your friend about our adventures?"

David gave a perplexed nod. "I will be happy to," he asserted. "But why have you decided this now?"

Rabbi Ben sat back, directing his attention to the bridegroom. "Peter," he said, "I do not mean to take away from the importance of tomorrow's grand event by speaking of these matters. I hope that you will consider this sidestep as part of the grander scheme which has brought all of us together."

Pete leaned forward, eager for whatever the rabbi had to share. "Whatever is important to you is important to me," he replied. "If it weren't for all of you . . ." He stopped, his throat constricted. "Well . . . who knows where Honey and I would be today if we had not met you?"

Rabbi Ben took a deep breath. "Very well, then," he said. "I must tell all of you about something I have just learned. Mel took me into town so I could call home to New York. I felt I should check on things there, and I am so glad I did! But first of all you need to understand what has transpired to bring my colleagues and myself back into David's life."

With this, he gave a quick description of the quest the rabbis had recently assigned to the archaeologist. As he did so, Ken's eyes grew wide with incredulity.

"The breastplate of the high priest?" he gasped. "Now, that would be some find! I suppose if Dave succeeds, you are going to send him on a quest for the high priest himself!"

Ken meant this as a joke, but when the group laughed more uproariously than he expected, the professor studied them in disbelief. "Come on!" he said. "*Do* you plan such a quest?"

"Perhaps we should tell Ken the entire story now," David suggested, grinning broadly. "I don't think we will get anywhere with this until we do."

Rabbi Ben wiped tears of laughter from his old eyes. "I think you are right," he said. "But let's give him the condensed version. I am eager to tell you of my phone call."

It would take some time for the entire story to be told, what with four rabbis, two Montanans, and the professor all contributing their parts. The moon had climbed high above the western ridge and was on the decline, making room for the sun, which would soon be appearing over the eastern rim of the forest, when a bleary-eyed Ken squinted, trying to sort things out.

"You have asked me to comprehend a great deal," he said. "I think I understand the nature of the Consortium, your goals, and the nature of Dave's work for you. I also understand that you have this Mr. Cohen under protective care, and not even Dave knows where."

"That is right," Rabbi Ben affirmed.

Leaning forward, his elbows on his knees, Ken rested his chin in his hands, deep in thought. "So far, I think I am with you. But, explain again . . . how does the murder of Senator Jefferson tie in with all of this?"

Carl Jacobs elucidated. "Shortly before his death, our agency in Jerusalem was notified that the senator had been given an item that might be of interest to our purposes. He was to deliver it to us in New York." Carl's round face saddened. "As you can imagine, it never made it to us."

Ken sat back and crossed his arms. "You believe he was killed for the article he was transporting?"

"Very possibly," Rabbi Ben sighed.

Ken glanced at his colleague. David was sobered, as he had been in Columbus, by the idea of getting mixed up in such matters.

"Sounds pretty sticky, Dave," Ken commented.

"To say the least," David agreed. "And now, whether you like it or not, you're involved too."

Ken looked at the floor, a chill working across his shoulders. "So what's this about a witness to the murder?" he asked, his voice raspy.

Pete and Mel were on edge, ready for the breaking news, when Carl Jacobs interrupted. "Is it safe to speak of this?" he asked Rabbi Ben.

"I think it is necessary," their friend replied. "It ties in with this evening's phone call."

The rabbis glanced at one another, and Katz glowered in his private stew.

Rabbi Ben cleared his throat. "A small boy, a child of the D.C. streets, witnessed the murder in the subway tunnel. What none of you know, because I just learned it myself, is that he was recently sent to the same safe house where Zachary Cohen is staying."

The rabbis were astonished at this information. "When was he taken there?" Carl asked.

"Just a couple of nights ago," Ben said. "The CIA felt that the case's Middle East connection called for Goldstein's help."

"Goldstein?" Mel repeated. "That name's new to me."

Pete nodded.

"A member of the board of the World Trade Center," Levine said. "And a fervent ally of Israel. We use his home often in dealing with many sensitive matters."

"Well put," Rabbi Ben replied. "The child is there now and seems to have taken a liking to our Mr. Cohen. For the first time, he is opening up regarding what he saw. But he is still quite traumatized by his experience. And then, they have learned that his mother was found dead."

Levine and Jacobs shook their heads. "Foul play?" Rabbi Katz guessed.

"Not necessarily," Rabbi Ben said. "She was apparently . . . how do you say . . . a *crack addict*."

The term came off the old rabbi's tongue awkwardly, unused to such topics as he was.

Mel, however, was all too familiar with such matters. "In that case, the boy's troubles did not start with what he saw in that subway," he deduced. "Has he been able to bring forth anything helpful?"

"Not really. I spoke with Zachary, and the most he has gotten from him is bits and pieces from the boy's bad dreams. Something about spiders coming after him . . . spiders and soldiers. He calls the killers 'soldiers' and says they have spiders on their arms."

Pete and Mel looked at each other quizzically, and the others shrugged.

"That's one mysterious little guy," Pete said, his brow furrowed.

Rabbi Ben agreed. "Well, here is another mystery," he said. At this, he dipped a hand into his plaid shirt pocket and pulled out the folded fax received at the convenience store. Opening it, he showed the men a crude black-and-white copy of the photo that Laad Girzim had relayed to the Temple Gallery. "This is a facsimile printout of a digital photo, which Mr. Goldstein received through the Internet from our headquarters in Jerusalem. The item it portrays may be what Senator Jefferson was carrying the day he died."

All the men leaned in close, forming a circle about the fax spread on Rabbi Ben's lap. David reached for it, his hands itching.

"May I?" he asked, and the older man nodded.

"What on earth is that?" Pete asked.

The photo gave a clear enough depiction of the animal on the cedar lid, its face staring mutely at them with empty eyes. Around the perimeter of the lid were intricate, decorative etchings of fruits and flowers, marred here and there by gouges.

"The Jordanians call it the 'Jeremiah Box,'" Ben replied.

Uriel Katz gasped and the other rabbis went white with wonder.

Huddled over the paper, the scholars were lost in historic possibilities.

Only Pete and Mel were alert to anything else at that moment. In a mutual flash of recognition, they looked at each other, their eyes asking, "Did you hear that?"

Above their friends' studious ponderings, the faintest sound of engines whisked through the dusk beyond, like the sound of chainsaws—or motorcycles—where there should be none.

CHAPTER 13

Marlon Goldstein did not know exactly why Zachary Cohen was staying at his posh upstate New York retreat. He only knew that the guest was important to the Consortium, and for Marlon, that was enough.

It was a sunny morning as the two men sat together beside the aqua waters of Goldstein's main swimming pool. Both were early risers and the day often found them chatting as they walked the grounds of the estate or sat over coffee on one of the verandas that graced the house. During Cohen's tenancy, Goldstein had deduced that he was a student of some sort, possibly training to be a teacher in one of the Consortium's yeshivas in Brooklyn or Jerusalem. Goldstein enjoyed Zachary's talk of life in Israel, of what it was like to grow up there as a post–World War II native, and of the unique spiritual challenges that went with being raised as a Christian, yet devoted to his Jewish heritage.

Why it was necessary that he be harbored in the safe house, Goldstein did not ask.

For several months, the rabbis had drifted in and out of the estate, sometimes all four of them staying with Zachary in the adjoining rooms off the mezzanine. Never had the young man been left on his own, at least one of his teachers being with him at all times. When the rabbis had left for Montana, they had impressed upon Marlon that Zachary's security must never be slackened, that they would be returning as soon as the Wester wedding was completed, and that they planned to bring back a permanent bodyguard for their ward.

Zachary sipped at a steaming cup of coffee, leaning back in one of the chaise lounges beside the pool. On another lounge, Marlon rested, his eyes scanning the line where the treetops that bordered the acreage touched the blue sky above. "Looks like another warm day," the host said. "I wonder what the weather is like where the rabbis are?"

A smile stretched Zachary's lips. "Can you imagine our rabbis in Montana? I've never been there, but I would bet they feel like fish out of water."

Marlon slapped his knee and laughed aloud. "Can you just see our dear old scholars joining in the folksy activities? Do you suppose they've really been wearing the western clothes they argued about?"

Zachary laughed with him, remembering the noisy "discussions" the old fellows engaged in, regarding that issue. "Rabbi Benjamin and Rabbi Katz really went at it over that," he recalled.

Marlon nodded. "Not only the clothes but the entire notion of going at all!"

The two would never forget the ill will that raged between the rabbis as they wrangled over the propriety and/or wisdom of attending the "mixed" wedding. Back and forth they had sparred, Jacobs and Levine swaying this way and that over the issue, depending on whether Katz or Benjamin had the best argument. Of course, Katz toed the ultra-orthodox line that it was improper for a rabbi even to attend a ceremony for the union of a Jew and a non-Jew such as Honey and Pete, let alone perform one.

Rabbi Katz contended that their mere presence at such a hybrid event gave silent endorsement to the union, while Rabbi Benjamin felt that to stay away would be a slap in the face to the couple who had done so much to further the Consortium cause. Pete was, in fact, a hero, Benjamin argued. He and his brother had literally saved the lives of the yeshiva scholars whom the Arab terrorist had targeted.

"To say nothing of the fact that Ms. Aronstam provided us with one of the crucial links in our research that brought us to Mr. Cohen," Dr. Jacobs threw in.

"But then," Rabbi Levine said, "Uriel does have a point. Perhaps we could just send them a gift, and let it go at that."

Jacobs had rankled. "That would be hypocrisy! Better to have nothing to do with any of it, if we would sink to that!"

Benjamin countered that there were many examples in the Scriptures where a leader of Israel had deviated from the strictest path for the sake of a higher cause. "We are told in the Torah that we are to make the stranger feel welcome in our land and not to shun him. Peter certainly deserves our salute at this important time in his life. Why, even the Persian king Cyrus was hailed by our ancestors as a savior of our people and was spoken of in the most glowing terms by our prophets and poets. Peter may not be a Jew, but he has certainly been a savior of Israel!"

This argument had been the most difficult for Katz to top. He had not even tried, though it did not completely win him over. In the end, they decided that the four of them should go to Montana as much to enlist the aid of Mel Wester for their high priest's bodyguard as to attend a wedding.

While Marlon Goldstein had not been directly privy to these interchanges, he had been aware of the tension that accompanied the rabbis' decision to head west. When a strange e-mail had come over his private computer just last night, showing the digital photo of the odd cedar box, he had been most anxious for the rabbis to return. Hoping that Zachary might know what it was about, he had shown him the picture, but the guest had given no insight.

This morning, the communiqué still haunted the host. Growing serious, he said, "Zack, I know that the Consortium deals in very sensitive matters. As a defender of their cause, I long ago decided to offer my assistance in any way I could, without asking many questions. But . . ." He paused, his brow knit. "I could not help but wonder why the e-mail I received last night was sent at the request of the royal house of Jordan. I assume it came via Jerusalem to my computer because of the fire walls that the Consortium and my own DSL lines have built in against surveillance. The Jerusalem contacts, likewise, requested that we fax it to the rabbis from our own fax station. Obviously, the pictured artifact is politically sensitive, to the point that the queen of Jordan could not trust the transmission to her own household's equipment."

Zachary squirmed. Goldstein was a very perceptive man, and not in the least ignorant of precautionary communication techniques.

"You are probably right," he said. "But I must be honest with you. The rabbis do not tell me everything. My job here is to keep focused on my studies. If there is any tie-in, they probably would not choose to divert my interests with such knowledge."

Marlon straightened, looking at his guest apologetically. "Forgive me," he said. "I was out of line asking you to speculate on such matters. I guess I get too much of a Sherlockian thrill, sniffing out clues—a risky pastime in my position."

A tense silence passed between them, but Marlon could not resist making one more observation. "I wonder if all of this ties in somehow with the death of Senator Jefferson? After all, he had just returned from Jordan when he was . . ."

Zachary cleared his throat, feeling quite uncomfortable. With a sigh, the younger Jew looked his host straight in the eye. "Mr. Goldstein, I wish I could help assuage your curiosity. But this is not my department."

Marlon knew he had gone too far, and his face reddened with embarrassment. "Again, I am sorry," he said. "I should never . . ."

Zachary raised a hand to hush him. "It is all right, Marlon. It must be hard on you, living each day with protected witnesses in your house, international mysteries and all. I would have a hard time keeping my questions to myself, were I in your position."

Marlon appeared grateful for the pardon, as Zachary continued, "Speaking of mysteries, let me just say that Senator Jefferson's death has come to dominate much of my thinking, what with the witness sleeping right next door." Shaking his head, he corrected himself. "I should say, 'quartered' next door. The boy does not sleep nearly as much as I would like."

Marlon took a sip of his coffee and lingered over the steam that rose from the rim. "Is he still having bad dreams?" he asked.

"Not quite as violent as the first night," Zachary replied. "But he still lives in terror of spiders . . . spiders everywhere. What do you suppose that is all about?"

Marlon set his cup down and rubbed his chin thoughtfully. "As I told you when Lamar arrived, the authorities in D.C. assigned a child psychologist to the case," he said, "but the results were vague. No one has been able to break through his trauma."

Zachary stifled a yawn, feeling the need for at least one solid, unbroken night of slumber. "Someone needs to do that," he said. "God knows, I've tried. But whatever he saw in the subway tunnel is shut up dark and hard within his soul."

Suddenly, as Zachary said this, the thought occurred to him that, in truth, only God could bring the darkness to light. And God was moved by two things: faith and prayer.

Zachary had faith. Now he needed to pray.

Honey Aronstam, soon to be Honey Wester, sat up on the couch and stretched in the sunlight just beginning to filter into the dusky living room of her log home. She turned to look at her sleeping friend Roberta, who, like herself, had finally managed to get some much-needed rest in anticipation of this, the "big day."

The two women had not been left alone to handle the fears prompted by the sound on the porch and the buzzing cycles in the woods beyond. Pete and Mel had slipped away from the bachelor party when they first heard the bikes, checking up on the women and looking around the grounds for any sign of trespass.

When they found none, they promised to be back, should they hear anything again.

Pete, of course, had found it very hard to leave his bride-to-be. He was, after all, used to spending his nights with her. But for the sake of his guests and for the sake of propriety, he knew he should return to the cabin.

Holding Honey tenderly, he planted a kiss on her forehead and told her he would see her in the morning. "Good night, my soon-to-be Mrs. Wester," he said, giving her a wink and bowing to her gallantly.

Honey had had no trouble sleeping from that moment until the first rays of sun warmed the window.

Now she was wide awake, her heart tripping with the excitement of the day ahead. She swung her bare feet out from under the quilt and, wrapping her cotton robe around her, she padded to the kitchen. In moments the smell of homebrewed coffee and the sound of her activity woke Roberta.

"What a night!" the older woman called out, sitting up on the bearskin rug and yawning. "I could use ten more hours of sleep!"

Honey laughed and brought her friend a mug of coffee, complete with the whole sweet cream Roberta always enjoyed. "As soon as you're able, come join me on the porch," Honey teased.

Roberta sat crossed-legged in her pajamas, savoring the coffee as Honey exited. The bride-to-be was gone but a few moments when she poked her head back inside the screen door.

"I think I found the source of the clatter we heard on the porch last night," Honey announced. She held up a ragged broom, which Pete often left propped against the front wall, the one he used to sweep off the veranda. "This was lying on the deck," she said. "It must have blown over in the wind."

Roberta laughed. "All that fuss over a broom?" But then she looked quizzical. "Wind? I don't recall any wind last night."

Honey thought a moment and then shrugged. Roberta stood up stiffly, rubbing her back from the ache of sleeping on the floor.

"Well," Honey said nonchalantly, "at least we know there was no bogeyman lurking about."

Roberta shuffled out the door, blinking in the bright morning light. She hesitated to dampen Honey's mood, but she wondered privately how the broom had come to land on the floor. As she sat down on the porch swing, she gave the area a quick scan. It did seem that nothing was amiss, so she tried to think of other things.

Together the women rehearsed the plans for the rest of the day. Every detail that could be taken care of ahead of time had been attended to. Since it was Roberta's job to see that the bride and groom had as little stress upon themselves as possible, she had offered to make flapjacks for the couple and all the guests and had done her homework on just what else was appropriate to serve the rabbis. There would be no bacon, of course; in fact, she had decided to keep everything vegetarian, figuring that was the safest route to avoid offending anyone. So, too, with the feast that would be laid out on long tables in the yard following the ceremony. Several of Honey's neighbors had volunteered to bring hot dishes and cold salads, as well as drinks and other desserts, and they seemed to take Roberta's stipulations regarding the menu restrictions in stride.

The men had set up the tables yesterday, and Roberta had brought floral arrangements for the altar and the table where the wedding cake would be placed. The cake, of course, had also arrived yesterday, transported carefully in Roberta's four-by-four and stored in a large cooler out back.

Since this wedding was the culmination of ten years' companionship, the couple had decided that the observance of certain traditions would be dispensed with. The groom, for instance, would be seeing the bride throughout the day, prior to the wedding. To try to do otherwise would be awkward and rather silly. Nor would he be carrying her over the threshold of a house she had called her own for a decade.

Also, since Honey's parents had died years ago, her cousin Ken would be giving her away. Her only other living relative was an aunt, Ken's mother, in Columbus, but she was too elderly to come. As for Pete, his parents, as well, were gone.

Music was to be provided by a small band from the nearby town of Libby. There would be no soloist, but the leader of the band, who was a fine fiddle player, had agreed to play "The Holy City" in commemoration of the climactic events that had encouraged this union.

As for the ceremony itself, except for the fact that it would be performed beneath the unique *chuppah*, a Jewish-style canopy made from the heirloom quilt, all other ethnic or religious connotations bowed to the simple formula the justice of the peace had chosen. Honey had insisted, however, that the traditional breaking of the glass, which had accompanied all Jewish weddings in her family, should be included in this one. Pete would take the crystal goblet from which they drank their wedding toast, wrap it in a piece of fine linen, place it on the ground, and stomp on it.

As the two women enjoyed the peace of the early morning, which would all too soon be invaded by hungry men, Honey explained to Roberta that the breaking of the glass was symbolic of the destruction of the Temple in Jerusalem by Roman invaders, and that it was meant to remind the couple that nothing would be completely joyous in life until the Temple was rebuilt.

When Roberta considered this, tears came to her eyes. "I have never heard anything so beautiful!" she said. "Though I am not Jewish, my Bible teaches me that the Messiah will set up his kingdom with that Temple at the center. So even Christians long for that day!"

Honey, who had never admired anyone more than she admired Roberta, smiled warmly at this acknowledgment. For a long moment, she was caught away in memories of her time in the Holy City. "You know," she said, "nothing has been the same for me since I went to Jerusalem. I am sure our time there was unusual in the fact that we met and worked with men of faith from both Judaism and Christianity. My head and heart have been so full this past year! It almost seemed, in those few days together, that bridges of understanding were built that the world at large would do well to cross. Anymore, I do not know why Christians and Jews must be divided."

Roberta observed her younger friend's thoughtful countenance, and a lump came to her throat. She had never been one to push her beliefs on anyone, but she could tell Honey was seeking without a shepherd. "Perhaps, dear girl, you caught a glimpse of what Saint John in the Revelation called 'the new heaven and the new earth.' Perhaps you and your friends were privileged to see the foreshadowing of John's prophecy of the New Jerusalem, coming down from heaven, adorned like a bride adorned for her husband."

Honey was taken aback. She had never heard of such things and did not even know how to respond. Her face flushed, she stammered, "I . . . I can only say that all of this is uncharted territory for me and Pete. We are humbled by what we have experienced, and I hope that we will understand our part in it someday."

Roberta sighed. Clapping herself on her knees, she straightened and said, "Well, there will not even be a wedding if we don't get busy." With this, she headed across the yard toward her car, where she had stored white linens for the tables.

As she opened the rig and gathered the cloths in her arms, Honey exclaimed, "I think I hear the men coming!"

Up the trail that led from the cabin, the sounds of voices and laughter could be heard. In moments the Wester brothers appeared where the trail turned down toward the open yard, leading the group.

"Good morning!" Pete hailed the women. "You have a hungry groom on your hands!"

Honey blushed and restrained herself from rushing for Pete's arms. There should be some holding back today, she realized.

Roberta thought the best way to keep the two apart was to keep them busy. "Honey, you get upstairs now, and get your gown in order. Pete, you set the table for breakfast, and Mel, tidy up the porch, won't you?"

There was really no tidying to do on the veranda, but Roberta suggested Mel could water the potted plants and take that ugly broom to the shed. She greeted the rabbis and led them into the living room, where she invited them to make themselves at home. As for David and Ken, she put them to work helping Pete set the table. Placing the linens on the sideboard, she took a pitcher of water back out to Mel and told him to water the pansies more heavily than the marigolds.

Mel looked bewildered and studied the flowers clumsily. "Which are the pansies?" he asked, looking straight at a cluster of orange 'golds.

"Men!" Roberta huffed. "You're all helpless!"

Taking Mel by the arm, she led him from pot to pot, naming the colorful contents. "And these are Mexican pansies," she said, pointing to a particularly vivid cluster.

As she bent over these flowers, her eyes were caught by something stuck between the clay vessel and the log wall.

"What on earth?" she said, reaching down and pulling out a round, paper-wrapped parcel.

"That's where Pete usually leaves the broom," Mel noted. "What have you found?"

Roberta shrugged, turning the strange, palm-sized item over in her hand. "Someone must have thrown this at the house," she said. "That would explain how the broom got knocked over."

Mel reached for the object and held it gingerly. A piece of brown string was wound around the parcel, and the white wrapper was smudged with dirt.

"Feels like a rock," he said. Glancing through the window, he saw that everyone else was busy, and he stepped off the porch into the side yard, Roberta following him.

"Open it!" she said.

"Okay, okay," he muttered. "That's what I had in mind."

Hardly concerned for all the training he had had in the handling of evidence as an L.A. detective, Mel took his pocketknife from his jeans and cut through the twine. Fumbling with the wrapper, he peeled it away from what was indeed a piece of river rock.

"Does it say anything?" Roberta spurred him.

Mel handed her the rock and opened the paper, which was fairly large and folded several times.

As he did so his skin bristled. "I was afraid of this!" he groaned.

Glancing over his shoulder to be sure no one else saw, he showed Roberta the paper on which was scrawled a large black swastika.

"Oh, Lord!" she gasped. "Not now! Not again!"

The woman trembled all over, her eyes reddening with fear and anger.

Mel put a comforting arm about her shoulders. "They don't need to know," he said, referring to the wedding party. "Nothing's going to ruin this day, if I have any say in the matter!"

Roberta nodded, her face still crimson. "I hate that emblem!" she wept.

"We all do," Mel agreed.

Roberta sighed. "No, you don't understand. My son is one of them—a neo-Nazi. He runs with a bunch of them in Spokane!"

This was common knowledge in the valley, and Mel, who had heard the rumor, felt bad for her. "They're cropping up all over the world," he said. "I'm sorry, Mrs. Barrett."

The kindly woman tried to compose herself. "Oh, but how I hate that symbol!" she growled. "The last time I saw it, my son had one tattooed on his arm! He said he intended to earn a new one every month 'til his arms were full of them, just like his buddies!"

Mel was stunned, as though an electric prod had jabbed him. "They wear them all over their arms?" he repeated. "You're sure?"

Roberta was shaken by his sudden intensity. Taking a deep breath, she muttered, "Yes, I'm sure!"

"And the gang competes for these tattoos? How do they earn them?"

Roberta lowered her head as a shiver passed through her. "I never inquired," she admitted. "That was something I didn't want to know."

CHAPTER 14

Folks from all over the Bull River Valley and from the towns of Noxon, Thompson Falls, and Plains began to ascend Cricket Creek Road from the highway a couple of hours before the Wester wedding. The earliest arrivals were the musicians from Libby, who were old chums of Pete's hippy days, and families whose rigs were laden with food for the feast to follow.

Honey had been shuffled off to her room in the loft by a motherly Roberta, who was determined that the bride should be exempt from the frustrations that inevitably attended last-minute preparations. The raven-haired beauty sat on the edge of the large log-post bed, which would from this night hence be the legitimate marriage bed of Mr. and Mrs. Wester, and she stared into a full-length floor mirror that hung in an ornate antique frame.

Honey knew she was beautiful. No one had ever needed to remind her of this fact, though she carried her beauty with a calm grace that belied such knowledge. She had chosen to wear her shiny black hair in an intricate braided design, pulled back on the sides in a French weave and knotted at the neck in a large chignon. Throughout the design were woven strands of dried flowers, and, instead of a veil, she would wear a simple circlet of flowers, like a tiara.

As she sat on the bed, waiting in her slip for Roberta to appear and help her into her gown, she ran a loving hand down the creamy white lace of the wedding dress, which was laid out upon the bedspread. One tradition she had honored was to keep the groom from seeing the gown before the wedding. She had purchased it weeks ago, during a shopping trip in Spokane. She had picked it out of a catalog and ordered it custom-made at the Marcus Department Store on Riverside Street, one of the most posh outlets in the big city, where the clerk in the Bridal Shoppe had taken all her measurements and had written them down meticulously. On pins and needles, Honey had awaited the arrival of the gown, which she had arranged to be delivered to Roberta's address. For one thing, she figured no delivery truck from Spokane and no UPS truck from anywhere else would find its way up Cricket Creek Road. For another, she figured the gown would be safe from the groom's prying eyes, as long as Roberta had it.

The day it had arrived, Roberta had fetched her and taken her to the big house at the other end of the Barrett acreage. When Honey pulled the gown out of the garment bag, its satiny folds resplendent beneath delicate lace, both women had sighed aloud.

"Fabulous!" Roberta had exclaimed. "I've never seen anything prettier!"

"You think so?" Honey had cried. "Oh, I do think so! Isn't it wonderful?"

Holding it up to her shoulders, she had twirled round and round in a flurry of sweeping satin.

"Try it on!" Roberta pleaded. "It will look better on you than in your arms!"

Fidgety as a couple of schoolgirls, the two got her into the gown, Roberta's fingers all aflutter as she closed a myriad of tiny cloth-covered buttons up the back, and Honey praying all the while for an exact fit.

At last Roberta clapped. "It is you!" she cried. "If any dress was ever a woman, this is you!"

And it was. Feminine to the nth degree, the full, densely gathered skirt, which was covered with a rose-pattern mesh, complemented the fitted bodice, which was adorned with an old-fashioned V-shaped yoke of the same fabric. A high neck went perfectly with quaint poof-shoulders that topped long, tight sleeves, again of mesh.

The moment the women saw Honey in the dress, they decided she must wear her hair up, off her shoulders. The gown would be shown to best advantage that way, Roberta said, as Honey held her long tresses away from her neck.

A wide satin ribbon served as the belt, which would be tied about her small waist in a graceful bow at her back. Finishing touches of creamy stockings and eggshell-colored pumps completed the picture.

The gown and accessories lay on Honey's bed, awaiting the moment when she would don them for the most important person in her life, her beloved Pete.

Honey rose from the bed and went to the dormer window, which gave a view of the front yard. Ruffled white muslin curtains covered the lower multipaned sash, so that she had to stand on tiptoes in her creamy white stockings to get a good look at what was going on below. A few trucks and cars were making their way into the yard, parking near the woods closest to the drive. Women were bringing baskets and coolers of food and drink to the tables that extended from the porch all along a raised flower bed that ran the length of the yard. Across the grass, on a small stage constructed by Pete of stained two-by-fours and planks, the Libby band was just setting up its little sound system, which consisted of a portable microphone, a small amplifier, and a couple of medium-sized speakers.

The late-thirtyish fellows in the band, with their long hair and hippy-throwback looks, reminded her of how she and Pete had met, at a gathering of back-to-the-earth types outside Seattle. Not exactly the Rainbow Family, the big meeting had its share of radicals and offbeat types but was mainly a fair for the exchange of information and ideas—"networking" they called it—for people who wanted to learn about natural foods and simpler life-styles.

She would always remember, as if it were yesterday, the first time she saw Pete—tall, blond, and tan, his shoulder-length hair pulled back, just as it was to this day, in a ponytail, his piercing blue eyes sizing her up with an intelligent and inquisitive look. She had fallen for him instantly. Pete had been standing in front of a display of hand-powered carpentry tools, something he could never resist, as Honey had passed by on her way to a quilting display. He had managed to locate her repeatedly throughout the day, popping up at the oddest places—at a baking show where some old fellow showed how to grind raw wheat with a mortar and pestle, and at an herbalist's lecture on the use of aromas in evoking various moods.

Honey knew he was trying to find a way to speak with her and that he must be feeling awkward about it. She had purposely dropped something—she could not even remember what—near where he stood, so that he would pick it up for her, inviting conversation.

She laughed to herself at the memory, thinking just how corny and unoriginal her move had been. But it had worked. Within a few weeks, they were making plans to move to Montana, where Pete would fulfill his dream of living off the land and off his earnings as a freelance carpenter, ultimately building the home they dreamed of together.

"And tonight," she whispered to herself, "I shall be Mrs. Peter James Wester . . . the happiest woman on earth!"

This, too, she figured was a corny thought, and not in the least original. But maybe that was how things became corny and unoriginal—because they were sentiments common to the human race. Tonight she would become a member of the universal sorority of women-in-love, those women who were lucky enough to have found the right men and to have made them their own.

This knowledge did not diminish her joy but made her feel a part of something hugely wonderful.

Honey longed for a glimpse of Pete. Wouldn't he be stepping up to help the boys set up the mike, or crossing the yard to help somebody carry something? As she wondered this, she also wondered how a woman could still be so captivated by the mere sight of a man, after ten years of closeness.

When a soft knock came at the bedroom door, Honey jumped, her first thought being that Pete had come to see her. On second thought, however, she figured it was Roberta, here to help with her gown.

Stepping to the door, she was about to open it when Rabbi Ben's fatherly voice called, "Is the bride lonely in there?"

Gasping, Honey spun toward the closet, where she grabbed for her robe. "Oh, Rabbi! I'll be out in a moment," she replied. Quickly, she bundled herself in her cotton skimmer and cracked the door to the loft hallway.

Rabbi Benjamin and his friends were all there, bunched like schoolboys and looking rather skittish about being near a woman's bedroom. "We just wanted to give the bride our fondest wishes for a life of happiness," Rabbi Ben said, and the others, even Katz, nodded effusively.

"Oh, you dears!" she said with a sigh, leaning out the door modestly. "You will never know what your attendance today means to me!"

Rabbi Ben looked hesitantly at his plaid shirt and jeans. "Actually, we are also wondering how you wish for us to dress." He stood there, his hands spread out from his sides, as though very confused about himself. "Shall we continue to wear these getups?"

Honey stifled a laugh. "Oh my!" she giggled. "I never did much like those clothes on you! Sorry, gentlemen!"

The quartet of bearded faces reddened.

"Neither did we, actually," Katz said with a glower.

Levine nudged him. "Speak for yourself, Uriel," he quipped. "I have grown rather fond of blue jeans."

All of them laughed, but at last Honey said, "When I invited you to my wedding, I meant it to be 'come as you are.' I really would like for my dear New York rabbis to look the part!"

Rabbi Ben glanced at his colleagues and then, with a look of concern and a low voice, he said, "We do not wish to cause you any trouble. We might draw unwelcome attention."

The bride felt a lump rise to her throat. How kind and selfless these men were! And what a burden of responsibility they carried everywhere they went in the world!

Honey reached out into the hall and placed a reassuring hand on Rabbi Ben's arm. "Please," she said, "you would do Pete and me the greatest of honors if you would be our rabbis. I want people to notice you, because I am proud of you!"

The men shuffled, a bit embarrassed.

"I understand that you might feel awkward endorsing this wedding—what with Pete being a Gentile and all," she guessed.

At this, Katz stiffened, and the others lowered their eyes. Honey went on. "We knew this might be a problem for you, and so we have not asked you to participate in any liturgical way. But"—she paused, looking at them lovingly—"do you know what would give us the greatest pleasure and honor?"

The men studied her shyly, ready to fulfill any wish she spoke.

"We have some volunteers who have offered to hold up the four posts of the chuppah. But we would be most honored if you would take over that task." She spoke softly and sincerely. "Would you be willing to do this?"

The men were old enough to be her grandfathers. They were orthodox conservatives. But they were men. When she gave them all that disarming look, they melted.

Rabbi Ben studied his colleagues' enamored expressions, and clearing his throat, he spoke for them. "It would be our honor, Ms. Aronstam, to hold the wedding canopy of Israel's most beautiful bride!"

The sky over the Bull River Valley had never been so gorgeous as it was the afternoon of Honey and Pete's wedding. Deep aqua in color, it was swirled with the faintest of wispy clouds, forming a crystalline dome that appeared to be held in place by the spires of dark green pines. The temperature was absolutely perfect as the day neared 4:00 P.M., the scheduled time of the event.

A wedding is always a time of reflection for all who attend. It is a time for the young to think to their futures, for the old to look back on their pasts, and for those in the prime of life to consider the opportunities that lie on their doorsteps.

Such it was for the many who attended the Wester wedding, and especially for those who had shared the Jerusalem experience with the happy couple. For them, nothing was seen through the same eyes as it would have been before their time in Israel—not even something so commonplace as a wedding.

For Mel, today held an odd mix of feelings. As he waited in the house with Pete, for whom he would be the best man, he was happy for his brother. Though, as Ken had said, Pete was slow on the uptake, Mel was happy that his brother had come to his senses a year ago, that he had left the white supremacists, that he had won Honey, and that he would be honoring his duty to her.

Unused to wearing a suit, he tried to appear comfortable, but he was also edgy over the discovery of the rock and the swastika. All afternoon, from the time the guests took their seats until the final toast, he would be casting sideways glances toward the forests and hills around the house, and he would have one ear tuned for the sound of trespassers.

But confounding even these thoughts was something the rabbis had sprung on him in front of everyone at the bachelor party, just last night. Sometime toward morning, after the talkative men had shared with Ken the entire story of their Jerusalem adventures, the rabbis had presented their proposition to Mel, the one they had planned together the day David showed them the old-timey postcard on which the ex-cop had announced he was looking for work.

"Don't you sometimes hanker for those days of adventure?" Ben had asked perceptively. "The time has come for us to return our priestly candidate to Jerusalem, where he will complete his studies. How would you like to go back to Israel with us, as our young priest's bodyguard?"

Mel had lunged at the opportunity. The footloose cop, with no place to go, suddenly had an opportunity for world travel and exotic responsibility unmatched by anything even InterPol or the U.S. Secret Service could offer. If he had ever envied Pete for his having found a woman to love, the ex-cop now knew he could leave Montana for something more in keeping with himself, a die-hard man of action.

If Mel faced this day full of anticipation for his future, another wedding guest was equally eager. David Rothmeyer had made it through spring quarter at the university feeling that time moved at a snail's pace. Ever since the day the rabbis had met with him in Columbus, inviting him to launch out on a quest that would surely rival the search for the priest, he had itched to begin.

Then, last night, he had also been surprised by an announcement the rabbis hurled his way. He knew that he would soon be going to Jerusalem to work on the Second Copper Scroll. What he had not realized, until last night, was that Father Ian McCurdy would be joining him. David could think of no more prestigious authority with whom to share this sensitive and demanding research.

As the lanky professor sat with the other guests on folding chairs lined up in rows across the Wester lawn, only one other thing filled his mind. He had never been much for weddings, especially since the loss of his beloved wife. Love stories and romance movies were hard to take, and he avoided get-togethers that required mixing with couples. But ever since he had met Britta Hayworth, the doors of his grief-encrusted heart had creaked open, permitting thoughts of love and possible happiness to peek inside. Today, more than ever, he missed the perky little blonde who had thrown his stubborn bachelorhood into a cocked hat.

He furtively hoped that his new assignment in Israel would not prevent his seeing her, as they had planned, at Christmas.

As for Ken Aronstam, who waited at the back of the gathering to walk Honey down the aisle, his thoughts were also a mix on this grand day. Happy for his cousin, proud of his future in-law, Pete, and delighted to be part of the ceremony, he did, nonetheless, feel like the odd-man-out. After all, apart from Roberta he was the only houseguest who had not shared in the Jerusalem experience, the only one who had not been privy to the quest for Zachary Cohen, and the only one who would return to Columbus with no reason to anticipate a new future.

Ken would go home to his classes, his fellow professors, and his quiet life, wondering what it was all for. Not so surprising, then, that a twinge of jealousy and envy colored his more joyful feelings this day.

But at last the moment had arrived when all thoughts should be on the big event, the reason for which everyone had congregated. The folksy leader of the Libby band, an accomplished fiddler, had just brought his group through a fine rendition of melodic love songs. Holding his violin tenderly, he lowered his eyes and bowed his head, taking a deep breath. When he began to play "The Holy City," his instrument quivering with emotion, the justice of the peace walked forward from the back of the gathering and stood to one side at the front.

To the audience's amazement, the New York rabbis were the next to walk up the center aisle. Very few present had known anything about their visit to the Wester property, and as they appeared today in their long Hassidic suit coats, their side curls and beards accentuated by their strange hats, a low murmur rose from the crowd.

Those who knew the unsung lyrics to "The Holy City" were especially baffled by this appearance. If the rabbis themselves knew the song, they did not object—not at this moment when they acted out of love for the couple. The fact that it referred to the crucifixion of Christ did not prevent them from fulfilling their agreement to hold the wedding canopy.

Assembling at the front, they bent over and picked up the poles wrapped together in the antique quilt and carefully unfurled the chuppah, holding the four posts high in the air.

Jerusalem, Jerusalem!
Lift up your gates and sing,
Hosanna in the highest.
Hosanna to your King!

Uriel Katz surely cringed as he heard the song in his head. What in the world was he doing here? How had he let Horace rope him into this? But he knew he had agreed, along with his colleagues, to perform this service! A swirl of doubts and confusion filled his orthodox mind. In truth, nothing had been the same since the day Zachary Cohen entered their lives. The line separating the faiths they espoused had become uncomfortably blurred, and Uriel did not know how to act.

Glancing at Horace Benjamin's uplifted face, he was galled to see that he seemed not at all ruffled by the contradictions in which they were embroiled. Grinding his teeth, Uriel took a deep breath and tried to steady his hands as they slipped on the peeled-fir post.

Roberta, who sat with her neighbors in the crowd, was astonished at what she witnessed. Her heart surged with the music. As she, too, listened to the lyrics in her head, she could not help but recall her midnight talk with Honey. She had told her that Saint John's Revelation spoke of a New Jerusalem, something the couple's time in Israel might have foreshadowed.

Roberta's skin tingled in goose flesh as the violinist played on:

And once again the scene was chang'd
New earth there seem'd to be,
I saw the Holy City
Beside the tideless sea;
The light of God was on its streets
The gates were open wide,
And all who would might enter
And no one was denied.
No need of moon or stars by night,
Or sun to shine by day,
It was the new Jerusalem
That would not pass away. . . .

Tears flooded Roberta's eyes. *How glorious!* she thought. *They are coming together, despite themselves!*

The best man and the groom were now taking their places, descending from the porch of the house. Pete stepped beneath the chuppah, looking more dashing than he ever had in his entire life. His long hair was pulled back neatly, caught by a black satin ribbon, and his tailored black suit had a bit of a western flair, the yoke trimmed in the same satin ribbon, the buttons capped with mother-of-pearl, and the silky shirt beneath the same cream color as the bride's gown. High-heeled boots, shined to black perfection, finished the look.

Chin held high, he turned his eyes toward the far end of the aisle, and by his expression, anyone could tell his heart was so full it could burst.

As the music swelled to its climax, the violinist drew his bow more powerfully across the strings:

Jerusalem! Jerusalem
Sing for the night is o'er
Hosanna in the highest
Hosanna for evermore!

As the final tones resonated across the gathering of wedding guests, the atmosphere was dense with inexpressible feeling. After a suitable pause, the little band began to play the wedding march.

Had there ever been such a unique nuptial ceremony? No one could deny the beauty of it. Nor could they deny the beauty of the bride as she stepped forth, leaning on Ken Aronstam's arm.

Everyone in the crowd, the four rabbis, the justice of the peace and the groom, had their eyes riveted on Honey. As she drew near to Pete and Ken passed her slender arm to her intended, the audience was breathless.

No one moved, no one spoke a whisper as the ceremony proceeded, the two promising all those things couples have promised for eons, gazing into one another's eyes just as couples have gazed since time immemorial. In finale, they toasted each other with a crystal goblet. When Pete wrapped the glass in linen, set it on the ground, lifted his foot, and brought it down with a crash, to represent the destruction of the Temple, the Montana crowd shouted and clapped. Whether or not they understood the meaning, they sensed the importance of the gesture and lent their endorsement to it.

Following that symbolic move, Pete swept his bride into his arms. The kiss he gave her was full of such meaning as he had never bestowed before. Honey was now truly his, the official Mrs. Wester!

As the crowd cheered, applauding the bride and groom, who walked back up the aisle in their first seconds of marriage, Mel followed, ready to fulfill the rest of his obligations as best man. He would toast the groom before the wedding cake was cut and would lead the crowd in a few jokes and jibes.

But all the while, he would be aware of the woods beyond, and the lurkers who might be observing the festivities from a distance. If there was any mayhem in the offing, Mel was determined to short-circuit it. As he had told Roberta, this day would go off without a hitch, if he had any say in the matter.

CHAPTER 15

As Mel neared the border of Idaho, heading toward Spokane on I-90, he knew he was being tailed. Whoever drove the gray Camaro that kept popping up along the nighttime horizon in his rearview mirror had apparently picked up his scent somewhere near Wallace, Idaho. That was the first time Mel had actually noticed the tracker.

Mel's red Suburban was an easy target as it passed down the well-lit interstate. He had wondered, when he bought it, if it was wise to own such an eye-grabber. But he was not a cop anymore, he had reasoned. He had no need to drive some boring department-green set of wheels. Now, for the first time since purchasing the flashy rig, he regretted it.

Weaving in and out of traffic, following just within range of sight so that Mel could not be sure whose headlights shone through the rear window, the shadower had not become overtly obvious until the town of Kellogg. That was where Mel purposely pulled off into a truck stop, got out and used the rest room at the convenience store, then returned to the car. When, a few seconds after Mel pulled back onto the highway, the gray phantom again showed itself in the rearview mirror, the ex-cop had no doubt: he was being followed.

His passengers, the two professors and four rabbis, were due to be delivered to a Spokane hotel to spend a restful night before catching planes for home tomorrow morning. Mel would be flying out to the East Coast in a few days. After he tied things up in Bull River, he would be leaving Montana to take up his new assignment as the priest's bodyguard.

That is, if everything went as planned. For now he gripped the steering wheel and tried not to let on that he was nervous about anything. He kept one ear on his passengers' small talk, while both eyes darted from the road to the side and rearview mirrors, all the way past the state border patrol station at Post Falls and on down the busy interstate.

Whoever the tracker was, he had been contacted by someone in Montana, someone who knew Mel's whereabouts and itinerary. The ex-cop did not even question the notion that there had been spies at the wedding, either in the woods nearby or among the guests themselves. Somebody, singular or plural, was motivated to see where the Suburban went, and Mel had no doubt that it was his rabbinical passengers who were that somebody's main interest.

He considered it one of the smartest moves he had ever made to leave his cell phone with the leader of the Libby band. Pete's old friends were going to be spending the night in the same cabin where the bachelor party had been held before returning home tomorrow morning. They were going to give the honeymoon couple due privacy in the main house but welcomed the offer of the cabin before loading up their gear and driving home.

When Mel learned that they would be staying, he had taken the bandleader, Rory Mason, aside. While the wedding guests enjoyed cake and punch, he had shown the old hippy the rock and the paper swastika.

"Uncool!" Rory had exclaimed, his bright brown eyes flashing with anger. "Most likely bestowed by some of Pete's old Aryan buddies, huh? Not surprising, I guess. They're probably still real burned over their honchos being hauled outa here in handcuffs."

Mel agreed as the middle-aged hippy expostulated, "Do you 'spose they knew the Jewish rabbis were here even before they made their appearance at the wedding?"

Mel shrugged. "Maybe . . . maybe not." He frowned at the rock and the paper in his hand. "They left these tokens of their affection last night, long before the rabbis appeared in their traditional garb. But maybe some yahoos just didn't like the idea of Pete marrying a Jew. And yeah, you're right . . . the whole thing of Pete deserting the Aryans and seeing the light has, for sure, left a sour taste in a lot of folks' mouths."

Rory pushed his long gray-streaked hair back from a youthful face. "Well, how can we help?" he asked. "Me and my guys will be happy to do whatever we can."

Mel had flashed a smile of gratitude, pulling his cell phone from his suitcoat pocket and handing it to Rory. "Know how to use one of these?" he asked. "I have a hunch I'm not gonna get all the way to Spokane and back without being tailed. Even if I do, you might want to reach someone in the outside world before morning."

Rory did not like the sound of that, but when Mel told him about the noises in the woods and the light he had seen on the hill the night before, the musician understood.

"We'll be on top of things," he said after Mel explained how to use the phone. "Thanks for the notice."

Mel had clapped the hippy on the shoulder. "You're a good man," he said. "Coulda used you on the force. But . . . I guess that's not your style."

Rory laughed and held up two fingers in a peace sign.

Then Mel drew close and talked low. "One more thing," he said, glancing over at the wedding party. "Try to leave Pete out of this, okay? At least for tonight."

Now as Mel drove into Spokane, he remembered that last injunction with a smirk. He glanced again in the rearview mirror and saw that the gray Camaro was a definite presence as the Suburban veered off the exit and headed for the Rivercrest Inn.

Big brother, you owe me! he thought to himself.

The lobby of the Rivercrest Inn was very quiet tonight. Mel and his companions were among only a few customers checking in. The blond cop stood at the counter while Rabbi Ben paid for the rooms, refusing to let the professors or Mel pick up their own tabs.

The four rabbis had booked two rooms for themselves; Rothmeyer and Aronstam would share a double suite, and Mel would sleep on a cot in the same quarters, despite Rabbi Ben's insistence that he should have his own accommodations.

As the bellhop, dressed in a casual polo shirt bearing the hotel logo, piled the suitcases on a brass pushcart, Mel watched the front entryway with a keen eye. He had lost track of the gray Camaro after pulling into the hotel parking lot, but undoubtedly the shadower had seen him turn in. Surely any moment the stranger would walk into the hotel as though he belonged there.

"I'll be up in a few," Mel said, waving his friends off. "I want to locate a newspaper stand."

The rabbis, heading for the elevators, bid good night and told him they would see him at breakfast in the morning. The professors suggested a nightcap in the lounge. "Go ahead," Mel said. "If I don't join you soon, I'll see you in the room."

As soon as he was left alone, he crossed the marble-tiled lobby and headed down a carpeted corridor that led to the main-floor lavatories. Standing in the shadows behind a tall potted plant, he watched the front door.

Sure enough, in a few moments a weasely looking fellow in a dark turtleneck pullover entered the hotel. Tight jeans held up by a wide black belt and huge chrome belt buckle in the shape of a tractor emphasized his scrawniness. His beardless face was noteworthy for the dark circles beneath the eyes and the pockmarks across the cheeks. Mel figured his head was shaved beneath his John Deere baseball cap. Something about him seemed familiar, something in the eyes, the forehead. As Mel watched him sidle up to the counter, cocky as a banty rooster, it struck him that, despite the stranger's repulsive appearance, he bore a strong resemblance to sweet little Roberta Barrett.

Good Lord! Mel thought. *Don't let this be her son!*

Mel tried to anticipate the tracker's plan. He had undoubtedly watched from the darkness outside the hotel windows as the rabbis and the professors checked in. Did he think he could get a room here and achieve something useful with regard to these enemies of Aryanism? It occurred to Mel, not for the first time, that the rabbis and Dr. Rothmeyer, to say nothing of Mel himself, were notorious media celebrities. Though it had been a full year since their faces had been seen on national television or in magazines, anyone with an interest in their escapades could recognize them. If this was Ronald Barrett, Roberta Barrett's son, and if he was in any way connected with the fringe groups who had once been headquartered on the Wester property, he and his cohorts probably knew more than enough about the Jerusalem contingent. Any number of things might motivate their desire to spy on the Westers and their friends, from outright revenge to political expediency. After all, whatever the rabbis were about, it was directly opposed to groups who hated Israel.

Looking at the skinny errand boy who had been commissioned to follow them here, Mel could have been less than concerned. After all, just how much of a threat could be posed by a bony super-race wannabe? Mel's street smarts told him better, however. He had learned long ago not to judge an adversary's effectiveness solely by his appearance.

Carefully, Mel watched the little man, wondering what he hoped to accomplish at the front desk. The night clerk, seeing that another patron had approached the counter, stepped out from the office. He gave the newcomer a doubtful look and asked if he had a reservation. To Mel's surprise, the little guy reached into his pocket, pulled out a credit card, and placed it on the counter, indicating that there was a room reserved for him. When the clerk turned his back to run the card through a machine, leaving the man free to give a quick perusal of the night register, which lay open on the desk, Mel realized the weasel's cleverness.

He's getting our room numbers! he deduced.

Sure enough, the clerk returned with a frown, plopped the credit card on the counter, and told the patron no reservation had been made in that name. The little guy feigned bewilderment, and Mel heard him say there must be some mistake. Was there a phone he could use so he could call his travel agent? The clerk, sizing him up, did not offer the desk phone but pointed toward the hallway that led to the rest rooms, the same hallway where Mel was lurking.

As the little fellow headed toward the pay phones arrayed on the wall across from Mel's hideout, the cop made a quick dash for the rest room, bolted through the door, and pretended to be washing his hands. He knew the weasel had no intention of making a call, but that he would probably tinker with one of the phones a few seconds and then duck into the lavatory himself to kill time.

Mel made a quick survey of the rest room and found that they would be alone, which suited him just fine. Standing against the wall toward which the main door would swing open, he listened for the sound of the man's boots on the floor outside. Here he came.

The door swung back, just missing Mel's nose, and as the weasel stood aimlessly in the middle of the room, the big cop made his move. Quick as a cat, he lunged for the culprit, grappling him to the floor in one fell swoop that knocked the air from the small man's lungs and knocked the John Deere cap from his bristly pate. Once down Mel wrapped his head in an armlock and gripped his squirming body between his legs.

"Quiet, Ronnie boy," he growled. "Let's not make a scene, now!"

"Who . . . wha' . . . ?" the stunned skinhead gasped. "How do you know me?"

Mel had his head in such a viselike hold that the weasel could barely turn to see who had him.

"Well, I didn't, but I do now," Mel admitted. "Good guess, huh?"

The weasel squirmed some more, and Mel gripped him tighter. "What say we strike a deal, Ronnie?" he snarled. "You be a nice quiet boy, and I'll ease up on ya. Okay?"

Ron let out a big sigh, as if to say "Uncle."

Mel tentatively loosened his arm hold, and when Ron did not struggle, he knelt beside him, releasing the scissor lock. "Now, superstar," Mel said, "I'm going to sit here while we talk, weasel to man, okay? No funny stuff. You make a move and I'll slice you to ribbons." With this, Mel pulled out a small buck knife from his hip pocket and flashed the open blade before Ron's fear-filled eyes.

"First, let me make it clear that I don't like being followed," Mel said. "Gotta say, you did a dang good job of it, but I know you've been with me since Wallace."

Barrett avoided Mel's gaze, and the cop grabbed his chin, jerking his face toward him. "I'm not even going to try to guess what you're up to!" he spat. "Let's just say that I know you're in way over your head, Ronnie baby! You think this is about some game on the highway, some game with motorcycles and flashlights in the big dark woods? You should be so lucky!"

At this, Mel grabbed Ron's slender right arm and ripped back the sleeve of his form-fitting shirt. "Aha! Am I surprised!" he laughed. "Looky here, will ya!" There in bold black contrast to his Aryan white skin was the image of a swastika tattooed on his forearm. "I suppose you were out to win yourself another one of these tonight? Am I right?"

Ron cringed. "How . . . how . . ."

"How do I know?" Mel smirked. "Let's just say I'm gifted with a sixth sense!"

The cop knew he had been lucky to have privacy to this point, in the men's latrine, but he couldn't count on it lasting all night. Leaping to his feet, he grabbed Ron by the collar and stood him up like a rag doll.

"My sixth sense tells me lots of things, like you have some buddies who recently took a trip to Washington, D.C. Am I right?"

Ron's eyes bugged out and his face went even whiter.

"Ah, so my gift is operating in top form!" Mel quipped. "Since I'm on a roll, let me continue. I'll bet those fellows won themselves more tattoos than they have arms for, right? Wanna be like them, do ya? Wanna spend the rest of your life in the slammer, or better yet, end it in the frying pan?"

Barrett was shaking now, holding on to Mel's strong arm for dear life, even as that arm threatened to strangle the breath from him.

"Show me how smart you are, Ronnie boy," Mel suggested as they walked toward the bathroom door. "How 'bout you and me go for a ride in my shiny Suburban, you know . . . the one you've been lusting after since Wallace? Let's go down and see the public servants at the SPD. You tell them nice, informative things, and they might work the deal of a lifetime for you."

As Mel reached the rest-room door to lead his charge into the hall, the little worm began to squirm. "Rat? You want me to rat on my friends?" he whimpered. "No way, man!"

Mel held him at arm's length and shook his head. "Very well, Einstein," he said. "Oops, Einstein was a Jew, wasn't he? That won't do. Very well, Elmer Fudd—now there's a whitey for you! I guess we can just go turn you in to the SPD without bothering with nice stories. They don't care if you fry for your friends. Just gives them one less skinhead to worry about."

At this, Ron reached for the edge of the sink, helplessly pulling against Mel's advance toward the door.

"What's up, buddy?" Mel asked. "Having second thoughts?"

Ron nodded his head violently. "Yeah, yeah, okay! Whatever you want!"

Mel grinned at him in mock adoration and brushed him off with pain-inducing pats. "Now, there's a smart Aryan!" He laughed. "Keep this up and you'll make me a believer!"

CHAPTER 16

It was the middle of the night in the Spokane police station. Though the building was part of a large county complex dominated by a huge Victorian gingerbread courthouse, there was nothing old-fashioned about this law-enforcement headquarters. Mel was used to the cutting-edge technology of the L.A. department, but he could see that this relatively small-town office was as modern and high-tech as any.

As he sat in a waiting room off the main lobby, he stifled a yawn. He should, after all, have been sound asleep in the Rivercrest Inn.

He had brought Barrett to the SPD an hour ago; the authorities had listened to his story and that of Barrett, and they now had the weasel in a holding tank, "on suspicion."

As Mel had watched Barrett being hauled away, the cop in charge of the night desk had asked him to sit in the waiting room while he made a quick phone call. What that was about, Mel could not imagine. When the night officer appeared in the doorway of the waiting room, Mel snapped alert.

"I have just contacted the FBI," the officer said. When Mel looked surprised, the officer explained that there was an FBI office located in one of the high-rises downtown. "They want you to report there in the morning," he instructed.

When no further explanation was forthcoming, Mel said, "Any certain time? I am supposed to take some friends to the airport."

The officer suggested he go to the Bureau as soon as he

had fulfilled that obligation, but that he was not, under any circumstances, to tell anyone what had come down this evening.

After creeping back to the hotel room, where Rothmeyer and Aronstam were sound asleep, Mel spent a restless night tossing and turning, adrenaline pumping through his veins as he wondered what all this would lead to. He also hoped all was well with the boys at the Wester cabin. When dawn arrived without any call from Rory, he figured things were cool back home.

Complying with orders, he said nothing to his companions about what had happened in the night, as he saw them safely off at the airport. Returning to town, he found Riverside Avenue and the twenty-story building where the FBI office was located. He parked his Suburban in the ajacent garage, and headed for the main entrance.

Checking his reflection in the tall tinted windows that framed the front door, he smoothed his shirt and tried to look less weary. "Here goes nothing," he told himself.

When he located the Bureau office and presented himself to the clerk, he was surprised at the quick reception.

"Oh yes, Mr. Wester," the clerk said, a look of admiration on his no-nonsense face, "there are some gentlemen waiting for you. Come this way."

As the day proceeded he would piece together that the wheels of law enforcement had moved very quickly during the night, the FBI and other agencies cooperating. He would learn that Barrett, ready to finger his buddies, had led the local police and the FBI to the very door where the skinheads holed up in the Spokane Valley. Due to teamwork of unprecedented swiftness and efficiency, the suspects and their boss had been located, nabbed, and incarcerated within hours of Barrett's informing.

What Mel had not anticipated was that, due to the international nature of Senator Jefferson's work, the CIA had immediately been called in on the case. As he followed the clerk to an interior office, he was amazed to find familiar faces waiting for him. Morris and Dalton, the same CIA agents who had worked on last year's Aryan bust, had been flown in from D.C. during the night and were eager to meet with Mel.

Standing up the instant they saw him, the two dignified men-in-black thrust out their hands in greeting. Mel returned the gesture with a quizzical look, to say nothing of surprise.

"Mr. Wester!" Morris said. "We trust you remember us."

"Of course," Mel replied. "How could I forget?"

Dalton gave a toothy smile. "Seems you've done it again," he marveled. "Gone and proven yourself invaluable to your country's security!"

Mel shook his head. "If that is the result of my efforts, I am happy to be of service," he said. "But really, I was just trying to protect some friends."

Dalton and Morris glanced knowingly at each other. "Ah, the rabbis," Morris said. "We just left a message for them in upstate New York."

Mel should not have been surprised that the CIA knew the rabbis' destination. But he would never get used to the idea that there were forces in the world that knew most everything there was to know about most everybody.

"Why, if I might ask, did you try to contact them?" Mel inquired.

"For the same reason that we are meeting with you," Dalton replied. "They have information of importance to our nation, just as you do."

Mel made no sense of this. "I sincerely doubt that the rabbis and I share that much mutual knowledge," he said. "Their interests are much more esoteric than mine."

Dalton shrugged. "Exactly," he said. "We need both kinds."

Mel was utterly bewildered. At last, when the agents added nothing helpful, he swallowed hard. "So why are you here? In fact, why am *I* here?"

The two men gestured to a chair, and as Mel sat down, they took seats across from him. "You and your brother were invaluable to us last year," Morris began. "We would like to enlist your help again. Apparently you continue to have a sense for some of the Aryan activity in the Northwest. We . . ."

Mel interrupted. "Now wait a minute!" he exclaimed. "Just because I spotted Ron Barrett in my rearview mirror, and intercepted whatever dirt he had planned against my friends, that does not make me an expert in Aryan activities!"

Dalton was bemused. "It does seem, Mr. Wester, that you have an uncanny knack for getting in their way . . . if you get my drift."

Mel was chagrined. "Maybe I just have a way of getting in over my head!" he muttered.

Morris studied Mel's deflated expression. "Put it any way you want," he said. "Your government considers you an unusually useful citizen. You and your brother . . ."

Mel straightened. "Just hold on! Leave Pete out of this! He just got married, for goodness' sake!" At this, he paused, and a smirk crossed his face. "But why am I telling you this? You undoubtedly know already!"

Morris and Dalton shook their heads. "Actually, no," Dalton said. "We were not aware of that. He married the Jewish girl?"

"Come on!" Mel snapped. "I don't buy this!"

The agents shrugged. "Believe it or not," Morris objected, "we really aren't that invasive! We try to keep up with what's material to our purposes. A wedding in the woods isn't particularly useful."

Mel looked at them suspiciously. "So how did you know it was in the woods?" he said through gritted teeth.

Dalton looked smug. "Of course, it would be useful if it drew the attention of . . . shall we say 'unsavory sorts.' "

"And it *did* draw that attention, didn't it?" Morris added.

Mel was cornered. "Okay," he conceded. "You're way ahead of me. What is it you want from me?"

"Well," Dalton went on, "if you have nothing better to do these days, we would like for you to be available . . . on call, shall we say. Don't take a day job, as they say." The agent flashed that toothy grin again, and Mel felt very uneasy.

"I . . . I do have plans," he said.

Morris rubbed his chin. "Do they involve a trip back east?"

Mel sighed.

"Because if they do," Morris went on, "we'd like to enlist your services in getting Barrett's four murderous buddies to our nation's capital."

Now Mel figured he was one up on the agents. "To be identified by an eyewitness to the murder of Senator Jefferson?" he guessed.

Morris and Dalton seemed genuinely surprised. "Aha!" Dalton exclaimed. "The rabbis have been letting you in on some sensitive stuff!"

Mel folded his arms and said nothing.

"Then," Morris added, "it won't surprise you that when the rabbis get home, they will find they have been asked to meet us in D.C. It seems the interest in this case goes way beyond our nation's borders."

Two days later, little Lamar Jackson sat in a small auditorium on the eighth floor of the J. Edgar Hoover Building, Washington, D.C. The headquarters of the Federal Bureau of Investigation was a landmark familiar to the boy, who had spent most of his six years on the streets of the capital city. Never had he been inside the block-long building, however, until today.

Waiting with Lamar on one row of the cushioned theater seats were two people who already felt like family to the child, more family than he had ever had before that fateful morning in the subway station. Although his mother had been found dead shortly after that climactic day, the friends who sat with him this afternoon—Zachary Cohen and Marlon Goldstein—had given him a sense of security that had gone a long way toward helping him overcome his grief and trauma.

In fact, so important were these men to Lamar, that when the authorities left word for the rabbis at Goldstein's compound, summoning them to D.C., the old fellows requested that Cohen and their host be included in the party.

An FBI agent stood at one end of the row, glancing at his watch and at the door that opened from a hallway at the back of the auditorium. He appeared very calm, but his steely eyes betrayed tension, as though whomever he awaited was unnervingly late.

Lamar's short legs swung back and forth with childish energy, and he watched the well-lit stage at the foot of the little arena with anxiety of his own. He had been told that in a few moments a line of men would cross the stage and stand before the dark backdrop beneath placards numbered one through six. He would be asked if any of the men looked familiar, if any of them might be the ones who had murdered Senator Jefferson. He had been assured that the men would be in handcuffs and ankle chains, that they would not even be able to see him, as the footlights and the darkened auditorium would prevent them from identifying anyone beyond the stage. Not only this, but a thick shield of bulletproof glass separated the stage from the seating area, and the men would not even be able to hear anyone talk beyond that partition.

Lamar sat like a diminutive shadow between Zachary on his left and Marlon on his right. The rabbis were seated down the row next to Zachary, Rabbi Ben on the aisle where the FBI agent stood, still eyeing his watch and the door.

At last the agent breathed a sigh of relief. Lamar and his companions turned to look at the entrance where three men were arriving. The rabbis were grateful to see Mel, whose white-blond hair caught the hall light and whose broad shoulders and tall physique nearly filled the doorway. Behind him were the two CIA agents who had called for the rabbis' presence here, as well as that of Lamar.

As Mel and his hosts entered the row of seats behind the others, the rabbis stood up in greeting. The mood in the room was still tense, but Wester's arrival somewhat alleviated the heaviness.

"We meet again," Agent Morris said pleasantly as the four rabbis shook his hand and Dalton's.

Rabbi Benjamin nodded toward Mel. "It seems our boy here has proven himself a hero once again," he said.

Dalton and Morris looked admiringly at the ex-cop. "If I were a believing man, I'd say he's your guardian angel," Morris acknowledged.

Gratitude filled the rabbis' faces. "When you took us to the plane in Spokane, you said nothing about your night's adventure," Carl Jacobs noted. "Are you always so secretive?"

Mel's mind flashed to all the things he had hidden from the rabbis: the rock on Pete's porch, the noises and lights in the Wester woods. And now this . . .

"Not usually," he hedged. "I'd been watching Ron Barrett tail us for miles, but I didn't want to worry you. Ends up his plan was to follow us to the airport and report your destination to his Aryan boss. I suppose you've heard all about it by now."

Rabbi Ben gestured toward the FBI agent in the aisle. "Our friends here at the bureau have informed us of how close a call we had," he said. "We can never repay you, Melvin. Once again, we are in your debt."

Mel shrugged. "All in a day's work," he said with a laugh. "Like they say, 'Cops never really retire; they just get more tired.' "

The group got a chuckle out of this. Even the somber FBI man grinned a little. When Lamar's round face broke into a big smile and he giggled out loud, Mel snapped him a quick salute. "From what I hear, you're the true hero!" he said.

Rabbi Ben endorsed this enthusiastically. "Please meet Lamar Jackson," he said. "And with him is our friend, Marlon Goldstein." Ben paused, realizing that the next introduction was the weightiest of all.

"And this," he said, "is Mr. Zachary Cohen."

Besides the four rabbis, only the two men meeting each other knew the importance of this introduction. Marlon Goldstein had tried in vain to imagine just who Cohen was and why his security was so critical. As for the agents in the room, they were only involved in the apprehension and arraignment of the murderous thugs whose identity and location Ronald Barrett had been plea-bargained into pinpointing. Beyond the chance that Senator Jefferson's assassins would be brought to justice, they only hoped that Mel's brave act of intervention might lead to further infiltration and breakup of terrorist rings.

As Mel reached out and shook the hand of the priestly candidate, a thrill of wonder and a sense of destiny gripped him. "Glad to meet you, Mr. Cohen," he said.

Zachary, who had been told he would be meeting his permanent bodyguard, studied Wester's firm jaw, intelligent eyes, and stalwart physique with humble admiration. "I am grateful that you were there for our rabbis," he said. "We can never repay you for your loyalty."

Mel's face reddened. "It was nothing," he said, turning his gaze to the floor.

The FBI agent cleared his throat and addressed Dalton and Morris. "Have the suspects been readied?" he asked.

"Yes," Dalton replied. "They were being lined up as we entered the auditorium."

"Very well," the agent said. "Will you all sit down, please?"

When everyone was seated, the FBI agent spoke into a little mike attached to his lapel. "Lights, please," he said, addressing someone behind the scenes.

At this, the auditorium was darkened, and the footlights on the stage were made brighter. The little audience grew very quiet, and Lamar grabbed onto Zachary's arm.

A door to the right of the stage opened and a rugged-looking cop with a holstered sidearm walked across the platform, taking a position at the far end.

Behind him followed a line of men in orange jumpsuits, their ankles shackled with iron bands, between which were slung short chains so that they were forced to walk with a choppy gait. Their wrists, likewise, were cuffed, and all of them had shaved heads.

Mel, familiar with this procedure, knew that one or two of these fellows were probably officers, undercover cops infiltrating skinhead ranks. Another one or two were probably from some local penal institution. If the eight in the lineup included the actual assassins, only Lamar Jackson would be able to identify them.

As Mel sat in the darkness, considering all that had happened in the last few hours, he felt as though he were in a dream—a rather morbid dream, to be sure. He squirmed in the padded seat. Despite the grisly nature of the case, he tried not to grin from ear to ear as he realized how jealous his big brother would be to have missed out on this escapade.

The FBI agent fiddled with his mike again and called out to the men on the stage to take their places on the footprints painted on the platform. Glancing down, the men located the white prints and did as they were told, placing themselves about two feet apart.

Mel glanced at little Lamar, who still held on to Cohen's arm. As the men positioned themselves, Cohen whispered something in the child's ear, and the boy hesitantly scooted forward on his seat. Mel could see that Lamar's lower lip quivered as he gripped the back of the chair in front of him, pulling himself up for a good look at the stage.

The men arrayed across the platform looked much alike at first appearance. All were about the same build and height. Their orange jumpsuits concealed their bodies entirely so that one could only distinguish them by their faces.

Again Cohen whispered something to Lamar, and the boy slowly nodded his head. Raising a hesitant hand, he began to point to various members of the lineup. The first, who stood beneath placard number two, was a young man with a bright red mustache; the second, who stood beneath placard number four, was about the same age, with piercing dark eyes; the third, beneath placard number five, was a stout fellow with crooked teeth. Finally, the tallest and biggest of the lot, an older, brutish-looking character with a broad nose and flat, knife-scarred face, stood beneath placard number seven.

"Are you sure?" Mel heard Zachary ask.

Lamar placed a finger on his quivering lip and nodded, blinking back tears.

At this, Zachary turned to the agent in the aisle. "He has identified the second, fourth, fifth, and seventh," he said.

The agent stepped into the row of seats in front of Lamar. Sitting down to one side, so that the boy could still see the stage, he spoke firmly but kindly. "Son," he said, "what you have done is very brave. I am going to ask you to be even braver. Okay?"

The boy perched on the edge of his seat, fearful but proud. "Okay," he croaked.

The agent continued. "Your friend, Mr. Cohen, tells me that you saw something scary on the bad men's arms. Is that right?"

Lamar nodded, taking a shuddery breath.

"The men on the stage have long sleeves. We did this on purpose because we wanted you to identify them without seeing their arms," the man went on. "Now we are going to roll up their sleeves. If you recognize the same pictures you saw that awful day, will you point them out to us?"

Lamar looked at Zachary, his eyes wide with horror. "It's all right," Cohen assured him. "They can't see you or hear you. The bad guys can't get at you."

Lamar turned back to the agent and nodded again, drawing his lower lip under his top teeth to keep it from trembling.

The agent used his mike again, directing the cop with the holstered weapon to push up the sleeves of the men's jumpsuits. Quickly, the cop complied, stepping behind each man and pushing his sleeves up beneath his armpits.

All of the men were tattooed. Mel figured the stand-ins had been specifically chosen for this fact. It would be up to Lamar to say whether any of them wore the "spiders" that had haunted his nightmares.

The reaction was instantaneous. As soon as number two's sleeves were raised, the child drew back and cowered against Zachary, but by the time numbers four, five, and seven had been exposed, the boy took courage. "I knew they were the ones!" he gasped. "See! They have spiders on their arms!"

Indeed, the four Aryans' forearms and biceps were laden with black designs. Of course, as Mel had suspected, the "spiders" were actually swastikas, just like the one that novice Ron Barrett boasted.

The agent looked at Lamar proudly, and reaching over the back of his seat, he clapped the boy on the knee. Lamar's anxious expression melted as the man told him he had just helped to put away some very bad dudes.

Zachary embraced Lamar's slender shoulders and hugged him tight. As the rabbis congratulated the little hero and Marlon Goldstein gave a thumbs-up, Mel reached forward and held his hand up in front of the boy's face.

"Give me five!" Wester said, to which Lamar slapped his open palm heartily.

At last the agent stood and spoke again into his mike, directing the cop onstage to haul the Aryans away. "Take suspects number two, four, five, and seven to the tank. Have them booked on suspicion of the murder of Senator Calvin Jefferson!"

CHAPTER 17

David Rothmeyer was in the depths of jet lag as he rode the small commuter bus from the Tel Aviv airport into Jerusalem. Despite the weariness and disorientation that a transatlantic flight brought on, he was enthralled with the sights of the evening skyline, thrilled to be back in the most marvelous city on earth.

The bus curved down the highway that hugged Mount Zion, following the ancient trail that had been carved into the hillside above the Kidron Valley by feet, wheels, hooves, and tires over the last fourteen millennia. To David's right, the spectacular walls that had seen countless wars and conquerors, that had been built and torn apart and rebuilt countless times by invaders and victors, loomed majestically above the road. The descending sun in the west cast this side of Jerusalem in shadow, giving the dusky walls a bluish cast. Soon, he knew, a full moon would be stationing itself over Mount Zion, arising from the east to see the Holy City through yet another night, and it would paint another color on the cityscape, a silvery patina unlike what the moon bestowed anywhere else on the planet.

David's keen eyes read the stones in the walls like others would read a history book. In the variety of shapes and sizes, the walls' strata delineated the periods of Jerusalem's past. Along the lowest levels were the crudest of stones, what few were left from the period of the early tribes and chieftains fourteen thousand years before; above them were finer pieces from the time of the early kings; the Herodian and Roman stones were always the easiest to spot, being the most ostentatious and enormous, with nicely notched edges that gave them a framed appearance. Above these, from the Byzantine period, were smaller, cruder stones, still better worked than the most primitive; then came the work of the Crusader masons, who were best at salvaging and recycling the stones and rubble of early periods, making their work noteworthy for its eclectic, jumbled appearance. The Ottomans gave the walls their last bit of spit and polish, as Suleiman the Magnificent and his ilk sought to reclaim the grandeur of Jerusalem at its most glorious. Here and there could be seen the even patching, the artistic masonry of the Ottoman craftsmen.

Since Suleiman's time, however, there had been little change in the appearance of the walls. What David looked on tonight, as his motorized conveyance made its way around the perimeter of the ancient city, was what travelers and locals had looked on for the past five hundred years.

As the bus neared the junction where the Hinnom Valley intercepted the Kidron, the road led around the southern foot of the Old City, the part of Jerusalem that contained most of the history with which the world was familiar. To the left, across the Hinnom, a structure strangely out of place in this Middle Eastern landscape loomed up in quixotic silhouette. A windmill marked the site of one of the first villages built outside the walls of the ancient city, an experiment that nineteenth-century Zionists from Europe had attempted. Failing beneath pressure from invading bedouins and bandits, the test had been abandoned, the villagers had withdrawn to inside the Old City walls, and the site had lain in disrepair until the late twentieth century, when artists had reclaimed it as a studio colony.

This windmill was what David had been watching for. Its location on the southern slope of the Hinnom Valley told him he was very close to his destination. The antique building that housed the Consortium headquarters lay across the narrow valley from this landmark, and as the bus neared the area, David hailed the driver.

"I will get out here!" he called toward the front of the commuter van.

The driver shot a glance into the rearview mirror, wondering why a passenger would want to disembark at this point, rather than waiting a few more minutes to arrive at Jaffa Gate, one of the main entrances to the Old City. With a shrug, he slowed the van and stopped in a wide spot where a long, snaking set of stone stairs ascended through dense foliage to a small gate high in the city wall.

"Will this do?" he asked.

"Wonderful!" David replied, walking down the aisle with his two suitcases. Before exiting, he handed the driver a hefty tip and clapped him on the shoulder. "Great to be home!" he said.

David skipped down the two steps toward the van door and, grabbing the chrome handle by the exit, swung his long legs and his bags to the ground. As the door closed and the van pulled away, he stood for a moment just staring up at the glimmering gray of the moon-washed walls. Scanning the tops, where Crusader parapets were notched, he sought the balcony where he had spent many an evening studying, researching on his laptop computer, visiting with the rabbis, or just gazing out over the historic landscape.

Yes, there it was, the first glimpse of his home away from home, the actual home of his heart. Not to waste another precious second, he turned for the stairs that would lead him toward the gate nearest the old house. As he did so, however, a movement on the balcony caught the corner of his eye. Glancing up, he saw the figure of a tall, lean gentleman who had just stepped onto the veranda.

Instantly he recognized him as the best friend of Father Ian McCurdy, John Cromwell. So the Oxfordians had beat him to Jerusalem! David lifted a hand and waved energetically to the dignified man.

"Dr. Rothmeyer?" Cromwell called down, his voice easily carrying through the still night.

"John Cromwell?" David hollered.

"The same!" the Britisher replied. "We have been waiting for you!"

"Is Ian there?"

"He is," John replied. "And as always, the press is on his heels!"

Oh no! David thought. Had the media tracked the old scholar to Jerusalem? Poor Father McCurdy never had much peace from the press.

No sooner had John announced this, however, than the old priest appeared on the balcony. Enthusiastically, he waved down at the American, and as David returned the greeting, he suddenly wondered if his eyes were playing tricks on him. Stepping up beside Ian, her bright blonde curls gleaming in the moonlight, was the "press" John referred to.

"Britta?" David cried. "Is that you?"

"Of course!" she called. "The star reporter gets to do one more story on the Oxford maverick!"

David's heart leaped in his chest. Jerusalem had a way of creating a dream for the soul, and this was a dream he wanted never to end.

"I'll be right up!" David called. Light-footed, he bounded up the stairs more like a college boy than a tenured professor.

The wonderful old house felt like a familiar friend. As David opened the creaking iron gate that led off a winding cobblestone street to the massive oak door, he had never felt more at one with a place. Of course, it helped that a smiling beauty waited for him, standing on the stone porch with her arms open.

David rushed up the path toward her, set his suitcases on the steps, and embraced her, sweeping her small body up in his arms and holding her to his heart. For the moment, neither he nor she cared that a couple of elderly gents might be watching from the doorway. David set her down and, after reading joy on her sweet face, bent over her, kissing her anxiously.

Father McCurdy raised a hand to his mouth, hiding a grin, and John Cromwell politely cleared his throat. David and Britta withdrew from each other, their faces a matching shade of red.

"Uh, gentlemen!" David greeted, stepping toward them. "Great to see you!" He stuck out a hand and received their gracious handshakes.

Father McCurdy made a quick deduction and teasingly asked in his Irish brogue, "Would we be far afield if we guessed that you and the wee newswoman here struck up more than a friendship during your stay in this romantic city?"

David looked at Britta adoringly. "Actually, I was quite taken with Ms. Hayworth when we met in Germany," he admitted. "And I was further charmed by her when we visited you at Oxford. I do think, however, that Jerusalem sealed my fate. A beautiful woman and the Holy City is a potent combination!"

By now Britta's face was crimson, and John Cromwell intervened. Gesturing from the entryway, he said, "Won't you come in, Professor? Let me take your bags."

David grabbed his suitcases and entered the house. "I think I can manage," he said. "Thanks, anyway. I presume I will be staying in my old room?"

Father McCurdy nodded. "The housekeeper retired early tonight. But she said that you would know your way."

"Good old Anya!" David said. "I look forward to her cooking!"

With this, he headed for the winding stairs that led to his little suite. "I'll just freshen up," he said. "The evening is still young. Will I join you in the parlor or on the veranda?"

John voted for the veranda. "You can tell us about the attractions seen from the balcony," he suggested.

"I'd like that," David said. Then, giving Britta a wink, he added, "If I can take my eyes off this attraction, that is."

CHAPTER 18

It was all coming back to David now. Not that it had ever entirely left him.

The wonder and the mystery that was Jerusalem infused his spirit as he gripped his briefcase and hurried to the Consortium laboratory the next morning. With him was his colleague, Father Ian McCurdy, the most notorious and respected living member of the Cave Scroll team, and accompanying both of them were Ian's friend and supporter, John Cromwell, and the delightful Britta Hayworth. Today they were going to press forward with the work that McCurdy and his deceased mentor, Father Ducharme, had never completed. They were going to study the enigmatic Copper Scroll, which Ian had kept hidden in a vault at the British Museum for half a century, and which Britta and David had ferreted out during months of international sleuthing.

This was the mysterious scroll referred to in another and better-known document, likewise made of copper and found at Qumran in the 1950s. It was the opinion of most Cave Scroll scholars that the First Copper Scroll contained a list of treasures taken from the Temple before the Roman invasion of 70 C.E. That document seemed to detail the hiding places of those treasures throughout ancient Palestine. The problem was that the First Copper Scroll was written in very cryptic language, the geographical locations of the inventory vague enough that it would require a key to interpret them. That interpretation, the scroll said, was contained in a second document, apparently the one Ian and his mentor had found.

A year ago David's quest for the high priest of Israel had taken a major leap when McCurdy's mysterious scroll proved to contain a crucial link in the genealogical record. That link, the mention of the name of the legitimate high priest living when the document was inscribed, tied together strands of the genealogy from times previous, and linked them with a much later record from Germany at the time of the Holocaust. Once the needed names were in place, it remained only for some modern person to be connected with them. Zachary Cohen proved to be that person.

David would never forget the day the last piece of the scroll's tightly wound inner core was opened and the ancient priestly name was found. Such a celebration there was in the Consortium laboratory, the old rabbis dancing a jig about the stainless-steel table as the British and American professors congratulated one another!

Today the same two professors hiked toward their assignment with the same energy and zeal they had felt that day. Who knew what they might learn as they set about to explicate more words and phrases of the priceless document? Of course, their primary interest would be to fulfill the immediate wishes of the rabbis, who hoped the scroll would give clues as to what had become of two articles critical to temple function: the Ashes of the Red Heifer and the Priestly Breastplate, particularly the oracular counters, the Urim and Thummim that went with the breastplate. Anything they might find in the scroll that related to these particular items would be most exciting.

Just before David had tied up business at the university and left Columbus, he had received a phone call from the rabbis. They would be arriving in the Holy City in a couple of days, bringing with them Zachary Cohen and his new bodyguard. They had important news to tell, but they would not divulge it over the phone. All they would say was that Mel Wester had proven himself invaluable to the cause once again, and they did believe he had been brought to them by "divine providence."

When David told Father McCurdy and the others about that message, the old Irishman had smiled knowingly. "Such a thing should not surprise us," he had said. "We must all get used to the idea that God is in charge of everything related to this business!"

David and Britta had made no reply. They had both seen enough evidence for such a statement a year ago, and though it went against their secular mind-set, they had been obliged to concede that something bigger than all of them orchestrated their Jerusalem experience.

As the four entered the front door of the Temple Gallery building, Shalom Diamant, the gallery curator, awaited them eagerly. "Professors!" he greeted David and Ian, shaking their hands. "And Mr. Cromwell! Such a pleasure to have you here again!"

Turning to Britta, he said, "This must be Ms. Hayworth. I am pleased to meet you."

Britta's presence might have troubled Diamant. After all, no woman, other than the female members of the Consortium Gallery staff, had ever set foot in the laboratory. McCurdy and Rothmeyer had phoned ahead, however, to get clearance for "the young woman who had helped to persuade the Oxford professor to release his scroll to Israel." It was also no small feather in her cap that she was "the cousin of the priestly candidate, Zachary Cohen."

As the foursome followed Diamant past the reception desk, through the fabulous gallery with its collection of replica furnishings and implements to be used in the future temple, David saw the amazement in Britta's eyes. "This is what I told you about," he whispered. "Isn't it wonderful?"

The young Briton was spellbound, clutching David's arm as they passed under the eyeless gaze of the high priestly manikin that displayed the special woven vestments. After taking a few more turns and arriving at a small outer courtyard, they waited for Diamant to unlock the door to the subterranean chamber that housed the lab.

As the door creaked open on the dark room, and Diamant switched on the bank of fluorescent lights that ran the length of the ceiling, the professors were surprised.

"Why, it is exactly as we left it!" Ian marveled.

"Yes," Diamant replied. "We kept your work covered with a sheet, and except for an occasional dusting in the room, no one has touched a thing since you worked on the scroll a year ago."

David stepped up to the long steel table where the strips of corroded copper lay in exactly the same configuration as when he and Ian had found the name of Cohen's forefather. "What of the other work that was ongoing here? Surely the geneticists and others have continued their research."

"They removed their machines and equipment to adjoining rooms," he answered, indicating doors that led off this chamber to others the professors had never seen. "What little they have done since you were here did not require so much space. Since the priestly candidate was located, their work has only supplemented the testing and cataloging of levitical and kohathic specimens carried on in various labs around the world."

Britta was intrigued. "Around the world?" she repeated. "So there are labs related to this one in other countries?"

"Oh, yes," Diamant said. "For years we have been collecting the names of priestly and levitical males from every race and nation. We find cohens and levites who are Chinese, Ethiopian, Irish . . . you name it. When we learned that they all have the same distinguishing genetic marker, we began collecting, studying, and storing saliva samples." At this he paused, seeing her incredulous expression. "Yes, I know," he laughed. "Sounds like the Twilight Zone. Truth stranger than fiction, right? But believe me, Ms. Hayworth, it *is* true!"

David understood her astonishment. "It gets better," he said with a chuckle. "Wait 'til they tell you about the cows they've been cloning!"

"Cloning!" she exclaimed.

Diamant was uneasy. "The professor jests," he said. "We have been attempting to raise a perfect heifer, but cloning? No!" Seeing that Britta was still bewildered, he turned to Rothmeyer. "Surely the young lady knows about the red heifer?"

David shrugged. "I have not gone into it with her."

Diamant looked at Ian. "And our friend from Oxford?"

Ian nodded. "Not to worry, Diamant. I have been filled in."

Britta shot a skeptical and somewhat angry look at David, and the professor lifted his hands. "Don't hold it against me, Britta," he said. "I haven't told Ian about the Jeremiah Box, either."

The Irishman and the British girl both scowled. "The Jeremiah Box? What is that?" they grumbled.

Diamant shook his head and rolled his eyes. "I think we had better have a little conference before we proceed," he said. Pulling up some stools from beneath a counter that ran the length of one lab wall, he offered everyone a seat. "It seems we all know a little, but no one knows enough. David, why don't you begin by telling about the red heifer while I go put on some coffee."

It was approaching midnight in the underground lab. After a long conversation in which David and Shalom Diamant explained what they knew about the Ashes of the Red Heifer, the enigmatic Jeremiah Box, and David's new assignments, the group had delved into the work of unlocking the mysteries of the Second Copper Scroll.

Even though Britta was not a linguist or an archaeologist, she was able to assist the scholars by taking their dictation as they proceeded with the arduous task of reading and translating the shards spread out on the table. Shalom Diamant likewise helped, by locating and reading what appeared to be corresponding portions of the original Copper Scroll, the entire transcript of which had been published in various scholarly journals over the years.

It was at the end of that First Copper Scroll that the very existence of the second had been divulged. After the reader waded through a detailed treasure list with location descriptions obscure enough that a key was required to fully understand them, the scroll ended by saying, "In the tunnel which is in Sechab, to the north of Kochlit, which opens toward the north and has graves in its entrance: a copy of this text and its explanation and its measurements and the inventory . . . item by item."

It was this item-by-item explanation that the scholars this night set out to make some sense of.

The inventory list in the first scroll was done in clear bookkeeping style, each item cataloged and quantified, with the vague location indicated. Columns of items were followed by series of letters of which no one had ever known the meaning: they could have been coded valuations of the goods, or they could have related to the names of individuals responsible for each cache. In all, the First Copper Scroll contained sixty-four such lists, or caches.

As Diamant read from the scholarly translations of the first scroll, the professors found that the second seemed to correlate nicely, taking each cache and explicating the locations more precisely. Scholars had always suspected, based on various placenames in this scroll, that the treasures had been widely distributed, caches being hidden everywhere throughout ancient Palestine, from Jericho to the region closest to Damascus, with some of the caches being located in the center of old Jerusalem itself. This seemed to be confirmed by what the men found as they worked through the difficult paleograms on the corroded copper.

Not that the explications were simple, however. Even with the added information they gave, it would take years of archaeological work to pinpoint the various sites with precision. In fact, as the professors went through the lists of containers, chests of gold and silver talents, tithe vessels, pots, pitchers, golden artifacts, sacred garments, etc., it became obvious that the bulk of the treasure might never be found.

While the hours passed they began to despair of finding any reference to the sacred items on which the rabbis had hoped to get a lead. As midnight drew on, David took a swig of Diamant's hot coffee, stifled a yawn, and read yet another line of the difficult script. Bending close to one of the shards, he translated: "'As to the furnishings of the Holy Place, behold, they are in the King's Tower.'"

Rothmeyer frowned and squinted at the lines again, wondering if he had heard himself correctly. McCurdy and Cromwell blinked their weary eyes and cocked their heads.

"What did you say?" Diamant marveled. "Did you say 'furnishings of the Holy Place,' the apartment that led to the Holy of Holies? Why, that would be the golden menorah! The table of showbread! The altar of incense! We had thought all of those things were taken by the Romans!"

Ian agreed. "Of course! After all, the menorah is plainly visible on the Arch of Titus in Rome—booty of the conquerors!"

David bent closer to the shard, Ian and John crowding in around him.

"Take a look," David said. "Maybe the late hour is playing tricks on me!"

The Oxfordian leaned over the table as the younger professor gave him room.

"Yes . . . yes," Ian surmised. "I would translate this the same way. It does indeed refer to the Holy Place!"

Together the professors turned to Diamant, who was anxiously scanning the translation of the original scroll for any such reference. His perplexed look answered for him. "I am sure there is nothing here to correlate with what you have just read," he said.

Ian nodded. "Nor will you find such a thing, though you search for the rest of your life!" he agreed. "Scholars of the Copper Scroll have always noted that it makes no mention of such furnishings, nor of the Ashes of the Red Heifer or the Priestly Breastplate." Straightening, the old man lifted a finger and shook it to make his point. "No, gentlemen," he asserted, "the statement which David has just read is an anomaly! It is very important, because it has no corollary in the first scroll, a scroll of which this is supposed to be a companion and an explanation!"

David rubbed his chin. "Why, then, is it stated at all? The First Copper Scroll tells us that this one gives an explanation 'item by item.' It says nothing about additional items, and I would think that articles as important as the Temple furnishings would have at least been alluded to in the first."

Ian was beginning to pace, a sign that the old gentleman was sufficiently excited that the late hour and his long day of work no longer sapped his strength. He rubbed his hands together, and John Cromwell watched him with a knowing smile. "He is on to something," he whispered to the others. "Just wait."

Sure enough, in a few seconds McCurdy made a pronouncement. "Aha!" he cried, waving his finger in the air. "Let us see that section again, Diamant, where the first scroll divulges the fact of the second scroll's existence."

Diamant quickly turned to the closing lines of the translation. "You mean this?" he said, handing a printout to Ian.

"Exactly!" McCurdy cried again, jabbing his finger at the page over and over. "Listen to this!" Reading, he quoted, "' . . . a copy of this text and its explanation and its measurements and the inventory . . . item by item.'"

Looking at his companions, he became impatient. "Don't you see? There is a missing phrase between the words 'inventory' and 'item by item.' Why, that could be anything! We simply cannot read it, because it is illegible! Perhaps"—he paused, tingling with possibilities—"perhaps, even *intentionally* illegible!"

The others pondered this, their expressions a mix of wonder, doubt, and skepticism. At last it was Britta who dared to postulate. "Are you saying, Father McCurdy, that the scribe wanted the reader to be left with some question as to what that illegible phrase might refer? And that the reader, especially of that day and age, would have easily guessed that he referred to the holiest of artifacts?"

Ian looked at the young woman admiringly. "Astute as always, Ms. Hayworth!" he said.

David was not so quick to accept the proposition. "Well," he warned, "we must avoid drawing premature conclusions. Besides, where is this King's Tower that the text designates? What does it matter if we have an anomaly, if we do not know the location?"

McCurdy considered this patiently. "You are right, Professor. Perhaps we should read on. But if we find more such peculiar sections, we can be sure the scribe purposely scattered them among the others to indicate their special status."

David cleared his throat and bent over the fragments again. For several long minutes he read, line after line of dry inventory, locations, and quantities. Sitting back, he rubbed his spine and shrugged. "No more mention of the King's Tower," he said. "I am mystified."

"Do go on!" Diamant urged him. "We are nowhere near finished with this!"

David sighed and proceeded, stumbling through the arduous assignment with a foggy brain, until he came upon another sensational notation. "Listen to this!" he exclaimed, carefully translating the phrases. "'Now, as to the Holy Ark, do not seek it, for until the day of purification, he who approaches it will surely die. The other furnishings, they are in the King's Tower, with the priest's *breastplate*.'"

Not only was the reference to the ark awe-inspiring, but the last word stuck in David's throat. Barely did he croak it out before the others, including Britta, closed in upon him. "Breastplate!" Diamant cried. "Are you sure, Dr. Rothmeyer?"

David nodded. "Yes . . . definitely!" He pointed to the exact word, and Ian nearly wept for joy. "Well done, my boy!" he cried. "Just what the rabbis have hoped for!"

Diamant was nearly salivating. "S-so," he stammered, "this King's Tower . . . Where do you suppose that is?"

Ian shook his head. "We are certain to find out!" he said. "We have not been brought this far to fail now!" Then, patting David on the back, he spurred him. "Go on, my boy! Read!"

David hunched over the table again, his heart pounding with adrenaline as he pulled a desk lamp closer to his workspace. "'As to the breastplate, think not to find the word of the Lord. For it shall only appear when my servant is ready to proclaim it.'"

The group stared at the shards blankly, wondering what this could mean. John Cromwell, remembering his Anglican liturgy, repeated, "'The Word of the Lord' . . . that is a most important phrase," he said. "When our priests use that term, they invoke the congregation's most profound attention."

"Yes," Father McCurdy said, "it is the same in our Roman Catholic tradition."

Diamant nodded. "And in ours," he said. "Whenever a prophet used the phrase, he was saying that he was speaking for God."

Britta squirmed on her stool and dared to offer a suggestion. "This may be over the top," she said, "but is it possible that in this context . . . with the breastplate and the priest and all . . . that the scribe is referring to the objects the high priest used to divine the will of God?"

The men considered this with amazement. "The Urim and Thummim!" David exclaimed. "Why, of course! 'Think not to find the word of the Lord,'" he quoted, "'for it will only appear when my servant is ready to proclaim it'!"

"'Servant' . . . ," Ian marveled. "Why, that must refer to the high priest himself!"

At this, the entire group fell silent, the subterranean chamber still as a tomb, as they considered the implications.

"The scribe is speaking of Zachary Cohen . . . our own Zachary!" Britta gasped.

"So he is," Ian agreed. "What a weight of responsibility our boy carries!"

David meant no disrespect, but as the group continued to ponder this, he went on reading, unable to resist the challenge.

"Listen to this!" he cried again. "I am beginning to feel that we are on a celestial scavenger hunt!"

The others bent in around him once more, jostling for a view.

"The author of this scroll has created a riddle for us," he said. "Something like what Samson did to the Philistines!"

"Go on!" Ian implored. "Tell us!"

David moved his finger along the piece of scroll, not touching it but raised just above each crabbed letter. "'When you find the casket of the prophet, which is in the hands of Cyrus, you will also find . . .'"

The professor paused, chagrined.

"Yes? Yes?" Ian pleaded.

"I am almost embarrassed!" Rothmeyer said with an ironic chuckle. "Here goes . . . 'you will also find the *map* to the King's Tower'!"

The members of the group glanced at one another in astonishment. Muttering among themselves, they did not give the reading good reviews.

"Casket?" Britta said with a grimace. "That's creepy!"

"Cyrus?" Diamant said with a frown. "The Persian king who conquered Babylon? He had been dead for centuries when this was written!"

"And this King's Tower," John said with a bit of a sneer. "We're to believe there's actually a map to the bloody place?"

David grew defensive. "I'm only telling you what it says!" he insisted.

It was much too late now to deal with all of this. Tension filled the air until Ian wisely suggested, "We do not doubt your word, David. I think we all feel some strain. Perhaps it is time to turn in?"

Collectively, they gave a sigh. Preparing to leave, they moved toward the laboratory door. As Diamant opened it, they all breathed deeply of the refreshing night air, then followed the curator back through the gallery and out onto Rebi Josef Street.

"See you in the morning, Mr. Diamant," David said.

"Certainly, Professor," Diamant replied, waving them all off.

As the gallery door closed and the huddled entourage walked slowly back toward the Consortium house, they spoke little. Their minds and hearts were full of mystery, and they doubted they would sleep at all, tonight.

CHAPTER 19

As the research had proceeded in the Jerusalem laboratory, another sort of inquiry was being pursued in Washington, D.C. A small room near the detention cells in the FBI building was the scene of an investigation as intense as that in which David Rothmeyer was engaged, and even more emotional.

Seated at a gray table in the nondescript room, his wrists bound with handcuffs, was Frank Paddock, the oldest of the four suspects identified by Lamar Jackson in the murder of Senator Jefferson. With him was a yuppie-looking attorney with slicked-back hair and wire-rimmed glasses, a graduate of Georgetown University who had just begun his first year of practice. On his eel-skin briefcase, which lay open on the table, was a little brass nameplate: "James Pickerell, P.C."

Also seated at the table were Rabbi Benjamin and Mel Wester. Perched on a high stool at one end of the room was CIA agent Morris, and pacing the floor was his partner, Agent Dalton.

"We're not here to question you about the murder," Dalton reiterated, glaring at the big Aryan. "We have enough ammo against you and your buddies to send you all to the chair!"

The young lawyer shifted nervously in his own chair and glanced at his client out of the corner of one eye. The big thug stared mutely at the tabletop like a kid in the wrong classroom.

"Don't I get to defend myself?" Paddock muttered.

His attorney looked flustered. Apparently this little interview didn't call for defense. He put a finger down his stiff white Pierre Cardin collar, trying to loosen it. "Just what do you want of my client?" the preppy lawyer asked.

Dalton stopped pacing and leaned on the table, his hands palm down on the gray linoleum surface. "Like I said," he growled, "we have reason to believe that Frank and his friends waylaid the senator in order to take something he had that day, something in the briefcase he always carried to work, and which was not found at the crime scene."

The smooth-faced lawyer brightened, a clever argument flashing through his mind. Raising a well-manicured finger, he said, "Ah, but wasn't the senator killed by a passing train? Wasn't his body . . . or what remained of it . . . found crushed upon the subway tracks? Just how likely would it be that anything he carried would have survived such demolition? The briefcase could be strewn in shreds from the subway station to Alexandria! The cops would never have found it."

Dalton and Morris looked at each other sideways, surprised at the young fellow's sharpness.

The lawyer, noting their reaction, gained confidence. "In light of this," he said boldly, "I think there is no real argument even for a murder! The senator simply fell in front of the train, and my client had the misfortune of being in the vicinity."

Dalton flashed angry eyes at the cocky advocate. "Now hold on, Mr. Pickerell!" he barked. "You know good and well the senator was shot before he was thrown on the tracks!"

Pickerell smiled smugly. "Do tell!" he quipped. "If the body was as badly mangled as the coroner says, evidence for cause of death is up for grabs." At this, he shrugged and, reaching for his own briefcase, casually slammed the lid shut. "Why don't we call it a day, gentlemen?" he said, pushing on the bridge of his trendy wire-rims. "You don't have squat to hang on my client!"

Dalton bristled. "Save your arguments in that regard for the court! The eyewitness to the *shooting* pulled Frank and his boys out of a lineup, slick as anything! We're not here to lay that groundwork again!"

The lawyer smirked. "A six-year old kid . . . a *black street kid* to boot! How far do you think his testimony will go before a jury!"

The thug grinned from ear to ear, and reaching over, he clapped the student on the shoulder. "Hey, Jim, you're not half bad!" he exclaimed.

No one missed the fact that as the Aryan gave his "attaboy" the Georgetownian cringed. Dalton sidled up to the lawyer. Leaning over him, both hands on the arms of his chair, he breathed into his face. "You sure this is a hole you want to crawl into, whiz kid? You could get a reputation as a skinhead lover!"

Mel took in this entire interchange with agitation. Glancing at Rabbi Ben, he saw that his old face was etched with worry. "Hey, boys," he said, after clearing his throat, "aren't we getting a little off the track? No pun intended."

Agent Morris winced, his own face contorted in a sorry grin. "Wester's right, Dalton," he agreed. "We're here to locate some important material. I think we'd better stick to that. Like you said, let's leave the rest to the court."

Dalton straightened, crossing his arms as he resumed pacing. The attorney studied his closed briefcase in silence, his cheeks flushed with what Mel figured was a bizarre mix of feelings. *James Pickerell probably wonders how he got into all of this. Just like me*, Mel thought.

As to how Mel had gotten into this, aside from being enlisted by Morris and Dalton, Rabbi Ben had requested he be with him as this interview took place. The only rabbi allowed in the chamber, he felt he would have been out of his element without Mel's expertise.

The rabbis believed that the senator had borne in his briefcase the article which the queen of Jordan had intended for them. A bonded transport company had made an appointment with Goldstein's estate to deliver a parcel from Senator Jefferson's office the day he was due to return from his diplomatic trip. A courier was supposed to take the package from Washington, D.C., to upstate New York, and from there the rabbis would have gotten it into the proper hands for study.

The item had never made it to Calvin Jefferson's office, let alone to Goldstein's estate. The plan had been interrupted by the assassins, and the rabbis suspected strongly that those assassins knew the parcel's whereabouts.

Pickerell squirmed, a look of desperation clouding his face. At last he brightened again. "Now, wait just a minute!" he said. "You obviously have your ideas of what this meeting is all about. But if I am to be this man's attorney"—he glanced sideways at the thug—"I must consider that anything we discuss ultimately relates to his fate. Any discussion of any article the senator was carrying relates to what became of the senator. Therefore, since we deny any knowledge of what preceded his death, this entire interview is off bounds for my client."

Mel was amazed at the young fellow's persistence. He thought that if he were ever in trouble, this would be the guy to have on his side. Still, he knew the kid was barking up the wrong tree.

Dalton, who seemed unprepared to respond to the whiz kid, looked grateful when Mel pulled his chair closer to the table and said, "If I may, I would like to interject something."

Dalton sighed and waved a hand toward the room. "Be my guest," he said.

Mel read the brass label on the young lawyer's valise. "You're a bright boy, James," he said, staring straight at him. "But based on my own experience with the LAPD, your defense is worth about as much as Bozo here is paying for it."

The Aryan bristled, his broad jaw clenching. The attorney tried not to look his way.

"You think you're going to win points with any jury because the prosecution's only witness is a 'little black street kid'? Well, let me tell you, Jimmy boy, in this day and age, that's one of the things the prosecution can take to the bank!" Mel turned from the student and glared at the steely eyed hood who faced him across the table. "To say nothing of the fact that this guy's as guilty as Macbeth's wife! How do you live with the stink of blood on your hands, slimeball?"

Morris waved a finger in the air. "Okay, Wester. Simmer down."

Mel clenched and unclenched his fists. "Like I was saying, I was nearly put away a few years ago by the fact that a bunch of 'street kids' testified against me. It didn't matter that my best friend, killed before my eyes, was the best black cop in L.A. My word meant nothing because I was white! Now, here's Super Whitey, right? You think his testimony is going to stand up against Lamar Jackson's? No way!"

The thug lurched across the table, slamming his handcuffed wrists onto the surface. His face nearly flush with Mel's, he growled, "Listen to yourself, blondie! Why don't you join us? You've suffered the oppression of the mud-people, just like we all have!"

The instant Frank made that move, the agents leaped behind him, trying to pull him off. The door to the room swung open and a husky armed guard rushed in to help. In seconds, the encounter was quelled, the guard yanking a night stick against the Aryan's thick neck.

Dalton and Morris straightened. "It's okay," Morris said, and the guard hesitantly pulled back. When he had left the room, and stood watching through the tiny barred window on the door, Mel sank into his chair. Letting go a big sigh, he sneerd at Frank Paddock.

"I don't join you because you're stupid!" Mel replied through gritted teeth.

Rabbi Ben reached out and patted Mel on the arm, trying to calm him.

"Enough, now," Dalton warned. Then, looking at Pickerell, whose eyes were as wide as platters behind his wire-rims, he said, "Wester's point should be well taken. Your client had best be thinking about what he can do to cover himself . . . not how weak or strong the prosecution's case could be."

Glowering at the thug, Dalton added, "Not that I wouldn't love to see you put away for the rest of your unnatural life!"

Frank hunkered back, and his attorney stared meekly at the floor. The room was silent for the first time, until the Georgetownian finally said, "May I have a moment alone with my client?"

Dalton flashed a triumphant look at his partner, and Morris motioned to Mel and Rabbi Benjamin to follow them out to the corridor. When the door shut behind them, the guard stood in front of it, and Mel leaned against the hall wall, his hands in his pockets. Rabbi Ben, feeling very much out of place, stood beside him quietly; Morris glanced repeatedly at his watch and Dalton continued to pace.

Five minutes later Morris nodded to the guard, who again opened the door, and the four men entered the room. The attorney leaned back from intense discussion with his client, and Dalton barked, "Time's up, James! What will it be?"

As Ben and Mel took their seats again, the young lawyer tried to look mature. "Frank wants to know what would happen if he said he had seen the briefcase."

Dalton squinted at the Aryan, and Morris grinned. "He'd be making a wise decision," he said.

The lawyer reached for his briefcase and flipped the latches open. "Now, note that we might concede he had 'seen' the briefcase . . . maybe even *took* the briefcase. That does not mean he *killed* the senator."

Dalton hovered over the attorney and glared at Frank. "Of course not!" he said sarcastically.

"Nor does it mean," the attorney continued, "that my client killed, or knows anything about the killing of, Senator Jefferson."

"Heaven forbid!" Dalton spat.

Morris leaned forward on his stool. "That is for the jury to decide," he said.

"Understood," the attorney agreed. "Well . . . so, tell us . . . just what would it mean for my client, and his friends, if they knew anything about the briefcase, which happened to be lying at the scene of the death, perhaps on the platform, waiting to be taken to the lost and found?"

Dalton crossed his arms and sneered. "It would mean they were model citizens!" he mocked. "Especially if they took the briefcase to the authorities, like the good boys we know they are!"

Morris choked back a laugh. "But we know they didn't do any such thing, James," he said. "So what now?"

The Aryan looked doubtfully at his attorney, as if he hoped the kid knew what he was doing.

"Say the briefcase had nothing valuable in it, so they just tossed it away," James suggested.

At this, Rabbi Benjamin, who had been very much in the background, stiffened visibly. Mel glanced at him and gave him a reassuring wink. "It's okay," he whispered.

Dalton clenched his jaw and studied Pickerell knowingly. "Clever boy!" he said. "So what does your client say were the 'less-than-valuable' items in the briefcase?"

Pickerell observed Frank cautiously. "Go ahead, Paddock. Tell them what you told me."

Frank scooted forward in his chair and cleared his throat. "Me and the guys, we just saw this briefcase, you know. Lying on the floor by the tracks, you know."

He rolled his eyes toward his lawyer, who nodded at him.

"We thought, geez, someone lost their briefcase, you know . . ."

Dalton raised a hand to his mouth and coughed.

"Go on, Frank," James said.

"We was in a hurry, you know." Paddock swallowed. "We just took a quick look inside, you know . . . to see . . . if it was worth the bother . . . to turn it in . . . you know."

Rabbi Benjamin sat forward, his hands folded tightly on his lap.

"Go on," James said again.

"Well . . ." The Aryan looked at the ceiling, as though trying very hard to remember. "There was this bunch of papers. They didn't mean nothin' to us."

Rabbi Ben pulled on the tips of his beard and studied the thug anxiously.

"Papers, of course," James agreed. "And what did you do with the papers?"

"Well," Frank proceeded, "we saw that they belonged to a senator, so we decided to take them to headquarters, you know, to our boss. He'd know what to do with 'em, we figured."

Dalton and Morris glanced knowingly at each other. "Your boss?" Dalton said smugly. "And that would be the gentleman currently residing in maximum security with Ron Barrett."

Paddock sank back into his chair. "This ain't workin'!" he cried, lifting his shackled hands to his face. "I don't wanna get the boss in trouble!"

Pickerell fidgeted and reached out to calm his client. "Go ahead, Frank. Like we talked about. It won't hurt."

Frank took a deep breath. "I guess Jimmy's right," he croaked. "You know who the boss is! Heck . . . you probably know more about my people than I do!"

Dalton rounded the table and leaned close to the brute. "Likely so," he said, a victorious grin stretching his lips. "So what did the Spokane boss do with the senator's papers?"

Frank slumped, his chin resting on his chest. "He . . . he burned 'em!"

The agents froze. They had not anticipated this. "He *burned* them?" Morris growled. "After he made copies, right?"

Frank shrugged. "Don't think so. He was plumb mad. Just tore 'em up and lit 'em with a cigarette lighter." At this, he shivered a little, as though the memory frightened him. "Said we'd failed 'im," he went on. "We didn't bring him nothin' meanin'ful, he said."

Either Frank was a very good actor, or he truly believed that much of what he said, that he and his friends had not found anything of value in that briefcase.

Dalton and Morris looked almost as miserable as their suspect. Obviously, they had anticipated that something critical to national security was in the senator's possession. Whether or not it was, it was gone now.

But Rabbi Ben was not satisfied. Raising a hand, he caught the agents' attention. "Do you mind if I ask Mr. Paddock a question?" he said.

Dalton and Morris glanced at each other. "Why not?" Morris said.

Rabbi Ben leaned forward, studying the Aryan intently. Chances were very good, Mel thought, that the old gentleman had never directly spoken to such an enemy in his life.

"Mr. Paddock," the old rabbi began, "do you believe in God?"

Frank's bloodshot eyes looked bewildered. As he focused on the rabbi, however, his hackles rose. "You talkin' to me, Jew boy?" he spat.

Rabbi Ben's face twitched, but he carried on. "Because if you believe in God, you will want to recall that he hears every word you say. And if you believe that . . ."

Frank glanced away, his jaw tightening.

"If you believe that," the elder proceeded, "you will want to tell the truth."

Mel shuddered. *Dear Rabbi Ben!* he thought. *He is too good for this world!*

But the rabbi was not concerned for the impression he made. "I am going to ask you one thing," he said to Frank, "and nothing more."

The old fellow continued to stare at his enemy's averted face. "Was there anything else in that briefcase? Anything at all?"

James Pickerell had not anticipated such a question. He was about to counsel his client that he need not answer when Frank shrugged, his mouth opening in a surprisingly soft voice. "Nothin' but junk," he grumbled. "Souvenir Jew junk," he said. "Sure nothin' we wanted!"

Pickerell was astonished. "Frank, you didn't tell me. . . . You said there were only papers!"

The client looked at his attorney with rigid indignation. "You think I don't know junk when I see it? It was nothin', Jimmy. Nothin' at all!"

Rabbi Ben tensed like a cat, his old hands gripping the lapels of his long black coat like claws. "What was this 'Jew junk'?" he managed to ask.

"Some old box!" Frank growled. "Souvenir garbage! Who needs it?"

The older man turned to Mel with desperate eyes. "The box, Melvin!" he gasped. "They have our box!"

Mel reached out and patted his friend on the knee. "It's okay, Rabbi. Hold steady!"

The ex-cop knew that the least thing could throw this off. Act too anxious, and they'd never get what they wanted.

Gently, he pressed for more information. "Of course, it was probably nothing, like you say. But humor us here, Frankie. What did you do with the box?"

The Aryan looked at his attorney with hot, stress-filled eyes. "Will it help me to tell them?" he asked.

James was in over his head. All he could do was shrug. "I guess it can't hurt, Frank," he replied. "We're clutching at straws either way."

The Aryan thought hard. "You know that little jerk who tracked you to the hotel?" he asked.

Mel squinted. *You mean, the weasel?* he wanted to say. Instead he asked, "Barrett? Ronald Barrett?"

"Yeah," Frank said. "He liked the stupid box. Said his girlfriend would love it. So the boss gave it to him in payment for puttin' us up at his house."

Mel remembered the story of how the police and the FBI had descended on Barrett's place in the Spokane Valley, snagging Frank, the boss, and his friends without a hitch.

When Wester sat back with a satisfied look, Frank got more nervous. "What, blondie?" he snarled. "Does this make you happy?"

Mel crossed his arms smugly, and Rabbi Ben's old eyes glinted with hope. The agents studied them with amazement. "A box?" Morris said. "Does that sound like something you're after?"

Rabbi Ben smiled gloriously. "It is a start, gentlemen!" he exclaimed. "It is, at least, a start!"

CHAPTER 20

David paced the moonlit terrace of the old Consortium house, which overlooked the Hinnom Valley. It must have been three o'clock in the morning. He had not slept a wink, the cryptic instructions on the Copper Scroll obsessing him since he had left the laboratory with Father McCurdy and the others.

About half an hour ago, he had finally left his rumpled bed, where he had tossed away the intervening hours. Not changing out of his pajamas, he had wrapped a bathrobe about himself and dragged his slippered feet up the winding stone stairway to the terrace. It seemed everyone else in the house was sound asleep. No light shown under any of the doorways he had passed, and he stood absorbed in thought, undisturbed by any sound.

His own thoughts were disturbing enough. Over and over he reviewed the lines from the scroll in his mind, its enigmatic phrases haunting him. ". . . do not look for the Holy Ark, for until the day of purification, he who approaches it will surely die." What, he wondered, was this futuristic "day of purification"? The phrase had an apocalyptic ring to it.

But then, so did much of the writing of the Cave Scrolls. Scholars had pondered, for years, the meaning of the War Scroll, for instance, with its Armaggedon-like allusions to the end of the world and the final war between the Sons of Light and the Sons of Darkness. Did the "day of purification" find its parallel in such references?

David walked back and forth upon the veranda, clasping

and unclasping his hands in contemplation. Some scholars had chalked the War Scroll and similar Essene writings up to allegory. But no one could seriously believe that the two Copper Scrolls were allegorical. They were too precise, too concerned with detail, location, and measurement, to be taken for fable or symbolism.

That being the case, David marveled, there really must be a King's Tower, where the most fabulous finds in Middle Eastern history might be buried. For that matter, if they were ever found, they would be the most fabulous finds in *human* history! In that unknown place were supposedly hidden furnishings of Herod's temple, the most fabulous building in the world, items even from the Holy Place that somehow escaped the Romans' plunder.

Not only furnishings, but the very *breastplate* of that temple's overseer, the breastplate of the high priest, was supposedly buried there!

But *where* was *there*? Where was this mysterious King's Tower? The scroll did not say, other than to indicate, in a most aggravating way, that yet another key to the puzzle existed: a map . . . in a casket!

David stopped his pacing and shook his head. It was at this reference that the evening's research had come to an abrupt halt. At first David's companions had not even trusted his interpretation of that part of the scroll. It seemed too far-fetched, too bizarre. As the professor remembered Britta's reaction, he grimaced. "A casket?" she had exclaimed. "That's creepy!"

And it was. All of David's work had suddenly taken on a ghoulish, Halloween-ish tenor when he had read those phrases.

Not only did the scroll seem to be taking them on a Dungeons and Dragons skeet chase, but the clues themselves seemed all out of context. Why, for instance, did the scroll refer to the Persian king Cyrus? What did he have to do with anything remotely related to the Essenes and their treasure? And who was this prophet whose casket contained more clues?

About the moment David began to despair of making any sense of the riddle, Britta again came to mind. Now there was a girl with a clear head, he thought, and with her feet planted firmly in reality. She seemed to have a way of getting past "anomalies," as Ian called them, to see actual possibilities. David had been amazed at her interpretation of the phrase "word of the Lord." Her quick mind had sorted through the context to make perfect sense of the reference. What else could "the word of the Lord" refer to, in this case, but the Urim and the Thummim?

David breathed with some relief. At least that portion of the scroll, if Britta's interpretation was correct, eased his workload somewhat. The wording made it clear that no one was to look seriously for the Urim and Thummim, because it would only appear when the high priest was ready for it. From the little David understood of Zachary's readiness, that might take a while.

As to the Ashes of the Red Heifer, the other item David was to locate, so far there was no reference to it. Perhaps it was also buried in this King's Tower, which would only be located if they found the mysterious "casket."

How David wished Britta might come up with a more pleasant interpretation of that term! On the other hand, he thought with a smirk, the meaning seemed all too clear without anyone's help. He was to look now for the tomb of some dead prophet. He was to find his casket and open it! Inside would be this map. . . .

David laughed to himself. Why was he surprised? Wasn't this the business of archaeology? Hadn't he opened many a tomb and grave in his years on Central American digs? What was so bizarre about this?

The professor wrapped his robe tight to his shoulders. A cool breeze wafted down from the heights of Mount Zion, spilling through the trees like a death rattle.

"Britta's right!" he said aloud. "This is creepy!"

Done with cogitating, he was just turning to leave the terrace when a shadow filled the doorway leading to the stairs inside. Starting, he felt the hair rise on the back of his neck.

"Did I hear my name spoken?" a woman's voice greeted him.

David relaxed instantly, blinking his eyes. "Britta?" he cried. "Is that you?"

The silhouetted girl stepped onto the terrace, illumined by moonlight. A smile lit her eyes. "Of course, silly!" She laughed. "Who else?"

"You should be asleep," David said, seeing that she was, like himself, in her robe and pajamas. Stepping close to her, he took her hands in his. "It is the middle of the night!"

"And what's your excuse?" she said. "Have you slept at all?"

David looked away. "Not a smidgen," he replied.

Britta led him to the low wall that edged the terrace. Breathing deep of the cooling air, she smelled the aroma of sage and myrtle that rose from the Hinnom Valley. "Isn't it wonderful?" she sighed. "Can you believe we are actually here . . . together?" She turned her deep blue eyes up at the tall man and he drew her head toward him, nesting it in the crook of his arm.

How small she is! he thought. *How . . .*

He was about to think the word "helpless," like any strong man would like to think. But he knew better. Of all women, Britta Hayworth was the least helpless!

Gazing down at her blonde curls, he lifted her face to his, longing for a kiss. When she smiled up at him, obviously willing, he leaned over her, pressing his mouth to hers.

Suddenly, however, he pulled back, glaring in agitation at the dark terrain.

"What is it?" Britta asked in surprise.

"Oh, I can't get that infuriating scroll out of my mind!" he exclaimed. "I agree with you. It's creepy! I don't relish looking for the tomb of some nameless prophet. For goodness' sake, we don't even know what time period or what culture to start with. The reference to Cyrus really throws things off!"

Britta stepped away and leaned over the low wall, studying the hills and distant shepherd fields just visible toward Bethlehem. "I knew you would be up here tonight, obsessing over all of this," she said. "I, too, have been trying to put the puzzle together." She turned to face him, resting against the wall. A teasing smile lit her face. "You may recall that I'm pretty good at putting clues together. Remember the British Museum?"

David nodded appreciatively. "I wish I could have been there when Ian realized you knew where he kept his stash!" he said with a chuckle. "Yes, if you could track down McCurdy's scroll in the bowels of British academia, you could track down anything!"

Britta crossed her arms. "Well, I may be clever, but you are Sherlock Holmes when it comes to sniffing out Israeli secrets. I think that, if we put our heads together, we'll figure this out."

David liked the sound of that and stepped toward the wall, bending over her. "I hope you don't mind if I take you literally, Ms. Hayworth," he teased. "I like putting my head and yours together."

Once more they kissed, but Britta was the one to pull away. "Seriously," she said with a smile, "I do have some thoughts that might be of interest to you."

"Everything about you interests me!" David replied, reaching for her. But she scooted out from under his arm, looking quite businesslike.

"Dr. Rothmeyer," she said firmly, "do you want to hear my ideas or don't you?"

David sighed and took the spot where she had just stood, leaning against the wall.

"Of course, Britta," he said. "Shoot."

"Well," she began, pointing into thin air, "I was thinking about what Diamant told us regarding the ashes."

". . . of the red heifer," David said.

"Right. . . . Now, listen. Remember that there was some legend of a prophet who took the ashes across the Jordan?"

"Jeremiah," David recalled.

"Okay," Britta went on. "Is it possible that the prophet referred to in the scroll is Jeremiah?"

David shook his head. "I thought of that," he said, "but it doesn't fit with the reference to Cyrus. That was a good generation or more removed from Jeremiah. In fact, it was about half a century after Jeremiah before Cyrus took over Babylon and freed the Jews."

Britta looked admiringly at David. "Wow! You've really learned this stuff, haven't you?"

David shrugged. "It's all part of my work for the rabbis. You wouldn't believe the library they had me read when I first started my research." He thought fondly on that time, when his room in this old building had always been strewn with dozens of books at various stages of reading and where hundreds more waited on the shelves. "I think I earned a Ph.D. in Hebrew studies that first month!"

Britta nodded. "So there's no chance the prophet is Jeremiah," she concluded.

David did not want to pass off her suggestion without a fair trial. "I won't say it's impossible," he said, "especially considering the legend that he took the ashes over the Jordan. But the biggest problem is that the last we hear from Jeremiah in the Scriptures, Jerusalem is doomed, and the Babylonians overrun it in short order. Meanwhile, he has escaped . . . to Egypt! That's apparently where he lived out his days. Why would his casket have ended up in Persian hands, at the opposite end of the earth?"

Britta lowered her head, disappointed. Then, suddenly, it was as if a light went off in her brain. "David!" she exclaimed. "Is it possible that we are misconstruing a word here?"

David looked bewildered. "Which word?" he asked.

"'Casket,'" she replied. "Does it have to mean a box for a dead person? Could it mean just a box—maybe even something quite small?"

All at once David felt as if an electric shock passed through him. It was one of those rare moments, like the time when many seemingly unrelated clues came together to point to Zachary Cohen. In a flash of perfect insight, he knew. "The Jeremiah Box!" he cried. "The Jeremiah Box!"

The two stood stunned for a moment, staring mutely at each other as the full import of the revelation dawned simultaneously in their minds.

Breathless, David began to pace again, almost running from one side of the terrace to the other, slamming fist into palm as thoughts and explanations tumbled from his brain in such rapid succession he could hardly keep up with them.

"How could we have missed it?" he cried. "Jeremiah took the ashes across the Jordan just before the Babylonians swept through the land. They must have been in a vial of some sort, but that vial would have rested in a protective container. . . ."

"A wooden box!" Britta declared.

"The box ended up in the hands of the court of Persian Babylon," David deduced.

"Clear across today's country of Jordan!" Britta added.

"Perhaps the Jews had it with them for centuries, but then . . ."

"The box was lost," she guessed.

"Or given away . . . perhaps as a decoy for its contents!" David was on a roll.

"Eventually it ended up closer to home," Britta went on.

"In the land of Jordan!"

"Meanwhile, the vial was hidden . . . ," Britta deduced.

"In the King's Tower?"

Britta shrugged. "Wherever that is!"

"But," David said, stopping and turning to her, "that is where we come in! The scroll says the box, when it is found, will have a . . ."

"Map!" Britta cried. "A map to the King's Tower!"

Britta smiled so wide her face felt as though it could split as David rushed at her and, lifting her off her feet, twirled her round and round.

As he did so, a scrambling sound ascended from the stairs inside. Ian McCurdy and John Cromwell suddenly appeared in the doorway, looking disheveled and astonished.

"What is happening?" Ian gasped.

"Are you all right?" Cromwell worried. "We heard . . ."

As soon as they came out on the terrace, they saw that everything was more than all right. Stopping, they backed away, afraid that they had interrupted a lovers' tryst—a rather ecstatic one, at that.

David laughed and set Britta down. She gripped the wall for support, trying to calm her dizziness, as David rushed at the old men and surprised each of them with a spontaneous hug.

The dignified Cromwell pulled away, smoothed his robe, and cleared his throat. "Are you quite certain you are all right?" he repeated.

"The best I have ever been!" David exclaimed. Wheeling about, his lanky arms spread like an eagle's wings, he danced in the moonlight. "The old and the new, the past and the present have come together again! Oh, Jerusalem!" he cried. "You are truly divine!"

CHAPTER 21

Pete sat in his brother's flashy red Suburban on a dirt street that ran toward a set of railroad tracks in a dingy part of Spokane. This section of the city's outskirts was technically a township of its own, known as Opportunity, Washington. As Pete hunched down in the driver's seat, watching the afternoon street, he thought the name was more wishful thinking than realistic.

Whatever "opportunity" this area offered, it had long since vanished from this particular neighborhood. Small houses, little better than shanties, sat oddly spaced on long, narrow lots, most of which had forgotten what a lawn was, if they ever knew. Weeds and stunted trees grew up along dilapidated fences, the only boundaries that distinguished one piece of property from another. Here and there a chained dog ran in a dirt track round and round a stake, or lay resigned in the door of a ramshackle doghouse. School would be out soon, filling the road with children returning to houses where, if they were lucky, at least one parent was present. The fathers were, more often than not, long gone, leaving single women to collect welfare checks and, if they were among the rare few, child support payments, from the mailboxes.

Opportunity was so named because it was situated on the broad, fertile plain that opened onto the Spokane Valley. At one time, this had been a great agricultural community, and there were still a few truck farms and huge vegetable gardens remaining from earlier times to attest to the fact. The railroad had once provided employment to the men who lived in Opportunity, but the sleek new Amtrak system held few jobs for locals, and activity along the line was not sufficient to discourage the weeds and litter that now encroached on the tracks.

Pete was not a Spokanite. When he came to town, which was only once or twice a year, he and Honey made the rounds of the warehouse and discount outlets, gathering up provisions for their backcountry lifestyle. Honey always insisted on at least one afternoon in the big department stores downtown and the malls beyond.

Today Pete and Honey's itinerary would not include discount shops, the downtown stores, or the malls. They were here for a special purpose, one that teased Pete with the taste of adventure he had experienced a year earlier.

Their plans for a Spokane trip had begun a few days ago, when they received a phone call, something unheard of in their low-tech lives. Had the call not been very important in nature, its intrusion into Pete's rustic world would have tempted him to throw Mel's cell phone into Cricket Creek.

The day after the wedding, as the Libby boys and their bandleader had prepared to leave Bull River, Rory had brought the little device to the big log house. He had fulfilled his promise not to interrupt the couple's honeymoon night with any worry about the rock with the swastika, the motorcycles, or the lights in the woods. But on departing the property and delivering the phone, he had quickly explained why Mel had wanted them to have it.

Handing the rock and the scrawled swastika to Pete, he had apologized for leaving him with a "downer." "Your brother didn't want me to trouble you last night," he explained. "But I'm sure it's best you know now what's been goin' down on your own place here."

Pete's stomach had tightened at the sight of the Nazi symbol. He had hoped that his days of dealing with such creeps were over, but he had always feared that hope was unrealistic.

"Thanks, buddy," he had replied, pulling a small wad of cash from his pocket in payment for the band's work. Rory had flashed him a peace sign as he turned to go, and Pete held up the rock, calling out, "You done good. And your music's not bad either!"

At first Pete had thought he would keep the news from Honey, but he was her husband now, and their marriage was already altering his perception of things. He knew that he should tell her about this, that they must face both good and bad together, in a way they never had before.

He had barely found her in the house, set her down in the living room and shown her the rock and paper, when the phone rang. As Honey sat holding the paper in shaking hands, staring at it in horror, Pete spoke with Mel, who was calling from Spokane.

Cryptically, the ex-cop explained what had transpired the night before, with Ron Barrett, his Aryan cronies, and the law. Mel was on his way to FBI headquarters in Washington, D.C., he said. Would Pete be willing to pick up his car from the Spokane garage? He had left word with the attendant that his brother would be coming for it sometime that week.

Then, just this morning, Rabbi Ben and Mel, together, had called from upstate New York. Now that Mel had been enlisted as Zachary Cohen's bodyguard, they would be transporting the priestly candidate back to Jerusalem, where he was due to complete his training with the yeshiva scholars. A great deal had transpired since Mel had left Spokane, all pertaining to the strange box depicted on the fax that Rabbi Ben had shown at the "bachelor party" the night before the wedding. Not only did they have a lead on its whereabouts, but they had received a communiqué from David Rothmeyer in Jerusalem illuminating its value. According to the professor, his research there pointed to the possibility that the box the senator had been carrying held clues to the location of the exact artifacts the rabbis were seeking!

The fact that Pete was going to Spokane to fetch Mel's car was a godsend of timing, Rabbi Ben declared. If the assassins could be believed at all, the precious box was in the home of Roberta Barrett's son, Ronald!

"Why not take Roberta to Spokane with you, for a nice, friendly visit with Ronnie's girlfriend?" Mel suggested wryly. "Barrett's not allowed visitors just now, but his girl's probably very lonely and depressed, what with her man being in jail and all. While you're in the house, see if there happens to be a pretty little box on the coffee table, or on some knickknack shelf."

How should he explain to Roberta about the box? Pete asked. She already had enough to deal with emotionally, since being notified of her son's arrest and incarceration. Rabbi Ben had suggested he tell her only that it was a priceless Israeli artifact, fallen into the hands of Israel's enemies and passed off to her unwitting son. She did not need to know anything more than that.

What should they do with the box, if they found it? Pete inquired. "We know we can trust you to guard it in utmost secrecy, until we say otherwise," Ben replied. "Let's take one step at a time."

Pete had swallowed hard, his throat tense with a sense of mounting intrigue. When he had hung up the phone, he called Honey to the sofa, where only days before, she had been handed the hateful signs of the enemy's threat: the rock and swastika. Today he clasped her small hands in his, fingered the gold ring on her left hand, and stared into her wary eyes.

"It seems we are being drawn into another mystery," he said with a nervous smile. Leaving out nothing, he told what Ben had shared about the box, about the murder of Senator Jefferson, and about the Consortium's new quests. "Strange, huh?" he concluded. "The last adventure started with your little music box, and now this one revolves around a box even more priceless."

Honey had sighed and, snuggling close, rested her head on Pete's shoulder. "I suppose I should be scared," she said, "but as long as you are with me, I don't feel afraid. Israel brought us together; we must do all we can to bring her dreams to pass."

Taking Pete's pickup from Bull River, the newlyweds and an amazingly calm Roberta had reached Spokane about noon. They had gone straight to the high-rise garage to get the Suburban. Just in case time got away from them, they did not want to chance having to leave it there another night. They retrieved Mel's car without incident, and headed back toward the eastern outskirts of the city, Honey driving with Roberta in the pickup, Pete following close behind in the Suburban.

Since Roberta did not approve of her son's lifestyle or his companions, she had been to Ron's Spokane address only a couple of times. The blocks in this seedy sector of flatland were not evenly laid out; the streets were winding and not well marked, but she had a fairly clear memory of the location. It did not take long to find the small tumbledown cottage on the dirt road two doors down from the track.

They had decided that Pete should wait with the car, while the two women went up to the door. Because Mel's rig was an eye-catcher, and because it might be recognized by Ron's associates, Pete had parked up across the tracks, on the other side of the road, where a grove of dusty maples formed a screen. He nervously blew through pursed lips as he watched the girls approach the house.

Dingy white, with peeling paint and frayed lace curtains at the windows, the place did not speak well for Ron's chosen path. Pete hunched down in the seat, a baseball cap pulled close to his eyes and his ponytail tucked up under the rim. Anxiously, he twined and untwined his fingers and rapped them on the steering wheel in a nervous staccato.

The women had reached the door and were now knocking. He doubted anyone was home. He wished he could *go* home!

For what seemed too long, the women stood on the front stoop of thick, uneven planks laid directly on the ground. They leaned this way and that, apparently trying to get a glimpse behind the door's window blind.

Just as they finally gave up and turned to leave, the door cracked open.

Pete lurched forward and grasped the steering wheel, pulling himself up for a view. He could barely make out the presence of a drab-looking female, probably in her early twenties. She peered out from the door, which she had opened a few inches, and must have recognized Roberta. Hesitantly, after the older woman made a few conciliatory gestures, the door opened wide enough to give Pete a better look.

The girl was a few pounds overweight, dressed in knee-length shorts and a smudged T-shirt. Her hair, dark at the roots and dishwater blonde elsewhere, appeared not to have been combed today and stood up in ragged spikes, as though she had recently attempted a punk look. He could see the dark circles beneath her eyes, even from this distance.

Roberta took advantage of the opening and gently pushed her way inside. Honey, a bit more reticent, nodded to the girl, who reluctantly let her pass.

Once the visitors had entered, the girl leaned out onto the porch and cast a wary glance up and down the street. Then she ducked inside and slammed the door.

It took a moment for the visitors' eyes to adjust to the dim interior. It took much less time for the smells of the house to reach their noses.

Ann Marie, Ronald Barrett's "significant other," made no apologies for the mess her place was in. She was probably used to it, Honey figured. But as the women stepped into the living room, it became apparent Ann Marie had more than given up housekeeping here.

Cardboard boxes and black shiny garbage bags were strewn across the floor, full of household effects and personal belongings.

Ann Marie was in the midst of moving out!

Honey and Roberta stood amazed amid the piles, wondering how to proceed. Their little "visit" was pretty meaningless under the circumstances. There was no way they were going to spot any priceless artifact in this confusion.

Ann Marie stood with a hand on one hip, her head tilted back, as with the other hand she fingered a cigarette, grabbed from a saucer on the sideboard. Holding it to her pale lips, she took a long drag and then exhaled a longer plume of smoke. The gray cloud rose to the ceiling and mingled with other odors in the house. Cat litter? Diapers? Macaroni and cheese? Apparently pets and kids hung out here, although, from what Honey understood, Ron was childless.

"I'd offer you a seat, Mrs. Barrett," Ann Marie said, flicking ashes on the skuzzy linoleum floor, "but as you can see, the seats are taken."

Roberta smiled rigidly and nodded. If there were chairs in the room, they were hidden behind boxes.

"My girlfriend—I watch her kids—she's coming by tonight to help me finish packing. Then I'm outta here," Ann Marie said with determination. "The kids'll be in here soon to eat their dinner, then I gotta get back to work."

Honey did not detect animosity in her abrupt tone. She just seemed defeated and tired—much too tired for her young years.

Roberta cleared her throat. "We should have called first," she said. "We didn't know . . ."

"Ah," the girl said, setting her cigarette down. "It's okay, Mrs. Barrett. I'm just sorry it had to turn out this way. You know . . . Ron and me? I do care for him, but . . . see, I just can't take any more of his"—she waved a hand in the air as if to catch the right word—"his . . . politics. Much as I admire a man who takes a stand, things are gettin' too weird . . . the cops and the raid and all. Wow! It's just . . ."

Roberta reached out and patted the girl on the arm, causing her to jolt. "You don't need to explain, Ann Marie," she said. "I know this is hard on you."

That last sentence provoked an unexpected reaction from the calloused girl. Tears welled up and brimmed in her eyes—eyes that Honey thought could be pretty if they didn't pretend such toughness.

"I . . . I've stuck with Ron through a lot of stuff, Mrs. Barrett," she stammered. "But this latest scrape . . . him in jail and all! I just need to get outta here and start over, ya know?"

Roberta looked helplessly at Honey, who was even more helpless to do anything.

"Ann Marie," Roberta said at last, mustering a firmness that surprised them all, "we are not here to judge you. Believe me, I love Ron, but I am not proud of him!"

At this confession, Ann Marie's shoulders slumped in relief. Some of the hard facade fell away, and she even smiled a little. Suddenly, she was moving about the room, trying to clear stuff from the sofa and chairs. "Here," she said, "let me get you some coffee."

Honey and Roberta looked askance at each other.

"Ann Marie," Roberta interrupted. "We really don't want to bother you. Listen, now, I want you to call me, you hear? Let me know where you go and what you're doing, will you?"

The girl quit her scramble and stood up straight, looking her could-have-been mother-in-law in the eyes. "Gee, Mrs. Barrett," she said, "I do wish things could have turned out different, ya know?"

"I know," Roberta replied. Then stepping to the door as though to leave, she stopped and wheeled about, as if a thought had just hit her. "Ann Marie, it occurs to me . . . since you're packing and all . . . have you run across something Ron was given recently? I'd kind of like to have it, if it's not too important to you."

Ann Marie looked eager to please. "Sure, Mrs. Barrett. What is it?"

"Well, some friends of his gave him a box, about the size of a shoe box, maybe smaller. From the Holy Land, I think." Roberta's eyes got big and round and she acted wistful. "I . . . I've always wanted to go to the Holy Land. Do you remember any such box?"

Ann Marie was clearly surprised. "Ron told you about that? The boss gave him that . . . some sort of 'reward for services rendered,' he told me." This last phrase was said with a sarcastic bite. Then, glancing around the room, she said, "Sure, I'd give it to ya. It didn't mean nothin' to me! But . . ." She shrugged. "I sent all Ron's stuff to the auction. I really didn't think you'd want any of it."

Roberta tried not to gasp, holding her hand to her throat.

Honey stepped up to her friend and smiled nonchalantly at Ann Marie. "There isn't much Roberta has ever mentioned about Ron's possessions, but that box did intrigue her. Could you tell us which auction house you sent it to?"

Ann Marie reached for her cigarette again. "Gee, I called them to come pick it up," she said, tapping her toe and straining her memory. "Let me think . . . oh, yeah! The truck said AAA Auction, up on Railroad Street. I remember I called them because they were the first ones listed in the yellow pages."

Roberta relaxed the hand on her throat and Honey nodded to the girl. "That's great!" she said. "We'll check it out!"

Ann Marie followed the women as they stepped onto the porch. She watched them go, tears welling again in her eyes. "It was nice seeing you, Mrs. Barrett," she called.

Roberta waved good-bye. "Yes, it was, Ann Marie! Now, you call me, okay?"

"Okay," the girl promised.

The women had just reached the pickup when Ann Marie hollered after them again, "Oh, yeah . . . one more thing . . . the auction is supposed to be tonight! If you hurry, you can get there before it starts."

CHAPTER 22

The run-down auction house sat near the crest of a hill on the main thoroughfare of Spokane's east railroad district. Once upon a time an auto repair shop, its front room was now filled, literally to the rafters and beyond, with old-timey collectibles—automobilia, railroadiana, old tin cans, pots and pans, dishes, knickknacks, dolls, magazines. You name it.

Hanging from hooks and lining high, dusty shelves were hunting trophies, so old and unkempt it was a wonder they did not disintegrate on patrons' heads: the usual deer and antelope mounts; a once-regal moosehead, undignified by a collection of John Deere and Cenex hats hanging from its antlers; a lynx, a couple of bobcats, a big cougar perched upon a papier-mâché rock ledge, caught for all time as though poised for a pounce; spread-winged eagles and other raptorial birds.

Pete, Honey, and Roberta had left Mel's Suburban about a mile away, on a side street of a college campus. It would not look out of place there, and the likelihood that it would be spotted by Ron's friends was remote. They had taken Pete's pickup to the sale, where it blended in just fine with the other rigs in the parking lot.

The auction was to begin at six o'clock. They arrived about an hour beforehand and made their way toward the registration booth, where a few other early arrivals were signing in and taking white numbered "paddles." The actual wooden paddles of bygone days, which bidders held up to make their bids, had been replaced in most such auction houses by long white cardstock strips, on which the attendant scrawled the registration numbers with black marker pen. While not as sturdy as the old-fashioned paddles, they had the advantages of fitting in a jeans pocket, having space on which to write and keep track of one's bids, and being disposable.

Pete, an old hand at the auction scene, sidled up to the registration desk and filled out the registration form, putting his address simply as "Montana." If he bought anything, he would avoid the 8 percent sales tax the locals had to pay. And he would deal only in cash, so he could avoid giving any personal information.

As he was thus occupied, Honey and Roberta ambled through the front room, trying to look casual. Inwardly, they were on pins and needles, wanting to rush into the auditorium and start pawing through the boxes.

They had all decided they would not appear too anxious or eager. "It's probably not a huge sale," Pete said. "They have one of these every week, so it's not like there'll be a big pile of stuff. If the box is there, we'll probably find it easily enough. But it's best to keep cool. Never know who might be looking for the same thing."

Roberta might have thought the last statement far-fetched, except that on the way to Spokane, Pete and Honey had given her a quick indoctrination regarding the likes of Ron's friends and various intelligence and counterintelligence communities that were pitted against one another behind the scenes of normal life. Not only had she learned about the mysterious box, but she had received a swift lesson in the realities of the terrorist world—a world she had hoped always to avoid, though her son had entered it months ago.

Chances were very good, however, that no one else knew Ann Marie had sent the ancient artifact to the auction. Unless the Montanans were being followed, something Pete would have picked up on by now, all they needed to do was locate the box and be sure their bid won.

Pete, having signed in, grabbed his paper paddle from the counter and motioned to the women to follow him. As the auditorium slowly filled with people, many of whom obviously knew each other and exchanged folksy greetings, the three out-of-towners wandered between tables loaded with items to be sold. The family that owned this auction barn spent their days preparing for such events, consigning goods, arranging them for display, and noting any reserves the consignors wanted to set. Most of the things they took in had no reserves; when the auction was under way, the auctioneer would tell the audience if someone had placed an absentee bid. Beyond this, it was an open market.

One long table facing the left-hand side of the rickety bleachers was arrayed with small dishes, bric-a-brac, and various cheap household items. Across an aisle from that table, facing the audience's right, were hand tools, small electrical appliances, and power tools. Pete knew that the auctioneer kept both men and women happy throughout the long evening by switching from side to side. Beneath these two tables were cardboard boxes of assorted items: handcrafts, knitting, dish sets, and other domestic goods on the one side; camping equipment, more tools, and miscellaneous hardware on the other.

The tables behind the front row were reserved for more valuable items—antique glassware, porcelain dolls, oil paintings, rifles and saddles, antique powder horns, and the like. Then there were the inevitable sets of occasional tables, the obsolete business machines, and unused exercise bikes.

Mixed in with all these things, whose twins had appeared and reappeared at similar auctions again and again, there were the "junk boxes," the unsorted stashes brought in for "whatever they might bring."

Normally, Pete would have seen half a dozen things he might try to get. Tonight, his eyes, and the eyes of his female companions, were peeled for one thing only.

First, they gave a quick scan to the entire collection. On the antique table, Honey spotted a small box, ornately carved and inset with mother-of-pearl designs. But she recognized it immediately as a recent East Indian item, something that could be purchased any day at any import market. Roberta lifted up a small shiny box with a brass clasp. Catching Honey's eye, she teased, "It's cedar! But unless we're looking for something that says 'Grand Canyon,' I doubt this is it."

The women snickered together as Pete picked up a nice wooden toolbox. "I think I'll bid on this if things get boring!" he quipped.

But no antique or even Middle Eastern box was on display.

Next, they began to pull out boxes from beneath the tables, sorting through linens, a pile of hand-knit potholders, a collection of *Popular Mechanics* magazines.

"Some of these bring a small fortune," Pete said, waving a 1962 copy in the air.

Honey hushed him, and they seriously plowed through more boxes.

The room was now noisy with people who were climbing up into the bleachers, ordering hot dogs and pretzels from the concession stand, jabbering about various sale items, and visiting in general.

A couple of grandmotherly looking women, who, by their focused expressions, appeared to be old pros at this auction business, rummaged through boxes nearby. Clearing a little space on one of the long tables, they set out a few items to contemplate.

"Mostly junk, Marge," one of them said.

The other agreed. "That's why they call 'em 'junk boxes,'" she replied with a laugh.

The Montana women kept busy with sorting of their own, until Roberta grabbed Honey's arm and nodded toward the two strangers. Honey, primed to see the artifact, stopped still. "What?" she whispered, glancing at what they had arrayed on the table. "I don't see anything!"

"No, not yet," Roberta replied. "But some of that is Ron's stuff. I recognize some of the record albums, and there . . . see that flashlight? I gave him that for Christmas!"

Pete, seeing their interchange, walked over, trying to be nonchalant. With his eyes, he asked what they had found.

Honey nodded toward the two pickers. "They're into Ann Marie's stuff," she said softly. Pointing at numbers written on the boxes, she added, "It's Lot 14."

Bit by bit, the older women pulled things out and put them back. Roberta counted the boxes. "There's about ten of them," she said. Then, noting the rapidly filling room and glancing at her watch, she announced, "We don't have time to go through them all!"

Pete walked to the end of the table and slid out one cardboard carton. "Come on," he called to Honey and Roberta. "You each grab one!"

The girls complied, and soon all three of them were bent over, pawing through Ann Marie's castoffs.

Suddenly, Honey poked Pete in the ribs. He raised his head and cleared his throat. Roberta looked up and followed his gaze.

There, in front of the two auction mamas, was a pile of wooden bowls, and next to it, an unusual carved box with the depiction of a cow on the lid.

Honey put a hand to her mouth, stifling a little shriek, and Roberta gasped. Pete instantly ducked back down, pretending to have found something amazing. "Yeah!" he cried. "It's great, isn't it!"

Honey and Roberta recovered quickly. "Yes, Pete!" Honey exclaimed. "You've wanted one of those for ages!"

In his hand he held the first thing he'd grabbed, an obviously used electric toothbrush. The women down the way glanced at him, and then at each other, shaking their heads.

As soon as they had turned away, Pete nodded toward the stands, and his companions followed him to a space on the bleachers still not taken by the crowd. The likable auctioneer was just entering from the registration area, chatting with people in the aisle.

The three Montanans' eyes were glued to the two auction mamas and the precious box, which still sat in front of them, next to the wooden bowls. Their hearts in their throats, they watched as one of the women picked up the box and turned it over, obviously looking for some sort of trademark or artist's name. It was clear from her expression that she thought this item had been wrongly placed in a "junk box."

Together, the women studied the priceless treasure, toying with the ornate brass clasp on the edge. Honey tensed. "It's fragile, don't you think?" she whispered. "I hope they don't break it!"

Pete sat rigidly on the plank bench, his right leg twitching nervously, bouncing up and down on the ball of his foot.

The auctioneer, a slight, balding fellow with a black leather vest and thick glasses, was now ascending the platform, taking a seat on the high stool behind his tall desk. He raised the gavel in his hand and let it fall, once, twice, three times. "Good evening, folks!" he called out. "We got lotsa good stuff here t'nite! Let's get this thing goin', now!"

The two auction mamas shuffled the wooden bowls into the box they were sorting, and the Montanans watched as they cleverly hid the Jeremiah Box deep beneath a pile of dishtowels in another box from Ann Marie's lot. The savvy women knew better than to leave it out for the world to see, and they could live in hopes that the auctioneer would sell the things beneath the tables by the boxful, without taking time to display it all.

Apparently satisfied with their ruse, they headed for the bleachers, taking seats a couple of rows down from the Montanans, as other people scurried to fill the few vacant places left in the stands. Honey leaned forward, trying to make out their words as they spoke softly to each other.

She thought one of them said the word "import." The other shrugged, and Honey caught the word "Mexican." The woman was saying that she had seen tons of that sort of thing in Tijuana. When the other one said it appeared to be very old, her friend laughed and reminded her how clever the tourist industry was at making things look antique.

Roberta had apparently caught as much of the conversation as Honey had and nudged her, giving her a wink and a thumbs-up.

Soon the air was filled with the yodeling chant of the auctioneer as he called for bids on the front tables. His two "spotters," a rotund man in a flannel shirt, whose button had popped off his protruding stomach, and a sweet-looking white-haired woman with a cane, watched for raised paddles. "Yeah!" "Yeah!" they called out as they held items aloft, one by one. Back and forth, from doilies to fishing reels, from teacups to seed spreaders, the barker and his attendants directed the audience's focus.

Though the auctioneer moved through the collections at a heady clip, for Pete, Honey, and Roberta, the evening dragged by like a funeral dirge. It seemed the old fellow would never get to the items beneath the tables.

Pete had procured three German-sausage hot dogs, three Cokes, and three small bags of popcorn for his party, and they had downed them all. Roberta's back was getting sore from her sitting on the flat plank, and she rubbed it tenderly. Three hours had passed, but the women two rows down were still having a high time, successfully bidding and outbidding competitors in the stands. They had acquired an amazing assortment of goods, with no apparent theme—everything from old *Life* magazines and Elvis memorabilia to bags of crochet needles, *Star Wars* cards, and a Porta Potty—by the time the auctioneer finally started on the boxes.

As he went from one carton of hardware to another, the next hour went by. The crowd was thinning out, families taking grumpy children home to bed, old men taking grumpy wives home to bed, and young couples having spent their week's pay with no more expendable resources.

By this time the auctioneer himself was getting tired. He saw no great purpose in prolonging the affair, especially since all this stuff had to be carted away before the house could shut down. The boxes of "women's stuff" were least interesting to him personally, and he raced through them like an old workhorse heading for the barn.

As he did so, Pete, Honey, and Roberta perked up. What was unenticing to the auctioneer was what they had come three hundred miles to find.

The women two rows down were still full of energy. It was obvious they had waited this long for the wooden box, and they would not go home until it had been sold—they hoped to them.

Box after box of Ann Marie's trash and treasures was pulled up from beneath the table. The rotund man with the gaping flannel shirt displayed the contents by tipping each box forward and rummaging through it with a disinterested hand. If he happened to stumble across something remotely appealing, he gave it a quick show—a bright piece of macramé, a plush toy, a planter shaped like a mushroom.

At last the box of dishtowels emerged. Pete pulled his cardboard paddle from his hip pocket and got ready to flash it. Roberta and Honey leaned together tensely, praying beneath their breath.

The old auctioneer hollered at the spotter, "Whadda we got there, Elmore?"

"Buncha dishrags!" Elmore called out. "Nice uns!"

The women two rows down smiled covertly and the Montanans braced themselves.

"Whaddamy bid?" the auctioneer cried, or rather yawned. He was ready to wind this up.

"Yeah-bid, yeah-bid, abid-bid-bid, whaddamybid, a-bid-bid-bid . . . Well, where'll ya start, girls?" he addressed the females of the audience. "Good towels, gooduns, here. Yeah, whaddamybid? Well, cummon, now, whaddayasay, ten dollars! Well, five! Well, two!"

One of the auction mamas shot her paddle in the air, and the white-haired spotter pointed at her, shouting, "Yeah!"

"I got two-two, whaddamybid, say three-three—"

Pete shot his paddle skyward, and the fat spotter jerked a finger at him, crying, "Yeah!"

"Well—three-three, say four—cummon—good towels, ladies, four, amIbid four?"

When someone, somewhere, beat the woman two rows down by bidding the four, towels suddenly became fashionable. Bids were popping up all over.

"Five, six, seven . . . good towels, ladies!"

The women below bid eight, Pete bid nine, and things stalled.

Ten dollars seemed to be a sticking point. The women consulted one another and turned around, wondering just who was ahead of them.

"Am I bid ten?" the auctioneer cried. "Cummon ladies . . . ten-ten-ten."

The auction mama shot her paddle skyward again, and they were off and running. She apparently suspected that Pete had seen her put the wooden box deep in the towels. Perhaps the spotter suspected something, too, for he started rummaging through the pile of rags with a vengeance.

Suddenly, he pulled forth the cedar case, and the audience gasped.

"Whatcha got there, Elmore?" the auctioneer cried.

"Purdy little box," Elmore replied, holding it in the air.

The women two rows down shot an angry look back at Pete and then slumped down in their bleacher.

"A little treasure, folks!" the auctioneer cried. Then, glaring at the crafty women, added, "*Buried* treasure to boot!" Taking a deep breath, he seemed to pick up steam.

"So, whaddamy bid for these towels *and* this little box?" he went on. "Ten! Ten! Say twelve . . . fifteen . . . twenty . . . whaddawehavehere? Thirty?"

People were leaving the stands now, traipsing up to the table to take a better look at the box. Some stood shaking their heads, some looked curious, others were just beginning to be enthused.

Honey leaned back, clasping her hands together over her knees and trying to keep her pulse in check. Roberta gave her a worried look, and Pete kept bidding.

Half a dozen speculators had now made offers, and the bidding had reached $75. The emboldened auctioneer stepped up the increments, going in bounds of $25 and higher. "Whaddamybid? $100 . . . $125 . . . $150 . . . $200 . . ."

At last, the frenzy began to subside. Pete had brought a lot of cash. The others had reached their limits. By the time the bidding was narrowed again, to Pete and the auction mamas, the price was $300 and climbing.

The women two rows down flashed bitter eyes at the Montanan. What did he know that they did not?

But they had run out of money. They couldn't go higher.

"Four hundred?" the auctioneer cried. "I have $350. Do I hear $400?"

The women had stalled, but the auctioneer continued to fish. "Well, then, $375!" he cried. "Cummon ladies! It must be some special box, all right! Do I hear $375?"

The women angrily glared at the old fellow and he shrugged. Raising his gavel he called out, "Going once! Going twice! SOLD! To the man with the ponytail!"

CHAPTER 23

It was nearly midnight in Bull River Valley. Pete and Honey had just arrived home from Spokane, having dropped Roberta off at her house. Still amazed at what they had been through in the big city, and the success of their venture, they could not wait to let the rabbis know of their achievement. Though it was two hours later in upstate New York, they decided to put through a call to Rabbi Ben before he left for Jerusalem.

It was cool in these mountains in late spring. After Pete had built a little fire in the fireplace, the newlyweds shared the bearskin rug, Honey holding the priceless Jeremiah Box in her lap and Pete punching in the numbers on Mel's cell phone. He was starting to think he could get used to the convenience of this gizmo.

The number he dialed, which Ben had relayed to him the last time they spoke, rang directly through to the rabbi's room, bypassing all the security blocks set up on the main line. A groggy voice answered, "Horace Benjamin, here."

"Rabbi Ben!" Pete exclaimed. "It's Pete. Are you ready for some good news?"

"Peter!" the old man cried. "Yes, yes! What has happened?"

Pete chose his words with care, still leery of cyberspace eavesdroppers. "The lost has been found!" he announced cryptically.

"Oh, that *is* good news!" Ben exclaimed. "So you were successful in your little visit?"

"All of us did our part," Pete replied. "We ended up at an auction. It was nip and tuck for a while. We wondered if we'd ever see the thing, let alone actually manage to get it!"

"An auction!" the rabbi gasped. "My, my! When I think of the places that wonderful object has been . . . how many hands it has passed through!"

"Yes," Pete agreed. "It is a miracle it has survived!"

Rabbi Ben was quiet on the other end. Pete began to wonder if they had been disconnected. Then he realized the old man was sniffling, apparently choking back tears.

"You okay?" he asked.

The old man managed to speak. "We have witnessed many miracles," he said. "Just when I think I cannot be more amazed, I am surprised once again!"

Pete said nothing, he himself overcome with a sense of unworthiness. "I . . . I am just glad we could help," he said at last.

Honey, picking up on her husband's sober tone, reached over to touch his knee. Her own eyes were welling with tears as she tenderly held the precious box.

Pete took a deep breath. "Well, sir," he said, "what's next? How shall we get this to you?"

Rabbi Ben was sitting on the edge of his bed now, rubbing his teary eyes. "We have given that much thought," he said. "Knowing how things tend to turn out in our ventures, we figured you would be successful, and so we have discussed this at length."

Honey anxiously leaned toward the phone, trying to hear the rabbi's voice. Pete held the receiver out so they could share it.

Rabbi Ben's tone was resigned as he broached the topic. "You know we are leaving for Israel in a few hours," he said. "As much as we would love to see the item and take it to our own laboratory, we have decided that it is best not to transport it internationally—not now, anyway. It has caused too much mayhem already. For now we feel it is best to get it into the hands of a scholar in the United States—someone qualified to study it and trustworthy enough to keep it until we feel it is safe to have it in our possession."

The newlyweds looked at each other, baffled.

"Who, besides Rothmeyer, is qualified to do such work?" Pete asked.

Ben spoke softly. "Dr. Rothmeyer himself has made an astute suggestion. As with all things related to this business, we believe that God has gone before us, preparing the way before we knew what we needed."

"Yes?" Pete spurred him on. "You have a prospect?"

"Dr. Rothmeyer believes that your wife's cousin, Dr. Aronstam, would be a fine choice for this assignment. After much prayer, the Consortium believes Kenneth has been brought to us for this very purpose. We would like for you to get the item to him."

Honey gasped. "Ken? My Ken?"

Rabbi Ben heard her on the line. "Mrs. Wester!" he exclaimed. "Is that you?"

"Yes, Rabbi," Honey replied. "I hope you do not mind that I have been listening in."

"I am happy that you are!" Rabbi Ben answered. "Do you think that Dr. Aronstam would be willing to help?"

Honey laughed softly. "If the truth were told, I think Ken has felt a wee bit left out of our Jerusalem circle. I know he would be honored, Rabbi! Have you spoken to him?"

"Now that we have the item for him to study," Rabbi Ben said, "I will contact him in the morning. Are you ready to take a quick trip to Columbus?"

Honey smiled up at Pete, who had heard all of this. He took the receiver again and answered enthusiastically. "You bet we'll go, Rabbi! Honey and I never planned a honeymoon, but between Spokane and Columbus, I'm giving her more than she bargained for!"

The last time Honey had entered the hall of the anthropology building at Midwest University, she had been on the run for her life. Pete's wrong turn into the world of the white supremacists had nearly cost him his beloved, and had nearly cost his beloved everything.

It did not escape the couple's notice that their adventure into the world of the rabbis had begun, as this one had, with a little wooden box. For years Honey had kept a music box on the mantel of the fireplace in Bull River. That music box, which had been hers since childhood, contained a secret. When Pete had accidentally broken the box, knocking it off the shelf and sending it crashing to the floor, his relationship with Honey had crashed with it. That accident had inadvertently led him to finding the box's secret—a little piece of tattered yellow cloth.

The cloth, whose safety was a responsibility passed on to Honey by her family, was a Jewish badge forced upon her great-grandfather when he was a prisoner of the Nazi death camp of Dachau, Germany. Upon the badge he had inscribed, at the risk of his life, a document that was a key to the identity of the future High Priest of Israel.

Fleeing Pete's Aryan Nations friends, who suspected her possession of a secret crucial to Israel, Honey had escaped to Columbus, hoping her cousin, the chairman of the anthropology department, could help her. What followed had led to the incredible events in Jerusalem, an experience that, it seemed, was still in the making.

The Westers hung close together as they entered the building and introduced themselves at the reception desk.

"Hello," Honey greeted the secretary. "I don't know if you remember me."

The secretary glanced up, a look of recognition crossing her face. "Why, yes," she said. "You are Dr. Aronstam's sister."

Honey smiled. "Cousin," she said. "Though he is more like a brother to me."

The prim woman stood up and walked toward the counter. "Didn't Dr. Aronstam just attend your wedding?" she recalled.

"Yes," Honey replied. Turning to her groom, she said, "This is my husband, Pete Wester. We decided to make Columbus part of our honeymoon. I thought Pete should see my hometown."

Of course, Pete had been to Columbus just a year ago, trying to track Honey down as she fled a pair of Aryan hoodlums. But the secretary knew nothing of that, nor of anything related to their international escapade.

"So you want to see Ken," the secretary surmised. "He has a pretty light class load this summer, but he does happen to be in his office right now."

She reached for the phone to buzz the professor, but Pete stopped her. He knew very well where Ken's office was. He and Mel had hidden in a nearby broom closet just a year ago, waiting to rummage through the professor's desk in search of clues as to Honey's whereabouts. Gesturing to the hallway that led to the administration offices, he smiled. "We'll just go on back and surprise him, if that's okay."

The secretary gave a befuddled shrug. "Very well," she said.

Honey and Pete ambled back to the office at the end of the hall, the largest and most prestigious of the lot. As they passed by one with a sign that said "Away on Research Assignment," they glanced knowingly at each other. "Dave's office," Pete said.

Between that door and Ken's was the door to the broom closet. "That's where Mel and I nearly suffocated," Pete recalled.

Honey proudly took his hand. Cradled in her other arm was a bundle that contained the Jeremiah Box. She was about to deliver it to David Rothmeyer's boss.

Brace yourself, Ken! she thought as Pete knocked on the chairman's office door. *Your life is about to change forever!*

CHAPTER 24

Zachary Cohen walked across the dewy grass of the Goldstein estate's horse pasture, the moisture of the sun-glinted field clinging to his loafers and the cuffs of his khaki Docker pants. Over his back was slung a cardigan sweater, and in one hand was a small travel bag. He could have taken the long way around from the mansion's back veranda, following the wide graveled path that led to the stables, but he was in a hurry.

The limousine that had brought him to the safe house in upstate New York a year ago was waiting in front of the mansion to speed him and the rabbis to the airport, where they would board a plane for Israel. Before he left, Zachary wanted to spend a few moments with his special friend, little Lamar Jackson.

Well before he had reached the stables, where the horses were receiving their morning grooming, he could hear the high-pitched laughter of the small boy. The stables were Lamar's favorite place in this wonderland of recreational pastimes. The child enjoyed the swimming pools, the fish ponds, the fabulous dogs in the master's kennels, a nine-hole miniature golf course, the tennis, badminton, and handball courts. But the horses were his favorite indulgence, second only to the kitchen of the main house, where he could often be found hanging out with the cooks and sampling their fare.

Lamar had become fast friends with the stablemaster's son, a boy of about his own age. Together they enjoyed free run of the estate, and Marlon Goldstein had recently told Lamar he was welcome to stay here until a suitable family was located to give him his own home. Even when that happened, Goldstein had told him, he would be welcome to come back to visit as often as he liked.

Despite Lamar's love of this place, it would be hard on the little boy when he learned that the man who had helped him through the nightmare of his trauma would be leaving. That man was Zachary, and he did not relish bidding farewell to this child whom he had so quickly come to love.

Cutting across the grassy circle, Zachary headed for the first opening of the long row of stables. A tall black man in riding pants and a red shirt with brass buttons was busy brushing out the mane of an elegant chestnut mare. Lamar and his little friend Montel, the groom's son, straddled the top of a six-foot-high board fence that separated this stable from the next. In Lamar's hand was a rope made into a lasso, and he was trying vainly to cast the loop over a hitching post across the stall. His repeated failure provoked peals of laughter from him and his companion.

Lamar did not see Zachary's approach, his back being to the doorway. Zachary was glad for this and leaned against the opening a moment, just watching the child. Andrew, the groom, nodded to him, and then toward the children, giving a thumbs-up gesture. Zachary smiled, pleased to see that his little charge was happy.

The groom's motion must have caught Lamar's eye. Turning about, the boy saw that Zachary had come and he leaped down from the fence with the agility of a squirrel. "Zach'ry!" he cried, running up to the handsome man and throwing his arms about his waist.

Zachary bent down and lifted the youngster in his arms, planting a kiss on his round cheek.

"You're all dressed up," the boy noted. Then his eyes fell on the travel bag Cohen had set on the ground. "You goin' somewhere?"

"That's what I came to tell you," Zachary said. "I have to take a long trip, and I will be gone for a good while."

Lamar clung to Zachary's neck as the man carried him out onto the gravel road. He reluctantly set him down and took his hand. Together they walked in silence a ways.

"Where you goin'?" the boy asked.

"To a very wonderful place, Lamar," Cohen said. "But I will miss you very much!"

The boy's eyes were big and round. He discerned something in Zachary's tone that troubled him. "When will I see you again?" he asked.

Zachary sighed. "I'm not sure, Lamar. But perhaps I will send for you sometime. Would you like that?"

Lamar nodded eagerly. "Sure, Zach'ry! I would like that!"

Cohen blinked back tears he did not want the boy to see and tried to change the subject. "I hear that Mr. Goldstein is going to get you a tutor—someone to teach you reading and writing."

Lamar was less than enthused and kicked absently at a pebble in the road. "I never been to school," he said. "Sounds boring!"

"Well, Montel goes to school. He's pretty smart, you know. You want to be smart like him, don't you?"

Lamar shrugged. "Guess so," he grunted. Then the child suddenly brightened. "Andrew says I might get to live in his house!"

Zachary stopped and looked down at the child. "What's that you say?" he asked.

"Andrew . . . he says Mr. Goldstein might let me live with him and Montel . . . and Mrs. Andrew."

Zachary had met Andrew's wife once or twice, a lovely young woman. "You mean Caroline?" Cohen corrected. "Why, Lamar! I had not heard this! That would be wonderful! Just wonderful!"

Zachary could not have been more pleased. The head stablemaster and his little family lived in a fine stone cottage right here on the estate. Lamar would not have to leave, ever! Relieved that he would not be abandoning the child to some unknown fate, Zachary reached down and joyously swept him into his arms again.

Lamar giggled and, considering it his turn, planted a juicy kiss on Cohen's cheek.

Zachary hugged him tight. "I will still miss you," he said, choking back tears. "Don't you go having any more of those spider dreams, you hear?"

Lamar shook his head firmly. "No, sir!" he promised. "Those bad guys are put away!"

Zachary set him down again and walked with him back to the stable. The boy hugged him once more and then ran to the fence, where he scrambled up to sit beside Montel.

Cohen grabbed his travel bag and gave another thumbs-up to Andrew. "Take good care of my kid!" he ordered.

Andrew, deducing that Lamar had told him about the upcoming arrangement, smiled broadly. "Will do, sir," he said. "It will be my pleasure!"

As Zachary headed back for the house and the waiting limousine, he felt as though a huge weight had been lifted from his shoulders. Lamar was safely cared for, and he could turn his entire focus to his most pressing duties.

Those duties involved the greatest responsibility in the world. The high priesthood of Israel was weight enough to carry, and he had yet to figure out how he would bear it.

CHAPTER 25

Somewhere over the Atlantic Ocean, it was sunset. Mel sat in a wide leather recliner near the rear of the first-class section of a jetliner, his husky legs stretched out until his black boots were tucked under the seat ahead of him. The flight attendant had just come by, picking up the trays from the evening meal of kosher veal and new potatoes.

A year ago Mel had been on such a plane, he and Pete crammed into economy-class seating, on their way to Dachau, Germany. This time, the ex-cop sat beside the enigmatic Zachary Cohen, a few rows behind Rabbi Ben and his colleagues.

It took a lot to make this sociably direct, no-nonsense Wester feel shy or uneasy. To his great consternation, being in the presence of the mysterious Cohen had that effect. Not that Zachary was unfriendly or elusive. He actually impressed Mel as very natural. He often attempted to engage Wester in conversation, but for the first time in his life, the ex-cop found himself at a loss for easy words.

This strange condition troubled Mel no end. He had been aware of it since he first met Cohen at the FBI headquarters. In the short time since then, he had been with the priestly candidate nearly round-the-clock, taking meals with him and the rabbis at Goldstein's estate, and being quartered next door to him in the guest rooms.

Mel was, after all, the priest's bodyguard! He had better get used to the fact that he was Zachary's shadow, the overseer of his physical safety. But no matter how often they were in company together, Mel still found himself with the aggravating affliction of awe.

Wester was not an especially religious man, though his experiences in Jerusalem and with the Consortium had certainly enlivened whatever seeds of faith lay dormant within him. He did grasp the fact that this Cohen was a very special figure; he believed, though he did not understand it all, that Zachary was a key to Israel's future and, apparently, the future of the world. He did not know how to begin learning about him; he would not have known what questions to ask him, even if he had the nerve. His was what theologians called a "blind faith" indeed!

Fact was, for the first time in his life, Mel felt stupid! He had no choice but to ride out this experience in the hopes the fog would clear, that his spiritual ineptitude would not trip him up, and that he would somehow be worthy of the great trust the rabbis had placed in him.

Just now, however, as the flight attendant came by again, bringing the dessert tray, he was as tongue-tied as a new kid in school. Zachary sat next to the window, Mel on the aisle. The simplest things eluded him, like whether Zachary should order dessert first, or did the stewardess work from the aisle out?

"Go ahead," he said to Cohen, sweeping his hand toward the tray in a gesture of deferment. As he did so, however, he clumsily knocked the teapot, sending a splash of hot liquid to the floor. "Uh, sorry," he stammered.

Zachary smiled and nodded to the flustered attendant. "I'll have the apple pie," he said.

Mel scrunched back in the seat as the attendant passed the fragrant pie in front of him, then nearly forgot to order for himself. "Uh, the . . ." He was pointing at a small silver goblet of sugared pudding. "Custard?" the stewardess guessed.

"Yeah . . . yes," Mel managed.

He also managed to ask for the small pitcher of cream that sat beside it and was relieved when the dessert sat safely on his lap tray.

You're really losing it, Wester! he thought to himself. *Get a grip!*

Zachary was not blind to Mel's embarrassment. No one who watched the two interact could have missed the fact that the bodyguard felt more like an awkward appendage than a soul mate.

Zachary could have ignored the matter, could have pretended not to notice, or could have hoped Mel would lighten up of his own accord. But as the two sat in silence, eating their desserts, he thought the direct approach couldn't make matters any worse.

"Listen, Wester," Zachary began. Then he paused. "May I call you Mel?"

Mel jerked sideways, looking at Zachary in surprise. "Uh, sure," he replied. Then, clearing his throat, "Why not?"

"And you may call me Zack. All my friends do." Cohen smiled, then added, "Well, of course the rabbis don't. They never will. If you are 'Melvin,' I will always be 'Zachary' to them! In fact, sometimes I expect Rabbi Benjamin to call me 'Zacharias,' or something!"

If it was possible to choke on custard, Mel choked. "Yeah," he said with a grin. "I know what you mean."

Zachary thought the bodyguard's rigid demeanor slackened slightly.

"Anyway, Mel," he went on, "I think we need to clear the air, here. I have a hunch—correct me if I'm wrong—that you have been a bit spooked by all this 'priest' stuff. *Capiche?*"

Mel could scarcely believe his ears. Had his clumsiness been so obvious?

He set his spoon on the tray, lifted his coffee cup, and took a short swig. "You've got that right!" he said, blowing softly through pursed lips. "I hate to admit it, but I feel a little out of my element." Then he rolled his eyes and shook his head. "No, I'll be frank. I feel like I stepped into an episode of the *The X-Files* about a year ago, and I don't know how to get back!" With a grateful sigh, he added, "Fact is, I feel like a dang fool!"

Mel's heart swelled. *Wow! That felt good!* he thought.

Zachary read his relief. Leaning toward him, he spoke softly, so as not to be overheard. "Would it help if I told you you've got nothing on me? If *you* feel in over your head, how do you think *I* feel?"

Mel gulped. Had he heard that right? Was Mr. Cohen having his own struggles? Suddenly, in the flash of time it took for Zachary's words to sink into Mel's brain, the walls of fear and bewilderment began to crumble. The one person who seemed the most out of Mel's league had stepped down to his level. Cohen was admitting frailty and confusion of a magnitude that Mel, caught up in his own fog, had never considered.

Blinking his eyes, Mel spoke the first words that came to mind. "I . . . I never gave any thought to how you feel," he confessed. "I figured you, of all people, had a handle on all of this!"

Zachary laughed. "Well," he declared, "you are alone in that assumption. To tell the truth, not even the rabbis have figured out how I fit in. I am an enigma to them, as much as I am to myself."

Mel frowned. "What do you mean?" he asked.

"How frank may I be?" Cohen countered.

Mel shrugged. "Hey," he said, "you're in no danger from me! I'd be the last to pass judgment on your credentials!"

Zachary leaned back in his seat and stared at the ceiling, apparently formulating a statement. "This is how bad it is," he began, sitting up and lifting a finger. "In a few moments, all the observant male Jews on this plane are going to stand up. They are going to enter the aisles and they are going to say their evening prayers. They are all going to face in different directions, because none of them will be able to agree on exactly which way Jerusalem is from here. And then they will lift shawls, *tallithim*, over their heads and shoulders."

Mel nodded. "Yes, I have seen the rabbis do this many times."

"Okay," Zachary went on. "You will see me perform the same ritual. But neither you, nor any of my fellow Jews, will know the quandary that I carry in my heart as I do this."

Mel was incredulous. "*You?*" he gasped.

"Yes, me!" Zachary confessed.

Mel could make no sense of this. "Surely you are a believer!" he exclaimed.

Zachary hushed him. "Of course I am!" he said. "I believe everything in the Torah and the Prophets!" Then he leaned back again and sighed. "My problem is that I do not stop there."

Mel studied Cohen's pensive face. The sense of bewilderment was settling over him again as he tried to imagine what that pronouncement meant. *Hey, pal,* he wanted to say, *you're really spooking me now!*

Instead, a strange possibility suddenly dawned on him. Managing to sound intelligent, he said, "You know, Pete and I, we went to Sunday school when we were kids. I remember the teacher saying that our Bible went beyond the Bible of the Jews. Is that what you're getting at?"

Now it was Zachary's turn to be surprised. Turning to Mel, he scrutinized him. "Pretty profound, Wester!" he exclaimed. "Which seminary did you say you went to?"

Mel laughed. But then he grew concerned again. "Now wait a minute!" he said. "Are you saying what I think you're saying? This is a joke, right?"

Zachary hung his head. "Maybe it would be easier if it were," he replied. "I think you're on to me."

Mel raised a hand and waved it back and forth. "Hold on! If you're saying what I *think* you're saying, we have a real problem."

Zachary looked gratefully at Mel. "*We?*" he gasped. "Do you know how good that sounds? I'd like nothing better than to share this problem with someone else!"

Mel crossed his arms. "Thanks a lot," he groaned. "So you're telling me you are a Christian . . . a Jewish Christian? Is that possible?"

Zachary laughed. "Well, let's see. There have been a few from time to time—Peter, James, John, Paul . . . shall I go on?"

Mel felt more foolish than ever. "Yeah—to say nothing of the founder himself."

"Right! Jesus!" Zachary agreed. "So I guess it's not so far out, huh?"

Mel slumped farther back in the seat. "Oh, brother!" he said. "Do the rabbis know about this?"

"They do," Zachary answered. "I'm a real problem, you see."

Mel was amazed. "They sure don't let on," he said.

"So far, they've avoided it by burying me in a year of study—history, ritual, glossary, you know. I've been a good student."

"But now . . ."

"Now we're getting close to having to face this," he explained. "The only things I have left to learn are the hands-on use of the implements which were involved in historic temple ritual."

Mel remembered seeing the brass censers, bowls, and other items displayed in the Temple Gallery, and he grimaced as he considered what many of them were for.

The two men sat silently for a long while, Zachary relieved to have shared his unearthly burden, and Mel in a greater quandary than ever.

Hey, buddy, he thought, *I can try to protect your body, but don't expect me to save your soul!*

The sun was disappearing behind the tail of the plane as the wings dipped toward Europe's southwest coast. Zachary was now rising, stepping over Mel's outstretched legs and heading for the aisle. He lifted the hatch door on the stowaway bin overhead and pulled out a neatly folded shawl.

All about the plane, others were doing the same, men of many countries joining one another in little clusters, most dressed in the familiar black coats of the Hassidim. As Zachary predicted, they faced slightly different directions, depending on their opinions of exactly where Jerusalem lay on the eastern horizon. Each raised his shawl over his head, tallithim of white, light gray, or ivory, all with broad stripes of dark blue or black across the bottoms and wide fringes to recall to them the Law of the Lord.

Prayer books, called *siddurim*, were held in clean hands, most of them dark blue in color with gold Hebrew letters on the cover. They were read from right to left, as the language demanded, and though the chorus of voices had different accents, all were unified in the never-lost tongue of the ancient Jews.

The prayers were accompanied by a traditional bobbing and swaying motion, as the men bent their knees, then their torsos, then straightened their legs, in one long, fluid gesture, over and over.

Mel watched Zachary as he stood in the aisle, his shawl covering his bowed head, his prayer book held reverently before him.

With words from the time of Moses, he quoted the *Shema*, the most hallowed prayer of Judaism. By the intent look on his face, Mel knew Cohen cherished each syllable, and, perhaps for Mel's benefit, he repeated it in English:

Hear, O Israel:
The Lord our God is one Lord:
And Thou shalt love the Lord thy God
with all thine heart,
and with all thy soul,
and with all thy might.

CHAPTER 26

It was the middle of the night in the reference library of the anthropology department at Midwest University. Ken Aronstam had used his personal set of keys to enter the building and to unlock the library door. He sat now at a long table in the center of the room, surrounded by piles of books written by respected archaeologists, and thick binders of theses and dissertations written by graduate students over the years.

With him at the table were Pete and Honey Wester, neither students nor scholars, but no strangers to such a setting. Only a year ago they had stood over David Rothmeyer in a hotel room in Germany as he deciphered a strange document unearthed at the Dachau death camp.

Ken, knowing the schedule of the building janitorial staff, and wanting no strangers observing his sensitive work, had waited until the night crew had completed their rounds and left the building before he entered. The smell of fresh wax applied to the floor by the cleaning staff mingled with the aromas of virgin olive oil and canned lighter fluid, elements that Ken brushed ever so gently into the surface of the lid on the ancient Jeremiah Box.

Honey watched in amazement as the wood took on new life beneath the professor's touch. Ken raised his balding head and glanced at his cousin through his wire-rimmed glasses. "Sometimes our work as archaeologists is more like antique restoration than science," he said. "But I'm not trying to make this old box pretty."

Pete leaned across the table, squinting at details on the

artifact not noticeable before, which took on clarity beneath the deft brush. "Wow!" he exclaimed. "I thought most of that was just mars and scratches. Is that writing I see?"

Ken nodded. "Could be," he said. "Boxes were often used in antiquity for the keeping of records or the sending of messages."

He sat back in his chair and reached for a large, colorful book full of photos. The spine read "Royal Containers—Dharma Dynasty." He flipped through the book for an example. "See here?" he said, turning the volume around and laying it open on the table. The photo depicted a beautiful polychrome box, inlaid with precious stones, pearl, and ivory. On the lid, much like on the Jeremiah Box, there was an etching of a creature, in this case an elephant. Around the edge were intricate figures, which, at first glance, appeared to be just so much fancy scrollwork.

"Those are actually letters," he said, pointing to tiny designs bunched between carvings of leaves and vines. "Paper, or papyrus, was extremely rare and even unheard of in many ancient societies. They kept records on anything carvable. The more important the record, the more permanent the material on which they wrote it."

Honey perked up. "Didn't the Greeks write on clay tablets?" she asked.

Ken smiled patiently. "You're probably thinking of the Babylonians with their cuneiform writing. But, yes, I'm sure all ancient societies used whatever was affordable and available—leaves, bark, hide, wooden tablets, wax, and, as you say, clay. For the most important messages and records, say inscriptions to the gods or kings, stonemasons etched on stone or marble."

Ken flipped through the book, which showed a variety of inscribed boxes. "Because writing was reserved for the scribal professions and the privileged class, it was often considered an art form, and empty spaces on artifacts—these boxes, for instance—were used to advantage as a place for lettering."

Returning his attention to the lid of the Jeremiah Box, he continued cleaning, scrutinizing the designs with the trained eye of a paleographic linguist. As he did so, he continued to teach, which was his most usual activity. "Boxes were often given as gifts, just as they are today," he said. "In fact, our practice of giving gifts in boxes goes way back into antiquity. Boxes are, after all, containers, and so these fancy wooden and stone boxes shown in the book most likely contained some kind of gift when they were delivered to friends and loved ones, or to higher-ups whom the givers wanted to impress."

"The fancier the box, the more valuable the gift," Honey deduced.

"Exactly," Ken replied.

Running his hand tenderly over this rather drab example, he added, "But fanciness did not always guarantee quality contents. Nor did plainness mean the contents were common. This box, for instance, probably never had many jewels or decorations. What few it had are missing. But it was basically a utilitarian casket anyway. It must have been used often."

Pete pointed to an indentation in the interior of the box's base, which sat to one side of Ken's workspace. "It looks like it was meant to carry a bottle," he noted.

"The one the rabbis are looking for, right?" Honey deduced.

"They are hoping so," Ken said. Then shrugging, he said, "Whether it did or not, it was important enough to get Senator Jefferson killed!"

Honey winced and looked at Pete. "And I thought my music box was special!"

Ken smiled. "It was, Honey. Without that little star hidden in that box, the rabbis would still be looking for their priest. Now they are hoping this box will further their mission."

The newlyweds leaned close together, more and more intrigued as the professor went on.

"Regarding the giving of gifts, you know how we attach little tags or give cards with our presents?"

"Sure," Honey said. "Sometimes that's the best part."

"True," Ken replied. "Well, it was not so different for our ancestors. They often had inscriptions put on the gift boxes—little love poems, kind words to the recipient, and so forth. Or sometimes instructions for the use of the gift."

The couple was amazed. "So do you think there are instructions on this box for the use of the ashes?" Pete asked.

"That's possible," Ken said. "But most likely not. I would imagine that the priests were so highly trained, they should not have needed any such thing."

Pete frowned. "Then what would the writing be?"

"That's what I hope to find out," Ken said.

Pete looked eager. "So, Professor," he said, "just how do you go about determining what's on the box? Will the letters just speak for themselves and everything be spelled out?"

Ken shook his head. "It's a little more complicated than that. First of all, see this little notch here?" He turned the box over and pointed to a place on the bottom where it appeared a small sliver of wood had recently been removed.

"Yes," Pete replied. "That looks fresh."

"It is," Ken said. "I took the liberty of removing a tiny slice today. I sent it to the lab with one of my grad students. He doesn't know where it came from, but I told him to have a carbon-14 reading on it by morning."

Honey brightened again. "That's how they figure out how old something is, right?"

"Right," Ken said. "Though the system has its limitations, it's good for vegetable matter, like wood. Papyrus scrolls, for instance, can be dated that way."

"So after you get the results, what then?" Pete asked.

"I can begin to look at the lettering on the box with greater understanding, knowing the time period in which it may have been written. I will begin by assuming it was inscribed shortly after the wood was processed."

Honey shrugged. "Aren't these figures Hebrew?" she asked, recalling her synagogue classes.

"I would say so," Ken said cautiously.

"Then what difference does the time frame make?" she inquired. "Isn't Hebrew Hebrew?"

"Language changes," Ken said. "Writing styles change, and so do the meanings of words. It is important to have some frame of reference before I start transcribing."

Pete sighed. "Takes more patience than I would have!" he exclaimed. "Can't you just give us a quick reading? Do you see any familiar words?"

Ken sat back and looked sternly at his new cousin-in-law. "Science demands patience," he said. "Sure, I could give you some ideas of what I think. But what point would there be? It is better to go about this the right way. It avoids unnecessary disappointment. To say nothing of outright errors!"

Pete accepted the correction. "Okay. So once you determine the time frame, what next?"

"That's where the latest technology is our greatest asset," Ken enthused. "What we do is make a digital scan of each side of the box. We feed that into our computer and overlay the scanned image with a digital program of the language from that period. The computer sorts through the images on the box and locates matching figures in the program. It tells us what the images most probably say by filling in missing or damaged characters with likely matches. It even gives alternate possibilities!"

Pete laughed. "Now that's the kind of archaeology I could live with!"

Honey nudged her husband. "Careful, Pete," she teased. "You might become a tech-head yet."

Ken agreed. "Yeah, Pete," he laughed. "For someone who won't have a telephone, you're speaking dangerously!"

The night was fast fading. Dawn would be creeping in the library windows in a couple of hours. Ken handed Pete the brush and pushed the base of the artifact across the table toward him. "If you want to be an archaeologist," he said, "how about starting now? Maybe between the two of us, we can get this box cleaned up before morning."

CHAPTER 27

Laad Girzim, Antiquities Curator to the Royal House of Jordan, got out of the limousine that had carried him from the palace to the entrance of his childhood home. When he left the car, he did not emerge in front of a posh residence, nor even in front of a house. The car let him off in front of a small gift shop, around which were parked taxicabs and buses, in a dusty lot, miles from nowhere.

The gift shop was not a residence either. He walked past it and directly through a cluster of outbuildings and picnic tables, where tour groups and individual sightseers were preparing to take a long hike. Their destination: the cavernous city of old Petra, in Jordan's southern sector.

The mysterious red-rock ruins of a civilization that had flourished twenty-six centuries ago were still home to thousands of Bedouins, whose abodes were in the natural caves and man-carved rooms of the "secret valley."

Laad had grown up in this enigmatic place, which had been the backdrop for everything from a once-thriving colony, to hideaways of escaped prisoners, shelters for war refugees, and even a Hollywood film or two. That any child could grow up in this isolated place and go on to succeed in the outside world was a rarity. Laad was one of the few such rarities to claim the honor.

He owed his success to his grandmother, who, as a child herself, had been privileged to visit Amman, the capital, more than once. She had traveled there with her father, a glass artisan of such amazing ability that his work had caught the eye of a clever exporter. An American businessman had seen the uniqueness of his wares and had paid him handsomely to let him market them abroad. In time the artist himself had become a commodity, the businessman arranging shows for him throughout Jordan, putting him up in fine hotels, and showing him the world that lay just beyond the boundaries of his isolated valley.

The artisan's daughter, Laad's grandmother, had accompanied her father on such excursions a couple of times. That had been enough to convince her that she should see to it that any son of hers would get an education, that any son of hers would have choices other Petran children did not know existed.

As it turned out, she had no sons, only daughters. Although she had been allowed to go with her father to Amman, she had never been educated and had no freedoms other than what her limited world gave her. So it was with the girls born to her, brought up not only in the traditionally restrictive Muslim world, but in the even more confining society within the red-rock walls.

But not so for her grandson—no! When Laad came along, she saw to it that he was sent to the visitors' center every morning, at the head of the valley, that he boarded a school bus with the children of the closest modern village, and that he learned to read and write.

Laad proved himself an unusually able student. Perhaps due to his Petran surroundings, he took a keen interest in all things ancient. Eventually, his skill and aptitude led him to work for Jordan's antiquities minister, and ultimately to procure that position for himself.

Today, as he left the handsome limo, trekked past the wealthy tourists in their Nike hiking shoes and Liz Claiborne sunglasses, he was aware of his special status. A man of many worlds, he knew this most arcane of Jordanian sites like the back of his hand; he also knew some of the most secret corners of Jordan's royal palace. He could take a plane to most of the far-flung cities from which these tourists hailed and would have been on familiar turf; yet he could also step into the rocky hovels of families within Petra's poverty-stricken valley, and he would know many a native by name. He was at home in a university classroom, had even guest lectured around the world, but he also knew how to call a herd of goats down to the valley floor after a day of following them through the red-rock hills.

As a youngster, Laad had been embarrassed to board the school bus when it picked him up. He had been ashamed of his poor family, his strange upbringing. But he had long ago outgrown such foolishness. He had come to appreciate his unique heritage, to even be proud of it.

He made it home too rarely to suit him these days. He had not come back to Petra since Ramadan, two years ago. He was returning today because he had received word that his grandmother wanted desperately to see him, that she had something she wanted to tell him.

One broad dirt path ran toward Petra's natural gateway, a narrow aperture between towering scarlet cliffs. Alongside this path, to the left, lay a shallow gorge, which was used like a racetrack by local Arab horsemen. As Laad passed by, visitors were lined up to watch the spectacle of darkly handsome riders on glorious Arabian horses tearing up and down the sunken course, their headscarves flying behind them, their fluid robes flapping in the violent, dusty breeze raised by their galloping steeds. How much of this activity was for the tourists' benefit, and how much simply for the joy of it, not even Laad was certain. He knew, however, that the young men would have raced their fabulous animals had no one been watching, just as Father Ishmael's desert-dwelling sons had done for countless generations.

The sights and sounds of this ancient pastime filled Laad with wistful sentiment. The pounding of the hooves, the heaving of the horses' lungs, the snap of leather whips, the cheering of the onlookers—whether the gawking tourists or the delighted Bedouin youngsters perched on rocks across the gorge—all signaled the proximity of home. As Laad identified with the noble horsemen, whose swarthy looks and athletic builds were typical of his people, he proudly considered that no more handsome humans existed anywhere else on the planet.

Laad himself was a handsome man. He wore glasses and was not especially athletic, having devoted himself to a life of study; but he had dark good looks, like these fellows on horseback, piercing black eyes, and a quick mind that was not easily fooled. Like his artistic great-grandfather and his determined grandmother, he reflected his heritage with the same strength of purpose manifested by these strapping riders. All were children of Ishmael, and all exhibited Ishmael's temperament, to one degree or another.

Laad picked up his pace as he entered the narrow slit that led to ancient Petra. Though it was midday, the long canyon, whose narrow floor snaked between sheer rock walls, was dusky with shadow. Tourists were warned to be out of Petra and away from this labyrinthine corridor before sunset, as bandits were known to hide within its folds, lying in wait for the unsuspecting. Yes, Laad knew there was a sinister side to the native cleverness, one with a gypsy-like disrespect for the naive or unwary among visitors and fellow Arabs alike.

He placed a protective hand over the zippered fanny-pack on his hip and scanned the natural causeway for suspicious sorts. Behind him he could hear the laughter and chatter of tourists just entering the echoing passage.

Ahead, the concourse opened onto the most famous and photographed area of Petra, the "Treasury Building," an elaborate edifice hand hewn into a high canyon wall. The Treasury Building was so named because archaeologists, upon "discovering" it years before, had assumed that the ornate multi-columned carving was the facade of an ancient royal bank. More recent speculations said it was the temple to some god or goddess.

Its proximity was heralded by smaller facades carved into the walls of the causeway. Exploding light from flashbulbs bounced through the passageway as tourists photographed the ruins along the dark approach. Laad breathed a little easier, knowing that any potential thieves lurking in the shadows would be discouraged for the moment.

Though he was a native, he would be glad to reach his grandmother's dwelling, and quickly moved through the open area in front of the Treasury Building. Turning right, beyond the large courtyard, he began the mile-long hike that led home. As he went he passed dozens of tables and stands where Bedouin women and children peddled native jewelry and trinkets, haggling with customers who knew better than to pay the asking price for anything. The marketplace, which spread for miles through the twisting hills, would be rolled up and hauled inside at sunset, when the natives retreated to the natural caves that pockmarked the sloping heights.

Laad's grandmother lived in one of those caves. As he watched for the trail he knew so well, one that rose precipitously toward his boyhood home, a high-pitched whistle caught his ear. Glancing toward the summit of one hill, he saw the silhouette of a young Arab boy with a wooden staff in his hand. That could have been Laad himself when he was that age, he thought.

The boy stood still as a statue, whistling a few more times, and within seconds, the sound of skittering hooves and bleating animals filled the hillside. There were probably a hundred such goatherds on surrounding ridges, but these creatures discerned the distinctive whistle of their particular master and heeded only his summons. Dozens of flop-eared goats appeared on the high horizon, running eagerly toward the boy. White, black, and speckled, they raised a dust cloud as they gathered behind the herdsman, following him down the steep trail toward home.

Home! Laad thought. *It is good to be home!*

At last he found the familiar path that led to his grandmother's cave. High above, the opening could be seen, and before it sat an old woman in vivid Bedouin dress. Though she was elderly and poor of sight, she recognized her grandson approaching from that distance.

"Laad!" she called, waving her walking stick in the air.

"Grandmother!" he replied, hurrying up the trail. "I am coming!"

The old matriarch sat beneath a shelter of branches and reeds, erected in front of the cave. It did little to protect from wind and rain, but it was good for shade against the blazing sun that dominated the desert sky. To Laad's surprise, another woman, equally aged, sat beside his grandmother.

Fatima! Laad marveled. *What is* she *doing here?*

Fatima, one of his grandmother's lifelong friends, was known as a prognosticator, a seer of some note, whose reputation for discerning the future reached beyond the boundaries of this isolated valley. Ironically, her natural eyes saw little at all. She was nearly blind, and waved to Laad only because his grandmother had announced his arrival.

As Laad approached, the mystery of the matriarch's urgent summons thickened. He knew that Fatima's notoriety brought all sorts of people to this valley, hoping for an audience with her. Wealthy foreigners offered to pay her handsomely for her services as they asked for advice on their love lives, businesses, even international politics. Never had she accepted any payment, however, for what she considered to be "a gift from Allah"—a gift that would become "polluted" by such trafficking. Even Jordanian statesmen had called on her from time to time, in person, or through emissaries, seeking her counsel as a prophet. So it was with good reason that Laad took her presence seriously.

By the time he reached the cave, his grandmother had managed to stand up. She leaned her frail body against her staff and reached out to embrace him.

Though in the Muslim value system women were considered lesser beings than men, age brought the benefit of respect for both sexes. But it was love that caused Laad to fervently return his grandmother's embrace, and not just respect.

Fatima remained seated. Not only did her blindness constrain her, but it was proper for a seer to remain at ease before a seeker.

Laad supposed he was perceived as such, though he did not know what he had come to seek.

"Son, son, sit down!" Grandmother insisted. "Fatima has much to tell you! It is for this that I have called you from the city . . . from the royal palace!"

"It is good to see you, Grandmother," Laad said as he took a seat on the dusty carpet spread beneath the shelter. He knew that the old woman emphasized his royal position to remind Fatima of his specialness and, hence, of her own.

"And you, Fatima," he added.

The prophetess nodded blindly, bowing toward him. Rows of silver coins suspended from chains about her neck jingled as she did so. Both women were dressed in flowing velvet gowns of many colors, the traditional garb of the Petran woman. The coins and other jewelry they so proudly sported were a mark of status to potential suitors. Though these ladies would not be receiving offers of marriage at this stage in their lives, they had worn these gaudy ornaments—necklaces, waist chains, bracelets, anklets, earrings—since girlhood, as economic protection in the event of divorce or widowhood.

Laad was surprised at how little conversation preceded the purpose of his summons. It was clear that Grandmother was eager to get down to business, that something of great urgency had transpired, and that nothing transcended it in importance.

As she reached out and patted Fatima on the knee, assuring her that nobody else was within earshot, Laad quickly surveyed his beloved cave home. A small clay oven dominated the interior, serving as a cook stove, a light on dark evenings, and heat in the winter. Smoke from the short chimney had darkened the cave's ceiling over the years, despite his grandmother's annual cleaning spree. But the rainbow colors of the natural rock were still vivid. Laad remembered how, as a child, he had lain on his bed, a pallet of goatskins spread out on a niche carved into the cave wall. Many an evening he had rested there, tracing the variegated strata with his eyes, as the light from the clay stove cast hypnotizing shadows about the room. Next thing he would know, it would be morning, and he would wonder where the night had gone.

How he would love to stretch out just now, in that cool, round room, and drift into a blissful nap. But he had not come to sleep. Fatima was leaning toward him, her weathered, leathery face close to his, her milky eyes staring at him as though she could see him just fine.

"Young man," she said, her voice dry as the desert breeze. She pressed a finger onto his knee, heedless of her position as a woman in a man's world. "I have something to tell the queen. Your grandmother assures me you have the queen's ear."

Laad was stunned. "She does, does she?" he said, trying not to laugh.

Grandmother stiffened, lifting her chin proudly.

"Indeed, he does!" she reiterated. "Now you listen, son."

With this, Fatima drew back, heaved a deep sigh, and turned her blind eyes heavenward. "I have seen a troublesome thing and a mighty!" she groaned.

Her tone sent a shiver through Laad, and he gripped his hands together nervously.

"Tell the queen to cast her eyes toward the west, toward the city of kings who have been our enemies!"

Laad frowned. He had barely had time to adjust to Fatima's presence, let alone prepare himself to receive a prophecy. "Excuse me," he croaked. "Should I be writing this down?" He fumbled with the zipper on his hip bag, ready to find a pencil and notepad, when Fatima reached out again and poked him firmly, this time on the forehead. "Ouch!" he complained, rubbing his brow. Grandmother corrected him with sparking eyes, and he lowered his head.

"No writing!" Fatima growled. "Only listen! Allah will write on your brain!"

Laad sat back, stunned to silence.

Suddenly, the old seer was speaking, her tone portentous. "I have seen what the king did, how he returned what the ancient ones took from our enemies. And now, behold, it will not be long. Our enemies will rise above us, those whom our king befriended. And they will be our enemies no longer, but only enemies of our brothers!"

Laad was astonished. Did she speak of the mysterious box, the one that the queen, at her husband's dying request, had given to the senator? The one for which Calvin Jefferson had been killed?

He leaned close. "Yes, Mother," he urged the prophetess. "I am listening!"

Fatima smiled, realizing that Laad understood. "Tell the queen to prepare herself, and the king's heir! The sons of Israel will be hindered no longer!" Then, raising both hands, as though the next words held the world, she pronounced, "The crown of Jerusalem is theirs!"

Laad quivered, turning his eyes to his grandmother, whose own eyes were closed in wonder.

"Mother?" he asked the old seer. "May I inquire?"

Fatima nodded. "You may."

"What you say is troublesome indeed. This is an evil thing for our people—this triumph of Israel! Our Arab brothers desire Jerusalem! They say Allah has given it to them! Should it not be theirs?"

The old woman bowed her head and shook it back and forth, incredulous herself at the riddle of her words.

"The clouds beneath Allah's footstool are very thick," she whispered. "I cannot see past them to even touch his toe. But such is his will, this prophecy. Peace to those who accept it. Calamity to those who fight it!"

CHAPTER 28

Ken Aronstam sat before a computer screen in the laboratory of Midwest University's anthropology department. On the monitor a series of images flashed, each a virtual 3-D of the Jeremiah Box, turning this way and that in a dizzying sequence, as the computer's special digital linguistics program analyzed the etchings on the ancient wood.

Once again it was late at night, after the custodial staff had left the building. The professor had pulled the shades on the windows of the basement facility and used only a few overhead lights for his work.

With him again were his cousin Honey Wester and her husband. Though it was the summer session of the school year, she wore a light cardigan in this cool room. She drew it tight to her chest not so much for warmth, however, as for comfort. The surroundings were eerie, especially at this time of night.

The room smelled dusty, not because it was unclean, but because that was the nature of much of the material studied here: old bits of pottery, corroded artifacts from a hundred different times and cultures, pieces of petrified vegetation from the remains of ancient meals. Skeletal remnants of beasts and even of humans, unearthed by students at various digs, were on display around the room, the sockets of their hollow eyes staring down from high shelves and dark corners. Burial items, such as bronzes from Burma, ivory cartouches from Egypt, or pinion-nut necklaces from the bogs of the Olympic Peninsula, spoke of death and the disruption of graves, which the original guardians believed were sealed for all time.

Intermingled with these "finds" were the tools of the scientists who studied such things: trowels, small picks and brushes for delicate excavation; wire grates on wooden frames for the sifting of dirt and matter; baskets and boxes for the sorting and cataloging of the collections. Added to all this were reams and reams of notebooks recording the exact sources of the items: in which level of which quadrant of which "tel," or ancient site, each had been found. Such information was invaluable to the understanding of ancient cultures, giving keys to the dates and uses of the items. The records also contributed to the body of knowledge making up the disciplines of anthropology, archaeology, and related sciences that were a cross between detective work and grave robbery.

Ken's task this evening was nothing unusual. The analysis of inscriptions on ancient artifacts was a common activity in this lab. David Rothmeyer had told him that Honey and Pete had been with him when he painstakingly interpreted the writing on the Dachau Document. But, Ken knew thay had never seen such techniques as he employed tonight.

"Dave had to do without the help of a digital program when he transcribed the information at Dachau," Ken said. "I am sure the Consortium has such a program in their Jerusalem laboratory, but from what Dave has told me about the Copper Scroll, it is too badly corroded to benefit from this sort of technology."

Pete was amazed as he watched the sorting and flashing of rapidly moving windows on the monitor.

"So what will this tell you?" he asked.

Ken tried to give a simple explanation. "Well," he said, "the results of the carbon-14 test confirm that the box was created from wood processed during the time of the prophet. Strangely, though, the inscription does not appear to be from that period. This program should help us pinpoint the era during which the etching was made."

Pete pulled up a stool and sat beside the professor. "That is because language changes," he remembered.

Ken nodded. "Yes," he replied. "Plus, if we are to read an inscription, we must begin by knowing just what language we are reading. I told you I thought it was probably Hebrew, but there are some things about the writing that baffle me. I do not want to jump to a premature conclusion that could lead me down the wrong path."

Honey scrutinized the box, which lay to one side of the computer. "What is it about the writing that baffles you?" she asked.

Ken clicked and scrolled around the screen, following the work of the program as he patiently explained. "It appears to be written by a non-Hebrew," he said. "I do not know if this is simply a matter of penmanship style, as we might call it. But I think it is more."

Honey studied the etching closely. Small figures, which might have been letters, appeared here and there among an elaborate scrollwork of leaves and vines that twisted all along the edge of the lid and the sides of the box. This peculiar decorative border framed the small figure of the highly stylized horned cow, who stared straight out from the lid of the box, its head planted squarely atop its chest and forequarters, with no hindquarters visible. The eyes of the cow had apparently been inset at one time with gems, but these had fallen out or had been stolen countless years ago.

"It's hard to tell the lettering from the design," Honey said. "But I think I make out a few characters here and there. They do look Middle Eastern but appear to be more cursive than the blocky Hebrew I learned as a kid."

Ken smiled approvingly. "Very good, Honey!" he praised her. "My analysis exactly."

Honey's eyes widened. "Wow! Really?"

Pete was also getting the idea. "Okay," he said, "so you have determined that the writing is not from Jeremiah's time. Does the program just read the scanned photo and tell you what time it was written?"

Ken chuckled. "I wish it were that easy. No, we humans still have to help our 'artificial intelligences' with some things. I have told the program to look for matches that would fit the time of the Essenes, who wrote about the Cave Scrolls. After all, the copper scroll David has been working on talks about this box and what it should reveal."

Pete comprehended. "Ah, so you figure maybe the clues in the scroll were written by the same people who wrote the words on the box!"

Ken sighed. "I doubt that," he said. "Like I pointed out, the lettering appears to be done by a non-Hebrew. But it's a starting place. Sometimes in these archaeology games we have very little to go on. We may run on nothing but hunches. If we're lucky, the hunches pay off. If they don't, we try something else."

Honey winked at her cousin teasingly. "Doesn't sound all that scientific to me!"

Ken was not offended. "Tell me about it!" He laughed. "But, then, when we do get lucky—when our hunches do lead from one discovery to another—there's nothing more rewarding."

Honey sparked to that. "We know what you mean," she said. "When we were with David, his work seemed to take on a life of its own. It was uncanny!"

Ken looked away from the screen. "Yeah, I know," he said. "Dave told me about some of that when we were in Montana. I've never had quite that sort of experience. I must admit, I was a little jealous of you all."

Honey glanced at her husband, who sensed they had struck a nerve in the professor. "Well, Ken," Pete said, "maybe this assignment will be like that. Maybe you'll get a taste of Rothmeyer's adventure."

Ken shrugged and focused on the screen again. "So," he sighed, "what do we have here?"

The windows and the images had ceased churning, flashing, and scrolling. A steady, unmoving view of the Jeremiah Box was suspended above a single line of type, which throbbed at the bottom of the screen like the landing lights of a hovercraft.

"*Habiru Nabataean*," the caption read.

Ken sat back, amazed at the confirmation. "Aha!" he said. "That makes sense!"

Honey and Pete scooted forward and stared at the strange words. "What is that?" Pete asked. "Looks like Latin."

Ken laughed again. "Actually, no, though Latin is the universal language of scholarship. *Habiru Nabataean* means the dialect of Hebrew spoken in the region of Nabataea or Petra, across the Jordan from Judea. Specifically, that would be the region south of the Dead Sea, across the river. The cursive quality of the script on the box is a relative of the Arabic script we see today in Jordan and other Muslim countries."

Honey was disappointed. "Then the box was not inscribed by anyone connected with David's copper scroll."

Ken shrugged again. "Like I said, we can't rush to conclusions. Very possibly the people who wrote the scroll *were* connected with the etcher of the box. Who's to say the Essenes didn't have their sympathizers outside Palestine?"

As Honey and Pete considered this, Ken began typing again on the keyboard. "I guess the only way we can put the puzzle together is to see just what the box has to say."

Reaching into his briefcase beneath the desk, he pulled out a diskette and plopped it into the "A" drive. With a click of the "enter" key, he sat back and listened to the whirring of the hard drive.

"Okay," he said. "The program is now overlaying a *Habiru Nabataean* translator onto the digital scan of the Jeremiah Box. Given the age and wear on the box, this could take a while, but sometime before dawn, we should begin to see a readout of the inscription."

Glancing up at an amazed Honey, he pointed to a Bunsen burner on the lab counter. Above it, on a faculty shelf, was a jar of instant coffee. "I could use some caffeine," he said. "It's going to be a long night."

CHAPTER 29

A few days after Laad Girzim made his visit to the red-rock valley of Petra, another trip was being made to another red-rock structure on the west side of the Jordan Valley.

One of the most famous and often photographed of the natural phenomena in Israel, the high mesa of Masada, whose name means "mountain citadel," was the destination of a group of travelers who had come out from Jerusalem. In an air-conditioned van, driven by Shalom Diamant, most of the Consortium contingent were heading for the ancient fortification at the south end of the Dead Sea, where King Herod had built a pleasure palace two millennia ago.

The four rabbis, along with David Rothmeyer, Britta Hayworth, Ian McCurdy, and John Cromwell, were accompanying Dr. Kenneth Aronstam to the world-renowned landmark.

Yes, Ken Aronstam had finally come to Israel!

The events that had brought the head of the Midwest University anthropology department to the Holy Land had transpired so quickly, he had barely had time to adjust to the idea of the journey before he found himself here.

Ken would never forget the moment, just three nights ago, when he and the Wester couple, during one of their clandestine research sessions, had discovered that the intricate design on the lid and sides of the Jeremiah Box contained an amazing message. Embedded among the swirls and flourishes of the border was an inscription verifying David's interpretation of the Copper Scroll: that the box was the "prophet's casket" with a "map to the King's Tower." The inscription explained that the etching of the heifer on the lid actually contained the promised map.

As Ken rode in a middle seat of the sleek van, which Diamant drove down the desert highway bordering the Dead Sea, he studied the dry wadis and ancient desert terrain that were the predominant features of the southern Jordan Valley. Despite his exhausting jet lag, he was enthralled. A tingle went up his spine as he realized that this very highway, or the version of it that was here two thousand years before, was depicted on the cover of the enigmatic cedar box. The right side of the heifer's body, which was to the observer's left, was rendered in highly stylized outline and was intended to represent the west bank of the Dead Sea, the head of the heifer sitting north of that body of saline water.

More astounding than this, however, was an apparent reference to the Ashes of the Red Heifer! While the Copper Scroll had indicated that the high priest's breastplate and some other treasures would be found in the King's Tower, it made no mention of the essential ashes. To everyone's amazement, the inscription on the box seemed to allude to that necessary item, which legend said Jeremiah hid in the desert.

Ken, reading haltingly to the amazed Westers as the computer program sifted through the scribbles on the digital photo, had felt the sparse hair on his own head rise: "'The contents of this box shall be found where friends of the prophet hid them, in the King's Tower, at the end of the sacred river, beneath the foot of the sacrifice.'"

"You're kidding!" Pete had exclaimed. "That has to mean the vial of ashes the rabbis have been looking for!"

Contacting the Consortium rabbis immediately, the professor had explained that he had some important information to show them, which required transporting the box to Israel. In a few hours Honey and Pete were driving him to the Columbus airport, seeing him off on a transoceanic flight to Israel before they returned to Montana. At no time was the precious box out of Ken's hands during that trip. He had not even stowed it in the overhead bin above his plane seat but had kept it in a small valise on his lap. In no communication with the rabbis had the word "box" or "ashes" or anything related to them been spoken. Ken would be traveling alone, with as little protection as Senator Calvin Jefferson had had, and the senator had been killed for that box!

Serious as all of this business was, however, it had its light moments. Ken's face broke into a grin at the memory of that last night in the anthro lab.

David, who sat between him and Britta in the van, noticed his amused look. "You seem to be quite pleased with yourself today," Rothmeyer teased. "Maybe the rabbis have praised you too much for your discovery. It's gone to your head."

"Sure, Dave. It's high time you had to share your glory with your old department chairman." Ken laughed. "Seriously, though, I was just remembering Honey's observation when we figured out that the heifer's foot was supposed to be resting on Masada."

David, the rabbis, and the others leaned in close as Ken pulled the box out from the valise cradled on his lap and pointed to the likeness of the mesa depicted beneath the heifer's right foot. Ken chuckled again. "Once we had figured out that the 'sacrifice' in the inscription refers to the heifer itself, and then pieced together that the 'sacred river' leading to the King's Tower has to be the Jordan, we realized the squarish item on which the heifer's foot rests is, in fact, Masada—Herod's desert tower."

David nodded. "Yes, that's why we're heading there now. So what's the joke?"

Ken chuckled. "Honey's eyes got real big when we figured this out. But she was a little embarrassed. 'Wow,' she said, 'and here I thought that was the cow's salt lick!' "

The travelers burst out laughing, the rabbis guffawing in breathless glee. "Well," said Rabbi Ben, wiping his eyes with his handkerchief, "I hope we find more than a salt lick for all our trouble!"

Outside the van, a brisk, hot breeze was kicking up yellowish sand along the road. Masada was just becoming visible across miles of hazy desert air, arising like a ghostly red tower behind a gauzy veil. The vanload of passengers became very still at the sight. As Diamant pulled into the parking lot, about a half mile from the base, all the riders were leaning toward the van's right-hand windows, their necks craned to take in the majestic height of the natural monument.

And "monument" it was, for this landmark was more than an amazing bit of geography. To Israel and all the world, it represented the bravery and heroism of a thousand men and women who had given up their lives rather than surrender to enslavement or martyrdom at the hands of Rome. Since the rebirth of the state of Israel in 1948, annual commemorative services had been held there by the Israeli military—with multigun salutes, speeches by dignitaries extolling the example of those brave patriots, and sometimes even fireworks.

The story was well known to all the passengers and to most of the educated world. A couple of generations after Herod built his pleasure spa on Masada, the inhospitable mountaintop became a Jewish rebel stronghold. When Rome overran Jerusalem in 70 C.E., burning the Jewish temple and dismantling the remains, a group of Israeli Zealots had holed up in the ruins atop the mesa. Men, women, and children refused to give in to the demands of the conquerors, preferring life on the isolated mountain, and potential starvation, to chains or death at the hands of their captors. The legend of their brave defiance, and of their ultimate choice to end their own lives and the lives of their families rather than succumb to Rome, was one of the most moving and heroic in human history.

Today another group of heroes had arrived at the mountain fort. These were just as invested in the future of Israel as their ancient counterparts had been. Though they had not been required to surrender their lives for their beliefs, they were nonetheless dedicated to the fulfillment of Israel's sacred purposes.

As they emerged from the van, stepping out of its air-conditioned luxury into the stifling heat of the tourist depot, their hearts raced with a sense of destiny. With only the words of the box as their guide, they were about to take a trip into the unknown.

What they might find there was uncertain, but the quest deserved the same sort of devotion the Zealots had exhibited two thousand years before.

Although some tourists chose to walk the switchbacked "Snakepath" trail that led to the top of Masada thirteen hundred feet above the valley floor, most preferred the safely engineered lift that ran on thick cables from the tourist station to the mesa's zenith. David and Britta might have chosen the hike, but deferred to the needs of the elderly members of the Consortium group.

As the tram rose higher and higher above the desert floor, the rabbis and their guests gazed out the windows upon an amazing vista. Of course, the old gentlemen had been to this place many times in their lives, but it never failed to impress them with its physical majesty and historical significance.

"Be prepared for a few jolts of the gondola," Shalom Diamant warned the passengers, who held on to grip bars that ran the length of the ceiling. "It is windy today, and even without wind, the gondola passes over seams in the cable. Do not be alarmed. This is one of the safest trams in the world."

Britta smiled excitedly up at David, who had encircled her waist with his free arm as he held the bar overhead.

As the conveyance moved up the shuddering wire toward the disembarking station near the mountaintop, Diamant's dramatic voice filled the confining space! Before taking the post of curator of the Temple Gallery, he had been an Israeli tour guide and had led many an expedition to Masada. Today his recital of the story of the Zealots was rendered as fluently as when it had been part of his routine.

Gesturing toward the base of the mesa, he pointed out several areas where enormous rock rings were laid out on the ground. Within these rings lay the debris of ancient structures, broken down by millennia of weather and pilfering.

"There are eight of these circles about the base of Masada," Diamant said. "These are the ruins of the Roman camps, which General Silva ordered built here for the capture of any Jews who might attempt to escape the mountaintop. Thousands of Roman soldiers were committed to stay here for whatever time it would take to wear the Zealots down."

David interjected, "Didn't I read somewhere that Silva was actually sent to Palestine from Belgium?"

Diamant nodded. "As I recall, yes. He was taken off a Roman campaign in Europe and assigned to Masada. He was one of Rome's most valuable commanders." Diamant cleared his throat and continued with his history. "As you will see when we arrive at the top of the mesa, an enormous ramp was built up the west side by Silva's men." Diamant expounded, "Actually, it was not the Romans who built the ramp but Jewish slaves—thousands of them—overseen by Roman taskmasters. Some of their skeletons have been found where they fell beneath the slave drivers' whips. They were simply buried in place, becoming part of the ramp itself."

The passengers were very quiet as they contemplated such cruelty. Suddenly, however, they were jolted out of their sad reveries by an unexpected bump and shift of the tram. Gasps and nervous laughs filled the car as the gondola lurched and then resumed its ascent.

"No problem," Diamant said as casually as possible. Gripping his part of the overhead bar a little tighter, he continued, "When we reach the top, you will see that the Roman ramp is the result of one of the largest earthmoving endeavors in human history, requiring nine months of work by those thousands of slaves, and countless yards of soil, rubble, and rock for its construction."

When Diamant reached this part of his tale, a common question arose. It was David who posed it, though it had undoubtedly been posed by thousands of visitors over the intervening millennia, and even by locals two thousand years ago.

"But why?" David shrugged. "Why would the Romans go to so much trouble, just to prove a point? They could have easily posted a few sentries about the base of the mountain and waited the rebels out. Eventually they would have surrendered, or starved."

The gondola was just pulling into the disembarking station when Diamant replied, "When I was a tour guide, the answer I always gave to that question is the same every Israeli has been handed for generations: 'The Romans were too proud to let the Zealots defy them. They would enslave them or kill them, nothing less.'" With a sigh, he conceded, "I guess, however, that

I can be honest with all of you. That response was never any more satisfactory to me than it was to my thinking guests."

David agreed. "Right! After all, just how aware would the Roman world have even been of a few holdouts locked atop an isolated desert mountain? Rome could have told the world anything! Who would have disputed the empire's word?"

The rabbis looked a little nervous. "Do you think that we have not all wondered these things?" Rabbi Ben admitted.

Dr. Jacobs laughed sardonically. "Yes, but it has never been politically correct to question the story."

Britta's eyes sparkled with intrigue. "Maybe the Romans suspected the Zealots had the treasures we're looking for!"

Father McCurdy considered this briefly. "Possibly," he said, rubbing his chin. "But unless they figured the entire missing wealth of the Jerusalem temple had been moved here, I can't imagine what would have commanded such interest. They must have known such a hoard could not have been brought to this single place in secrecy! As for the few items we hope to find here, precious as they are to Israel, they would not have been worth such expense and manpower to the Romans."

The gondola rocked to a stop at the exit port. Diamant slid the door open and the riders stepped onto a ledge that led to a narrow, winding set of sandstone stairs.

"We will begin our ascent on foot now," Diamant said. "Are you all up for that?"

Everyone nodded eagerly, and Ken, holding his valise safely beneath one arm, said, "You bet! I, for one, have come a very long way for this!"

CHAPTER 30

Blasts of hot afternoon wind scoured the mountain's tabletop as the visitors from the Consortium emerged from the winding stairway. As was true almost every day of the year, there were dozens of tourists walking through the ruins of the ancient baths, palace, and royal post office that remained from Herod's glorious era. The great builder king had spared no expense in putting together this desert retreat, though his family used it for only a few years, and he himself had come but rarely.

Archaeologists had made good progress toward a realistic reconstruction of the Herodian buildings in the last few years. Piles of numbered rocks remained to be placed where the scholars figured they had once been part of tumbled walls, but the walls themselves were about half rebuilt in several places.

Diamant, ever a guide by nature, took his guests through a quick overview of the ruins, showing them the synagogue that had been used here during the time of the Zealots, the spas and baths of Herod, with their intricate mosaic floors and faux marble walls still much intact. The spas were quite modern, considering the technology of the day. They had recessed plumbing and underfloor heating systems, fountains, and every possible convenience. The "post office" was a favorite of tourists, with its dozens of tiny cubbyholes built along the western wall, closest to Jerusalem. The cubbyholes were not for letters, however, as one might expect. They were literally "pigeon holes," tiny birdhouses for the king's many carrier pigeons, which delivered and retrieved messages to and from the capital.

Against the wall where the post office was mounted was the gargantuan Roman ramp—a glacis of countless tons of dirt and debris carved from the surrounding hills and hauled here over the better part of a year. As David looked down from the height of the mesa to the slope that hundreds had died to build, he shook his head. *It doesn't compute*, he told himself. *No group of mere holdouts was worth this effort!*

The Consortium group was not here as tourists, but they had determined beforehand to appear as ordinary as possible to the strangers they would encounter. They had deliberately come toward the end of the day, planning to stay on the mountaintop after the last tram had returned to the base. Permission for this had been granted by the Israel Antiquities Authority in Jerusalem, and the base depot had agreed to send them a tram when Diamant called for one on his cellular phone.

As Diamant led them around, recounting history, the group had one goal: to ferret out the hiding place of the priceless artifacts, which the carver of the Jeremiah Box and the scribe of the Second Copper Scroll had meant someone to find. Rothmeyer, McCurdy, and Aronstam pretended to listen to the guide as they scanned the area for anything that might trigger a thought, a possibility, a clue never before seen. Though thousands of people came and went here every year, some with archaeological background, it was safe to say that nobody had ever come with the same understandings these scholars had.

Yet, as they wandered about, they felt as if they had been dropped on an alien planet and told to find something there. They had brought the only assisting record available, the Jeremiah Box. Beyond a vague idea of what they sought, however, they had no notion where to begin.

Or so they thought. Suddenly, however, David's ears were pricked by something Diamant was saying. "Yes," he said, answering a question from Britta, "the Zealots of Masada were likely connected with other desert groups up and down Palestine. For some time now scholars have thought that the Essenes of Qumran and En-Gedi, just a few miles north of here, had goals and purposes in common with the people of Masada."

Now, this was a topic dear to David's heart. His months of study in seeking the Second Copper Scroll, and his more recent endeavors to translate it, had necessitated a knowledge of the Essenes.

Leaving McCurdy and Aronstam for a moment, he wandered back over to the rabbis and Britta, who were gathered around Diamant. "Are you talking about the warrior class of the Essenes?" he asked.

"That's right, David," Diamant said. "You know better than I that the Essenes were not a bunch of hermit monks. Their War Scroll and similar documents portray them as ready to lay down their lives for their beliefs, and to fight to the death to defend them."

David gazed off, deep in thought.

"What is it?" Britta asked, touching his arm. "You always get that look when you've had a revelation."

David shook himself. "Prophets get revelations," he said. "Scientists just get lucky."

The others gathered around David now. "What's on your mind?" Ben asked as McCurdy and Aronstam joined the group.

"I am just putting some things together that have been stored in my files for a while," David replied.

Britta looked knowingly at the others. "He means his brain," she explained. "His brain is like a file cabinet!"

David hushed her. "Okay, okay," he said. "Let me sort this out." He held up one hand, his fingers separated like numerals. Touching one at a time, he listed his thoughts. "The Essenes and the Zealots had a lot in common: there was a warrior class at Qumran, and the Zealots of Masada were definitely of the warrior class. These groups were probably in communication with each other . . . who knows, they may have even used carrier pigeons, like Herod! Both groups believed the Temple had been polluted and wanted to see it cleansed, and both groups were probably involved in the hiding and the recording of the Temple treasures throughout Palestine."

He paused for a second, and Father McCurdy broke in. "It has been speculated that the men of Masada, like some of the Essenes, were previous Temple officials, possibly guards or police. The camp at Qumran is even laid out like a miniature Temple!"

David nodded. "That's right! These are the similarities. The differences are that the Zealots did the legwork . . ."

Britta chimed in, "And the Essenes kept the records!"

Diamant was becoming agitated. There were strangers wandering about the mesa, and he did not want them listening in. "Step this way," he said to his group, loudly enough to be heard beyond the Consortium circle. "The baths are quite interesting."

At this, he led the group toward the central bathing house, which, at the moment, was empty. Once he had brought them down the steep steps to the inside, the group sat together on the benches lining the frescoed walls. If any other visitors came along, they would probably go away, seeing that these people had stopped here with their guide.

"We can't be too careful," Diamant said. "Go on, David."

"Thanks, Shalom," David replied. "Sometimes I forget myself."

Diamant nodded and spurred him on. "You were on a roll . . . don't stop now."

David rubbed his forehead and snapped his fingers. "There's something here," he said with a sigh. "There's something to be gained from these facts that will help us. I just know it. I feel it, but I can't put my finger on it!"

Britta sensed his frustration, much like the night they had stood together, two insomniacs on the Jerusalem rooftop.

"It will come," she assured him.

Suddenly, he lurched upright, as though a light had gone off in his head. This look Britta also knew, as did McCurdy and all those who had worked with Rothmeyer in the past year.

"What?" Ben cried.

"What is it?" Levine and Jacobs echoed. Even Uriel Katz urged him with, "Tell us, tell us!"

David held up his hands for silence. "Listen to this! If the men of Masada really were Temple police, they would not be unlike the security forces to whom we entrust our national secrets. Right?"

The Israelis, Britons, and Americans all agreed. "Of course!" Ken exclaimed. "They would be like the Secret Service in the U.S."

"Or the Queen's Guard in England," Cromwell said.

"Or the Mossad in Israel," the rabbis added.

"And what is required of such people in their profession?" David asked them, taking on a teacherly role.

"Secrecy!" McCurdy cried. "Utter secrecy!"

"To the point of death, if need be," Cromwell added somberly.

Everyone digested this for a moment. Then Britta summed it up. "Are you saying, David, that the Zealots of Masada were protecting a secret—a secret of such magnitude that they would have been expected to die for it rather than betray their country?"

David sighed, looking intently into her blue eyes. "That is exactly what I am saying. That is the only reason they would have come up here in the first place, the only reason they would have taken their own lives and the lives of their families! Thousands of other Jews went into slavery; some even fought their own countrymen to save their own skins. What was so special about the people of Masada?"

An evening breeze was pushing the hot daytime air off the tabletop outside, sending an eerie echo down into the sunken bathhouse. Britta cuddled close to David on the bench.

McCurdy croaked softly, "We are probably all thinking the same thing right now."

The group looked about at one another, each seeing his or her own thoughts mirrored in the others' eyes.

Cromwell put those thoughts into words. "The people of Masada were responsible for burying the treasures throughout the land and for reporting the whereabouts to the Essenes . . ."

"In code!" Rabbi Katz interrupted.

"Yes," Levine gasped. "The code of the Copper Scroll!"

"And only the Zealots of Masada had the key to the code . . . ," Ken deduced.

"The *Second* Copper Scroll!" David concluded. "Each of those two scrolls was recorded by an uneducated man . . . not a scribe like the monks of Qumran. Some coppersmith at Masada made the records the best he could and then they were delivered to the Essenes for safekeeping. It is possible the monks did not even know what they possessed! Only the Zealots of Masada were worth all the effort the Romans put into their capture. No one else was worth that much. Everyone else was expendable!"

Britta's eyes grew misty as she listened to the moaning wind above. "So the Romans never intended to kill the people of Masada."

"Not before they wrung their secrets from them!" McCurdy agreed.

Ken hung his head. "It was up to them to kill themselves."

For a long while the bathhouse was silent, each member of the group in private rumination.

At last, however, Uriel Katz spoke up. "So where does this leave us?" he asked. "We may have come up with some good revisionist history, but are we any closer to finding what we came for?"

Diamant fidgeted with the buttons on his vest. "As I told you in the tram, I have never been satisfied with the standard version of the Masada legend. It was written by Josephus, a Jew hired by Rome to tell the history of the Jews. On the positive side, I suppose, it is flattering to the Jewish people, a concession the Romans allowed the writer. On the negative side, it is devoid of true scholarship." He shrugged. "Still, it is all we have to work with."

"Very well," David said, "remind us of the details, and let us see if we can make something of them."

Diamant leaned back against the wall and clasped one knee with his hands. "Supposedly, when the Romans arrived on the mountaintop, finding only corpses and no army, they were told what had preceded them by a couple of women, who, along with a group of children, had escaped the mass suicide. Actually, the account was given by the younger of the two women, both of whom were related to Eleazar, the Zealot leader."

Ken clenched his jaw. "Ah . . . now, isn't that handy? The children were probably his as well. Just how did the leader's family happen to be the only ones to survive?"

"It gets better," Diamant said with a sardonic smile. "Apparently the women and children had planned their escape sometime beforehand, showing that the mass suicide was planned well in advance. They had even stashed jugs of water in the underground cavern where it is said they hid. When the Romans reached the mountaintop, the story goes, they began to search for survivors, calling out loudly for anyone to come forth. The women emerged from the cavern, and the younger proceeded to report, without missing a word, the entire long, poetic speech which Eleazar had given his people—the speech that supposedly convinced all of them to take their lives."

David leaned forward. "Ah, yes," he said. "I remember reading that speech. It goes on for pages. How in the world that woman could have remembered all of it, and then related it so perfectly . . . well, it seemed . . ."

"Canned?" Ben offered.

David was shocked at the rabbi's use of the idiom. "You said it." He laughed. "I didn't!"

"Exactly!" Diamant agreed. "As popular as that tale is, I think many people have wondered about it. But her version, and Josephus's, is that Eleazar gave such a stirring address on patriotism that, within moments, over nine hundred men, women, and children had sacrificed themselves to its ideals."

Now Uriel Katz began to bristle. "Wait just a minute!" he objected. "Perhaps it *was* all planned beforehand. Perhaps, as you say, the woman's report was 'canned.' Still, this does not negate the fact that the people sacrificed themselves for the welfare of Israel!"

The group was stunned by the correction. Uriel Katz was right, they knew. Red-faced, they stared at their laps or fidgeted nervously.

David nodded. "Sorry, Rabbi," he said. "For once, I must say, I agree with you. We have gotten carried away."

Rabbi Ben, likewise, conceded. "Thank you for reminding us of that truth. Never let it be said that Horace Benjamin makes light of genuine martyrdom!"

Katz raised his chin, surprised and pleased at their affirmation.

But Ken was off onto another train of speculation. Lifting a finger, he interjected, "Diamant, did you say that the women and children hid out in a cavern?"

"Yes," the guide replied. "I believe Josephus's words were something to the effect that they hid in 'caverns underground.' "

Ken glanced at the rabbis. "Have there ever been sonograms or infrared readings made of this area?"

McCurdy stepped in. "Indeed, there have," he said. "I keep on top of all the archaeological news from Israel, and I have read of such research. In fact, as I recall, the ground here has been combed by high-tech readings, but it has not revealed anything extraordinary. Certainly nothing of the magnitude of the Qumran scriptorium, for instance."

Ken's brow furrowed. "Maybe I'm catching some sort of religious bug from all of you, but I am beginning to think that our labors are never allowed to prove fruitless." Caressing his valise, he said, "I do not believe that we have found this box for no reason. Nor do I believe for one moment that those zealous women of Masada were hiding below ground merely to escape death."

David scrutinized his friend's expression. "What are you getting at?" he asked.

"Well," Ken proceeded, "if the mass suicide was planned in advance, and the women's hiding place was selected in advance, and the women, who just happened to be fairly well-educated members of the leadership, had rehearsed their story to the nth degree, it has to be that they were up to something more than met the Romans' eyes."

Diamant started. "Oh, speaking of what met the Romans' eyes, the story also goes that the Zealots created a pyre of all their belongings before they killed themselves, so that the Romans would find no booty for their trouble."

Ken pursed his lips. "That fits," he said. "Sure, that fits! Listen, if you wanted to keep something from a thief, wouldn't it be clever to distract him with something else—say, the appearance of poverty? If the Romans were deceived into thinking that the Zealots had destroyed everything to spite them, I doubt they would have spent any time searching further."

Jacobs bolted upright, sitting as straight as a poker. "Oh, I understand!" he cried. "You are saying that the women had the most precious treasures with them . . ."

". . . in the underground caverns Josephus speaks of!" Diamant added.

As this concept sank in, the group tensed, of one mind as to the implications. "Why," Ben exclaimed, "all that remains is for us to locate those caverns!"

"Yes," Jacobs agreed. "That is what we must do! Why, they could be very close by," he said, studying the sunken bathhouse. "We could be sitting over them as we speak!"

McCurdy gave a nervous smile. "Gentlemen!" he interrupted. "Not so hasty! As I said, Masada has been read like a grid. Nothing like you describe has been found. The largest so-called cavern is the reservoir Herod dug out, to capture rainwater for his fancy spigots!"

"And the reservoir reveals nothing?" Ken inquired.

"Nothing," Father McCurdy said. "If there ever were treasures buried there, they were absconded with long ago!"

A mood of disappointment descended on the group. Diamant, looking deflated, suggested that perhaps they should take lodging down the mountain and return in the morning. Perhaps something useful would occur to them overnight.

"Is it too late to catch the regular tram?" Rabbi Levine asked.

"Probably not," Diamant replied, looking at his watch. "But, if so, we can always phone for one."

Haltingly, the group rose and began to file up the narrow stairs from the bathhouse. David followed Britta, Ken close behind him. When they reached the outside, they saw that the remaining tourists were hurrying to the exit port to catch the last tram of the day.

David stood for a moment at the head of the stairs, feeling the blessed coolness of the evening breeze. The heat of the day, which had still been scalding when they entered the bathhouse, had all but entirely dissipated.

As the rest of the group hastened to catch up with the tourists, not wanting to be left behind, the lanky professor was loath to go. Catching Britta by the arm, he drew her to him.

"Come on, Dave," she giggled. "We don't have time for romance!"

Ken, the eternal bachelor, passed by them, shaking his head. "Between you and the Westers," he grumbled, "I feel very old."

David clutched the little blonde to him. "We have kissed on a Jerusalem rooftop," he whispered. "Let's make it a habit to kiss in every exotic place on earth!"

With a smile, Britta sank into his arms, ready to oblige.

But he did not want to rush this experience. "Just look at this!" he marveled, sweeping one hand across the horizon. "Sunset on Masada! Have you ever seen anything more fabulous?"

Britta turned about and leaned her head back in the crook of his elbow, gazing upon the ancient fortress. The sun, sinking toward the west, cast a mauve-and-apricot hue over everything, and the ragged rocks of the tumbled ramparts looked almost like people silhouetted in prayer.

"It is glorious!" she sighed, lifting her face to his for that promised kiss.

But there it was again—that look he too often got. He was lost in study, she knew, his perceptive eyes having spotted something he could not let go.

Suddenly, he slackened his hold on her and even stepped back a pace or two.

Trying not to be offended, Britta gave him the benefit of the doubt. "What now, Dave?" she said in frustration. "Or should I ask?"

He did not reply immediately. He was looking at the western ramparts, where a stream of orange sunlight was just passing across a narrow aperture. For a long moment, the sun's rays were captured in that fissure, creating a fiery finger that thrust itself directly toward another crevice in the earth. David did not think to excuse himself but, leaving Britta standing alone in the middle of the mesa, ran to the site where the finger had touched down.

Throwing himself to his knees, he took out his pocketknife and scribed a large X where the light indicated.

Britta, seeing what he was up to, raced to his side. "Oh no, Dave," she said. "This is too simple. It can't be this simple!"

"Call Ken," he cried. "Get the others!"

Shaking her tousled curls, she put her hands on her hips. When he glared up at her, she gasped and took off running.

"Ken! Rabbis! Everyone!" she hollered. "David needs you!"

Rothmeyer stayed in his kneeling position until the sun had moved on, leaving the X in shadow. For a split second, he questioned himself. Britta was right. This was too easy.

Standing up, he shook his head. *Rothmeyer,* he thought, *must you be so determined to make a fool of yourself?*

As he stood there, staring down at the X, he wondered what he should say to his colleagues. Yes, here they came, ready to hear something marvelous, the older men shuffling as quickly as their legs could carry them, with Uriel, Ken, and Shalom in the lead.

"What's going on?" Aronstam cried.

"What have you found?" Diamant shouted.

As for the rabbis and McCurdy and Cromwell, they just wheezed and panted to a standstill, gathering about him and the ridiculous X at his feet.

He figured it was best to be honest. "Sorry, fellas," he apologized. "It's been a long day. It was nothing."

Rabbi Katz flashed angry eyes at him. "We've missed the tram now. Diamant will have to phone for one. It will be a good hour . . ."

"Oh, shush!" Rabbi Ben spat. "Let the man talk."

David shook his head. "No, really, Ben," he said. "I have nothing to say. It was silly of me. I should have listened to Britta."

The men turned to the young woman, awaiting an explanation. She shrugged nervously. "Well," she covered, "it was a good idea, but . . ."

"What happened, Britta?" Ken insisted.

"Oh, I guess I should speak for myself," David admitted. "You'd think I was at Stonehenge or something. I guess I'm just so anxious for an answer, I was about to take anything."

"Stonehenge?" Cromwell asked. "What does Stonehenge have to do with this?"

Britta intervened. "Let me speak as a Briton," she said. "Everyone knows the theories that say Stonehenge was like a big calendar, that the stones were arranged thus and so to give the years, months, days, and even the hours, as the sun cast shadows across the monoliths."

Ken chuckled. "Okay, I get it!" Putting his hand over his heart, he waxed poetic. "'And then the famous archaeologist saw a ray of light from the departing sun pass through the ancient rocks . . .'"

David cringed. “Touché!” he replied. “So we’ve had our little joke on Rothmeyer. Sorry, guys!”

They all had a good laugh and, a couple of them slapping the professor on the back, they headed toward the exit port. “Maybe it’s not too late to catch the tram, after all,” Diamant said hopefully, dragging David along.

But as they neared the station, they realized Ken was not with them. Raising his eyes to the west again, David shielded them against the lowering sun. In the middle of the mesa, Ken could be seen standing alone, his bald head shining red in the evening glow.

“Come on!” David hollered. “We’re not waiting for you!”

Britta caught David’s sleeve. “Not so fast, Dave,” she said. “Maybe he’s on to something.”

David sighed in disgust. “He’s just being a clown,” he said. “Mimicking me . . .”

“No, look!” she exclaimed. “He’s taken the Jeremiah Box out of his briefcase!”

David squinted in Ken’s direction. Indeed, he had the box in his hands and was holding it up to the departing light, turning this way and that.

“Okay, friends,” David called out to the others. “Better come back! Ken’s up to no good!”

“Really, Dr. Rothmeyer!” Rabbi Katz objected. “Enough is enough!”

Jacobs squared his shoulders and turned back, waving his companions to follow. “We didn’t bring Dr. Aronstam all the way from Columbus to ignore him!” he growled. “Let’s see what he has to say!”

Against their better judgment, the others followed suit, David and Britta going with them.

“What have you found now?” Jacobs asked, waddling up to Ken as quickly as his pudgy legs could move.

Ken stood on the graying landscape, holding the Jeremiah Box before him like a compass. “I had a thought. Crazy, probably, but I figured it was worth a try. If I didn’t do this, I’d always wonder.”

David could see that Ken was dead serious. Stepping toward him, he tried to make sense of his actions.

“See these notches on the edge of the lid?” Ken said.

“Sure,” David replied as the others gathered close.

“I think we all figured these were just mars, accidental nicks that happened to the box over the years,” Ken said.

“Yes,” Ben agreed. “That is what we thought.”

“Well,” Ken went on, “there are some of those, for sure, but look . . . look at these grooves, one on each side of the lid.”

He pointed to four distinct notches, spaced unevenly on each edge.

"Now," he said, holding the box squarely before him, "say we line up the groove on the west side with that fissure David was so in love with."

David cleared his throat and Ken winked at him.

"Of course, we will need an eastern coordinate to complete the alignment," he said. "Stand back a little. I am looking to see if there is another fissure in the ramparts that might be the complement."

The group muttered in amazement and began to scan the wall to the east. "There!" Britta cried. "Is that one?"

Ken and the others followed her pointing finger. "Sure looks like one!" David admitted.

"Great!" Ken exclaimed, spotting the site. Adjusting the angle of the box, he said, "I must move back a ways."

The group followed him, like football players huddled about their quarterback, as he moved backward down the field.

"There," he said. "Does that do it?"

He placed the box on the ground, again turning it just so, and the others agreed: the left and right notches seemed to be aligned with the distant fissures.

"That's nowhere near David's X," McCurdy objected.

"Maybe the sun has nothing to do with it," Cromwell guessed.

David shrugged. "Fine by me. What about the other notches?"

"Well," Ken explained, "if we're lined up east-west, the other notches would position us on a north-south reading."

At this the group began to scan the ramparts again. It was Diamant who first spotted a northern fissure. "There!" he cried. "Just over the top of Herod's Hanging Palace."

He referred to a phenomenal piece of architecture, which Herod had defied the laws of gravity to create—an incomparable house carved into the north face of Masada through sheer sandstone. Not even visible from on top, it could only be seen from the desert below, and was accessible only by hazardous stairs down the face of the cliff, most of which had fallen away over the centuries.

"Very good!" Ben cried. "I see it!"

And now Uriel Katz was waving his arms in uncharacteristic enthusiasm. "There!" he called out from some distance away. "There is an aperture to the south!"

"Wonderful!" Ken replied. Picking up the box, he moved several paces to the west. "Stand aside," he said to his companions. "I can't see."

At last he figured he had the northern and southern fissures aligned with the top and bottom notches on the lid. Taking a deep breath, he bent over and placed the Jeremiah Box on the ground.

A unison gasp went up from the huddled gathering. Uriel Katz, the youngest of the rabbis, came running and skid to a halt, kicking up yellow dust.

"What is it?" he cried.

To everyone's astonishment, the box rested directly on David's X.

Standing straight and puffing out his meager chest, David crossed his arms and looked smugly at his admiring colleagues. "I guess we'll need to get some shovels," he said with a laugh.

CHAPTER 31

The Consortium van pulled out of the large parking lot at the base of Masada about an hour after most other tourists had departed. A few lingering visitors, those who had not come here on tour buses, still pawed through the gift shops and used the latrine in the depot. They, too, would be leaving when the shopkeepers began to bring their wares in off the sidewalk.

Of course, the Consortium team could not simply begin digging atop the ancient Herodian site. As soon as David had made his joking comment, the group had decided it was best to rub out the X drawn on the ground, to descend the mountain as soon as Diamant could get a tram to return for them, and to be in Jerusalem before nightfall. Such was the influence of the rabbis, that a quick, early morning visit to the Israel Antiquities Authority should get them a special visa to have the mountain closed to tourists for a couple of days, and they would begin their excavation.

That was, if nothing interfered.

A dark-eyed youth stood over a bin of posters in the shop nearest the parking lot. He pretended to be arranging the long rolled-up pictures more neatly in their cardboard barrel, but his attention had actually been fixed on the rabbis and their colleagues since they had returned from the mountain in their specially scheduled tram.

As they drove away in their van, the young clerk turned to his boss and, without a word, gave him a nod. At this, the shopkeeper picked up the handset of the phone on his counter and quickly keyed in a number in Jerusalem.

"Ramal, here," he said in a subdued voice, a Lebanese tinge to his international English. "They have now departed. Yes . . . yes . . . I am certain. Yes, Mr. Hamir, I am confident that these are the people who intercepted our plans last year. Yes . . . I am aware of that, sir . . . the mountain falls under Israeli authority . . . but . . . sir . . . you yourself have said it is a contested site. . . . That is right, sir." At this he listened a moment, then laughed, a little too loudly for his assistant's comfort.

The youngster grabbed a broom and distracted a group of tourists by brushing past them, asking them to please move aside. He came near the counter and gave his boss a warning look, rolling his eyes in the direction of the customers.

The proprietor turned his back and cupped his hand over the mouthpiece, placing his lips close to the speaker. "That is right . . ." The clerk heard him chuckle. "Qumran is also under Israeli control! But we are effectively disputing that! Yes . . . very well . . . they will probably be going to the Israel Antiquities Authority in the morning. They appear to be quite eager. Right, sir. . . . You are very welcome. . . . What's that, sir? No, I have no idea what they are after. . . . You are welcome, sir. No problem!"

The shopkeeper put the handset back in the cradle and turned to help a couple of patrons. As he placed their money in the till and wrapped their purchases, he caught the clerk's eye. With a nod barely perceptible to the customers, he winked at his assistant.

"Bring in the silk scarves from the rack and sweep the sidewalk, won't you?" he instructed him.

The boy flashed a smile and saluted. The boss was glad the customers did not see his enthusiastic gesture.

Later that night, on the other side of the Jordan River, Laad Girzim paced the balcony of his sumptuous apartment in sleepless agitation. He had just returned to Amman from his visit to Petra, and he could not put to rest the revelations that the old seer, Fatima, and his grandmother had bestowed upon him.

Leaving his residence, which was in one wing of the royal palace, he descended a short set of stairs to the king's gardens, which lay in the enormous central courtyard shared by the royal family and all the palace staff. He thought of how many years he had been privileged to live in this fabulous place, yet how rarely he had ever entered the garden at night.

"That is because you used to sleep at night!" he chastised himself. "Now you are a creature of the dark!"

It was true that his life and his work used to be very pleasant, orderly, predictable. He worked with history, artifacts, scholars—things that did not change and did not threaten. While there were mystery and challenge to his duties, they had never before been a source of trouble.

Not until that American evangelist came to Jordan! The one who had played with the king's heart and mind. The visit of the longhaired preacher had changed everything. Everything!

Laad had no idea just what the preacher had said to the king to make him behave so strangely. He knew that the king had always been the kindliest of Arab sovereigns to his neighbors, particularly to Israel. But he had never had a special open-door policy to Christian leaders. Why he had allowed the evangelist to actually conduct a crusade in Amman was a mystery to all Jordanians. In an unheard-of gesture of tolerance, the king had permitted the preacher a full week in Amman University's public arena. The gathering place, the largest in Jordan, had been packed by thousands, mostly of Muslim background, who had gone to hear the strange American. While most of the audience was there out of curiosity, even, in many cases, outright contempt and mockery, the evangelist's visit had taken its toll.

Laad had gone to hear him once. He had been captivated by the man's charismatic, flamboyant style, by the music of a fifty-piece orchestra, the singing of a very large woman in flowing scarves and blonde, bouffant hair. But the evangelist's words had been the most astonishing part of the program.

Laad remembered very little of the preacher's exact message. Whenever he would quote from the Hebrew or Christian Scriptures, Laad's mind had closed reflexively. But he did remember something that hit home—directly home. The evangelist had said that some Bible interpreters believe the ancient prophets of Israel predicted that Jordan would befriend the Jews, that Jordan would even hide them in time of trouble. The description of the hiding place sounded like Laad's boyhood surroundings, perhaps the red-rock caverns of Petra!

Much more than this, he did not remember. And even this he had chosen to discount as clever talk, the sort of trickery that could mesmerize the masses and bend them to the speaker's will.

Laad had tried to put the evangelist's visit out of his mind after the man returned to the United States. But, apparently, the king had not been able to do so. In fact, Laad counted the peculiar change in the king to be directly related to the preacher's visit, to the hours the two had sequestered themselves in the king's private quarters. Laad remembered passing down the hall of the palace's east wing, one day during the man's visit, and seeing the two of them emerging from a private council chamber. Several of the preacher's staff were with them, and they were huddled about the king like old comrades.

Laad swallowed hard, even now, as he remembered seeing tears on their faces, the king's hands uplifted, as he nodded and agreed to something they were saying.

"Lord God Allah!" Laad muttered to himself. Shaking his head, he tried to cast the memory from him, though he knew it would never be expunged.

Then the king had taken ill. Or perhaps he had been ill for a long while and the world did not know. Perhaps, Laad pondered, perhaps he had actually summoned the preacher to his side because he was ill.

Whatever the case might be, Laad knew that things had begun to change in the palace from the moment the preacher arrived. Evening prayers included more frequent references to the prophets Moses and Jesus than were traditionally spoken. The king seemed kindlier than ever to the women in his charge, though he had always been a gentleman. And, to the dismay of the Arab world, he publicly embraced the leadership of Israel as brothers!

One might have thought the foolishness would stop after the king died. When his son took the throne, tenderness toward the enemy should have ceased. But, to this point, there was no great change in the government's approach to things.

During the transition from father to son, the queen had called for Laad. She had told of the king's urgent request that the mysterious box be found and that the artifact be transferred to "certain rabbis" in the United States.

The rest, as they say, was history . . . Laad's personal history.

A warm blush of moonlight spilled over the platter-sized poppies in the king's garden. The night was temperate, the aromas of the garden sweet and soothing. But Laad's mind was so full of tumbling confusion, he could enjoy nothing.

In one hand, he gripped a copy of the photo that the queen had sent with him to Jerusalem. Again and again he studied it, as though for the first time. There was nothing in it he had not seen before. But his perception of it now was different from when he had delivered it to the eerie Israeli gallery.

He knew now that the box was very ancient, going back at least twenty-five centuries, and that it had once contained something very precious to the Jews.

He knew this because his grandmother had told him.

For the hundredth time, his shoulders tensed at the memory of her revelation. Stopping dead in his meandering tracks, he clenched the paper in his fist, wishing he could wad it into a meaningless ball and cast it from him forever.

As he stood there, in haunting rumination, the sound of soft footsteps and the sweep of leaves caused him to wheel about.

"Who goes there?" he croaked.

"Is that you, Mr. Girzim?" a woman's voice called out.

Stunned, Laad stammered, "Y-your Majesty!" Bowing in the traditional manner, straight from the waist, lowering his head and keeping his heels together, he touched his forehead, his chest, and then his knees with the fingertips of his right hand. This done, he continued to keep his head bowed and his eyes downcast as she placed her hand on his shoulder.

Slowly he stood up, still cautious to avert his gaze, as he awaited her instructions.

"It is a lovely night, Mr. Girzim," she said. The tone called for a response, and Laad readily agreed. "It is, Your Majesty," he said, standing stiffly and looking at the ground.

He knew she was not alone. He could hear the rustling of chaperones between the overhanging plants that bordered the walk behind her. Only one other time, when he had been summoned to her stateroom, where he received orders to find the box, had he ever spoken with her one on one. Even that day, her guards had stood outside the half-open door, and a couple of female attendants had kept watch from behind a grillwork screen.

"How was your visit to Petra?" she asked kindly.

Laad barely let his eyes catch a glimpse of her. Though she was middle-aged, she was truly one of the loveliest women imaginable, he thought! Her coloring, blonde and blue-eyed, was unusual in Jordan, and her speech had never lost its American accent. The story of her romance with the king and the eventual marriage would have made a wonderful novel, he thought, and he sometimes wondered how she fared in this alien land, now that she was a widow. For wealth and accommodations, she lacked nothing, he knew, but she must have often missed her own people and the ways she grew up with. He noted, for instance, that though she often wore the long gowns typical of Jordanian matrons, her chest and arms laden with lovely chains and jewels, she never wore a veil like those that concealed the faces of more conservative women.

Yet she never let on that she missed America. Her courtly demeanor and gracious cheerfulness, and her ability to recall small, personal details about commoners like Laad would have made her seem at home anyplace in the world.

"I thank you for asking, my queen," he said. "I enjoyed my visit very much."

Perhaps his voice betrayed his weary ponderings. The queen glimpsed the paper he had crumpled in his left hand as he hastily saluted her entrance. She seemed to recognize a corner of the photo and looked at it in curiosity.

"Ah," she sighed, "I see that you have been obsessing over the same things I have. Strange, isn't it, how that old box haunts the soul?"

Laad was astonished at her perceptiveness. "My queen," he said, bowing his head again, "I did not mean to trouble you with this." He tried to fold the paper so he could stick it in a pocket, but his hands shook.

The queen shrugged. "I did not need to ask. The entire Arab world considers the Jews to be their foremost enemies, do they not?"

Laad nodded. "And so," he reflected, "you believe that the king's heart was turned toward Israel in those last days?"

"He had always been generous to them," she said. "But yes, absolutely! It was about the time that the evangelist came that he publicly declared himself their friend!" Then suddenly she looked as though a light filled her head. "Why, yes! How could I have overlooked this!"

"Your Majesty?" Laad puzzled.

"I recall that the evangelist told my husband he would go down in history as a great deliverer! He would become known, the preacher predicted, as the 'second Cyrus'!"

Laad was amazed. "The Persian king who freed the Jews and returned them to their homeland!"

"Yes," the queen affirmed. "Over twenty-five hundred years ago!"

Laad looked away, lost in contemplation.

"This registers deeply within you, Mr. Girzim. I can see that," the queen observed.

Laad was awestruck. "Your words are very much like those spoken by my grandmother and her friend, an old woman of Petra," he said.

The queen looked at him respectfully. "Are you free to share what your grandmother said?" she asked.

Laad thought a moment. "Some of it, my queen," he replied.

A twitch of a smile worked at a corner of the queen's mouth. "Very well, I will settle for 'some of it,'" she conceded.

"Most of my people are illiterate," he said. "But that does not mean they are ignorant. As you may know, societies that do not rely on the written word develop quite a facility for oral history and tradition."

"I am aware of this," the queen acknowledged.

"The keeping of the histories often falls to the matriarchs in such cultures," he went on. "Such is the case among my people."

Seeing that the queen was eager to hear more, he took courage. "Your words about Cyrus remind me of what the old woman recounted to me, of the history of Petra, and Jordan as a whole. Apparently we have a long tradition of being somewhat less hostile to the Hebrew people than other nations have been. When we were known as the lands of Moab and Edom, we did not war against the Children of Israel as they entered Canaan."

"What they now call Israel, and we call Palestine," the queen noted.

"Right," Laad said. "And for three hundred years, we were at 'peace' with them."

The queen smiled shyly. "I remember my Sunday School lessons," she said. "But it is good to have them brought back to me."

Laad laughed. "Very well," he said. "Then you remember that the prophet Moses watched Joshua and the Children of Israel enter Canaan from the height of Mount Nebo."

"I do," she said. "I have also seen the fountain near Petra that gushes out of solid rock. The place is called Wadi Musa, the Valley of Moses, where he supposedly struck the rock and brought forth water for his people."

"Yes," Laad said. "I visited it many times as a youth."

"I am with you," she said. "Go on."

"Well," he proceeded, "according to my grandmother and the other old woman, our valley of Petra has often been a hideout for Hebrew refugees. Supposedly, the prophet Jeremiah hid there toward the end of his life, when the Babylonians were on the march."

The queen's eyes grew large. "Jeremiah?" she gasped. "The one for whom the box is named?"

"Who else?" he exclaimed. Then he grew very somber and she wondered if he would speak again. At last, taking a deep breath, he continued. "Now, my queen, here is the strangest thing of all. According to my grandmother, our people also hid a handful of survivors from Masada, after the Romans took the mountain. My grandmother and her friend showed me a cave where they were hidden."

The queen leaned close as they walked slowly down the path, as though leaning on his very words.

"That cave is known among my people as the Cave of Jeremiah," he said.

Halting, the queen raised a hand to her throat.

"Now . . . can you imagine what they showed me on the wall of that cave?" Laad asked.

"Some sort of pictographs?" she guessed.

"Two, to be exact." Holding the paper up to the moonlight, he pointed to the heifer in the photo and then to the likeness of Masada at its foot.

"Truly?" she exclaimed. "The same images?"

"The same!" he replied.

Her brow knit, she asked, "What do you make of this?"

Laad shrugged. "A message, to the effect that whatever was once inside that box, apparently a vial, brought there by the prophet, was taken back to Masada. This is a legend of my people."

The queen interpreted, "Whatever the prophet Jeremiah had brought to the cave had been returned to the refugees of Masada," she concluded. "And they, in turn, took it back with them to Masada after the Romans left."

"Exactly!" Laad said. "After they entrusted the box to the Petrans for safe-keeping!"

When the queen looked perplexed, he explained, "It is my hunch that the box bears a record of the vial's whereabouts."

The queen shook her head and drew a light scarf about her shoulders. "Are you certain we are not making too much of this . . . perhaps letting our imaginations run wild?"

Laad looked at her sadly. If only she knew the fuller story, the prophecy Fatima had given. But he dare not share that—not now. If it were true, she would know . . . the whole world would know soon enough.

"There seems to be no other explanation," he said. "Besides, what could be wilder than to believe a box has such power that it could give our enemies command over us? My grandmother told me that the sheiks took the box for themselves, to control its power. Generations of our leaders have tried to keep that box out of Israel's hands?" Swallowing hard, he added, "And now a leader of your own people, an American statesman, has been murdered for that box!"

The queen was horrified. "Mr. Girzim, what do you think the vial contained? What was taken to Masada that was so threatening to our people for all those years?"

The curator was baffled. "I have no idea," he said. "This is what keeps me awake at night."

The two walked a few more steps, the weight of the mystery crushing in upon them. At last the queen said a hard thing. "You realize, of course, what my husband would have you do with this information."

Laad did not want to consider this. "I guess I do," he said. Turning to her, he looked straight into her eyes for the first time.

"He would have you help them," she said. "He would have you do whatever must be done to help Israel fulfill its destiny."

CHAPTER 32

If the queen and Laad Girzim had hoped their commiserating in the garden might ease their minds, it did nothing of the sort. After the queen had made her statement regarding her late husband's wishes, Laad and she had bid good night, each returning to their rooms to wile away the rest of the night hours in hopeless ponderings.

Laad had barely attained a measure of sleep when his alarm clock told him his workday had begun. After hastily showering, shaving, and dressing, he made his way to his office in a nearby building. His secretary, a pleasant older man who had once been a valet to visiting ambassadors, had coffee ready for him—the thick, bitter coffee so beloved by Jordanians. Upon bringing it to Laad's desk in a small pot, the secretary poured a steaming portion into a minuscule cup and placed a tablespoon of cream in it, just as his boss liked.

Laad did little more than nod to the man, not out of discourtesy, but out of weariness. "What's on the agenda today?" he asked.

Teasing, the secretary replied, "A meeting with the museum cleaning crew. They're going to begin repainting the walls, and they need your advice on colors."

Horrified, Laad bristled. "Spare me! I have been out of town. I have a mountain of paperwork here!"

"I knew that," the secretary said with a twinkle in his eye. "I was only joking. I made sure you'd have no appointments today."

Laad sighed. "Thank you, Buscar."

The paperwork took two hours, between phone calls and other demands. It was ten o'clock before Laad got to the overnight e-mails.

"I have already read the professional updates," the secretary said, sticking his head in the door. "Nothing very earthshaking."

"Good, Buscar," Laad sighed. "I need the earth to be very stable today."

The secretary backed toward the door, bowing his tall, lean body deferentially. "If you need me for anything . . ."

"Yes, yes, Buscar," Laad said, with a wave of his hand.

As the computer monitor hummed to life, Laad clicked on the browser and then on the little envelope that brought up the e-mail screen. Ding, ding, ding . . . one after another, the titles of seventeen e-mails announced themselves in a long column. Laad did as he always did, the electronic version of sorting and tossing mail. He could tell the spam messages from the legitimate ones quicker than he could read them and instantly relegated them to the delete bin.

Most of the other messages could be forwarded to the secretary's computer for further sorting, filing, and tossing. As usual, only a couple merited his personal attention.

One he had been waiting for, a letter from his staff in the field, was read with zest. Yes! The geologists had finally arrived to analyze the strange, golf-ball-shaped rocks that littered the desert south of the Dead Sea. The notorious cities of Sodom and Gomorrah had once existed there, legend had it. For years, scientists had tried to determine what had caused the unique rubble of heat-baked rock that spread as far as the eye could see. Not exactly lava, yet charred on the outside and local white on the inside, the rounded rock fragments were unlike anything found anywhere else on the planet. Under Girzim's administration, headway had been made in funding further study, and he had recently dispatched a team of students from the university in Amman to begin work there.

Pleased that something was going right, Laad whipped off a quick, congratulatory reply to his fieldworkers, scrolled through a couple of other items, and then came to the listings of current regional digs, posted weekly by the Mideast Archaeology Cooperative.

The expedition to the Sodom region was now posted as ongoing, having first appeared on last week's roster. The work of Israeli archaeologists at Dan, north of Galilee, was winding down. Ever since the celebrated find of the stele on which the name of King David appeared, the only item ever found with his family name, and the only item ever verifying the Bible story of that most famous of Hebrew kings, that dig had been written up in almost every scholarly journal. Of course, there was always something flaring up around Mount Moriah in Jerusalem. For several years, the Jews had been digging around in the Byzantine layers at the base of the mount. More than once, their efforts had nearly sparked full-scale war in the Old City. Laad hardly gave such matters in that area more than a cursory reading, since they were so commonplace.

But, here, now . . . what was this? Blinking his eyes, he reread the heading of the most recently listed item, something even Buscar had not seen: "IAA Denies Consortium Application at Masada." The dateline was Jerusalem and the story had just been posted!

Laad knew that the Consortium was the agency in charge of the place where he had delivered the photo for the queen. A chill ran up his spine as he read the headline again, and then digested the brief bulletin, which linked the mysterious Jewish group with a proposed dig at Masada:

> Jewish rabbis made application to the Israel Antiquities Authority early this morning to begin excavation atop the ancient site of the Herodian fortress at Masada. Purpose of their proposed dig was stated as "preliminary survey of suspected depository of Jewish artifacts; layer date 70 C.E. +/–."
>
> In an unprecedented move on the part of the IAA, application was denied, due to objection from the Palestinian Antiquities Authority, Jerusalem. "This denial is unlawful," said Mr. Shalom Diamant of the Temple Consortium Gallery, Rebi Josef Street, Old City, Jerusalem. "There is no basis for such denial, as Masada and environs fall under the authority of Israel and have always been available for study to Jewish scholars."
>
> The Consortium intends to appeal to Chief Rabbi Mikel Horowitz to overrule the denial. When this publication asked the IAA why they had rejected the application, they stated that politically sensitive objections from the PAA needed to be addressed. PAA director Amal Hamir was unavailable for comment, but his aide stated, "Studies at Masada do, by their very nature, overlap with studies at Qumran and En-Gedi. The PAA is currently disputing the IAA's claim of rights to all work at Qumran and En-Gedi and hence to any studies to be done at Masada."
>
> According to Diamant, "Masada has always been under Israeli control. Nothing short of a redrawing of international boundary lines in the West Bank can change that."
>
> The IAA was unavailable for comment on this point.

Laad took his glasses off and rubbed his eyes. Exasperated, he felt that he was being funneled against his will into an unholy alliance.

"They know," he groaned under his breath. "The Jews have figured it out."

His mind chased this thought with one he dare not speak aloud: *And they need my help!*

All his instincts, his training from childhood, the nature of the blood that flowed in his veins, recoiled at the idea. He was an Arab. By profession he was just a historian, a simple curator of old things. He had never meant to get involved in international politics. But he could not deny the facts of timing and of insight that had placed him in this position. Something higher and bigger than he seemed determined to drive him into the embrace of his enemies!

His hands were cold and clammy as he fumbled through his desk drawer for a stale pack of cigarettes, a habit he had forsaken months ago. Finding it, he tapped the side of the carton until a slender white cylinder toppled into his left hand. He did not light the cigarette but let it hang between his lips like a pacifier.

He could have stood up and walked to his secretary's door, but his knees felt weak. Instead, he reached for his desk phone and dialed him. They could hear each other through the wall, as well as over the phones, as they spoke. "Buscar," Laad said.

"Yes, sir," the secretary replied. "May I help you?"

"Call me a taxi. I am going to Jerusalem."

Perhaps Laad should have paid more heed to the shifting arenas of conflict in Israel and the West Bank. If he had been aware of what had transpired during the night when he was walking with the queen in the garden, he might not have so quickly decided to make a trip to Jerusalem.

As it was, he had missed the news story of the missile that had been shot from the Golan Heights into the Galilee region, just north of Tiberias, at about three o'clock in the morning. This sort of incident was all too familiar to those living in the Middle East. The seesaw of contention that rarely let up for more than a few days at a time was a bewildering mishmash of seemingly haphazard behavior to the international community, but it could make life extremely unpredictable to those living in the region.

When he had made his last trip to Jerusalem, Laad had been obliged to stay at the Allenby/King Hussein checkpoint overnight. The tension at that time revolved around the assassination of Senator Jefferson, whose return from Jordan had made his death a matter of international focus on the Middle East, and on Jordan in particular. Because Laad was a member of the royal household, and for fear that his movements might be traced to the Israeli agency her husband was attempting to help, the queen had forbade him to identify himself to anyone.

This time Laad had brought his ID papers with him, his credentials as a member of the palace staff. He was carrying no secret material, as he had last time, and it was not out of order for him to come and go from neighboring countries.

Still, last night's incident had so enraged the sensibilities of Palestinians and Israelis that passage through the area was highly monitored.

While the route from Amman to Jerusalem was reasonably direct, crossing the Jordan River at Allenby/King Hussein Bridge and proceeding up a winding mountain course, the boundaries declared by international law to be no man's land, Palestinian territory and reserved Israeli settlement areas wove back and forth across that route in a confusing patchwork. Laad's taxi was obliged to stop at checkpoints, slowing the trip with stops and starts.

Fortunately, Laad's credentials gave him quicker entrée than other travelers received, and he arrived in the tension-filled Holy City by four o'clock in the afternoon.

"Drive straight to the Damascus Gate," he told the cabby.

Fifteen minutes of walking down the narrow Via Dolorosa in the Arab Quarter brought him to the scalloped, Islamic-style entrance of the Palestinian Antiquities Authority. Showing his identification papers to the man at the front desk, he asked to see Mr. Hamir. "It is urgent," he said. "I am here under the authority of the queen of Jordan."

The receptionist stepped into an adjoining office and in a few seconds another man emerged with him, looking as tired as Laad himself felt.

He must have had a rough night too, Laad thought. *Perhaps there is a virus circulating among our profession*.

Amal Hamir, Ph.D. in Archaeology and Middle Eastern Studies, was a familiar character in Laad's circle of associates. The two of them had run into each other many times at conventions, seminars, and even field digs, where their interests coincided.

When Amal saw the Jordanian waiting in his lobby, he was astonished. "Girzim!" he exclaimed. "This is a pleasant surprise!"

Giving one another the traditional Muslim embrace, they planted light kisses on each other's cheeks, left and right.

"What brings you to Jerusalem?" Amal asked.

Laad smiled, hiding his anxieties nicely. "I would say I happened to be in the area, but you know how unlikely that would be," Laad joked. "Under normal circumstances, of course, I would have called ahead."

Amal nodded to the receptionist to hold his calls and, placing a friendly hand on Laad's back, directed him into his private office.

Taking a seat behind the desk and gesturing to Laad to be seated across from him, he said, "And these are not normal circumstances?"

Laad drew a solid breath. "No, Hamir," he said. "They are not."

The older man, whose swarthy face was blotched with dark freckles from years on desert digs, and whose hair was thinning over a shining head, peered over the rims of his reading glasses, which he wore at all times on the tip of his nose. "Very well, Laad," he said familiarly. "What may I do to help you?"

Laad placed his valise on his lap and looked straight at Amal. "I read the morning communication from the Cooperative," he began.

Amal shrugged. "Yes?"

"I am here to ask you to reconsider your objection to the Jewish proposal for work at Masada."

His eyes widening, Hamir leaned back in his chair. "And just why should I do that?" he asked. "I saw this as a marvelous opportunity to begin staking our claim in that area. I feel that my reasoning was sound."

Laad nodded. "Of course, Amal," he said, following suit by using the familiar name, "I agree. Your step is well considered, and, I might add, quite clever. The PAA's dispute regarding work at Qumran and En-Gedi would doubtless overlap with anything done at Masada. I have no quarrel with that."

Amal leaned forward again, elbows on the desk. "What then?"

Laad cleared his throat. He had rehearsed this part of the conversation all the way to Israel. He must get it right.

"In order for you to understand my request, I need to share something with you which I do not want repeated in some upcoming dispatch from the Cooperative." He looked steadily at Amal. "Do you understand?"

The official shrugged again, lifting his hands. "My lips are sealed," he said.

Laad nodded. "Without going into specifics, I must tell you that some recent and rather esoteric research in my country has led to some intriguing finds, from the same period which the Jewish agency wishes to study." He lifted a finger to drive home a point. "Now, I am not saying that the two investigations necessarily overlap. There may be no correlation whatever. But there is enough reason to speculate that I would like very much to see what the Jews are up to."

Amal was quizzical. "Let me understand," he said. "Are you saying that the study of Jordanian history might somehow be advanced by a look at Masada?"

Laad nodded firmly. "I am," he said.

Hamir was bewildered. "So why don't you just apply yourself for access to the mountain? Why rely on the Jews?"

Laad had anticipated this question. "First," he said, "my speculations are only hunches at this point. Second, strange as it might sound, we would not know where to begin, or even what to look for. The Jews are on to something, which may or may not relate to our studies. But it must be granted, they are ahead of us in all research regarding Masada."

Amal chuckled dubiously. "Girzim!" he laughed. "This is a most unscientific approach to things!"

Laad laughed with him, then said, "Now, now, Amal. You and I may be honest with one another. Just how much of our profession is based on science, and how much on dumb luck?"

Amal rolled his eyes, chuckling again. Then he sat back once more, studying Laad for an uncomfortable moment, his fingers intertwined and his forefingers tapping his lower lip.

Jordan and the Palestinians had a strange relationship. While the Jordanians had always been supportive of the Palestinian demand for a homeland, they also maintained diplomatic relations with Israel and with her strongest ally, the United States. Therefore, while the Palestinians felt a kinship with Jordan, going back over centuries of bloodlines and political alliance, there was an uneasiness between them, a blend of trust and suspicion.

At last, Amal spoke. "Very well, my friend," he conceded. "I shall retract my objection to the Jews' application . . . under certain conditions."

Laad was pleased with this response, but dubious of the implications. "What conditions?" he asked.

"I make the retraction, only if you, personally, are permitted to oversee their work."

Laad started. This was beyond anything he had hoped for.

But Amal quickly tempered the offer. "*And*, provided you agree to report all findings directly to me."

Laad shifted tensely. "Of course, my report will be available for the entire scholarly community," he hedged, "just as the Jews' would be."

Amal read his uneasiness. "No, no, my friend," he reiterated. "I mean, you shall report to me *before* you report to anyone else."

Laad reasoned with himself. How bad could this be? If he was "overseeing" the dig, he could pick and choose just *what* to report. If he happened to overlook something, well, who would be the wiser?

With a nod, he complied. "Certainly, Mr. Hamir. I have no quarrel with that. If the Jews are willing to accept my mediation, I am pleased to help."

Hamir did not like his quick acceptance of these requirements. Still, playing along, he reached for his telephone and rang the receptionist in the front room. "Ali, get ahold of the IAA. Tell them I am withdrawing my objection to the Masada application, on condition that our Jordanian colleague is permitted to be present all the way along."

Hanging up the phone, he turned a gimlet eye on his guest. "I hope you find all you are seeking," he said. Then, feigning munificence, he added, "I will be sure to be on hand when your work nears completion."

Laad did not care for the sound of that. Pretending gratitude, he begged off. "You are too kind, Amal. That is not necessary. I will see that you get my report . . ."

But Amal was not to be derailed. "I *will* be on hand," he said. "I would not want the enemy to take the credit for your work. The world must see that the Palestinians and Jordanians support one another."

CHAPTER 33

As Laad was paying his visit to the PAA, the atmosphere was glum at the Consortium house on the wall of the Old City. What had begun as a day of high hopes and anticipation had quickly turned sour at the unexpected denial of the team's application.

Arising early, eager to head for the IAA, the rabbis, David, Ken, and the British contingent had eaten a hasty breakfast on the balcony overlooking the Hinnom Valley. Full of chatter about their good fortune the night before, they were all certain some unseen hand was guiding their endeavors. With energetic feet, they had walked the few blocks to the gallery, picked up Shalom Diamant, and then made it to the IAA offices on King David Street shortly after the agency opened.

Only moments later they had left the Antiquities Authority in stunned disappointment.

It seemed someone from the PAA had called the IAA before they got there, demanding that any work on Masada be denied until Palestinian interests could be addressed.

Who on earth could have notified the PAA of their visit to the desert mountain, they could not imagine. Even if someone at Masada recognized them as Consortium scholars, why would they have wanted to interfere with their studies? Worst of all, why would the IAA deny their rightful access on the basis of a Palestinian whim?

Of course, the team's reaction to the denial was one of anger. Uriel Katz had barked the loudest, but David, Ken, and

Father McCurdy had had their say in no uncertain terms. Still, no matter how they had argued, implored, even threatened to go above the IAA's heads, the denial stood.

Leaving the agency, the old rabbis and their colleagues had walked back down King David Hill, their staccato steps fueled by disgust and embarrassment. Even Rabbi Ben, usually the most even-tempered of the lot, was red-faced with disappointment.

Britta, shocked at the sudden turn of events, had hung close to David, her blonde head downcast as she kicked at the occasional pebble on the sidewalk. "I can scarcely believe it!" she said in her British way. "Surely this can't be happening."

"Oh, but it is!" Rabbi Katz spat. "But then, should we really be surprised? Our efforts at the Consortium are a joke among our own people, to say nothing of a threat to our enemies!"

For once, Rabbi Ben agreed with his colleague. "I am afraid you are right," he said. "Perhaps if we had sent David and Ken, as American archaeologists, and if we had stayed behind the scenes, we would have gotten our license."

David and Ken had looked at each other sideways, feeling very helpless.

The rest of the morning was spent in depressing ambivalence. After Diamant had gone his way, back to the gallery, threatening to report this injustice to the Mideast Archaeology Cooperative, David and Ken sat on the balcony wondering if they should make plans to return to the States; McCurdy and Cromwell stayed cloistered in the parlor, huddled over a slow-moving game of chess. The rabbis sulked and paced, and paced some more, alternately thinking they should go to the chief rabbi, they should quit altogether, even that they should sneak back up to the mountain incognito and begin their dig!

"Now, that's the silliest thing you've ever come up with!" Katz growled at Carl Jacobs. "Besides, the last time we went anywhere 'incognito,' you had me in cowboy boots and a ten-gallon hat! Nothing doing! I'll have none of it!"

At last, as the day waned with no meaningful action, Britta, who had spent the afternoon working a crossword puzzle under a corner lamp, stood up and quietly slipped past the grumpy men. She had heard Zachary and Mel enter the house a while ago. Having arisen after the group left for the IAA, they had spent the day at the yeshiva and were now probably in the exercise room working out before supper. Britta wanted to find her cousin and fill him in on what had happened. *After all*, she thought, *this impacts him more than all of us!*

Britta had seen little of Zachary since he had arrived in Jerusalem from New York. What time they had had to interact had been when the group went to the airport to pick him up. For a year, she had lived with the knowledge that her own flesh-and-blood kin was in line for the highest appointment in Israel. Due to the security around him, however, they had never been able to really communicate. During the trip from the Tel Aviv airport, they had shared the car with the rabbis and Mel Wester, and ever since, she had been busy helping David with his research. Now she would let nothing interfere with getting his attention.

Hurrying down the hall, she went to the basement stairs, then hastened to the exercise room that the rabbis had installed specially for their young candidate. Since Zachary's activities were even more restricted in Jerusalem than they had been at the New York estate, the rabbis had planned well in advance for his arrival, taking into consideration all of his needs. Most of his physical activity was limited to the weightlifting and aerobics he could engage in here.

Britta could hear Zachary and Mel Wester joking and laughing as they worked out together. *What a contrast to the gloomy old men upstairs!* she thought.

Sticking her head in the little gym, she caught Mel's eye.

"Hi!" he called to her. "Supper on?"

Men! Britta thought. *The sight of a woman always makes them think of either food or . . .*

She suddenly remembered that David had never given her the promised kiss on top of Masada. She would have to call in that debt one of these evenings.

"No," she said. "Supper's not my department. You'll have to talk to Anya. But"—she sniffed—"come to think of it, something was smelling awfully good up there."

Zachary, sweaty and prone on the weight bench, placed his 200-pound barbells in the iron cradle above his head and pulled himself to a sitting position. "What's up, cuz?" he greeted her.

Britta became very serious. "Dry yourselves off, boys," she said. "The rabbis need you."

Bewildered, the two men grabbed towels off the exercise bike and followed Britta upstairs. The moment they entered the hallway, they met up with David and Ken, just coming down from the roof.

"What's happening?" David asked.

"Don't know," Mel answered with a shrug as they wandered into the parlor.

Uriel Katz was still arguing with Carl Jacobs, looking angrily at the floor as though he would like to kick something. Zachary stepped past him and stood in the middle of the room. "How's it going?" he asked, observing all the disgruntled faces.

"We've reached a rock wall!" Rabbi Katz said with a glower. "We have no way to turn!"

Zachary whipped the towel off his shoulder and wiped a sheen of sweat from his forehead. Mel, waylaying a chill, untied a sweatshirt about his waist, pulled it on over his head, and sat down on the arm of the sofa.

"Nothing can be that bad," Zachary said.

"Ask them!" Katz barked, pointing to his colleagues.

In a jumble of quick talk, everyone constructed a version of what had transpired that morning. When it had all been reported, Zachary sat down on the footstool by the ever-burning fireplace. "Well," he replied thoughtfully, "I sure expected your application to go through without a hitch. Sorry, fellas."

The rabbis nodded, Rabbi Ben shaking his snowy head sadly.

"Maybe because I wasn't there, it's easy for me to offer the most obvious solution," Zachary stated.

Rabbi Ben was dubious. "Solution?" he said. Then brightening, he turned to the others. "Ah, the boy thinks as I do! We should go to the chief rabbi!"

Jacobs shrugged and Levine bristled. "What could it hurt, Menachem?" Jacobs muttered. "It is worth a try."

Zachary chuckled and held up a hand. "Not so fast, Rabbis," he said. "I wasn't thinking any such thing." Then he paused and reconsidered. "Well, maybe, in a way, I was . . . I was thinking we should pray."

The old men looked at him quizzically. Rabbi Ben tried to interpret. "Prayer is a very good suggestion. We should all have thought of that," he said. "But what do you mean about the chief rabbi?"

Zachary smiled. "That is what we call *Mesheach Yeshua* in our synagogue," he replied. "Messiah Jesus is our Chief Rabbi!"

Suddenly, the crowded room sizzled with a variety of responses. Jacobs and Levine were ruffled by the suggestion; Katz was, of course, offended; Rabbi Ben looked sorry that he had needed that explanation; McCurdy and Cromwell perked up; Britta and the Americans were ready to try anything.

As for Zachary Cohen, he had studied under the rabbis for a year. For the first time, he was being given an opportunity to teach them something.

"Father God!" he suddenly spoke aloud, his face uplifted and his eyes closed.

Everyone reacted with a start. Some stared at Zachary mutely, others lowered their heads in reverence, in bewilderment, in desperation. No one, regardless of his or her personal persuasion, would be so disrespectful as to interrupt him.

"Father God," he repeated, "Father of us all, you have been our guide since birth, our ever-present help in time of trouble! You have brought all of us to this, your Holy City, where the prophets ministered and were martyred, where Abraham offered Isaac, where your dear Son, Yeshua, was crucified. We, O Father, do not pretend to know all your plans, but we know your guidance has ever overshadowed your people, Israel! Your plans will go forward. Nothing will stop them. You brought us across the Red Sea; you defeated our enemies in war and brought us into this place as our eternal homeland. You will plant your Temple on Mount Zion."

Zachary's shoulders slumped with the weight of his own words, his head bowed in awe, his hands cupped in his lap as if in expectation. "Father God . . . it was here that you raised up your only Son, Yeshua, and set him at your right hand for all time. He oversees our work today, whether we acknowledge him or not. Now, most holy Father, we know you have brought our little team this far, with miracle after miracle, just as you brought the Children of Israel into their inheritance. We believe"—his hands were now upraised—"we believe you will overcome our enemies once again and fulfill your purposes for us!"

Zachary drew his hands together over his bowed head and was quiet for a long moment. The others dared not breathe as they awaited his next words. "We claim this now," he said, drawing his hands into fists before him. "This moment!" he cried, pounding his fists into his knees. "In the name of thy holy Messiah, Yeshua, AMEN!"

The group was transfixed.

Barely had they emerged from the prayer's last words when a jangling, nerve-wrenching sound broke in . . . the ringing of a telephone.

Father McCurdy leaned away from the chessboard over which he had hunched in prayer and picked up the receiver of the old dial phone sitting near the fireplace. "Hello," he said. "Yes . . . this is he. Is that you, Diamant? What's that . . . you sound so far away. Yes . . . he what?"

McCurdy looked as though an electric prod had stunned him. "What's that you say?" His hand quivered as he gripped the mouthpiece and listened intently. "Very well," he croaked. "Yes . . . that is most amazing. I shall tell them. Right away!"

Obviously shaken, Father McCurdy hung up the phone and then stared into space, as though he had seen an angel.

"Diamant just received word from the IAA," he managed to say. "The PAA has withdrawn its objection to our application. The Antiquities Curator for the Royal House of Jordan has been assigned to cooperate with our excavation at Masada. We may begin tomorrow!"

CHAPTER 34

What an evening! The group staying at the Consortium house was aflame with joy and hope, until the idea of going to bed and trying to sleep was no more than an afterthought.

When word had come that the dig could proceed, under the mediating authority of Jordan, the rabbis were ecstatic. Jordan had proven to be their friend, in no uncertain terms. Despite what the PAA had in mind, the team perceived the Jordanian presence as a buffer to Arab animosity.

The group ate heartily of Anya's kosher duckling, and then made a merry hike up to the Jaffa Gate and straight up to Ben Yehuda Street, where the late-night shops were open, and where almost every night, except the high holy days, was a party. Celebrating, laughing, joking, they toasted their good fortune from one sidewalk bistro to another, the rabbis stopping to dance a Yiddish jig on each street corner. David and Britta twirled to the reveling of street musicians, while Shalom Diamant, who had joined the group at dinner, tossed obscene amounts of money at immigrant violinists, jugglers, and pantomime artists. Zachary, Mel, and Ken had a glorious time feasting on the baked goods and pastries offered by sidewalk vendors and spending a little money in the shops.

Yes, Zachary had gone out tonight. The rabbis did not restrain him, believing that if God was so much with him that his prayers could open the doors to Masada and the hearts of the enemies, they did not need to fret over him so much. Of course, they must not become lax in their duties and so insisted that Mel continue to stick close to him.

Which was fine with Zachary. Mel and he had become good friends since their talk on the airplane. Ken and Dave were also great guys, and Zachary, or Zack, as they called him, had never had so much fun.

Only one person, out of the entire lot, exhibited less than giddy behavior tonight. *Poor old Uriel Katz*, Zachary thought. What was it about him that he could never just lighten up? And why did Zack think of him as "old"? Rabbi Katz was only in his forties, a first-generation, post-Holocaust native of Israel, much younger than the other three rabbis. Yet his personality had aged him, and no one thought of him as young.

At home, after the joyous outing, Zachary plopped down on the edge of his bed. A smile had frozen on his face. He had laughed so much tonight, his sides still ached. He wondered if it would do any good to lie down and try to sleep. Dawn would be creeping through his window much too soon to give adequate rest.

He pulled off his shoes, then decided to just rest on top of the crisply made-up bed while his pounding heart and the raucous echoes in his mind simmered down. The sounds of others still moving about the house told him they were no more interested in sleep than he.

Gradually, however, a tentative stillness settled over the place, broken now and then by the shuffle of feet in and out of bathrooms, the running of water in sinks, the low chatter of muted conversation among those who defied bedtime. At last, Zachary curled up and fell into a deep slumber, still dressed in his street clothes.

It must have been two o'clock in the morning when a rap at his bedroom door woke him with a start. His eyes popping open, he lay there a few seconds, wondering if he had dreamed the knocking sound. When it came a second time, soft, hesitant, Zachary rose up stiffly and rubbed his eyes. "Who is it?" he called.

There was no answer. Feeling a little grouchy, he tried to work up some enthusiasm. *The guys are still up*, he thought. *They want me to come down for more palaver*.

"Coming," he replied to the third knock. He dragged himself to the door and opened it a crack, peering into the dimly lit hallway with bleary eyes.

What returned his gaze was the last thing he would have wished to see. "Rabbi Katz?" he groaned. "Is that you?"

"It is." The little man's voice had none of its usual gruffness, no hint of demanding imposition. "May I speak with you, Mr. Cohen?"

Squinting at him in bewilderment, Zachary stepped back, pulling the door open. "Of course." As the diminutive fellow entered the room, Zachary glanced up and down the hall, wondering if anyone else was about.

Closing the door, he turned to face his unexpected guest. "What is wrong, Rabbi? Is there an emergency? Are the others okay?" Suddenly, an awful possibility suggested itself. "Rabbi Ben? Is he well?"

Katz gave a weak smile. "Everyone is fine," he replied. "I should not be surprised that you would think only an emergency would bring me here. I have not been your closest friend."

Zachary noted that the rabbi was still in his street clothes, like himself. But it appeared he had not gone to bed at all.

"Have a seat," Zachary offered, clearing an armchair of a pile of *Jerusalem Posts*. "To what do I owe the honor of this call?"

Zachary sat down on the bed and smoothed his rumpled hair. He wished he had brushed his teeth. But the other man did not seem to be the least bit focused on his host's grooming.

"Let me get straight to the point," Rabbi Katz began, in a deliberate tone that was more typical of him. "I have been out walking. In fact, I only now came back to the house."

Zachary had not noticed his absence. The busy, noisy group had not really missed the standoffish fellow.

"It is not a night for sleeping," Zachary agreed.

Rabbi Katz's face was more pensive than Zachary had ever seen it. Somehow, though, the anger that usually lay behind his owlish eyes was not evident. To Zachary's amazement, the little rabbi swallowed hard, and began a couple of times to speak but halted and faltered miserably. The host refrained from reaching out to him, though he felt the man could use some comforting.

"What is it, Rabbi?" he asked. "You are troubled about something?"

Zachary was astonished to see tears welling up along the man's lashes, about to spill down his cheeks. The rabbi blinked and sniffled, pulling out a linen handkerchief from his vest pocket.

"I . . . I do not know where to begin," he confessed. "As you know, I pride myself on my education. Why"—his eyes glistened—"as a boy, I was the star pupil of my yeshiva. When I moved to Brooklyn to teach, I was the favored rabbi of my synagogue, and I was on my way to becoming the chief rabbi!"

"Of Brooklyn?" Zachary marveled. "My, I had no idea!"

"Indeed," Katz said. "I have had a great deal to be proud of in my life."

Zachary could have taken this as boasting, but the man's tone belied that attitude. He seemed, rather, to be ashamed of himself.

"I am sure that you have perceived my animosity all these months," Katz continued.

Zachary looked at the floor. "You have not embraced my candidacy with the greatest warmth," he replied.

The rabbi actually laughed a little. "That is an understatement, if I ever heard one!" he said. Then sobering, "You are right, for sure. But I have had good reason, Mr. Cohen, to resent you."

Zachary listened respectfully. "Go on, sir," he said.

"You see," Katz explained, "the people of my synagogue and of the yeshiva where I taught had great expectations for me. Everything about my background, my Cohen name (Katz is a derivative of Cohen, you know), my learning . . . and yes, I will be frank . . . my abilities, seemed to qualify me for the position you have attained: candidate for the high priesthood."

Zachary was stunned. Shaking his head, he apologized. "I am sorry . . . I had no idea . . ."

Uriel Katz raised a hand. "It is all right," he said. "I have been forced to accept that my Cohen lineage is not sufficiently pure. When all of the evidence pointed to you as the proper candidate, what could I do but go along?"

Zachary did not know what to say. "What else prevented your endorsement of me?" he asked.

The older man quivered, his hands clasping the tassels on his vest. "Your doctrine, of course!" he exclaimed. "A Messianic Jew as high priest? A *Christian*? Why the very idea has been anathema to me!"

Zachary was relieved to hear the admission. "Ah, good!" he said.

Rabbi Katz was shocked. "Good?" he repeated. "You are not offended?"

The young candidate smiled. "Offended? Of course not, Rabbi! It is good to have someone else address this issue, other than the continual nagging of my own soul!"

Katz had not anticipated this response. Amazed, he seemed to relax a bit.

"In fact," Zachary went on, "if you, with all your learning, have any insights for me, I am open to suggestion."

Katz laughed ironically. "Dear boy," he said, "I have come to you for advice tonight. And you seek advice of me? Surely, you would not betray your beliefs, no matter what the cost!"

Silence hung between them, as Zachary studied his visitor's conflicted expression. "Of course I would not," Zachary affirmed. "Nor do I sense that you would want such a thing of me. Just why are you here, Rabbi?"

Katz fidgeted, cocking his ear toward the door, as if fearing eavesdroppers.

"Rabbi . . . ," he said. Then, looking sheepish, "I shall call you Rabbi, young man, for you are as much a teacher as I have ever been."

Zachary, surprised, accepted the compliment as Katz went on.

"We, my colleagues and I, know that you are a teacher come from God. No man can pray as you have prayed tonight, no man can move the heart of God as you have done, opening the way for us against our enemies, unless God be with him."

Zachary was quiet a moment. "There is a question buried in your endorsement," he guessed. "What you really want to know is what to do with my doctrine, am I right?"

The older man shifted, tears welling in his eyes again.

Zachary leaned toward him, feeling as though he were in a time warp. "You know," he said, "your visit puts me in mind of another great leader of Israel who paid a visit to a young rabbi one night. The ruler's name was Nicodemus, and he slipped out under cover of darkness to pay a call on Yeshua, Jesus the Nazarene."

The rabbi listened in amazement. "Truly?" he asked.

"Yes," Zachary said with a smile. "And his words to the young rabbi were much like yours to me." He paused, giving this time to sink in. "Would you like to know Yeshua's answer?" he asked.

"Indeed, I would," Katz replied, moving to the edge of his seat.

"He said that except a man be born again, he cannot see the kingdom of God."

Katz frowned. "'Born again,' yes! I have heard this term applied to certain modern Christians. This is actually a very old idea?"

Zachary tried not to chuckle. "It was first spoken by my Chief Rabbi," he answered.

Katz recalled the conversation that preceded Zachary's prayer earlier in the day. He smiled, knowing that Zachary spoke of Jesus.

"Amazing!" he said. "But just what did he mean? How can a person be 'born again'? Surely he did not speak of physical rebirth!"

Zachary's eyes widened, and he looked at his questioner proudly. "You are ahead of Nicodemus!" he said. "He did not pick up on that fact right off."

Rabbi Katz was actually humbled. "So," he said with a sigh, "what else did Jesus say?"

"Well," Zachary went on, "he said, 'That which is born of the flesh is flesh, and that which is born of the Spirit is spirit.'"

Uriel Katz liked the sound of that. "I have read such things in the Talmud," he said. "Even the prophets spoke like that!"

"Of course!" Zachary said. "Jesus was, after all, a student of Israel, as well as a teacher. Where do you think he learned these things?"

Katz was amazed, perching on the edge of his seat like a hungry bird. "So how have we missed this?" he asked. "One can actually achieve a new birth?"

"*Achieve* is not exactly the idea," Zachary explained. "Jesus said it had nothing to do with our own will, but the will of the Father."

Standing up, he went to the window of his third-story room and pulled up the blind, letting the evening air come whooshing through the open grillwork. "Jesus might have done something like this," he said, "when he spoke to Nicodemus. For it is recorded that he said, 'The wind blows where it wants to, and you hear the sound of it but cannot tell where it comes from or where it is going. So it is with everyone who is born of the Spirit.' "

Rabbi Katz lifted his face to the warm breeze that flapped past the open blind. His heart swelled to the words. But then, he shook his head, his sharply trained sense of reason taking precedence. "I . . . I still don't understand. How can these things be?"

Zachary wondered if this were a dream. It seemed he was replaying the exact scene he had read a hundred times, and just now he had reached the part where Jesus felt frustrated. Without even thinking about it, he found himself speaking as the Nazarene would have. "Are you an Israeli teacher," he sighed, facing Katz with his arms crossed, "and you do not understand these things? If you can't grasp physical analogies, how will you grasp the spiritual?"

He walked to the bed and sat down again. Uriel Katz looked like a schoolboy who had been corrected by the headmaster. Zachary's heart went out to him as it suddenly occurred to him why Jesus had said what he did next.

"Rabbi Katz," he began, "perhaps it would help if I gave you an example from our own history. Do you remember when the Children of Israel were wandering in the wilderness, and a swarm of vipers came into the camp, a veritable plague of poisonous snakes?"

Katz nodded. "Of course I remember."

"And what did Moses do to save them?"

The rabbi did not hesitate, knowing the story very well. "He made an image of a serpent out of bronze, and he lifted it up on a pole so all the people could see."

"Yes," Zachary said. "And he told them . . ."

". . . that if they looked upon the image, if they trusted in the image, they would not die."

The little rabbi tried to sort this out but needed help.

"Think back to your yeshiva catechisms," Zachary said. "What did the bronze serpent represent?"

"Sin," Katz recited. "Yes . . . the sin of the people, captured and condemned."

"That is right," Zachary agreed. "Moses wanted them to see that God had forgiven them their sin, had condemned it and killed it. They must believe this, or go on in their misery."

Katz remembered the mysterious lesson from his early days at synagogue school. Still, he understood it no better now than then.

Zachary read his confusion. "If you are like most of us, you wonder how God could make such an offer. Didn't it require justice, a sacrifice of some pure creature?"

Katz was surprised at Zachary's easy reading of his mind. "Exactly!" he said. "I always wanted to ask my teachers about that!"

Zachary sighed. "Well, Jesus addressed that issue when he said to Nicodemus, 'As Moses lifted up the serpent in the wilderness, even so must I be lifted up, that whoever believes in me shall not perish, but have eternal life.' "

Rabbi Katz was bewildered. "But that is terrible!" he objected. "Jesus was saying that he himself was the likeness of sin?"

Zachary did not argue. "Could not the same be said of every lamb and goat and bull our people sacrificed years ago? Were they not taking on the sins of the people?"

Katz was astonished. "I . . . I guess so," he admitted.

Zachary moved on. "The problem was, they had only so much staying power. The sacrifices were only good so long as no one sinned again. In a very real way, Rabbi, Jesus took on the sins of the whole world. He was raised up on a cross, like the serpent on a pole, and was condemned for the sins of all the world, for all time! Jesus himself became the sacrifice his Father required!"

The little rabbi shuddered at the thought. Suddenly, the tears that had threatened to undo him all evening came spilling over his thin cheeks. "Dear God!" he cried, lifting his hands to his face. "What is happening to me?"

Zachary could refrain no longer from reaching out to his guest. Leaning across the short distance between the bed and the rabbi's chair, he placed a hand on Katz's knee.

"Nicodemus probably wept, just like you are doing," he said softly. "One thing is for sure: he became a believer that night, a disciple of the Chief Rabbi."

Rabbi Katz nodded his head, quaking from head to toe as Zachary continued. "That night, Jesus said to Nicodemus the words that are the mainstay of my faith: 'For God so loved the world that he gave his only begotten Son, that whosoever believes in him should not perish but have everlasting life.' "

Suddenly, Katz was grasping Zachary's hands, bowing his head to his knees, pressing his tear-stained face against the young man's pliant fingers.

"It is a very short step to take, Rabbi," Zachary said. "A small step from darkness to light. Do you wish to take it?"

"I do!" Katz groaned.

Zachary's own face was wet with tears as he led Uriel Katz to the gate of life. "Jesus said, 'Behold, I stand at the door and knock. If any man hears my voice and opens the door, I will come in and dine with him, and he with me.' "

Katz raised his face, which glistened with tears in the lamplight, and then he released Zachary's hands and brought his own tense fists to his chest.

"Here is my door, Yeshua!" he cried. Then throwing his arms wide, "I open it to you!"

CHAPTER 35

The next morning, Ramal, the shopkeeper at the Masada depot, and his youthful assistant watched the unloading of two vans full of archaeologists, their colleagues, and equipment in the gravel parking lot. Seething with frustration and indignation, Ramal also watched as sentries from the Israel Antiquities Authority turned away busloads of tourists and guarded the road signs that announced, "Masada, Herod's Desert Fortress, Closed Today."

Tour guides on the buses coming out from Jerusalem, Jericho, Eilat, and other points were used to such detours. They always had a Plan B in the eventuality that the stops they had scheduled might be shut down for one reason or another. Of course, each morning their tour agencies checked the daily updates in the papers and on-line, but they could not rely on the information being up-to-the-minute.

Sites could be shut down for a variety of reasons, from needed repairs to unanticipated outbreaks of violence in the politically sensitive region. Site closures due to archaeological digs were usually announced further ahead than this one had been, but even that courtesy could not always be counted on. Scientists had a way of stumbling onto new finds, which required the quarantining of sites from the feet, prying hands, and eyes of the public, with no notice whatever.

Such was the case this morning, the tour guides were told. Scholars from Jordan, Israel, America, England, and Ireland were cooperating here today. The guards were sorry, they told them, but they would have to come another time. Did the sentries have any idea when the site would be reopened? guides asked. No, there had been no word about that, was the reply. "Check back tomorrow," the sentries suggested.

And so, tours coming up from Eilat and points south would go on to the Dead Sea, to frolic in the briny water, and would then move on up to En-Gedi and Qumran; those coming from points north would retrace their journey and head for Hebron, Jericho, or points east.

As for the shopkeepers of Masada, however, they did not have a Plan B. Except for the hope that the archaeologists might do a little buying, this was a worthless day.

Ramal picked up his telephone and angrily punched in the number of Mr. Hamir at the PAA. His assistant, lazily arranging the wares on the sidewalk, knew he was asking what had gone amiss, how it was that not only the Israelis had gotten leave to dig on the mountain, but that they were being supported by the Jordanians. The answer was apparently less than satisfactory, for he slammed the receiver down with a crash and told his assistant not to bother with setting up. "Pull the blinds!" he spat. "We are closed today, just like Masada itself!"

The transporting of the entire team of archaeologists, their colleagues, and all their equipment up the mountain would require three trams. Laad Girzim had also requested the royal house of Jordan to commission a group of militia to stand guard around the site, and had cleared this with the IAA. Leaving Amman in the middle of the night, the soldiers had arrived at the base of the mountain well before Laad had come out from Jerusalem.

Of course, the IAA had likewise asked the Israeli Army to dispatch troops to guard the mission. In a spirit of mutual cooperation, soldiers from Jerusalem had linked up with the Jordanian troops, and the entire company, numbering about one hundred, had already nearly completed the hike up the arduous, snaking footpath to the mesa's top, their Uzis and rifles on their backs.

It had been a short night for the eager Consortium team. Barely had they slept before they awoke at 5:00 A.M., ate breakfast, and then drove down the Dead Sea Highway at dawn. None the worse for wear after their evening on Ben Yehuda Street, they were a merry lot, jabbering, joking, and anticipating all the way.

If they noticed a change in Uriel Katz—signified by an uncharacteristic cheerfulness and atypical chatter—they passed it off as the result of too much partying, coupled with the anticipation of a treasure hunt.

As for Katz himself, he certainly noticed the change. He tried to suppress it but found it bubbling up from somewhere inside himself, nearly embarrassing him with its unexpected eruptions.

To his own amazement, the abrupt, bored, angry Katz seemed to be no more. Even the more positive aspects of his personality—his studious, cautious, reserved nature—appeared to have taken a backseat to more childlike effusiveness. Like people he had heard of in love songs and silly romances, he was acting and feeling as if he were in love.

Katz had never been in love.

Katz had never had a real childhood.

Katz had never felt loved.

Yes, he thought to himself, *that's it! I feel love . . . loved . . . loving! For the first time in my life!*

He lifted a hand to his smiling lips and sank into the high-backed seat in the middle of the van. He was surrounded by friends, colleagues. He wondered if they noticed anything new about him. He hoped they did, and he hoped they didn't. He did not know how to deal with himself, how to explain himself to *himself*, let alone explain himself to *them*. It was best for now to keep a lid on all this newness.

If possible.

He wished Zachary were here! His situation was rather like that of a baby being delivered, and then being taken away from the doctor, the mother, the father, before even getting a good feeding. How he longed to sit again with Zachary and learn more . . . more!

Feeble as his fledgling faith was, however, he knew something very real had happened to him. He knew, if he knew nothing else, that God the Father loved him, and that knowledge would get him through the day.

So transforming was that certainty, however, that keeping a lid on it was extremely difficult. It seemed to have an energy of its own, beyond Uriel's ability to contain. "*Like springs of living water . . .*"

Where had he read such words? Oh, the Song of Solomon! he remembered. Yes, that was fitting, for Solomon's song was a love song. And Uriel was in love, loved, loving!

Out of the corner of one eye, he saw that Horace Benjamin was looking at him. Oh, he did not need this! The most awkward thing about what had happened to him was that he would have to explain himself to Horace, and Horace Benjamin was the last person on earth to whom he wanted to admit anything.

Fortunately, for Uriel Katz, the day's agenda would not allow for such a confessional. If he were to have the inevitable unveiling, at least it could wait.

As the vans were being unloaded at Masada, Shalom Diamant crossed the parking lot to greet the Jordanian archaeologist with long steps, his hand outstretched. Only Diamant, of all the Jerusalem group, had ever met the royal curator.

"This is amazing!" he said, shaking Laad's hand warmly. "I was astonished when the IAA told me you had offered to help us." Calling his friends over, he said in a private tone, "Mr. Girzim is the man who brought us the photo of the box!" Then, drawing Rabbi Ben forward, he added softly, "And this is Horace Benjamin, who received a fax of the photo while he was in America."

Rabbi Ben greeted Laad with a fervent handshake. "I hope that you have expressed our gratitude to your lovely queen," he said. "The kindness of the Jordanian people will surely be blessed by God Almighty!"

Laad rankled at that endorsement. This was, after all, a Jew who praised him. Jews did not worship Allah, he thought, yet they presumed to speak for him.

Nonetheless, Laad graciously accepted the thanks. "When I read about your application being denied," he explained, "I knew my queen would want me to do what I could to help you."

The rabbis were mystified by this second intervention on the part of the Jordanian royal house. Laad easily read the question in their eyes. "I wish I could explain her desire to aid you. Let us just say that she follows in the footsteps of her late husband."

He did not volunteer that the queen really knew little about today's venture. He did not say that his intervention on their behalf had been his own decision—that some unseen power seemed to be compelling him to aid them. He did not understand this, so why should he expect them to?

The Britons and the Americans rode in the first two trams, with the equipment, Laad, and the rabbis in the third. On the way, Laad inquired of the rabbis just what it was they sought.

"Certain artifacts from our Temple period," Rabbi Ben offered evasively. "There may be nothing here at all. But we have reason to believe there may."

Laad understood his reticence. "You are wise to be cautious in what you reveal," he said. With keen eyes, he scanned the tram's interior. "In fact," he asked, "can we be certain there are no monitoring devices in this gondola?"

The rabbis appreciated his concern for secrecy. "These transports are checked regularly for any sort of vandalism, tampering, or wiring devices, including 'bugs,'" Rabbi Ben assured him. "It is part of the Israeli government's duty to check for such intrusions and endangerments at tourist sites. We ordered a sweep of the trams last evening when we knew we were coming out. I believe we may be sure of our security in that respect."

This last phrase caught Laad's attention. "You may be certain you are secure with respect to my presence, as well, Rabbi Benjamin. It was for reasons of security, for instance, that I had Jordanian militia go ahead of us."

"We appreciate these safeguards," Carl Jacobs said. Gesturing out the window toward the line of troops that had nearly made it to the top of the mesa, he said, "If you will look, you will find that your soldiers are also in company with Israelis."

Laad studied the distant foot soldiers, finding that the Jordanians, in their brown field uniforms, did indeed hike side by side with Israelis outfitted in olive green.

"Very good," he said with a smile.

Levine picked up on the theme. "Was it for security's sake that you faxed the photo from Jerusalem instead of from Amman?"

Laad nodded soberly. "Correct," he said. "We already had good reason to believe there was someone in the palace who was aware of Senator Jefferson's mission, that he was transporting something of value to Israel's cause. Otherwise, just why was he assaulted?"

Carl Jacobs cringed as Menachem Levine deduced, "And that someone had contacts in the U.S. who commissioned the murder."

"Yes," Laad said. "It must be so."

Rabbi Ben frowned. "I take it, from your continued caution, that you have no clue as to who, within the palace, is responsible for those communications."

Laad's face reddened. "None, sir. But as the media has faithfully reported, our government is shamed by the suspicion which the act has cast upon our country. The queen, and our new king, have made it a priority to ferret out the traitors, whoever they may be. Unfortunately," he said, shaking his head, "so far there is no answer."

The tram swayed gently as it neared the top. Laad studied the old men around him, amazed at their resilience. "I must assume, gentlemen," he said, "that you have somehow managed to retrieve the cedar box."

The statement filled the air within the confining compartment with an almost tangible tension. The rabbis had known Laad would get to this. The Jordanian's life, like theirs, had become irrevocably intertwined with the mysterious box.

Benjamin, Jacobs, and Levine looked silently at one another, wondering what to say. They did not look to Katz, figuring they knew he would never choose to reveal a Consortium secret to an Arab. To their amazement, however, it was he who, at last, had the boldness to reply.

His eyes sparkling with an unexplained confidence, Uriel said, "Show our friend the box, Horace. God brought Mr. Girzim to assist us. We should not tie his hands by keeping him in the dark."

Astonished, Rabbi Ben took a grateful breath and, with Jacob's and Levine's blessings, brought forth the box from the valise, which Ken Aronstam had transferred to him. Gently, he unwrapped the linen binder and showed the contents to Laad.

The Jordanian was awestruck. "Yes, this is it!" he cried. "I was commissioned to find it in the archives before the senator arrived."

His eyes were full of questions as he stroked the carved lid. "So, shall I deduce that this box has somehow led you to Masada?"

Rabbi Ben smiled, returning it to the valise. "You may," he said. "And we hope Masada will lead us further."

Laad sighed. "I will not ask for a recounting of how you came to obtain it."

"Nor would we tell you if you did ask," Levine replied with a chuckle. "Not just yet, anyhow."

Laad nodded. "Very well. But would I be foolish to assume that you hope to find the vial that once rested within the box?"

The rabbis squirmed under his probing gaze. Rabbi Ben finally shrugged. "We would be foolish to deny it," he said.

Laad leaned back, remembering the story his grandmother had told of the Masada refugees and the Jeremiah cave. He, too, had secrets he was not ready to share.

One thing he knew he must tell his new colleagues, however. Leaning forward again, he grew very serious. "My friends," he said, "you have honored me by the trust you place in me. It would be wrong of me not to confess to you that I was allowed to help you today on condition that I would report all of our findings to the PAA."

Scarcely believing their ears, the rabbis were stunned. Uriel Katz would normally have become undone, bristling with animosity and badgering his colleagues with I-told-you-sos. As it was, he did grow tense, but he managed to bite his tongue.

Rabbi Ben scrutinized the Jordanian. Despite his own agitation, he was as diplomatic as possible. "Shall we assume that this admission means you will do no such thing?" he asked hopefully.

Laad bowed his head and clicked his heels together in salute. "You may not only assume, gentlemen," he replied. "You may be certain!"

The tram was nearing the arrival port. Ben looked at the Jordanian in amazement. "I feel we can believe you, Mr. Girzim," he said. "Perhaps someday you will tell us why your queen has chosen to befriend us."

Laad gave a befuddled smile. "I shall be happy to do so," he said, "when I understand it all myself. For now let us just say that she honors her husband's commitments."

So it was that there were many riddles, many unexplained feelings and compulsions among the members of the team as they reached the arrival platform. When they emerged into the hazy light of early morning, then trekked, one by one, up the winding stairs chiseled into the sandstone face, the group was much quieter than during the road trip.

The going was treacherous, as they each carried various tools and equipment for the dig, and the soldiers, who awaited them above, weapons slung over their shoulders, looked more like an occupying army than attendants at an excavation.

At last the team reached the tabletop of Masada, entering like actors on a pewter stage. An odd assortment of characters manned this cast for the unusual drama about to be played out. The opening scene had a mystical quality as the actors took their places where some of the most astonishing performances in human history had been witnessed.

Quietly they went about the business of setting up the props—laying out shovels, picks, electronic survey equipment, sensitive seismometers, dust pans, tiny brushes, and wire-mesh screens. The tools of the profession were about to become both the instruments of history and the keys to the future.

Depending on what was found today.

Away from the eyes of the soldiers, who were now stationed around the perimeter of the plateau, the rabbis handed the cedar box to the archaeologists. Ken Aronstam took the precious little casket to the middle of Masada's tabletop and held it before him like a compass. When he had aligned the notches on the lid with the portals on the mesa's rim, David Rothmeyer knelt at his feet, just where the X had been two evenings before.

Horace Benjamin, Carl Jacobs, Menachem Levine, Uriel Katz, Britta Hayworth, John Cromwell, Shalom Diamant, and Laad Girzim stood in shuddering stillness, as David placed a battery-powered sonogram to the ground and asked Father McCurdy to turn on the portable generator.

Tense with hope, David moved the instrument back and forth over the ground, studying the readout on the sonogram screen. A mass of black, needled lines traced across the dinky backlit monitor, a meaningless scribble to the untrained eye.

Suddenly, just as the sun burned off the haze of the eastern horizon, blasting the cast with orange light, David cried, "Yes! There is a void beneath us! A cave! Let's get at it!"

CHAPTER 36

Zachary Cohen awoke when the first rays of sunlight crept through his window. The fact that the blinds usually covered that window upon his rising reminded him—as if he needed reminding—of the amazing night he had spent with Rabbi Katz.

"Jesus may have done something like this," he had told Katz as he opened the blinds, letting the unseen breeze give its object lesson.

Truly, it had been an astonishing sensation, the feeling that he could so clearly understand something the Messiah had done, what the Master would do, as though the Master actually moved through him, spoke through him. *The work of the Holy Spirit!* he thought. *This is what it feels like!*

How he hoped he would experience such a thing again! And again!

Yes! Zachary had led someone to the Lord! Not just any someone, but someone so obstinate, so contrary, that he was the last person on earth from whom such a decision had been expected.

If nothing else had ever completely convinced Zachary of his calling, this might: not the fact that he had been an instrument used of God (any yielded soul could be that), but that a brittle prickly pear like Uriel Katz, could-have-been Chief Rabbi of Brooklyn, one of the key leaders of the Temple movement, had accepted his testimony.

Somehow, overnight, this experience had cauterized the wounds of fear and uncertainty that had haunted Zachary for a year. He still did not know how to reconcile the various doctrines that faced off in his soul, but this morning, upon rising, he believed he would understand soon enough.

After Rabbi Katz had left the room, Zachary had finally gotten out of his street clothes and crawled under the covers for a couple of hours of shuteye. The house was very quiet by the time he had stretched, breathed in the soft, sunlit breeze that spilled through the window, and decided to get up. He knew that the rabbis and their friends had already left. He had slept through their hushed departure, but he knew they had planned to be on their way to Masada long before sunrise.

Suddenly, at the thought of what they might find there, he knew he must act. Very shortly, he would have to make the ultimate decision—to serve as high priest, or to reject the opportunity on the basis of conflicting beliefs. Last night notwithstanding, he must resolve the issues that had hounded him for many months.

After throwing back the covers, he leaped from bed, rushed through a shower, groomed, dressed, and hurried downstairs. Mel was in the parlor, ready to join him for breakfast and then shadow him throughout the unplanned day.

"Hi, Zack!" Mel greeted, having dropped the "Mr. Cohen" approach somewhere on Ben Yehuda Street. "What's on the docket for today?"

Zachary smiled tensely. Mel was too fine a guy to inspire resentment, but this thing about having a bodyguard could get annoying. How nice it would be to move about freely once again!

Wester followed his charge to the breakfast table, where Anya had left a plate of kosher sweet rolls and a carafe of coffee for the late risers. As they enjoyed the hot brew and baked goods, Zachary announced, "I am going up to King David Street. There is a meeting there once a week, and I haven't been for ages."

Mel's reaction was one of concern. "Meeting? Like . . . *people?*"

Zachary bristled. "I guess that is the definition of 'meeting,'" he said. "Some old friends of mine get together each Tuesday noon."

Mel picked up on his aggravation and raised his hands defensively. "Hey, Zack, I'm just doing my job here. If you don't want me around, I can go home."

Zachary sighed. "Of course I want you around! I just wish you could be my buddy, not my . . ."

"Baby-sitter?" Mel said, cracking a smile.

"You got it!" Zachary grumbled.

Mel scooted forward, leaning his elbows on the table. "Tell you what," he said, "how about if we just go ahead and be friends. We don't have to tell the rabbis!"

Zachary's face reddened. Laughing lamely, he said, "Sorry, Mel. Sure. Sounds like a plan. But . . . I don't suppose that means . . ."

"I'll give up the guardian role? No . . . don't think so."

With a shrug of surrender, Zachary relaxed a little.

"So," Mel inquired, "what exactly is this meeting we two buddies are about to attend?"

Zachary pursed his lips. "Well," he said, "since you volunteered for this assignment, you can't back out! It's a Bible study, Mel, and a prayer meeting."

The ex-cop's eyes widened. "Oh boy!" he said, squirming. "How do I get myself into these things?"

The trek across Hinnom Gorge, past the ancient windmill, then west past the modern hotels and gift shops to King David Street, was filled with lively sounds and vivid color. The summer landscape was a riot of greens, poppy reds, morning-glory yellows. The huge deciduous trees that lined the boulevard were all in leaf, and the flowering trees were a lush delight. City traffic, honking cabs, clusters of artists on the lawns of the Montefiore colony, and chattering tourists admiring the sights could bring the sleepiest soul to life.

Mel tried not to look too protective as he walked beside Zachary. Most of the people they passed, as they headed toward the newer part of town, appeared to be business sorts, in suits and tailored dresses, many with briefcases. Shiny-faced tourists were caught up in their plans and groups. No one made the bodyguard suspicious.

King David Street was a boulevard reminiscent of a specific era of Jerusalem's history. The tree-lined avenue was part of the heritage bestowed by wealthy Jewish and Egyptian investors after the turn of the twentieth century. Though the buildings were a blend of Middle Eastern styles, the occupying culture of the post–WWI British Mandate period had also imbued them with a distinctly imperial ambiance, and English design held sway in imposing symmetry and post-Victorian elegance.

One of the most legendary of the buildings on this street was the King David Hotel. As the two men arrived on the sidewalk in front of this seven-story landmark, Zachary told Mel a little of the history of the place, how it had been bombed in 1946 by Jewish militants connected to the Haganah, whose followers were still making headlines today. Nearly one hundred people had been killed during that bombing, which took out the west wing where the Mandate had its headquarters. Most of them had been British administrators, but many others, Jews included, had also lost their lives to that political statement.

That bombing had been followed by the famous Black Sabbath, on which the British retaliated by arresting twenty-seven hundred people throughout the country, and putting them in an internment camp. This, of course, led to more violence, ultimately causing the Britons to throw up their hands and withdraw from Israel, unable to control the rapidly growing dissent.

"Doesn't sound much different from what goes on here most any given day," Mel noted. "There's always some sort of uprising. Only the players change."

Zachary agreed. "Jerusalem was named 'City of Peace' sheerly from hope, not from experience," he said.

Across the street from the King David was another hotel, this one a direct contribution of the British. Two sprawling wings led to a very tall central tower, which looked much like a fat Muslim minaret. The Three Arches Hotel, it was called, but Mel quickly noticed the sign over the main entrance. "The YMCA?" he said with a laugh. Then quoting from the lyrics to a pop song, he said, "I wonder if it's 'fun to stay' here?"

Zachary had anticipated this. "It probably was, in its heyday," he said. "This was *the* gathering place of the displaced British, away from their Anglican homeland, missing their churches and their social set. The Young Men's Christian Association was really big in England and the U.S. in those days."

When Zachary turned down the driveway that circled a huge fountain that had been converted to a flower bed, Mel's eyes grew wide. "Is the YMCA our destination?" he asked.

"The meeting is up those stairs," he replied, pointing to a door in the west wing where a small group of people was just entering.

As they headed that way, Mel puzzling over the idea of Jews worshiping in a Christian building, he stopped to read a bronze placard mounted beside the hotel entry. "*Here is a place whose atmosphere is peace, where political and religious jealousies can be forgotten, and international unity fostered and developed.* Field Marshall Edmund Lord Allenby."

Impressed, he thought it was a wonderful sentiment, if it was true.

As he hurried to catch up with Zachary, he saw that one of the men who was heading for the door had stopped on the stairs, obviously happy to see them approach. A very Orthodox-looking fellow, wearing a short-sleeved black dress shirt, traditional side locks, long black beard, and yarmulke, he hailed them.

"Zachary Cohen!" he called. "Is it really you?"

"It is, Rabbi!" Zachary replied.

As Zachary joined him on the stairs, they embraced warmly, giving the traditional kisses on the cheeks, and then the rabbi held him at arm's length, studying him up and down. "It has been so long, Zachary!" he protested. "You left without a word! Where have you been?"

Zachary shrugged. "I guess you could say I have been on a spiritual journey, Rabbi," he said. Then turning to Mel, who was just now ascending the stairs, he added, "And this is my traveling partner, Mel Wester."

The rabbi shook Mel's hand and invited them inside. "Welcome," he said. "We are just starting." Handing them a couple of Bibles, he led them to the group, which was just taking seats in a small circle of folding chairs near the back of the room.

"I think we were in Acts when you left, Zachary," he said. "We have now made it to Hebrews. Some very tough passages for Jews to digest. I hope you will lend us all the insight you have."

Zachary wanted to say he was here to *receive* insight, not to give it.

As the group began to sing an opening chorus, Mel looked in bewilderment at the Bible the rabbi had handed him. Zachary noted his perplexed expression.

"What is it?" he whispered.

"This book has the New Testament as well as the Old. I thought you guys just read the Old," Mel replied.

"Not here," Zachary explained. "These folks are part of a Messianic congregation. We embrace the entire truth, not just the first half."

CHAPTER 37

Mel Wester was nervous. He had never been to a Bible study before, let alone a prayer meeting.

The fifteen or so people gathered in the meeting hall of the YMCA were pleasant enough, several of them looking a little like Pete and Honey, like hippie holdovers in long hair, long dresses, beads, the works. When they went around the group introducing themselves, he learned that most of that sort had come from America in recent years, Jews who had been born abroad—Children of the Diaspora come home, they said. Their testimonies were remarkably similar. They had come to Israel seeking their roots, their "identities." They had fallen in love with their own Jewish heritage, but had not found total fulfillment until they realized that Yeshua was the Messiah they had been seeking. Now, they said, they were "completed Jews."

Mel didn't know what to think of all that. The term "completed Jew" seemed rather odd. Had they been *incomplete* before?

Others present were businessmen and -women on their lunch breaks. They ate from brown bags as they participated in the discussion, and they would have to excuse themselves to return to work before the prayer session began.

Mel could not help but notice that few present were much past middle age. Most were in their twenties and thirties. The rabbi who sat beside Zachary, and whose name was Ernie Silverman, was no more than forty-five. Mel wondered what his story was, though the man did not go into it. It was obvious he was highly educated, and by his accent, was probably an Israeli-born Jew, first-generation post-Holocaust, like Uriel Katz.

Mel had just sat through a rambling discussion of an esoteric text out of the New Testament book of Hebrews, a long dissertation on Jewish and Christian doctrines, the authorship of which was uncertain. All of it was above his head, though the group gathered in the meeting hall seemed profoundly captivated by it.

Mel had often seen clusters of Jewish students in the restaurants and bistros of Jerusalem. Debate and the matching of scholarly wits was their favorite pastime, and they enjoyed the heated sparring about as much as young Americans enjoyed a good game of football. The Messianic Jews gathered in the YMCA followed suit, only they were dealing with writings that the orthodox would consider doctrinally spurious and these people seemed, for the most part, to be in agreement over them.

The discussion—what little of it Mel understood—dealt with things he had never even heard of, let alone had an opinion regarding. The book of Hebrews dealt with the transition from Judaism to Christianity, dividing time and human history into the period of the "old" and "new covenants," between the time when the ancient Jews attempted to attain holiness by the keeping of voluminous laws, and the time of Christ's atonement.

The writer of Hebrews contended that the old ways had never sufficed for the permanent cleansing of the nation or of individuals, but that Messiah's death had served to suffice for all time.

This much Mel understood on an intellectual level.

As the others enjoyed their discussion, Mel's eyes wandered to a large bulletin board on the wall next to the gathering. Displayed were posters with pictures of the ancient Temple, the priesthood, calendars of holy days, charts of genealogies. There was also a picture of the large tentlike enclosure the Israelites had carried with them during the days of Moses, during their wilderness wanderings, a sort of portable temple called the "tabernacle."

Though today's lesson did not deal with these posters, Mel deduced that the Temple had been built on the same pattern as the tabernacle, with courtyards, an altar of sacrifice, and a central structure that housed the holiest place. Long arrows were drawn from this structure to the wide margin of the paper, pointing to renderings of the Ark of the Covenant and other items that had been housed in this enclosure. A single figure of a man was also pointed out, a man in full priestly regalia, a miterlike bonnet on his head and a breastplate with colorful stones. Mel knew this must be the High Priest, and his skin tingled as he realized that Zachary Cohen was supposed to follow in his footsteps.

Glancing at Zachary, Mel saw that he was intent on getting the most he could out of the meeting. Though Mel was out of his league when it came to discussing the Bible, he was the only one present who knew just how personal all of this was to the young man next to him. When Zachary began to speak out on matters regarding the priesthood, Mel fidgeted, hoping he would not go too far.

"I have been pondering all of this for months," Cohen said. "In fact, my long absence relates to a period of study I have undergone—a spiritual quest, you might say—regarding these very things."

It was obvious that everyone here admired Zachary. The bright, handsome fellow had been missed, and they were curious.

"I would love to tell you everything that has happened to me this past year . . ."

This reinforced Mel's agitation, and he sent unheeded warning glances Zachary's way. The bodyguard relaxed a little when Zachary said, "But for now I would just like to throw some things out for discussion. 'Unsolved mysteries,' I call them. Do you mind?"

Rabbi Silverman was intrigued. "By all means, Zack," he said. "We are all ears!"

Zachary took a deep breath. "Okay," he said. "I have studied Hebrews, and everything related to it, all my adult life. This past year it has become particularly important to me to get a grasp on some things."

The group listened eagerly.

"I am sure many of you have wondered about these same issues. So, here goes. . . . The writer of Hebrews says, 'It is not possible that the blood of bulls and of goats should take away sins.' "

The listeners agreed.

"Then he also says, 'We are made holy by the death of Messiah Yeshua, for all time.' "

These words sparked a chorus of "Amens!" and "Hallelujah, brothers!" from the zealous gathering. Mel noticed that some of them actually had tears in their eyes, and a few raised their hands in spontaneous worship.

The ex-cop shifted uncomfortably in the folding steel chair. *Come on, Zack*, he thought. *Let's get outta here!*

But Zachary was only beginning. Seeing that his friends were in tune with him, he went on, "Now, people, here's the rub. Most of you probably already know where I'm going with this. Don't tell me you haven't had the same questions . . ."

He could see from their faces that some of them anticipated his next topic.

"Go ahead, Zack," Silverman prodded.

"We have all studied how the prophets of the Old Covenant looked forward to the time of Yeshua. But . . ." He swallowed. "What would we do with the fact that those same prophecies say blood sacrifices are supposed to be reinstated?"

Zachary blew out a long breath between pursed lips. "There, I've said it. I've pondered this for months. Any advice?"

Ernie Silverman nodded, a gleam in his eye. Several of the group seemed to be in tune with the rabbi's reaction.

"You have been gone too long!" someone teased.

"Amen!" another chimed in.

Zachary, frustrated by the suspense, held his hands up. "Wha-a-a-t?" he asked in a Yiddish twang, evoking a round of laughter. "Lay it on me!"

Silverman began by reminding Zachary of a guest speaker who had addressed the congregation a couple of years earlier, a man who had written a book on hidden codes in the Bible.

"Yeah, I remember," Zachary replied. "There were a lot of books on that topic going around back then. As I recall, this fellow had done a study looking for Yeshua's name in the Torah."

"*And* in the Prophets!" somebody added.

"Okay," Zachary admitted. "I guess I missed something."

"Probably not," Silverman said. "I think you were here for all his lectures. It wasn't until after you left that our group here got to looking into this further."

Zachary was intrigued. "Did you find something helpful?"

Silverman and the others smiled, as though they had a mutual secret. "We think we did," he replied. "Remember how the speaker said it wasn't until computers came along that we even had the technology to do such a study?"

"Yes," Zachary recalled. "He had created a program that could search out such words as Messiah, Jesus, Nazarene, etcetera, and had found them embedded in a variety of mathematical sequences throughout the words of Scripture."

"Exactly!" Silverman enthused, his youthful face brightening. "All throughout the Old Covenant, in the very books that speak of Messiah's coming, the name is found. Even phrases like 'Jesus is my Name' are embedded."

Zachary rubbed his chin thoughtfully. "That is all well and good," he said. "But . . ."

"What does it have to do with your question?" the rabbi said.

"Right." Zachary nodded.

"Well," the rabbi asked, "do you think the name is missing from those books where the animal sacrifices are spoken of? Do you think the prophets left him out of those writings?"

Zachary shrugged. "Not likely," he figured.

"Indeed not!" Silverman exclaimed. "His name brackets and undergirds those prophecies. It is as though God is telling us, 'When I speak of sacrifice, I speak of my Son. Woven into the very words themselves is the name of the ultimate sacrifice. Someday he will stand in the holy place. No other sacrifice will be necessary!'"

Zachary absorbed these words in speechless amazement. Should he pinch himself to see that he did not dream this?

For a long, drawn-out moment, he sat stone still, staring into space as though his soul had left his body. All about him his friends whispered silent prayers.

At last, he managed to speak. "But . . . why are we only learning this now? Without the electronic capabilities we have today, we would never know these things! Why, now, is it revealed?"

Silverman smiled calmly. "God reveals what is needed 'when the fullness of time has come,'" he said. "When the prophets spoke of Jesus' first coming, few understood their words until he stood in flesh before them. Perhaps it is the same with this. Perhaps we did not need to know until now!" The rabbi leaned forward and placed a hand on Zachary's knee. Peering into the younger man's tear-filled eyes, he added, "Perhaps you, Zachary, needed to know, now."

Soft "Amens!" "Praise Yeshuas!" and "Hallelujahs!" arose from the circle. Zachary raised his hands, his lips moving in silent thanksgiving, as the others worshiped quietly.

Mel looked about him tensely, feeling very much out of place. When people began to leave their seats, gathering around Zachary, placing their hands on his head and shoulders, praying in louder voices, the bodyguard became more anxious still.

He was supposed to protect the future of Israel, but this situation was beyond him. Bible study, prayer meeting, weird talk of priests and computers. And now they were laying hands on Zachary!

There's a lot here that's beyond me, he thought. *Hey, good buddy, say a little prayer for me while you're at it!*

CHAPTER 38

The void beneath the X on the top of Masada would not be broken into easily. Although blistering heat on the mountain had given way to cooler breezes that swirled across the plateau beneath a providential cloud cover, the work of pick and shovel was still backbreaking.

With all of the men lending a hand, however, the little fissure, to which the finger of light had pointed the evening before, gradually became a wide crack. By midmorning, it was obvious that the seam was the juncture of two large stones, about eight inches thick, part of a patio of some building long gone, or the pavement of an avenue that ran between Herodian structures, now leveled.

As the crew took a break, sitting on the rubble of nearby walls, snacking on falafel and hummus sandwiches, Father McCurdy observed that, for all the archaeology that had gone on here, it was peculiar that no one had ever recorded the evidence of these missing structures.

"Perhaps Silva and his troops scavenged Masada for anything of value," suggested Diamant. "Perhaps they burned the limestone buildings like they did at Mount Zion."

"Yes," said Rabbi Ben, "Masada is reminiscent of the condition in which the Romans left Temple Mount. They did a good job of leveling and obliterating all signs of structures existing there in 70 C.E. Except for records of the day, we would have little idea of what Herod's temple was like."

McCurdy sighed. "You know," he said, "Jesus prophesied such total destruction. In the Gospel of Matthew he told his disciples, when they were admiring the great stones of the Temple, that one day there would not be one stone left atop another."

As the priest quoted from the Christian Scriptures, Carl Jacobs and Menachem Levine looked sideways at each other. Laad Girzim was more than a little uncomfortable, finding that he must cooperate not only with Jews but with Christians.

Rabbi Ben nodded to Father McCurdy graciously, then glanced at Rabbi Katz, expecting the usual disapproving look. When he received none, he wondered if he had been imagining that the normally testy rabbi had been acting strangely today.

"But," Diamant objected, "modern scholars attribute such statements to early Christian editors. How could Jesus have known such a thing?"

Father McCurdy rolled his eyes. "Come now, friend," he said, "shall we say the same of the prophet Isaiah, who foretold the birth, life, and resurrection of the same man? For years *modern scholars* said that those prophecies were edited in after Jesus had come and gone. The Cave Scrolls confirmed for all time, by *modern* dating methods, that Isaiah's words were written centuries before Jesus!"

Diamant did not reply, and Cromwell looked at his colleague proudly.

David, however, sensed another squabble brewing. He wrapped the remainder of his sandwich in a baggy and stuffed it in his backpack. "I think a more intriguing question is why none of the scholars who have surveyed Masada ever discovered the void which we have located."

McCurdy thought a moment. "The most thorough investigation here was done in the 1960s. The equipment they used was not sensitive enough to read through thick slabs of rock. Besides, if they were looking for caves, they would probably have limited their search to the areas of natural ground, not paved ones, like this."

"Good observation," David agreed. He stretched his tall body and picked up a shovel. "The day is half gone," he said. "I, for one, would like to get in and out of that cave before dark!"

This, no one disputed. Laad eagerly joined him, and the rest of the crew followed.

They had decided that the next step would be to separate the stones, which nested into each other, apparently forming an interlocking lid over a storage hole. Whatever had been kept here in Herodian times must have been valuable, for it took several men to open the lid.

The combined strengths of David, Ken, Ian, Cromwell, Diamant, Laad, and the rabbis, making use of iron pry bars, finally lifted one and then the other of the rock slabs, pivoting them up and away from the opening. Even Britta did what she could, squeezing planks, from earlier excavation sites, beneath the rocks, so that, should they slip, they would not settle back into place.

As the second slab came to rest alongside the pit, a gust of wind, as though from some deep subterranean tunnel, came whooshing up and out, sending a swirl of dust and debris into the air. The crew fell back, choking and coughing, then stepped cautiously forward and stared into the chamber.

It took a few seconds for the dust to settle enough that they could make out what lay below. To their disappointment, nothing but an empty cavern presented itself to their hopeful gazes.

David stood on the ledge, studying the void with a trained eye. "The wind that escaped from below," he said, "indicates there is another opening to this cavern, possibly on the side of the mountain. I have witnessed the same phenomenon in the Andes, when we opened ancient cave tombs. The Indians used the tombs as fronts to elaborate tunnel systems, where they hid their treasures."

Britta stepped close to David and peered below, huddling against his side. "Rather spooky, isn't it?" she said with a shudder.

David put an arm around her slender shoulders. "Depends on how you look at it," he said.

"Nice one!" McCurdy agreed. "What you're saying is that the Zealots may have done something similar here, right, laddie?"

"I think it's worth a look," David replied.

No sooner had the suggestion been made than they were all ready to lower themselves into the cavern. David held them back, however, suggesting that someone should watch the entry. "It isn't safe for all of us to risk unknown dangers, with no one to go for help," he added.

The rabbis and Laad Girzim selected a couple of sentries, one Israeli and one Jordanian, from among the troops assigned to protect the mission. The young men, considered the most responsible and trustworthy of the lot, hastened to stand guard, their loaded weapons on their shoulders. Strong and confident, they stationed themselves beside the pit. The team disappeared down a dark corridor that led off the chamber, flashlights their only barrier against total darkness.

The labyrinthine tunnel was suffocatingly dry. It had none of the musty, mildewy odor of caves in damper climates, but was permeated by a perpetual, leaching breeze that filtered through the twisting corridor from some unseen aperture at the far end.

As the eleven invaders wormed their way through, hunched beneath the low ceiling, nothing greeted them except sandstone walls, glowing yellow in the beams of their battery-energized torches.

The older men in the group had the most difficulty with this mission.

"Not a place for the claustrophobic," McCurdy observed.

"I think I must have a touch of that ailment," Cromwell replied. "I'll certainly be pleased to see the sky again!"

"As for me," the portly Jacobs grumbled, "I'll just be glad to straighten my aching back!"

David, who was at the head of the group, called over his shoulder, "I'll let you know the minute I see anything hopeful!"

Britta, who thought of this adventure as quite romantic, held on to David's hand as he reached behind him. Ken Aronstam, who followed her, was absorbed in studying the tunnel walls.

"Amazing!" Ken suddenly exclaimed. "Even at this elevation, there is evidence of ancient sea life! Look!"

The group stopped and gathered as close to him as space permitted, staring at a tiny multilegged crustacean fossilized in the limestone.

"From the Paleozoic period," Ken pronounced. "Proof that this entire area was once underwater!"

McCurdy snorted. "Isn't our science clever?" he said with an ironic tone. "We come up with the most elaborate names for the things we understand the least. Perhaps the story of Noah, which every child understands, explains it all."

Aronstam looked at McCurdy in bewilderment. "You can't be serious!" he laughed. "That was just a legend to account for some frightening flood that covered as much earth as the ancients knew about. Probably the Tigris-Euphrates Valley was inundated in a catastrophic monsoon, or some such thing."

McCurdy shrugged. "I suppose it is also believable that tropical jungles found in the polar icecap were planted there by aliens?"

Aronstam tried to be smug, but instead, just lowered his flashlight and nodded to David. "Let's get on with this," he grumbled.

Laad Girzim didn't know what to make of his new colleagues. His own world of study, in the Jordanian desert, was full of enigmas and contradictions. His coworkers did not squabble over them but tried to interpret them at face value. What was it about the Judeo-Christian Scriptures that fostered such antipathy?

Still, he was here because of those very Scriptures. Though he knew very little about the Bible, he knew that something in its teachings was what this mission was all about. Stranger still, he knew that he had become involved with these squabblers through no personal choice.

"I am no archaeologist, Dr. Rothmeyer," Levine called out. "But it appears to me that this is not a man-made tunnel. It is natural, am I right?"

David replied over his shoulder, "For the most part, yes, Rabbi. I am sure this mountain is riddled with such natural voids. However, there is some evidence of human remodeling. See the chinks and cutouts here and there?"

Indeed, tools had left their marks on the walls, apparently opening impassable sections and smoothing out protrusions.

Diamant interpreted. "My guess would be that one of the main uses of this particular tunnel was as an escape route, in the event of attack on the mesa. Probably Herod himself ordered the work done as a protection for his family."

"Yes," McCurdy said, agreeing with his challenger, "that fits. From what I've read, Herod lived in constant fear of uprisings. Why, his development here was as much a fortress as a getaway spa."

As the team batted these ideas about, David's flashlight beam suddenly widened, dispersing into an alcove. "Hey, guys," he announced, "looks like a good place to rest up ahead."

Inspired to move more quickly, the group breathed a sigh of relief as they approached a room-sized cave, its ceiling high enough that even David could stand up.

Swinging their lights about the little cavern, they were astonished to see proof-positive of previous human habitation. Rocks, which had probably once littered the approach and the floor itself, had been piled here and there, forming crude bench and table bases. Upon these were ancient pieces of lumber, remarkably well preserved, apparently hauled in here for tabletops and seating space. Within natural niches along the walls were piles of disintegrated fiber, sticks, and the remains of what appeared to be leather. As the archaeologists studied these materials, they identified them as woven fabric and stuffing for what must have been makeshift beds.

McCurdy was enthralled. "This is what I used to love about digs in Palestine," he said. "The dry climate does little to destroy such finds."

Britta, who had spent months studying McCurdy for an exposé in the *London Times*, sparked to his comment. "Isn't that one reason that the Cave Scrolls lasted for two thousand years?"

McCurdy nodded. "That, and the fact that the Essenes hid them well."

Standing in the center of the room, Britta wrapped her arms around herself as she watched the busy archaeologists. "I just hope you don't go finding skeletons, or some such thing," she said.

Diamant shrugged. "Prepare yourself for the possibility," he said. "The remains of about twenty-five people, including warriors, their women, and even a fetus, were found in a cave on the side of this very mountain!"

Britta groaned. "Oh, please. Let's not go grave hunting."

Then, looking quizzical, she said, "But I thought the seven holdouts whom Silva found were the only survivors. Had the twenty-five escaped the mass suicide as well?"

Diamant shook his head. "From what the archaeologists could determine, the corpses were placed in the cave at some point previous to the suicide. Perhaps they were casualties of the assault that riddled the mountain for months previous."

"That's right," David said. "I remember reading that the Romans sent volleys of artillery and flaming torches onto the mesa, and even used a battering ram on the Herodian fortress, to flush out the rebels."

Britta found a convenient rock pile on which to sit. "I don't know what all of you find so charming about your profession," she muttered.

She had just sat down, closing her eyes against the eeriness of the place, when Uriel Katz, who had been very quiet to this point, suddenly emitted a shriek. "God of Abraham, Isaac, and Jacob!" he cried. "Do I see what I think I'm seeing?"

The little man, ever the loner, had busied himself with studying the cave walls, as the others were investigating the ancient bedding. Rushing over to him, Benjamin, Jacobs, and Levine gasped in astonishment.

"Look here, will you!" Rabbi Ben exclaimed, holding his flashlight up to a distinct pictograph, etched in the limestone near the ceiling.

Britta leaped to her feet as Ken, David, and Laad wheeled about. Rushing toward the rabbis, everyone raised their flashlights to the wall so that it blazed with clarity. There, before their awe-filled gazes, was the image of the red heifer, larger, but identical in form to the one on the Jeremiah Box.

Fumbling in his backpack, Ken pulled out the box, unwrapped the linen binder with shaking hands, and held the little casket up for comparison. "Good Lord!" he cried.

"Exactly!" Rabbi Katz agreed. "The Lord *is* good!"

As the group, in marveling wonder, glanced from the box to the wall, from the wall to the box, Laad Girzim pushed between them like a wedge, until he stood inches from the picture. Only when Britta noticed that his head was bowed and his shoulders were shaking did the group focus on him. Placing a hand on his back, she inquired, "Are you all right, Mr. Girzim?"

It took a moment for the Jordanian to compose himself. At last he managed to speak, though his voice was choked with tears. "It was a picture like this that convinced me I should help you!" he cried.

The others were bewildered. "Of course, Mr. Girzim," Ben replied. "We have all been led by the picture on the box."

"No, no," he said, turning about and facing them. "I do not speak of the box. I saw this very picture on the wall of another cave, only days ago."

"Another cave?" David asked. "But where?"

Laad broached to them the subject of his visit with his grandmother and her old friend. "They showed me the cave, in my own town of Old Petra, where the prophet Jeremiah is said to have hidden. There, on a similar wall, was this exact image!"

Blinking his teary eyes, he pulled out a handkerchief from his hip pocket and blew his nose. Frustrated that they did not seem to grasp the obvious, he said firmly, "Gentlemen, you will find what you are seeking if you will dig beneath the foot of the heifer!"

Ken gasped. "Just as the inscription on the box told us!"

Suddenly, a jolt of comprehension shocking them to action, the group grabbed picks, trowels, and shovels, and as Laad moved aside, they began to do as he said. True to his prediction, they found that a thin veneer of camouflaging limestone concealed a doorway, all filled in with rubble. As the Jordanian intently watched, they removed rock after rock. Their pulses pounding, they dodged tumbling debris and scrambled for a look into an opening near the top.

David, who was at the front of the group, groaned as the others pressed in on him. "Stand back!" he commanded. "The rest of these rocks could give way any moment! Do you all want to go falling, face first, into who knows what?"

Collecting themselves, the crew stepped back. As David straightened his shoulders and dusted himself off, Laad raised a hand to his mouth, concealing a grin, and tried not to laugh aloud.

"That's better," David growled, mustering some dignity. Then, waving them all aside, he said, "Now I shall have a look, if you don't mind."

David climbed up on the rock pile and, leaning carefully into the aperture, thrust his light inside.

What seemed to the onlookers an inordinate length of time, but was actually only seconds, elapsed before David pronounced, "Well done, Rabbi Katz and Mr. Girzim! We do have a find here!"

Now was no time to stand on ceremony. As a body, the group rushed at the professor again. "Come on, Dave," Ken insisted. "Let's get on with it!"

David scrambled down from the pile and, eager as anyone else, began to pull the remaining rubble aside. In moments, everyone lending a hand, the opening was complete.

Then, abruptly, they all hesitated.

Ben, interpreting the pause, said, "This is it, dear friends. Whatever lies in that chamber, we have all invested a good part of our lives and our energies into finding it. We must not let fear overcome us now!"

David, looking at his crew, and then at the hole in the wall, gave a quick nod. Together, they moved forward, flashlights ablaze, squeezing shoulder to shoulder into the chamber.

What met their eyes was beyond astonishing. Within a natural cavern, the size of a typical bedroom, were piled several pieces of gold-leaf furniture: small tables, footstools, straight-backed armchairs, all similar to what could be seen in the museums of Cairo, Amman, Damascus, and other royal cities. Scattered among them were burlap bags, marvelously preserved, of gold and silver artifacts, jewel-encrusted goblets, candelabrum, serving pieces—any one of which would have done justice to the tombs of ancient Egypt or the archives of Rome.

Had any stranger been dropped into this scene from the outside and asked to interpret it, he would have assumed he had entered the staging area of a B movie. Here were the beautiful blonde, the lanky archaeologist, the cute rabbis, the helpful Arab. Here were the gaudy treasures from some long-lost civilization, papier-mâché, he would have assumed, spray-painted to look like precious metal.

But these were not actors. This was not a stage.

This was real. The treasures were real.

The overwhelmed expressions, the speechless awe, were real.

Most amazing was the presence of a tall, seven-branched candlestand of solid gold; a long table that must be the table of showbread; and an incense altar—all apparently from the apartment adjacent to the Temple's inmost sanctum.

"Oh, Lord Jehovah!" Rabbi Ben exclaimed. "The scroll was right!"

"Treasures from the Holy Place!" Carl whispered.

"But, how is it possible?" Levine marveled. "These things were taken by the Romans when they ransacked the Temple!"

Uriel grinned from ear to ear. "The Romans were left with copies!" he cried. "These have to be the originals!"

The rabbis laughed aloud, clapping one another on the back, as if to congratulate themselves for their ancestors' sleight of hand.

Meanwhile, Britta tiptoed through the piles of bagged artifacts, eyeing them as though she were in a dream. "Is it all right to touch anything?" she asked, bending over a chest of golden dishes.

The rabbis looked at one another and shrugged silently. "You *will* be very careful, Ms. Hayworth," Jacobs replied.

As Britta picked up one small goblet and turned it over and over in trembling hands, Ken commented, "These are but a tiny fraction of the wealth of the ancient Temple. Most of it *was* hauled away by Titus, was it not?"

"Correct," Diamant confirmed. "As we recounted earlier, he even burned the limestone of the Temple compound to melt the gold from the buildings."

Overcome with emotion, Ben cleared his throat and reminded them, "Wondrous as this is, we are here to locate two things, and two things only."

"Right you are!" Cromwell said. "But where shall we begin?"

The men thought a moment, and David suggested, "Perhaps if we try to think as the guardians of these treasures would have thought, we will come up with a starting point."

At this, Laad, who had remained close to the entrance, stepped forward. "Though you have not admitted to seeking the vial that once rested in the Jeremiah Box," he said, "I have good cause to believe that it would have been hidden in this cave some time after these other items were placed here. As you can see, the furnishings have been piled neatly, not in haste, as though the ones who stored them had time to organize and arrange them. As for the vial, I would expect to find it close to this door, and since the box was missing, the bottle would be in some sort of protective container."

The group, following his suggestion, turned toward the cave's front wall and scanned the area. As they did so, however, Britta, who had continued to sort through the chest of golden serving pieces, pulling them out and placing them one by one upon the ground, thought otherwise.

"Not to be contrary, Mr. Girzim," she said, "but perhaps the one who hid the vial wanted to put it with the other most important artifact we are seeking."

David, who knew her best, discerned the tone of suppressed excitement in her voice. Turning to her, he also saw the teasing twinkle in her eye that meant she had some great thing to say.

"What is it, Britta?" he asked, walking toward her.

The girl clamped one hand over her mouth, restraining a squeal, and bounced up and down on the balls of her feet. Pointing to the chest, she said with a laugh, "Perhaps our anonymous Zealot thought he was clever, putting these things among the dishes!"

As David bent over the chest, peering inside, his legs went weak. Slumping to his knees, he raised his hands to his face and blinked awe-filled eyes.

The rabbis rushed toward him, Laad Girzim, McCurdy, Cromwell, and Aronstam pushing close behind.

Britta, whose blue eyes had never shone so much as they did at this moment, pointed her flashlight into the chest. There, on the bottom, lay a breastplate, embroidered with solid gold and inset with twelve magnificent gems. And nestled beside it, on a velvet pillow, lay an alabaster bottle etched with the image of a calf—the little urn of the Ashes of the Red Heifer.

CHAPTER 39

No more rapturous celebration had ever taken place upon Masada than the little party that ensued where the stash of treasures was found.

With tenderness and honor befitting the most hallowed items on earth, the rabbis lifted the vial and its pillow, along with the breastplate, from the ancient storage chest, tenderly carried them into the adjoining chamber, and set them on the old table, which refugees had constructed of rocks and planks in the middle of the room. Their companions illumined their cautious passage with their flashlights, and when the rabbis had deposited the precious objects on the crude altar, the flashlights were set about them, pointing upward so as to reflect off the sandstone ceiling.

"Rabbi Ben," David said somberly, "don't you think we should check the contents of the vial? Perhaps, God forbid, it is empty! Whatever the case, it is best we know now."

The old rabbi looked to his colleagues. "Go ahead, Horace," Katz agreed. "Among all of us, you are the most deserving of this honor."

Jacobs and Levine agreed, and so Rabbi Benjamin, quivering from head to toe, reached for the vial. Trying to control his shakes, he managed to remove the alabaster stopper, which resisted nearly to the breaking point. When at last it gave in to his gentle twisting and pulling, coming forth with a pop, the group gasped.

Huddling about him, they all tried to get a look, but only Rabbi Benjamin could see what was deposited inside.

Lips trembling, he feared to speak. "Yes," he said with a sigh, returning the stopper to its place and the vial to its pillow, "there is a good amount of gray dust in the bottle!"

Laad cleared his throat inquisitively, hoping for an explanation of the strange substance. But the group remained in a huddle, just gawking at the priceless finds.

At last, Carl Jacobs suggested they make a ring around the table.

"Come, Mr. Girzim," he said. "Celebrate with us! Then we shall tell you our secrets, and you shall tell us yours."

Obediently, Laad complied, and there they all stood—rabbis, Americans, British, Irish, Arab—like mesmerized worshipers.

Scarcely a breath was drawn, until Jacobs silently took Rabbi Benjamin and Rabbi Levine by the hand, one to each side of him. They, following suit, took the hands of their closest neighbors, and so on, until the entire group of eleven friends was linked in a companionable circle.

Then Dr. Jacobs began to shift from foot to foot, lifting one and then the other, in simple rhythm. Soon all the rabbis were softly singing, kicking their feet and swaying, urging the others, by example, to join in.

"*Hava nagila!*" they began to chant, the minor chords of the world's most famous song of joy gradually swelling as it was repeated again and again.

"*Hava nagila, hava nagila, hava nagila, v' nis m' cha!*"

"Come let us rejoice and be glad!"

The group was circling now, mimicking the rabbis with splaying feet and bouncing knees.

"*Hava n'ra n'na, hava n'r n'na, hava n'ra n'na, v' min m' cha!*"

"Arise, brothers, with a joyful heart!"

The ring was picking up speed, bodies twisting this way and that, fringes flying on tunic borders, side locks bouncing, eyes sparkling, girl laughing, men weeping.

"*U ru, u ru, a chim! U ra a chim b' lev sa me ach . . . b'lev sa me ach!*"

"Come let us rejoice and be glad! Arise, brothers, with a joyful heart!"

Round and round and round the room they went, round and round the little altar, until they were all asweat, teary faced, and hoarse.

Hearts pounding to the point of pain, they fell at last in a joyous, circular heap, and David, embracing his beloved Britta, planted upon her lips the kiss he had promised their first night on Masada.

Dusk would soon be descending on the earth above. The sheen of sweaty exuberance still shone on their faces as the rabbis and the Jordanian shared their secrets in an atmosphere of unprecedented trust. Seated about the cave floor, the revelers revealed their cherished legends, the quests that had absorbed them, the tales held sacred for ages. Stories of the ashes, the Petran cave, the fearful sheiks who had stolen the box, the prophet and the Masada refugees . . . All was told, nothing was held back.

"And when our priest is installed," Rabbi Ben said, "you and your queen must be our guests!"

Laad bowed, his heart warm with joy. "Nothing could honor us more," he said.

At last the group got to their feet.

There were decisions to be made: what to do with what they had found. Oh, the vial and breastplate must remain their secret! That, no one disputed. As to the rest of the finds, some thought it best to seal them away for another day; others thought it best to report them to the world, to turn them over to the IAA so they might be put in safekeeping.

"You can be sure the authorities will be waiting for us when we descend the mountain," Shalom warned them. "We do not want it to appear we came here for nothing!"

Laad nodded gratefully. "Mr. Hamir, of the PAA, assured me he would be 'on hand' to check on my work. I must have something to report."

At last, after much talk and much debate, an agreement was reached. They would go forth with a few of the smaller items, just to satisfy the waiting world. They would report that there was more, much more, to be brought down.

And they would leave it to the IAA to do that. If God was in the work of the Temple, he would see to it that the treasures were kept safe for the future, and he would put them in their rightful places in good time.

Meanwhile, they all concurred that the very existence of the vial and breastplate was "classified" information, much too sensitive to entrust to outsiders. "How about if they were hidden again, among the dishes?" Britta suggested. "We can haul a few such crates down with us. Surely, they will not insist on digging through them all. We can demand the right to study a few pieces and get them safely back to headquarters. The rest can be left to the IAA."

The men decided they liked the sound of this.

"It's worth a try," David said. "Okay, Rabbis?"

"Okay!" Rabbi Ben agreed.

The exhausted invaders began to gather up a few of the bags, light crates of artifacts, as Britta had suggested, and the smallest pieces of furniture. The precious vial was secreted back into the chest where it had sat for two thousand years, put to rest on its pillow, and nested against the breastplate. Golden goblets and dishes were piled atop the holy articles before Ken and David each grabbed a side handle and carried the chest between them.

Together the group headed back through the Herodian chamber.

As they had predicted, it was dusk when they emerged from the underground void. "Sir," one of the sentries greeted David as he climbed onto the plateau, "the PAA and the IAA sent word that they are waiting below."

David dusted himself off and smiled bleakly at the young man. "Why am I not surprised?" he said.

Buscar, the tall, dignified secretary to the Curator of the Antiquities of the Royal House of Jordan, was having an easy day of it. With Laad Girzim having taken off for Jerusalem, Buscar would have time to catch up on work he never got to when the boss was around. Mainly, he hoped to start sorting out old material from the steel file cabinet in the boss's office.

It was a wonder the cabinet hadn't broken under its own weight, he thought, as he pulled the top drawer open and found that the files were so full, not one more shred of paper could have been squeezed in without popping the rivets.

When Mr. Girzim was not present, Buscar made himself quite at home in the sumptuous inner office. A big-screen TV sat in one corner, and a full liquor bar in another. Laad used the bar to entertain visiting dignitaries who might happen to drop in and kept precise tabs on the supply; Buscar would not indulge in the contents. But he did flick on the television, to entertain himself as he worked. As always, it was tuned to CNN International, which the boss usually had broadcasting softly in the background so that he could keep abreast of developments that might affect his work in this politically volatile region.

Laad would never have suspected that Buscar would have preferred an Israeli soap opera. The secretary spoke fluent Hebrew and enjoyed watching the American-styled romances that showed Israel was headed down the slippery trail of decadence blazed by its Western mentors. Of course, had any of the palace staff dropped by, Buscar would have aimed the remote control at the screen and returned to CNN. It would not be wise to let his fellow Muslims see that he indulged in such fleshly fantasies.

He resisted the temptation, however, and let the screen flash onto the well-known set of the newsroom that came over the satellite feed station into the palace.

Before entering the boss's office, he had poured himself a cup of espresso from his own carafe. He set it on the brass tray that was supported by carved legs in front of the sofa, then went to the file cabinet to yank out a handful of burgeoning folders. Where to start, he wondered. He could begin at the beginning of the drawer, which was arranged according to the alphabet of the international language, English. *Amman Archaeology Association*, said the first file. But he would much rather sort through something interesting.

As he pondered this he also pondered what could have caused Mr. Girzim's sudden departure for Jerusalem. It was not like him to leave so abruptly without explaining himself to his secretary, especially not if he was going into such alien territory as the Israeli capital.

Buscar could remember only one other time when this had happened. It had followed shortly after the assassination of the American senator Calvin Jefferson. It had struck Buscar as strange that a Jordanian official, like Laad, would go into Israel, a country allied with the United States, when the entire world suspected some sort of Jordanian complicity in the senator's death.

Buscar had phoned certain contacts at the Jordanian border station when his boss made that untimely trip. Laad had apparently slipped through the checkpoint, possibly with an alias and, arousing no suspicions, had gone on his way. But Buscar had done his duty, reporting anything that smacked of behavior traitorous to the Muslim cause originating at his assigned post—the palace in Amman.

For Buscar was not only the secretary to the palace curator; he was, unbeknownst to the royal house, a spy for a web of international terrorists committed to the cause of Allah—specifically, the cause of Allah as interpreted by a certain Sheik Abu Matif, a shadowy Muslim radical whose headquarters location was a well-guarded secret. One day, Buscar believed, Sheik Matif would reveal himself to the world as the Great Savior of Righteousness. For now, Matif lived in shadow, awaiting the time of his revelation. That was not to say he was powerless, however. Matif ruled over a machine of terrorism, the enormity of which only the most sophisticated international police had any clue.

It was true that notorious Muslims rose to the forefront of public notice from time to time. They appeared, to the general public, to be elusive characters, hard to expose, hard to comprehend, protected by vast networks of safe houses, encampments, and munitions depots. But, these were children, compared to Matif. These were, in fact, Matif's puppets.

Buscar had never met Matif. His work for the cause was so region-specific, so tiny by comparison to Matif's universal plan, that he could only hope his efforts contributed something to the larger cause.

Buscar had a unique background, which made him valuable to Matif. Before going to work for the Jordanian Antiquities Authority, he had served for years as a valet to countless foreign ambassadors. He had been in an unusual position to learn all sorts of things about the Great Satan, the Western imperialists whose values posed a direct assault on the principles of Muslim fundamentalism. Since he had secured himself a position within the Jordanian palace, he was even more useful to Matif's cause.

Due to his position, for instance, he had been able to report to his co-conspirators the peculiar liaison that the previous king had developed with the American evangelist. He had not known what to make of that friendship, or how meaningful it might be to the sheik, but he had reported it, just in case.

He had also reported his suspicion that Senator Jefferson's brief visit to Amman, following as it did on the heels of the king's death, did not bode well for the Muslim cause. "My hunch is that the senator is bearing information helpful to the Great Satan," he reported, "perhaps even to Israel itself!"

When Calvin Jefferson had promptly been intercepted and murdered, Buscar had felt, for the first time, that he did not serve Matif in vain.

Buscar had no reason to believe he would unearth any treachery today. The mundane task of cleaning a file cabinet was less than glamorous. He decided to begin by randomly grabbing a handful of files from the center of the drawer. Yes, the Ms through the Qs would do nicely. Taking the folders to the sofa, he sat down, placed them on the brass tray, and began to look through them.

Opening the first M file, labeled *Masada,* he found the usual sorts of things Laad would have filed regarding a regional site: a map of the old Herodian structures, a list of scholars who had worked there, their addresses, and so on. There was not much here to toss out. Masada had not been a popular dig site for a couple of decades, so the material in the file was old but as current as was to be had.

One paper in the file did strike Buscar as peculiar: a digital photo of some sort of box. Apparently quite old, the box's most noticeable characteristic was the etching of a cow on the lid. Buscar looked at it in curiosity. Making nothing of it, he replaced it in the file, but not before he noticed it had a notation on the bottom: "F3, R2, S5."

Buscar recognized this as the format used for recording locations of items in the royal archives. "Floor three," he whispered, "row two, shelf five." Apparently Laad had placed this photo in the Masada file because it related to study he had done on the Herodian fortress.

The secretary did not recall Laad ever discussing Masada in the office. But, then, Buscar was not privy to everything Mr. Girzim researched. Shrugging, he placed it in the folder and moved on.

There were several M, *N*, and O files, and two *P* files, all thick enough to take a while to sort. But here was a Q file, and it was quite thin. Might as well take care of it, so he could feel he was accomplishing something.

Buscar was pleased to see that there was only one item in this file, two sheets stapled together, the top one being the cover of a fax transmission. To his surprise, he found that, across one corner of the cover sheet, Laad had written: "Sent at queen's request."

This explained why the item was in the Q file, Buscar figured. "Q for queen," he said aloud, grinning at his boss's filing rationale.

When he read the sheet, however, his grin faded.

The cover sheet indicated that the fax had been sent from an office supply company in Jerusalem, a place where anyone could enter and, for a small fee and the cost of the long-distance phone connection, send a fax anywhere in the world. The date of the fax fit with the time frame during which Laad had made his last trip to Jerusalem.

Interestingly, the destination phone number was only a United States country code, followed by a row of asterisks, making it impossible to know the recipient's location. Buscar realized that this meant the receiving phone had a built-in security device that blocked the number from being printed out or otherwise recorded by the originating machine. The only thing he knew for sure was that the terminal was somewhere in the U.S.

Bewildered, Buscar turned back the cover sheet to see what Laad had transmitted to the Great Satan. To his astonishment, he found that the second page contained the same photo that had been filed under *Masada*!

Leaning back into the sofa cushions, he held the picture to the light, studying it intently. *What in the world could this be about?* he wondered. Why would anything filed under *Masada* have been faxed from Jerusalem to the United States—and at the request of the queen of Jordan, no less?

Buscar scratched his pointed chin and, leaning forward again, reached for his cup of espresso. Indeed, he had a mystery on his hands, and he had a strong hunch his boss had never intended him to unearth it.

It occurred to him that there might be a tie-in here with the deceased king's friendship with Israel. Perhaps he should report this peculiar find to the sheik's henchmen. But then, what, exactly, would he report? Until he knew more, it would be absurd to tell them about an obscure fax to an unknown number.

Returning the papers to the folder, he had decided to simply keep his eyes and ears open, when, suddenly, the television in the corner seemed to speak directly to him. Until that moment, he had paid no heed to the news being broadcast from CNN International. Now, it appeared, the reporters were dealing directly with the subject at hand.

"In an unprecedented show of international cooperation," the announcer was saying, "archaeologists from Israel, the United States, Britain, and Jordan unearthed some fabulous finds at the ancient fortress of King Herod near the Dead Sea early this morning. Masada, most famous as the place of the last stand of Jewish Zealots against Rome in the first century, has proven to be the hiding place of furnishings and artifacts which may date from the time of the Jewish temple, destroyed in 70 C.E."

Buscar gawked at the screen. There, for all the world to see, were priceless treasures and ornamental items being brought forth from trams that had just descended the mountain. Reporters and cameramen were eagerly getting the story from the scholars and the soldiers who had guarded them. A cute British woman with hair as golden as the treasures themselves proudly displayed one crate of plates and goblets before they were hauled off to a waiting van. A tall American professor and his academic colleague discussed possible interpretations of the find, and with them were a number of Jewish rabbis. Buscar recognized them as the same men interviewed a year ago, when an Arab attempt to bomb a boys' school went awry.

So sudden and unexpected were these images that Buscar barely had time to get the gist of the story before he was stunned to see Laad Girzim's face flash onto the screen.

"Traitor!" Buscar cried. "Now the world shall know what a traitor you are!"

Buscar reached for the phone to call his contacts in Damascus and alert them to the treachery afoot in the royal house of Jordan. But now the CNN camera pulled back, revealing that Laad stood side by side with the head of the Palestinian Antiquities Authority. Mr. Hamir, whom Buscar knew to be a friend of Sheik Matif, appeared very pleased with what had transpired today.

Confounded, Buscar listened as Hamir announced that the PAA supported Girzim's cooperation with the dig, and that a Palestinian-Jordanian study on the finds would soon be forthcoming.

Buscar's hand, which had just picked up the phone, went numb. For a long moment, he held the receiver, the dial tone vibrating into dead air, until, in speechless confusion, he returned it to the cradle.

Yes, he considered, there was a mystery here! But it was a mystery so far over his head, he could not ask the right questions, let alone find any answers.

As the report continued, promising that CNN would follow up on all future developments, Buscar glared at the files on the tray table. Fumbling with the M and Q folders, he bit his lower lip.

He had no way of understanding the complicity he had just witnessed, but he had a strong hunch that the box was behind it all. He also had a hunch that if that box was missing from the archives, it had been given to Senator Calvin Jefferson. Furthermore, he would lay odds that it was for that box that Senator Jefferson had been killed!

Just to satisfy himself that he was not hallucinating, he picked up the phone again and called a clerk in the royal museum.

"Buscar here," he said, his authoritative tone laced with tension. "I want you to bring me something. Yes . . . an item from the archives . . . Number F3 R2 S5. Yes, I will wait. Phone me when you find it."

Buscar hung up and sat back, drumming his fingers on the file folders resting in his lap.

This would take a while. He closed his eyes, trying to put the pieces of the puzzle together. Fifteen minutes passed, and the phone rang.

"Buscar, here," he repeated. "Yes . . . what? How can that be? No . . . no, don't bother. It must have been misplaced. Too much ineptitude in your department! No . . . don't bother! Perhaps we can do without it. Yes . . . I will check with Mr. Girzim. Good-bye."

Again Buscar hung up the phone, this time congratulating himself on his confirmed suspicion.

Staring at the incongruous images on the TV screen—the apparent cooperation between enemies—he felt as if he were watching a disjointed dream.

Political demarcations, once clearly drawn, seemed suddenly blurred.

Just who *was* "the enemy" anyway?

CHAPTER 40

The parlor of the Consortium house was filled with warmth, from the crackling fire on the grate to the jubilant conversation and laughter of the occupants. Not since David Rothmeyer had first met the rabbis in New York City over a year ago had he seen them so starry-eyed with wonder and fulfillment.

Under the scrutiny of the world press, the rabbis had departed Masada with their team, returning to Jerusalem by late evening. The finds, including the furnishings from the Holy Place, were still being hauled out of the Herodian tunnel by the young soldiers who had protected the scholars. Under the direction of the IAA, but allowing controlled access by the PAA, they would be quartered for study at a laboratory near Hebrew University.

Laad Girzim had departed for Amman, promising Mr. Hamir that he would send the PAA a full report of the team's experiences. As to the finds themselves, he assured Hamir that nothing was hidden, and that what they brought forth from the tunnel was all there was to see.

Hamir was still mystified as to how anything on Masada related to the history of Jordan, but Laad told him he would include that in a supplementary report, once the finds were cataloged and studied. He would be on hand, he told Hamir, to sort out Jordan's interests.

The rabbis, taking a "few samples" from the find "for their own study," had delivered the crate of golden dishes to their underground lab, where they had stored them for safekeeping.

But not before removing the coveted vial and breastplate. Those items they had secreted in the old house, where, this night, they would be reunited with the Cohen priesthood.

The team, luxuriating after a grand meal and a bottle of wine, recounted their experiences for Zachary and Mel.

Describing the moment when they had located the tunnel's hidden chamber, Carl Jacobs roared with laughter, quoting the most memorable statement of the day. "And then, Mr. Girzim said, 'Gentlemen, you will find what you are seeking if you will dig beneath the foot of the heifer!' "

"You should have seen Dave!" Ken jibed. "Squished up against the rocks as we all tried to climb over him!"

Britta defended her beloved professor. "Now, Ken, that's not nice!" she said, trying not to laugh herself. "What do you think we must have looked like, scrambling atop him?"

"I don't care how I *looked*!" David retorted. "It was how I *felt* that mattered! The whole bunch of you nearly broke all my bones!"

Zachary appreciated the account, but as the group chatted on, his eyes kept traveling to a certain valise, which sat squarely in front of the fireplace, begging to be opened. Rabbi Ben, noting his eager expression, at last announced, "We could talk on all night, but we have come together for one special purpose." Gesturing to Zachary, he said, "Mr. Cohen, shall we step over to the table?"

Anya had cleared away the supper dishes and replaced the soiled tablecloth with fresh linen. Zachary stared in speechless wonder as Rabbi Ben set the valise on the dining table and flipped the latches.

All of Zachary's friends stood with him, these dear ones who knew just who he was and how he was connected with the things he was about to see. Respecting the awesomeness of the moment, they were very quiet.

Rabbi Ben reached into the valise and, with cautious, reverent hands, lifted out the alabaster vial, the sacred Ashes of the Red Heifer, cradled on its pillow. As he placed it on the table, Ken handed him the Jeremiah Box, and everyone watched as the vial, for the first time in two and a half millennia, was returned to its container.

When the vial nestled perfectly into the box's hollowed-out interior, a gasp of delight went up from the group.

Zachary's eyes had never been so wide. "Wonderful!" he said. "Is this the first time you tried the box on for size?"

"It is," Ben said. "We wanted you to share in the moment."

Zachary blinked back tears. "May I?" he said, reaching out to touch the vial.

"Of course!" Ben said. "It is yours, after all!"

No one needed an explanation of that comment. In truth, the vial and the other item in the valise did belong to Zachary, in a way no one else on earth could claim.

His fingers were cold with trepidation as he tentatively stroked the little bottle. Quickly, he withdrew his hand, overcome with the mystery of the moment.

"To think," he said hoarsely, "some grandfather of mine, so far back in time that we do not know his name, last used this bottle!"

Menachem Levine echoed his wonder. "That is right! Someone even before your ancestor who is named in the First Copper Scroll, for that man was denied his rightful heritage."

"Furthermore," Carl Jacobs added, "except for the people at Petra and Masada, the last person to touch the vial was the prophet Jeremiah!"

Zachary bowed his head.

A hush fell over the little group as Rabbi Benjamin reached into the valise once again, this time bringing out a square piece of multi-colored tapestry, about the span of a man's hand in width. Woven of fine linen yarn, its colors were still amazingly vivid, though the peculiar vestment had been stored away for twenty centuries. Blue, purple, and scarlet, the magnificent cloth was framed with embroidery of gold, so dense as to be almost solid, and worthy of the designation breast*plate*. Set into the tapestry, and secured by backings and pegs of gold, were twelve precious stones, gleaming with brilliant color, representing the twelve tribes of Israel.

At each corner of the breastplate were eyelets, inset with golden rings, through which ribbons had once passed, to secure the piece to the high priest's upper body.

Zachary leaned over the table, studying the breastplate with astonished eyes. "I have tried to envision this precious item a million times!" he exclaimed. "I never really imagined how beautiful it would be!"

Rabbi Ben slipped one hand into the breastplate, showing Zachary that it was actually made double. "See," he said, "it is a pocket. On the inside, possibly in another pouch, the priest carried the oracle of Israel, by which he could determine the will of God!"

Every fiber of Zachary's being thrilled to the notion. "The Urim and Thummim!" he marveled.

Inquiringly, he looked at Ben. The old rabbi shook his head. "No, Zachary, they are not here. And so, you see, our work is not yet done."

Trying not to show much disappointment, Zachary sighed deeply. He thanked Rabbi Ben for sharing the sacred treasures, then returned to his place by the fire, the group following his lead and taking seats about the room.

"How I wish Mel and I could have been with you!" he said. "Tell me, have you come up with any plausible scenario for just how these wonderful things came to be at Masada?"

Father McCurdy jumped at the chance to summarize what the team had discussed on the way home from the King's Tower. "As you know," he said, "things have been quite ajumble over the past weeks, as we have attempted to sort out the clues along the way. On the trip back from Masada, we all had our ideas, and we talked long and hard about how to piece the puzzle together."

"Yes," said Carl Jacobs, "between two copper scrolls, a cedar box, a vial, and then the information Mr. Girzim gave us, we have had a lot of information."

"And a lot of confusion!" Britta added.

Zachary frowned. "Regarding Mr. Girzim, I am also confused. You told me about the drawing of the cow on the tunnel wall. Just how did he know it pointed to a sealed doorway?"

McCurdy picked up again. "That's where things got really interesting . . ."

Rabbi Katz laughed. "As though they were dull before?"

McCurdy raised his hands. "Touché," he said. "Now, let me explain. We ourselves could have deduced as much from the picture on the tunnel wall, considering that the box told us we would find the vial at the foot of the heifer. However, there could be no doubt when Girzim told us about an exact replica of the drawing on a cave in the valley of Petra! A pictograph matching the one in the tunnel!"

Zachary shook his head. "Amazing! What do you make of that?"

McCurdy replied, "As I said, we had many sources of clues, and we needed to put them in order. It was not until we learned of the Petran pictograph that things began to come together. Let me see," he said, rubbing his chin, "where to begin?"

David stepped in. "Let's start with the scrolls. After all, that's all we had at first."

McCurdy nodded. "Very well. This is what we deduced: the people at Masada were hiding something. What they hid was not so much a bunch of treasures as the knowledge of their whereabouts, scattered throughout Palestine."

Diamant added, "In fact, we came up with the novel idea that it was to keep their secret secure that the Zealots were willing to give up their lives."

McCurdy agreed. "Exactly," he said. "And they needed a way to record their secret, a way to keep a list of the treasures and their locations."

"Ta da!" Britta sang. "The Copper Scrolls!"

Zachary smiled. "Go on!"

"Well," McCurdy proceeded, "apparently the people, or person, who etched the Copper Scrolls did so during the time the Zealots were staked out on Masada. Whether the rebels were able to sneak the scrolls down to Qumran and hide them before the Romans came, or whether someone had been picked to survive the mass suicide and escape after the Romans left, we cannot know."

"But," David explained, "somehow they fulfilled their mission to hide the inventory list in the caves at Qumran, where no one, until the Cave Scroll team, ever found them."

Britta could not resist a good tease. "Even then, a certain renegade scholar smuggled the Second Scroll to the British Museum, where he kept it for half a century!"

Father McCurdy winced. "You made my life miserable enough in the past, Ms. Hayworth," he said good-naturedly. "You do not need to continue the practice!"

Britta laughed and David winked at her.

"I would like to add," the professor said, "that Father McCurdy's suppositions are highly believable. It is quite possible that the person, or people, who took the scrolls to Qumran escaped the mountain by way of the very tunnel we were in. As I pointed out, there has to be an opening at the far end which causes all the air movement through the corridor. Perhaps, by dead of night, someone exited through that opening, crept down the mountain, managed to skirt the Roman camps, and headed north."

"Or, perhaps," Ken reiterated, "they waited for the Romans to leave and finished their mission afterward."

Zachary followed along. "Okay," he said, "so we have a couple of scrolls, inventory lists, hidden to the north. What about the cedar box?"

"To understand how the cedar box was incorporated into the story, we must look again at what we learned from the Second Copper Scroll," McCurdy said, his professorial voice ringing forth as though he were in an Oxford classroom. "We know the Second Scroll is a key to the earlier one, giving the explanation of where the treasures were hidden. What cued us to the fact that it also dealt with items not listed in the First Scroll, was the first anomaly it contained."

"Anomaly?" Zachary asked.

"Something out of order, or not expected," David replied. "When we were reading through the Second Copper Scroll, we found it followed the first quite nicely, only with broader information. It was not until we came to references to extraneous items, not mentioned in the First Copper Scroll, that we knew we were on to something even more important."

"The furnishings of the Holy Place," Zachary deduced.

"Exactly!" Britta enthused. "The scroll said those items would be found in the King's Tower!"

"Yes," McCurdy said. "Another anomaly! We had no clue where the King's Tower was until our American professor came across the most cryptic statement on the scroll."

David was red-faced, remembering his embarrassment that night. "The crew didn't like my translation, I'll tell you!" he said.

"That's for sure!" Cromwell spoke up. "All that about caskets and maps! I was ready to go back to England!"

Zachary was quizzical. "Caskets?"

David grinned. "Well, one, actually. Let's not make it any worse than it was."

Britta squirmed. "Do tell them about my interpretation, won't you?"

David nodded. "Of course, Ms. Hayworth," he said, saluting her. "But first, let me tell them mine."

Zachary held up a hand. "Just get on with it!" he laughed.

"Well, we were getting close to the end of the scroll when suddenly a peculiar line appeared. 'When you find the casket of the prophet,' it said, 'which is in the hands of Cyrus, you will also find the map to the King's Tower'!"

Zachary was as bewildered as the team had been that night in the laboratory. "Does sound creepy," he agreed. "What did you make of it?"

"Well," David went on, "we wrestled with the concepts well into the night. At last it was Ms. Hayworth who came up with the idea that 'casket' might, in this case, simply mean a 'small box.' "

Zachary's eyes widened. "The Jeremiah Box!" he cried.

"Right-o!" Cromwell exclaimed.

Zachary thought a moment. "And the bit about Cyrus? He was well after the time of Jeremiah."

"David pointed that out, when we were sorting this through," Britta said. "We came up with a possible scenario that the box had ended up in the court of the Persian Babylonians, way back then, and eventually wound up closer to home, in Jordan."

"However," David said, "we had to do a little revisionist history on that notion when Dr. Aronstam concluded that the words on the box were etched during the first century."

"Apparently the box had been in the possession of the Jews until then," McCurdy said. "But the scroll's statement still makes sense, because it is highly plausible that the Zealots would have used the term 'Cyrus' for any friendly territory east of the Jordan."

Zachary was thoroughly bewildered. "Hold on!" he groaned. "You've lost me. Are you saying that the Zealots were prophesying the fact that the Jordanians would end up with the box? I have a little trouble with that!"

McCurdy shook his head. "We have gotten ahead of ourselves," he said, holding up his hands. "We have not told you what Mr. Girzim revealed to us, which fits perfectly with the words of the scroll."

Succinctly, he relayed what Girzim learned at Petra—the legend of the Jeremiah Cave, how the Zealots who escaped Masada were hidden there, and how the locals gave them the vial, which the prophet had stashed there for safekeeping.

Taking a deep breath, McCurdy went on, "At this point, from what we can deduce, the refugees transferred the cedar box to the Petrans, in the hope they would protect it as they had protected the vial. Though Arab chieftains later absconded with the box, the Zealots had taken it east of the Jordan, as a record of the whereabouts of the King's Tower, for the scroll said it would be found 'in the hands of Cyrus.' What they did not anticipate was that they would locate the Ashes of the Red Heifer once they got there!"

Zachary tried to follow this. "How, then," he asked, "did the vial get back at Masada?"

David stepped in. "Apparently, the refugees, hoping to bring the most precious priestly articles together in one place, took the bottle from Petra back to the King's Tower after the Romans left. Before leaving Petra, they drew the heifer on the wall of the Jeremiah Cave, again with the foot pointing to the mesa, and then duplicated the same pictograph in the Herodian tunnel, pointing to the door!"

Zachary leaned back, clasping one knee. "Clever!" he exclaimed. "It does seem the only explanation!"

Ken spoke up eagerly. "And it also fits with what I deciphered from the inscription on the box."

Mel, who sat on an ottoman near the fire, joined in. "Pete and Honey helped you with that, right?"

"Yes," Ken said with a smile. "We had a great time burning the midnight oil, using the university's lab and digital equipment!"

David chuckled with his colleague over his clandestine maneuverings.

"Anyway," Ken went on, "turns out the inscription in the box's border was a Petran form of Hebrew, a kind of Arabic-styled writing. Apparently someone in Petra, all those centuries ago, helped the refugees cloak their instructions in the flouncy decoration."

"So," Zachary prodded him, "what did it say?"

"It established the fact that the etching on the lid contained a map to the King's Tower, and went on to say that the original contents of the box would be found where"—here he held up his fingers like quotation marks—" 'friends of the prophet' hid them."

David nodded. "This also explains why the Copper Scrolls made no reference to the Ashes of the Red Heifer. The scribe who wrote the scrolls did not know that the ashes would be found by refugees in Petra!"

Zachary nodded, heaving a sigh. "I think I follow all of this. And the breastplate? Was it mentioned in the Second Scroll?"

"Indeed," Father McCurdy said. "It was one of the anomalies, popping up with no prior reference in the First Copper Scroll. The second talked about the furnishings that would be found in the King's Tower, along with the priest's breastplate."

Mel grew curious. "I have never heard you mention the Ark of the Covenant. Was there any reference to it?"

"Only one," McCurdy replied. "The Second Scroll said we should not look for it, because it will not be revealed until the day of purification."

Mel shrugged. "Whatever that is!"

At this, the rabbis offered their insight. "For centuries, our traditions have taught us that Messiah will not come until we are pure enough to receive him," Ben said.

"True!" Jacobs replied. "Perhaps this is saying something similar. Until Israel is ready, the Ark will not be regained."

Silence settled over the group as they soberly reflected on this teaching.

Then Rabbi Benjamin studied Zachary for a long moment. "There is something else you should know, Mr. Cohen," he said. "The Second Scroll also tells us that we will not find the 'Word of the Lord' until God's servant is ready to proclaim it."

Zachary was bewildered. "The Word of the Lord?" he repeated. "What should we make of that?"

Rabbi Katz thrilled to the topic. "We have deduced that this refers to the 'oracle' which the high priest used to determine the will of the Almighty."

Zachary stammered, "The . . . the Urim and Thummim!"

The rabbis' silence answered for them.

McCurdy finally broke in, continuing with his plausible scenario of events that had transpired at Masada. "Regarding the Urim and Thummim, we have our theory as to what the Zealots might have had in mind for the oracle. Here we get into the details of what became of the two women and the children whom the Romans found surviving in a cave—the story Josephus recounted so gloriously in his *History of the Jews*."

Zachary sat on the edge of his seat. "Lay it on me!" he said. "I've been wanting to know about them. I assume they were hiding in the Herodian tunnel?"

To his surprise, McCurdy shook his head. "Quite doubtful," he replied. "For one thing, there is no way they could have emerged in front of the Romans, as Josephus reports, if they were hidden in the tunnel. The entryway atop the mesa was sealed with enormous paving stones, which it took all of us to remove."

Diamant joined in. "We do not know just where they were hidden, but it had to be in one of the many hollows that riddle the mountain. And they had to be close enough to the surface to hear the Romans when they went calling out for survivors."

"So," Zachary concluded, "it was others who went east to Petra and north to Qumran, escaping through the far end of the tunnel, as you suggested."

"Right," McCurdy said. "We know, from the account of Josephus, that there were only two women, one very old, and five children who presented themselves to the Romans, hardly the sort who could have pulled off such feats."

"But," David continued, raising a finger, "that is not to say they were mere cowards, who saved their own hides when their friends were dying."

"Not at all!" Diamant agreed. "We have deduced that their survival, along with their detailed account of what transpired among their fellows, was well rehearsed, and long planned by the community as a whole."

Ken threw in, "We also found it fitting that they were, according to Josephus, related to Eleazer, the Zealot commander—probably his wife, his mother, and his own children!"

Cromwell chuckled. "Such is the reward of leadership. Nepotism prevails even among the most righteous!"

Zachary laughed. "Very well. So what was the purpose of their survival? Surely, considering the bravery of all their kind, they had more in mind than mere escape."

"We agree," Rabbi Levine chimed in. "We believe it may have had something to do with the missing oracle."

Zachary squinted. "How do you conclude that?"

Father McCurdy explained. "We know that they purposely separated the oracle, the Urim and Thummim, from the breastplate. They might have felt that the tiny items would be safer in their possession than buried somewhere to be lost to all posterity."

Zachary pondered this. "I can see that," he said. "The little family was preserved to keep the oracle within reach, to keep them on their persons, so to speak."

Cromwell nodded. "Makes perfect sense! Something so small could have been hidden in a hemline, in a pouch, or most anywhere, without arousing Roman suspicion."

Jacobs chuckled. "Rather like Rachel, who hid the household gods beneath her skirts," he said, recalling an episode from Genesis.

Mel had been quietly taking all of this in. But his practical, street-savvy mind rebelled with questions. Clearing his throat, he said, "Okay, guys, I'm with you to a point. But aren't you giving these Zealots way too much credit? How could they have planned all this and carried it off without a hitch? For instance, how did they expect all their little clues and maps and hidden scrolls to ever be found? What made them think anyone would ever be able to piece the clues together?" He shifted in agitation. "I don't know . . . seems pretty farfetched to me!"

Zachary sympathized with Mel's objections. "I may not be quite so skeptical as my friend here," he said, "but I can understand his doubts. Besides," he wondered, "what made the women and children think they wouldn't be hauled off into slavery, or worse, killed on the spot? What good would that do their attempts to preserve the oracle?"

Rabbi Ben smiled. "Do not apologize for having intelligent skepticism," he said. "Do you think that we have not all asked the same questions?"

Father McCurdy agreed. "Absolutely!" he exclaimed. "But how to answer your concerns? I could play the role of spiritual adviser, which comes with this backward collar," he said, pointing to his clerical choker, "in which case I would advise you that those ancient believers put a lot of trust in God. They had what I call 'shoeleather faith,' meaning that they did all they could, under the circumstances, to fulfill their mission, and then left the rest to the Almighty."

Rabbi Levine agreed. "And see, here we are tonight, having unearthed the very clues they entrusted to fate, and now proceeding to interpret them. Was their faith not rewarded?"

Mel looked at the floor, giving no argument.

"Or," McCurdy went on, "I could go with practical deduction and try to imagine what they thought could realistically be expected."

David rallied to that statement. "May I, Father?" he said. "I really like what we came up with here!"

"Certainly, Professor," McCurdy deferred. "Be my guest."

David straightened his shoulders, an excited gleam in his eye. "We got to thinking what we would have anticipated, had we been in the women's shoes," he began.

"Or sandals," Ken teased.

"Okay," David said, with a nod. "Sandals . . . Anyway, let's reconstruct the situation. Here's Silva, having spent years and the equivalent of multiplied millions of dollars of Caesar's cash, to flush out a bunch of rebels. His mission, we believe, was not just to prove a point, but to wring the Jews' secret from them, to locate the fabulous revenue which they had hidden in the landscape."

Zachary nodded. "With you, so far."

"Now," David went on, "the Zealots knew that Silva would be devastated when he got to the top and found they had all killed themselves off. They knew that if he got back to Rome with this explanation of his failure, no one would believe him. After all, there was no precedent for such self-sacrifice among the Romans."

"Gotcha," Zachary said. "Go on."

"That explains why Silva is recorded as going around the mountaintop desperately calling out for someone, anyone, to appear, who would tell him what happened. He would need witnesses to take back to Rome, to verify the truth of the matter."

"Otherwise," Ken broke in, "he would lose his head!" At this, the department chairman drew a finger across his throat, like a blade, making an obnoxious, guttural sound.

The group roared with laughter, until David proceeded. "That's right," he said. "We all know what happened to Roman generals who failed the emperor!"

Zachary was floored. "Are you saying that the Zealots expected that the Romans would spare the lives of the hideouts?"

McCurdy grew very serious. "Not only that, but that they would take them to Rome!"

"Living insurance policies!" Ken quipped.

Zachary blinked in amazement. "Not as slaves?"

"Indeed not!" Diamant said. "Silva had seen that they would rather kill themselves than be put in chains. If he wanted their story told, he would have to treat them well."

Zachary leaned back, laughing in delight. "Wow!" he cried. "It just gets better and better."

Mel, likewise, was grinning from ear to ear. "I've got to hand it to you, people," he said. "Your story is as good as anyone could come up with. And I think it's probably true. Every word!"

As the group congratulated themselves, again laughing and chatting over their prowess, a new light went off in Zachary's head. "Wait a minute!" he exclaimed. "Are we saying, then, that the oracle ended up in . . ."

"Rome," McCurdy said with a nod.

At the sound of the word, a hush filled the room. The group had reached this conclusion on the way back from Masada. Now that their priestly candidate had caught on, they wondered what he would think.

All eyes were on Zachary as he pondered this latest unfolding. "So," he said at last, taking a deep breath, "do you plan to go there?"

David looked very weary. Ken shrugged. The rabbis, McCurdy, and Cromwell shook their heads in exhaustion.

"We wouldn't know where to begin, but it appears we have no choice," David said at last. "'No rest for the wicked,' my grandmother used to say!"

The group laughed hollowly.

Then, Rabbi Ben, continuing to study his young candidate, made a sobering pronouncement. "All of this has been hashed about among the crew here," he said. "We are all willing to do what must be done. But . . . ," he sighed, "if the scroll is to be believed, we will not find what we are looking for until you, my boy, are ready for it to be found."

"That is right," Uriel Katz said sympathetically. "Remember, the scroll tells us that we will not find the 'Word of the Lord . . .' "

Zachary nodded, repeating the phrase with him, " '. . . until God's servant is ready to proclaim it.' "

In a split second of time, the world of spirit and flesh collided in Zachary's soul. His heart and mind, which had been battered about for months over this very issue of readiness, felt the crunching imperative for decision.

As the others in the room held their breath, awaiting a word from him, Zachary gazed at the floor, his eyes tracing the complex design of the oriental carpet as it glowed in the fire's hypnotic light. How he wished the twisted strands of reasoning within his own being would form such a perfect pattern!

Did anyone here comprehend the valley of choice that lay before him? Did a single one of them fully understand that the role he would play, should he take the priestly path, would impact not only their future, but the future of all humanity beyond the walls of this one house?

Mel Wester watched his friend's protracted hesitation, remembering the strange meeting at the YMCA, and the evident catharsis Zachary had expressed. Although these things were still very new to the ex-cop, he was enough in touch with Zachary to know he had reached a telling point in his spiritual quest this day.

With shaky knees, Zachary stood up and, crossing the room, clasped and unclasped his hands. The eyes of the gathering did not leave him as he approached the personal and private crossroads only he could clearly see.

At last he bowed his head and closed his eyes. Then, taking a confirming breath, he nodded, and when he opened his eyes again, he turned to Rabbi Benjamin. "I am ready," he announced. "For the first time since you found me and told me who I am, I am truly ready!"

CHAPTER 41

A sleek Italian limousine, chartered from the airport at Rome, maneuvered through the congested downtown streets of the Eternal City with a facility that confirmed the driver's experience with the area. Young people on motor scooters, daring delivery men in tiny paneled vans, well-to-do couples in classy sedans, bobbed back and forth over the vague dividing lines on the cobblestone boulevards leading through one of the older shopping areas.

It was nearly ten o'clock at night, yet the streets were still as lively as at midday, with vendors filling orders, adventuresome parties making nightclub rounds, and tourists taking in the evening sights. As David Rothmeyer rode with his colleagues—the rabbis, McCurdy, Cromwell, Ken Aronstam, and Britta Hayworth—in the luxury automobile, he watched the boisterous street life outside the tinted windows with amusement. David had heard New York referred to as the "city that never sleeps," but it couldn't be any noisier or more active than this Italian metropolis, he thought.

David never failed to be amazed at the twists and turns his life had taken, ever since he had first heard of the Temple Consortium. Only a year ago he had been a rather dull professor of Central American anthropology and obscure languages. The most exciting places he had ever seen were buried beneath jungle growth so dense, it took a machete to penetrate them. And they were only exciting to people like himself, who thought the world of long-dead Indians was fascinating.

It was true that his former field of interest had its merits, but it certainly did not compare to the quests he had been on since, for intrigue, or for impact on humanity.

This trip to Rome was yet another step down a path he had long ago accepted as prophetic. David Rothmeyer had not taken a plunge of spiritual commitment comparable to Zachary Cohen's or Uriel Katz's, but neither he nor anyone else in the car would come to the end of this adventure without much soul-searching.

As always, the little collection of scholars who traveled together were the most unlikely of colleagues. They had gotten used to the notion that they, though Jews and Christians, were meant to cooperate. They had spent so much time in close quarters, working on such emotionally and spiritually charged matters, that most of the time they forgot their differences. It was not until they saw themselves reflected in the perplexed gazes of onlookers, or caught a glimpse of their group in some window or mirror, that they were reminded of just how uncommon their collaborative friendship was.

The uniqueness of their mutual vision was brought home to them once again as they headed for an old *palazzo*, a house of bygone Italian aristocracy. The mansion now served as headquarters for the Interfaith Center for Ecumenical Studies. Headed by an Anglican bishop from Australia, it was one of a number of endeavors borne of late twentieth-century efforts to bring unity among divergent Christian faiths. This particular agency was meant primarily to be a bridge for understanding between the Roman Catholic tradition, the Church of England, and the Episcopal Church worldwide; though, as the visitors were to learn, it embraced Christians of all persuasions.

Father McCurdy, who had visited Rome on several occasions, had come up with the idea that, since the team had no notion where to begin their quest, they might start by touching base with this institution. "At least they will make us feel at home," he asserted.

The rabbis, who might have chafed at the idea once upon a time, were only a little dubious. "You think they will not slam the door in the faces of a bunch of Hassidics?" Levine joked. "After all, surely even their ecumenism has its limits!"

Katz shrugged. "Perhaps we should take comfort in the fact that the pope recently traveled to Israel and gave the church's apologies for its role in our persecution."

Rabbi Ben eyed Katz closely. For days now he had been astonished at the little man's about-face. No longer could he resist inquiring. "I agree with you, my friend," he said. "But since when are you so open-minded?"

Rabbi Katz sank back into the limousine's deep seat and said no more. As for Rabbi Ben, he decided, then and there, that he would get to the bottom of Katz's personality change, as soon as there was an opportunity.

The limousine was nearing the neighborhood of the Palazzo Bontiface.

McCurdy gave the team a little of the house's history. "You probably recognize the name," he said. "The Bontifaces have been world renowned since the Middle Ages for their shipping industry. Many steamers and luxury liners bear the family crest on their flags and prows."

Britta nodded. "I have heard of the 'sinking of the *Bontiface*,'" she said. "That was some big ship during World War II, wasn't it?"

"It was," McCurdy said. "Unfortunately, the Bontifaces supported Mussolini at that time. His defeat spelled the doom of their vast enterprise. Today the name is but a holdover of fame, with little substance."

"And what of the house we are going to visit?" Carl Jacobs asked, peering out the window at the multistoried buildings on the avenue. "Is it still owned by the same family?"

"I read somewhere that they bequeathed it to the City of Rome," Father McCurdy replied. "The agency simply rents space there. And, Carl, if you're wondering where the mansions are on this boulevard, you might not recognize them. We are passing by many such palazzos right now."

The group stared out at the nondescript "palaces" that lined the street. Except for the fact that each one was several stories high, painted in a distinctive shade of pastel, and well maintained, they were not especially eye-catching.

"Are you disappointed?" McCurdy asked with a smile. "Just you wait. The car will soon turn down a lane and then . . . well, you will see!"

Sure enough, the car slowed to a stop, waited for oncoming traffic to provide a break, and then turned sharply into a narrow opening between two of the towering houses. An amazed gasp went up from the passengers at the revelation of what the street-side facades hid from public view.

Tucked amid a number of aristocratic domiciles was a magnificent common courtyard, complete with an ornate multitiered fountain, a circular drive whose glistening cobblestones were flecked with gleaming crystal chips, and flourishing flower beds that lined every walk. Elaborate cut-glass lamps, suspended from artful wrought-iron posts, lit the drive, as the limo swung to a stop before one grand door.

"The Palace of Bontiface!" McCurdy announced.

Pale green in color, the house was trimmed in a creamy white, with sumptuous cascades of flowers spilling from window boxes, and dense vines tenaciously hugging the stuccoed walls. Five stories high, it was nonetheless invitingly warm, its maroon enameled door set deep beneath a columned Moorish-style portico, roofed in red-clay tile.

Dazzled, the limo's occupants emerged from the car and waited on the sidewalk. Rabbi Ben instructed the chauffer to remain parked where he was until they came out again. Their bags were in the trunk, and he did not know where the team would be staying for the night.

The group followed McCurdy up the walkway to the towering door. To their amazement, he did not knock or ring a doorbell but put his hand to the bronze latch and entered, bold as he pleased. Answering their shocked expressions, he explained. "The first two floors are a museum to the Bontiface enterprise. The agency rents the top three floors. Bishop Ashcraft's secretary told us to buzz him at the elevator door, and he would send down a lift."

An enormous curved stairway, wide enough for six people shoulder to shoulder, led from the lobby to the second floor. On either side of the first step, framing the ascent, were life-size busts of the Bontiface forebears, and throughout the lobby, which was all sheathed in white marble, were other family statues and busts done in Renaissance style.

The little elevator, a 1920s afterthought, clanked to a stop when it reached the lobby. Just as its old iron door creaked open, revealing an interior that would hold two or three at the most, hurried footsteps could be heard coming down the marble stairs.

"Ian!" a man's voice rang out. "How good to see you!"

Descending the flight was a trim, middle-aged man in a black clerical suit, his backward collar a match to McCurdy's. Thrusting out their hands, the two priests, one of the Anglican and one of the Roman faith, greeted each other warmly.

"Jim!" Ian exclaimed. "You did not need to come down!"

"It is my pleasure!" Bishop Ashcraft said. Pointing to the antiquated elevator, he objected, "Besides, my secretary should not have expected you to use that accident-waiting-to-happen!"

Father McCurdy turned to his team, and leading the bishop from one to the other, introduced the rabbis, the professors, Cromwell, and Britta. "Bishop Ashcraft was a fellow at Oxford about twenty years ago," he said. "One of my students, actually, in Middle Eastern Studies."

Ashcraft greeted the group enthusiastically. "I hope Ian has not been as hard on you as he was on us poor cadets!" he joked.

"He is a tough old bird!" David quipped.

"But an invaluable asset to our cause," Rabbi Ben added.

"And a cause I want to hear all about!" Bishop Ashcraft said, gesturing to the stairway. "I hope you don't mind a little climb. We'll arrive at our destination much more quickly by taking the stairs than by waiting on the old iron horse."

The group was happy to comply. "It will feel good to exercise after our trip," Britta said.

The third floor said more than words could express about the agency's agenda. A modern-looking reception area doubled as the institute's library. A collection of more than ten thousand volumes of Christian classics, church history, interdenominational Bible commentaries, biographies of great Christian leaders, and so on, lined shelves that ascended two stories in height and required a mezzanine, as well as rolling ladders, to reach them all. The shelves, suspended from the walls by a framework of steel pipe, placed no weight on the five-hundred-year-old parquet floor.

David, though by no means an expert in such studies, recognized many names on the spines of the well-maintained books: Luther, Calvin, Wesley, Spurgeon, Brainerd, Unger, Albright, Moody, Graham, Saint Augustine, Thomas à Kempis, Matthew Henry, Saint Jerome, Mother Teresa, on and on they went—names familiar to almost any educated person. Here were multivolumed sets of language studies; Greek, Hebrew, and Latin translations of holy works; slim devotionals and fat prayer books going back through centuries of meditation and liturgy; hymnals chronicling the worship style of the church for two thousand years.

Ashcraft, seeing the scholars' salivating looks, smiled proudly. "Most major works concerning Christianity will be found here," he said. "And, Rabbis, I hope one day to be able to say the same for biblical studies in general."

The Jewish gentlemen nodded graciously. "Does your center serve as a school?" Rabbi Ben asked.

"Indeed!" Ashcraft replied. "This floor and the two above us have classrooms and guest rooms for anyone who wishes to take in our offerings, or anyone who just wishes a private spiritual retreat. Teachers from all over the Christian world come here to share their knowledge and their insights with students from every background. Last year we enrolled four hundred men and women in our courses."

Placing a friendly hand on Ben's back, he led the team toward an elegant carved door off the reception area. "Come this way," he said. "I have tea waiting for you in the parlor. And, oh yes, you will be staying, won't you? I have beds made up in several of the guest rooms."

Ian looked for his companions' reactions. Everyone seemed to be fascinated by the surroundings, and the rabbis, especially, were grateful for a place to rest.

David nodded to Father McCurdy. "Ken and I can go back down and get the bags," he said.

As the two American professors descended the sweeping marble steps, Ken was very quiet.

"Impressive, huh?" David said.

"I'll say!" Ken exclaimed. "All those books! I had no idea so much had been written about one religion!"

David nodded. "I had no idea about a lot of things, when I got hooked up with this bunch! Sometimes, I think my head will burst if I have to broaden my horizons any further!"

Ken shrugged. "I've always thought I was pretty smart, you know. Chairman of the Department of Anthropology and Ancient Languages!" He shook his head. "I used to laugh when people called theology the 'mother of all sciences.' "

"Yeah," David said. "Me too. Maybe theology will have the last laugh yet!"

CHAPTER 42

It was past midnight, the summer moon shining in a full silver orb above the Eternal City. David Rothmeyer and Britta Hayworth stood on a balcony overlooking the Bontiface gardens, a private retreat enjoyed by the family that had lived here for half a millennium.

The enormous domicile, whose back was to the boulevard, and whose face was to the common court where the limousine had parked, wrapped around this central garden in an architectural embrace. No one, save those inside the house, had access to this pleasant place, which had been maintained by countless gardeners, masons, and handymen over the years. A blend of Mediterranean styles, it boasted Greco-Roman columns along four porticoes, Moorish tile work in its patio and walls, and Renaissance fountains, sculptures, and murals in every nook. To say nothing of the flora. Every colorful variety of flower to be seen in Rome was duplicated here, along with palm trees, flowering fruit trees, and aromatic herbs.

Even at this time of night, the sleepy song of finches, canaries, and little tree frogs, and the occasional chatter of rousing parrots rode upward with the music of the splashing fountain and the fragrance of irises and roses on the evening breeze.

"Is this romantic enough?" David asked his sweetheart as he enfolded her in his arms.

Britta, her back to the tall man, leaned her head into the crook of his elbow and entwined her own arms through his, folding them against her chest. Her lips curled in a satisfied smile. "It will do," she sighed.

The wall sconces in the guest parlor behind them mixed a warm glow with the moonlight spilling over the balcony. In this private sanctum, the noises of the boulevard were almost entirely muted. But from somewhere in a neighboring palazzo a violin could be heard, the sweet lullaby of a wakeful musician, blessing the evening like a prayer.

"This may be our only chance to kiss in this exotic city," David said, lifting her chin with his fingers.

Britta turned around within his embrace and rose up on tiptoes, waiting.

David studied her dreamy countenance, and bending down, pressing her to him, he kissed her deliciously. Heart thrumming, she then sank against him, and he rested his cheek on her head, as together they stood for a long while, lost in the gift of their mutual love.

"Darling," he said, "you realize that, however this adventure ends, ours is only beginning."

Britta snuggled more persistently against him and heaved a happy sigh. "Oh, I do hope so, David," she said. Then, raising worried eyes to him, she said, "I do hope our feelings are not merely the product of all the exciting places we have been . . . all the thrilling experiences . . ."

David placed a finger to her lips. "Don't even think it!" he said. "If I had met you in a freshman seminar, it would not have mattered! I love you, Britta!"

Their next kiss, though just as tantalizing as the previous, would not last so long. To their dismay, the sound of someone clearing his throat interrupted their ecstasy. Pulling away from each other, they straightened their clothes and David drew out a handkerchief, wiping lipstick from his face.

"Ian," he said. "You aren't sleeping tonight?"

McCurdy laughed softly. "No more than you two," he teased. "Sorry to interrupt, young people. But we need to talk to you."

Just entering the parlor was Bishop Ashcraft, his normally neat hair rumpled and his clerical suit exchanged for robe and pajamas. "I am glad to find you still awake," he said. "I hope you don't mind my bothering you at this late hour."

"Please," David said, gesturing to the seating area. "Come in, Bishop. What's happening?"

Ashcraft, bleary-eyed behind his wire-rimmed glasses, took a seat next to Father McCurdy. Britta and David sat down across from them. "I enjoyed our chat tonight, ever so much!" the bishop said.

David nodded. "No more than we!" he acknowledged.

The earlier visit in the bishop's living room, over tea and cookies, had been a risky "unveiling." For the first time since enlisting Ken Aronstam and sharing with Laad Girzim, the rabbis and their team had explained their mission and revealed their experiences to an outsider, a man who McCurdy was convinced could be trusted, and who might be able to help them. After recapping their adventure, to date, and explaining all their findings, they had told the bishop they had no clue where to begin the quest in Rome.

"And you are hoping I might be able to advise you?" Ashcraft had surmised.

With hopeful eyes, the team had watched as he sat back in his chair, overwhelmed by all they had shared.

"Gentlemen, and lady," he had said, nodding to Britta, "I am astonished that you would come to me with this marvelous tale, and I am truly honored. I know that it must have taken great courage for you to do so. Except for Ian, you are meeting me for the first time."

The rabbis had not argued this point. They had indeed put themselves at this stranger's mercy. The bishop had risen from his chair and paced the parquet floor, rubbing his smooth chin. "I assume you have come to me in the hopes that I might be able to shed some light on your search for this 'oracle'—the Urim and Thummim."

"'Word of the Lord,'" Rabbi Ben said, squirming a little. "That is what the Copper Scroll calls it."

"Very well," Ashcraft acknowledged. "'Word of the Lord.'" Standing in the middle of the room, the kind man had only shrugged. "I will need to give this much thought," he had said. "At first blush, I come up with nothing. Nothing in what you say rings any bells with me, other than bells of excitement."

The group laughed with him, but their disappointment was unconcealed.

Sad that he could offer no ready help, the bishop suggested that they let him sleep on this. "Perhaps I will awake in the night with some revelation," he had said, half in jest.

That had been a couple of hours ago. Obviously, neither McCurdy nor Ashcraft had slept a wink. Perhaps the other members of the team managed to doze in their guest rooms, but the bishop, though weary, appeared eager for the dawn.

"Let me get right to the point," he said, looking seriously at his three guests. "When I went to bed, saying that perhaps I would get a revelation, I was being facetious. But I did pray as I lay down to sleep. I tossed and turned, thinking back to what I know of Roman and Jewish history. I would like to tell you that I know for certain that the treasures Titus took from Jerusalem are hidden away in the Vatican Archives, or in the catacombs beneath this city! But," he said with a shrug, "I am sorry to say, I know no such thing."

McCurdy laughed. "Of course, that would be too obvious!" he said. "Besides, too much time elapsed between the destruction of Jerusalem and the building of the Vatican, as we know it."

"Some fourteen hundred years," Ashcraft confirmed.

McCurdy agreed. "What transpired during that interim were countless upheavals, conquests, demolitions, and bloodbaths. The likelihood that the church ended up with those treasures is remote to the point of foolishness!"

Bishop Ashcraft nodded, grateful for the support. "I am glad you were not expecting the sensational," he said. Then, taking a deep breath, he squared his shoulders. "Perhaps, however, your specific goal is not beyond reach."

The guests brightened. "You have come up with a possibility?" David asked.

"Maybe," Ashcraft said, his tone heavy with reserve. Shifting in his seat, he explained, "As I lay in bed, trying to calm my mind, it occurred to me that I had a pile of tourist brochures lying on my nightstand. I had been looking through them yesterday, planning for your arrival."

When he saw their quizzical expressions, he explained. "I always like to plan at least one day with my guests, if they have time, for sightseeing. I try to choose places I think they would find the most interesting. There is so much to see in Rome, it would take a lifetime . . ."

Father McCurdy nodded. "Go on, Jim."

"Well," he continued, "I had put together a nice little itinerary. Coliseum, Saint Peters, Forum, Arch of Titus, you know . . ."

"Yes," McCurdy spurred him on.

"This evening, as I wrestled with your request, I suddenly sat up and turned on the lamp by my bed. It occurred to me that I had marked one site which I myself have never seen. Jewish sites are quite rare in this Catholic stronghold, but I had noticed one listing I thought our rabbis might enjoy."

As the guests leaned forward eagerly, the bishop pulled out a rumpled brochure from the pocket of his robe. Opening it, he adjusted his wire-rims and searched for the name of an obscure place in the list of tourist attractions.

"Ah, here it is!" he said, pointing to his pencil mark. "Listen to this! 'One of the few Jewish sites in Rome, this privately owned grotto claims to date back to the time of the Diaspora. Relics from the destruction of Jerusalem are said to have been housed here from earliest times.' "

David, Britta, and McCurdy tensed with excitement. "Amazing!" Ian cried. "What is the name of this place?"

The bishop took off his wire-rims, rubbing misty tears from his eyes. "I don't want to make too much of this, my friends," he said, "but the name does suggest hope." Looking down again at the brochure, he read, "'*Il Santuario della Parola de Signore*—Shrine of the Word of the Lord.'"

CHAPTER 43

Short of ordering several taxicabs, the city bus line was the easiest way for Bishop Ashcraft to take his guests across town. As the rabbis and company piled into the crowded transport for a ride through busy boulevards, tourists and locals stared at them curiously. Indeed, they were an odd mix, in their backward collars, Hassidic getups, tweed sport coats, and jeans.

But the least of their concerns were the questions they raised in the minds of onlookers. Today, far-fetched as it seemed, they just might be nearing the fulfillment of the grandest dream of the ages, the fulfillment of the vision of Israel!

It was a rainy day as they made their trek cross town. Water coated the bus windows, running in rivers down the panes, lending a mystical quality to the passing scenery. David and Ken stood in the middle of the crowded bus, holding on to the grip bar near the ceiling and looking at nothing in particular. Britta, Cromwell, the rabbis, and the priest and the bishop had found seats and watched the street with preoccupied gazes. All their thoughts were focused on what might lie at the end of the journey.

When the bus neared the Coliseum area, Bishop Ashcraft stood up stiffly and reached for the grip bar. "We'll get off here," he told his guests.

Umbrellas under their arms, the rabbis eagerly pushed their way through to the front of the bus, their broad-brimmed hats brushing against strangers in the way. Bishop Ashcraft tipped his smaller fedora to the offended passengers, silently apologizing for his companions, and followed the rabbis meekly.

Once outside, ten umbrellas popped open, and the group huddled together, looking like a black mushroom in full bloom. The bishop, who stood in the middle, took out his brochure again, the one with the directions to the sites, and turning the map this way and that, got his bearings. "If you like, I can take you to the Coliseum now," he said. When they all shook their heads anxiously, he smiled. "I didn't think so. Well, then," he said, turning about, his eyes scanning the rain-soaked hills beyond the parking lot, "the directions are quite vague, but the best I can figure, the grotto is up there somewhere."

Like obedient sheep, rather than trailblazers, the rabbis fell in behind the bishop. With their team, they undertook a very wet trek across the busy lot, where taxis wheeled in and out. To their right, between the old Forum area and the arena, stood the notorious Arch of Titus. The famous carving of the Jewish slaves being brought into Rome, the loot from the Temple being hauled with them as booty, seemed, under the circumstances, a poetic irony.

No one said a word as the group looked up at the menorah and the other treasures portrayed there. They all knew that this depiction had been a basis of replicas on display in the Temple Gallery. They also believed that the original menorah had been found in the secret chamber on Masada.

The rabbis smiled covertly at one another and followed the bishop, who quickly moved on, leading the group across the main avenue and heading toward a set of winding stone stairs cut into the green hillside.

Daring college kids, on their first forays in Europe, were heedless of the rain and splashed up and down the steps with youthful zest. The bishop's guests, dodging the rambunctious youngsters, ascended the stairs more slowly and came at last to a neighborhood of steep, twisting streets. While Bishop Ashcraft consulted his map, the shivering group huddled beneath their umbrellas, Britta clinging to David as much for warmth as for love as the rain ran through the cobblestone joints like miniature rivers.

According to the tour brochure, there were several historic sites in this locale, including the Church of Saint Peter in Chains, which supposedly sat over the cave where Peter was held before his execution. Between the cheap tourist shops and espresso huts, numerous chapels and grottoes attracted visitors who were willing to hike up the approaches to find them.

Today other tourists were few. Die-hard tour guides darted with their meager groups in and out of doorways, sheltering their clients from the wind and persistent rain. Shopkeepers were grateful for the weather, which made sightseers linger inside.

Bishop Ashcraft's company, however, would have come here in a snowstorm.

"Are we getting close?" Rabbi Ben asked.

"I think so," Ashcraft replied. "We need to find a lane called La Strada di Morte."

"Street of Death?" David interpreted. "Doesn't appeal to me."

The others laughed, and the bishop explained, "That's where Peter was supposedly led from prison to be martyred in the Coliseum."

Sobered, the group grew quiet and said little as they followed their leader up and down the rain-drenched avenues.

Suddenly, Britta squealed, "Is that it?"

She pointed to a small placard mounted on the side of an old building a few feet ahead. At the juncture of one cobblestone street and a little alley, it was nearly hidden by a flowering vine.

"I think you're right!" the bishop said. "Let's go."

Encouraged, the group clung together, following their guide. They turned into the dirt lane, which seemed, at first, to lead only to a sloping bank of vegetation.

"If anything's here, it doesn't get many visitors," Ken quipped.

Making their way down the muddy causeway, they read the signs on the doors of the obscure buildings. "Nothing here," Carl Jacobs said in disappointment.

For a while, they all stood still, listening to the rain drip forlornly off their umbrellas. They were about to turn to leave when Rabbi Katz spotted a small white gate set into a wall. Stepping away from the group, he went to investigate.

"Horace," he called. "What do you think?"

Rabbi Benjamin begrudgingly followed him. "What is it, Uriel?" he asked, impatient.

Katz stood silent, his mouth agape, as he pointed to a Star of David emblazoned on a stone partition beyond the gate. Above it, on a simple bronze sign shaped like an arrow, were words written in Italian, Hebrew, and English: "Shrine of the Word of the Lord."

With a surge of joy, Rabbi Benjamin gestured to his companions. "Come, come!" he cried. "We have found it! It is here!"

In a rush of wet feet and bobbing umbrellas, the others joined them. Eager, they all would have plunged through the gate had Rabbi Ben not stopped them. Holding up a hand, he called for discretion. "This is a house of God," he said, "whether we find what we want or not."

Caught up short, the group collected itself and followed Rabbi Ben's lead through the modest portal. The bronze sign directed them to the left, through a passageway that took them around the wall. Once on the other side, they were amazed at what greeted them.

A lovely natural grotto protected a fragrant garden. Beyond the shrubbery and flowering plants, a small cave sheltered an unusual shrine. A peculiar-looking place, it was a hodgepodge of Judaica, with small menorahs, mezuzahs, miniature Torahs, and Stars of David in every chink and cranny, all aglow with candles and strings of glittering lights, in a rather tasteless but exuberant display of adoration. Brass censers emitted potent aromas, and in the middle, just beneath the cave's arching ceiling, an altar was erected, profusely adorned with fresh-cut flowers.

Bishop Ashcraft gathered his guests together and spoke softly. "According to the brochure, this place is privately owned. That means it has no support from the government or the Church. It may get some funding from local synagogues, but it is probably the provenance of one family."

His assumption was about to be confirmed. As the group wandered through the grotto, closing their umbrellas beneath the green arbor, the sound of children playing spilled down steep steps that led from a home on the ridge above the grotto. In a frolic, three young boys scrambled down the wet stairs, skidding to a muddy halt when they saw the visitors.

Surprised, they stood stone still, their eyes wide as saucers, until the eldest, about eight years old, called out, "*Mama! Turistos! Turistos!*"

The scent of spaghetti sauce issued from the kitchen of the house, which was visible through dripping tree branches. A squeaking screen door said that "Mama" was coming, and the boys glanced toward her. "*Vicente! Tomas! Ramon!*" she called in Italian. "If you are teasing me again, you shall get a spanking, and no lunch . . ."

By now she had reached the bottom step, and she went red-faced with embarrassment. Her floury hands, which she had been wiping on her apron, flew to her mouth. "Pardon, signores and signora!" she cried, breaking into English, which she assumed they would understand. "I thought my boys . . . Get now!" she growled at her sons. Whipping a dishtowel from her shoulder, she snapped it at them, and they scrambled up the steps, where they hid behind the rain-soaked foliage.

Rabbi Ben caught the bishop's eye. Squeamish, he shook his head, indicating they should be going. Bishop Ashcraft frowned at him and then turned to the woman. "Madam," he said, "I see that we have come at an inconvenient time. Perhaps another . . ."

The woman protested. "No, no, Padre. We are happy to have you! Please, signore . . ." She pointed to a row of benches near the cave, bidding them to stay awhile.

"Vicente!" she cried. "The pamphlets! Bring them, quickly!"

Rabbi Ben sat down next to Ashcraft, while the others found seats as well and leaned close to him. "Bishop," he whispered, "we appreciate your efforts. But this place . . . well, you can see, it cannot be what we are looking for."

The bishop placed a hand on Rabbi Ben's arm. "Very well, Rabbi," he sighed. "I will deal with her."

Ashcraft rose and went back over to the woman, who was fumbling with her apron strings, trying to remove the soiled garment and prepare herself to give them a tour.

"Madam, really, it is all right," he said. "We will be going . . ."

"No, no! Please!" she insisted. "You have come far, in the rain, no? You will stay, just a few moments?"

To the bishop's surprise, one of the boys had slipped back down the stairs and was going from turisto to turisto holding out a cup and collecting offerings. The group, obviously feeling obliged, dipped into their pockets and gave him some change.

With a sigh, the bishop conceded, and returned to his friends.

The woman, having wiped most of the flour from her hands and smoothed her hair, looked less bedraggled as she stepped to the front of the gathering. The eldest of the three children happily passed out leaflets to the visitors, while his brothers sneaked into the back row of benches and watched the proceedings.

"Signores and signora," the woman began, taking on an amazingly professional air, "welcome to the Shrine of the Word of the Lord. As you can see from the brochure which Vicente is giving you, this is a Hebrew chapel, a memorial to the first Jews of the Diaspora." She took a deep breath and continued with a spiel she had obviously given many times. "The Diaspora, or the dispersion of the Jews from Palestine, was instigated by the Romans in the year seventy."

Suddenly, she seemed to catch herself. Looking at the rabbis, she smiled shyly. "But, sirs, I am telling you nothing which you do not already know! Let me skip ahead."

Gesturing to the house on the hill, she said, "This old home is built over the tomb of one of the mothers of Israel, a certain Miriam, wife of Eleazar. Her legend has been kept by my family for centuries, as well as her sacred gravesite."

Turning about, she continued, "You see this cave behind me? Deep within it is Miriam's tomb. She came to the Eternal City after the destruction of Jerusalem, as a special agent of the Roman army. Under the direction of General Silva, who took Masada, she was brought to Rome. At his command, she gave the account of the Zealot heroes to Josephus, the Jewish historian, hired by Rome to write the story of his people."

As she talked on, David's spine tingled. Glancing at his companions, he saw that they, too, were mesmerized. It almost seemed they were in a dream, that David and the others must have fallen asleep at last in the bishop's house, and they were all having the same magnificent fantasy.

But, no, this was no dream. The rain dripping off the leaves above, slithering down David's shirt collar, was all too real. Reaching up, he wiped his neck and leaned forward, letting the water fall on his back as he listened intently to the woman's story.

"The legend goes that Miriam, her mother, and her five little sons"—she stopped and smiled, gesturing to her own boys—"children just like these, were brought to Rome, not in chains, but in an amazing show of mercy on the part of their captors, to give their tale of Masada."

David peered over at Ken, who looked askance at this interpretation of Silva's motivation. The rabbis, likewise, looked sideways at one another, trying not to smile.

The woman, caught up in her rhetoric, did not notice their reaction. "The legend asserts that Miriam was given a house and land, in payment for her brave journey to Rome and her preserving of the story of the Zealots. This garden is part of her homestead, as is the tomb in which she lies."

David looked at the cave, trying to be gracious. *Clever Miriam*, he thought. *You did well!*

The woman was almost finished. As she concluded, she encouraged the visitors to read the brochure at their leisure. "As you will see," she said, "the story goes that Miriam brought with her certain valuable treasures from Masada, though, to this day, the only items accounted for are those which she held dearest. They have been entrusted to my family, descendants of Miriam and her husband, Eleazar, to protect for all time."

Now, the woman gestured to the altar, overspread with flowers. "Miriam called these items the 'Word of the Lord.' They are mysterious," she said. "They do not look like much, not so grand as the treasures of the Vatican. But to me and my family, they are priceless."

Stepping back, she invited the group to come forward and take a look.

Weak-kneed, Rabbi Ben stood up, Uriel Katz assisting him with a supporting arm. Together, the two men approached the hallowed altar. Behind them came Jacobs, Levine, and then the others.

They did not know what they would see. They did not know if this was a sideshow, a cruel joke on hopeful believers. They did not know if God had truly led them here, or if he was testing them.

One by one, they drew near as the woman removed the concealing flowers to expose a small glass case upon the altar.

The papal archives were full of relics, housed in just such cases—fingers and toes of saints, pieces of wood from Roman crosses, splinters from Paul's shipwrecked boat, bones of martyrs and bishops and popes. The public passed by them every day, marveled at them, joked about them, prayed to them, scoffed, worshiped, laughed, adored. No one knew whether they were really genuine. It took faith to accept them, to trust they had any power at all.

Not so this relic. Not so the two little ivory counters that gleamed in the crystal box on this Italian altar. Not so the little white stones on which were written the "yea" and "nay" of the Almighty. There could be no doubt that these were the original Word of the Lord, the oracle referred to in the Second Copper Scroll. There could be no doubt, if the observer knew the facts, if the worshiper knew the full story, if the adorer was informed.

So it was that the visitors to the shrine this day trembled as they looked.

For they had found the Urim and Thummim, the oracle of the High Priest of Israel. And they had come to take it home.

CHAPTER 44

Buscar, the Jordanian secretary, hung up the phone in his office. In utter frustration, he shook his head, his ears still ringing from the biting words heard through the receiver.

It had been a week since his boss, Laad Girzim, had returned from Masada, a week of the man's evasiveness regarding his highly broadcast venture in Israel and his work with the Jewish rabbis. Today Buscar had felt obliged to do something. Much soul-searching, and the pressing weight of duty to the Muslim cause, finally persuaded him to call Mr. Hamir, the head of the Palestinian Antiquities Authority.

Just moments ago he had told him of the mysterious digital photo and fax he had found filed under Q for *Queen*, and under M for *Masada*, in Girzim's file cabinet. "I suspect this has something to do with what drove him to cooperate with the Jews," Buscar told Hamir. "I researched the reference number on the photo and found that it relates to an ancient box which has apparently been in the possession of our leaders for centuries. I do not know its purpose, but it is missing from the archives."

Hamir had seemed doubtful. "You think that a mere box would have provoked such an alliance between your royal house and the Temple Movement?" he asked angrily. "Please, Mr. Buscar, let us be reasonable!"

Buscar's face had burned as he received this scurrilous rebuke. "I . . . I am only doing my job, Mr. Hamir," he said. "Perhaps I should have called the people in Damascus instead?"

Incensed, Hamir had flown into a rage. "Do you think you can threaten me, Buscar?" he cried. "Mind your position!

Next time you think to report something to me, let it be something of substance!"

The Palestinian had then slammed down his phone, causing Buscar to jump.

Eyes hot, the tall, thin Arab held his head in his hands. *Very well, Mr. Hamir,* he thought, *you may be sure I will never call you again!*

At the other end of the disconnected line, Hamir felt a migraine coming on.

He rose from his desk in his stuffy office and walked out into the Via Dolorosa. He thought anxiously over the past months, of the plot to assassinate Senator Calvin Jefferson, which had been coordinated with allies in the United States. The Palestinian Liberation Organization, at Sheik Matif's suggestion, believed that the Jordanians had sent sensitive material with Jefferson, to be handed over to the enemies of Allah, material that would somehow assist the State of Israel. Though the assassins had done their job faultlessly, they claimed to have found nothing of importance among the papers in Jefferson's briefcase.

Now should the PLO believe that the contraband secret had gotten through to the enemy after all? Was Hamir supposed to report to his superiors that an old box was the valuable item the senator had carried, that the box had held the key to strange treasures on Masada, which Israel risked political furor to locate?

What were these treasures, anyway? What was the box? And why, in the name of Allah, had the skinheads in the subway tunnel let it slip through their fingers?

Hamir leaned against a wall on the ancient street and pulled a cigarette from his shirt pocket. Lighting it, he lifted it to his lips with shaky fingers and took a long drag, trying to calm his nerves. He closed his eyes and let the familiar sounds of the old city envelop him.

As he did, certain scenes from the day at Masada returned to him with new clarity. He realized now that the rabbis' calm reserve, as they had taken interviews from the press, masked a secret triumph. He remembered how they had whisked a couple of boxes of artifacts into their van before they casually sped away.

Clenching and unclenching one fist, Hamir pounded it into his thigh.

No, he thought, *I will not report this. What would I say anyway? Who would believe me? And besides, it is too late. Whatever our enemies were after, they have found it!*

Two weeks later, the old Consortium house on the city wall was full of activity, joy, and laughter. The time had come for the rabbis to present their priestly candidate to the Sanhedrin, a ruling body based on ancient tradition, of seventy prominent orthodox elders from throughout Israel.

The Chief Rabbi of Jerusalem, Mikel Horowitz, would be overseeing the proceedings, as the candidate was subjected to examinations from the council. The austere and prestigious gathering, while not directly involved in the location of this candidate, had been apprised of the Consortium's progress all along the way, and this day, Zachary Cohen would be approved or disapproved by majority vote of the elite body.

The search for the heir to the Aaronic priesthood was no new thing. It had been in process, in one form or another, for nearly half a century. David Rothmeyer and company had been brought in on it only when modern advances in technology indicated the goal was within reach. Though they were latecomers to the endeavor, Rothmeyer, McCurdy, Aronstam, and the others had made the greatest strides and had secured the candidate by their gallant efforts. They deserved applause, and today, they would be honored by admission to the highly secretive and exclusive convention.

Not only had these scholars been invited, but at the Consortium's request, the chief rabbi had permitted the inclusion of any other trustworthy persons who had contributed to the quest. Though today's proceeding was not an inauguration ceremony—for that could only be performed in the future temple—it was the event at which the candidate would be confirmed or rejected. Depending on how confident the rabbis were of his election, they were free to invite any persons who had helped bring him to this point.

Therefore, in addition to the entire Consortium team—the rabbis, Diamant, the laboratory crew, the American professors, the British contingent, the delightful Ms. Hayworth, and Mel Wester—the old house was full of guests whom Zachary and the rabbis wanted to honor for their assistance. Pete and Honey Wester had been flown in from Montana; with them was their friend, Roberta Barrett, who had helped to locate the Jeremiah Box; Marlon Goldstein from New York had brought little Lamar Jackson, the brave boy whose testimony had led to the capture of the senator's assassins and the tracking down of the box; Father McCurdy's sister Emily had been flown in from Dublin, in gratitude for her contribution and bravery at Dachau a year ago. Laad Girzim was here, and even the queen of Jordan would be arriving in time for the proceedings.

Not to be forgotten were Zachary Cohen's parents, Reginald and Deborah, and last but not least were Bishop Ashcraft and the faithful Italian woman, the keeper of the Shrine of the Word of the Lord. A letter of introduction from Jerusalem's chief rabbi, which Rabbi Benjamin had carried with him to Rome, followed by Israel's promise of a lifetime stipend to support the family who had protected the oracle all these years, had convinced her to release the ancient treasure to the Chosen People.

Then there was Zachary's personal rabbi, Ernie Silverman. Swearing him to secrecy, Zachary had insisted he be included. "After all," Cohen had told him, "though you had no idea what I was facing, you helped me make the biggest decision of my life!"

As the guests, many of whom were meeting for the first time, mingled and visited in the parlor and on the balcony of the old house, Zachary Cohen was preparing to be presented to the elders of Judaism. With him in his private suite were Uriel Katz, Horace Benjamin, and Zachary's best friend, Mel Wester. Levine and Jacobs were playing host downstairs, which allowed Rabbi Ben and Rabbi Katz to speak freely.

Rabbi Ben waved his hands in the air joyously, telling Zachary of a wonderful discovery he had made. "And so, I decided then and there to get to the bottom of Uriel's strange transformation!" he enthused. "I was not prepared for what he told me!"

Zachary, sitting on the bed where he was tying his shoelaces, smiled knowingly. "Yes?" he urged him. "And what did he say?"

"I shall never forget it!" Rabbi Ben exclaimed. "The little scoundrel said to me, 'I have been like Nicodemus. I went to Zachary by night, asking him the secrets of eternity. And now I am born again!'"

Katz grinned from ear to ear, and Rabbi Ben's eyes welled with tears. "So do you know what I answered him?"

"Tell me." Zachary laughed.

"I said, 'It is nice to know I am not alone!'"

At this, the two rabbis hugged rapturously, nearly breaking into a jig, and Zachary slapped his thighs with hilarity. "Oh, Rabbi Ben, it is so good to hear this!" he exclaimed. "I remember how you used to sneak into our meetings at the YMCA. I thought there was hope for you then. I am thrilled to hear I now have two brothers in Christ among the Consortium!"

The two rabbis sat down with Zachary, one on either side. Rabbi Ben patted him on the knee. "Give it time, my boy. The others are not far behind!"

"Jacobs and Levine?" he marveled.

Rabbi Ben nodded. "Their hearts are tender. They only need a little courage."

Zachary closed his eyes in gratitude. To all of this, Mel had not a word to say. Seated in a corner of the room, he observed the three men with a prick of envy, wishing he might feel as they did. But there was still much he did not understand. He wondered now if he would ever get the chance to ask Zachary those questions Uriel Katz had asked.

Rabbi Ben studied his candidate proudly. "Relax, if you can, my boy," he said. "We believe this day will go smoothly."

"Give me the agenda again," Zachary requested.

"The examination is threefold," the old rabbi explained. "The first two parts are directed at the Consortium. We will be asked to give our evidence of your genealogical and physical purity. To this we will give a summary account of how we narrowed the search down to your name. Regarding your health and bodily condition, we will show the results of the physical you underwent recently."

Rabbi Ben clapped Zachary on his strong back. "Of course, you are rather puny, but we hope they will see past that."

The four men in the room laughed heartily at this. Mel, leaning forward, said with a chuckle, "If he were any punier, he wouldn't need a bodyguard!"

Zachary ran a hand through his dark hair and asked nervously, "So the third part is the doctrinal exam?"

Uriel Katz spoke up. "We have seen a list of the questions. We are not permitted to tell you what they are, but you do not need to worry."

"Right," Rabbi Ben said. "The council had little to go on in this regard, as we have only vague traditions concerning the inquiries that were made two thousand years ago. But, as Uriel says, you need not worry. The Sanhedrin decided that only a few matters needed to be addressed—and these are probably no harder than what you answered at your bar mitzvah. They will ask you about the nature of God . . ."

Omniscient, omnipresent, omnipotent, Zachary thought to himself.

". . . the nature of sin . . ."

Pride, self-will, that which separates us from our Creator . . .

". . . the nature of redemption . . ."

At this, Zachary hesitated. And then, it occurred to him that there was no real difference between the proclamations of the Old and New Covenants.

A pure sacrifice, he thought.

". . . and the hope of Israel."

The Messiah!

Zachary grasped his knees and bowed his head. Taking a deep breath, he said, "To all of this, I can respond justly. But, friends, I must warn you of something."

The two rabbis looked at him with furrowed brows. "What is it?" Rabbi Ben asked.

Zachary sighed. "If the day comes that I actually stand in the Holy Sanctuary, to speak to the people of Israel, I will feel it my duty to point them to Yeshua, the Messiah, the ultimate sacrifice. I can do no less."

The older men nodded soberly, and Mel's heart swelled with amazement. Never had he known a braver man than Zachary Cohen.

"And," the priest continued, "I shall use the oracle to confirm the truth before Israel and the nations. I shall ask the Urim and the Thummim what the Word of the Lord is in this matter. I know that you have spent much time and money researching the sacrificial system, the implements, and so on. But"—he raised a pointed finger—"should my beliefs be confirmed, there will be no blood sacrifices in my temple!"

Impressed by his confident directive, Rabbi Ben sighed gratefully. "We do not dispute this, nor would we want to," he said. Then, standing, "The time grows short, Mr. Cohen. We will meet you downstairs."

Zachary stood up and received their parting embrace. As the two gentlemen left the room, he shut the door behind them and turned to finish dressing.

He had nearly forgotten Mel's presence, until the husky ex-cop stepped up to him and, in a kindly gesture, adjusted his suit collar. Zachary caught the look of wistful sadness in his friend's eyes.

"Why the long face, Wester?" he said. "This is the day we've all waited for!"

"Yeah," Mel said, looking at the floor. "But it's also a good-bye. You won't be needing me much longer."

Zachary was stunned. "What are you talking about?" he asked. "I'll need you now more than ever! I intend to be quite a controversial character, don't you know. I expect to develop a lot of enemies!"

Mel's mouth fell open. "So you'll still want a Gentile hanging around when you're the big-time Jewish honcho? I don't really fit the M.O.!"

Zachary laughed. "Hey," he said, "do you think they're expecting a Messianic Jew to step into the high priest's shoes? I don't fit the M.O. either!"

EPILOGUE

To the north of the Western Wall courtyard, a small doorway gives access to labyrinthine tunnels and echoing chambers. On any given day, hundreds of tourists come and go through that door, walking on compacted ground that has felt the tread of the most important leaders of the Hebrew race. In recent years, the tunnels have been scrutinized, opened up and analyzed by Jewish archaeologists, and the consensus has been reached that the subterranean chambers were once dedicated to the utilitarian uses of the ancient Israelite priesthood.

On this particular day, the modern Sanhedrin of Judaism was gathering in one of the largest of those caverns. No television cameras were present, no media of any kind was privy to what would transpire within the hidden vault called the Hall of Polished Stones.

This chamber, based on descriptions of a similar meeting hall in the ancient rabinnical writings, had recently been refurbished and decorated for the most holy purposes of the religion. Lacking the fulfillment of a new temple, which would one day look down from Mount Moriah, Jewish leaders were content to meet here.

In ancient times Hebrew elders had convened daily in the Hall of Polished Stones, to interview, accept, or reject candidates for the general priesthood, which had thousands of positions. In that hall they also decided the acceptability of each new high priest, of which there was only one at any time.

Today, for the first time in nearly two millennia, a potential high priest would be interviewed.

David Rothmeyer and his companions, along with all the guests of the Consortium, entered the narrow doorway one by one and followed the rabbis toward the chamber. The musty smell of ancient earth and bone-dry stone greeted their noses as their eyes adjusted to the dim light. From some indiscernible distance, the sound of solemn music could be heard, which grew louder the farther they went.

Their footsteps echoing through the hallways, the gathering wound back and back, until the tunnel widened into a broad, light-filled chamber. Tall menorahs, lit by flaming candles, shone forth from all corners of the natural cave, their warm glow glancing off the walls with each breath of air that managed to enter.

The music was very clear now, its mellow minor chords typical of any synagogue. David had to bow his head to enter the low doorway of yet another room, this one enormous. Greeting the rabbis and their guests were young men who appeared to be yeshiva students, all done up in tallithim, yarmulkes, and poyim. Perhaps they were from the same boys' school that Pete and Mel had rescued only a year ago, David thought.

The youngsters handed out programs to the guests, on which were emblazoned the Star of David and the Golden Menorah. The title on the creamy white paper was "Sanhedrin Convention for High Priestly Interview," and below this, "Candidate, Zachary Cohen."

David, along with Britta and Ken Aronstam, took a seat in the second row of the stone benches, which were arrayed on either side of a central aisle. In the front row, the rabbis were seated, along with Diamant and others of the Consortium staff. Across the aisle from David sat McCurdy and Cromwell. All the honored guests sat behind, including Laad Girzim, who escorted the beautiful queen of Jordan.

The echoing chamber was a sight to rival any chapel of the Vatican. Completely sheathed in polished alabaster, the walls were a gleaming white; the floor was a checkerboard of black and gray marble, which glistened in a pampered sheen. Scattered across the ceiling were fabulous hanging lamps; made of wrought brass and lit with fat candles, they were inset with colored glass that caused them to cast a rainbow of colors through the room.

Censers filled the chamber with a sweet aroma, not too strong, for there was poor ventilation here.

At the head of the room, on a very large platform, two semicircles of chairs faced the center. At the back of the stage, on a higher riser, a taller, more elegant chair stood, looking much like a throne. To the side of this, a little lower, was yet another. None of the chairs on the stage were yet filled. David did a quick count, and finding that each semi-circle contained thirty-five seats, he figured these were for the seventy Sanhedrin members.

A long interlude passed as the crowd sat silent. All present had a private moment to consider what had brought them here, what role each of them had played.

David glanced about the room, his heart full of a hundred feelings as he studied the faces of his wonderful friends. There were the newlyweds, handsome Pete and lovely Honey, their hands entwined and their gazes lost in memories. There was Ian McCurdy, the notorious rebel of the Cave Scroll team—what would David, or any of them, have done without him? Brave Mel Wester was one of the truest heroes David would ever know; he was proud to count him among his comrades. And, of course, the rabbis! David's lips spread in a smile as he considered how blessed he was to have gotten that strange letter a year ago.

David did not know some of them so well. One he wished he had met before was the dear boy who had bravely told his story of horror to the right people. Little Lamar Jackson, who sat wide-eyed with wonder as he took in the glory of this place, had a lifetime ahead to learn just how important he was. For now, as Marlon Goldstein placed an arm about his slender shoulders, the boy sat still as a statue, his plump mouth open in awe.

The music, which was provided by a string quartet offstage, came to a close. A movement at the rear of the room indicated proceedings were about to begin. Heading a line of ostentatious-looking gentlemen, the Chief Rabbi of Jerusalem entered the aisle. His long gray beard, typical of his orthodox caste, lay resplendent against a black tunic, his shoulders overspread with a striped and fringed shawl. Slowly he walked up the aisle as a cantor mounted one corner of the platform and prepared to sing.

The Sanhedrin, which followed, took seats in the two semicircles, as the chief rabbi sat on the tall chair to the back of the stage.

Just as the singer began, his warm voice calling the faithful to worship, three yeshiva students came forward, bearing golden platters on which were three precious items. David's heart skipped a beat as the vial of the Ashes of the Red Heifer, the Breastplate of the High Priest, and the crystal box containing the Oracle were placed reverently on an altar at center stage.

A thrill went through the crowd as they looked upon the long-lost treasures.

Finally, when the chief rabbi nodded toward the rear of the room, the priestly candidate came forward, dressed in a fine suit, his tallith over his shoulders. Hands folded before him, he approached the council, and as he stood before the chief rabbi, he raised his mantle over his bowed head in deference. Only when the rabbi nodded and gestured to the chair nearest him did Zachary take his place.

Now the cantor began a familiar refrain, and everyone stood up in response.

Hear, O Israel, the Lord your God is one Lord;
There is no other god like him.

"Amen," said the crowd and sat down again.

A rustling of programs preceded the chief rabbi's introduction. Addressing the congregation from his throne, he said, "This is a momentous day in the history of Israel! We are gathered here this day to look into the qualifications of the first candidate for the high priesthood to come before us in two thousand years. In preparation for the rebuilding of our holy sanctuary, which our people have wept for all these generations, we are ready to select its overseer. Without a high priest, we have no use for a temple. Without a temple, Jerusalem is a crown without a star, the Messiah has no place from which to reign, and Israel is a dream unfulfilled!"

How those words struck a chord in David's heart! They were the exact ones that Rabbi Ben had spoken to him the day they met in New York City, the day the Consortium enlisted him into their service. The chief rabbi went on to say that there would be three inquiries: genealogical, physical, and spiritual. But David was mesmerized by his opening statement.

The professor had long ago accepted the fact that he had been brought along this path, not of his own will, but under the direction of a force unseen. He had kept busy with his work, with his growing love affair with Britta, with his scholarly investigations. But today it came home to him in a new way just how miraculous this adventure had been.

Rabbi Ben was now standing, going forward to address the matters of Zachary's genealogy, the doctor's certification of Zachary's health, and so on. The old scholar was making a great case for the fact that God himself had overseen their quest, telling of the amazing connections between the Copper Scrolls, the Dachau document, etc. "All of you are aware that the divine providence," he was saying, "only recently brought us to the Ashes of the Red Heifer, the Breastplate, and the Oracle." He was gesturing to the amazing treasures on the altar. "Is this alone not confirmation of our candidate?"

David's head registered all of these proceedings, but in his heart another work was going on.

Suddenly, he gripped Britta's hand so hard she jolted.

"What is it, David?" she whispered, giving him a startled look.

Embarrassed, he shook his head. "Nothing," he said softly.

David's eyes were riveted on Zachary, who sat ready for the inquisition. A year ago the professor had found this remarkable young fellow at a Messianic gathering in the courtyard just outside. As David gazed upon the holy man, that fact and others, fragments of truth like flashes of disjointed light, suddenly came together in one kaleidoscopic burst.

This man believes Jesus is the Messiah! he remembered. *If I believe in Zachary, I must believe in . . .*

For David Rothmeyer, secular Jew, disenchanted seeker of lost things, reality took on a new dimension in that instant.

When he had introduced himself to Zachary Cohen, those many months ago, he had recognized then that his life would never be the same. Remembering his first words to the priest, they suddenly became a prayer, a prayer to Zachary's God:

My name is David Rothmeyer. You don't know me, but I have been looking for you for a long time!

BOOK GROUP DISCUSSION GUIDE

Note: These study questions may "give away" the plot. Please read the sections in the book before looking at the questions that go with them, so as not to spoil your reading experience. See www.ellentraylor.com for additional questions.

1. What items do the rabbis want David to find, and why? Why don't they just create new ones, rather than go on a quest for the originals? Be specific.
2. What is Zachary Cohen's dilemma? Do you think it can realistically be solved? How?
3. Discuss the phrase "word of the Lord." Why is this such a universal saying, and what does it mean?
4. How prevalent is the Neo-Nazi Movement? (You may want to look into this and see how it is growing today.)
5. What is the legend of Masada? Why do the characters question it?
6. What conclusion do Laad and the queen come to? Why does the queen want to help Israel? (This is a work of fiction, but what do you know about Jordan's relationship to Israel?)
7. Discuss Zachary's prayer when the rabbis' plans appear to be blocked. The prayer seems to bring the necessary answer, yet God had already solved the problem before Zachary prayed. Discuss the nature of prayer.
8. Read John chapter 3 in the New Testament. How is Uriel Katz's experience with Zachary similar to Nicodemus's experience with Jesus? What does it mean to be "born again"? How does Katz's experience change him?
9. Discuss "Messianic Judaism." What is it? Do you consider it a valid belief system? Why/why not? What answer does Zachary discover in the Messianic meeting? Do you think the discovery is believable? Discuss.
10. Discuss the network of evil in the book. Who are the spies in the Jordanian palace, at Masada, etc.? How far-reaching is the network? Do you think such an international scenario is likely?
11. What climactic moment faces Zachary in Chapter 40? How has he prepared for it, and what choice does he make?
12. How does Zachary conclude that the Old and New Covenants are alike?
13. What does David experience at Zachary's ceremony? In what way is it true that God didn't "know" David, until then?